EX LIBRIS

UNIVERSITATIS SANCTI JOANNIS

THE ILLUSTRATED
TREASURY OF
CHILDREN'S
LITERATURE

THE ILLUSTRATED
TREASURY OF
CHILDREN'S
LITERATURE

Edited and with an introduction by Margaret E. Martignoni
formerly Superintendent of Work with Children
Brooklyn Public Library, New York

COMPILED WITH THE ORIGINAL ILLUSTRATIONS UNDER THE DIRECTION OF
P. EDWARD ERNEST

STAFF EDITORS: DORIS DUENEWALD • EVELYN ANDREAS • ALICE THORNE

GROSSET AND DUNLAP · PUBLISHERS · NEW YORK

ACKNOWLEDGMENTS

Grateful acknowledgment is made to the following publishers, authors, illustrators and other copyright holders, for permission to reprint copyrighted materials:

LOUISE ANDREWS — "Table Manners-1," from *Goops and How to Be Them*, by Gelett Burgess, copyright, 1900, 1928, by Gelett Burgess, by permission of Louise Andrews.

APPLETON-CENTURY-CROFTS, INC. — Drawings by A. B. Frost for "The Wonderful Tar Baby," from *Uncle Remus, His Songs and His Sayings*, by Joel Chandler Harris, copyright 1908, 1920, by Esther La Rose Harris, used by permission of Appleton-Century-Crofts, Inc.

ARTISTS AND WRITERS GUILD, INC. — Illustrations by F. Rojankovsky, from *The Ugly Duckling*, copyright 1945 by Artists and Writers Guild, Inc., used by permission. Illustrations by Everett Shinn, from *Poems of Childhood*, by James Whitcomb Riley, copyright 1943 by Artists and Writers Guild, Inc., used by permission.

PAMELA BIANCO — Illustrations from *Flora*, by permission of Pamela Bianco.

THE BOBBS-MERRILL COMPANY, INC. — "The Raggedy Man," "An Impetuous Resolve," from *Rhymes of Childhood*, by James Whitcomb Riley, and "Extremes," from *The Book of Joyous Children*, by James Whitcomb Riley, copyright 1902, used by special permission of the publishers, The Bobbs-Merrill Company, Inc.; "The Discovery of Oz, the Terrible," from *The Wizard of Oz*, by L. Frank Baum, copyright 1900, 1903, by L. Frank Baum and W. W. Denslow; copyright 1928, 1931, by Maud G. Baum, used by special permission of the publishers, The Bobbs-Merrill Company, Inc.; excerpt from *Augustus Goes South*, by LeGrand, copyright 1940, used by special permission of the publishers, The Bobbs-Merrill Company, Inc.

BRANDT & BRANDT — Excerpt from *Penrod*, published by Doubleday & Co., Inc., copyright, 1914, 1942, by Booth Tarkington.

MARGARET WISE BROWN — "The Shy Little Horse," copyright 1938 by Margaret Wise Brown, reprinted from *The Fish With the Deep Sea Smile*, by permission of Roberta B. Rauch.

THORNTON W. BURGESS — "Two Happy Little Bears," by permission of the author.

JONATHAN CAPE, LIMITED — Excerpt from *Bambi*, by Felix Salten, by permission of Jonathan Cape, Limited, London.

CASSELL & CO., LTD. — Excerpt, "Freedom Again," from *Lassie Come-Home*, by Eric Knight.

CHILD LIFE MAGAZINE — "Mud," by Polly Chase Boyden, from *Child Life Magazine*, copyright 1930.

COWARD-McCANN, INC. — "The Fisherman and His Wife," from *Tales From Grimm*, by Wanda Gág, illustrations by Wanda Gág, copyright 1936 by Wanda Gág, by permission of Coward-McCann, Inc.; illustration by Wanda Gág reprinted from "Hansel and Gretel," from *Tales From Grimm*, by Wanda Gág, copyright 1936 by Wanda Gág, by permission of Coward-McCann, Inc.; illustrations by Berta and Elmer Hader from *A Picture Book of Mother Goose*, by Berta and Elmer Hader, copyright 1944 by Berta and Elmer Hader, reprinted by permission of Coward-McCann, Inc.

CURTIS BROWN, LTD. — Excerpt "Freedom Again," from *Lassie Come-Home*, by Eric Knight, copyright 1940 by Jere Knight Lindtner, reprinted by permission of the author's estate;

The Horse Who Lived Upstairs, by Phyllis McGinley, copyright 1944 by Phyllis McGinley, reprinted by permission of the author; excerpt, "Eeyore Loses a Tail and Pooh Finds One," from *Winnie-the-Pooh*, by A. A. Milne, illustrated by E. H. Shepard; "The Engineer" and "The End" from *Now We Are Six*, "Hoppity" and "Halfway Down" from *When We Were Young*, by A. A. Milne, illustrated by E. H. Shepard; illustrations by E. H. Shepard for excerpt, "Mr. Toad," from *The Wind in the Willows*, by Kenneth Grahame.

INGRI AND EDGAR PARIN D'AULAIRE — "The Three Aunts," from *East of the Sun and West of the Moon*, by Ingri and Edgar Parin d'Aulaire, reprinted by permission.

WALTER DE LA MARE — "Dream Song" and "Some One" by permission of the author.

J. M. DENT & SONS, LTD. — Excerpt, "Quiet," from *Lad: A Dog*, by Albert Payson Terhune; "The Sleeping Beauty" and illustration by D. J. Watkins-Pitchford, and "Dick Whittington" and illustration by D. J. Watkins-Pitchford, from *Fairy Tales of Long Ago*, edited by M. C. Carey; "The Tinder-Box" and illustration by Maxwell Armfield, "The Steadfast Tin Soldier," "The Little Match Girl," "The Emperor's New Clothes," and "The Ugly Duckling," from *Hans Andersen's Fairy Tales*, translated by Mrs. E. Lucas; illustrations by Charles Folkard from *The Land of Nursery Rhyme*, As Seen by Alice Daglish and Ernest Rhys, by permission of J. M. Dent & Sons, Ltd., London.

THE DIAL PRESS, INC. — "Pandora, The First Woman," from *Stories of the Gods and Heroes*, by Sally Benson, by permission of The Dial Press, Inc., copyright 1940 by Sally Benson.

DODD, MEAD & COMPANY, INC. — "How Thor Found His Hammer," reprinted by permission of Dodd, Mead & Company from *Norse Stories*, by Hamilton Wright Mabie; illustrations by Walter Crane for "Puss in Boots," from *Cinderella Picture Book*; illustrations by Walter Crane for "The Three Bears," from *Mother Hubbard Picture Book*, reprinted by permission of Dodd, Mead & Company; illustrations by Jessie Wilcox Smith from *A Child's Book of Stories*, by P. W. Coussens; illustrations by Percy J. Billinghurst from *A Hundred Fables of Aesop*; reprinted by permission of Dodd, Mead & Company.

DOUBLEDAY & COMPANY, INC. — Excerpt from *The Velveteen Rabbit*, by Margery Williams Bianco, reprinted by permission of Doubleday & Co., Inc.; excerpt from *Copper-Toed Boots*, by Marguerite de Angeli, copyright 1938 by Marguerite de Angeli, reprinted by permission of Doubleday & Co., Inc.; excerpt from *Poppy Seed Cakes*, by Margery Clark, copyright 1924 by Doubleday & Co., Inc.; excerpt from *Paul Bunyan and His Great Blue Ox*, by Wallace Wadsworth, copyright 1928 by Doubleday & Co., Inc.; "How the Rhinoceros Got His Skin" from *Just So Stories*, by Rudyard Kipling, copyright 1912 by Rudyard Kipling, reprinted by permission of Mrs. George Bambridge and Doubleday & Company, Inc.; "Taxis," "General Store," "Woods," from *Taxis and Toadstools*, by Rachel Field, copyright 1926 by Doubleday & Co., Inc.; "Mother," from *Fairies and Chimneys*, by Rose Fyleman, copyright 1920 by Doubleday & Co., Inc.

E. P. DUTTON & CO., INC. — "Hoppity," "Halfway Down," from *When We Were Very Young*, by A. A. Milne, illustrated by Ernest H. Shepard, copyright 1924 by E. P. Dutton & Co., Inc., renewal, 1952, by A. A. Milne; "The Engineer" and "The End" from *Now We Are Six*, by A. A. Milne, illustrated by Ernest H. Shepard, copyright 1927 by E. P. Dutton & Co.; excerpt, "Eeyore Loses a Tail and Pooh Finds One," from *Winnie-the-Pooh*, by A. A. Milne, illustrated by Ernest H.

Shepard, copyright 1926 by E. P. Dutton & Co., Inc., renewal, 1954, by E. P. Dutton & Co., Inc.; excerpt, "Quiet," from *Lad: A Dog*, by Albert Payson Terhune, copyright 1919, 1926, renewal 1947 by E. P. Dutton & Co., Inc.; "The Sleeping Beauty" and "Dick Whittington" from *Fairy Tales of Long Ago*, edited by M. C. Carey, illustrated by D. J. Watkins-Pitchford; "The Tinder-Box" from *Hans Andersen's Fairy Tales*, translated by Mrs. E. Lucas, illustrated by Maxwell Armfield; "The Steadfast Tin Soldier," "The Little Match Girl," "The Emperor's New Clothes," "The Ugly Duckling" from *Hans Andersen's Fairy Tales*, translated by Mrs. E. Lucas; illustrations by Charles Folkard from *The Land of Nursery Rhyme*, As Seen by Alice Daglish and Ernest Rhys, by permission of the publisher, E. P. Dutton & Co., Inc.

FABER & FABER — "Dream Song," and "Some One," by Walter de la Mare; *New World for Nellie*, by Rowland Emett, from *Nellie Come Home*.

C. B. FALLS — Illustration from *Mother Goose*, by C. B. Falls, by permission of C. B. Falls.

GORDAN GRANT — Illustrations from *Penrod*, by Booth Tarkington; by permission of Gordon Grant.

THE JOHNNY GRUELLE COMPANY — Excerpt "Raggedy Andy's Smile," from *Raggedy Andy Stories*, copyright 1920 by P. F. Volland Co., copyright renewed 1947 by Myrtle Gruelle, copyright 1948 by The Johnny Gruelle Company, by permission.

ROBERT HALE, LTD. — *The Horse Who Lived Upstairs*, by Phyllis McGinley, copyright 1944 by Phyllis McGinley.

HARCOURT, BRACE AND COMPANY, INC. — *New World For Nellie*, by Rowland Emett, copyright 1952 by Harcourt, Brace and Co., Inc., by permission of Harcourt, Brace and Co., Inc., New York, "The Fir Tree," from *It's Perfectly True and Other Stories*, by Hans Christian Andersen, copyright 1938 by Paul Leyssac, by permission of Harcourt, Brace and Co., Inc., and estate of Paul Leyssac; illustrations by Richard Bennett from *It's Perfectly True and Other Stories*, copyright 1938 by Paul Leyssac, by permission of Harcourt, Brace and Co., Inc.

HARPER & BROTHERS — *Pelle's New Suit*, by Elsa Beskow; illustration by Ilonka Karasz from *The Twelve Days of Christmas*, copyright 1949 by Ilonka Karasz; excerpts from *The Adventures of Tom Sawyer* and *The Adventures of Huckleberry Finn*, by Mark Twain; "The Force of Need," from *Pepper and Salt*, by Howard Pyle, by permission of Harper & Brothers.

GEORGE G. HARRAP & CO., LTD. — "Cinderella," "Aladdin," "Puss in Boots," and "The Princess and the Pea," from *The Arthur Rackham Fairy Book*, by Arthur Rackham, with illustrations therefrom; illustration by Arthur Rackham from "Red Riding-Hood," illustration from "The Little Match Girl" by Arthur Rackham from *Fairy Tales by Hans Andersen*; illustrations by Arthur Rackham from *The Pied Piper of Hamelin*; by permission of George G. Harrap & Co., Ltd., London.

JOHN A. HARTELL — Illustrations from *Over In The Meadow* by John A. Hartell, by permission of John A. Hartell.

WILLIAM HEINEMANN, LTD. — Excerpt from *The Velveteen Rabbit*, by Margery Williams Bianco; illustration by Edmund Dulac from "The Emperor's New Clothes," from *Stories from Hans Andersen*, by permission of William Heinemann, Ltd.

HENRY HOLT & CO., INC. — "Dream Song," and "Some One," by Walter de la Mare, from *Collected Poems* by Walter de la Mare, copyright 1920 by Henry Holt & Co., Inc., copyright 1948 by Walter de la Mare, used by permission of the publishers.

HOUGHTON MIFFLIN COMPANY — Illustration by Gustaf Tenggren from *Heidi*, by Johanna Spyri.

ALFRED A. KNOPF, INC. — "Little Lisa" from *Fairy Tales from the North*, by Einar Nerman, copyright 1946 by Einar Nerman; illustration by Warren Chappell from *Peter and the Wolf*, by Serge Prokofieff, copyright 1940 by Alfred A. Knopf, Inc.; illustration by Richard Bennett from *Legends of Paul Bunyan*, compiled by Harold W. Felton, copyright 1947 by Alfred A. Knopf, Inc.; illustrations by C. Lovat Fraser from *Nursery Rhymes with Pictures By C. Lovat Fraser*; by permission of Alfred A. Knopf, Inc.

JOHN LANE THE BODLEY HEAD, LTD. — Illustrations by Walter Crane from "Puss in Boots," from *Cinderella Picture Book*, and from "The Three Bears," from *Mother Hubbard Picture Book*.

J. B. LIPPINCOTT COMPANY — Excerpt from *My Friend Flicka*, by Mary O'Hara, published by J. B. Lippincott Co., copyright 1941 by Mary O'Hara; "Animal Crackers," from *Songs for a Little House* by Christopher Morley, published by J. B. Lippincott Company, copyright 1917, 1945, by Christopher Morley; "Playing," from *Manners Can Be Fun*, by Munro Leaf, published by J. B. Lippincott Company, copyright 1936 by Munro Leaf; "A Kitten," "Jill Came From the Fair," from *Over the Garden Wall*, by Eleanor Farjeon; published by J. B. Lippincott Company, copyright 1933 by Eleanor Farjeon.

LITTLE, BROWN & COMPANY — Excerpts from *Little Women*, by Louisa May Alcott; "Peter Finds a Name," from *The Adventures of Peter Cottontail*, by Thornton W. Burgess, copyright 1941 by Thornton W. Burgess; by permission of Little, Brown & Company.

LONGMANS, GREEN & CO., INC. — "The Half-Chick" from *Green Fairy Book*, by Andrew Lang, copyright 1948 by Longmans, Green & Co., Inc.; "Drakestail," from *Red Fairy Book*, by Andrew Lang, copyright 1948 by Longmans, Green & Co., Inc.; also illustrations by H. J. Ford from the following fairy tales: "The Emperor's New Clothes," "The Steadfast Tin Soldier," "Rumpelstiltskin," "The Brave Little Tailor," and "Aladdin"; by permission of Longmans, Green & Company, Inc., New York, and Longmans, Green & Company, Limited, London.

THE MACMILLAN COMPANY — *The Lion-Hearted Kitten*, by Peggy Bacon, copyright 1950 by The Macmillan Company, used with publisher's permission; "Baucis and Philemon," from *A Book of Myths*, copyright 1942 by The Macmillan Company, used with publisher's permission; "Lazy Jack," "Jack and the Beanstalk," "Henny-Penny," "The Story of the Three Bears," from *English Fairy Tales*, by Flora Annie Steel, copyright 1918 by The Macmillan Co. and used with publisher's permission; illustrations by Hedvig Collin from *East of the Sun and West of the Moon*; illustrations by Francis D. Bedford from *A Christmas Carol*, by Charles Dickens, copyright 1946 by The Macmillan Company; excerpt from *The Story of Peter Pan*, from Daniel O'Connor's Barrie's Play, copyright 1950 by The Macmillan Co.; excerpt from *Pinocchio* by C. Collodi, illustrated by Attilio Mussino, copyright 1929 by The Macmillan Company, by permission of the publisher, New York and London.

THE MACMILLAN COMPANY OF CANADA, LTD. — "How the Rhinoceros Got His Skin," from *Just So Stories*, by Rudyard Kipling.

THE MACMILLAN COMPANY, LIMITED — Illustrations by John Tenniel from *Alice's Adventures in Wonderland* and *Through the Looking Glass* by Lewis Carroll.

INTRODUCTION

Perhaps the purest joy in the family relationship lies in the privilege of *sharing*. Precious hours that parents and children spend in each other's company are remembered longest and with the greatest delight. Those little excursions made together, the useful and beautiful things built together, and—perhaps, best of all—the books explored together, all form a chain of experiences which give a child a much needed sense of security and a feeling of being wanted and loved.

What has become of the old-fashioned family reading hour? Once an established custom in the American home, the reading hour has in recent years become more and more of a rarity. Yet most families are not happy about the growing tendency on the part of individual members to pursue their own interests independently of the rest of the clan. Nor do they find any other than chilly comfort in the fact that, while radio and television are bringing families together again in the living room, the arbitrary selection and rapid pace of most of the programs usually prevent sharing in the best sense of the word. Thoughtful parents are turning to books and reading as an ideal family experience. There is an old saying among book lovers that reading together leads to reading separately. Boys and girls are great imitators. In families where everybody reads children are likely to grow up with a

real affection for books and a genuine confidence in the printed page as a source of information and pleasure.

But, where to begin with the family reading program? How can the average family keep on hand a library of sufficient diversity to permit browsing which will suit the taste of all ages? The answer is, of course, that the average family cannot. Even those fortunate enough to own a wide variety of fine books sometimes find selection a very real problem. *The Illustrated Treasury of Children's Literature* has been compiled to meet just such a need.

Designed primarily for family use and for reading aloud with children, every selection has already earned the approval of real live boys and girls. Each is a work of true literary distinction in its own right. Many stories are complete in themselves while others are carefully chosen excerpts from some of the greatest books in the English language. The selections have been made largely from the works of English and American writers because these have produced the greatest wealth of literature for children. Books like Mark Twain's *The Adventures of Tom Sawyer* and Robert Louis Stevenson's *Treasure Island* have already earned a secure niche in the annals of universal literature. But continental authors who have endeared themselves to American youth have not been neglected.

Switzerland is represented by *Heidi,* Italy by *Adventures of Pinocchio,* Russia by *Peter and the Wolf* and Germany, Spain, France and the Scandinavian countries by fairy tales.

One of the most distinguished features of the *Treasury* is the art work. Illustrations have been chosen from the most beautiful and distinctive editions of the books selected and in many cases are as famous as the stories they depict. Randolph Caldecott, Kate Greenaway, and Leslie Brooke are among the most honored names of early artists for children. Boys and girls will pore over their pictures just as they delight in the intricate and lacy creations of Reginald Birch and the action and sweep of N. C. Wyeth's drawings. Nor are the moderns excluded, as work by Leonard Weisgard, Gustav Tenggren, Kurt Wiese, Wanda Gág and many, many others will prove. All in all, eighty-five top ranking artists are represented in the *Treasury* and a veritable art education awaits boys and girls in its pages.

There is something for all ages. Very little children will nod happily to the cadences of *Baa, Baa, Black Sheep, The Three Little Kittens, Little Miss Muffet* and numerous other Mother Goose rhymes. They will revel in the gaily illustrated ABC jingles. From these they can go on to such delightfully different nursery classics as *The Story of Babar* and *The Tale of Peter Rabbit.* Six- and seven-year-olds will find Margery Clark's *The Poppy-Seed Cakes,* illustrated by Maud and Miska Petersham, a continual source of laughter and bliss. Also included for this wide-awake age are excerpts from the world-famous A . A . Milne story, *Winnie-the-Pooh,* and many modern tales such as *The Horse Who Lived Upstairs* by Phyllis McGinley.

Eight, nine and ten is the fairy tale age. What a wealth of fantasy is in store in the *Treasury* for the delectation of this group. *Cinderella, The Three Bears, The Ugly Duckling, Hansel and Gretel*—to name only a few of the traditional tales. These are supplemented by selections from *Alice's Adventures in Wonderland, The Wizard of Oz, The Wind in the Willows, The Jungle Book,* and many other modern fanciful stories with much the same appeal as the fairy tales. Older boys and girls have not been forgotten. To them the *Treasury* brings adventurous living in scenes from *David Copperfield, The Good Master, Lassie Come-Home, My Friend Flicka,* and many others.

While the *Treasury* is a real boon to family reading, it is not necessarily restricted thereto. Many a child will haul the volume from the shelf and spend countless happy hours threading his way through its rich hoard. There is something for his every mood. Laughter lurks in the rollicking nonsense limericks of Edward Lear and the fantastic creations of Dr. Seuss. Poetry is here in abundance, from the familiar everyday world of Christopher Morley's *Animal Crackers* and Dorothy Aldis' *Naughty Soap Song* to the exquisite imagery of Christina Rossetti, Shelley or Shakespeare. Pageantry and breath-taking adventure beckon from the pages of the *Robin Hood* and *King Arthur* stories while home and family constitute the appeal of *Swiss Family Robinson* and *Little Women.*

The very best in children's literature is represented in the *Treasury* and its enjoyment is not restricted to the children alone. Parents and other adults will thoroughly enjoy introducing boys and girls to this great literature heritage and exploring with them the best of contemporary writing for children. Having savored these pleasures, both child and parent will be ready to reach out for the full-length editions from which these selections have been made. Yes, reading together leads to reading separately. *The Illustrated Treasury of Children's Literature* will help to point the way.

MARGARET E. MARTIGNONI

CONTENTS

THE ILLUSTRATED
TREASURY OF
CHILDREN'S
LITERATURE

Mistress Mary,
Quite contrary,
How does your garden grow?
With silver bells,
And cockleshells,
And pretty maids all in a row.

Lucy Locket, lost her pocket,
Kitty Fisher found it;
There was not a penny in it,
But a ribbon round it.

Little Miss Muffet
Sat on a tuffet
Eating of curds and whey;
There came a big spider,
And sat down beside her,
And frightened
Miss Muffet away.

Illustrations by Kate Greenaway

A diller, a dollar,
    a ten o'clock scholar,
What makes you
    come so soon?
You used to come
    at ten o'clock,
But now you come at noon.

Georgie Porgie,
    pudding and pie,
Kissed the girls
    and made them cry,
When the boys
    came out to play,
Georgie Porgie ran away.

Little Jack Horner sat in a corner,
    Eating his Christmas pie;
He put in his thumb,
    And pulled out a plum,
And said, "What a good boy am I!"

Illustrations by Kate Greenaway

Three little kittens
    lost their mittens,
And they began to cry,
"Oh, mother dear, we sadly fear
Our mittens we have lost!"
"What! lost your mittens,
    you naughty kittens!
Then you shall have no pie."
"Meow, meow, meow!"

The three little kittens
    found their mittens,
And they began to cry,
"Oh, mother dear, see here, see here,
Our mittens we have found."
"What! found your mittens,
    you good little kittens,
Then you shall have some pie."
"Purr, purr, purr."

Illustrations by Leonard Weisgard

Diddle diddle dumpling, my son John,
Went to bed with his breeches on,
One shoe off and one shoe on;
Diddle diddle dumpling, my son John.

Old Mrs. McShuttle
Lived in a coal-scuttle,
Along with her dog
   and her cat;
What they ate I can't tell,
But 'tis known very well,
That none of the
   party were fat.

Illustrations by Leonard Weisgard

Rock-a-bye, baby,
  on the tree top!
When the wind blows
  the cradle will rock,
When the bough breaks
  the cradle will fall,
And down will come baby,
  cradle and all.

Hey, diddle, diddle!
  The cat and the fiddle,
The cow jumped
  over the moon;
The little dog laughed
  To see such sport,
And the dish ran away
  with the spoon.

Illustrations by Leonard Weisgard

What are little
    girls made of?
What are little
    girls made of?
Sugar and spice and
    all that's nice;
And that's what little
    girls are made of.

What are little
    boys made of?
What are little
    boys made of?
Snakes and snails and
    puppy-dogs' tails;
And that's what little
    boys are made of.

Illustrations by Leonard Weisgard

Illustration from a drawing by Pelagie Doane

Twinkle, twinkle, little star,
How I wonder what you are!
Up above the world so high,
Like a diamond in the sky!

When the blazing sun is gone,
When he nothing shines upon,
Then you show your little light,
Twinkle, twinkle, all the night.

8

Peter, Peter, pumpkin-eater,
Had a wife and couldn't keep her;
He put her in a pumpkin shell,
And there he kept her very well.

Hickory, dickory, dock!
The mouse ran up the clock;
The clock struck one,
And down he run,
Hickory, dickory, dock.

Pease porridge hot,
   pease porridge cold,
Pease porridge in the pot,
   nine days old.
Some like it hot,
   some like it cold,
Some like it in the pot,
   nine days old.

Illustrations by Leonard Weisgard

Pussy-cat, pussy-cat,
 where have you been?
I've been to London
 to visit the queen.
Pussy-cat, pussy-cat,
 what did you there?
I frightened a little mouse
 under the chair.

Donkey, donkey,
 old and gray,
Ope your mouth
 and gently bray.
Lift your ears and
 blow your horn,
To wake the world
 this sleepy morn.

Illustrations by Françoiso

10

Pat-a-cake, pat-a-cake,
  baker's man,
Bake me a cake as fast
  as you can,
Pat it and prick it and
  mark it with T,
And put it in the oven
  for Tommy and me.

Jack be nimble,
  Jack be quick,
Jack jump over
  the candlestick.

Illustration from a drawing by Charles Folkard

Three young rats with black felt hats,
Three young ducks with white straw flats,
Three young dogs with curling tails,
Three young cats with demi-veils,
Went out to walk with two young pigs
In satin vests and sorrel wigs;
But suddenly it chanced to rain,
And so they all went home again.

Illustration from a drawing by Françoise

Mary had a little lamb,
  Its fleece was white as snow,
And everywhere that Mary went
  The lamb was sure to go.

It followed her to school one day,
  Which was against the rule;
It made the children laugh and play
  To see a lamb at school.

13

Illustration by Charles Folkard

I saw a ship a-sailing,
   A-sailing on the sea;
And, oh! it was all laden
   With pretty things for thee!

There were comfits in the cabin,
   And apples in the hold;
The sails were made of silk,
   And the masts were made of gold.

The four-and-twenty sailors
   That stood between the decks,
Were four-and-twenty white mice,
   With chains about their necks.

The captain was a duck,
   With a packet on his back;
And when the ship began to move,
   The captain said, "Quack! quack!"

Illustration by Charles Folkard

The Queen of Hearts, she made some tarts,
  All on a summer's day;
The Knave of Hearts, he stole the tarts,
  And took them clean away.

The King of Hearts called for the tarts,
  And beat the Knave full sore;
The Knave of Hearts brought back the tarts,
  And vowed he'd steal no more.

Illustration from a drawing by C. Lovat Fraser

Doctor Foster went to Gloster,
    In a shower of rain;
He stepped in a puddle, up to the middle,
    And never went there again.

How far is it to Babylon?
    Threescore miles and ten.
Can I get there by candlelight?
    Yes, and back again.

Illustration from a drawing by C. Lovat Fraser

Hot cross buns!
   Hot cross buns!
One a penny, two a penny,
   Hot cross buns!

If you have no daughters,
   Give them to your sons;
One a penny, two a penny,
   Hot cross buns!

My maid Mary, she minds the dairy,
   While I go hoeing and mowing each morn;
Gaily run the reel and the little spinning wheel,
   While I am singing and mowing my corn.

Illustration by C. B. Falls

Hark, Hark, the dogs do bark!
The beggars are coming to town,
Some in rags, and some in tags,
And some in velvet gowns.

Illustration by C B. Falls

Baa, baa, black sheep, have you any wool?
Yes, sir; yes, sir, three bags full:
One for my master, one for my dame,
And one for the little boy that lives down the lane.

Illustration from a drawing by C. B. Falls

Tom, Tom, the piper's son,
He learned to play when he was young,
But all the tunes that he could play
Was "Over the hills and far away."

Three wise men of Gotham
Went to sea in a bowl.
If the bowl had been stronger
My song had been longer.

Illustration by C. B. Falls

Little Boy Blue, come blow your horn,
The sheep's in the meadow, the cow's in the corn;
But where is the boy that looks after the sheep?
He's under a haycock, fast asleep.
Will you wake him?   No, not I;
For if I do, he'll be sure to cry.

Illustration by C. B. Falls

Ride a cock-horse
　　To Banbury Cross,
To see a fine lady
　　Upon a white horse,

With rings on her fingers
　　And bells on her toes,
And she shall have music
　　Wherever she goes.

Illustrations from drawings by C. B. Falls

Little Bo-Peep has lost her sheep,
   And can't tell where to find them;
Leave them alone and they'll come home,
   And bring their tails behind them.

Little Bo-Peep fell fast asleep,
 And dreamt she heard them bleating;
But when she awoke, she found it a joke,
 For they were still a-fleeting.

Then up she took her little crook,
 Determined for to find them;
She found them indeed, but it made her
  heart bleed,
 For they'd left their tails behind them.

It happened one day, as Bo-Peep did stray
 Unto a meadow hard by:
There she espied their tails side by side,
 All hung on a tree to dry.

Then she heaved a sigh, and wiped her eye,
 And ran o'er hill and dale-o,
And tried what she could, as a shepherdess should,
 To tack to each sheep its tail-o.

Hickety, Pickety, my black hen,
She lays eggs for gentlemen;
Sometimes nine, sometimes ten—
Hickety, Pickety, my black hen.

Illustration by Berta and Elmer Hader

Illustration by C. B. Falls

There was a crooked man, and he went a crooked mile,
He found a crooked sixpence against a crooked stile:
He bought a crooked cat, which caught a crooked mouse,
And they all lived together in a crooked little house.

Illustration by C. B. Falls

Daffy-Down-Dilly has come up to town,
In a yellow petticoat, and a green gown.

27

Jack Sprat could eat no fat,
   His wife could eat no lean,
And so between them both, you see,
   They licked the platter clean.

Jack ate all the lean,
   His wife ate all the fat,
The bone they picked it clean,
   Then gave it to the cat.

Bow-wow, says the dog;
   Mew, mew, says the cat;
Grunt, grunt, goes the hog;
   And squeak, goes the rat.

Tu-whu, says the owl;
   Caw, caw, says the crow;
Quack, quack, says the duck;
   And moo, says the cow.

Illustrations from drawings by Charles Folkard

28

Three blind mice, see how they run!
   They all ran after the farmer's wife,
Who cut off their tails with the carving-knife;
   Did you ever see such a thing in your life
     As three blind mice?

Humpty Dumpty
  sat on a wall,
Humpty Dumpty
  had a great fall;
All the king's horses
  and all the king's men
Cannot put Humpty
  Dumpty together again.

Illustrations from drawings by Charles Folkard

I had a little nut tree, nothing would it bear
But a silver nutmeg and a golden pear;
The King of Spain's daughter came to visit me,
All on account of my little nut tree.

Illustrations by Berta and Elmer Hader

Barber, barber,
shave a pig,
How many hairs will
make a wig?
Four and twenty,
that's enough.
Give the barber a
pinch of snuff.

Little Tommy Tucker
  Sang for his supper.
What shall he eat?
  White bread and butter.

How shall he cut it
  Without e'er a knife?
How shall he marry
  Without e'er a wife?

Illustrations by Berta and Elmer Hader

Jack and Jill
  went up the hill
To fetch a pail
  of water;
Jack fell down and
  broke his crown
And Jill came
  tumbling after.

Illustration by C. Lovat Fraser

Old Mother Hubbard went to the cupboard,
To get her poor dog a bone;
But when she got there the cupboard was bare,
And so the poor dog had none.

She went to the barber's to buy him a wig;
When she came back he was dancing a jig.
"Oh, you dear merry Grig! how nicely you're prancing!"
Then she held up the wig, and he began dancing.

She went to the fruiterer's to buy him some fruit;
When she came back he was playing the flute.
"Oh, you musical dog! you surely can speak:
Come sing me a song"—and he set up a squeak.

The dog he cut capers and turned out his toes;
'Twill soon cure the vapors he such attitude shows.
The dame made a curtsey, the dog made a bow;
The dame said, "Your servant"; the dog said, "Bow-wow!"

Simple Simon met a pieman
    Going to the fair;
Says Simple Simon to the pieman,
    "Let me taste your ware."

Says the pieman to Simple Simon,
    "Show me first your penny";
Says Simple Simon to the pieman,
    "Indeed I have not any."

Simple Simon went a-fishing
    For to catch a whale;
All the water he had got
    Was in his mother's pail.

Illustration by C. Lovat Fraser

Illustration by Berta and Elmer Hader

Little Robin Redbreast
    sat upon a tree,
Up went Pussycat and
    down went he;
Down came Pussycat
    and away Robin ran;
Says little Robin Redbreast:
    "Catch me if you can!"

Little Robin Redbreast
    jumped upon a wall;
Pussycat jumped after him,
    and almost had a fall.
Little Robin chirped and sang,
    and what did Pussy say?
Pussycat said "Mew" and
    Robin jumped away.

Brownie Year Book

PALMER COX

Illustrations by Palmer Cox

JANUARY

Throughout the year the Brownie Band
   For pleasure travels o'er the land:
   In January, when the snow
   Lies on the hills and valleys low,
   And from the north the chilly breeze
   Comes whistling through the naked trees,
   Upon toboggans long they ride
   For hours down the mountain side,
   Until the broadening light of day
   Compels them all to quit their play.

PALMER COX

FEBRUARY

When ice has coated
   lake and stream,
And skating is
   the common theme
Of which the youthful
   people speak
By night and day
   from week to week;
The Brownies
   are not left behind
But manage well
   their sport to find.

MARCH

When March arrives
   with sweeping gales
That bend the trees
   and split the sails,
And people have
   a lively chase
For hats that will not
   keep their place,
Then to the field
   the Brownies bring
Their home-made kites
   and balls of string.

APRIL

When fall the drenching
    April showers
To start the grass
    and bud the flowers,
Each cunning Brownie
    must be spry
To keep his scanty
    garments dry;
For they know where
    in wood or field
The friendly tree
    will shelter yield.

MAY

When flowers spring
    on every side,
In gardens fair,
    and meadows wide,
The Brownies quickly
    take the chance
That's offered
    for a merry dance.
They place the tapering
    pole upright
To which they fasten
    ribbons bright.

JUNE

In sunny June when skies are bright,
    And woods and water do invite
    The people from their tasks away
    To sport themselves by night and day,
    The Brownies are not slow to take
    A ride upon a pleasant lake,
    Or follow fast by rock and tree
    A stream that hastens to the sea;
    Though dangers may the band surround
    Before the night has circled round.

JULY

When July has
    its visits paid,
And trees afford
    a grateful shade,
And stretched across
    from tree to tree
The hammocks swing
    above the lea,
The Brownies
    are not slow to find
Where people
    through the day reclined.

AUGUST

To swim and sport
    in August mild
Though water may be
    calm or wild,
Gives pleasure
    to the Brownie band
Who haste at night
    to reach the strand,
That they may plunge
    into the wave
To swim and dive,
    or like a stave,
To float on water,
    to and fro.

SEPTEMBER

When fish in lake
   and river bright
At tempting bait
   are prone to bite,
And people from
   the rock or boat,
Watch bobbing corks
   that drifting float;
The Brownies
   also take delight,
And spend the mild
   September night
In landing fish
   of every kind.

OCTOBER

When woods are tinged
   with all the glow
October on the woods
   can throw,
And game is plenty
   on the tree
And every kind
   of weapon free;
The Brownies
   imitate the way
Mankind does creep
   upon the prey.

NOVEMBER

November's winds
    are keen and cold,
As Brownies know
    who roam the wold
And have no home
    to which to run
When they have had
    their night of fun,
But cunning hands
    are never slow
To build a fire
    of ruddy glow.

DECEMBER

When comes the month
    that calls to mind
The day so dear
    to all mankind,
The people living,
    West or East,
Begin to talk
    about the feast
That will be spread
    for young and old,
While songs are sung
    and stories told.

Two Happy Little Bears

THORNTON W. BURGESS

Illustrations by Phoebe Erickson

Teeny Bear and Weeny Bear were the liveliest babies in the Green Forest, and Mother Bear was sure they were the most mischievous. There was no guessing what they would do next. They often disobeyed their mother although they didn't mean to disobey. They would just forget. There is nothing so easy to do as to forget.

This morning Mother Bear had sent the cubs up in a tree and told them to stay in it until she came back. At first the cubs didn't mind staying up in that tree. Climbing about in a big tree was fun, and this was a big tree. They tried to see which could climb the highest. They chased each other up and down.

When they grew tired of playing, each curled up in a crotch of the tree for a nap. But it was a short nap. It was the scolding of Chatterer the Red Squirrel that woke them. He was in the next tree calling them names and shrieking at them as only he can. He is the

43

noisiest, sauciest person in all the Green Forest.

"It would be fun to catch that fellow and stop his noise," said Teeny Bear.

"Come on," cried Weeny Bear.

They forgot what Mother Bear had said about staying up in that tree. They scrambled down to the ground, ran over to the other tree and tried to see who could climb it fastest. When they reached the place where Chatterer had been, he wasn't there. He had run out to the tip of a long limb, made a flying leap to the tip of a limb of another tree, caught it and pulled himself up and now was making fun of the two little bears.

"He isn't worth catching," said Teeny Bear. "Let's go back."

So they scrambled down to the ground. "Let's go find Mother," said Weeny Bear, forgetting that they were supposed to stay up in a tree.

Off they started to look for Mother Bear. They followed her footprints for a little way, then lost them and just wandered about. It was just their good luck that at last they found her. They heard a growling and grumbling and other sounds a little way off. They stole toward those sounds and at last, peeping out from behind a big stump, they saw Mother Bear. She was part way up a dead tree.

At first they couldn't make out what she was doing. She seemed to be fighting that tree. She was clinging to it with her feet and one paw. With the big claws of the other paw she was trying to tear that tree apart. She had made an opening big enough to get her paw in. She would pull out a pawful of something and eat it. Then she would lick that paw off, all the time grunting with pleasure. She would strike at something the cubs couldn't see and snarl and growl, then plunge her paw into that hole again, or try to tear it bigger. And all the time there was a humming sound, an angry hum.

The two little bears moved nearer and nearer until they were at the foot of that dead tree almost under Mother Bear. Just then she tore out a big piece of that tree and it fell almost on Weeny Bear. Clinging to it was a big piece of honeycomb dripping with golden honey. The two little bears sniffed at it. Then they tasted. Right then and there Teeny Bear and Weeny Bear forgot everything but this wonderful new food. Never had they tasted anything like its sweetness. A Bee stung Weeny on the nose. She didn't mind. Another stung Teeny. He didn't even know it. Mother Bear tore out more comb and dropped it. In no time at all they were the stickiest, sweetest, happiest little bears in all the Great World. They were too happy to even remember that they had disobeyed and might be spanked. But they weren't spanked. You see Mother Bear was just as happy with all that sweetness as they were.

The Tale of Peter Rabbit

BEATRIX POTTER

Illustrations by Beatrix Potter

Once upon a time there were four little Rabbits, and their names were—

Flopsy,
Mopsy,
Cotton-tail,
and Peter.

They lived with their Mother in a sand-bank, underneath the root of a very big fir-tree.

"Now, my dears," said old Mrs. Rabbit one morning, "you may go into the fields or down the lane, but don't go into Mr. McGregor's garden: your Father had an accident there; he was put in a pie by Mrs. McGregor.

"Now run along, and don't get into mischief. I am going out."

Then old Mrs. Rabbit took a basket and her umbrella, and went through the wood to the baker's. She bought a loaf of brown bread and five currant buns.

Flopsy, Mopsy, and Cotton-tail, who were good little bunnies, went down the lane to gather blackberries.

But Peter, who was very naughty, ran straight away to Mr. McGregor's garden, and squeezed under the gate!

First he ate some lettuces and some French beans; and then he ate some radishes.

And then, feeling rather sick, he went to look for some parsley.

But round the end of a cucumber frame, whom should he meet but Mr. McGregor!

Mr. McGregor was on his hands

and knees planting out young cabbages, but he jumped up and ran after Peter, waving a rake and calling out, "Stop thief!"

Peter was most dreadfully frightened; he rushed all over the garden, for he had forgotten the way back to the gate.

He lost one of his shoes among the cabbages, and the other shoe amongst the potatoes.

After losing them, he ran on four legs and went faster, so that I think he might have got away altogether if he had not unfortunately run into a gooseberry net, and got caught by the large buttons on his jacket. It was a blue jacket with brass buttons, quite new.

Peter gave himself up for lost, and shed big tears; but his sobs were overheard by some friendly sparrows, who flew to him in great excitement, and implored him to exert himself.

Mr. McGregor came up with a sieve, which he intended to pop upon the top of Peter; but Peter wriggled out just in time, leaving his jacket behind him.

And rushed into the tool-shed, and jumped into a can. It would have been a beautiful thing to hide in, if it had not had so much water in it.

Mr. McGregor was quite sure that Peter was somewhere in the

tool-shed, perhaps hidden underneath a flower-pot. He began to turn them over carefully, looking under each.

Presently Peter sneezed—"Kertyschoo!" Mr. McGregor was after him in no time,

And tried to put his foot upon Peter, who jumped out of a window, upsetting three plants. The window was too small for Mr. McGregor, and he was tired of running after Peter. He went back to his work.

Peter sat down to rest; he was out of breath and trembling with fright, and he had not the least idea which way to go. Also he was very damp with sitting in that can.

After a time he began to wander about, going lippity—lippity—not very fast, and looking all around.

He found a door in a wall; but it was locked, and there was no room for a fat little rabbit to squeeze underneath.

An old mouse was running in and out over the stone doorstep, carrying peas and beans to her family in the wood. Peter asked her the way to the gate, but she had such a large pea in her mouth that she could not answer. She only shook her head at him. Peter began to cry.

Then he tried to find his way straight across the garden, but he became more and more puzzled. Presently, he came to a pond where Mr. McGregor filled his water-cans. A white cat was staring at some gold-fish; she sat very, very still, but now and then the tip of her tail twitched as if it were alive. Peter thought it best to go away without speaking to her; he had heard about cats from his cousin, little Benjamin Bunny.

He went back towards the tool-shed, but suddenly, quite close to him, he heard the noise of a hoe—scr-r-ritch, scratch, scratch, scritch. Peter scuttered underneath the bushes. But presently, as nothing happened, he came out, and climbed upon a wheelbarrow, and peeped over. The first thing he saw was Mr. McGregor hoeing on-ions. His back was turned towards Peter, and beyond him was the gate!

Peter got down very quietly off the wheelbarrow, and started running as fast as he could go, along a straight walk behind some black-currant bushes.

Mr. McGregor caught sight of him at the corner, but Peter did not care. He slipped underneath the gate, and was safe at last in the wood outside the garden.

Mr. McGregor hung up the little jacket and the shoes for a scare-crow to frighten the blackbirds.

Peter never stopped running or looked behind him till he got home to the big fir-tree.

He was so tired that he flopped down upon the nice soft sand on the floor of the rabbit-hole, and shut his eyes. His mother was busy cooking; she wondered what he had done with his clothes. It was the second little jacket and pair of shoes that Peter had lost in a fort-night!

I am sorry to say that Peter was not very well during the evening.

His mother put him to bed, and made some camomile tea; and she gave a dose of it to Peter!

"One table-spoonful to be taken at bed-time."

But Flopsy, Mopsy, and Cotton-tail had bread and milk and black-berries, for supper.

Pelle's New Suit

ELSA BESKOW

Illustrations by Elsa Beskow

There was once a little Swedish boy whose name was Pelle. Now, Pelle had a lamb which was all his own and which he took care of all by himself.

The lamb grew and Pelle grew. And the lamb's wool grew longer and longer, but Pelle's coat only grew shorter!

One day Pelle took a pair of shears and cut off all the lamb's wool. Then he took the wool to his grandmother and said: "Granny dear, please card this wool for me!"

"That I will, my dear," said his grandmother, "if you will pull the weeds in my carrot patch for me."

So Pelle pulled the weeds in Granny's carrot patch and Granny carded Pelle's wool.

Then Pelle went to his other grandmother and said: "Grandmother dear, please spin this wool into yarn for me!"

"That will I gladly do, my dear,"

said his grandmother, "if while I am spinning it you will tend my cows for me."

And so Pelle tended Grandmother's cows and Grandmother spun Pelle's yarn.

Then Pelle went to a neighbor who was a painter and asked him for some paint with which to color his yarn.

"What a silly little boy you are!" laughed the painter. "My paint is not what you want to color your wool. But if you will row over to the store to get a bottle of turpentine for me, you may buy yourself some dye out of the change from the shilling."

So Pelle rowed over to the store and bought a bottle of turpentine for the painter, and bought for himself a large sack of blue dye out of the change from the shilling.

Then he dyed his wool himself until it was all, all blue.

And then Pelle went to his mother and said: "Mother dear, please weave this yarn into cloth for me."

"That will I gladly do," said his mother, "if you will take care of your little sister for me."

So Pelle took good care of his little sister, and Mother wove the wool into cloth.

Then Pelle went to the tailor: "Dear Mr. Tailor, please make a suit for me out of this cloth."

"Is that what you want, you little rascal?" said the tailor. "Indeed I will, if you will rake my hay and bring in my wood and feed my pigs for me."

So Pelle raked the tailor's hay and fed his pigs.

And then he carried in all the wood. And the tailor had Pelle's suit ready that very Saturday evening.

And on Sunday morning Pelle put on his new suit and went to his lamb and said: "Thank you very much for my new suit, little lamb."

"Ba-a-ah," said the lamb, and it sounded almost as if the lamb were laughing.

"Thank you very much for my new suit, little lamb"

The Poppy Seed Cakes

MARGERY CLARK

ERMINKA AND THE CRATE OF CHICKENS[1]

"Erminka, I need eighteen duck eggs. I think I shall go to market for them," said Erminka's mother.

"May I go with you? May I carry the little basket? And may I carry some eggs? And oh, Mother!" said Erminka, "may I wear the red topped boots?"

"Will you be very careful, Er-minka, and not upset anything, if you wear the red topped boots?"

"I will be careful, Mother, if I may wear my red topped boots," said Erminka. "I look so beautiful in my nice red topped boots."

"Your brother's red topped boots," reminded Erminka's mother.

"Well, Erminka," said Erminka's

[1] From "The Poppy Seed Cakes," by Margery Clark, illustrated by Maude and Miska Petersham

mother, as she locked the kitchen door. "I am ready to go to market now. I think I will buy some gooseberries, too. Then we can have gooseberry tarts."

"May I make some tarts, too, and have a tea-party?" Erminka asked.

"Yes, indeed!" said her mother.

Erminka and her mother started for the market. They went down a hill and across the tracks and up two blocks until they came to a big red shed.

It was the market. Inside, the farmers and the farmers' wives were selling vegetables and fruit and chickens and flowers and one farmer had five little white pigs for sale.

Erminka's mother saw many friends among the farmers' wives.

"How do you do, Mrs. Smith?" she would say. "Have you any sweet butter this morning?"

"How do you do, Mrs. Gray? Have you any nice fresh buttermilk?"

"Good morning, Mrs. Popolovski! Have you any nice little cabbages today?"

Erminka grew tired of visiting with all these friends. She wandered off by herself.

She saw a crate full of chickens. "You nice chickens!" she said. "Wouldn't you like to see my red topped boots?"

"Yes, indeed!" said the chickens.

Erminka opened the door of the crate with the toe of her red topped boot.

As soon as the crate was open, five white chickens flew past Erminka. The market was upset. Everyone stopped buying apples and selling eggs and ran after the chickens.

The chickens flew wildly about the market in all directions. One chicken fluttered out of the front door of the market and down the street. Only a baby chicken was left in the crate.

The market master and the farmers caught the chickens and put them back in the crate.

"I did not mean to let the chickens run away, Mother," said Erminka. "But it looked so easy to open the door of the crate with the toe of my red topped boot."

"Your brother's red topped boot," reminded Erminka's mother.

In the evening after supper Erminka's mother said to Erminka's father, "What do you think Erminka did to-day at the market?"

"I do not know," said Erminka's father, as he puffed on his long pipe. "Had it something to do with the red topped boots?"

"Yes!" said Erminka and her mother at the same time. "How did you guess so quickly?"

LITTLE

Dorothy Aldis

Illustration by Helen D. Jameson

I am the sister of him
And he is my brother.
He is too little for us
To talk to each other.

So every morning I show him
My doll and my book;
But every morning he still is
Too little to look.

GROWN UP

Dorothy Aldis

Illustration by Helen D. Jameson

I'm growing up, my mother says—
Today she said I'd grown;
The reason why is this: Now I
Can do things all alone.

And though I'm glad that I don't need
Someone to brush my hair
And wash my hands and face and button
Buttons everywhere,

Although I'm very glad indeed
To help myself instead,
I hope that I won't have to try
To TUCK MYSELF IN BED.

NAUGHTY SOAP SONG

Dorothy Aldis

Illustration by Helen D. Jameson

Just when I'm ready to
Start on my ears,
That is the time that my
Soap disappears.

It jumps from my fingers and
Slithers and slides
Down to the end of the
Tub, where it hides.

And acts in a most diso-
Bedient way
AND THAT'S WHY MY SOAP'S GROWING
THINNER EACH DAY.

MERRY PHILLIS

Kate Greenaway

Illustration by Kate Greenaway

You see, merry Phillis, that dear little maid,
    Has invited Belinda to tea;
Her nice little garden is shaded by trees—
    What pleasanter place could there be?

There's a cake full of plums, there are strawberries too,
    And the table is set on the green;
I'm fond of a carpet all daisies and grass—
    Could a prettier picture be seen?

A blackbird (yes, blackbirds delight in warm weather,)
    Is flitting from yonder high spray;
He sees the two little ones talking together—
    No wonder the blackbird is gay!

THE END

A. A. Milne

When I was One,
I had just begun.

When I was Two,
I was nearly new.

When I was Three,
I was hardly Me.

When I was Four,
I was not much more.

When I was Five,
I was just alive.

But now I am Six, I'm as clever as clever.
So I think I'll be six now for ever and ever.

HALFWAY DOWN

A. A. Milne

Halfway down the stairs
Is a stair
Where I sit.
There isn't any
Other stair
Quite like
It.
I'm not at the bottom,
I'm not at the top;
So this is the stair
Where
I always
Stop.

Halfway up the stairs
Isn't up,
And isn't down.
It isn't in the nursery,
It isn't in the town.
And all sorts of funny thoughts
Run round my head:
"It isn't really
Anywhere!
It's somewhere else
Instead!"

Illustrations by Ernest H. Shepard

THE ENGINEER

A. A. Milne

Let it rain!
Who cares?
I've a train
Upstairs,
With a brake
Which I make
From a string
Sort of thing,
Which works
In jerks,
'Cos it drops
In the spring,
Which stops
With the string,
And the wheels
All stick
So quick
That it feels
Like a thing
That you make
With a brake,
Not string. . . .

So that's what I make,
When the day's all wet.
It's a good sort of brake
But it hasn't worked yet.

HOPPITY

A. A. Milne

Christopher Robin goes
Hoppity, hoppity,
Hoppity, hoppity, hop.
Whenever I tell him
Politely to stop it, he
Says he can't possibly stop.

If he stopped hopping,
He couldn't go anywhere,
Poor little Christopher
Couldn't go anywhere . . .
That's why he *always* goes
Hoppity, hoppity,
Hoppity,
Hoppity,
Hop.

Illustrations by Ernest H. Shepard

FIVE LITTLE SISTERS   *Kate Greenaway*

Five little sisters walking in a row;
Now, isn't that the best way for little girls to go?
Each had a round hat, each had a muff,
And each had a new pelisse of soft green stuff.

Five little marigolds standing in a row;
Now, isn't that the best way for marigolds to grow?
Each with a green stalk, and all the five had got
A bright yellow flower, and a new red pot.

SCHOOL IS OVER   *Kate Greenaway*

School is over,
    Oh, what fun!
Lessons finished,
    Play begun.
Who'll run fastest,
    You or I?
Who'll laugh loudest?
    Let us try.

58

IN A GO-CART
Kate Greenaway

In go-cart so tiny
   My sister I drew;
And I've promised to draw her
   The wide world through.

We have not yet started—
   I own it with sorrow—
Because our trip's always
   Put off till to-morrow.

IT WAS TOMMY
Kate Greenaway

It was Tommy who said,
   "The sweet spring-time is come;
I see the birds flit,
   And I hear the bees hum.

"Oho! Mister Lark,
   Up aloft in the sky,
Now, which is the happiest—
   Is it you, sir, or I?"

59

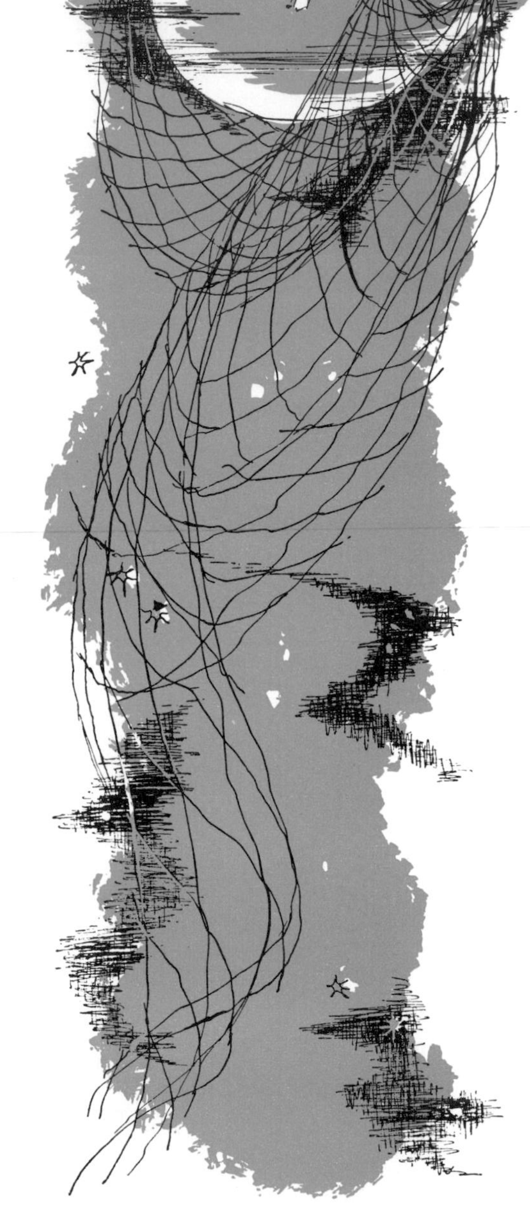

WYNKEN, BLYNKEN, AND NOD

Eugene Field

Illustrations by Meg Wohlberg

Wynken, Blynken, and Nod one night
   Sailed off in a wooden shoe,—
Sailed on a river of crystal light
   Into a sea of dew.
"Where are you going, and what do you wish?"
   The old moon asked the three.
"We have come to fish for the herring fish
   That live in this beautiful sea;
Nets of silver and gold have we!"
        Said Wynken,
        Blynken,
        And Nod.

The old moon laughed and sang a song,
   As they rocked in the wooden shoe;
And the wind that sped them all night long
   Ruffled the waves of dew.
The little stars were the herring fish
   That lived in that beautiful sea—
"Now cast your nets wherever you wish,—
   Never afeard are we!"
So cried the stars to the fishermen three,
        Wynken,
        Blynken,
        And Nod.

All night long their nets they threw
    To the stars in the twinkling foam,—
Then down from the skies came the wooden shoe,
    Bringing the fishermen home:
'Twas all so pretty a sail, it seemed
    As if it could not be;
And some folk thought 'twas a dream they'd dreamed
    Of sailing that beautiful sea;
But I shall name you the fishermen three:
            Wynken,
            Blynken,
            And Nod.

Wynken and Blynken are two little eyes,
    And Nod is a little head,
And the wooden shoe that sailed the skies
    Is a wee one's trundle-bed;
So shut your eyes while Mother sings
    Of wonderful sights that be,
And you shall see the beautiful things
    As you rock in the misty sea
Where the old shoe rocked the fishermen three:—
            Wynken,
            Blynken,
            And Nod.

MUD

Polly Chase Boyden

Illustration by Willy Pogany

Mud is very nice to feel
    All squishy-squash between the toes!
I'd rather wade in wiggly mud
    Than smell a yellow rose.

ANIMAL CRACKERS

Christopher Morley

Illustration by John Hull

Animal crackers, and cocoa to drink,
That is the finest of suppers, I think;
When I'm grown up and can have what I please
I think I shall always insist upon these.

What do *you* choose when you're offered a treat?
When Mother says, "What would you like best to eat?"
Is it waffles and syrup, or cinnamon toast?
It's cocoa and animals that *I* love the most!

The kitchen's the cosiest place that I know:
The kettle is singing, the stove is aglow,
And there in the twilight, how jolly to see
The cocoa and animals waiting for me.

Daddy and Mother dine later in state,
With Mary to cook for them, Susan to wait;
But they don't have nearly as much fun as I
Who eat in the kitchen with Nurse standing by;
And Daddy once said he would like to be me
Having cocoa and animals once more for tea!

THE SUGARPLUM TREE

Eugene Field

Illustration by Meg Wohlberg

Have you ever heard of the Sugarplum Tree?
   'Tis a marvel of great renown!
It blooms on the shore of the Lollipop Sea
   In the garden of Shut-Eye Town;
The fruit that it bears is so wondrously sweet
   (As those who have tasted it say)
That good little children have only to eat
   Of that fruit to be happy next day.

When you've got to the tree, you would have a hard time
   To capture the fruit which I sing;
The tree is so tall that no person could climb
   To the boughs where the sugarplums swing!
But up in that tree sits a chocolate cat,
   And a gingerbread dog prowls below—
And this is the way you contrive to get at
   Those sugarplums tempting you so:

You say but the word to that gingerbread dog
   And he barks with such terrible zest
That the chocolate cat is at once all agog,
   As her swelling proportions attest.
And the chocolate cat goes cavorting around
   From this leafy limb unto that,
And the sugarplums tumble, of course, to the ground—
   Hurrah for that chocolate cat!

There are marshmallows, gumdrops, and peppermint canes,
   With stripings of scarlet or gold,
And you carry away of the treasure that rains
   As much as your apron can hold!
So come, little child, cuddle closer to me
   In your dainty white nightcap and gown,
And I'll rock you away to that Sugarplum Tree
   In the garden of Shut-Eye Town.

THE GOOPS [1]

Gelett Burgess

The Goops they lick their fingers,
    And the Goops they lick their knives;
They spill their broth on the tablecloth—
    Oh, they lead disgusting lives!
The Goops they talk while eating,
    And loud and fast they chew;
And that is why I'm glad that I
    Am not a Goop—are you?

[1] From "Goops and How to Be Them," by Gelett Burgess

Henny-Penny[1]

One day Henny-penny was picking up corn in the rickyard when—whack!—an acorn hit her upon the head. "Goodness gracious me!" said Henny-penny; "the sky's a-going to fall; I must go and tell the King."

So she went along, and she went along, and she went along till she met Cocky-locky. "Where are you going, Henny-penny?" says Cocky-locky. "Oh! I'm going to tell the King the sky's a-falling," says Henny-penny. "May I come with you?" says Cocky-locky. "Cer-tainly," says Henny-penny. So Henny-penny and Cocky-locky went to tell the King the sky was falling.

They went along, and they went along, and they went along, till they met Ducky-daddles. "Where are you going to, Henny-penny and Cocky-locky?" says Ducky-dad-dles. "Oh! we're going to tell the King the sky's a-falling," said Hen-ny-penny and Cocky-locky. "May I come with you?" says Ducky-daddles. "Certainly," said Henny-penny and Cocky-locky. So Hen-ny-penny, Cocky-locky, and Ducky-daddles went to tell the King the sky was a-falling.

So they went along, and they

[1] From "English Fairy Tales," retold by Flora Annie Steel, illustrated by Arthur Rackham

went along, and they went along, till they met Goosey-poosey. "Where are you going to, Henny-penny, Cocky-locky, and Ducky-daddles?" said Goosey-poosey. "Oh! we're going to tell the King the sky's a-falling," said Henny-penny and Cocky-locky and Ducky-daddles. "May I come with you?" said Goosey-poosey. "Certainly," said Henny-penny, Cocky-locky, and Ducky-daddles. So Henny-penny, Cocky-locky, Ducky-daddles, and Goosey-poosey went to tell the King the sky was a-falling.

So they went along, and they went along, and they went along, till they met Turkey-lurkey. "Where are you going, Henny-penny, Cocky-locky, Ducky-daddles, and Goosey-poosey?" says Turkey-lurkey. "Oh! we're going to tell the King the sky's a-falling," said Henny-penny, Cocky-locky, Ducky-daddles, and Goosey-poosey. "May I come with you, Henny-penny, Cocky-locky, Ducky-

daddles, and Goosey-poosey?" said Turkey-lurkey. "Oh, certainly, Turkey-lurkey," and Henny-penny, Cocky-locky, Ducky-daddles, and Goosey-poosey. So Henny-penny, Cocky-locky, Ducky-daddles, Goosey-poosey, and Turkey-lurkey all went to tell the King the sky was a-falling.

So they went along, and they went along, and they went along, till they met Foxy-woxy, and Foxy-woxy said to Henny-penny, Cocky-locky, Ducky-daddles, Goosey-poosey, and Turkey-lurkey, "Where are you going, Henny-penny, Cocky-locky, Ducky-daddles, Goosey-poosey, and Turkey-lurkey?" And Henny-penny, Cocky-locky, Ducky-daddles, Goosey-poosey, and Turkey-lurkey said to Foxy-woxy, "We're going to tell the King the sky's a-falling." "Oh! but this is not the way to the King, Henny-penny, Cocky-locky, Ducky-daddles, Goosey-poosey, and Turkey-lurkey," says Foxy-woxy; "I know the proper way;

shall I show it to you?" "Oh, certainly, Foxy-woxy," said Henny-penny, Cocky-locky, Ducky-daddles, Goosey-poosey, and Turkey-lurkey. So Henny-penny, Cocky-locky, Ducky-daddles, Goosey-poosey, Turkey-lurkey, and Foxy-woxy all went to tell the King the sky was a-falling. So they went along, and they went along, and they went along, till they came to a narrow and dark hole. Now this was the door of Foxy-woxy's burrow. But Foxy-woxy said to Henny-penny, Cocky-locky, Ducky-daddles, Goosey-poosey, and Turkey-lurkey, "This is the short cut to the King's palace: you'll soon get there if you follow me. I will go first and you come after, Henny-penny, Cocky-locky, Ducky-daddles, Goosey-poosey, and Turkey-lurkey." "Why of course, certainly, without doubt, why not?" said Henny-penny, Cocky-locky, Ducky-daddles, Goosey-poosey, and Turkey-lurkey.

So Foxy-woxy went into his burrow, and turned to wait for Henny-penny, Cocky-locky, Ducky-daddles, Goosey-poosey, and Turkey-lurkey. Now Turkey-lurkey was the first to go into the burrow. He hadn't got far when—

"Hrumph!"

Foxy-woxy snapped off Turkey-lurkey's head and threw his body over his left shoulder. Then Goosey-poosey went in, and—

"Hrumph!"

Off went her head and Goosey-poosey was thrown beside Turkey-lurkey. Then Ducky-daddles waddled down, and—

"Hrumph!"

Foxy-woxy had snapped off Ducky-daddles' head and Ducky-daddles was thrown alongside Turkey-lurkey and Goosey-poosey. Then Cocky-locky strutted down into the burrow and he hadn't gone far when—

"Hrumph!"

But Cocky-locky *will* always crow whether you want him to do so or not, and so he had just time for one "Cock-a-doo-dle-d—" before he went to join Turkey-lurkey, Goosey-poosey, and Ducky-daddles over Foxy-woxy's shoulder.

Now when Henny-penny, who had just got into the dark burrow, heard Cocky-locky crow, she said to herself:

"My goodness! it must be dawn. Time for me to lay my egg."

So she turned round and bustled off to her nest; so she escaped, but she never told the King the sky was falling!

The Story of the
Three Bears[1]

Once upon a time there were three Bears, who lived together in a house of their own, in a wood. One of them was a Little Wee Bear, and one was a Middle-sized Bear, and the other was a Great Big Bear. They had each a bowl for their porridge; a little bowl for the Little Wee Bear; and a middle-sized bowl for the Middle-sized Bear; and a great bowl for the Great Big Bear. And they had each a chair to sit in; a little chair for the Little Wee Bear; and a middle-sized chair for the Middle-sized Bear; and a great chair for the Great Big Bear. And they had each a bed to sleep in; a little bed for the Little Wee Bear;

[1] "From English Fairy Tales," retold by Flora Annie Steel. Illustrations from drawings by Walter Crane

and a middle-sized bed for the Middle-sized Bear; and a great bed for the Great Big Bear.

One day, after they had made the porridge for their breakfast, and poured it into their porridge-bowls, they walked out into the wood while the porridge was cooling, that they might not burn their mouths by beginning too soon, for they were polite, well-brought-up Bears. And while they were away a little girl called Goldilocks, who lived at the other side of the wood and had been sent on an errand by her mother, passed by the house, and looked in at the window. And

then she peeped in at the keyhole, for she was not at all a well-brought-up little girl. Then seeing nobody in the house she lifted the latch. The door was not fastened, because the Bears were good Bears, who did nobody any harm, and never suspected that anybody would harm them. So Goldilocks opened the door and went in; and well pleased was she when she saw the porridge on the table. If she had been a well-brought-up little girl she would have waited till the Bears came home, and then, perhaps, they would have asked her to breakfast; for they were good Bears —a little rough or so, as the manner of Bears is, but for all that very good-natured and hospitable. But she was an impudent, rude little girl, and so she set about helping herself.

First she tasted the porridge of the Great Big Bear, and that was too hot for her. Next she tasted the porridge of the Middle-sized Bear, but that was too cold for her. And then she went to the porridge of the Little Wee Bear, and tasted it, and that was neither too hot nor too cold, but just right, and she liked it so well, that she ate it all up, every bit!

Then Goldilocks, who was tired, for she had been catching butter-flies instead of running on her errand, sate down in the chair of the Great Big Bear, but that was too hard for her. And then she sate down in the chair of the Middle-sized Bear, and that was too soft for her. But when she sate down in the chair of the Little Wee Bear, that was neither too hard, nor too soft, but just right. So she seated herself in it, and there she sate till the bottom of the chair came out, and down she came, plump upon the ground; and that made her very cross, for she was a bad-tempered little girl.

Now, being determined to rest, Goldilocks went upstairs into the bedchamber in which the three Bears slept. And first she lay down upon the bed of the Great Big Bear, but that was too high at the head for her. And next she lay down upon the bed of the Middle-sized Bear, and that was too high at the foot for her. And then she lay down upon the bed of the Little Wee Bear, and that was neither too high at the head, nor at the foot, but just right. So she covered herself up comfortably, and lay there till she fell fast asleep.

By this time the Three Bears thought their porridge would be cool enough for them to eat it properly; so they came home to breakfast. Now careless Goldilocks had left the spoon of the Great Big Bear

standing in his porridge.

"Somebody has been at my porridge!"

said the Great Big Bear in his great, rough, gruff voice.

Then the Middle-sized Bear looked at his porridge and saw the spoon was standing in it too.

"Somebody has been at my porridge!"

said the Middle-sized Bear in his middle-sized voice.

Then the Little Wee Bear looked at his, and there was the spoon in the porridge-bowl, but the porridge was all gone!

"Somebody has been at my porridge, and has eaten it all up!"

said the Little Wee Bear in his little wee voice.

Upon this the Three Bears, seeing that some one had entered their house, and eaten up the Little Wee Bear's breakfast, began to look about them. Now the careless Goldilocks had not put the hard cushion straight when she rose from the chair of the Great Big Bear.

"Somebody has been sitting in my chair!"

said the Great Big Bear in his great, rough, gruff voice.

And the careless Goldilocks had squatted down the soft cushion of the Middle-sized Bear.

"Somebody has been sitting in my chair!"

said the Middle-sized Bear in his middle-sized voice.

"Somebody has been sitting in my chair, and has sate the bottom through!"

said the Little Wee Bear in his little wee voice.

Then the Three Bears thought they had better make further search in case it was a burglar, so they went upstairs into their bedchamber. Now Goldilocks had pulled the pillow of the Great Big Bear out of its place.

"Somebody has been lying in my bed!"

said the Great Big Bear in his great, rough, gruff voice.

And Goldilocks had pulled the bolster of the Middle-sized Bear out of its place.

"Somebody has been lying in my bed!"

said the Middle-sized Bear in his middle-sized voice.

But when the Little Wee Bear came to look at his bed, there was the bolster in its place!

And the pillow was in its place upon the bolster!

And upon the pillow——?

There was Goldilocks' yellow head—which was not in its place, for she had no business there.

"Somebody has been lying in my bed,— and here she is still!"

said the Little Wee Bear in his little wee voice.

Now Goldilocks had heard in her sleep the great, rough, gruff voice of the Great Big Bear; but she was so fast asleep that it was no more to her than the roaring of wind, or the rumbling of thunder. And she had heard the middle-sized voice of the Middle-sized Bear, but it was only as if she had heard some one speaking in a dream. But when she heard the little wee voice of the Little Wee Bear, it was so sharp, and so shrill, that it awakened her

at once. Up she started, and when she saw the Three Bears on one side of the bed, she tumbled herself out at the other, and ran to the window. Now the window was open, because the Bears, like good, tidy Bears, as they were, always opened their bed-chamber window when they got up in the morning. So naughty, frightened little Goldilocks jumped; and whether she broke her neck in the fall, or ran into the wood and was lost there, or found her way out of the wood and got whipped for being a bad girl and playing truant no one can say. But the Three Bears never saw anything more of her.

The Wolf and the Seven Kids[1]

There was once an old nanny goat who had seven kids, and she was just as fond of them as a mother is of her children. One day she was going into the woods to fetch some food for them, so she called them all up to her and said, "My dear children, I am going out into the woods. Beware of the wolf! If once he gets into the house, he will eat you up—skin, and hair, and all. The rascal often disguises himself, but you will know him by his rough voice and his black feet."

The kids said, "Oh, we will be very careful, dear mother. You may be quite happy about us."

Bleating tenderly, the old goat went off to her work. Before long, someone knocked at the door and cried, "Open the door, dear children! Your mother has come back and brought something for each of you."

But the kids knew quite well by the voice that it was the wolf.

"We won't open the door," they cried. "You are not our mother. She has a soft, gentle voice, but yours is rough, and we are quite sure that you are the wolf."

So he went away to a shop and bought a lump of chalk, which he ate, and it made his voice soft.

He went back, knocked at the door again, and cried, "Open the door, dear children. Your mother has come back and brought something for each of you."

But the wolf had put one of his paws on the window sill, where the kids saw it, and they cried, "We won't open the door. Our mother has not got a black foot as you have. You are the wolf."

Then the wolf ran to a baker and said, "I have bruised my foot. Please put some dough on it." And when the baker put some dough on his foot, he ran to the miller and said, "Strew some flour on my foot."

The miller thought, "The old wolf is going to take somebody in," and refused.

But the wolf said, "If you don't do it, I will eat you up." So the miller was frightened, and whitened his paws. People are like that, you know.

Now the wretch went for the third time to the door, and knocked and said, "Open the door, children. Your dear mother has come home and has brought something for each of you out of the wood."

The kids cried, "Show us your feet first, so that we may be sure you are our mother." He put his

[1] A fairy tale by the Brothers Grimm.   Illustration by Art Seiden

paws on the window sill, and when they saw that they were white they believed all he said and opened the door.

Alas, it was the wolf who walked in. They were terrified and tried to hide themselves. One ran under the table, the second jumped into bed, the third into the oven. The fourth ran into the kitchen, the fifth got into the cupboard, the sixth into the washtub, and the seventh hid in the tall clockcase. But the wolf found them all but one and made short work of them. He swallowed one after the other, except the youngest one in the clockcase, whom he did not find. When he had satisfied his appetite, he took himself off and lay down in a meadow outside, where he soon fell asleep.

Not long afterwards the old nanny goat came back from the woods. Oh, what a terrible sight met her eyes! The house door was wide open. Tables, chairs, and benches were overturned. The washing bowl was smashed to atoms, the covers and pillows torn from the bed. She searched all over the house for her children, but nowhere were they to be found. She called them by name, one by one, but no one answered.

At last when she came to the youngest, a tiny voice cried, "I am here, dear mother, hidden in the clockcase."

She brought him out and he told her that the wolf had come and eaten all the others. You may imagine how she wept over her children.

At last in her grief she went out, and the youngest kid ran by her side. When they went into the meadow, there lay the wolf under a tree, making the branches shake with his snores. They examined him from every side, and they could plainly see movements within his distended body.

"Ah, heavens!" thought the goat, "is it possible that my poor children, whom he ate for his supper, should be still alive?"

She sent the kid running to the house to fetch scissors, needles, and thread. Then she cut a hole in the monster's side, and hardly had she begun when a kid popped out its head. And as soon as the hole was big enough, all six jumped out, one after the other—all alive and without having suffered the least injury, for in his greed the monster had swallowed them whole. You may imagine the mother's joy! She hugged them and skipped about like a tailor on his wedding day.

At last she said, "Go fetch some stones, and we will fill up the brute's body while he is asleep."

Then the seven kids brought a lot of stones as fast as they could carry them, and stuffed the wolf with them till he could hold no more. The old mother quickly sewed him up, without his having noticed anything or even moved.

At last when the wolf had had his sleep out he got up, and as the stones made him feel very thirsty he wanted to go to a spring to drink. But as soon as he moved, the stones began to roll about and rattle inside him. Then he cried:

"What's the rumbling and tumbling
That sets my stomach grumbling?
I thought 'twas six kids, flesh and
bones,
Now I find it's nought but rolling
stones."

When he reached the spring and stooped over the water to drink, the heavy stones dragged him down, and he was drowned miserably. When the seven kids saw what had happened, they came running up and cried aloud, "The wolf is dead! The wolf is dead!" And they and their mother capered and danced around the spring in their joy.

Johnny-Cake[1]

Once upon a time there was an old man, and an old woman, and a little boy. One morning the old woman made a Johnny-cake, and put it in the oven to bake. "You watch the Johnny-cake while your father and I go out to work in the garden." So the old man and the old woman went out and began to hoe potatoes, and left the little boy to tend the oven. But he didn't watch it all the time, and all of a sudden he heard a noise, and he looked up and the oven door popped open, and out of the oven jumped Johnny-cake, and went rolling along end over end, towards the open door of the house. The little boy ran to shut the door, but Johnny-cake was too quick for him and rolled through the door, down the steps, and out into the road long before the little boy could catch him. The little boy ran after him as fast as he could clip it, crying out to his father and mother, who heard the uproar, and threw down their hoes and gave chase too. But Johnny-cake outran all three a long way, and was soon out of sight, while they had to sit down, all out of breath, on a bank to rest.

On went Johnny-cake, and by-and-by he came to two well-diggers who looked up from their work and called out: "Where ye going, Johnny-cake?"

He said: "I've outrun an old man and an old woman, and a little boy, and I can outrun you too-o-o!"

"Ye can, can ye? we'll see about that," said they; and they threw down their picks and ran after him, but couldn't catch up

[1] From "English Fairy Tales," collected by Joseph Jacobs, illustrated by John D. Batton

with him, and soon they had to sit down by the roadside to rest.

On ran Johnny-cake, and by-and-by he came to two ditch-diggers who were digging a ditch. "Where ye going, Johnny-cake?" said they. He said: "I've outrun an old man, and an old woman, and a little boy, and two well-diggers, and I can outrun you too-o-o!"

"Ye can, can ye? we'll see about that!" said they; and they threw down their spades, and ran after him too. But Johnny-cake soon outstripped them also, and seeing they could never catch him, they gave up the chase and sat down to rest.

On went Johnny-cake, and by-and-by he came to a bear. The bear said: "Where are ye going, Johnny-cake?"

He said: "I've outrun an old man, and an old woman, and a little boy, and two well-diggers, and two ditch-diggers, and I can outrun you too-o-o!"

"Ye can, can ye?" growled the bear, "we'll see about that!" and trotted as fast as his legs could carry him after Johnny-cake, who never stopped to look behind him. Before long the bear was left so far behind that he saw he might as well give up the hunt first as last, so he stretched himself out by the roadside to rest.

On went Johnny-cake, and by-and-by he came to a wolf. The wolf said: "Where ye going, Johnny-cake?"

He said: "I've outrun an old man, and an old woman, and a little boy, and two well-diggers, and two ditch-diggers, and a bear, and I can outrun you too-o-o!"

"Ye can, can ye?" snarled the wolf, "we'll see about that!" And he set into a gallop after Johnny-cake, who went on and on so fast that the wolf too saw there was no hope of overtaking him, and he too lay down to rest.

On went Johnny-cake, and by-and-by he came to a fox that lay quietly in a corner of the fence. The fox called out in a sharp voice, but without getting up: "Where ye going, Johnny-cake?"

The bear stretched out to rest

78

He said: "I've outrun an old man, and an old woman, and a little boy, and two well-diggers, and two ditch diggers, a bear, and a wolf, and I can outrun you too-o-o!"

The fox said: "I can't quite hear you, Johnny-cake won't you come a little closer?" turning his head a little to one side.

Johnny-cake stopped his race for the first time, and went a little closer, and called out in a very loud voice: *"I've outrun an old man, and an old woman, and a little boy, and two well-diggers, and two ditch-diggers, and a bear, and a wolf, and I can outrun you too-o-o!"*

"Can't quite hear you; won't you come a *little* closer?" said the fox in a feeble voice, as he stretched out his neck towards Johnny-cake, and put one paw behind his ear.

Johnny-cake came up close, and leaning towards the fox screamed out: "I'VE OUTRUN AN OLD MAN, AND AN OLD WOMAN, AND A LITTLE BOY, AND TWO WELL-DIGGERS, AND TWO DITCH-DIGGERS, AND A BEAR, AND A WOLF, AND I CAN OUTRUN YOU TOO-O-O!"

"You can, can you?" yelped the fox, and he snapped up the Johnny-cake in his sharp teeth in the twinkling of an eye.

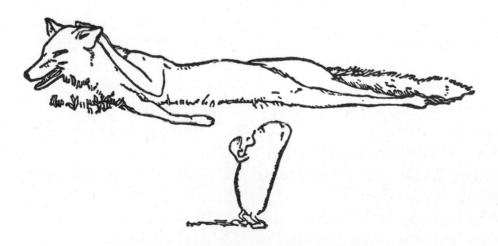

"Come a little closer," said the fox

The Story of the Three Little Pigs[1]

Once upon a time when pigs spoke rhyme
And monkeys chewed tobacco,
And hens took snuff to make them tough,
And ducks went quack, quack, quack, O!

There was an old sow with three little pigs, and as she had not enough to keep them, she sent them out to seek their fortune. The first that went off met a man with a bundle of straw, and said to him:

"Please, man, give me that straw to build me a house."

Which the man did, and the little pig built a house with it. Presently came along a wolf, and knocked at the door, and said:

"Little pig, little pig, let me come in."

To which the pig answered:

"No, no, by the hair of my chiny chin chin."

The wolf then answered to that:

"Then I'll huff, and I'll puff, and I'll blow your house in."

So he huffed, and he puffed, and he blew his house in, and ate up the little pig.

The second little pig met a man with a bundle of furze and said:

"Please, man, give me that furze to build a house."

Which the man did, and the pig built his house. Then along came the wolf, and said:

"Little pig, little pig, let me come in."

"No, no, by the hair of my chiny chin chin."

"Then I'll puff, and I'll huff, and I'll blow your house in."

So he huffed, and he puffed, and he puffed, and he huffed, and at last he blew the house down, and he ate up the little pig.

The third little pig met a man with a load of bricks, and said:

"Please, man, give me those bricks to build a house with."

So the man gave him the bricks, and he built his house with them. So the wolf came, as he did to the other little pigs, and said:

"Little pig, little pig, let me come in."

"No, no, by the hair on my chiny chin chin."

"Then I'll huff, and I'll puff, and I'll blow your house in."

Well, he huffed, and he puffed,

[1] From "English Fairy Tales," collected by Joseph Jacobs. Illustration by L. Leslie Brooke

and he huffed and he puffed, and he puffed and huffed; but he could *not* get the house down. When he found that he could not, with all his huffing and puffing, blow the house down, he said:

"Little pig, I know where there is a nice field of turnips."

"Where?" said the little pig.

"Oh, in Mr. Smith's Home-field, and if you will be ready to-morrow morning I will call for you, and we will go together, and get some for dinner."

"Very well," said the little pig, "I will be ready. What time do you mean to go?"

"Oh, at six o'clock."

Well, the little pig got up at five, and got the turnips before the wolf came (which he did about six), who said:

"Little pig, are you ready?"

The little pig said: "Ready! I have been and come back again, and got a nice potful for dinner."

The wolf felt very angry at this, but thought that he would be up to the little pig somehow or other, so he said:

"Little pig, I know where there is a nice apple tree."

"Where?" said the pig.

"Down at Merry-garden," re-

plied the wolf, "and if you will not deceive me I will come for you at five o'clock to-morrow and get some apples."

Well, the little pig bustled up the next morning at four o'clock, and went off for the apples, hoping to get back before the wolf came; but he had further to go, and had to climb the tree, so that just as he was coming down from it, he saw the wolf coming, which, as you may suppose, frightened him very much. When the wolf came up he said:

"Little pig, what! are you here before me? Are they nice apples?"

"Yes, very," said the little pig. "I will throw you down one."

And he threw it so far, that, while the wolf was gone to pick it up, the little pig jumped down and ran home. The next day the wolf came again, and said to the little pig:

"Little pig, there is a fair at Shanklin this afternoon, will you go?"

"Oh yes," said the pig, "I will go; what time shall you be ready?"

"At three," said the wolf. So the little pig went off before the time as usual, and got to the fair, and bought a butter-churn, which he was going home with, when he saw the wolf coming. Then he could not tell what to do. So he got into the churn to hide, and by so doing turned it round, and it rolled down the hill with the pig in it, which frightened the wolf so much, that he ran home without going to the fair. He went to the little pig's house, and told him how frightened he had been by a great round thing which came down the hill past him. Then the little pig said:

"Hah, I frightened you, then. I had been to the fair and bought a butter-churn, and when I saw you, I got into it, and rolled down the hill."

Then the wolf was very angry indeed, and declared he *would* eat up the little pig, and that he would get down the chimney after him. When the little pig saw what he was about, he hung on the pot full of water, and made up a blazing fire, and, just as the wolf was coming down, took off the cover, and in fell the wolf; so the little pig put on the cover again in an instant, boiled him up, and ate him for supper, and lived happy ever afterwards.

Drakestail[1]

Drakestail was very little, that is why he was called Drakestail. But tiny as he was he had brains, and he knew what he was about, for having begun with nothing he ended by amassing a hundred crowns. Now the King of the country, who was very extravagant and never kept any money, having heard that Drakestail had some, went one day in his own person to borrow his hoard, and, my word, in those days Drakestail was not a little proud of having lent money to the King. But after the first and second year, seeing that they never even dreamed of paying the interest, he became uneasy, so much so that at last he resolved to go and see His Majesty himself, and get repaid. So one fine morning Drakestail, very spruce and fresh, takes the road, singing:

"Quack, quack, quack, when shall I get my money back?"

He had not gone far when he met friend Fox, on his rounds.

"Good-morning, neighbor," says the friend, "where are you off to so early?"

"I am going to the King for what he owes me."

"Oh! take me with thee!"

Drakestail said to himself, "One can't have too many friends . . ." "I will," says he, "but going on all-fours you will soon be tired. Make yourself quite small, get into my throat—go into my gizzard and I will carry you."

"Happy thought!" says friend Fox.

He takes bag and baggage, and, presto! is gone like a letter into the post. And Drakestail is off again, all spruce and fresh, still singing:

"Quack, quack, quack, when shall I have my money back?"

He had not gone far when he met his lady-friend Ladder, leaning on her wall.

"Good-morning, my duckling,"

From the "Red Fairy Book," edited by Andrew Lang, illustrated by H. J. Ford

says the lady friend, "whither away so bold?"

"I am going to the King for what he owes me."

"Oh! take me with thee!"

Drakestail said to himself, "One can't have too many friends . . ." "I will," says he, "but with your wooden legs you will soon be tired. Make yourself quite small, get into my throat—go into my gizzard and I will carry you."

"Happy thought!" says my friend Ladder, and nimble, bag and baggage, goes to keep company with friend Fox.

And "Quack, quack, quack." Drakestail is off again, singing and spruce as before. A little farther he meets his sweetheart, my friend River, wandering quietly in the sunshine.

"Thou, my cherub," says she, "whither so lonesome, with arching tail, on this muddy road?"

"I am going to the King, you know, for what he owes me."

"Oh! take me with thee!"

Drakestail said to himself, "We can't be too many friends . . ." "I will," says he, "but you who sleep while you walk will soon be tired. Make yourself quite small, get into my throat—go into my gizzard and I will carry you."

"Ah! happy thought!" says my friend River.

She takes bag and baggage, and glou, glou, glou, she takes her place between friend Fox and my friend Ladder.

And "Quack, quack, quack." Drakestail is off again singing.

A little farther on he meets comrade Wasp's-nest, maneuvering his wasps.

"Well, good-morning, friend Drakestail," said comrade Wasp's-nest, "where are we bound for so spruce and fresh?"

"I am going to the King for what he owes me."

"Oh! take me with thee!"

Drakestail said to himself, "One can't have too many friends . . ." "I will," says he, "but with your battalion to drag along, you will soon be tired. Make yourself quite small, go into my throat—get into my gizzard and I will carry you."

"By Jove! that's a good idea!" says comrade Wasp's-nest.

And left file! he takes the same road to join the others with all his party. There was not much more room, but by closing up a bit they managed . . . And Drakestail is off again singing.

He arrived thus at the capital, and threaded his way straight up the High Street, still running and singing "Quack, quack, quack, when shall I get my money back?" to the great astonishment of the

Drakestail meeting his friends on his journey

good folks, till he came to the King's palace.

He strikes with the knocker, "Toc! toc!"

"Who is there?" asks the porter, putting his head out of the wicket.

"'Tis I, Drakestail. I wish to speak to the King."

"Speak to the King! . . . That's easily said. The King is dining, and will not be disturbed."

"Tell him that it is I, and I have come he well knows why."

The porter shuts his wicket and goes up to say it to the King, who was just sitting down to dinner with a napkin round his neck, and all his ministers.

"Good, good!" said the King laughing. "I know what it is! Make him come in, and put him with the turkeys and chickens."

The porter descends.

"Have the goodness to enter."

"Good!" says Drakestail to himself, "I shall now see how they eat at court."

"This way, this way," says the porter. "One step further . . . There, there you are."

"How? what? in the poultry yard?"

Fancy how vexed Drakestail was!

"Ah! so that's it," says he. "Wait! I will compel you to receive me. Quack, quack, quack, when shall I get my money back?" But turkeys and chickens are creatures who don't like people that are not as themselves. When they saw the newcomer and how he was made, and when they heard him crying too, they began to look black at him.

"What is it? what does he want?"

Finally they rushed at him all together, to overwhelm him with pecks.

"I am lost!" said Drakestail to himself, when by good luck he remembers his comrade friend Fox, and he cries:

Reynard, Reynard, come out of your earth,
Or Drakestail's life is of little worth.

Then friend Fox, who was only waiting for these words, hastens out, throws himself on the wicked fowls, and quick! quack! he tears them to pieces; so much so that at the end of five minutes there was not one left alive. And Drakestail, quite content, began to sing again:

"Quack, quack, quack, when shall I get my money back?"

When the King, who was still at table, heard this refrain, and the poultry woman came to tell him what had been going on in the yard, he was terribly annoyed. He ordered them to throw this tail of a drake into the well, to make an end of him.

And it was done as he commanded. Drakestail was in despair of getting himself out of such a deep hole, when he remembered his lady friend, the Ladder.

Ladder, Ladder, come out of thy hold,
Or Drakestail's days will soon be told.

My friend Ladder, who was only waiting for these words, hastens out, leans her two arms on the edge of the well, then Drakestail climbs nimbly on her back, and hop! he is in the yard where he begins to sing louder than ever.

When the King, who was still at table and laughing at the good trick he had played his creditor, heard him again reclaiming his money, he became livid with rage.

He commanded that the furnace should be heated, and this tail of a drake thrown into it, because he must be a sorcerer.

The furnace was soon hot, but this time Drakestail was not so afraid; he counted on his sweetheart, my friend River.

River, River, outward flow,
Or to death Drakestail must go.

My friend River hastens out, and

errouf! throws herself into the furnace, which she floods, with all the people who had lighted it; after which she flowed growling into the hall of the palace to the height of more than four feet. And Drakestail, quite content, begins to swim, singing deafeningly:

"Quack, quack, quack, when shall I get my money back?"

The King was still at table, and thought himself quite sure of his game; but when he heard Drakestail singing again, and when they told him all that had passed, he became furious and got up from table brandishing his fists.

"Bring him here, and I'll cut his throat! Bring him here quick!" cried he.

And quickly two footmen ran to fetch Drakestail.

"At last," said the poor chap, going up the great stairs, "they have decided to receive me."

Imagine his terror when on entering he sees the King as red as a turkey cock, and all his ministers attending him standing sword in hand. He thought this time it was all up with him. Happily, he remembered that there was still one remaining friend, and he cried with dying accents:

Wasp's-nest, Wasp's-nest, make a sally,
Or Drakestail nevermore may rally.

Hereupon the scene changes.

"Bs, bs, bayonet them!" The brave Wasp's-nest rushes out with all his wasps. They threw themselves on the infuriated King and his ministers, and stung them so fiercely in the face that they lost their heads, and not knowing where to hide themselves they all jumped pell-mell from the window and broke their necks on the pavement.

Behold Drakestail much astonished, all alone in the big salon and master of the field. He could not get over it. Nevertheless, he remembered shortly what he had come for to the palace, and improving the occasion, he set to work to hunt for his dear money. But in vain he rummaged in all the drawers; he found nothing; all had been spent.

And ferreting thus from room to room he came at last to the one with the throne in it, and feeling fatigued, he sat himself down on it to think over his adventure. In the meanwhile the people had found their King and his ministers with their feet in the air on the pavement, and they had gone into the palace to know how it had occurred. On entering the throne-room, when the crowd saw that there was already someone on the royal seat, they broke out in cries of surprise and joy:

The King is dead, long live the King!
Heaven has sent us down this thing.

Drakestail, who was no longer surprised at anything, received the acclamations of the people as if he had never done anything else all his life.

A few of them certainly murmured that a Drakestail would make a fine King; those who knew him replied that a knowing Drakestail was a more worthy King than a spendthrift like him who was lying on the pavement. In short, they ran and took the crown off the head of the deceased, and placed it on that of Drakestail, whom it fitted like wax.

Thus he became King.

"And now," said he after the ceremony, "ladies and gentlemen, let's go to supper. I am hungry!"

Why the Bear Is Stumpy-tailed[1]

Long ago on a winter afternoon, a bear met an old fox, who was carrying a string of fish on his back.

"My!" said the bear. "Where did you get such a fine string of fish?"

Now the fox was as sly as sly could be. He didn't want the bear to know that he hadn't caught the fish himself.

"Ha!" he said with a sly smile. "I caught them myself! I caught them just a little while ago. And I'm thinking how good they will taste for supper. Why don't you catch some yourself?"

The bear was getting hungry, and he wanted some fish at once. So he asked, "What's the best way to catch them?"

The sly fox said, "Go down to the river and cut a hole in the ice. Then put your tail in the hole and wait for the fish to bite.

"When the fish bite your tail, it may sting and hurt a little. But you must sit there as long as you can.

"The longer you sit and keep your tail in the river, the more fish you'll catch. When you think you have caught enough, pull out your tail. Give a hard pull and a strong pull, too.

"Now remember what I've told you."

"Thanks, Brother Fox," said the bear. "It's a queer way to catch fish, but I'll do it, and I surely hope the fish will bite."

"Ha! Ha!" laughed the sly old fox, as the bear ran toward the river.

The hungry bear soon reached the river and cut a hole in the ice. Then he sat so that his tail hung down in the water. While he waited for the fish to bite, he got

[1] From "Popular Tales from the Norse," by Peter Christian Asbjörnsen and Jorgen Moe. Illustrations by John Averill

colder and colder. After a while his tail began to sting and hurt.

It kept stinging and hurting, but the bear didn't get up, because he believed the fish had started to bite.

Late in the afternoon he thought that he had caught enough fish on his tail. Then he tried to stand up and pull out the fish he thought he had caught.

But the bear couldn't stand up straight. The water in the hole had turned to ice, and the part of the bear's tail that hung in the river was caught fast.

He was getting as angry as could be when he remembered what the sly fox had told him. So he gave a hard pull and a strong pull, too.

All of a sudden the bear's tail came out of the ice—but only a part of it, and the shorter part at that! The rest of it stayed fast in the ice.

This happened a long time ago, but to this very day all the bears on earth have short tails.

Slovenly Peter

DR. HEINRICH HOFFMAN

THE CROW-BIDDY [1]

There was once a man and his wife, who one fine morning found an egg. "Well," said the wife, "wait till it is hatched: and some beautiful bird will certainly come from it!"

And when the egg was hatched, what did they have?—A great Chicken, and a very naughty one. But the man and his wife said, "O what a lovely bird!"

And the Chicken began to crow and make a dreadful noise. And the man said—"How sweetly our dear Bird sings!"

And when the Crow-Biddy snatched at everything on the dinner-table, and spilt the cream, the good wife said, "What an appetite the dear thing has!"

And when he tore up his school-books, and threw them away, they said, "Oh! our Pet knows everything!"

And when he broke all the plates and dishes, they said, "How lively the dear thing is!"

After a time the cock beat the man, but he only said, "How strong and stout he is growing!"

One day the cock went into the street, and threw stones at the lamps and windows, and husband and wife both said, "Indeed there is nobody like him in the whole town."

But then came a soldier, and caught the cock, and locked him up in a dark prison. This time the husband and wife said nothing.

They locked him up in a dark prison

[1] From "Slovenly Peter," by Dr. Heinrich Hoffman

The Twelve Days of Christmas

On the first day of Christmas my true love sent to me a partridge in a pear tree.

On the second day of Christmas my true love sent to me two turtledoves, and a partridge in a pear tree.

On the third day of Christmas my true love sent to me three French hens, two turtledoves, and a partridge in a pear tree.

On the fourth day of Christmas my true love sent to me four calling birds, three French hens, two turtledoves, and a partridge in a pear tree.

On the fifth day of Christmas my true love sent to me five gold rings, four calling birds, three French hens, two turtledoves, and a partridge in a pear tree.

On the sixth day of Christmas my true love sent to me six geese alaying, five gold rings, four calling birds, three French hens, two turtledoves, and a partridge in a pear tree.

On the seventh day of Christmas my true love sent to me seven swans aswimming, six geese alaying, five gold rings, four calling birds, three French hens, two turtledoves, and a partridge in a pear tree.

On the eighth day of Christmas my true love sent to me eight maids amilking, seven swans aswimming, six geese alaying, five gold rings, four calling birds, three French hens, two turtledoves, and a partridge in a pear tree.

On the ninth day of Christmas my true love sent to me nine ladies dancing, eight maids amilking, seven swans aswimming, six geese alaying, five gold rings, four calling birds, three French hens, two turtledoves, and a partridge in a pear tree.

On the tenth day of Christmas my true love sent to me ten lords aleaping, nine ladies dancing, eight maids amilking, seven swans aswimming, six geese alaying, five gold rings, four calling birds, three French hens, two turtledoves, and a partridge in a pear tree.

On the eleventh day of Christmas my true love sent to me eleven pipers piping, ten lords aleaping, nine ladies dancing, eight maids amilking, seven swans aswimming, six geese alaying, five gold rings, four calling birds, three French hens, two turtledoves, and a partridge in a pear tree.

On the twelfth day of Christmas my true love sent to me twelve drummers drumming, eleven pipers piping, ten lords aleaping, nine ladies dancing, eight maids amilking, seven swans aswimming, six geese alaying, five gold rings, four calling birds, three French hens, two turtledoves, and a partridge in a pear tree.

Illustration from a drawing by Ilonka Karasz

Aesop's Fables
The Shepherd Boy and the Wolf

Illustration by Percy J. Billinghurst

help chase the marauder away, only to find the sheep grazing peacefully and no wolf in sight.

So well had the trick worked that the foolish boy tried it again and again, and each time the villagers came running, only to be laughed at for their pains.

But there came a day when a wolf really came. The shepherd screamed and called for help. But all in vain! The neighbors, supposing him to be up to his old tricks, paid no heed to his cries, and the wolf devoured the sheep.

Application: LIARS ARE NOT BE-LIEVED EVEN WHEN THEY TELL THE TRUTH.

Every day the shepherd boy was sent with his father's sheep into the mountain pasture to guard the flock. It was, indeed, a lonely spot at the edge of a dark forest, and there were no companions with whom he could pass the long, weary hours of the day.

One day, just to stir up some excitement, he rushed down from the pasture, crying "Wolf! Wolf!" The villagers heard the alarm and came running with clubs and guns to

The Lion and the Mouse

Illustration by Boris Artzybasheff

A lion was asleep in his den one day, when a mischievous mouse for no reason at all ran across the out-stretched paw and up the royal nose of the king of beasts, awakening him from his nap. The mighty beast clapped his paw upon the now thoroughly frightened little

creature and would have made an end of him.

"Please," squealed the mouse, "don't kill me. Forgive me this time, O King, and I shall never forget it. A day may come, who knows, when I may do you a good turn to repay your kindness." The lion, smiling at his little prisoner's fright and amused by the thought that so small a creature ever could be of assistance to the king of beasts, let him go.

Not long afterward the lion, while ranging the forest for his prey, was caught in the net which the hunters had set to catch him. He let out a roar that echoed through the forest. Even the mouse heard it, and recognizing the voice of his former preserver and friend, ran to the spot where he lay tangled in the net of ropes.

"Well, your majesty," said the mouse, "I know you did not believe me once when I said I would return a kindness, but here is my chance." And without further ado he set to work to nibble with his sharp little teeth at the ropes that bound the lion. Soon the lion was able to crawl out of the hunter's snare and be free.

Application: NO ACT OF KINDNESS, NO MATTER HOW SMALL, IS EVER WASTED.

The Farmer's Boy

AN OLD NURSERY POEM

Illustrations from drawings by Randolph Caldecott

When I was a farmer, a Farmer's Boy,
    I used to keep my master's HORSES,
With a GEE-wo here, and a GEE-wo there,
    And here a GEE, and there a GEE,
    And everywhere a GEE;
Says I,   My pretty lass, will you come to the banks
        of the Aire oh?

When I was a farmer, a Farmer's Boy,
    I used to keep my master's LAMBS,
With a Baa-baa here, and a Baa-baa there,
    And here a Baa, and there a Baa,
    And everywhere a Baa;
With a Gee-wo here, and a Gee-wo there,
    And here a Gee, and there a Gee,
    And everywhere a Gee;
Says I,   My pretty lass, will you come to the banks
        of the Aire oh?

When I was a farmer, a Farmer's Boy,
      I used to keep my master's HENS.
With a CHUCK-CHUCK here, and a CHUCK-CHUCK there,
      And here a CHUCK, and there a CHUCK,
      And everywhere a CHUCK;
      With a BAA-BAA here, and a BAA-BAA there,
      And here a BAA, and there a BAA,
      And everywhere a BAA;
      With a GEE-WO here, and a GEE-WO there,
          &c., &c., &c.
Says I,   My pretty lass, will you come to the banks
      of the Aire oh?

When I was a farmer, a Farmer's Boy,
      I used to keep my master's PIGS,
With a GRUNT-GRUNT here, and a GRUNT-GRUNT there,
      And here a GRUNT, and there a GRUNT,
      And everywhere a GRUNT;
With a CHUCK-CHUCK here, and a CHUCK-CHUCK there,
      And here a CHUCK, and there a CHUCK,
      And everywhere a CHUCK;
      With a BAA-BAA here, and a BAA-BAA there,
          &c., &c., &c.
      With a GEE-WO here, and a GEE-WO there,
          &c., &c., &c.
Says I,   My pretty lass, will you come to the banks
      of the Aire oh?

When I was a farmer, a Farmer's Boy,
      I used to keep my master's DUCKS,
With a QUACK-QUACK here, and a QUACK-QUACK there,
      And here a QUACK, and there a QUACK,
      And everywhere a QUACK;
With a GRUNT-GRUNT here, and a GRUNT-GRUNT there,
          &c., &c., &c.
      With a CHUCK-CHUCK here, &c.
      With a BAA-BAA here, &c.
      With a GEE-WO here, &c.

Says I,   My pretty lass, will you come to the banks
of the Aire oh?

When I was a farmer, a Farmer's Boy,
I used to keep my master's DOGS,
With a Bow-bow here, and a Bow-wow there,
And here a Bow, and there a Wow,
And everywhere a Wow;
With a QUACK-QUACK here, and a QUACK-QUACK there,
&c.,   &c.,   &c.
With a GRUNT-GRUNT here, &c.
With a CHUCK-CHUCK here, &c.
With a BAA-BAA here, &c.
With a GEE-WO here, &c.

Says I,   My pretty lass, will you come to the banks
of the Aire oh?

When I was a farmer, a Farmer's Boy,
I used to keep my master's TURKEYS,
With a GOBBLE-GOBBLE here, and a GOBBLE-GOBBLE there,
And here a GOBBLE, and there a GOBBLE;
And everywhere a GOBBLE;
With a SHOUTING here, and a POUTING there,
&c.,   &c.,   &c.
With a Bow-wow here, &c.
With a QUACK-QUACK here, &c.
With a GRUNT-GRUNT here, &c.
With a CHUCK-CHUCK here, &c.
With a BAA-BAA here, &c.
With a GEE-WO here, &c.

Says I,   My pretty lass, will you come to the banks
of the Aire oh?

When I was a farmer, a Farmer's Boy,
    I used to keep my master's CHILDREN,
With a SHOUTING here, and a POUTING there,
    And here a SHOUT, and there a POUT,
    And everywhere a SHOUT;
With a BOW-BOW here, and a BOW-WOW there,
    &c.,   &c.,   &c.
With a QUACK-QUACK here, &c.
With a GRUNT-GRUNT here, &c.
With a CHUCK-CHUCK here, &c.
With a BAA-BAA here, &c.
With a GEE-WO here, &c.
Says I,   My pretty lass, will you come to the banks
    of the Aire oh?

Over in the Meadow

AN OLD NURSERY POEM

Illustrations from drawings by John A. Hartell

Over in the meadow in the sand in the sun
Lived an old mother turtle and her little turtle
                    one
Dig said the mother *We dig* said the one
So they dug all day in the sand in the sun

Over in the meadow where the stream runs blue
Lived an old mother fish and her little fishes
two
Swim said the mother *We swim* said the two
So they swam all day where the stream runs blue

Over in the meadow in a hole in a tree
Lived an old mother owl and her little owls
                    three
Tu-whoo said the mother *Tu-whoo* said the three
So they tu-whooed all day in a hole in a tree

Over in the meadow by the old barn door
Lived an old mother rat and her little ratties
four
Gnaw said the mother *We gnaw* said the four
So they gnawed all day by the old barn door

Over in the meadow in a snug beehive
Lived an old mother bee and her little bees
five
Buzz said the mother *We buzz* said the five
So they buzzed all day in a snug beehive

Over in the meadow in a nest built of sticks
Lived an old mother crow and her little crows
                              six
Caw said the mother *We caw* said the six
So they cawed all day in a nest built of sticks

Over in the meadow where the grass grows so even
Lived an old mother frog and her little froggies
seven
Jump said the mother *We jump* said the seven
So they jumped all day where the grass grows so even

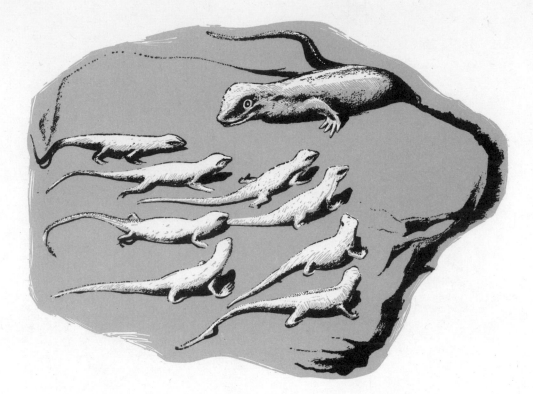

Over in the meadow by the old mossy gate
Lived an old mother lizard and her little lizards
eight
Bask said the mother *We bask* said the eight
So they basked all day by the old mossy gate

Over in the meadow by the old scotch pine
Lived an old mother duck and her little ducks
nine
Quack said the mother *We quack* said the nine
So they quacked all day by the old scotch pine

Over in the meadow in a cozy wee den
Lived an old mother beaver and her little beavers
                              ten
Beave said the mother *We beave* said the ten
So they beaved all day in a cozy wee den

Nonsense Alphabet
Edward Lear

Illustrations by Edward Lear

A was an ape,
Who stole some white tape,
And tied up his toes
In four beautiful bows.

a Funny old ape!

B was a bat,
Who slept all the day,
And fluttered about
When the sun went away.

b Brown little bat!

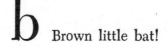

111

C was a camel:
You rode on his hump;
And if you fell off,
You came down such a bump!

c What a high camel!

D was a dove,
Who lived in a wood,
With such pretty soft wings,
And so gentle and good!

d Dear little dove!

E was an eagle,
Who sat on the rocks,
And looked down on the fields
And the far-away flocks.

e Beautiful eagle!

F was a fan
Made of beautiful stuff;
And when it was used,
It went puffy-puff-puff!

f Nice little fan!

G was a gooseberry,
Perfectly red;
To be made into jam,
And eaten with bread.

g Gooseberry red!

H was a heron,
Who stood in a stream:
The length of his neck
And his legs was extreme.

h Long-legged heron!

I was an inkstand,
Which stood on a table,
With a nice pen to write with
When we are able.

i Neat little inkstand!

J was a jug,
So pretty and white,
With fresh water in it
At morning and night.

j Nice little jug!

K was a kingfisher:
Quickly he flew,
So bright and so pretty!—
Green, purple, and blue.

k Kingfisher blue!

L was a lily,
So white and so sweet!
To see it and smell it
Was quite a nice treat.

l Beautiful lily!

M was a man,
Who walked round and round;
And he wore a long coat
That came down to the ground.

m Funny old man!

N was a nut
So smooth and so brown!
And when it was ripe,
It fell tumble-dum-down.

n Nice little nut!

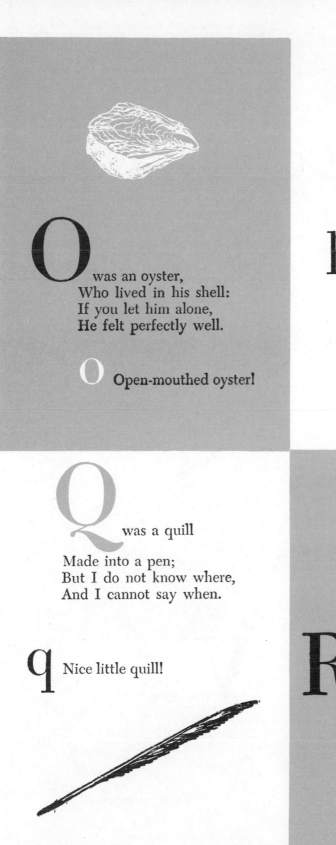

O was an oyster,
Who lived in his shell:
If you let him alone,
He felt perfectly well.

O Open-mouthed oyster!

P was a polly,
All red, blue, and green,—
The most beautiful polly
That ever was seen.

p Poor little polly!

Q was a quill

Made into a pen;
But I do not know where,
And I cannot say when.

q Nice little quill!

R was a rattlesnake,
Rolled up so tight,
Those who saw him ran quickly,
For fear he should bite.

r Rattlesnake bite!

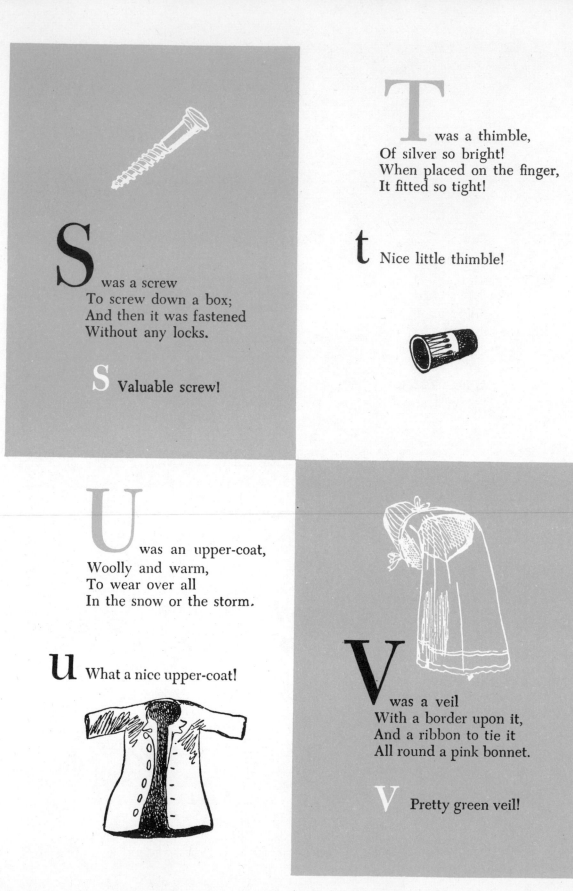

S was a screw
To screw down a box;
And then it was fastened
Without any locks.

S Valuable screw!

T was a thimble,
Of silver so bright!
When placed on the finger,
It fitted so tight!

t Nice little thimble!

U was an upper-coat,
Woolly and warm,
To wear over all
In the snow or the storm.

u What a nice upper-coat!

V was a veil
With a border upon it,
And a ribbon to tie it
All round a pink bonnet.

V Pretty green veil!

W was a watch,
Where, in letters of gold,
The hour of the day
You might always behold.

W Beautiful watch!

X was King Xerxes,
Who wore on his head
A mighty large turban,
Green, yellow, and red.

X Look at King Xerxes!

Z was a zebra,
All striped white and black;
And if he were tame,
You might ride on his back.

Z Pretty striped zebra!

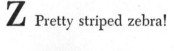

Y was a yak,
From the land of Thibet:
Except his white tail,
He was all black as jet,

y Look at the yak!

THE OWL AND THE PUSSY-CAT

Edward Lear

Illustrations by Edward Lear

The Owl and the Pussy-cat went to sea
   In a beautiful pea-green boat:
They took some honey, and plenty of
   money
   Wrapped up in a five-pound note.
The Owl looked up to the stars above,
   And sang to a small guitar,
"O lovely Pussy, O Pussy, my love,
   What a beautiful Pussy you are,
      You are,
      You are!
   What a beautiful Pussy you are!"

Pussy said to the Owl, "You elegant fowl,
   How charmingly sweet you sing!
Oh! let us be married; too long we have
   tarried;
   But what shall we do for a ring?"
They sailed away, for a year and a day,
   To the land where the bong-tree grows;
And there in a wood a Piggy-wig stood,
   With a ring at the end of his nose,
      His nose,
      His nose,
   With a ring at the end of his nose.

"Dear Pig, are you willing to sell for one
   shilling
   Your ring?"   Said the Piggy, "I will."
So they took it away, and were married
   next day
   By the Turkey who lives on the hill.
They dined on mince and slices of quince,
   Which they ate with a runcible spoon;
And hand in hand, on the edge of the sand,
   They danced by the light of the moon,
      The moon,
      The moon,
   They danced by the light of the moon.

LIMERICKS

Edward Lear

Illustrations by Edward Lear

There was an Old Man with a nose,
Who said, "If you choose to suppose
That my nose is too long, you are certainly
  wrong!"
That remarkable Man with a nose.

There was a Young Lady of Welling,
Whose praise all the world was a-telling;
She played on the harp, and caught sev-
  eral Carp,
That accomplished Young Lady of Wel-
  ling.

There was an Old Man of Marseilles,
Whose daughters wore bottle-green veils;
They caught several Fish, which they put
  in a dish,
And sent to their Pa at Marseilles.

THE WALRUS AND THE CARPENTER

LEWIS CARROLL

Illustrations from drawings by Sir John Tenniel

The sun was shining on the sea,
  Shining with all his might:
He did his very best to make
  The billows smooth and bright—
And this was odd, because it was
  The middle of the night.

The moon was shining sulkily,
  Because she thought the sun
Had got no business to be there
  After the day was done—
"It's very rude of him," she said,
  "To come and spoil the fun!"

The sea was wet as wet could be,
  The sands were dry as dry.
You could not see a cloud, because
  No cloud was in the sky:
No birds were flying overhead—
  There were no birds to fly.

The Walrus and the Carpenter
  Were walking close at hand;
They wept like anything to see
  Such quantities of sand:
"If this were only cleared away."
  They said, "it *would* be grand!"

"If seven maids with seven mops
  Swept it for half a year,
Do you suppose," the Walrus said,
  "That they could get it clear?"
"I doubt it," said the Carpenter,
  And shed a bitter tear.

"O Oysters, come and walk with us!"
  The Walrus did beseech.
"A pleasant walk, a pleasant talk,
  Along the briny beach:
We cannot do with more than four,
  To give a hand to each."

The eldest Oyster looked at him,
  But never a word he said:
The eldest Oyster winked his eye,
  And shook his heavy head—
Meaning to say he did not choose
  To leave the oyster bed.

But four young Oysters hurried up,
  All eager for the treat:
Their coats were brushed, their faces
    washed,
  Their shoes were clean and neat—
And this was odd, because, you know,
  They hadn't any feet.

Four other Oysters followed them,
  And yet another four;
And thick and fast they came at last,
  And more, and more, and more—
All hopping through the frothy waves,
  And scrambling to the shore.

The Walrus and the Carpenter
  Walked on a mile or so,
And then they rested on a rock
  Conveniently low:
And all the little Oysters stood
  And waited in a row.

"The time has come," the Walrus said,
  "To talk of many things:
Of shoes—and ships—and sealing wax—
  Of cabbages—and kings—
And why the sea is boiling hot—
  And whether pigs have wings."

"But wait a bit," the Oysters cried,
  "Before we have our chat;
For some of us are out of breath,
  And all of us are fat!"
"No hurry!" said the Carpenter.
  They thanked him much for that.

"A loaf of bread," the Walrus said,
  "Is what we chiefly need:
Pepper and vinegar besides
  Are very good indeed—
Now, if you're ready, Oysters dear,
  We can begin to feed."

"But not on us!" the Oysters cried,
  Turning a little blue.
"After such kindness, that would be
  A dismal thing to do!"
"The night is fine," the Walrus said,
  "Do you admire the view?

"It was so kind of you to come!
  And you are very nice!"
The Carpenter said nothing but
  "Cut us another slice.
I wish you were not quite so deaf—
  I've had to ask you twice!"

"It seems a shame," the Walrus said,
  "To play them such a trick,
After we've brought them out so far,
  And made them trot so quick!"
The Carpenter said nothing but
  "The butter's spread too thick!"

"I weep for you," the Walrus said;
  "I deeply sympathize."
With sobs and tears he sorted out
  Those of the largest size,
Holding his pocket handkerchief
  Before his streaming eyes.

"O Oysters," said the Carpenter,
  "You've had a pleasant run!
Shall we be trotting home again?"
  But answer came there none—
And this was scarcely odd, because
  They'd eaten every one.

HUMPTY DUMPTY

Lewis Carroll

Illustration by Sir John Tenniel

Humpty Dumpty
    sat on a wall:
Humpty Dumpty
    had a great fall.
All the King's horses
    and all the King's men
Couldn't put Humpty Dumpty
    in his place again.

TWEEDLEDUM AND TWEEDLEDEE

Lewis Carroll

Illustration by Sir John Tenniel

Tweedledum and Tweedledee
    Agreed to have a battle;
For Tweedledum said Tweedledee
    Had spoiled his nice new rattle.

Just then flew down a monstrous crow,
    As black as a tar barrel,
Which frightened both the heroes so,
    They quite forgot their quarrel.

123

Father William

LEWIS CARROLL

Illustrations from drawings by Sir John Tenniel

"You are old, Father William," the young man said,
  "And your hair has become very white;
And yet you incessantly stand on your head—
  Do you think, at your age, it is right?"

"In my youth," Father William replied to his son,
  "I feared it might injure the brain;
But now that I'm perfectly sure I have none,
  Why, I do it again and again."

"You are old," said the youth, "as I mentioned before,
    And have grown most uncommonly fat;
Yet you turned a back somersault in at the door—
    Pray, what is the reason of that?"

"In my youth," said the sage, as he shook his gray locks,
    "I kept all my limbs very supple
By the use of this ointment—one shilling the box—
    Allow me to sell you a couple."

"You are old," said the youth, "and your jaws are too weak
    For anything tougher than suet;
Yet you finished the goose, with the bones and the beak—
    Pray, how did you manage to do it?"

"In my youth," said his father, "I took to the law,
    And argued each case with my wife;
And the muscular strength, which it gave to my jaw,
    Has lasted the rest of my life."

"You are old," said the youth, "one would hardly suppose
    That your eye was as steady as ever;
Yet you balanced an eel on the end of your nose—
    What made you so awfully clever?"

"I have answered three questions, and that is enough,"
    Said his father; "don't give yourself airs!
Do you think I can listen all day to such stuff?
    Be off, or I'll kick you downstairs!"

WOODS

Rachel Field

Illustration by Rachel Field

Whenever the woods I walk among
Are very green and very young,
With leaves a-twinkle on every tree,
The heart begins to dance in me,
And my feet to caper from tree to tree
Over the sun-patched greenery.

But when the woods I walk among
Are very old, with mosses hung
In thin festoons of tattered gray,
And the green seems high and far away,
Oh, then I tiptoe from tree to tree,
For a hush is on the heart of me.

GENERAL STORE

Rachel Field

Illustration by Rachel Field

Someday I'm going to have a store
With a tinkly bell hung over the door,
With real glass cases and counters wide
And drawers all spilly with things inside.
There'll be a little of everything:
Bolts of calico; balls of string;
Jars of peppermint; tins of tea;
Pots and kettles and crockery;
Seeds in packets; scissors bright;
Kegs of sugar, brown and white;
Sarsaparilla for picnic lunches,
Bananas and rubber boots in bunches.
I'll fix the window and dust each shelf,
And take the money in all myself,
It will be my store and I will say:
"What can I do for you to-day?"

MOTHER

Rose Fyleman

When mother comes each morning
  She wears her oldest things,
She doesn't make a rustle,
  She hasn't any rings;
She says, "Good-morning, chickies,
  It's such a lovely day,
Let's go into the garden
  And have a game of play!"

When mother comes at tea-time
  Her dress goes shoo-shoo-shoo,
She always has a little bag,
  Sometimes a sunshade too;
She says, "I am so hoping
  There's something left for me;
Please hurry up, dear Nanna,
  I'm dying for my tea."

When mother comes at bed-time
  Her evening dress she wears,
She tells us each a story
  When we have said our prayers;
And if there is a party
  She looks so shiny bright
It's like a lovely fairy
  Dropped in to say good-night.

TAXIS

Rachel Field

Illustration by Rachel Field

Ho, for taxis green or blue,
  Hi, for taxis red,
They roll along the Avenue
  Like spools of colored thread!

    Jack-o'-Lantern yellow,
    Orange as the moon,
    Greener than the greenest grass
    Ever grew in June.
    Gayly striped or checked in squares,
    Wheels that twinkle bright,
    Don't you think that taxis make
    A very pleasant sight?
    Taxis shiny in the rain,
    Scudding through the snow,
    Taxis flashing back the sun
    Waiting in a row.

Ho, for taxis red and green,
  Hi, for taxis blue,
I wouldn't be a private car
  In sober black, would you?

THE FAIRIES

William Allingham

Illustrations by Charles Folkard

Up the airy mountain,
  Down the rushy glen,
We daren't go a-hunting,
  For fear of little men;
Wee folk, good folk,
  Trooping all together;
Green jacket, red cap,
  And white owl's feather!

Down along the rocky shore
  Some make their home,
They live on crispy pancakes
  Of yellow tide-foam;
Some in the reeds
  Of the black mountain-lake,
With frogs for their watch-dogs,
  All night awake.

THE VILLAGE BLACKSMITH

Henry Wadsworth Longfellow

Illustration by Jacob Landau

Under a spreading chestnut-tree
  The village smithy stands;
The smith, a mighty man is he,
  With large and sinewy hands;
And the muscles of his brawny arms
  Are strong as iron bands.

His hair is crisp, and black, and long,
  His face is like the tan;
His brow is wet with honest sweat,
  He earns whate'er he can,
And looks the whole world in the face,
  For he owes not any man.

Week in, week out, from morn till night,
  You can hear his bellows blow;
You can hear him swing his heavy sledge,
  With measured beat and slow,
Like a sexton ringing the village bell,
  When the evening sun is low.

And children coming home from school
  Look in at the open door;
They love to see the flaming forge,
  And hear the bellows roar,
And catch the burning sparks that fly
  Like chaff from a threshing floor.

He goes on Sunday to the church,
  And sits among his boys;
He hears the parson pray and preach,
  He hears his daughter's voice
Singing in the village choir,
  And it makes his heart rejoice.

It sounds to him like her mother's voice,
  Singing in Paradise!
He needs must think of her once more,
  How in the grave she lies;
And with his hard, rough hand he wipes
  A tear out of his eyes.

Toiling,—rejoicing,—sorrowing,
  Onward through life he goes;
Each morning sees some task begin,
  Each evening sees it close;
Something attempted, something done,
  Has earned a night's repose.

Thanks, thanks to thee, my worthy friend,
  For the lesson thou hast taught!
Thus at the flaming forge of life
  Our fortunes must be wrought;
Thus on its sounding anvil shaped
  Each burning deed and thought!

OH, FAIR TO SEE

Christina Rossetti

Oh, fair to see
Bloom-laden cherry tree,
  Arrayed in sunny white:
  An April day's delight,
Oh, fair to see!

Oh, fair to see
Fruit-laden cherry tree,
  With balls of shining red
  Decking a leafy head,
Oh, fair to see!

MILKING TIME

Christina Rossetti

When the cows come home the milk is
    coming;
Honey's made while the bees are hum-
    ming;
Duck and drake on the rushy lake,
And the deer live safe in the breezy brake:
And timid, funny, pert little bunny
Winks his nose, and sits all sunny.

BOATS SAIL ON THE RIVERS

Christina Rossetti

Boats sail on the rivers,
  And ships sail on the seas;
But clouds that sail across the sky
  Are prettier far than these.

There are bridges on the rivers,
  As pretty as you please;
But the bow that bridges heaven,
  And overtops the trees,
And builds a road from earth to sky,
  Is prettier far than these.

Illustrations by Meg Wohlberg

132

BE LIKE THE BIRD

Victor Hugo

Be like the bird, who
Halting in his flight
On limb too slight
Feels it give way beneath him,
Yet sings
Knowing he hath wings.

AN IMPETUOUS RESOLVE

James Whitcomb Riley

When little Dickie Swope's a man,
    He's go' to be a Sailor;
An' little Hamey Tincher, he's
    A-go' to be a Tailor:
Bud Mitchell, he's a-go' to be
    A stylish Carriage-Maker;
An' when *I* grow a grea'-big man,
    I'm go' to be a Baker!

An' Dick'll buy his sailor-suit
    O' Hame; an' Hame'll take it
An' buy as fine a double-rig
    As ever Bud kin make it:
An' nen all three'll drive roun' fer me,
    An' we'll drive off togevver,
A-slingin' pie-crust 'long the road
    Ferever an' ferever!

Illustrations by Meg Wohlberg

THE DUEL

Eugene Field

Illustrations by Meg Wohlberg

The gingham dog and the calico cat
Side by side on the table sat;
'Twas half-past twelve, and (what do you
    think!)
Nor one nor t'other had slept a wink!
    The old Dutch clock and the Chinese
    plate
    Appeared to know as sure as fate
There was going to be a terrible spat.
    (*I wasn't there; I simply state
    What was told to me by the Chinese
    plate!*)

The gingham dog went "bow-wow-wow!"
And the calico cat replied "mee-ow!"
The air was littered, an hour or so,
With bits of gingham and calico,
    While the old Dutch clock in the chim-
    ney-place
    Up with its hands before its face,
For it always dreaded a family row!
    (*Now mind: I'm only telling you
    What the old Dutch clock declares is
    true!*)

The Chinese plate looked very blue,
And wailed, "Oh, dear! what shall we do!"
But the gingham dog and the calico cat
Wallowed this way and tumbled that,
    Employing every tooth and claw
    In the awfullest way you ever saw—
And, oh! how the gingham and calico flew!
    (*Don't fancy I exaggerate—
    I got my news from the Chinese
    plate!*)

Next morning, where the two had sat
They found no trace of dog or cat;
And some folks think unto this day
That burglars stole that pair away!
    But the truth about the cat and pup
    Is this: they ate each other up!
Now what do you really think of that!
    (*The old Dutch clock it told me so,
    And that is how I came to know.*)

THE LION

Hilaire Belloc

Illustration by Meg Wohlberg

The Lion, the Lion, he dwells in the waste,
He has a big head and a very small waist;
But his shoulders are stark, and his jaws
    they are grim,
And a good little child will not play with
    him.

THE YAK

Hilaire Belloc

Illustration by Meg Wohlberg

As a friend to the children commend me
    the Yak.
  You will find it exactly the thing:
It will carry and fetch, you can ride on its
    back,
  Or lead it about with a string.

The Tartar who dwells on the plains of
    Thibet
  (A desolate region of snow)
Has for centuries made it a nursery pet,
  And surely the Tartar should know!

Then tell your papa where the Yak can be
    got,
  And if he is awfully rich
He will buy you the creature—or else he
    will not.
  (I cannot be positive which.)

TIME TO RISE

Robert Louis Stevenson

A birdie with a yellow bill
Hopped upon the window sill,
Cocked his shining eye and said:
'Ain't you 'shamed, you sleepy-head?'

SINGING

Robert Louis Stevenson

Of speckled eggs the birdie sings
    And nests among the trees;
The sailor sings of ropes and things
    In ships upon the seas.

The children sing in far Japan,
    The children sing in Spain;
The organ with the organ man
    Is singing in the rain.

RAIN

Robert Louis Stevenson

The rain is raining all around,
    It falls on field and tree,
It rains on the umbrellas here,
    And on the ships at sea.

Illustrations by Jessie Wilcox Smith

136

MY SHADOW

Robert Louis Stevenson

Illustrations by Jessie Wilcox Smith

I have a little shadow that goes in and out
    with me,
And what can be the use of him is more
    than I can see.
He is very, very like me from the heels up
    to the head;
And I see him jump before me, when I
    jump into my bed.

The funniest thing about him is the way
    he likes to grow—
Not at all like proper children, which is
    always very slow;
For he sometimes shoots up taller like an
    india-rubber ball,
And he sometimes gets so little that there's
    none of him at all.

He hasn't got a notion of how children
    ought to play,
And can only make a fool of me in every
    sort of way.
He stays so close beside me, he's a coward
    you can see;
I'd think shame to stick to nurse as that
    shadow sticks to me!

One morning, very early, before the sun
    was up,
I rose and found the shining dew on every
    buttercup;
But my lazy little shadow, like an arrant
    sleepy-head,
Had stayed at home behind me and was
    fast asleep in bed.

A KITTEN

Eleanor Farjeon

Illustration by Meg Wohlberg

He's nothing much but fur
  And two round eyes of blue,
He has a giant purr
  And a midget mew.

He darts and pats the air,
  He starts and cocks his ear,
When there is nothing there
  For him to see and hear.

He runs around in rings,
  But why we cannot tell;
With sideways leaps he springs
  At things invisible—

Then half-way through a leap
  His startled eyeballs close,
And he drops off to sleep
  With one paw on his nose.

JILL CAME FROM THE FAIR

Eleanor Farjeon

Illustration by Meg Wohlberg

Jill came from the Fair
With her pennies all spent.
She had had her full share
Of delight and content;
She had ridden the ring
To a wonderful tune,
She had flown in a swing
Half as high as the moon,
In a boat that was drawn
By an ivory swan
Beside a green lawn
On a lake she had gone,
She had bought a gold packet
That held her desire,
She had touched the red jacket
Of one who ate fire,
She had stood at the butt,
And although she was small
She had won a rough nut
With the throw of a ball,
And across the broad back
Of a donkey a-straddle,
She had jolted like Jack-
In-the-Box on a saddle—
Till mid frolic and shout
And tinsel and litter,
The lights started out
Making everything glitter,
And dazed by the noise
And the blare and the flare,
With her toys and her joys
Jill came from the Fair.

PRINCE TATTERS

Laura E. Richards

Illustration by Meg Wohlberg

Little Prince Tatters has lost his cap!
  Over the hedge he threw it;
Into the river it fell "kerslap"!
  Stupid old thing to do it!
Now Mother may sigh and Nurse may fume
For the gay little cap with its eagle plume.
"One cannot be thinking all day of such
    matters!
Trifles are trifles!" says little Prince Tatters.

Little Prince Tatters has lost his coat!
  Playing, he did not need it;
"Left it *right there,* by the nanny goat,
  And nobody never seed it!"
Now Mother and Nurse may search till
    night
For the little new coat with its buttons
    bright;
But—"Coat sleeves or shirt sleeves, how
    little it matters!
Trifles are trifles!" says little Prince Tatters.

Little Prince Tatters has *lost his ball!*
  Rolled away down the street!
Somebody'll *have to find it,* that's all,
  Before he can sleep or eat.
Now raise the neighborhood, quickly, do!
And send for the crier and constable, too!
"Trifles are trifles; but serious matters,
They must be *seen to,*" says little Prince
    Tatters.

EXTREMES

James Whitcomb Riley

Illustration by Meg Wohlberg

I

A little boy once played so loud
That the Thunder, up in a thunder-cloud,
Said, "Since *I* can't be heard, why, then
I'll never, never thunder again!"

II

And a little girl once kept so still
That she heard a fly on the window-sill
Whisper and say to a ladybird,—
"She's the stilliest child I ever heard!"

THE FLOWERS

Robert Louis Stevenson

Illustration from a drawing by Jessie Wilcox Smith

All the names I know from nurse:
Gardener's garters, Shepherd's purse,
Bachelor's Buttons, Lady's Smock,
And the Lady Hollyhock.

Fairy places, fairy things,
Fairy woods where the wild bee wings,
Tiny trees for tiny dames—
These must all be fairy names!

Tiny woods below whose boughs
Shady fairies weave a house;
Tiny tree-tops, rose or thyme,
Where the braver fairies climb!

Fair are grown-up people's trees,
But the fairest woods are these;
Where if I were not so tall,
I should live for good and all.

THE RAGGEDY MAN

James Whitcomb Riley

Illustrations from drawings by Everett Shinn

O The Raggedy Man! He works fer Pa;
An' he's the goodest man ever you saw!
He comes to our house every day,
An' waters the horses, and feeds 'em hay;
An' he opens the shed—an' we all ist laugh
When he drives out our little old wob-
    ble-ly calf;
An' nen—ef our hired girl says he can—
He milks the cow fer 'Lizabuth Ann.—
  Ain't he a' awful good Raggedy Man?
Raggedy! Raggedy! Raggedy Man!

W'y, The Raggedy Man—he's ist so good,
He splits the kindlin' an' chops the wood;
An' nen he spades in our garden, too,
An' does most things 'at *boys* can't do.—
He clumbed clean up in our big tree
An' shooked a' apple down fer me—
An' nother'n', too—fer 'Lizabuth Ann—
An' nother'n', too, fer The Raggedy Man.—
   Ain't he a' awful kind Raggedy Man?
   Raggedy! Raggedy! Raggedy Man!

An' The Raggedy Man, he knows most
    rhymes,
An' tells 'em, ef I be good, sometimes:
Knows 'bout Giunts, an' Griffuns, an' Elves,
An' the Squidgicum-Squees 'at swallers
    the'rselves!
An', wite by the pump in our pasture-lot,
He showed me the hole 'at the Wunks is
    got,
'At lives 'way deep in the ground, an' can
Turn into me, or 'Lizabuth Ann!
Er Ma, er Pa, er The Raggedy Man!
   Ain't he a funny old Raggedy Man?
   Raggedy! Raggedy! Raggedy Man!

The Raggedy Man—one time, when he
Was makin' a little bow-'n'-orry fer me,
Says, "When *you're* big like your Pa is,
Air *you* go' to keep a fine store like his—
An' be a rich merchant—an' wear fine
    clothes?—
Er what *air* you go' to be, goodness
    knows?"
An' nen he laughed at 'Lizabuth Ann,
An' I says "'M go' to be a Raggedy Man!—
   I'm ist go' to be a nice Raggedy Man!"
   Raggedy! Raggedy! Raggedy Man!

THE FORCE OF NEED

Howard Pyle

Illustration from a drawing by Howard Pyle

"Hey, Robin! Ho, Robin!
   Singing on the tree,
I will give you white bread,
   If you will come to me."

"Oh, the little breeze is singing
   To the nodding daisies white,
And the tender grass is springing,
   And the sun is warm and bright;
And my little mate is waiting
   In the budding hedge for me;
So, on the whole, I'll not accept
   Your kindly courtesy."

"Hey, Robin! Ho, Robin!
   Now the north winds blow;
Wherefore do you come here,
   In the ice and snow?"

"The wind is raw, the flowers are dead,
   The frost is on the thorn,
So I'll gladly take a crust of bread,
   And come where it is warm."

Oh, Children! Little Children!
   Have *you* ever chanced to see
One beg for crust that sneered at crumb
   In bright prosperity?

THE NIGHT BEFORE CHRISTMAS

Clement C. Moore

Illustrations from original cuts designed and engraved by Boyd

'Twas the night before Christmas, when
all through the house
Not a creature was stirring, not even a
mouse;
The stockings were hung by the chimney
with care,
In hopes that St. Nicholas soon would be
there;
The children were nestled all snug in their
beds,
While visions of sugar-plums danced in
their heads;
And mamma in her 'kerchief, and I in my
cap,
Had just settled our brains for a long
winter's nap,
When out on the lawn there arose such a
clatter,
I sprang from the bed to see what was the
matter.
Away to the window I flew like a flash,
Tore open the shutters and threw up the
sash.

The moon on the breast of the new-fallen
snow
Gave the lustre of mid-day to objects
below,
When, what to my wondering eyes should
appear,
But a miniature sleigh, and eight tiny rein-
deer,
With a little old driver, so lively and
quick,
I knew in a moment it must be St. Nick.
More rapid than eagles his coursers they
came,
And he whistled, and shouted, and called
them by name:
"Now, *Dasher!* now, *Dancer!* now, *Prancer*
and *Vixen!*
On, *Comet!* on, *Cupid!* on, *Donder* and
Blitzen!
To the top of the porch! to the top of the
wall!
Now dash away! dash away! dash away
all!"
As dry leaves that before the wild hurri-
cane fly,
When they meet with an obstacle, mount
to the sky,
So up to the house-top the coursers they
flew,
With the sleigh full of toys, and St. Nich-
olas too.

And then, in a twinkling, I heard on the
    roof
The prancing and pawing of each little
    hoof.
As I drew in my head, and was turning
    around,
Down the chimney St. Nicholas came with
    a bound.
He was dressed all in fur, from his head to
    his foot,
And his clothes were all tarnished with
    ashes and soot;
A bundle of toys he had flung on his back,
And he looked like a peddler just opening
    his pack.
His eyes—how they twinkled! his dimples
    how merry!
His cheeks were like roses, his nose like a
    cherry!
His droll little mouth was drawn up like
    a bow,
And the beard of his chin was as white as
    the snow;
The stump of a pipe he held tight in his
    teeth,
And the smoke it encircled his head like a
    wreath;
He had a broad face and a little round
    belly,

That shook, when he laughed, like a bowl-
    ful of jelly.
He was chubby and plump, a right jolly
    old elf,
And I laughed when I saw him, in spite of
    myself;
A wink of his eye and a twist of his head,
Soon gave me to know I had nothing to
    dread;
He spoke not a word, but went straight to
    his work,
And filled all the stockings; then turned
    with a jerk,
And laying his finger aside of his nose,
And giving a nod, up the chimney he rose;
He sprang to his sleigh, to his team gave a
    whistle,
And away they all flew like the down of a
    thistle.
But I heard him exclaim, ere he drove out
    of sight,
"Happy Christmas to all, and to all a good-
    night."

145

AT THE SEA-SIDE

Robert Louis Stevenson

Illustration from a drawing by Pelagie Doane

When I was down beside the sea
A wooden spade they gave to me
    To dig the sandy shore.

My holes were empty like a cup.
In every hole the sea came up,
    Till it could come no more.

THE LAND OF COUNTERPANE

Robert Louis Stevenson

Illustration from a drawing by Jessie Wilcox Smith

When I was sick and lay a-bed,
I had two pillows at my head,
And all my toys beside me lay
To keep me happy all the day.

And sometimes for an hour or so
I watched my leaden soldiers go,
With different uniforms and drills,
Among the bed-clothes, through the hills;

And sometimes sent my ships in fleets
All up and down among the sheets;
Or brought my trees and houses out,
And planted cities all about.

I was the giant great and still
That sits upon the pillow-hill,
And sees before him, dale and plain,
The pleasant land of counterpane.

THE BAREFOOT BOY

John Greenleaf Whittier

Blessings on thee, little man,
Barefoot boy, with cheek of tan!
With thy turned-up pantaloons,
And thy merry whistled tunes;
With thy red lip, redder still
Kissed by strawberries on the hill;
With the sunshine on thy face,
Through thy torn brim's jaunty grace;
From my heart I give thee joy,—
I was once a barefoot boy!

Prince thou art,—the grown-up man
Only is republican.
Let the million-dollared ride!
Barefoot, trudging at his side,
Thou hast more than he can buy
In the reach of ear and eye,—
Outward sunshine, inward joy:
Blessings on thee, barefoot boy!

Oh, for boyhood's painless play,
Sleep that wakes in laughing day,
Health that mocks the doctor's rules,
Knowledge never learned of schools,
Of the wild bee's morning chase,
Of the wild flower's time and place,
Flight of fowl and habitude
Of the tenants of the wood;
How the tortoise bears his shell,
How the woodchuck digs his cell,
And the ground-mole sinks his well;
How the robin feeds her young,
How the oriole's nest is hung;

Where the whitest lilies blow,
Where the freshest berries grow,
Where the ground-nut trails its vine,
Where the wood-grape's clusters shine;
Of the black wasp's cunning way,
Mason of his walls of clay,
And the architectural plans
Of gray hornet artisans!
For, eschewing books and tasks,
Nature answers all he asks;
Hand in hand with her he walks,
Face to face with her he talks,
Part and parcel of her joy,—
Blessings on the barefoot boy!

Oh, for boyhood's time of June,
Crowding years in one brief moon,
When all things I heard or saw,
Me, their master, waited for.
I was rich in flowers and trees,
Humming-birds and honey-bees;
For my sport the squirrel played,
Plied the snouted mole his spade;
For my taste the blackberry cone
Purpled over hedge and stone;
Laughed the brook for my delight
Through the day and through the night,—
Whispering at the garden wall,
Talked with me from fall to fall;
Mine the sand-rimmed pickerel pond,
Mine the walnut slopes beyond,
Mine, on bending orchard trees,
Apples of Hesperides!

Still as my horizon grew,
Larger grew my riches too;
All the world I saw or knew
Seemed a complex Chinese toy,
Fashioned for a barefoot boy!

Oh, for festal dainties spread,
Like my bowl of milk and bread;
Pewter spoon and bowl of wood,
On the door-stone, gray and rude!
O'er me, like a regal tent,
Cloudy-ribbed, the sunset bent,
Purple-curtained, fringed with gold,
Looped in many a wind-swung fold;
While for music came the play
Of the pied frogs' orchestra;
And, to light the noisy choir,
Lit the fly his lamp of fire.
I was monarch: pomp and joy
Waited on the barefoot boy!

Cheerily, then, my little man,
Live and laugh, as boyhood can!
Though the flinty slopes be hard,
Stubble-speared the new-mown sward,
Every morn shall lead thee through
Fresh baptisms of the dew;
Every evening from thy feet
Shall the cool wind kiss the heat:
All too soon these feet must hide
In the prison cells of pride,
Lose the freedom of the sod,
Like a colt's for work be shod,
Made to tread the mills of toil,
Up and down in ceaseless moil:
Happy if their track be found
Never on forbidden ground;
Happy if they sink not in
Quick and treacherous sands of sin.
Ah! that thou couldst know thy joy,
Ere it passes, barefoot boy!

THE HAYLOFT

Robert Louis Stevenson

Illustration from a drawing by Jessie Wilcox Smith

Through all the pleasant meadow-side
    The grass grew shoulder-high,
Till the shining scythes went far and wide
    And cut it down to dry.

These green and sweetly smelling crops
    They led in waggons home;
And they piled them here in mountain
        tops
    For mountaineers to roam.

Here is Mount Clear, Mount Rusty-Nail,
    Mount Eagle and Mount High;—
The mice that in these mountains dwell,
    No happier are than I!

O what a joy to clamber there,
    O what a place for play,
With the sweet, the dim, the dusty air,
    The happy hills of hay.

BED IN SUMMER

Robert Louis Stevenson

Illustration from a drawing by Tasha Tudor

In winter I get up at night
And dress by yellow candle-light.
In summer, quite the other way,
I have to go to bed by day.

I have to go to bed and see
The birds still hopping on the tree,
Or hear the grown-up people's feet
Still going past me in the street.

And does it not seem hard to you,
When all the sky is clear and blue,
And I should like so much to play,
To have to go to bed by day?

A THOUGHT

Robert Louis Stevenson

Illustration from a drawing by Tasha Tudor

It is very nice to think
The world is full of meat and drink,
With little children saying grace
In every Christian kind of place.

HAPPY THOUGHT

Robert Louis Stevenson

The world is so full of a number of things,
I'm sure we should all be as happy as
kings.

Aesop's Fables

THE LIONESS

Illustration from a drawing by Fritz Kredel

A great rivalry existed among the beasts of the forest over which could produce the largest litter. Some shamefacedly admitted having only two, while others boasted proudly of having a dozen.

At last the committee called upon the lioness.

"And to how many cubs do you give birth?" they asked the proud lioness.

"One," she replied sternly, "but that one is a lion!"

Application: QUALITY IS MORE IMPORTANT THAN QUANTITY.

THE WOLF AND THE GOAT

Illustration from a drawing by Fritz Kredel

A wolf saw a goat browsing near the edge of a high cliff. "My dear friend," he cried in his most sympathetic voice, "aren't you afraid you will get dizzy and fall and hurt yourself?" But the goat went on feeding.

The wolf tried again. "Isn't it terribly windy up there so high with no shelter at all?" But the goat went on plucking grass.

"Besides," shouted the wolf, "I am sure that you will find the grass far sweeter and more abundant down here."

Then the goat replied: "Are you quite sure, friend wolf, that it is my dinner you are so solicitous about, and not your own?"

Application: BEWARE OF A FRIEND WITH AN ULTERIOR MOTIVE.

THE CAT AND THE MICE

Illustration from a drawing by Fritz Kredel

A cat, grown feeble with age, and no longer able to hunt for mice as she was wont to do, sat in the sun and bethought herself how she might entice them within reach of her paws.

The idea came to her that if she would suspend herself by the hind legs from a peg in the closet wall, the mice, believing her to be dead, no longer would be afraid of her. So, at great pains and with the assistance of a torn pillow case she was able to carry out her plan.

But before the mice could approach within range of the innocent-looking paws a wise old gaffer-mouse whispered to his friends: "Keep your distance, my friends. Many a bag have I seen in my day, but never one with a cat's head at the bottom of it."

Then turning to the uncomfortable feline, he said: "Hang there, good madam, as long as you please, but I would not trust myself within reach of you though you were stuffed with straw."

Application: HE WHO IS ONCE DECEIVED IS DOUBLY CAUTIOUS.

154

THE WOLF AND THE CRANE

Illustration from a drawing by Fritz Kredel

A wolf, in gorging himself upon some poor animal he had killed, had got a small bone stuck in his throat. The pain was terrible, and he ran up and down beseeching every animal he met to relieve him. None of the animals, however, felt very sorry for the wolf, for, as one of them put it, "That bone which is stuck in the wolf's throat might just as well be one of mine."

Finally the suffering wolf met the crane. "I'll give you anything," he whined, "if you will help take this bone out of my throat."

The crane, moved by his entreaties and promises of reward, ventured her long neck down the wolf's throat and drew out the bone. She then modestly asked for the promised reward.

"Reward?" barked the wolf, showing his teeth. "Of all the ungrateful creatures! I have permitted you to live to tell your grandchildren that you put your head in a wolf's mouth without having it bitten off, and then you ask for a reward! Get out of here before I change my mind!"

Application: THOSE WHO LIVE ON EXPECTATION ARE SURE TO BE DISAPPOINTED.

THE FOX

AND THE GRAPES

Illustration by Boris Artzybasheff

Mister Fox was just about famished, and thirsty too, when he stole into a vineyard where the sun-ripened grapes were hanging up on a trellis in a tempting show, but too high for him to reach. He took a run and a jump, snapping at the nearest bunch, but missed. Again and again he jumped, only to miss the luscious prize. At last, worn out with his efforts, he retreated, muttering: "Well, I never really wanted those grapes anyway. I am sure they are sour, and perhaps wormy in the bargain."

Application: ANY FOOL CAN DESPISE WHAT HE CANNOT GET.

THE HEN AND THE FOX

Illustrations by Fritz Kredel

A fox was out looking for a late supper. He came to a henhouse, and through the open door he could see a hen far up on the highest perch, safe out of his reach.

Here, thought the fox, was a case for diplomacy. Either that or go hungry! So he gave considerable thought to just how he should approach his intended supper.

"Hello, there, friend hen," said he in an anxious voice. "I haven't seen you about of late. Somebody told me that you have

156

had a sick spell and I was sincerely worried over you. You look pale as a ghost. If you will just step down I'll take your pulse and look at your tongue. I'm afraid you are in for quite a siege."

"You never said a truer word, cousin fox," replied the hen. "It will have to be a siege, for I am in such a state that if I were to climb down to where you are, I'm afraid it would be the death of me."

Application: BEWARE OF THE INSINCERE FRIEND!

THE HARE AND THE TORTOISE

Illustration by Boris Artzybasheff

A hare was continually poking fun at a tortoise because of the slowness of his pace. The tortoise tried not to be annoyed by the jeers of the hare, but one day in the presence of the other animals he was goaded into challenging the hare to a foot race.

"Why, this is a joke," said the hare. "You know that I can run circles around you."

"Enough of your boasting," said the tortoise. "Let's get on with the race."

So the course was set by the animals, and the fox was chosen as judge. He gave a sharp bark and the race was on. Almost before you could say "scat" the hare was out of sight. The tortoise plodded along at his usual unhurried pace.

After a time the hare stopped to wait for the tortoise to come along. He waited for a long, long time until he began to get sleepy. "I'll just take a quick nap here in this soft grass, and then in the cool of the day I'll finish the race." So he lay down and closed his eyes.

Meanwhile, the tortoise plodded on. He passed the sleeping hare, and was approaching the finish line when the hare awoke with a start. It was too late to save the race. Much ashamed, he crept away while all the animals at the finish line acclaimed the winner.

Application: SLOW AND STEADY WINS THE RACE.

THE DOG AND THE SHADOW

Illustration by Percy J. Billinghurst

One day a dog stole a piece of meat out of a butcher shop, and on his way to a safe place where he could eat it without interruption he had to cross a footbridge over a clear stream. Looking down he saw his own reflection in the water.

Thinking that the reflection was another dog with another piece of meat, and being a greedy dog, he made up his mind to have that also. So he snarled and made a grab for the other dog's meat.

As his greedy mouth opened, out dropped the piece of meat and fell into the stream and was lost.

Application: GRASP AT THE SHADOW AND LOSE THE SUBSTANCE.

THE COUNTRY MOUSE AND THE TOWN MOUSE

Illustration by Percy J. Billinghurst

Once upon a time a country mouse who had a friend in town invited him, for old acquaintance's sake, to pay him a visit in the country. Though plain and rough and somewhat frugal in his nature, the country mouse opened his heart and store in honor of an old friend. There was not a carefully stored-up morsel that he did not produce from his larder—peas and barley, cheese parings and nuts—to please the palate of his city-bred guest.

The town mouse, however, turned up his long nose at the rough country fare. "How is it, my friend," he exclaimed, "that you can endure the boredom of living like a toad in a hole? You can't really prefer these solitary rocks and woods to the excitement of the city. You are wasting your time out here in the wilderness. A mouse, you know, does not live forever, one must make the most of life while it lasts. So come with me and I'll show you life and the town."

In the end, the country mouse allowed himself to be persuaded, and the two friends set out together on their journey to town. It was late in the evening when they crept stealthily into the city, and midnight before they reached the great house where the town mouse lived.

On the table of the splendid banquet room were the remains of a lavish feast. It was now the turn of the city mouse to play host. He ran to and fro to supply all the guest's wants. He pressed dish upon dish and dainty upon dainty upon him as though he were waiting on a king. The country mouse, for his part, pretended to feel quite at home, and blessed the good fortune that had wrought such a change in his way of life.

But in the midst of his enjoyment, just as he was beginning to feel contempt for his frugal life in the country, the sound of barking and growling could be heard outside the door.

"What is that?" said the country mouse.

"Oh, that is only the master's dogs," replied the town mouse.

"Only!" replied the visitor in dismay. "I can't say that I like music with my dinner."

At that moment the door flew open and a party of revelers, together with two huge dogs, burst into the room. The affrighted friends jumped from the table and concealed themselves in a far corner of the chamber. At length, when things seemed quiet, the country mouse stole out from his hiding place, and bidding his friend good-bye, whispered in his ear: "This fine way of living may do for those who like it. But give me my barley bread in peace and in security in preference to your dainty fare partaken with fear and trembling."

Application: A CRUST EATEN IN PEACE IS BETTER THAN A BANQUET PARTAKEN IN ANXIETY.

THE FOX AND THE CROW

Illustration by Percy J. Billinghurst

A crow, who had stolen a piece of cheese, was flying toward the top of a tall tree where he hoped to enjoy his prize, when a fox spied him. "If I plan this right," said the fox to himself, "I shall have cheese for supper."

So, as he sat under the tree, he began to speak in his politest tones: "Good day, mistress crow, how well you are looking today! How glossy your wings, and your breast is the breast of an eagle. And your claws—I beg pardon—your talons are as strong as steel. I have not heard your voice, but I am certain that it must surpass that of any other bird just as your beauty does."

The vain crow was pleased by all this flattery. She believed every word of it and waggled her tail and flapped her wings to show her pleasure. She liked especially what friend fox said about her voice, for she had sometimes been told that her caw was a bit rusty. So, chuckling to think how she was going to surprise the fox with her most beautiful caw, she opened wide her mouth.

Down dropped the piece of cheese! The wily fox snatched it before it touched the ground, and as he walked away, licking his chops, he offered these words of advice to the silly crow: "The next time someone praises your beauty be sure to hold your tongue."

Application: FLATTERERS ARE NOT TO BE TRUSTED.

The Husband Who Was to Mind the House[1]

Once on a time there was a man, so surly and cross, he never thought his Wife did anything right in the house. So, one evening, in haymaking time, he came home, scolding and swearing, and showing his teeth and making a dust.

"Dear love, don't be so angry; there's a good man," said his Goody; "to-morrow let's change our work. I'll go out with the mowers and mow, and you shall mind the house at home."

Yes, the Husband thought that would do very well.

So, early next morning, his Goody took a scythe over her neck, and went out into the hayfield with the mowers, and began to mow; but the man was to mind house, and do the work at home.

First of all, he wanted to churn the butter; but when he had churned a while, he got thirsty, and went down to the cellar to tap a barrel of ale. So, just when he had knocked in the bung, and was putting the tap into the cask, he heard overhead the pig come into the kitchen. Then off he ran up the cellar steps, with the tap in his hand, as fast as he could, to look after the pig, lest it should upset the churn; but when he got up, and saw the pig had already knocked the churn over, and stood there, rooting and grunting amongst the cream which was running all over the floor, he got so wild with rage that he quite forgot the ale barrel, and ran at the pig as hard as he could. He caught it, too, just as it ran out of doors, and gave it such a kick, that piggy lay for dead on the spot. Then all at once he remembered he had the tap in his hand; but when he got down to the cellar, every drop of ale had run out of the cask.

Then he went into the dairy and found enough cream left to fill the churn again, and so he began to churn, for butter they must have at dinner. When he had churned a bit, he remembered that their milking cow was still shut up in the byre, and hadn't had a bit to eat or a drop to drink all the morning, though the sun was high. Then all at once he thought 'twas too far to take her down to the meadow, so he'd just get her up on the housetop—for the house, you must know, was thatched with sods, and a fine crop of grass was growing there. Now the house lay close up against a steep down, and he thought if he laid a plank across to the thatch at the back he'd get the cow up.

But still he couldn't leave the churn, for there was his little babe crawling about on the floor, and "if I leave it," he thought, "the child is safe to upset it." So he took the churn on his back, and went out with it; but then he thought he'd better first water the cow before he turned her out on the thatch; so he took up a bucket to draw water out of the well; but, as he stooped down at the well's brink, all the cream ran out of the churn over his shoulders, and so down into the well.

Now it was near dinner time, and he hadn't even got the butter yet; so he thought he'd best boil the porridge, and filled the pot with water and hung it over the fire. When he had done that, he thought the cow might perhaps fall off the thatch and break her legs or her neck. So he got up on the house to tie her up. One end of the rope he made fast to the cow's neck and the other he slipped down the chimney, and tied round his own thigh; and he had to make haste, for the water now began to boil in the pot, and he had still to grind the oatmeal.

[1] From "East of the Sun and West of the Moon," by P. C. Asbjörnsen, illustrations from drawings by Hedvig Collin

So he began to grind away; but while he was hard at it, down fell the cow off the housetop after all, and as she fell, she dragged the man up the chimney by the rope. There he stuck fast; and as for the cow, she hung halfway down the wall, swinging between heaven and earth, for she could neither get down nor up.

And now the Goody had waited seven lengths and seven breadths for her Husband to come and call them home to din-ner; but never a call they had. At last she thought she'd waited long enough, and went home. But when she got there and saw the cow hanging in such an ugly place, she ran up and cut the rope in two with her scythe. But, as she did this, down came her Husband out of the chimney; and so, when his old dame came inside the kitchen, there she found him standing on his head in the porridge pot.

Lazy Jack[1]

Once upon a time there was a boy whose name was Jack, and he lived with his mother on a common. They were very poor, and the old woman got her living by spinning, but Jack was so lazy that he would do nothing but bask in the sun in the hot weather, and sit by the corner of the hearth in the winter-time. So they called him Lazy Jack. His mother could not get him to do anything for her, and at last told him one Monday, that if he did not begin to work for his porridge she would turn him out to get his living as he could.

This roused Jack, and he went out and hired himself for the next day to a neighboring farmer for a penny; but as he was coming home, never having had any money before, he lost it in passing over a brook.

"You stupid boy," said his mother, "you should have put it in your pocket."

"I'll do so another time," replied Jack.

Well, the next day, Jack went out again and hired himself to a cowkeeper, who gave him a jar of milk for his day's work. Jack took the jar and put it into the large pocket of his jacket, spilling it all, long before he got home.

"Dear me!" said the old woman; "you should have carried it on your head."

"I'll do so another time," said Jack.

So the following day, Jack hired himself again to a farmer, who agreed to give him a cream cheese for his services. In the evening Jack took the cheese, and went home with it on his head. By the time he got home the cheese was all spoilt, part of it being lost, and part matted with his hair.

"You stupid lout," said his mother, "you should have carried it very carefully in your hands."

"I'll do so another time," replied Jack.

Now the next day, Lazy Jack again went out, and hired himself to a baker, who would give him nothing for his work but a large tom-cat. Jack took the cat, and began carrying it very carefully in his hands, but in a short time pussy scratched him so much that he was compelled to let it go.

When he got home, his mother said to him, "You silly fellow, you should have tied it with a string, and dragged it along after you."

"I'll do so another time," said Jack.

So on the following day, Jack hired himself to a butcher, who rewarded him by the handsome present of a shoulder of mutton. Jack took the mutton, tied it to a string, and trailed it along after him in the dirt, so that by the time he had got home the meat was completely spoilt. His mother was this time quite out of patience with him, for the next day was Sunday, and she was obliged to do with cabbage for her dinner.

"You ninney-hammer," said she to her son; "you should have carried it on your shoulder."

"I'll do so another time," replied Jack.

Well, on the Monday, Lazy Jack went

[1] From "English Fairy Tales," retold by Flora Annie Steel, illustration from a drawing by Arthur Rackham

163

once more, and hired himself to a cattle-keeper, who gave him a donkey for his trouble. Now though Jack was strong he found it hard to hoist the donkey on his shoulders, but at last he did it, and began walking home slowly with his prize. Now it so happened that in the course of his journey he passed a house where a rich man lived with his only daughter, a beautiful girl, who was deaf and dumb. And she had never laughed in her life, and the doctors said she would never speak till somebody made her laugh. So the father had given out that any man who made her laugh would receive her hand in marriage.

Now this young lady happened to be looking out of the window when Jack was passing by with the donkey on his shoulders; and the poor beast with its legs sticking up in the air was kicking violently and hee-hawing with all its might. Well, the sight was so comical that she burst out into a great fit of laughter, and immediately recovered her speech and hearing. Her father was overjoyed, and fulfilled his promise by marrying her to Lazy Jack, who was thus made a rich gentleman. They lived in a large house, and Jack's mother lived with them in great happiness until she died.

Jack and the Beanstalk [1]

A long long time ago, when most of the world was young and folk did what they liked because all things were good, there lived a boy called Jack.

His father was bedridden, and his mother, a good soul, was busy early morns and late eves planning and placing how to support her sick husband and her young son by selling the milk and butter which Milky-White, the beautiful cow, gave them without stint. For it was summertime. But winter came on; the herbs of the fields took refuge from the frosts in the warm earth, and though his mother sent Jack to gather what fodder he could get in the hedgerows, he came back as often as not with a very empty sack; for Jack's eyes were so often full of wonder at all the things he saw that sometimes he forgot to work!

So it came to pass that one morning Milky-White gave no milk at all—not one drain! Then the good hard-working mother threw her apron over her head and sobbed:

"What shall we do? What shall we do?"

Now Jack loved his mother; besides, he felt just a bit sneaky at being such a big boy, and doing so little to help, so he said, "Cheer up! Cheer up! I'll go and get work somewhere." And he felt as he spoke as if he would work his fingers to the bone; but the good woman shook her head mournfully.

"You've tried that before, Jack," she said, "and nobody would keep you. You are quite a good lad but your wits go a-woolgathering. No, we must sell Milky-White and live on the money. It is no use crying over milk that is not here to spill!"

You see, she was a wise as well as a hard-working woman, and Jack's spirits rose.

"Just so," he cried. "We will sell Milky-White and be richer than ever. It's an ill wind that blows no one good. So, as it is market-day, I'll just take her there and we shall see what we shall see."

"But—" began his mother.

"But doesn't butter parsnips," laughed

[1] From "English Fairy Tales," retold by Flora Annie Steel, illustrations from drawings by Arthur Rackham and George Cruikshank

Jack. "Trust me to make a good bargain."

So, as it was washing-day, and her sick husband was more ailing than usual, his mother let Jack set off to sell the cow.

"Not less than ten pounds," she bawled after him as he turned the corner.

Ten pounds, indeed! Jack had made up his mind to twenty! Twenty solid golden sovereigns!

He was just settling what he should buy his mother as a fairing out of the money, when he saw a queer, little, old man on the road who called out, "Good-morning, Jack!"

"Good-morning," replied Jack, with a polite bow, wondering how the queer, little, old man happened to know his name; though, to be sure, Jacks were as plentiful as blackberries.

"And where may you be going?" asked the queer, little, old man. Jack wondered again—he was always wondering, you know—what the queer, little, old man had to do with it; but, being always polite, he replied:

"I am going to market to sell Milky-White—and I mean to make a good bargain."

"So you will! So you will!" chuckled the queer, little, old man. "You look the sort of chap for it. I bet you know how many beans make five?"

"Two in each hand and one in my mouth," answered Jack readily. He really was sharp as a needle.

"Just so, just so!" chuckled the queer, little, old man; and as he spoke he drew out of his pocket five beans. "Well, here they are, so give us Milky-White."

Jack was so flabbergasted that he stood with his mouth open as if he expected the fifth bean to fly into it.

"What!" he said at last. "My Milky-White for five common beans! Not if I know it!"

"But they aren't common beans," put in the queer, little, old man, and there was a queer little smile on his queer little face. "If you plant these beans over-night, by

morning they will have grown up right into the very sky."

Jack was too flabbergasted this time even to open his mouth; his eyes opened instead.

"Did you say right into the very sky?" he asked at last; for, see you, Jack had wondered more about the sky than about anything else.

"*Right up into the very sky*," repeated the queer old man, with a nod between each word. "It's a good bargain, Jack; and, as fair play's a jewel, if they don't— Why! meet me here to-morrow morning and you shall have Milky-White back again. Will that please you?"

"Right as a trivet," cried Jack, without stopping to think, and the next moment he found himself standing on an empty road.

"Two in each hand and one in my mouth," repeated Jack. "That is what I said, and what I'll do. Everything in order, and if what the queer, little, old man said isn't true, I shall get Milky-White back to-morrow morning."

So whistling and munching the bean he trudged home cheerfully, wondering what the sky would be like if he ever got there.

"What a long time you've been!" exclaimed his mother, who was watching anxiously for him at the gate. "It is past sun-setting; but I see you have sold Milky-White. Tell me quick how much you got for her."

"You'll never guess," began Jack.

"Laws-a-mercy! You don't say so," interrupted the good woman. "And I worritting all day lest they should take you in. What was it? Ten pounds—fifteen—sure it *can't* be twenty!"

Jack held out the beans triumphantly.

"There," he said. "That's what I got for her, and a jolly good bargain too!"

It was his mother's turn to be flabbergasted; but all she said was:

"What! Them beans!"

"Yes," replied Jack, beginning to doubt his own wisdom; "but they're *magic* beans. If you plant them over-night, by morning

they—grow—right up—into—the—sky—
Oh! Please don't hit so hard!"

For Jack's mother for once had lost her
temper, and was belabouring the boy for
all she was worth. And when she had finished scolding and beating, she flung the
miserable beans out of window and sent
him, supperless, to bed.

If this was the magical effect of the
beans, thought Jack ruefully, he didn't
want any more magic, if you please.

However, being healthy and, as a rule,
happy, he soon fell asleep and slept like a
top.

When he woke he thought at first it was
moonlight, for everything in the room
showed greenish. Then he stared at the
little window. It was covered as if with a
curtain by leaves. He was out of bed in a
trice, and the next moment, without waiting to dress, was climbing up the biggest
beanstalk you ever saw. For what the
queer, little, old man had said was true!
One of the beans which his mother had
chucked into the garden had found soil,
taken root, and grown in the night. . . .
Where? . . .

Up to the very sky? Jack meant to see
at any rate.

So he climbed, and he climbed, and he
climbed. It was easy work, for the big
beanstalk with the leaves growing out of
each side was like a ladder; for all that he
soon was out of breath. Then he got his
second wind, and was just beginning to
wonder if he had a third when he saw in
front of him a wide, shining white road
stretching away, and away, and away.

So he took to walking, and he walked,
and walked, and walked, till he came to a
tall shining white house with a wide white
doorstep.

And on the doorstep stood a great big
woman with a black porridge-pot in her
hand. Now Jack, having had no supper,
was hungry as a hunter, and when he saw
the porridge-pot he said quite politely:

"Good-morning, 'm. I wonder if you
could give me some breakfast?"

"Breakfast!" echoed the woman, who, in
truth, was an ogre's wife. "If it is breakfast you're wanting, it's breakfast you'll
likely be; for I expect my man home every
instant, and there is nothing he likes better
for breakfast than a boy—a fat boy grilled
on toast."

Now Jack was not a bit of a coward, and
when he wanted a thing he generally got
it, so he said cheerful-like:

"I'd be fatter if I'd had my breakfast!"
Whereat the ogre's wife laughed and bade
Jack come in; for she was not, really, half
as bad as she looked. But he had hardly
finished the great bowl of porridge and
milk she gave him when the whole house
began to tremble and quake. It was the
ogre coming home!

Thump! Thump!! THUMP!!!

"Into the oven with you, sharp!" cried
the ogre's wife; and the iron oven door was
just closed when the ogre strode in. Jack
could see him through the little peep-hole
slide at the top where the steam came out.

He was a big one for sure. He had
three sheep strung to his belt, and these

he threw down on the table. "Here, wife," he cried, "roast me these snippets for breakfast; they are all I've been able to get this morning, worse luck! I hope the oven's hot?" And he went to touch the handle, while Jack burst out all of a sweat wondering what would happen next.

"Roast!" echoed the ogre's wife. "Pooh! the little things would dry to cinders. Better boil them."

So she set to work to boil them; but the ogre began sniffing about the room. "They don't smell—mutton meat," he growled. Then he frowned horribly and began the real ogre's rhyme:

"Fee-fi-fo-fum,
I smell the blood of an Englishman.
Be he alive, or be he dead,
I'll grind his bones to make my bread."

"Don't be silly!" said his wife. "It's the bones of the little boy you had for supper that I'm boiling down for soup! Come, eat your breakfast, there's a good ogre!"

So the ogre ate his three sheep, and when he had done he went to a big oaken chest and took out three big bags of golden pieces. These he put on the table, and began to count their contents while his wife cleared away the breakfast things. And by and by his head began to nod, and at last he began to snore, and snored so loud that the whole house shook.

Then Jack nipped out of the oven and, seizing one of the bags of gold, crept away, and ran along the straight, wide, shining white road as fast as his legs would carry him till he came to the beanstalk. He couldn't climb down it with the bag of gold, it was so heavy, so he just flung his burden down first, and, helter-skelter, climbed after it.

And when he came to the bottom there was his mother picking up gold pieces out of the garden as fast as she could; for, of course, the bag had burst.

"Laws-a-mercy me!" she says. "Wherever have you been? See! It's been rainin' gold!"

"No, it hasn't," began Jack. "I climbed up—" Then he turned to look for the beanstalk; but lo, and behold! it wasn't there at all! So he knew, then, it was all real magic.

After that they lived happily on the gold pieces for a long time, and the bedridden father got all sorts of nice things to eat; but, at last, a day came when Jack's mother showed a doleful face as she put a big yellow sovereign into Jack's hand and bade him be careful marketing, because there was not one more in the coffer. After that they must starve.

That night Jack went supperless to bed of his own accord. If he couldn't make money, he thought, at any rate he could eat less money. It was a shame for a big boy to stuff himself and bring no grist to the mill. He slept like a top, as boys do when they don't overeat themselves, and when he woke . . .

Hey, presto! the whole room showed greenish, and there was a curtain of leaves over the window! Another bean had grown in the night, and Jack was up it like a lamp-lighter before you could say knife.

This time he didn't take nearly so long climbing until he reached the straight, wide, white road, and in a trice he found himself before the tall white house, where on the wide white steps the ogre's wife was standing with the black porridge-pot in her hand.

And this time Jack was as bold as brass. "Good-morning, 'm," he said. "I've come to ask you for breakfast, for I had no supper, and I'm as hungry as a hunter."

"Go away, bad boy!" replied the ogre's wife. "Last time I gave a boy breakfast my man missed a whole bag of gold. I believe you are the same boy."

"Maybe I am, maybe I'm not," said Jack, with a laugh. "I'll tell you true when I've had my breakfast; but not till then."

So the ogre's wife, who was dreadfully curious, gave him a big bowl full of porridge; but before he had half finished it he heard the ogre coming—

Thump! THUMP! THUMP!

"In with you to the oven," shrieked the ogre's wife. "You shall tell me when he has gone to sleep."

This time Jack saw through the steam peep-hole that the ogre had three fat calves strung to his belt.

"Better luck to-day, wife!" he cried, and his voice shook the house. "Quick! Roast these trifles for my breakfast! I hope the oven's hot?"

And he went to feel the handle of the door, but his wife cried out sharply:

"Roast! Why, you'd have to wait hours before they were done! I'll broil them— see how bright the fire is!"

"Umph!" growled the ogre. And then he began sniffing and calling out:

"Fee-fi-fo-fum,
I smell the blood of an Englishman.
Be he alive, or be he dead,
I'll grind his bones to make my bread."

"Twaddle!" said the ogre's wife. "It's only the bones of the boy you had last week that I've put into the pig-bucket!"

"Umph!" said the ogre harshly; but he ate the broiled calves and then he said to his wife, "Bring me my hen that lays the magic eggs. I want to see gold."

So the ogre's wife brought him a great, big, black hen with a shiny red comb. She plumped it down on the table and took away the breakfast things.

Then the ogre said to the hen, "Lay!" and it promptly laid—what do you think? —a beautiful, shiny, yellow, golden egg!

"None so dusty, henny-penny," laughed the ogre. "I shan't have to beg as long as I've got you." Then he said, "Lay!" once more; and lo and behold! there was another beautiful, shiny, yellow, golden egg!

Jack could hardly believe his eyes, and made up his mind that he would have that hen, come what might. So, when the ogre began to doze, he just out like a flash from the oven, seized the hen, and ran for his life! But, you see, he reckoned without his prize; for hens, you know, always cackle when they leave their nests after laying an egg, and this one set up such a scrawing that it woke the ogre.

"Where's my hen?" he shouted, and his wife came rushing in, and they both rushed to the door; but Jack had got the better of them by a good start, and all they could see was a little figure right away down the wide white road, holding a big, scrawing, cackling, fluttering, black hen by the legs!

How Jack got down the beanstalk he never knew. It was all wings, and leaves, and feathers, and cacklings; but get down he did, and there was his mother wondering if the sky was going to fall!

But the very moment Jack touched ground he called out, "Lay!" and the black hen ceased cackling and laid a great, big, shiny, yellow, golden egg.

So every one was satisfied; and from that moment everybody had everything that money could buy. For, whenever they wanted anything, they just said, "Lay!" and the black hen provided them with gold.

But Jack began to wonder if he couldn't find something else besides money in the sky. So one fine, moonlight, midsummer night he refused his supper, and before he went to bed stole out to the garden with a big watering-can and watered the ground under his window; for, thought he, "there must be two more beans somewhere, and perhaps it is too dry for them to grow." Then he slept like a top.

And lo, and behold! when he woke, there was the green light shimmering through his room, and there he was in an instant on the beanstalk, climbing, climbing, climbing for all he was worth.

But this time he knew better than to ask for his breakfast; for the ogre's wife would be sure to recognize him. So he just hid in some bushes beside the great white house, till he saw her in the scullery, and then he slipped out and hid himself in the copper; for he knew she would be sure to look in the oven first thing.

And by and by he heard—

Thump! THUMP! THUMP!

And peeping through a crack in the copper-lid he could see the ogre stalk in with three huge oxen strung at his belt. But this time, no sooner had the ogre got into the house than he began shouting:

"*Fee-fi-fo-fum,*
I smell the blood of an Englishman.
Be he alive, or be he dead,
I'll grind his bones to make my bread."

For, see you, the copper-lid didn't fit tight like the oven door, and ogres have noses like a dog's for scent.

"Well, I declare, so do I!" exclaimed the ogre's wife. "It will be that horrid boy who stole the bag of gold and the hen. If so, he's hid in the oven!"

But when she opened the door, lo, and behold! Jack wasn't there! Only some joints of meat roasting and sizzling away.

Then she laughed and said, "You and me be fools for sure. Why, it's the boy you caught last night as I was getting ready for your breakfast. Yes, we be fools to take dead meat for live flesh! So eat your breakfast, there's a good ogre!"

But the ogre, though he enjoyed roast boy very much, wasn't satisfied, and every now and then he would burst out with "*Fee-fi-fo-fum,*" and get up and search the cupboards, keeping Jack in a fever of fear lest he should think of the copper.

But he didn't. And when he had finished his breakfast he called out to his wife, "Bring me my magic harp! I want to be amused."

So she brought out a little harp and put it on the table. And the ogre leant back in his chair and said lazily:

"Sing!"

And lo, and behold! the harp began to sing. If you want to know what it sang about! Why! It sang about everything! And it sang so beautifully that Jack forgot to be frightened, and the ogre forgot to think of "*Fee-fi-fo-fum,*" and fell asleep and

did
NOT
SNORE.

Then Jack stole out of the copper like a mouse and crept hands and knees to the table, raised himself up ever so softly and laid hold of the magic harp; for he was determined to have it.

But, no sooner had he touched it, than it cried out quite loud, "Master! Master!" So the ogre woke, saw Jack making off, and rushed after him.

My goodness, it was a race! Jack was nimble, but the ogre's stride was twice as long. So, though Jack turned, and twisted, and doubled like a hare, yet at last, when he got to the beanstalk, the ogre was not a dozen yards behind him. There wasn't time to think, so Jack just flung himself on to the stalk and began to go down as fast as he could while the harp kept calling, "Master! Master!" at the very top of its voice. He had only got down about a quarter of the way when there was the most awful lurch you can think of, and Jack nearly fell off the beanstalk. It was the ogre beginning to climb down, and his weight made the stalk sway like a tree in a storm. Then Jack knew it was life or death, and he climbed down faster and faster, and as he climbed he shouted, "Mother! Mother! Bring an axe! Bring an axe!"

Now his mother, as luck would have it, was in the back-yard chopping wood, and she ran out thinking that this time the sky must have fallen. Just at that moment Jack touched ground and he flung down the harp—which immediately began to sing of all sorts of beautiful things—and he seized the axe and gave a great chop at the beanstalk, which shook and swayed and bent like barley before a breeze.

"Have a care!" shouted the ogre, clinging on as hard as he could. But Jack *did* have a care, and he dealt that beanstalk such a shrewd blow that the whole of it, ogre and all, came toppling down, and, of course, the ogre broke his crown, so that he died on the spot.

After that every one was quite happy. For they had gold and to spare, and if the bedridden father was dull, Jack just brought out the harp and said, "Sing!" And lo, and behold! it sang about everything under the sun.

So Jack ceased wondering so much and became quite a useful person.

And the last bean hasn't grown yet. It is still in the garden.

I wonder if it will ever grow?

And what little child will climb its beanstalk into the sky?

And what will that child find?

Goody me!

"Fee-fi-fo-fum, I smell the blood of an Englishman"

The Little Match Girl [1]

It was late on a bitterly cold New Year's Eve. The snow was falling. A poor little girl was wandering in the dark cold streets; she was bareheaded and barefoot. She had of course had slippers on when she left home, but they were not much good, for they were so huge. They had last been worn by her mother, and they fell off the poor little girl's feet when she was running across the street to avoid two carriages that were rolling rapidly by. One of the shoes could not be found at all, and the other was picked up by a boy who ran off with it, saying that it would do for a cradle when he had some children of his own.

So the poor little girl had to walk on with her little bare feet, which were red and blue with the cold. She carried a quantity of matches in her old apron, and held a packet of them in her hand.

Nobody had bought any of her during all the long day, and nobody had even given her a copper. The poor little creature was hungry and perishing with cold, and she looked the picture of misery.

The snowflakes fell on her long yellow hair, which curled so prettily round her face, but she paid no attention to that. Lights were shining from every window, and there was a most delicious odor of roast goose in the streets, for it was New Year's Eve. She could not forget that! She found a corner where one house projected a little beyond the next one, and here she crouched, drawing up her feet under her, but she was colder than ever. She did not dare to go home, for she had not sold any matches and had not earned a single penny. Her father would beat her, and besides it was almost as cold at home as it was here. They had only the roof over them, and the wind whistled through it although they stuffed up the biggest cracks with rags and straw.

Her little hands were almost dead with cold. Oh, one little match would do some good! If she only dared, she would pull one out of the packet and strike it on the wall to warm her fingers. She pulled out one. *R-r-sh-sh!* How it sputtered and blazed! It burnt with a bright clear flame, just like a little candle, when she held her hand round it.

Now the light seemed very strange to her! The little girl fancied that she was sitting in front of a big stove with polished brass feet and handles. There was a splendid fire blazing in it and warming her so beautifully, but—what happened? Just as she was stretching out her feet to warm them, the flame went out, the stove vanished—and she was left sitting with the end of the burnt match in her hand.

She struck a new one. It burnt, it blazed up, and where the light fell upon the wall, it became transparent like gauze, and she could see right through it into the room.

The table was spread with a snowy cloth and pretty china. A roast goose stuffed with apples and prunes was steaming on it. And what was even better, the goose hopped from the dish with the carving knife sticking in his back and waddled across the floor. It came right up to the poor child, and then—the match went out, and there was nothing to be seen but the thick black wall.

She lit another match. This time she was sitting under a lovely Christmas tree. It was much bigger and more beautifully decorated than the one she had seen when she peeped through the glass doors at the rich merchant's house on the last Christmas. Thousands of lighted candles gleamed under its branches. And colored pictures, such as she had seen in the shop windows, looked down at her. The little girl stretched out both her hands towards them—then out went the match. All the

[1] From "Hans Andersen's Fairy Tales," translated by Mrs. E. Lucas. Illustrations by Richard Bennett and Arthur Rackham

She struck the whole bundle of matches

Christmas candles rose higher and higher, till she saw that they were only the twinkling stars. One of them fell and made a bright streak of light across the sky.

"Now someone is dying," thought the little girl, for her old grandmother, the only person who had ever been kind to her, used to say, "When a star falls, a soul is going up to God."

Now she struck another match against the wall, and this time it was her grandmother who appeared in the circle of flame. She saw her quite clearly and distinctly, looking so gentle and happy.

"Grandmother!" cried the little creature. "Oh, do take me with you. I know you will vanish when the match goes out. You will vanish like the warm stove, the delicious goose, and the beautiful Christmas tree!"

She hastily struck a whole bundle of matches, because she did so long to keep her grandmother with her. The light of the matches made it as bright as day. Grandmother had never before looked so big or so beautiful. She lifted the little girl up in her arms, and they soared in a halo of light and joy, far, far above the earth, where there was no more cold, no hunger, and no pain—for they were with God.

In the cold morning light the poor little girl sat there, in the corner between the houses, with rosy cheeks and a smile on her face—dead. Frozen to death on the last night of the old year. New Year's Day broke on the little body still sitting with the ends of the burnt-out matches in her hand.

"She must have tried to warm herself," they said. Nobody knew what beautiful visions she had seen, nor in what a halo she had entered with her grandmother upon the glories of the New Year.

Red Riding Hood[1]

Once upon a time there was a sweet little maiden who was loved by all who knew her, but she was especially dear to her grandmother, who did not know how to make enough of the child. Once she gave her a little red velvet cloak. It was so becoming and she liked it so much that she would never wear anything else, and so she got the name of Red Riding Hood.

One day her mother said to her, "Come here, Red Riding Hood! Take this cake and bottle of wine to grandmother. She

[1] A fairy tale by the Brothers Grimm. Illustrations from drawings by Jessie Wilcox Smith and Arthur Rackham

is weak and ill, and they will do her good. Go quickly, before it gets hot. And don't loiter by the way, or run, or you will fall down and break the bottle, and there will be no wine for grandmother. When you get there, don't forget to say 'Good morning' prettily, without staring about you."

"I will do just as you tell me," Red Riding Hood promised her mother.

Her grandmother lived away in the wood, a good half hour from the village. When she got to the wood she met a wolf, but Red Riding Hood did not know what a wicked animal he was, so she was not a bit afraid of him.

"Good morning, Red Riding Hood," he said.

"Good morning, wolf," she answered.

"Whither away so early, Red Riding Hood?"

"To grandmother's."

"What have you got in your basket?"

"Cake and wine. We baked yesterday, so I'm taking a cake to grandmother. She wants something to make her well."

"Where does your grandmother live, Red Riding Hood?"

"A good quarter of an hour farther into the wood. Her house stands under three big oak trees, near a hedge of nut trees which you must know," said Red Riding Hood.

The wolf thought, "This tender little creature will be a plump morsel! She will be nicer than the old woman. I must be cunning and snap them both up."

He walked along with Red Riding Hood for a while. Then he said, "Look at the pretty flowers, Red Riding Hood. Why don't you look about you? I don't believe you even hear the birds sing. You are just as solemn as if you were going to school. Everything else is so gay out here in the woods."

Red Riding Hood raised her eyes, and when she saw the sunlight dancing through the trees, and all the bright flowers, she thought, "I'm sure grandmother would be pleased if I took her a bunch of fresh flow-ers. It is still quite early. I shall have plenty of time to pick them."

So she left the path and wandered off among the trees to pick the flowers. Each time she picked one, she always saw another prettier one farther on. So she went deeper and deeper into the forest.

In the meantime the wolf went straight off to the grandmother's cottage and knocked at the door.

"Who is there?"

"Red Riding Hood, bringing you a cake and some wine. Open the door!"

"Lift the latch," called out the old woman. "I am too weak to get up."

The wolf lifted the latch and the door sprang open. He went straight in and up to the bed without saying a word, and ate up the poor old woman. Then he put on her nightdress and nightcap, got into bed and drew the curtains.

Red Riding Hood ran about picking flowers till she could carry no more, and then she remembered her grandmother again. She was astonished when she got to the house to find the door open, and when she entered the room everything seemed so strange.

She felt quite frightened but she did not know why. "Generally I like coming to see grandmother so much," she thought. "Good morning, grandmother," she cried. But she received no answer.

Then she went up to the bed and drew the curtain back. There lay her grand-mother, but she had drawn her cap down over her face and she looked very odd.

"Oh grandmother, what big ears you have," she said.

"The better to hear you with, my dear."

"Grandmother, what big eyes you have."

"The better to see you with, my dear."

"What big hands you have, grand-mother."

"The better to catch hold of you with, my dear."

"But grandmother, what big teeth you have."

"The better to eat you with, my dear."

"Good morning, grandmother," cried Red Riding Hood

Hardly had the wolf said this than he made a spring out of bed and swallowed poor little Red Riding Hood. When the wolf had satisfied himself he went back to bed, and he was soon snoring loudly.

A huntsman went past the house and thought, "How loudly the old lady is snoring. I must see if there is anything the matter with her."

So he went into the house and up to the bed, where he found the wolf fast asleep. "Do I find you here, you old sinner!" he said. "Long enough have I sought you!"

He raised his gun to shoot, when it just occurred to him that perhaps the wolf had eaten up the old lady, and that she might still be saved. So he took a knife and began cutting open the sleeping wolf. At the first cut he saw the little red cloak, and after a few more slashes, the little girl sprang out and cried, "Oh, how frightened I was! It was so dark inside the wolf." Next the old grandmother came out, alive but hardly able to breathe.

Red Riding Hood brought some big stones with which they filled the wolf, so that when he woke up and tried to spring away, the stones dragged him back and he fell down dead.

They were all quite happy now. The huntsman skinned the wolf and took the skin home. The grandmother ate the cake and drank the wine which Red Riding Hood had brought, and she soon felt quite strong. Red Riding Hood thought to herself, "I will never again wander off into the forest as long as I live, when my mother forbids it."

Hansel and Gretel [1]

Close to a large forest there lived a wood-cutter with his wife and his two children. The boy was called Hansel and the girl Gretel. They were always very poor and had very little to live on. And at one time when there was famine in the land, he could no longer procure daily bread.

One night when he lay in bed worrying over his troubles, he sighed and said to his wife, "What is to become of us? How are we to feed our poor children when we have nothing for ourselves?"

"I'll tell you what, husband," answered the woman. "Tomorrow morning we will take the children out quite early into the thickest part of the forest. We will light a fire and give each of them a piece of bread. Then we will go to our work and leave them alone. They won't be able to find their way back, and so we shall be rid of them."

"Nay, wife," said the man, "we won't do that. I could never find it in my heart to leave my children alone in the forest. The wild animals would soon tear them to pieces."

"What a fool you are!" she said. "Then we must all four die of hunger. You may as well plane the boards for our coffins at once."

She gave him no peace till he consented. "But I grieve over the poor children all the same," said the man. The two children could not go to sleep for hunger either, and they heard what their stepmother said to their father.

Gretel wept bitterly and said, "All is over with us now."

"Be quiet, Gretel," said Hansel. "Don't cry! I will find some way out of it."

When the old people had gone to sleep, he got up, put on his little coat, opened the door, and slipped out. The moon was shining brightly and the white pebbles round the house shone like newly minted coins. Hansel stooped down and put as many into his pockets as they would hold.

Then he went back to Gretel and said, "Take comfort, little sister, and go to sleep. God won't forsake us." And then he went to bed again.

At daybreak, before the sun had risen, the woman came and said, "Get up, you lazybones! We are going into the forest to fetch wood."

Then she gave them each a piece of bread and said, "Here is something for your dinner, but don't eat it before then, for you'll get no more."

Gretel put the bread under her apron, for Hansel had the stones in his pockets. Then they all started for the forest.

When they had gone a little way, Hansel stopped and looked back at the cottage, and he did the same thing again and again.

His father said, "Hansel, what are you stopping to look back at? Take care and put your best foot foremost."

"Oh, father," said Hansel, "I am looking at my white cat. It is sitting on the roof, wanting to say good-by to me."

"Little fool, that's no cat! It's the morning sun shining on the chimney," said the mother.

But Hansel had not been looking at the cat. He had been dropping a pebble on the ground each time he stopped.

When they reached the middle of the forest, their father said, "Now, children, pick up some wood. I want to make a fire to warm you."

Hansel and Gretel gathered the twigs together and soon made a huge pile. Then the pile was lighted, and when it blazed up the woman said, "Now lie down by the fire and rest yourselves while we go and cut wood. When we have finished we will come back to fetch you."

[1] A fairy tale by the Brothers Grimm. Illustrations from drawings by Wanda Gág and Jessie Wilcox Smith

Hansel and Gretel sat by the fire, and when dinnertime came they each ate their little bit of bread, and they thought their father was quite near because they could hear the sound of an ax. It was no ax, however, but a branch which the man had tied to a dead tree, and which blew backwards and forwards against it. They sat there so long a time that they got tired. Then their eyes began to close and they were soon fast asleep.

When they woke it was dark night. Gretel began to cry, "How shall we ever get out of the wood?"

But Hansel comforted her and said, "Wait a little while till the moon rises, and then we will soon find our way."

When the full moon rose, Hansel took his little sister's hand and they walked on, guided by the pebbles, which glittered like newly coined money. They walked the whole night, and at daybreak they found themselves back at their father's cottage.

They knocked at the door, and when the woman opened it and saw Hansel and Gretel she said, "You bad children, why did you sleep so long in the wood? We thought you did not mean to come back any more."

But their father was delighted, for it had gone to his heart to leave them behind alone.

Not long afterwards they were again in great destitution, and the children heard the woman at night in bed say to their father, "We have eaten up everything again but half a loaf, and then we will be at the end of everything. The children must go away! We will take them farther into the forest so that they won't be able to find their way back. There is nothing else to be done."

The man took it much to heart and said, "We had better share our last crust with the children."

But the woman would not listen to a word he said. She only scolded and reproached him. Anyone who once says A must also say B, and as the father had given in the first time he had to do so the second. The children were again wide awake and heard what was said.

When the old people went to sleep Hansel again got up, meaning to go out and get some more pebbles, but the woman had locked the door and he couldn't get out. But he consoled his little sister and said, "Don't cry, Gretel. Go to sleep. God will help us."

In the early morning the woman made the children get up and gave them each a piece of bread, but it was smaller than the last. On the way to the forest Hansel crumbled it up in his pocket, and stopped every now and then to throw a crumb onto the ground.

"Hansel, what are you stopping to look about you for?" asked his father. "I am looking at my dove which is sitting on the roof and wants to say good-by to me," answered Hansel.

"Little fool," said the woman, "that is no dove! It is the morning sun shining on the chimney."

Nevertheless, Hansel kept strewing the crumbs from time to time on the ground. The woman led the children far into the forest, where they had never been in their lives before. Again they made a big fire, and the woman said, "Stay where you are, children, and when you are tired you may go to sleep for a while. We are going farther on to cut wood, and in the evening when we have finished we will come back and fetch you."

At dinnertime Gretel shared her bread with Hansel, for he had crumbled his upon the road. Then they went to sleep and the evening passed, but no one came to fetch the poor children.

It was quite dark when they woke up, and Hansel cheered his little sister. He said, "Wait a bit, Gretel, till the moon rises, and then we can see the bread crumbs which I scattered to show us the way home."

When the moon rose they started, but they found no bread crumbs, for all the

the little house was made of bread and roofed with cake. The windows were transparent sugar.

"Here is something for us," said Hansel. "We will have a good meal. I will have a piece of the roof, Gretel, and you can have a bit of the window. It will be nice and sweet."

Hansel reached up and broke off a piece of the roof to see what it tasted like. Gretel went to the window and nibbled at that. A gentle voice called out from within:

"Nibbling, nibbling like a mouse,
Who's nibbling at my little house?"

The children answered:

"The wind, the wind doth blow
From heaven to earth below."

And they went on eating without disturbing themselves. Hansel, who found the roof very good, broke off a large piece for himself, and Gretel pushed a whole round pane out of the window and sat down on the ground to enjoy it.

All at once the door opened and an old, old woman, supporting herself on a crutch, came hobbling out. Hansel and Gretel were so frightened that they dropped what they held in their hands.

But the old woman only shook her head and said, "Ah, dear children, who brought you here? Come in and stay with me. You will come to no harm."

She took them by the hand and led them into the little house. A nice dinner was set before them: pancakes and sugar, milk, apples, and nuts. After this she showed them two little white beds into which they crept, and they felt as if they were in heaven.

Although the old woman appeared to be so friendly, she was really a wicked old witch who was on the watch for children, and she had built the bread house on purpose to lure them to her. Whenever she could get a child into her clutches she cooked it and ate it, and considered it a

thousands of birds in the forest had picked them up and eaten them.

Hansel said to Gretel, "We shall soon find the way." But they could not find it. They walked the whole night and all the next day from morning till night, but they could not get out of the wood.

They were very hungry, for they had nothing to eat but a few berries which they found. They were so tired that their legs would not carry them any farther, and they lay down under a tree and went to sleep.

When they woke in the morning, it was the third day since they had left their father's cottage. They started to walk again, but they only got deeper and deeper into the wood, and if no help came they must perish.

At midday they saw a beautiful snow-white bird sitting on a tree. It sang so beautifully that they stood still to listen to it. When it stopped, it fluttered its wings and flew around them. They followed it till they came to a little cottage, on the roof of which it settled down.

When they got quite near, they saw that

grand feast. Witches have red eyes and can't see very far, but they have keen noses like animals and can scent the approach of human beings.

When Hansel and Gretel came near her, she laughed wickedly to herself and said scornfully, "Now that I have them, they shan't escape me."

She got up early in the morning before the children were awake, and when she saw them sleeping, with their beautiful rosy cheeks, she murmured to herself, "They will be dainty morsels."

She seized Hansel with her bony hand and carried him off to a little stable, where she locked him up behind a barred door. He might shriek as loud as he liked, she took no notice of him.

Then she went to Gretel and shook her till she woke, and cried, "Get up, little lazybones! Fetch some water and cook something nice for your brother. He is in the stable and has to be fattened. When he is nice and fat, I will eat him."

Gretel began to cry bitterly, but it was no use; she had to obey the witch's orders. The best food was now cooked for poor Hansel, but Gretel got nothing but the shells of crayfish.

The old woman hobbled to the stable every morning and cried, "Hansel, put your finger out for me to feel how fat you are."

Hansel put out a knucklebone, and the old woman, whose eyes were too dim to see, thought it was his finger. And she was much astonished that he did not get fat.

When four weeks had passed and Hansel still kept thin, she became very impatient and would wait no longer.

"Now then, Gretel," she cried, "bustle along and fetch the water. Fat or thin, tomorrow I will kill Hansel and eat him."

Oh, how his poor little sister grieved! As she carried the water, the tears streamed down her cheeks.

"Dear God, help us!" she cried. "If only the wild animals in the forest had eaten us, we should at least have died together."

"You may spare your lamentations! They will do you no good," said the old woman.

Early in the morning Gretel had to go out to fill the kettle with water, and then she had to kindle a fire and hang the kettle over it.

"We will bake first," said the old witch. "I have heated the oven and kneaded the dough."

She pushed poor Gretel towards the oven and said, "Creep in and see if it is properly heated, and then we will put the bread in."

She meant, when Gretel had gone in, to shut the door and roast her, but Gretel saw her intention and said, "I don't know how to get in. How am I to manage it?"

"Stupid goose!" cried the witch. "The opening is big enough. You can see that I could get into it myself."

She hobbled up and stuck her head into the oven. But Gretel gave her a push which sent the witch right in, and then she banged the door and bolted it.

"Oh! oh!" the witch began to howl horribly. But Gretel ran away and left the wicked witch to perish miserably.

Gretel ran as fast as she could to the stable. She opened the door and cried, "Hansel, we are saved! The old witch is dead."

Hansel sprang out, like a bird out of a cage when the door is set open. How delighted they were. They fell upon each other's necks and kissed each other and danced about for joy.

As they had nothing more to fear, they went into the witch's house, and in every corner they found chests full of pearls and precious stones.

"These are better than pebbles," said Hansel, as he filled his pockets.

Gretel said, "I must take something home with me too." And she filled her apron.

"But now we must go," said Hansel, "so that we may get out of this enchanted wood."

Before they had gone very far, they came to a great piece of water.

"We can't get across it," said Hansel. "I see no steppingstones and no bridge."

"And there are no boats either," answered Gretel, "but there is a duck swimming. It will help us over if we ask it." So she cried:

"Little duck that cries quack, quack,
Here Gretel and here Hansel stand.
Quickly take us on your back,
No path nor bridge is there at hand!"

The duck came swimming towards them, and Hansel got on its back and told his sister to sit on his knee.

"No," answered Gretel, "it will be too heavy for the duck. It must take us over one after the other."

The good creature did this, and when they had got safely over and walked for a while the wood seemed to grow more and more familiar to them, and at last they saw their father's cottage in the distance. They began to run, and rushed inside, where they threw their arms around their father's neck. The man had not had a single happy moment since he deserted his children in the wood, and in the meantime his wife had died.

Gretel shook her apron and scattered the pearls and precious stones all over the floor, and Hansel added handful after handful out of his pockets.

So all their troubles came to an end, and they lived together as happily as possible.

The History of Tom Thumb [1]

In the days of the great Prince Arthur, there lived a mighty magician, called Merlin, the most learned and skilful enchanter the world has ever seen.

This famous magician, who could take any form he pleased, was travelling about as a poor beggar, and being very tired, he stopped at the cottage of a ploughman to rest himself, and asked for some food.

The countryman bade him welcome, and his wife, who was a very good-hearted woman, soon brought him some milk in a wooden bowl, and some coarse brown bread on a platter.

Merlin was much pleased with the kindness of the ploughman and his wife; but he could not help noticing that though everything was neat and comfortable in the cottage, they both seemed to be very unhappy. He therefore asked them why they were so melancholy, and learned that they were miserable because they had no children.

The poor woman said, with tears in her eyes: "I should be the happiest creature in the world if I had a son; although he was no bigger than my husband's thumb, I would be satisfied."

Merlin was so much amused with the idea of a boy no bigger than a man's thumb, that he determined to grant the poor woman's wish. Accordingly, in a short time after, the ploughman's wife had a son, who, wonderful to relate! was not a bit bigger than his father's thumb.

The queen of the fairies, wishing to see the little fellow, came in at the window while the mother was sitting up in the bed admiring him. The queen kissed the child, and, giving it the name of Tom Thumb, sent for some of the fairies, who dressed her little godson according to her orders:

"An oak-leaf hat he had for his crown;
His shirt of web by spiders spun;
With jacket wove of thistle's down;
His trowsers were of feathers done.
His stockings, of apple-rind, they tie
With eyelash from his mother's eye:
His shoes were made of mouse's skin,
Tann'd with the downy hair within."

Tom never grew any larger than his father's thumb, which was only of ordinary size; but as he got older he became very cunning and full of tricks. When he was old enough to play with the boys, and had lost all his own cherry-stones, he used to creep into the bags of his playfellows, fill his pockets, and, getting out without their noticing him, would again join in the game.

One day, however, as he was coming out of a bag of cherry-stones, where he had been stealing as usual, the boy to whom it belonged chanced to see him. "Ah, ah! my little Tommy," said the boy, "so I have caught you stealing my cherry-stones at last, and you shall be rewarded for your thievish tricks." On saying this, he drew the string tight round his neck,

[1] From "English Fairy Tales," collected by Joseph Jacobs. Illustrations from drawings by L. Leslie Brooke

and gave the bag such a hearty shake, that poor little Tom's legs, thighs, and body were sadly bruised. He roared out with pain, and begged to be let out, promising never to steal again.

A short time afterwards his mother was making a batter-pudding, and Tom, being very anxious to see how it was made, climbed up to the edge of the bowl; but his foot slipped, and he plumped over head and ears into the batter, without his mother noticing him, who stirred him into the pudding-bag, and put him in the pot to boil.

The batter filled Tom's mouth, and prevented him from crying; but, on feeling the hot water, he kicked and struggled so much in the pot, that his mother thought that the pudding was bewitched, and, pulling it out of the pot, she threw it outside the door. A poor tinker, who was passing by, lifted up the pudding, and, putting it into his budget, he then walked off. As Tom had now got his mouth cleared of the batter, he then began to cry aloud, which so frightened the tinker that he flung down the pudding and ran away. The pudding being broke to pieces by the fall, Tom crept out covered all over with the batter, and walked home. His mother, who was very sorry to see her darling in such a woful state, put him into a teacup, and soon washed off the batter; after which she kissed him, and laid him in bed.

Soon after the adventure of the pudding, Tom's mother went to milk her cow in the meadow, and she took him along with her. As the wind was very high, for fear of being blown away, she tied him to a thistle with a piece of fine thread. The cow soon observed Tom's oak-leaf hat, and liking the appearance of it, took poor Tom and the thistle at one mouthful. While the cow was chewing the thistle, Tom was afraid of her great teeth, which threatened to crush him in pieces, and he roared out as loud as he could: "Mother, mother!"

"Where are you, Tommy, my dear Tommy?" said his mother.

"Here, mother," replied he, "in the red cow's mouth."

His mother began to cry and wring her hands; but the cow, surprised at the odd noise in her throat, opened her mouth and let Tom drop out. Fortunately his mother caught him in her apron as he was falling to the ground, or he would have been dreadfully hurt. She then put Tom in her bosom and ran home with him.

Tom's father made him a whip of a barley straw to drive the cattle with, and having one day gone into the fields, Tom slipped a foot and rolled into the furrow. A raven, which was flying over, picked him up, and flew with him over the sea, and there dropped him.

A large fish swallowed Tom the moment he fell into the sea, which was soon after caught, and bought for the table of King Arthur. When they opened the fish in order to cook it, every one was astonished at finding such a little boy, and Tom was quite delighted at being free again. They carried him to the king, who made Tom his dwarf, and he soon grew a great favourite at court; for by his tricks and gambols he not only amused the king and queen, but also all the Knights of the Round Table.

It is said that when the king rode out on horseback, he often took Tom along with him, and if a shower came on, he used to creep into his majesty's waist-coat pocket, where he slept till the rain was over.

King Arthur one day asked Tom about his parents, wishing to know if they were as small as he was, and whether they were well off. Tom told the king that his father and mother were as tall as anybody about the court, but in rather poor circumstances. On hearing this, the king carried Tom to his treasury, the place where he kept all his money, and told him to take as much money as he could carry home to his parents, which made the poor little fellow caper with joy. Tom went immediately to procure a purse, which was made of a water-bubble, and then returned to the treasury, where he received a silver threepenny-piece to put into it.

Our little hero had some difficulty in lifting the burden upon his back; but he at last succeeded in getting it placed to his mind, and set forward on his journey. However, without meeting with any accident, and after resting himself more than a hundred times by the way, in two days and two nights he reached his father's house in safety.

Tom had travelled forty-eight hours with a huge silver-piece on his back, and was almost tired to death, when his mother ran out to meet him, and carried him into the house. But he soon returned to court.

As Tom's clothes had suffered much in the batter-pudding, and the inside of the fish, his majesty ordered him a new suit of clothes, and to be mounted as a knight on a mouse.

Of Butterfly's wings his shirt was made,
His boots of chicken's hide;
And by a nimble fairy blade,
Well learnèd in the tailoring trade,
His clothing was supplied.
A needle dangled by his side;
A dapper mouse he used to ride,
Thus strutted Tom in stately pride!

It was certainly very diverting to see Tom in this dress and mounted on the mouse, as he rode out a-hunting with the king and nobility, who were all ready to expire with laughter at Tom and his fine prancing charger.

The king was so charmed with his address that he ordered a little chair to be made, in order that Tom might sit upon his table, and also a palace of gold, a span high, with a door an inch wide, to live in. He also gave him a coach, drawn by six small mice.

The queen was so enraged at the honours conferred on Sir Thomas that she resolved to ruin him, and told the king that the little knight had been saucy to her.

The king sent for Tom in great haste, but being fully aware of the danger of royal anger, he crept into an empty snail-shell, where he lay for a long time until he was almost starved with hunger; but at last he ventured to peep out, and seeing a fine large butterfly on the ground, near the place of his concealment, he got close to it and jumping astride on it, was carried up into the air. The butterfly flew with him from tree to tree and from field to field, and at last returned to the court, where the king and nobility all strove to catch him; but at last poor Tom fell from his seat into a watering pot, in which he was almost drowned.

When the queen saw him, she was in a rage, and said he should be beheaded; and he was again put into a mouse trap until the time of his execution.

However, a cat, observing something alive in the trap, patted it about till the wires broke, and set Thomas at liberty.

The king received Tom again into favour, which he did not live to enjoy, for a large spider one day attacked him; and although he drew his sword and fought well, yet the spider's poisonous breath at last overcame him.

King Arthur and his whole court were so sorry at the loss of their little favourite that they went into mourning and raised a fine white marble monument over his grave with the following epitaph:

Here lies Tom Thumb, King Arthur's
* knight,*
Who died by a spider's cruel bite.
He was well known in Arthur's court,
Where he afforded gallant sport;
He rode a tilt and tournament,
And on a mouse a-hunting went.
Alive he filled the court with mirth;
His death to sorrow soon gave birth.
Wipe, wipe your eyes, and shake your
* head*
And cry,—Alas! Tom Thumb is dead!

The butterfly carried Tom Thumb into the air

The Ugly Duckling [1]

The country was very lovely just then—it was summer. The wheat was golden and the oats still green. The hay was stacked in the rich low meadows, where the stork marched about on his long red legs, chattering in Egyptian, the language his mother had taught him.

Round about field and meadow lay great woods, in the midst of which were deep lakes. Yes, the country certainly was lovely. In the sunniest spot stood an old mansion surrounded by a deep moat, and great dock leaves grew from the walls of the house right down to the water's edge. Some of them were so tall that a small child could stand upright under them. In among the leaves it was as secluded as in the depths of a forest, and there a duck was sitting on her nest. Her little ducklings were just about to be hatched, but she was quite tired of sitting, for it had lasted such a long time. Moreover, she had very few visitors, as the other ducks liked swimming about in the moat better than waddling up to sit under the dock leaves and gossip with her.

At last one egg after another began to crack. "Cheep, cheep!" they said. All the chicks had come to life and were poking their heads out.

"Quack, quack!" said the duck, and then they all quacked their hardest and looked about them on all sides among the green leaves. Their mother allowed them to look as much as they liked, for green is good for the eyes.

"How big the world is, to be sure!" said all the young ones. They certainly now had ever so much more room to move about than when they were inside their eggshells.

"Do you imagine this is the whole world?" said the mother. "It stretches a long way on the other side of the garden, right into the parson's field, though I have never been as far as that. I suppose you are all here now?" She got up and looked about. "No, I declare I have not got you all yet! The biggest egg is still there. How long is this going to take?" she said, and settled herself on the nest again.

"Well, how are you getting on?" said an old duck who had come to pay her a visit.

"This one egg is taking such a long time!" answered the sitting duck. "The shell will not crack. But now you must look at the others. They are the finest ducklings I have ever seen. They are all exactly like their father, the rascal!—yet he never comes to see me."

"Let me look at the egg which won't crack," said the old duck. "You may be sure that it is a turkey's egg! I was cheated like that once and I had no end of trouble and worry with the creatures, for I may tell you that they are afraid of the water. I simply could not get them into it. I quacked and snapped at them, but it all did no good. Let me see the egg! Yes, it is a turkey's egg. You just leave it alone, and teach the other children to swim."

"I will sit on it a little longer. I have sat so long already that I may as well go on till the Midsummer Fair comes round."

"Please yourself," said the old duck, and away she went.

At last the big egg cracked. "Cheep, cheep!" said the young one and tumbled out. How big and ugly he was! The duck looked at him.

"That is a monstrous big duckling," she said. "None of the others looked like that. Can he be a turkey chick? Well, we shall soon find that out. Into the water he shall go, if I have to kick him in myself."

The next day was gloriously fine, and the sun shone on all the green dock leaves. The mother duck with her whole family went down to the moat.

[1] From "Hans Andersen's Fairy Tales," translated by Mrs. E. Lucas. Illustrations from drawings by Feodor Rojankovsky

Splash! into the water she sprang. "Quack, quack," she said, and one duckling after another plumped in. The water dashed over their heads, but they came up again and floated beautifully. Their legs went of themselves, and they were all there. Even the big ugly gray one swam about with them.

"No, that is no turkey," she said. "See how beautifully he uses his legs and how erect he holds himself. He is my own chick, after all, and not bad looking when you come to look at him properly. Quack, quack! Now come with me and I will take you out into the world and introduce you to the duckyard. But keep close to me all the time so that no one may tread upon you. And beware of the cat!"

Then they went into the duckyard. There was a fearful uproar going on, for two broods were fighting for the head of an eel, and in the end the cat captured it.

"That's how things go in this world," said the mother duck. She licked her bill, because she wanted the eel's head herself.

"Now use your legs," said she. "Mind you quack properly, and bend your necks to the old duck over there. She is the grandest of us all. She has Spanish blood in her veins and that accounts for her size. And do you see? She has a red rag round her leg. That is a wonderfully fine thing, and the most extraordinary mark of distinction any duck can have. It shows clearly that she is not to be parted with, and that she is worthy of recognition both by beasts and men! Quack, now! Don't turn your toes in! A well-brought-up duckling keeps his legs wide apart just like father and mother. That's it. Now bend your necks and say quack!"

They did as they were bid, but the other ducks round about looked at them and said, quite loud, "Just look there! Now we are to have that tribe, just as if there were not enough of us already. And, oh dear, how ugly that duckling is! We won't stand him." And a duck flew at him at once and bit him in the neck.

"Let him be," said the mother. "He is doing no harm."

"Very likely not," said the biter. "But he is so ungainly and queer that he must be whacked."

"Those are handsome children mother has," said the old duck with the rag round her leg. "They are all good looking except this one. He is not a good specimen. It's a pity you can't make him over again."

"That can't be done, your grace," said the mother duck. "He is not handsome, but he is a thoroughly good creature, and he swims as beautifully as any of the others. I think I might venture even to add that I think he will improve as he goes on, or perhaps in time he may grow smaller. He was too long in the egg, and so he has not come out with a very good figure." And then she patted his neck and stroked him down. "Besides, he is a drake," said she. "So it does not matter so much. I believe he will be very strong, and I don't doubt but he will make his way in the world."

"The other ducklings are very pretty," said the old duck. "Now make yourselves quite at home, and if you find the head of an eel you may bring it to me."

After that they felt quite at home. But the poor duckling which had been the last to come out of the shell, and who was so ugly, was bitten, pushed about, and made fun of by both the ducks and the hens. "He is too big," they all said. And the turkey cock, who was born with his spurs on and therefore thought himself quite an emperor, puffed himself up like a vessel in full sail, made for him, and gobbled and gobbled till he became quite red in the face. The poor duckling was at his wit's end, and did not know which way to turn. He was in despair because he was so ugly and the butt of the whole duckyard.

So the first day passed, and afterwards matters grew worse and worse. The poor duckling was chased and hustled by all of them. Even his brothers and sisters ill-used him. They were always saying, "If

only the cat would get hold of you, you hideous object!" Even his mother said, "I wish to goodness you were miles away." The ducks bit him, the hens pecked him, and the girl who fed them kicked him aside.

Then he ran off and flew right over the hedge, where the little birds flew up into the air in a fright.

"That is because I am so ugly," thought the poor duckling, shutting his eyes, but he ran on all the same. Then he came to a great marsh where the wild ducks lived. He was so tired and miserable that he stayed there the whole night. In the morning the wild ducks flew up to inspect their new comrade.

"What sort of a creature are you?" they inquired, as the duckling turned from side to side and greeted them as well as he could. "You are frightfully ugly," said the wild ducks, "but that does not matter to us, so long as you do not marry into our family." Poor fellow! He had not thought of marriage. All he wanted was permission to lie among the rushes and to drink a little of the marsh water.

He stayed there two whole days. Then two wild geese came, or rather two wild ganders. They were not long out of the shell and therefore rather pert.

"I say, comrade," they said, "you are so ugly that we have taken quite a fancy to you! Will you join us and be a bird of passage? There is another marsh close by, and there are some charming wild geese there. All are sweet young ladies who can say quack! You are ugly enough to make your fortune among them." Just at that moment, bang! bang! was heard up above, and both the wild geese fell dead among the reeds, and the water turned blood red. Bang! bang! went the guns, and whole flocks of wild geese flew up from the rushes and the shots peppered among them again.

There was a grand shooting party, and the sportsmen lay hidden round the marsh. Some even sat on the branches of the trees which overhung the water. The blue smoke rose like clouds among the dark trees and swept over the pool.

The retrieving dogs wandered about in the swamp—splash! splash! The rushes and reeds bent beneath their tread on all sides. It was terribly alarming to the poor duckling. He twisted his head round to get it under his wing, and just at that moment a frightful big dog appeared close beside him. His tongue hung right out of his mouth and his eyes glared wickedly. He opened his great chasm of a mouth close to the duckling, showed his sharp teeth, and—splash!—went on without touching him.

"Oh, thank Heaven!" sighed the duckling. "I am so ugly that even the dog won't bite me!"

Then he lay quite still while the shots whistled among the bushes, and bang after bang rent the air. Late in the day the noise ceased, but even then the poor duckling did not dare to get up. He waited several hours more before he looked about, and then he hurried away from the marsh as fast as he could. He ran across fields and meadows, and there was such a wind that he had hard work to make his way.

Towards night he reached a poor little cottage. It was such a miserable hovel that it remained standing only because it could not make up its mind which way to fall. The wind whistled so fiercely round the duckling that he had to sit on his tail to resist it, and it blew harder and ever harder. Then he saw that the door had fallen off one hinge and hung so crookedly that he could creep into the house through the crack, and by this means he made his way into the room.

An old woman lived here with her cat and her hen. The cat, whom she called "Sonnie," could arch his back, purr, and even give off sparks, though for that you had to stroke his fur the wrong way. The hen had quite tiny short legs, and so she was called "Chickie-low-legs." She laid good eggs, and the old woman was as fond of her as if she had been her own child.

In the morning the strange duckling was discovered immediately, and the cat began to purr and the hen to cluck.

"What on earth is that?" said the old woman, looking round, but her sight was not good and she thought the duckling

was a fat duck which had escaped. "This is a wonderful find!" said she. "Now I shall have duck's eggs—if only it is not a drake. We must wait and see about that."

So she took the duckling on trial for three weeks, but no eggs made their appearance. The cat was master of this house and the hen its mistress. They always said "We and the world," for they thought that they represented the half of the world, and that quite the better half.

The duckling thought there might be two opinions on the subject, but the cat would not hear of it.

"Can you lay eggs?" she asked.

"No."

"Have the goodness to hold your tongue then!"

And the cat said, "Can you arch your back, purr, or give off sparks?"

"No."

"Then you had better keep your opinions to yourself when people of sense are speaking!"

The duckling sat in the corner nursing his ill humor. Then he began to think of the fresh air and the sunshine, and an uncontrollable longing seized him to float on the water. At last he could not help telling the hen about it.

"What on earth possesses you?" she asked. "You have nothing to do. That is why you get these freaks into your head. Lay some eggs or take to purring, and you will get over it."

191

"But it is so delicious to float on the water," said the duckling. "It is so delicious to feel it rushing over your head when you dive to the bottom."

"That would be a fine amusement!" said the hen. "I think you have gone mad. Ask the cat about it. He is the wisest creature I know. Ask him if he is fond of floating on the water or diving under it. I say nothing about myself. Ask our mistress herself, the old woman. There is no one in the world cleverer than she is. Do you suppose she has any desire to float on the water or to duck underneath it?"

"You do not understand me," said the duckling.

"Well, if we don't understand you, who should? I suppose you don't consider yourself cleverer than the cat or the old woman, not to mention me! Don't make a fool of yourself, child, and thank your stars for all the good we have done you. Have you not lived in this warm room, and in such society that you might have learned something? But you are an idiot, and there is no pleasure in associating with you. You may believe me: I mean you well. I tell you home truths, and there is no surer way than that of knowing who are one's friends. You just set about laying some eggs, or learn to purr, or to emit sparks."

"I think I will go out into the wide world," said the duckling.

"Oh, do so by all means," said the hen. So away went the duckling. He floated on the water and ducked underneath it, but he was looked askance at and slighted by every living creature for his ugliness. Now the autumn came on. The leaves in the woods turned yellow and brown. The wind took hold of them, and they danced about. The sky looked very cold and the clouds hung heavy with snow and hail. A raven stood on the fence and croaked, "Caw, caw!" from sheer cold. It made one shiver only to think of it. The poor duckling certainly was in a bad case!

One evening, the sun was just setting in wintry splendor when a flock of beautiful large birds appeared out of the bushes. The duckling had never seen anything so beautiful. They were dazzlingly white with long waving necks. They were swans, and uttering a peculiar cry they spread out their magnificent broad wings and flew away from the cold regions to warmer lands and open seas. They mounted so high, so very high, and the ugly little duckling became strangely uneasy. He circled round and round in the water like a wheel, craning his neck up into the air after them. Then he uttered a shriek so piercing and so strange that he was quite frightened by it himself. Oh, he could not forget those beautiful birds, those happy birds. And as soon as they were out of sight he ducked right down to the bottom, and when he came up again he was quite beside himself. He did not know what the birds were, or whither they flew, but all the same he was more drawn towards them than he had ever been by any creatures before. He did not envy them in the least. How could it occur to him even to wish to be such a marvel of beauty? He would have been thankful if only the ducks would have tolerated him among them—the poor ugly creature.

The winter was so bitterly cold that the duckling was obliged to swim about in the water to keep it from freezing over, but every night the hole in which he swam got smaller and smaller. Then it froze so hard that the surface ice cracked, and the duckling had to use his legs all the time so that the ice should not freeze around him. At last he was so weary that he could move no more, and he was frozen fast into the ice.

Early in the morning a peasant came along and saw him. He went out onto the ice and hammered a hole in it with his heavy wooden shoe, and carried the duckling home to his wife. There he soon revived. The children wanted to play with him, but the duckling thought they were going to ill-use him, and rushed in his fright into the milk pan, and the milk spurted out all over the room. The woman shrieked and threw up her hands. Then he flew into the butter cask, and down into the meal tub and out again. Just imagine what he looked like by this time! The woman screamed and tried to hit him with the fire tongs. The children tumbled over one another in trying to catch him, and they screamed with laughter. By good luck the door stood open, and the duckling flew out among the bushes and the newly fallen snow. And he lay there thoroughly exhausted.

But it would be too sad to mention all the privation and misery he had to go through during the hard winter. When the sun began to shine warmly again, the duckling was in the marsh, lying among the rushes. The larks were singing and the beautiful spring had come.

Then all at once he raised his wings and they flapped with much greater strength than before and bore him off vigorously. Before he knew where he was, he found himself in a large garden where the apple trees were in full blossom and the air was scented with lilacs, long branches of which overhung the indented shores of the lake. Oh, the spring freshness was delicious!

Just in front of him he saw three beautiful white swans advancing towards him from a thicket. With rustling feathers they swam lightly over the water. The duckling recognized the majestic birds, and he was overcome by a strange melancholy.

"I will fly to them, the royal birds, and they will hack me to pieces because I, who am so ugly, venture to approach them. But it won't matter! Better be killed by them than be snapped at by the ducks, pecked by the hens, spurned by the hen-wife, or suffer so much misery in the winter."

So he flew into the water and swam towards the stately swans. They saw him and darted towards him with ruffled feathers.

"Kill me!" said the poor creature, and he bowed his head towards the water and awaited his death. But what did he see reflected in the transparent water?

He saw below him his own image, but he was no longer a clumsy dark gray bird, ugly and ungainly. He was himself a swan! It does not matter in the least having been born in a duckyard, if only you come out of a swan's egg!

He felt quite glad of all the misery and tribulation he had gone through, for he was the better able to appreciate his good fortune now and all the beauty which greeted him. The big swans swam round and round him and stroked him with their bills.

Some little children came into the garden with corn and pieces of bread which they threw into the water, and the smallest one cried out, "There is a new one!" The other children shouted with joy, "Yes, a new one has come." And they clapped their hands and danced about, running after their father and mother. They threw the bread into the water, and one and all said, "The new one is the prettiest of them all. He is so young and handsome." And the old swans bent their heads and did homage before him.

He felt quite shy, and hid his head under his wing. He did not know what to think. He was very happy, but not at all proud, for a good heart never becomes proud. He thought of how he had been pursued and scorned, and now he heard them all say that he was the most beautiful of all beautiful birds. The lilacs bent their boughs right down into the water before him, and the bright sun was warm and cheering. He rustled his feathers and raised his slender neck aloft, saying with exultation in his heart, "I never dreamt of so much happiness when I was the Ugly Duckling!"

The

Tinder

Box[1]

A soldier came marching along the high-road. One, two! One, two! He had his knapsack on his back and his sword at his side, for he had been to the wars and now he was on his way home. He met an old witch on the road. She was so ugly that her lower lip hung right down onto her chin.

She said, "Good evening, soldier! What a nice sword you've got, and such a big knapsack. You are a real soldier! You shall have as much money as ever you like."

"Thank you kindly, you old witch," said the soldier.

"Do you see that big tree?" said the witch, pointing to a tree close by. "It is hollow inside. Climb up to the top and you will see a hole into which you can let yourself down, right down under the tree. I will tie a rope round your waist so that I can haul you up when you call."

[1] From "Hans Andersen's Fairy Tales," translated by Mrs. E. Lucas. Illustrations by Richard Bennett and from a drawing by Maxwell Armfield

"What am I to do down under the tree?" asked the soldier.

"Fetch money," said the witch. "You must know that when you get down to the bottom of the tree you will find yourself in a wide passage. It's quite light there, for there are over a hundred blazing lamps. You will see three doors which you can open, for the keys are there. If you go into the first room you will see a big box in the middle of the floor. A dog is sitting on the top of it and he has eyes as big as saucers, but you needn't mind that. I will give you my blue-checked apron, which you can spread out on the floor. Go quickly forward, take up the dog, and put him on my apron. Then open the box and take out as much money as you like. It is all copper, but if you like silver better, go into the next room. There you will find a dog with eyes as big as millstones. But never mind that. Put him on my apron and take the money. If you prefer gold you can have it too, and as much as you can carry, if you go into the third room. But the dog sitting on that box has eyes each as big as the Round Tower. He *is* a dog, indeed, as you may imagine. But don't let it trouble you. You only have to put him on my apron. Then he won't hurt you, and you can take as much gold out of the box as you like!"

"That's not so bad," said the soldier. "But what am I to give you, old witch? You'll want something, I'll be bound."

"No," said the witch. "Not a single penny do I want. I only want you to bring me an old tinder box that my grandmother forgot the last time she was down there."

"Well, tie the rope round my waist," said the soldier.

"Here it is," said the witch. "And here is my checked apron."

Then the soldier climbed up the tree, let himself slide down the hollow trunk, and found himself, as the witch had said, in the wide passage where the many hundred lamps were burning.

Now he opened the first door. Ugh! There sat the dog with eyes as big as saucers staring at him.

"You are a nice fellow!" said the soldier, as he put him onto the witch's apron and took out as many pennies as he could cram into his pockets. Then he shut the box, put the dog on the top of it again, and went into the next room. Hallo! There sat the dog with eyes as big as millstones.

"You shouldn't stare at me so hard. You might get a pain in your eyes!" Then he put the dog on the apron, but when he saw all the silver in the box, he threw away all the coppers and stuffed his pockets and his knapsack with silver. Then he went into the third room. Oh, how horrible! That dog really had two eyes as big as the Round Tower, and they rolled round and round like wheels.

"Good evening," said the soldier, saluting, for he had never seen such a dog in his life. But after looking at him for a bit he thought, "That will do." And then he lifted him down onto the apron and opened the chest. Heavens! What a lot of gold! He could buy the whole of Copenhagen with it, and all the sugar pigs from the cake woman, all the tin soldiers, whips, and rocking horses in the world. That was money indeed! Now the soldier threw away all the silver he had filled his pockets and his knapsack with and put gold in its place. Yes, he crammed all his pockets, his knapsack, his cap, and his boots so full that he could hardly walk. Now, he really had got a lot of money. He put the dog back onto the box, shut the door, and shouted up through the tree, "Haul me up, you old witch!"

"Have you got the tinder box?"

"Oh, to be sure!" said the soldier. "I had quite forgotten it." And he went back to fetch it. The witch hauled him up, and there he was standing on the highroad again with his pockets, boots, knapsack, and cap full of gold.

"What do you want the tinder box for?" asked the soldier.

"That's no business of yours," said the

witch. "You've got the money. Give me the tinder box!"

"Rubbish!" said the soldier. "Tell me directly what you want with it or I will draw my sword and cut off your head."

"I won't!" said the witch.

Then the soldier cut off her head. There she lay! But he tied all the money up in her apron, slung it on his back like a pack, put the tinder box in his pocket, and marched off to the town.

It was a beautiful town. He went straight to the finest hotel and ordered the grandest rooms and all the food he liked best, because he was a rich man now that he had so much money.

Certainly the servant who had to clean his boots thought they were funny old things for such a rich gentleman, but he had not had time yet to buy any new ones. The next day he bought new boots and fine clothes. The soldier now became a fine gentleman, and the people told him all about the grand things in the town, and about their king, and what a lovely princess his daughter was.

"Where is she to be seen?" asked the soldier.

"You can't see her at all," they all said. "She lives in a great castle surrounded with walls and towers. Nobody but the King dares to go in and out, for it has been prophesied that she will marry a common soldier, and the King doesn't like that!"

"I should like to see her well enough," thought the soldier. But there was no way of getting leave for that.

He now led a very merry life. He went to theaters, drove about in the King's Park, and gave away a lot of money to poor people, which was very nice of him, for he remembered how disagreeable it used to be not to have a penny in his pocket. Now he was rich, wore fine clothes, and had a great many friends who all said what a nice fellow he was—a thorough gentleman— and he liked to be told that.

But as he went on spending money every day and his store was never re-newed, he at last found himself with only twopence left. Then he was obliged to move out of his fine rooms. He had to take a tiny little attic up under the roof, clean his own boots, and mend them himself with a darning needle. None of his friends went to see him because there were far too many stairs.

One dark evening when he had not even enough money to buy a candle with, he suddenly remembered that there was a little bit in the old tinder box he had brought out of the hollow tree, when the witch helped him down. He got out the tinder box with the candle end in it and struck fire. But as the sparks flew out from the flint, the door burst open and the dog with eyes as big as saucers, which he had seen down under the tree, stood be-fore him and said, "What does my lord command?"

"By heaven!" said the soldier, "this is a nice kind of tinder box, if I can get what-ever I want like this. Get me some money," he said to the dog, and away it went.

It was back in a twinkling with a bag full of pennies in its mouth. Now the soldier saw what a treasure he had in the tinder box. If he struck once, the dog which sat on the box of copper came. If he struck twice, the dog on the silver box came. And if he struck three times, the one from the box of gold.

He now moved down to the grand rooms and got his fine clothes again, and then all his friends knew him once more and liked him as much as ever.

Then he suddenly began to think, "After all, it's a curious thing that no man can get a sight of the Princess. Everyone says she is so beautiful! But what is the good of that when she always has to be shut up in that big copper palace with all the towers. Can I not somehow manage to see her?" Where is my tinder box?" Then he struck the flint and, whisk! came the dog with eyes as big as saucers.

"It certainly is the middle of the night,"

196

said the soldier, "but I am very anxious to see the Princess, if only for a moment."

The dog was out of the door in an instant, and before the soldier had time to think about it, he was back again with the Princess. There she was, fast asleep on the dog's back, and she was so lovely that anybody could see that she must be a real princess. The soldier could not help it, but he was obliged to kiss her, for he was a true soldier.

Then the dog ran back again with the Princess, but in the morning, when the King and Queen were having breakfast, the Princess said that she had such a wonderful dream about a dog and a soldier. She had ridden on the dog's back and the soldier had kissed her.

"That's a pretty tale," said the Queen.

After this an old lady-in-waiting had to sit by her bed at night to see if this was really a dream, or what it could be.

The soldier longed so intensely to see the Princess again that at night the dog came to fetch her. He took her up and ran off with her as fast as he could, but the old lady-in-waiting put on her galoshes and ran just as fast behind them. When she saw that they disappeared into a large house, she thought, "Now I know where it is," and made a big cross with chalk on the gate. Then she went home and lay down, and presently the dog came back with the Princess. When he saw that there was a cross on the gate, he took a bit of chalk, too, and made crosses on all the gates in the town. Now this was very clever of him, for the lady-in-waiting could not possibly find the gate when there were crosses on all the gates.

Early next morning the King, the Queen, the lady-in-waiting, and all the court officials went to see where the Princess had been. "There it is," said the King, when he saw the first door with the cross on it.

"No, my dear husband, it is there," said the Queen, who saw another door with a cross on it.

"But there is one! And there is another!" they all cried out.

They soon saw that it was hopeless to try to find it.

Now the Queen was a very clever woman. She knew more than how to drive in a chariot. She took her big gold scissors and cut up a large piece of silk into small pieces, and made a pretty little bag which she filled with fine grains of buckwheat. She then tied it onto the back of the Princess. And when that was done she cut a little hole in the bag, so that the grains could drop out all the way wherever the Princess went.

At night the dog came again, took the Princess on his back, and ran off with her to the soldier, who was so fond of her that he longed to be a prince, so that he might have her for his wife.

The dog never noticed how the grain dropped out all along the road from the palace to the soldier's window, where he ran up the wall with the Princess.

In the morning the King and the Queen easily saw where their daughter had been, and they seized the soldier and threw him into the dungeons.

There he lay. Oh, how dark and tiresome it was! And then one day they said to him, "Tomorrow you are to be hanged." It was not amusing to be told that, especially as he had left his tinder box behind him at the hotel.

In the morning he could see through the bars in the little window that the people were hurrying out of the town to see him hanged. He heard the drums and saw the soldiers marching along. All the world was going. Among them was a shoemaker's boy in his leather apron and slippers. He was in such a hurry that he lost one of his slippers, and it fell close under the soldier's window where he was peeping out through the bars.

"I say, you boy! Don't be in such a hurry," said the soldier to him. "Nothing will happen till I get there. But if you will run to the house where I used to live and fetch me my tinder box, you shall have a penny. You must put your best foot foremost."

The boy was only too glad to have the penny and tore off to get the tinder box. He gave it to the soldier and—yes, now we shall hear.

Outside the town a high scaffold had been raised, and the soldiers were drawn up round about it as well as crowds of the townspeople. The King and the Queen sat upon a beautiful throne exactly opposite the judge and all the councilors.

The soldier mounted the ladder, but when they were about to put the rope round his neck, he said that before undergoing his punishment a criminal was always allowed the gratification of a harmless wish, and he wanted very much to smoke a pipe as it would be his last pipe in this world. The King would not deny him this, so the soldier took out his tinder box and struck fire, once, twice, three times. And there were all the dogs—the one with eyes like saucers, the one with eyes like millstones, and the one whose eyes were as big as the Round Tower.

"Help me! Save me from being hanged," cried the soldier.

And then the dogs rushed at the soldiers and the councilors. They took one by the legs and another by the nose and threw them up into the air, and when they fell down they were broken all to pieces.

"I won't!" cried the King, but the biggest dog took both him and the Queen and threw them after all the others. Then the soldiers became alarmed, and the people shouted, "Oh, good soldier, you shall be our King and marry the beautiful Princess!"

Then they conducted the soldier to the King's chariot, and all three dogs danced along in front of him and shouted "Hurrah!" The boys all put their fingers in their mouths and whistled, and the soldiers presented arms. The Princess came out of the copper palace and became Queen, which pleased her very much. The wedding took place in a week, and the dogs all had seats at the table, where they sat staring with all their eyes.

The Steadfast Tin Soldier[1]

There were once five and twenty tin soldiers, all brothers, for they were the offspring of the same old tin spoon. Each man shouldered his gun, kept his eyes well to the front, and wore the smartest red and blue uniform imaginable. The first thing they heard in their new world, when the lid was taken off the box, was a little boy clapping his hands and crying, "Soldiers, soldiers!"

It was his birthday and they had just been given to him, so he lost no time in setting them up on the table. All the soldiers were exactly alike with one exception, and he differed from the rest in having only one leg. For he was made last, and there was not quite enough tin left to finish him. However, he stood just as well on his one leg as the others did on two. In fact he was the very one who became famous.

On the table where they were being set up were many other toys, but the chief thing which caught the eye was a delightful paper castle. You could see through the tiny windows right into the rooms. Outside there were some little trees surrounding a small mirror, representing a lake, whose surface reflected the waxen swans which were swimming about on it. It was altogether charming, but the prettiest thing of all was a little maiden standing at the open door of the castle. She too was cut out of paper, but she wore a dress of the lightest gauze, with a dainty little blue ribbon over her shoulders, by way of a scarf, set off by a brilliant spangle as big as her whole face. The little maid was stretching out both arms, for she was a dancer. And in the dance one of her legs was raised so high into the air that the tin soldier could see absolutely nothing of it, and supposed that she like himself had but one leg.

[1] From "Hans Andersen's Fairy Tales," translated by Mrs. E. Lucas. Illustrations by Richard Bennett and Arthur Szyk

"That would be the very wife for me!" he thought, "but she is much too grand. She lives in a palace, while I have only a box, and then there are five and twenty of us to share it. No, that would be no place for her. But I must try to make her acquaintance!" Then he lay down full length behind a snuffbox which stood on the table. From that point he could have a good look at the lady, who continued to stand on one leg without losing her balance.

Late in the evening the other soldiers were put into their box, and the people of the house went to bed. Now was the time for the toys to play. They amused themselves with paying visits, fighting battles, and giving balls. The tin soldiers rustled about in their box for they wanted to join the games, but they could not get the lid off. The nutcrackers turned somersaults and the pencil scribbled nonsense on the slate. There was such a noise that the canary woke up and joined in, but his remarks were in verse. The only two who did not move were the tin soldier and the little dancer. She stood as stiff as ever on tiptoe, with her arms spread out. He was equally firm on his one leg, and he did not take his eyes off her for a moment.

Then the clock struck twelve, when pop! up flew the lid of the snuffbox, but there was no snuff in it. No! There was a little black goblin, a sort of jack-in-the-box.

"Tin soldier," said the goblin, "have the goodness to keep your eyes to yourself." But the tin soldier feigned not to hear.

"Ah! you just wait till tomorrow," said the goblin.

In the morning when the children got up they put the tin soldier on the window frame, and whether it was caused by the goblin or by a puff of wind, I do not know, but all at once the window burst open and the soldier fell head foremost from the third story.

It was a terrific descent, and he landed at last with his leg in the air and resting on his cap, with his bayonet fixed between two paving stones. The maidservant and the little boy ran down at once to look for him, but although they almost trod on him they could not see him. Had the soldier only called out, "Here I am!" they would easily have found him. But he did not think it proper to shout when he was in uniform.

Presently it began to rain, and the drops fell faster and faster till there was a regular torrent. When it was over, two street boys came along.

"Look out!" said one. "There is a tin soldier. He shall go for a sail."

So they made a boat out of a newspaper and put the soldier into the middle of it, and he sailed away down the gutter. Both boys ran alongside clapping their hands. Good heavens! what waves there were in the gutter, and what a current, but then it certainly had rained cats and dogs. The paper boat danced up and down, and now

and then whirled round and round. A shudder ran through the tin soldier, but he remained undaunted and did not move a muscle. He looked straight before him with his gun shouldered. All at once the boat drifted under a long wooden tunnel, and it became as dark as it was in his box.

"Where on earth am I going now?" thought he. "Well, well, it is all the fault of that goblin! Oh, if only the little maiden were with me in the boat, it might be twice as dark for all I should care."

At this moment a big water rat, who lived in the tunnel, came up.

"Have you a pass?" asked the rat. "Hand up your pass."

The tin soldier did not speak, but clung still tighter to his gun. The boat rushed on, the rat close behind. Phew, how he gnashed his teeth and shouted to the bits of stick and straw, "Stop him! Stop him! He hasn't paid his toll. He hasn't shown his pass."

But the current grew stronger and stronger. The tin soldier could already see daylight before him at the end of the tunnel, but he also heard a roaring sound, fit to strike terror to the bravest heart. Just imagine: where the tunnel ended, the stream rushed straight into the big canal. That would be just as dangerous for him as it would be for us to shoot a great rapid.

He was so near the end now that it was impossible to stop. The boat dashed out. The poor tin soldier held himself as stiff as he could. No one should say of him that he even winced!

The boat swirled round three or four times and filled with water to the edge; it must sink. The tin soldier stood up to his neck in water and the boat sank deeper and deeper. The paper became limper and limper, and at last the water went over his head. Then he thought of the pretty little dancer whom he was never to see again, and this refrain rang in his ears:

"Onward! Onward! Soldier!
For death thou canst not shun."

Then the paper gave way entirely and the soldier fell through, and at the same moment he was swallowed by a big fish.

Oh, how dark it was inside the fish! It was worse even than being in the tunnel. And then it was so narrow! But the tin soldier was as dauntless as ever and lay full length, shouldering his gun.

The fish rushed about and made the most frantic movements. At last it became quite quiet, and after a time a flash like lightning pierced it. The soldier was once more in the broad daylight, and someone called out loudly, "A tin soldier!" The fish had been caught, taken to market, sold, and brought into the kitchen, where the cook cut it open with a large knife. She took the soldier up by the waist with two fingers and carried him into the parlor, where everyone wanted to see the wonderful man who had traveled about in the stomach of a fish. But the tin soldier was not at all proud. They set him up on the table, and—wonder of wonders! he found himself in the very same room that he had been in before. He saw the very same children, and the toys were still standing on the table, as well as the beautiful castle with the pretty little dancer.

She still stood on one leg and held the other up in the air. You see, she also was unbending. The soldier was so much moved that he was ready to shed tears of tin, but that would not have been fitting. He looked at her and she looked at him, but they said never a word. At this moment one of the little boys took up the tin soldier, and without rhyme or reason threw him into the fire. No doubt the little goblin in the snuffbox was to blame for that. The tin soldier stood there, lighted up by the flame and in the most horrible heat, but whether it was the heat of the real fire, or the warmth of his feelings, he did not know. He had lost all his gay color. It might have been from his perilous journey, or it might have been from grief. Who can tell?

He looked at the little maiden and she

looked at him, and he felt that he was melting away, but he still managed to keep himself erect, shouldering his gun.

A door was suddenly opened. The draft caught the little dancer and she fluttered like a sylph, straight into the fire, to the soldier, blazed up and was gone!

By this time the soldier was reduced to a mere lump, and when the maid took away the ashes next morning she found him in the shape of a small tin heart. All that was left of the dancer was her spangle, and that was burned as black as a coal.

The Elves and the Shoemaker [1]

There was once a shoemaker who through no fault of his own had become so poor that at last he had only leather enough left for one pair of shoes. At evening he cut out the shoes which he intended to begin upon the next morning, and since he had a good conscience, he lay down quietly, said his prayers, and fell asleep.

In the morning, when he had said his prayers and was preparing to sit down to work, he found the pair of shoes standing finished on his table. He was amazed and could not understand it in the least.

He took the shoes in his hand to examine them more closely. They were so neatly sewn that not a stitch was out of place, and were as good as the work of a master hand.

Soon afterwards a purchaser came in and, as he was much pleased with the shoes, he paid more than the ordinary price for them, so that the shoemaker was able to buy leather for two pairs of shoes with the money.

He cut them out in the evening, and the next day with fresh courage was about to go to work. But he had no need to, for when he got up the shoes were finished, and buyers were not lacking. These gave him so much money that he was able to buy leather for four pairs of shoes.

Early next morning he found the four pairs finished, and so it went on. What he cut out at evening was finished in the morning, so that he was soon again in comfortable circumstances and became a well-to-do man.

Now it happened one evening not long before Christmas, when he had cut out some shoes as usual, that he said to his wife, "How would it be if we were to sit up tonight to see who it is that lends us such a helping hand?"

The wife agreed and lighted a candle, and they hid themselves in the corner of the room behind the clothes which were hanging there.

At midnight came two little naked men who sat down at the shoemaker's table, took up the cutout work, and began with their tiny fingers to stitch, sew, and hammer so neatly and quickly that the shoemaker could not believe his eyes. They did not stop till everything was quite finished and stood complete on the table. Then they ran swiftly away.

The next day the wife said, "The little men have made us rich, and we ought to show our gratitude. They were running about with nothing on, and must freeze with cold. Now I will make them little shirts, coats, waistcoats, and hose, and will even knit them a pair of stockings. And you shall make them each a pair of shoes."

The husband agreed. And at evening, when they had everything ready, they laid out the presents on the table and hid themselves to see how the little men would behave.

Hiding, they watched the elves

[1] A fairy tale by the Brothers Grimm. Illustration from a drawing by George Cruikshank

At midnight they came skipping in and were about to set to work. But instead of the leather ready cut out, they found the charming little clothes.

At first they were surprised, then excessively delighted. With the greatest speed they put on and smoothed down the pretty clothes, singing:

"Now we're boys so fine and neat,
  Why cobble more for others' feet?"

Then they hopped and danced about, and leapt over chairs and tables and out the door. Henceforward they came back no more, but the shoemaker fared well as long as he lived, and had good luck in all his undertakings.

Rumpelstiltskin[1]

There was once a miller who was very poor, but he had a beautiful daughter. Now it once happened that he had occasion to speak with the King, and in order to give himself an air of importance he said, "I have a daughter who can spin gold out of straw."

The King said to the miller, "That is an art in which I am much interested. If your daughter is as skillful as you say she is, bring her to my castle tomorrow, and I will put her to the test."

Accordingly, when the girl was brought to the castle, the King conducted her to a chamber which was quite full of straw, gave her a spinning wheel and a reel, and said, "Now set to work. And if between tonight and tomorrow at dawn you have not spun this straw into gold, you must die." Thereupon he carefully locked the chamber door, and she remained alone.

There sat the unfortunate miller's daughter, and for the life of her did not know what to do. She had not the least idea how to spin straw into gold, and she became more and more distressed until at last she began to weep. Then all at once the door sprang open, and in stepped a little man who said, "Good evening, Mistress Miller. Why are you weeping so?"

"Alas," answered the maiden, "I've got to spin gold out of straw, and don't know how to do it."

Then the little man said, "What will you give me if I spin it for you?"

"My necklace," said the maid.

The little man took the necklace, sat down before the spinning wheel, and whir —whir—whir, in a trice the reel was full.

Then he fixed another reel, and whir—whir—whir, thrice round, and that too was full. And so it went on until morning, when all the straw was spun and all the reels were full of gold.

Immediately at sunrise the King came, and when he saw the gold he was astonished and much pleased, but his mind became only the more avaricious. So he had the miller's daughter taken to another chamber full of straw, larger than the former one, and he ordered her to spin it also in one night, if she valued her life.

The maiden was at her wit's end and began to weep. Then again the door sprang open, and the little man appeared and said, "What will you give me if I spin the straw into gold for you?"

"The ring off my finger," answered the maiden.

The little man took the ring, began to whir again at the wheel, and by morning had spun all the straw into gold.

The King was delighted at sight of the masses of gold, but was not even yet satisfied. So he had the miller's daughter taken to a still larger chamber full of straw, and

[1] A fairy tale by the Brothers Grimm. Illustration from a drawing by H. J. Ford

said, "This must you spin tonight into gold, but if you succeed you shall become my Queen." "Even if she is only a miller's daughter," thought he, "I shan't find a richer woman in the whole world."

When the girl was alone the little man came again and said for the third time, "What will you give me if I spin the straw for you this time?"

"I have nothing more that I can give," answered the girl.

"Well, promise me your first child if you become Queen."

"Who knows what may happen?" thought the miller's daughter, but she did not see any other way of getting out of the difficulty. So she promised the little man what he demanded, and in return he spun the straw into gold once more.

When the King came in the morning and found everything as he had wished, he celebrated his marriage with her, and the miller's daughter became Queen.

About a year afterwards a beautiful child was born, but the Queen had forgotten all about the little man. However, he suddenly entered her chamber and said, "Now, give me what you promised."

The Queen was terrified, and offered the little man all the wealth of the kingdom if he would let her keep the child. But the little man said, "No, I would rather have some living thing than all the treasures of the world."

Then the Queen began to moan and weep to such an extent that the little man felt sorry for her. "I will give you three days," said he, "and if within that time you discover my name you shall keep the child."

Then during the night the Queen called to mind all the names that she had ever heard, and sent a messenger all over the country to inquire far and wide what other names there were.

When the little man appeared the next day, she began with Caspar, Melchior, Balthazar, and mentioned all the names which she knew, one after the other. But at every one the little man said, "No. No. That's not my name."

The second day she had inquiries made all round the neighborhood for the names of people living there, and suggested to the little man all the most unusual and strange names. "Perhaps your name is Cowribs, or Spindleshanks, or Spiderlegs?"

But he answered every time, "No. That's not my name."

On the third day the messenger came back and said, "I haven't been able to find any new names, but as I came round the corner of a wood on a lofty mountain, where the fox says good night to the hare,

I saw a little house, and in front of the house a fire was burning. And around the fire a most ridiculous little man was leaping. He was hopping on one leg and singing:

'Today I bake; tomorrow I brew my beer;
The next day I will bring the Queen's child
here.
Ah! lucky 'tis that not a soul doth know
That Rumpelstiltskin is my name. Ho!
Ho!'"

You can imagine how delighted the Queen was when she heard the name! And soon afterwards when the little man came in and asked, "Now, Your Majesty, what is my name?" at first she asked, "Is your name Tom?"

"No."

"Is it Dick?"

"No."

"Is it, by chance, Rumpelstiltskin?"

"The devil told you that! The devil told you that!" shrieked the little man. And in his rage he stamped his right foot into the ground so deep that he sank up to his waist.

Then in his rage he seized his left leg with both hands and tore himself asunder in the middle.

The Fir Tree [1]

HANS CHRISTIAN ANDERSEN

Deep in the forest there stood such a pretty little fir tree. It grew in a nice spot; the sun could reach it, there was fresh air in abundance, and all around it were many taller comrades, firs as well as pines. But the little fir tree was in a great hurry to grow up. It paid no attention to the warm sunshine or the fresh air, and it took no notice of the farmers' children who went about chattering, and picking strawberries or raspberries. Often they would sit down by the little tree, with whole jug-

fuls of raspberries, or holding strawberries threaded on long straws, and exclaim, "Isn't that baby tree the sweetest thing you ever saw!" But the fir tree did not like to hear that at all.

The next year it had added a long section to its growth, and the following year one still longer. You can tell a fir tree's age by the number of new sections it has.

"Oh, I wish I were as tall as the others!" sighed the little tree. "Then I could spread my branches far and wide, and from my

[1] From "It's Perfectly True and Other Stories," by Hans Christian Andersen, translated by Paul Leyssac; illustrations by Richard Bennett and Arthur Szyk

top see what the world looks like. The birds would build their nests in my branches, and when the wind was blowing, I should be able to nod with as much dignity as the others."

It found no pleasure in the sunshine, nor in the birds, nor in the rosy clouds that went sailing over it morning and evening.

In winter, when the ground was covered with glistening white snow, a hare would often come hopping along, and jump right over it. How annoying that was! But two winters passed by, and in the third it was so tall that the hare was obliged to run round it.

"Oh, if I could but grow and grow, become tall and old! That's the only thing worth living for," thought the tree.

In the autumn the woodcutters would come and fell a few of the tallest trees; this happened every year, and the young fir, which was now quite grown up, trembled with fear when it saw the splendid big trees fall to the ground with a crash. Their branches were lopped off so that they looked all naked and thin; one could hardly recognize them. They were loaded on to timber-wagons, and horses dragged them away out of the forest.

Where were they going? What would happen to them?

In the spring, when the swallows and the stork arrived, the tree asked them, "Do you know where the other trees were taken? Did you meet them?"

The swallows knew nothing about it, but the stork looked thoughtful, nodded his head, and said, "Yes, I think I did meet them. Coming away from Egypt, I saw many new ships with splendid new masts. I daresay those were the trees you mean; they had a smell of fir about them. They wanted to be remembered to you; they looked grand, very grand."

"If only I too were big enough to fly over the sea! Tell me, what is this sea really, and what does it look like?"

"That would take too long to explain," said the stork, and he walked away.

"Enjoy your youth! Rejoice in your healthy growth, and in the young life that is within you!" said the sunbeams.

And the wind kissed the tree, and the dew wept tears over it, but the fir tree did not understand.

With the coming of Christmas, quite a number of very young firs were chopped down, some of them neither so tall nor so old as our tree, which was still restless and impatient to get away. These young firs, just the most beautiful ones, were not stripped of their branches—they were loaded on to timber-wagons and horses dragged them away out of the forest.

"Where are they going?" asked the fir

tree. "They are no taller than I am, in fact one of them was much smaller—why were they allowed to keep all their branches? Where are they going?"

"We know! We know!" chirped the sparrows. "We've peeped in at the windows down in the town. We know where they're going to. The greatest pomp and splendor imaginable awaits them there! We've peeped in at the windows, and we've seen them planted in the middle of a nice warm room, and decorated with the most beautiful things—gilded apples, gingerbread, toys, and many hundreds of bright candles!"

"And then?" asked the fir tree, quivering through all its branches. "And then? What happens then?"

"We haven't seen anything more than that, but it was too wonderful for words!"

"Was I born for such a glorious destiny, I wonder?" exclaimed the tree, trembling with delight. "That is even better than crossing the sea. I'm sick with longing. If it were only Christmas now! I'm as tall and well-grown as those trees which were taken away last year. Oh, if I were only loaded on to the wagon! Oh, that I were in that warm room in the midst of so much pomp and splendor! And then—? Then something still better, still more beautiful will happen, or why should they take such trouble to decorate me? Something still greater, still more splendid is bound to happen—but what? Oh, how I ache, how I yearn! I don't know myself what is wrong with me."

"Rejoice in me," said both the air and the sunshine. "Rejoice in your fresh youth out here in the open!"

But it did not rejoice at all. It grew and grew; winter and summer it stood there, ever green, dark green. The people who looked at it said, "What a beautiful tree!" And the following Christmas it was the first to be felled. The ax struck deep into its marrow, and with a profound sigh the tree fell to the ground. It suffered pain, it felt faint, and could not think of any happiness, for it was sad at parting from its home, from the place where it had grown up; it knew that it would never again see its dear old friends, the little bushes and flowers round about—perhaps not even the birds. It was anything but pleasant to say good-by.

The tree did not recover until it found itself unloaded in a yard with other firs and heard a man say, "This one's a beauty. This is the one we want."

Then two servants in smart livery arrived, and carried the fir tree into a beautiful great reception room. All round the walls hung portraits, and beside the tiled stove stood big Chinese jars with lions on their covers. There were rocking chairs, silk-covered sofas, large tables littered with picture books, and toys worth loads and loads of money—at least so the children said.

And the fir tree was planted in a big tub filled with sand; but no one could see it was a tub, for it was covered with green cloth, and stood on a great many-colored carpet. How the tree trembled! What was going to happen? Men servants and young ladies began to decorate it. On the branches they hung little nets cut out of colored paper, every net filled with sweets; gilded apples and walnuts hung down as if they grew there, and more than a hundred red, blue, and white candles were fastened to the branches. Dolls that looked exactly like real live children—the tree had never seen anything of the sort before—floated among the green branches, and up at the top was fixed a large star of gold tinsel; it was magnificent beyond words!

"Tonight," they all said, "tonight it will be lit up."

"Oh!" thought the tree. "If only it were already night! If only the candles were already lit! And later—what will happen then? Will trees from the forest come and look at me? Will the sparrows peep in at the windows? Shall I grow roots here and keep my decorations winter and summer?"

How little it knew! All those longings had brought on a very bad barkache—and it is just as bad for a tree to have a barkache as it is for us to have a headache.

At last the candles were lighted. What a blaze of splendor! The tree trembled so much in all its branches that one of the candles set fire to a twig—and what a scorching pain that was!

"Oh, dear!" cried the young ladies, and they quickly put out the fire. Now the tree did not even dare to quiver—it was awful! It was so afraid of losing some of its decorations, and felt quite overwhelmed with all that splendor. . . . And now at last the folding doors were flung open and dozens of noisy children came tumbling in as if they were going to upset the whole tree. The older people followed more calmly behind. The little ones stood quite speechless, but only for a minute—then they shrieked again with excitement, danced joyfully round it, and took down one present after another.

"What are they doing?" thought the tree. "What is going to happen?" The candles burnt right down to the branches and were put out as fast as they were burnt; then the children were allowed to plunder the tree. They rushed at it with such force that all the branches creaked; if it had not been fastened to the ceiling by the string and the gold star, it would have toppled over. The children danced round and round with their beautiful toys. No one looked at the tree except the old nurse who was peering about among the branches to see if by any chance a fig or an apple had not been forgotten.

"A story! A story!" demanded the children, pulling a little fat man towards the tree, and he sat down just beneath it. "Here we are in the green wood," he said, "and it will do the tree a lot of good to listen. But I shall only tell one story. Would you like the one about Hey-diddle-diddle, or the one about Humpty-dumpty who fell down the stairs, and yet ascended the throne and married the Princess?"

"Hey-diddle-diddle," cried some of them; "Humpty-dumpty," cried others; and there was a great deal of shrieking and shouting. Only the fir tree stood quite silent, and thought, "Am I not to be in this at all? Am I not to take part in anything?" But it had been in the evening's fun. It had played its part.

So the little fat man told about Humpty-dumpty who fell down the stairs and yet ascended the throne and married the Princess. And the children clapped their hands, shouting, "Another! another!" for they wanted the story of Hey-diddle-diddle too, but they had to be content with Humpty-dumpty.

The fir tree stood quite silent and thoughtful—never had the birds in the forest told such a story as that. "Humpty-dumpty fell down the stairs and yet married the Princess. Well! Well! that's the way things happen in the world," thought the fir tree, believing it must all have been true, because such a nice man had told the story. "Well, who knows? I, too, may fall downstairs and win my Princess!" And it looked forward to being decorated again the next day with candles and toys, tinsel and fruit.

"Tomorrow I shall not tremble," it

thought. "I shall rejoice in all my splendor. Tomorrow I shall hear the story of Humpty-dumpty again, and perhaps the one about Hey-diddle-diddle too." And it remained quiet and thoughtful all night.

In the morning the man came in with one of the servants.

"Now the festivities are going to begin again," thought the tree. But they dragged it out of the room, up the stairs to the attic, and there they put it in a dark corner where no daylight penetrated. "What does this mean?" thought the tree. "What am I to do in this place? What am I to hear?" And it leant against the wall, lost in deep thought. . . . It had time enough, for days and nights went by, and nobody came up. When at last someone did come, it was only to move some big boxes into the corner. The tree was so well hidden away that one might think it had been quite forgotten.

"It's winter outside now," thought the tree. "The ground is hard and covered with snow; I cannot be planted now, and that is probably why I am to be sheltered here until the springtime. How considerate of them! How kind people are! I only wish it weren't so dark here and so terribly lonely—not even a little hare! After all, it was nice in the forest when the snow covered the ground, and the hare sped by—yes, even when it jumped over me it was fun, but I didn't think so then. This loneliness is perfectly unbearable!"

" 'Eak! 'Eak!" squeaked a little mouse just then, running out on the floor, and followed by another one. They sniffed at the fir tree, slipping in and out among the branches.

"It's frightfully cold," said the two little mice, "otherwise it's very pleasant here. Don't you think so, you old fir tree?"

"I'm not old at all," answered the fir tree. "There are many much older than I."

"Where do you come from?" asked the mice, "and what do you know?"

Weren't they outrageously inquisitive? "Tell us about the most attractive place on earth; have you ever been there? Have you ever been in the larder, where there are cheeses on the shelves, and hams hang from the ceiling, where you can dance over tallow candles, and slip in thin and come out fat?"

"I don't know that place," replied the tree, "but I know the forest where the sun shines and the birds sing!" And it told all about its youth, and the little mice had never heard anything like it. They listened very attentively and said, "My, what a lot you must have seen! How happy you must have been!"

"I?" said the fir tree, thinking about what it had been saying. "Yes, after all, those days were rather pleasant." Then it told them all about the Christmas Eve when it had been decorated with sweets and candles.

"Oh!" said the little mice. "How happy you've been, you old fir tree!"

"I'm not old at all," said the fir tree. "It was only this winter that I came out of the forest; I'm in the prime of life, and I've only just stopped growing for the time being."

"How beautifully you tell things!" said the little mice; and the next night they brought four other mice to hear the tree tell all about its life, and the more the tree told, the more clearly did it remember everything, and thought, "Those really were quite happy days. But they may return—they may return once more. Humpty-dumpty fell down the stairs and still he won the Princess! Perhaps I too may marry a Princess!" And the fir thought of a most adorable little birch that grew out in the forest—for to the fir tree that little birch was a beautiful real Princess.

"Who is Humpty-dumpty?" asked the little mice. The fir tree then told them the whole story, for it remembered every word, and the little mice were so delighted that they almost leaped to the very top of the tree. The next night many more mice came, and on Sunday even two rats appeared—but they said the story was not amusing, which made the little mice rather sad, for now they did not think much of it either.

"Do you know only that one story?" asked the rats.

"Only that one," answered the tree. "I heard it on the happiest evening of my life, but I never knew then how happy I was!"

"It's a very boring story. Don't you know any about pork and tallow candles? Any larder stories?"

"No," said the tree.

"Thank you, then we shan't bother you any more," said the rats, and they returned to the bosom of their families.

Finally the little mice kept away too, and now the tree sighed: "After all, it was rather cozy when those nimble little mice sat round listening to what I told them. All that is over too; but I shall remember to enjoy myself when I'm taken out from here!"

But when would that happen?

Well, it happened one morning when people came to tidy up the attic. The boxes were moved. The tree was pulled out from the corner and thrown rather brutally on the floor, but at once one of the men dragged it towards the stairs where it saw daylight once more. "Now life is beginning again," thought the tree. It felt the fresh air and the first sunbeams —and now it was out in the courtyard. All happened so quickly that the tree quite forgot to look at itself, there was so much to see all round. The courtyard was next to a garden where all the flowers were in bloom; the roses hung in great fragrant clusters over the little fence, the lime trees were in full blossom, and the swallows flew high and low, twittering, "Kvee-ve-ve, kvee-ve-ve—my love has come!"—but it was not the fir tree they meant.

"Now I am really going to live!" exclaimed the fir tree, bursting with happiness, and it stretched out all its branches. Alas! they were all withered and yellow—

it found itself in a corner amongst weeds and nettles. The tinsel star was still fastened to the top, and sparkled in the bright sunshine.

Some of the merry children who had danced round the tree at Christmas-time, and had taken such a delight in it then, were playing in the courtyard. One of the smallest rushed at it and pulled off the gold star.

"Look what is still hanging on that ugly old Christmas tree!" he said, trampling on the branches that crackled under his feet.

And the tree looked at the beauty and splendor of the flowers in the garden, and then looked at itself, and wished it had remained in that dark corner of the attic. It thought of its fresh green youth in the forest, of the merry Christmas Eve, and of the little mice which had listened with so much pleasure to the story of Humpty-dumpty.

"All over and done with," said the poor tree. "Why didn't I enjoy them while I could? Done with! Done with!"

And the man came and chopped the tree up into small pieces; they made quite a heap. A great blaze flared up under the big copper, and the tree moaned so deeply that each moan was like a faint shot. The children were attracted by the sound, made a ring round the fire, gazed into it and shouted, "Bing! bang!" But at each explosion—which was a deep moan—the tree thought of a beautiful summer's day in the forest, or of a starry winter's night out there; it thought of Christmas Eve and of Humpty-dumpty, the only story it had ever heard and been able to tell . . . and by now the tree was burnt to ashes.

The boys played in the courtyard, and the youngest one wore on his breast the gold star which had decorated the tree on the happiest evening of its life.

Now that was done with, and the tree was done with, and the story is done with! done with! done with! And that's what happens to all stories.

The Princess and the Pea[1]

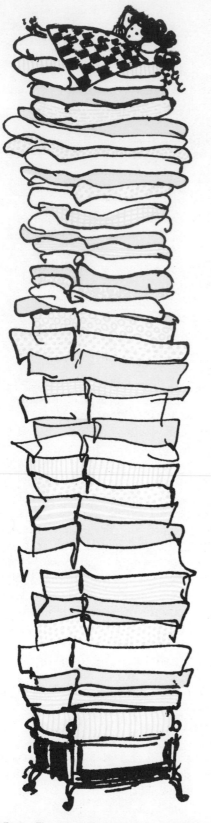

Once upon a time there was a prince, and he wanted a princess; but she would have to be a *real* princess. He travelled all round the world to find one, but always there was something wrong. There were princesses enough, but he found it difficult to make out whether they were *real* ones. So he came home again, and was very sad, for he would have liked to have a real princess.

One evening a terrible storm came on; it thundered and lightened, and the rain poured down in torrents. It was dreadful! Suddenly a knocking was heard at the gate, and the old King went to open it.

It was a princess standing out there before the gate. But what a sight she was after all the rain and the dreadful weather! The water ran down from her hair and her clothes; it ran down into the toes of her shoes and out again at the heels. And yet she said that she was a real princess.

"Yes, we'll soon find that out," thought the old Queen. But she said nothing, went into the bedroom, took all the bedding off the bedstead, and laid a pea at the bottom; then she took twenty mattresses and laid them on the pea, and then twenty eiderdown beds on top of the mattresses. On this the Princess was to lie all night. In the morning she was asked how she had slept.

"Oh, terribly badly!" said the Princess. "I have scarcely shut my eyes the whole night. Heaven only knows what was in the bed, but I was lying on something hard, so that I am black and blue all over."

Now they knew that she was a real princess, because she had felt the pea right through the twenty mattresses and the twenty eiderdown beds. Nobody but a real princess could be as sensitive as that.

So the prince took her for his wife, for now he knew that he had a real princess; and the pea was put in the Art Museum, where it may still be seen, if no one has stolen it. There, that is a real story!

[1] From "The Arthur Rackham Fairy Book," selected by Arthur Rackham. Illustration by Wade Ray

The Brave Little Tailor [1]

One summer morning a little tailor was sitting at his bench near the window, working cheerfully with all his might, when an old woman came down the street. She was crying, "Good jelly to sell! Good jelly to sell!"

The cry sounded pleasant in the little tailor's ears, so he put his head out the window and called out, "Here, my good woman! Come here, if you want a customer."

So the poor woman climbed the steps with her heavy basket, and was obliged to unpack and display all her pots to the tailor. He looked at every one of them and, lifting all the lids, applied his nose to each.

At last he said, "The jelly seems pretty good. You may weigh me out four half ounces, or I don't mind having a quarter of a pound."

The woman, who had expected to find a good customer, gave him what he asked for but went off angry and grumbling.

"This jelly is the very thing for me!" cried the little tailor. "It will give me strength and cunning." And he took down the bread from the cupboard, cut a big slice off the loaf and spread the jelly on it, laid it near him, and went on stitching more gallantly than ever. All the while the scent of the sweet jelly was spreading throughout the room, where there were quantities of flies. They were attracted by it and flew down to eat of it.

"Now then, who invited you here?" said the tailor, and drove the unbidden guests away. But the flies, not understanding his language, were not to be got rid of like that, and returned in larger numbers than before. Then the tailor, unable to stand it any longer, took from his chimney corner a ragged cloth.

"Now, I'll let you have it!" he said, and beat it among them unmercifully. When he ceased and counted the slain, he found seven lying dead before him.

"This is indeed somewhat," he said, wondering at his own bravery. "The whole town shall know about this."

So he hastened to cut out a belt, and he stitched it and put on it in large capitals: "Seven at one blow!"

"The town, did I say?" said the little tailor. "The whole world shall know it!" And his heart quivered with joy, like a lamb's tail.

The tailor fastened the belt round him and began to think of going out into the world, for his workshop seemed too small for his valor. So he looked about in all the house for something that would be useful to take with him, but he found nothing but an old cheese, which he put in his pocket. Outside the door he noticed that a bird had got caught in the bushes, so he took that and put it in his pocket with the cheese. Then he set out gallantly on his way, and as he was light and active he felt no fatigue.

The way led over a mountain, and when he reached the topmost peak he saw a terrible giant sitting there, and looking about him at his ease.

The tailor went bravely up to him, called out to him, and said, "Good day, comrade! There you sit looking over the wide world. I am on the way thither to seek my fortune. Have you a fancy to go with me?"

The giant looked at the tailor contemptuously and said, "You vagabond! You miserable little creature!"

"That may be," answered the little tailor, and undoing his coat he showed the giant his belt. "You can read there whether I am a man or not."

The giant read, "Seven at one blow!" And thinking it meant men that the tailor had killed, he at once felt more respect for the little fellow. But as he wanted to test

[1] A fairy tale by the Brothers Grimm. Illustrations from drawings by H. J. Ford

him, he took a stone and squeezed it so hard that water came out of it.

"Now you can do that," said the giant, "that is, if you have the strength for it."

"That's not much!" said the little tailor. "I call that play." And he put his hand in his pocket and took out the cheese and squeezed it till the whey ran out of it.

"Well," said he, "what do you think of that?"

The giant did not know what to say to it, for he could not have believed it of the little man. Then the giant took up a stone and threw it so high that it was nearly out of sight.

"Now, little fellow, suppose you do that!"

"Well thrown!" said the tailor. "But the stone fell back to earth again. I will throw you one that will never come back." So he felt in his pocket, took out the bird, and threw it into the air. And the bird, when it found itself at liberty, took wing, flew off, and returned no more.

"What do you think of that, comrade?" asked the tailor.

"There is no doubt that you can throw," said the giant. "Now we will see if you can carry."

He led the little tailor to a mighty oak tree which had been felled and was lying on the ground, and said, "Now, if you are strong enough, help me to carry this tree out of the wood."

"Willingly," answered the little man. "You take the trunk on your shoulders and I will take the branches with all their foliage. That is by far the biggest end."

So the giant took the trunk on his shoulders, and the tailor seated himself on a branch. And the giant, who could not see what he was doing, had the whole tree to carry, and the little man on it as well. And the little man was very cheerful and merry and whistled the tune, *"There were three tailors riding by,"* as if carrying the tree was mere child's play.

The giant, when he had struggled on under his heavy load a part of the way, was tired out and cried, "Look here, I must let go the tree!"

The tailor jumped off quickly. Then, taking hold of the tree with both arms as if he were carrying it, he said to the giant, "You see you can't carry the tree, though you are such a big fellow!"

They went on together a little farther and presently they came to a cherry tree. And the giant took hold of the topmost branches, where the ripest fruit hung, and pulling them downward gave them to the tailor to hold, bidding him eat. But the little tailor was much too weak to hold the tree, and as the giant let go, the tree sprang back and the tailor was thrown up into the air.

And when he dropped down again without any damage, the giant said to him, "How is this? Haven't you strength enough to hold such a weak sprig as that?"

"It is not strength that is lacking," answered the little tailor. "How should it to one who has slain seven at one blow? I just jumped over the tree because the hunters are shooting down there in the bushes. Why don't you jump it too?"

The giant made the attempt and, not being able to vault the tree, he remained hanging in the branches, so that once more the little tailor got the better of him.

Then said the giant, "As you are such a gallant fellow, suppose you come with me to our den and stay the night."

The tailor was quite willing and followed him. When they reached the den, there sat some other giants by the fire and all gladly welcomed him.

The little tailor looked round and thought, "There is more elbow room here than in my workshop."

The giant showed him a bed and told him he had better lie down on it and go to sleep. The bed, however, was too big for the tailor, so he did not stay in it but crept into a corner to sleep. As soon as it was midnight the giant got up, took a great staff of iron and beat the bed through with one stroke, and supposed he had made an end of that grasshopper of a tailor. Very early in the morning the giants went into the wood and forgot all about the little tailor, and when they saw him coming after them alive and merry, they were terribly frightened. And thinking he was going to kill them, they ran away in all haste.

So the little tailor marched on, always following his nose. And after he had gone a great way he entered the courtyard belonging to a king's palace, and there he felt so overpowered with fatigue that he lay down and fell asleep. In the meanwhile came various people, who looked at him very curiously and read on his belt, "Seven at one blow!"

"Oh," said they, "why should this great lord come here in time of peace? What a mighty champion he must be!"

Then they went and told the King about him. They thought that if war should break out what a worthy and useful man he would be, and he ought not to be allowed to depart at any price. The King then summoned his council and sent one of his courtiers to the little tailor to beg him, as soon as he should wake up, to consent to serve in the King's army. So the messenger stood and waited at the sleeper's side until he began to stretch his limbs and to open his eyes, and then he carried his answer back. "That was the reason for which I came," the little tailor had said.

"I am ready to enter the King's service."

So he was received into it very honorably, and a separate dwelling was set apart for him.

But the rest of the soldiers were very much set against the little tailor, and they wished him a thousand miles away.

"What shall be done about it?" they said among themselves. "If we pick a quarrel and fight with him, then seven of us will fall at each blow. That will be of no good to us."

So they came to a resolution, and went all together to the King to ask for their discharge.

"We never intended," said they, "to serve with a man who kills seven at a blow."

The King felt sorry to lose all his faithful servants because of one man. He wished that he had never seen him, and would willingly get rid of him if he might. But he did not dare to dismiss the little tailor for fear he should kill all the King's people and place himself upon the throne. He thought a long while about it, and at last made up his mind what to do.

He sent for the little tailor and told him that as he was so great a warrior he had a proposal to make to him. He told him that in a wood in his dominions dwelt two giants who did great damage by robbery, murder, and fire, and that no man dared go near them for fear of his life. But that if the tailor should overcome and slay both these giants the King would give him his only daughter in marriage and half his kingdom as dowry, and that a hundred horsemen should go with him to give him assistance.

"That would be a fine thing for a man like me," thought the little tailor. "A beautiful princess and half a kingdom are not to be had every day."

So he said to the King, "Oh yes, I can soon overcome the giants, and yet I have no need of the hundred horsemen. He who can kill seven at one blow has no need to be afraid of two."

So the little tailor set out and the hundred horsemen followed him.

When he came to the border of the wood he said to his escort, "Stay here while I go to attack the giants."

Then he sprang into the wood and looked about him right and left. After a while he caught sight of the two giants. They were lying down under a tree asleep, and snoring so that all the branches shook. The little tailor, all alert, filled both his pockets with stones and climbed up into the tree, and made his way to an overhanging bough so that he could seat himself just above the sleepers. And from there he let one stone after another fall on the chest of one of the giants.

For a long time the giant was quite unaware of this, but at last he waked up and pushed his comrade and said, "What are you hitting me for?"

"Are you dreaming?" said the other. "I am not touching you." And they composed themselves again to sleep, and the tailor let fall a stone on the other giant.

"What can that be?" cried he. "What are you casting at me?"

"I am casting nothing at you," answered the first, grumbling.

They disputed about it for a while, but as they were tired they gave it up at last, and their eyes closed once more. Then the little tailor began his game anew. He picked out a heavier stone and threw it down with force upon the first giant's chest.

"This is too much!" cried he, and sprang up like a madman and struck his companion such a blow that the tree shook above them. The other paid him back with ready coin, and they fought with such fury that they tore up trees by their roots to use for weapons against each other, so that at last both of them lay dead upon the ground. And now the little tailor got down. "What a lucky thing," he said, "that the tree I was sitting in did not get torn up, too! Or else I should have had to jump from one tree to another."

Then he drew his sword and gave each of the giants a few hacks in the breast, and went back to the horsemen and said, "The deed is done. I have made an end of both of them, though it went hard with me. In the struggle they rooted up trees to defend themselves, but it was of no use. They had to do with a man who can kill seven at one blow."

"Then are you not wounded?" asked the horsemen.

"Nothing of the sort!" answered the tailor. "They have not injured a hair."

The horsemen still would not believe it and rode into the wood to see, and there they found the giants wallowing in their blood, and all about them lying the up-rooted trees. The little tailor then claimed the promised boon, but the King repented of his offer and again sought how to rid himself of the hero.

"Before you can possess my daughter and the half of my kingdom," said he to the tailor, "you must perform another heroic act. In the wood lives a unicorn who does great damage. You must capture him."

"A unicorn does not strike more terror into me than two giants. Seven at one blow! That is my way," was the tailor's answer.

So taking a rope and an ax with him, he went out into the wood and told those who were ordered to attend him to wait outside. He had not far to seek. The unicorn soon came out and sprang at him, as if he would make an end of him without delay.

"Softly, softly!" said the tailor. "Most haste, worst speed." And he remained standing until the animal came quite near; then he slipped quickly behind a tree. The unicorn ran with all his might against the tree and stuck his horn so deep into the trunk that he could not get it out again, and so was captured.

"Now I have you," said the tailor, coming out from behind the tree. And putting the rope around the unicorn's neck, he took the ax and cut free the horn, and when all his party was assembled he brought the animal to the King.

The King did not yet wish to give him the promised reward and set him a third task to do. Before the wedding could take place the tailor was to secure a wild boar which had done a great deal of damage in the wood.

The huntsmen were to accompany him and help him.

"All right," said the tailor. "This is child's play."

But he did not take the huntsmen into the wood, and they were all the better pleased, for the wild boar had many a time before received them in such a way that they had no fancy to disturb him.

When the boar caught sight of the tailor he ran at him with foaming mouth and gleaming tusks to bear him to the ground, but the nimble hero rushed into a chapel which chanced to be near and jumped quickly out a window on the other side. The boar ran after him, and when he got inside the tailor shut the door after him, and there he was imprisoned, for the creature was too big and unwieldy to jump out the window too.

Then the tailor called the huntsmen that they might see the prisoner with their own eyes. And then he betook himself to the King, who now, whether he liked it or not, was obliged to fulfill his promise and give him his daughter and the half of his kingdom. But if he had known that the great warrior was only a little tailor he would have taken it still more to heart.

So the wedding was celebrated with great splendor and little joy, and the tailor was made into a king. One night the young Queen heard her husband talking in his sleep and saying, "Boy, make me that waistcoat and patch me those breeches, or I will wrap my yardstick about your shoulders!"

And as she perceived of what low birth her husband was, she went to her father the next morning and told him all, and begged him to set her free from a man who was nothing better than a tailor.

The King bade her be comforted, saying, "Tonight leave your bedroom door open. My guards shall stand outside, and when he is asleep they shall come in and bind him and carry him off to a ship that will take him to the other side of the world."

So the wife felt consoled, but the King's water bearer, who had been listening all the while, went to the little tailor and disclosed to him the whole plan.

"I shall put a stop to all this," said he.

At night he lay down as usual in bed, and when his wife thought that he was asleep she got up, opened the door, and lay down again. The little tailor, who only made believe to be asleep, began to murmur plainly.

"Boy, make me that waistcoat and patch me those breeches, or I will wrap my yardstick about your shoulders! I have slain seven at one blow, killed two giants, caught a unicorn, and taken a wild boar. And shall I be afraid of those who are standing outside of my room door?"

And when they heard the tailor say this, a great fear seized the guards. They fled away as if they had been wild hares and none of them would venture to attack him.

And so the little tailor all his lifetime remained a king.

The Bremen Town Musicians [1]

A certain man had an ass which for many years carried sacks to the mill without tiring. At last, however, its strength was worn out and it was no longer of any use for work. Accordingly, its master began to ponder as to how best to cut down its keep. But the ass, seeing there was mischief in the air, ran away and started on the road to Bremen. There he thought he could become a town musician.

When he had been traveling a short time, he fell in with a hound, who was lying panting on the road as though he had run himself off his legs.

"Well, what are you panting so for, Growler?" said the ass.

"Ah," said the hound, "just because I am old, and every day I get weaker. And also, because I can no longer keep up with the pack, my master wanted to kill me, so I took my departure. But now how am I to earn my bread?"

"Do you know what?" said the ass. "I am going to Bremen and shall there become a town musician. Come with me and take your part in the music. I shall play the lute, and you shall beat the kettle-drum."

The hound agreed and they went on.

A short time afterwards they came upon a cat sitting in the road, with a face as long as a wet week.

"Well, why are you so cross, Whiskers?" asked the ass.

"Who can be cheerful when he is out at elbows?" said the cat. "I am getting on in years and my teeth are blunted, and I prefer to sit by the stove and purr instead of hunting round after mice. Just because of this my mistress wanted to drown me. I made myself scarce, but now I don't know where to turn."

"Come with us to Bremen," said the ass. "You are a great hand at serenading, so you can become a town musician."

The cat consented and joined them.

Next the fugitives passed by a yard where a barnyard fowl was sitting on the door, crowing with all its might.

"You crow so loud you pierce one through and through," said the ass. "What is the matter?"

"Why, didn't I prophesy fine weather for Lady Day, when Our Lady washes the Christ Child's little garment and wants to dry it? But notwithstanding this, because Sunday visitors are coming tomorrow, the mistress has no pity, and she has ordered the cook to make me into soup. So I shall have my neck wrung tonight. Now I am crowing with all my might while I can."

"Come along, Red-comb," said the ass. "You had much better come with us. We are going to Bremen and you will find a much better fate there. You have a good voice, and when we make music together there will be quality in it."

The cock allowed himself to be persuaded and they all four went off together. They could not, however, reach the town in one day, and by evening they arrived at a wood, where they determined to spend the night. The ass and the hound lay down under a big tree. The cat and the cock settled themselves in the branches, the cock flying right up to the top, which was the safest place for him. Before going to sleep he looked round once more in every direction. Suddenly it seemed that he saw a light burning in the distance. He called out to his comrades that there must be a house not far off, for he saw a light.

"Very well," said the ass. "Let us set out and make our way to it, for the entertainment here is very bad."

The hound thought some bones or meat would suit him too, so they set out in the direction of the light. They soon saw it shining more clearly and getting bigger

[1] A fairy tale by the Brothers Grimm. Illustration from a drawing by George Cruikshank

and bigger, till they reached a brightly lighted robbers' den. The ass, being the tallest, approached the window and looked in.

"What do you see, old Jackass?" asked the cock.

"What do I see?" answered the ass. "Why, a table spread with delicious food and drink, and robbers seated at it enjoying themselves."

"That would just suit us," said the cock.

"Yes, if we were only there," answered the ass.

Then the animals took counsel as to how to set about driving the robbers out. At last they hit upon a plan.

The ass was to take up his position with his forefeet on the window sill, the hound was to jump on his back, the cat to climb up onto the hound, and last of all the cock was to up and perch on the cat's head. When they were thus arranged, at a given signal they all began to perform their music. The ass brayed, the hound barked, the cat mewed, and the cock crowed. Then they dashed through the window, shivering the panes. The robbers jumped up at the terrible noise. They thought nothing less than that the devil was coming in upon them and fled into the wood in the greatest alarm. Then the four animals sat down to table and helped them-

selves according to taste, and they ate as though they had been starving for weeks. When they had finished, they extinguished the light and looked for sleeping places, each one to suit his taste.

The ass lay down on a pile of straw, the hound behind the door, the cat on the hearth near the warm ashes, and the cock flew up to the rafters. As they were tired from the long journey, they soon went to sleep.

When midnight was past, and the robbers saw from a distance that the light was no longer burning and that all seemed quiet, the chief said, "We ought not to have been scared by a false alarm." And he ordered one of the robbers to go and examine the house.

Finding all quiet, the messenger went into the kitchen to kindle a light. And taking the cat's glowing, fiery eyes for live coals, he held a match close to them so as to light it. But the cat would stand no nonsense—it flew at his face, spat, and scratched. He was terribly frightened and ran away.

He tried to get out the back door, but the hound, who was lying there, jumped up and bit his leg. As he ran across the pile of straw in front of the house, the ass gave him a good sound kick with his hind legs; while the cock, who had awakened at the uproar quite fresh and gay, cried out from his perch, "Cock-a-doodle-doo."

Thereupon the robber ran back as fast as he could to his chief and said, "There is a gruesome witch in the house who breathed on me and scratched me with her long fingers. Behind the door there stands a man with a knife, who stabbed me, while in the yard lies a black monster who hit me with a club. And upon the roof the judge is seated, and he called out, 'Bring the rogue here!' So I hurried away as fast as I could."

Thenceforward the robbers did not venture again to the house, which pleased the four Bremen musicians so much that they never wished to leave it again.

The Story of Peter Pan

PETER'S SHADOW [1]

Sitting on the rug, he soaped his feet and then he soaped his shadow. But his feet and the shadow would not stick together. It is of no use to have a shadow if it will not stick to you. After trying and trying in vain, the poor little fellow put his face in his hands, and sobbed aloud.

It was then that Wendy awoke, and she sat right up in bed. Not at all afraid, she said, "Little boy, why are you crying?"

The boy sprang to his feet, and taking off his cap, bowed very low. Wendy bowed in return, though she found it a hard thing to do in bed.

"What's your name?" asked the little boy.

"Wendy Darling. What's yours?"

"Peter Pan."

"Where do you live?"

"Second turning to the right, and then keep on till morning."

This seemed to Wendy a very funny way of going home, but she was so sorry when she heard that Peter had no mother. But Peter was not crying for that.

Peter was crying because he could not get his shadow to stick on. This made Wendy smile, and she said firmly that soap

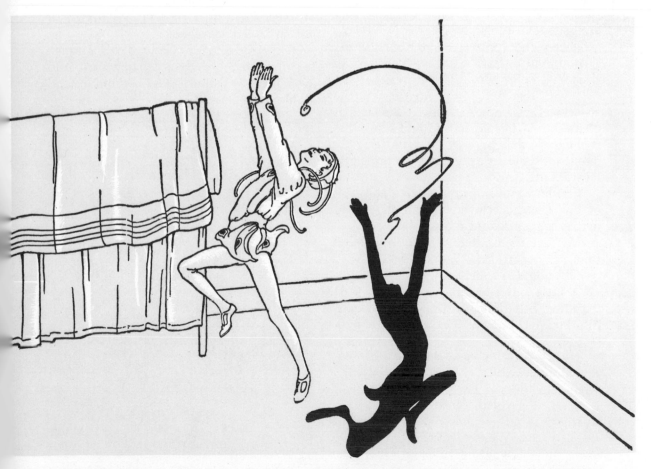

[1] From "The Story of Peter Pan," simplified from Daniel O'Connor's story of Sir J. M. Barrie's fairy play, illustrated by Alice B. Woodward

liked, but Peter did not know what she meant. Then, seeing the thimble on Wendy's finger, he thought she meant to give him that, and held out his hand for it.

Now Wendy saw at once that the poor boy did not even know what a kiss was. Being a nice little girl, she did not hurt his feelings by laughing at him, but just put the thimble on his finger.

Peter liked the thimble very much.

"Shall I give you a kiss?" he asked, and pulling a button off his coat, gave it to her with a grave face.

Wendy at once put it on a chain which she wore round her neck, and then she forgot that he did not know what a kiss was, and again asked him for one. At once he gave back the thimble.

"Oh, I didn't mean a *kiss*, I meant a thimble!" said Wendy.

"What's that?" he asked.

"It's like this," replied Wendy, and gently kissed his cheek.

"Oh," cried Peter, "how nice!" and he began to give her *thimbles* in return, and ever after he called a kiss a thimble, and a thimble a kiss.

was no good. The shadow must be sewn on.

"Shall I do it for you?" she asked, and jumped out of bed to get her work-box.

Then she set to work, and though it hurts a good deal to have a shadow sewn on to your feet, Peter bore it very bravely.

It was the right thing to do, for the shadow held on so well. Peter *was* pleased, and he danced up and down the room with delight. He saw the shadow dance on the floor as he flung his arms and legs about.

"Oh, how clever I am!" cried Peter, full of joy, and he crowed, for all the world just as a cock would crow.

"You are vain," said Wendy in a vexed tone, "of course *I* did nothing!"

"Oh, you did a little!"

"A little! If I am no use I can at least withdraw," she said, and she jumped back into bed and put her head under the bed-clothes.

"Oh, Wendy, please don't withdraw," Peter cried sadly. "I can't help crowing when I'm pleased with myself. One girl is of more use than twenty boys."

This was rather clever of Peter, and at these words, Wendy got up again. She even said she would give Peter a kiss if he

Dick Whittington [1]

In the reign of the famous King Edward III there was a little boy called Dick Whittington, whose father and mother died when he was very young, so that he remembered nothing at all about them, and was left a ragged little fellow, running about a country village. As poor Dick was not old enough to work, he was very badly off; he got but little for his dinner, and sometimes nothing at all for his breakfast; for the people who lived in the village were very poor indeed, and could not spare him much more than the parings of potatoes and now and then a hard crust of bread.

For all this Dick Whittington was a very sharp boy, and was always listening to what everybody talked about. On Sunday he was sure to get near the farmers, as they sat talking on the tombstones in the churchyard, before the parson was come; and once a week you might see little Dick leaning against the signpost of the village ale-house, where people stopped to drink as they came from the next market town; and when the barber's shop door was open, Dick listened to all the news that his customers told one another.

In this manner Dick heard a great many very strange things about the great city called London; for the foolish country people at that time thought that folks in London were all fine gentlemen and ladies, and that there was singing and music there all day long, and that the streets were all paved with gold.

One day a large wagon and eight horses, all with bells at their heads, drove through the village while Dick was standing by the signpost. He thought that this wagon must be going to the fine town of London; so he took courage and asked the wagoner to let him walk with him by the side of the wagon. As soon as the wagoner heard that poor Dick had no father or mother, and saw by his ragged clothes that he could not be worse off, he told him he might go if he would, so they set off together.

I could never find out how little Dick contrived to get meat and drink on the road; nor how he could walk so far, for it was a long way; nor what he did at night for a place to lie down to sleep in. Perhaps some good-natured people in the towns that he passed through, when they saw he was a poor little ragged boy, gave him something to eat; and perhaps the wagoner let him get into the wagon at night, and take a nap upon one of the boxes or large parcels in the wagon.

Dick, however, got safe to London, and was in such a hurry to see the fine streets paved all over with gold that I am afraid he did not even stay to thank the kind wagoner, but ran off as fast as his legs would carry him, through many of the streets, thinking every moment to come to those that were paved with gold; for Dick had seen a guinea three times in his own little village, and remembered what a deal of money it brought in change; so he thought he had nothing to do but to take up some little bits of the pavement and should then have as much money as he could wish for.

Poor Dick ran till he was tired, and had quite forgot his friend the wagoner; but at last, finding it grow dark, and that every way he turned he saw nothing but dirt instead of gold, he sat down in a dark corner and cried himself to sleep.

Little Dick was all night in the streets; and next morning, being very hungry, he got up and walked about, and asked everybody he met to give him a halfpenny to keep him from starving; but nobody stayed to answer him, and only two or three gave him a halfpenny, so that the poor boy was soon quite weak and faint for the want of victuals.

[1] From "Fairy Tales of Long Ago," edited by M. C. Carey, illustrations from drawings by D. J. Watkins-Pitchford

At last a good-natured looking gentleman saw how hungry he looked. "Why don't you go to work, my lad?" said he to Dick.

"That I would, but I do not know how to get any," answered Dick.

"If you are willing, come along with me," said the gentleman, and took him to a hay-field, where Dick worked briskly and lived merrily till the hay was made.

After this he found himself as badly off as before; and being almost starved again, he laid himself down at the door of Mr. Fitzwarren, a rich merchant. Here he was soon seen by the cook-maid, who was an ill-tempered creature, and happened just then to be very busy dressing dinner for her master and mistress; so she called out to poor Dick: "What business have you there, you lazy rogue? There is nothing else but beggars; if you do not take yourself away, we will see how you will like a sousing of some dishwater; I have some here hot enough to make you jump."

Just at that time Mr. Fitzwarren himself came home to dinner; and when he saw a dirty ragged boy lying at the door, he said to him: "Why do you lie there, my boy? You seem old enough to work; I am afraid you are inclined to be lazy."

"No, indeed, sir," said Dick to him, "that is not the case, for I would work with all my heart, but I do not know anybody, and I believe I am very sick for the want of food."

"Poor fellow, get up; let me see what ails you."

Dick now tried to rise, but was obliged to lie down again, being too weak to stand, for he had not eaten any food for three days, and was no longer able to run about and beg a halfpenny of people in the street. So the kind merchant ordered him to be taken into the house and have a good dinner given him, and be kept to do what dirty work he was able for the cook.

Little Dick would have lived very happily in this good family if it had not been for the ill-natured cook, who was finding fault and scolding him from morning to night, and besides, she was so fond of basting, that when she had no meat to baste, she would baste poor Dick's head and shoulders with a broom, or anything else that happened to fall in her way. At last her ill-usage of him was told to Alice, Mr. Fitzwarren's daughter, who told the cook she should be turned away if she did not treat him kinder.

The ill-humour of the cook was now a little amended; but besides this Dick had another hardship to get over. His bed stood in a garret, where there were so many holes in the floor and the walls that every night he was tormented with rats and mice. A gentleman having given Dick a penny for cleaning his shoes, he thought he would buy a cat with it. The next day he saw a girl with a cat, and asked her if she would let him have it for a penny. The girl said she would, and at the same time told him the cat was an excellent mouser.

Dick hid his cat in the garret, and always took care to carry a part of his dinner to her; and in a short time he had no more trouble with the rats and mice, but slept quite sound every night.

Soon after this his master had a ship ready to sail; and as he thought it right that all his servants should have some chance for good fortune as well as himself, he called them all into the parlour and asked them what they would send out.

They all had something that they were willing to venture except poor Dick, who had neither money nor goods, and therefore could send nothing.

For this reason he did not come into the parlour with the rest; but Miss Alice guessed what was the matter, and ordered him to be called in. She then said she would lay down some money for him, from her own purse; but her father told her this would not do, for it must be something of his own.

When poor Dick heard this, he said he had nothing but a cat which he bought for

a penny some time since of a little girl. "Fetch your cat then, my good boy," said Mr. Fitzwarren, "and let her go."

Dick went upstairs and brought down poor puss, with tears in his eyes, and gave her to the captain; for he said he would now be kept awake again all night by the rats and mice.

All the company laughed at Dick's odd venture; and Miss Alice, who felt pity for the poor boy, gave him some money to buy another cat.

This, and many other marks of kindness shown him by Miss Alice, made the ill-tempered cook jealous of poor Dick, and she began to use him more cruelly than ever, and always made game of him for sending his cat to sea. She asked him if he thought his cat would sell for as much money as would buy a stick to beat him.

At last poor Dick could not bear this usage any longer, and he thought he would run away from his place; so he packed up his few things, and started very early in the morning, on All Hallows' day, which is the first of November. He walked as far as Holloway, and there sat down on a stone, which to this day is called Whittington's stone, and began to

think to himself which road he should take as he went onwards.

While he was thinking what he should do, the Bells of Bow Church, which at that time had only six, began to ring, and he fancied their sound seemed to say to him:

"Turn again, Whittington,
Lord Mayor of London."

"Lord Mayor of London!" said he to himself. "Why, to be sure I would put up with almost anything now to be Lord Mayor of London, and ride in a fine coach, when I grow to be a man! Well, I will go back, and think nothing of the cuffing and scolding of the old cook, if I am to be Lord Mayor of London at last."

Dick went back, and was lucky enough to get into the house, and set about his work, before the old cook came downstairs.

The ship, with the cat on board, was a long time at sea, and was at last driven by the winds on a part of the coast of Barbary, where the only people were the Moors, whom the English had never known before.

The people then came in great numbers

to see the sailors, who were of different colour from themselves, and treated them very civilly; and, when they became better acquainted, were very eager to buy the fine things that the ship was loaded with.

When the captain saw this he sent patterns of the best things he had to the King of the country, who was so much pleased with them that he sent for the captain to the palace. Here they were placed, as it is the custom of the country, on rich carpets marked with gold and silver flowers. The King and Queen were seated at the upper end of the room, and a number of dishes were brought in for dinner. They had not sat long when a vast number of rats and mice rushed in, helping themselves from almost every dish. The captain wondered at this, and asked if these vermin were not very unpleasant.

"Oh, yes," said they, "very destructive; and the King would give half his treasure to be freed of them, for they not only destroy his dinner, as you see, but they assault him in his chamber, and even in bed, so that he is obliged to be watched while he is sleeping for fear of them.'

The captain jumped for joy; he remembered poor Whittington and his cat, and told the King he had a creature on board the ship that would dispatch all these vermin immediately. The King's heart leapt so high at the happiness this news gave him that his turban dropped off his head. "Bring this creature to me," said he; "vermin are dreadful in a Court, and if she will perform what you say I will load your ship with gold and jewels in exchange for her."

The captain, who knew his business, took this opportunity to set forth the merits of Mrs. Puss. He told His Majesty that it would be inconvenient to part with her, as, when she was gone, the rats and mice might destroy the goods in the ship—but to oblige His Majesty he would fetch her.

"Run, run!" said the Queen; "I am impatient to see the dear creature."

Away went the captain to the ship, while another dinner was got ready. He put Puss under his arm, and arrived at the place soon enough to see the table full of rats.

When the cat saw them she did not wait for bidding, but jumped out of the captain's arms, and in a few minutes laid almost all the rats and mice dead at her feet. The rest of them in their fright scampered away to their holes.

The King and Queen were quite charmed to get so easily rid of such plagues, and desired that the creature who had done them so great a kindness might be brought to them for inspection. Upon which the captain called: "Pussy, pussy, pussy!" and she came to him. He then presented her to the Queen, who started back, and was afraid to touch a creature who had made such a havoc among the rats and mice. However, when the captain stroked the cat and called "Pussy, pussy," the Queen also touched her and cried "Putty, putty," for she had not learned English. He then put her down on the Queen's lap, where she, purring, played with Her Majesty's hand, and then sung herself to sleep.

The King, having seen the exploits of Mrs. Puss, and being informed that her kittens would stock the whole country, bargained with the captain for the whole ship's cargo, and then gave him ten times as much for the cat as all the rest amounted to.

The captain then took leave of the royal party, and set sail with a fair wind for England, and after a happy voyage arrived safe in London.

One morning Mr. Fitzwarren had just come to his counting-house and seated himself at the desk, when somebody came tap, tap, at the door.

"Who's there?" says Mr. Fitzwarren.

"A friend," answered the other; "I come to bring you good news of your ship *Unicorn.*"

The merchant, bustling up instantly, opened the door, and who should be seen waiting but the captain and factor, with a

Dick bought a cat with a penny

cabinet of jewels, and a bill of lading, for which the merchant lifted up his eyes and thanked heaven for sending him such a prosperous voyage.

They then told the story of the cat, and showed the rich present that the King and Queen had sent for her to poor Dick. As soon as the merchant heard this he called out to his servants:

"Go fetch him—we will tell him of the same;
Pray call him Mr. Whittington by name."

Mr. Fitzwarren now showed himself to be a good man; for when some of his servants said so great a treasure was too much for Dick he answered: "God forbid I should deprive him of the value of a penny."

He then sent for Dick, who at that time was scouring pots for the cook and was quite dirty.

Mr. Fitzwarren ordered a chair to be set for him, and so he began to think they were making game of him, at the same time begging them not to play tricks with a poor simple boy, but to let him go down again, if they pleased, to his work.

"Indeed, Mr. Whittington," said the merchant, "we are all quite in earnest with you, and I most heartily rejoice in the news these gentlemen have brought you; for the captain has sold your cat to the King of Barbary, and brought you in return for her more riches than I possess in the whole world; and I wish you may long enjoy them!"

Mr. Fitzwarren then told the men to open the great treasure they had brought with them, and said: "Mr. Whittington has nothing to do but to put it in some place of safety."

Dick hardly knew how to contain himself for joy. He begged his master to take what he pleased, since he owed it to his kindness. "No, no," answered Mr. Fitzwarren, "this is all your own, and I have no doubt but you will use it well."

Dick next asked his mistress, and then Miss Alice, to accept a part of his good fortune; but they would not, and at the same time told him they felt great joy at his good success. But the poor fellow was too kind-hearted to keep it all to himself; so he made a present to the captain, the mate, and the rest of Mr. Fitzwarren's servants; and even to the ill-natured old cook.

After this, Mr. Fitzwarren advised him to send for a proper tradesman and get himself dressed like a gentleman; and told him he was welcome to live in his house till he could provide himself with a better.

When Whittington's face was washed, his hair curled, his hat cocked, and he was dressed in a nice suit of clothes, he was as handsome and genteel as any young man who visited at Mr. Fitzwarren's; so that Miss Alice, who had once been so kind to him, and thought of him with pity, now looked upon him as fit to be her sweetheart; and the more so, no doubt, because Whittington was now always thinking what he could do to oblige her, and making her the prettiest presents that could be.

Mr. Fitzwarren soon saw their love for each other, and proposed to join them in marriage; and to this they both readily agreed. A day for the wedding was soon fixed; and they were attended to church by the Lord Mayor, the court of aldermen, the sheriffs, and a great number of the richest merchants in London, whom they afterwards treated with a very rich feast.

History tells us that Mr. Whittington and his lady lived in great splendour, and were very happy. They had several children. He was Sheriff of London, also Mayor, and received the honour of knighthood by Henry V.

The figure of Sir Richard Whittington with his cat in his arms, carved in stone, was to be seen till the year 1780 over the archway of the old prison of Newgate, that stood across Newgate Street.

The Emperor's New Clothes[1]

Many years ago there was an Emperor who was so excessively fond of new clothes that he spent all his money on them. He cared nothing about his soldiers, nor for the theater, nor for driving in the woods except for the sake of showing off his new clothes. He had a costume for every hour in the day. Instead of say-ing as one does about any other king or emperor, "He is in his council chamber," the people here always said, "The Emperor is in his dressing room."

Life was very gay in the great town where he lived. Hosts of strangers came to visit it every day, and among them one day were two swindlers. They gave them-

[1] From "Hans Andersen's Fairy Tales," translated by Mrs. E. Lucas. Illustrations by Richard Bennett and H. J. Ford

selves out as weavers and said that they knew how to weave the most beautiful fabrics imaginable. Not only were the colors and patterns unusually fine, but the clothes that were made of this cloth had the peculiar quality of becoming invisible to every person who was not fit for the office he held, or who was impossibly dull.

"Those must be splendid clothes," thought the Emperor. "By wearing them I should be able to discover which men in my kingdom are unfitted for their posts. I shall distinguish the wise men from the fools. Yes, I certainly must order some of that stuff to be woven for me."

He paid the two swindlers a lot of money in advance, so that they might begin their work at once.

They did put up two looms and pretended to weave, but they had nothing whatever upon their shuttles. At the outset they asked for a quantity of the finest silk and the purest gold thread, all of which they put into their own bags while they worked away at the empty looms far into the night.

"I should like to know how those weavers are getting on with their cloth," thought the Emperor, but he felt a little queer when he reflected that anyone who was stupid or unfit for his post would not be able to see it. He certainly thought that he need have no fears for himself, but still he thought he would send somebody else first to see how it was getting on. Everybody in the town knew what wonderful power the stuff possessed, and everyone was anxious to see how stupid his neighbor was.

"I will send my faithful old minister to the weavers," thought the Emperor. "He will be best able to see how the stuff looks, for he is a clever man and no one fulfills his duties better than he does."

So the good old minister went into the room where the two swindlers sat working at the empty loom.

"Heaven help us," thought the old minister, opening his eyes very wide. "Why, I can't see a thing!" But he took care not to say so.

Both the swindlers begged him to be good enough to step a little nearer, and asked if he did not think it a good pattern and beautiful coloring. They pointed to the empty loom. The poor old minister stared as hard as he could, but he could not see anything, for of course there was nothing to see.

"Good heavens," thought he. "Is it possible that I am a fool? I have never thought so, and nobody must know it. Am I not fit for my post? It will never do to say that I cannot see the stuff."

"Well, sir, you don't say anything about the stuff," said the one who was pretending to weave.

"Oh, it is beautiful—quite charming," said the minister, looking through his spectacles. "Such a pattern and such colors! I will certainly tell the Emperor that the stuff pleases me very much."

"We are delighted to hear you say so," said the swindlers, and then they named all the colors and described the peculiar pattern. The old minister paid great attention to what they said, so as to be able to repeat it when he got home to the Emperor.

Then the swindlers went on to demand more money, more silk, and more gold, to be able to proceed with the weaving. But they put it all into their own pockets. Not a single strand was ever put into the loom, but they went on as before, weaving at the empty loom.

The Emperor soon sent another faithful official to see how the stuff was getting on and if it would soon be ready. The same thing happened to him as to the minister. He looked and looked, but as there was only the empty loom, he could see nothing at all.

"Is not this a beautiful piece of stuff?" said both the swindlers, showing and explaining the beautiful pattern and colors which were not there to be seen.

"I know I am no fool," thought the man,

"so it must be that I am unfit for my good post. It is very strange, though. However, one must not let it appear." So he praised the stuff he did not see, and assured them of his delight in the beautiful colors and the originality of the design.

"It is absolutely charming," he said to the Emperor. Everybody in the town was talking about this splendid stuff.

Now the Emperor thought he would like to see it while it was still on the loom. So, accompanied by a number of selected courtiers, among whom were the two faithful officials who had already seen the imaginary stuff, he went to visit the crafty impostors, who were working away as hard as ever they could at the empty loom.

"It is magnificent," said both the trusted officials. "Only see, Your Majesty, what a design! What colors!" And they pointed to the empty loom, for they each thought no doubt the others could see the stuff.

"What?" thought the Emperor. "I see nothing at all. This is terrible! Am I a fool? Am I not fit to be Emperor? Why, nothing worse could happen to me!"

"Oh, it is beautiful," said the Emperor. "It has my highest approval." And he nodded his satisfaction as he gazed at the empty loom. Nothing would induce him to say that he could not see anything.

The whole suite gazed and gazed, but saw nothing more than all the others. However, they all exclaimed with His Majesty, "It is very beautiful." And they advised him to wear a suit made of this wonderful cloth on the occasion of a great procession which was just about to take place. "Magnificent! Gorgeous! Excellent!" went from mouth to mouth. They were all equally delighted with it. The Emperor gave each of the rogues an order of knighthood to be worn in their buttonholes and the title of "Gentleman Weaver."

The swindlers sat up the whole night before the day on which the procession was to take place, burning sixteen candles, so that people might see how anxious they

were to get the Emperor's new clothes ready. They pretended to take the stuff off the loom. They cut it out in the air with a huge pair of scissors, and they stitched away with needles without any thread in them. At last they said, "Now the Emperor's new clothes are ready."

The Emperor with his grandest courtiers went to them himself, and both swindlers raised one arm in the air, as if they were holding something. They said, "See, these are the trousers. This is the coat. Here is the mantle," and so on. "It is as light as a spider's web. One might think one had nothing on, but that is the very beauty of it."

"Yes," said all the courtiers, but they could not see anything, for there was nothing to see.

"Will Your Imperial Majesty be graciously pleased to take off your clothes?" said the impostors. "Then we may put on the new ones, right here before the great mirror."

The Emperor took off all his clothes, and the impostors pretended to give him one article of dress after the other of the new ones which they had pretended to make. They pretended to fasten something around his waist and to tie on something. This was the train, and the Emperor turned round and round in front of the mirror.

"How well His Majesty looks in the new clothes! How becoming they are!" cried all the people round. "What a design, and what colors! They are most gorgeous robes."

"The canopy is waiting outside which is to be carried over Your Majesty in the procession," said the master of the ceremonies.

"Well, I am quite ready," said the Emperor. "Don't the clothes fit well?" Then he turned round again in front of the mirror, so that he should seem to be looking at his grand things.

The chamberlains who were to carry the train stooped and pretended to lift it from the ground with both hands, and they walked along with their hands in the air. They dared not let it appear that they could not see anything.

Then the Emperor walked along in the procession under the gorgeous canopy, and everybody in the streets and at the windows exclaimed, "How beautiful the Emperor's new clothes are! What a splendid train! And they fit to perfection!" Nobody would let it appear that he could see nothing, for then he would not be fit for his post, or else he was a fool.

None of the Emperor's clothes had been so successful.

"But he has got nothing on," said a little child.

"Oh, listen to the innocent," said its father. And one person whispered to the other what the child had said. "He has nothing on—a child says he has nothing on!"

"But he has nothing on!" at last cried all the people.

The Emperor writhed, for he knew it was true. But he thought, "The procession must go on now." So he held himself stiffer than ever, and the chamberlains held up the invisible train.

Cinderella [1]

There was once an honest gentleman who took for his second wife the proudest and most disagreeable lady in the whole country. She had two daughters exactly like herself. He himself had one little girl, who resembled her dead mother, the best woman in all the world. Scarcely had the second marriage taken place before the stepmother became jealous of the good qualities of the little girl, who was so great a contrast to her own two daughters. She gave her all the hard work of the house, compelling her to wash the floors and staircases, to dust the bedrooms, and clean the grates. While her sisters occupied carpeted chambers hung with mirrors, where they could see themselves from head to foot, this poor little girl was sent to sleep in an attic, on an old straw mattress, with only one chair and not a looking-glass in the room.

She suffered all in silence, not daring to complain to her father, who was entirely ruled by his new wife. When her daily work was done she used to sit down in the chimney-corner among the ashes, from which the two sisters gave her the nickname of "Cinderella." But Cinderella, however shabbily clad, was handsomer than they were, with all their fine clothes.

It happened that the King's son gave a series of balls, to which were invited all the rank and fashion of the city, and among the rest the two elder sisters. They were very proud and happy, and occupied their whole time in deciding what they should

[1] From "The Arthur Rackham Fairy Book," selected by Arthur Rackham, illustrations from drawings by Arthur Rackham

wear. This was a source of new trouble to Cinderella, whose duty it was to get up their fine linen and laces, and who never could please them, however much she tried. They talked of nothing but their clothes.

"I," said the elder, "shall wear my velvet gown and my trimmings of English lace."

"And I," added the younger, "will have but my ordinary silk petticoat, but I shall adorn it with an upper skirt of flowered brocade, and shall put on my diamond tiara, which is a great deal finer than anything of yours."

Here the elder sister grew angry, and the dispute began to run so high that Cinderella, who was known to have excellent taste, was called upon to decide between them. She gave them the best advice she could, and offered to dress them herself, and especially to arrange their hair, an accomplishment in which she excelled many a noted coiffeur. The important evening came, and she exercised all her skill in adorning the young ladies. While she was combing out the elder's hair this ill-natured girl said sharply, "Cinderella, do you not wish you were going to the ball?"

"Ah, madam"—they obliged her always to say madam—"you are only mocking me; it is not my fortune to have any such pleasure."

"You are right; people would only laugh to see a little cinder-wench at a ball."

After this any other girl would have dressed the hair all awry, but Cinderella was good, and made it perfectly even and smooth.

The sisters had scarcely eaten for two days, and had broken a dozen stay-laces a day in trying to make themselves slender; but to-night they broke a dozen more, and lost their tempers over and over again before they had completed their toilette. When at last the happy moment arrived Cinderella followed them to the coach, and after it had whirled them away she sat down by the kitchen fire and cried.

Immediately her godmother, who was a fairy, appeared beside her. "What are you crying for, my little maid?"

"Oh, I wish—I wish—" Her sobs stopped her.

"You wish to go to the ball; isn't it so?" Cinderella nodded.

"Well, then, be a good girl, and you shall go. First run into the garden and fetch me the largest pumpkin you can find."

Cinderella did not understand what this

had to do with her going to the ball, but, being obedient and obliging, she went. Her godmother took the pumpkin, and, having scooped out all its inside, struck it with her wand. It then became a splendid gilt coach, lined with rose-colored satin.

"Now fetch me the mouse-trap out of the pantry, my dear."

Cinderella brought it; it contained six of the fattest, sleekest mice.

The fairy lifted up the wire door, and as each mouse ran out she struck it and changed it into a beautiful black horse.

"But what shall I do for your coachman, Cinderella?"

Cinderella suggested that she had seen a large black rat in the rat-trap, and he might do for want of better.

"You are right. Go and look again for him."

He was found, and the fairy made him into a most respectable coachman, with the finest whiskers imaginable. She afterwards took six lizards from behind the pumpkin frame and changed them into six footmen, all in splendid livery, who immediately jumped up behind the carriage, as if they had been footmen all their days.

"Well, Cinderella, now you can go to the ball."

"What, in these clothes?" said Cinderella piteously, looking down on her ragged frock.

Her godmother laughed, and touched her also with the wand, at which her wretched, threadbare jacket became stiff with gold and sparkling with jewels, her woollen petticoat lengthened into a gown of sweeping satin, from underneath which peeped out her little feet, covered with silk stockings and the prettiest glass slippers in the world.

"Now, Cinderella, you may go; but remember, if you stay one instant after midnight your carriage will become a pumpkin, your coachman a rat, your horses mice, and your footmen lizards, while you yourself will be the little cinder-wench you were an hour ago."

Cinderella promised without fear, her heart was so full of joy.

Arrived at the palace, the King's son, whom some one, probably the fairy, had told to await the coming of an uninvited princess whom nobody knew, was standing at the entrance, ready to receive her. He offered her his hand, and led her with the utmost courtesy through the assembled guests, who stood aside to let her pass, whispering to one another, "Oh, how beautiful she is!" It might have turned the head of anyone but poor Cinderella, who was so used to being despised, but she took it all as if it were something happening in a dream.

Her triumph was complete; even the old King said to the Queen that never since her Majesty's young days had he seen so charming a person. All the Court ladies scanned her eagerly, clothes and all, and determined to have theirs made next day of exactly the same pattern. The King's son himself led her out to dance, and she danced so gracefully that he admired her more and more. Indeed, at supper, which was fortunately early, his admiration quite took away his appetite. Cinderella herself sought out her sisters, placed herself beside them, and offered them all sorts of civil attentions. These, coming as they supposed from a stranger, and so magnificent a lady, almost overwhelmed them with delight.

While she was talking with them she heard the clock strike a quarter to twelve, and, making a courteous *adieu* to the royal family, she re-entered her carriage, escorted gallantly by the King's son, and arrived in safety at her own door. There she found her godmother, who smiled approval, and of whom she begged permission to go to a second ball the following night, to which the Queen had invited her.

While she was talking the two sisters were heard knocking at the gate, and the fairy godmother vanished, leaving Cinderella sitting in the chimney-corner, rubbing her eyes and pretending to be very sleepy.

"Ah," cried the eldest sister spitefully, "it has been the most delightful ball, and there was present the most beautiful princess I ever saw, who was so exceedingly polite to us both."

"Was she?" said Cinderella indifferently. "And who might she be?"

"Nobody knows, though everybody would give their eyes to know, especially the King's son."

"Indeed!" replied Cinderella, a little more interested. "I should like to see her." Then she turned to the elder sister and said, "Miss Javotte, will you not let me go to-morrow, and lend me your yellow gown that you wear on Sundays?"

"What, lend my yellow gown to a cinder-wench! I am not so mad as that!" At which refusal Cinderella did not complain, for if her sister really had lent her the gown she would have been considerably embarrassed.

The next night came, and the two young ladies, richly dressed in different toilettes, went to the ball. Cinderella, more splendidly attired and more beautiful than ever, followed them shortly after. "Now, remember twelve o'clock," was her godmother's parting speech; and she thought she certainly should. But the prince's attentions to her were greater even than on the first evening, and in the delight of listening to his pleasant conversation time slipped by unperceived. While she was sitting beside him in a lovely alcove and looking at the moon from under a bower of orange-blossom she heard a clock strike the first stroke of twelve. She started up, and fled away as lightly as a deer.

Amazed, the prince followed, but could not catch her. Indeed, he missed his lovely princess altogether, and only saw running out of the palace doors a little dirty lass whom he had never beheld before, and of whom he certainly would never have taken the least notice. Cinderella arrived at home breathless and weary, ragged and cold, without carriage or footmen or coachman; the only remnant of her past magnificence being one of her little glass slippers; the other she had dropped in the ballroom as she ran away.

When the two sisters returned they were full of this strange adventure: how the beautiful lady had appeared at the ball more beautiful than ever, and enchanted every one who looked at her; and how as the clock was striking twelve she had suddenly risen up and fled through the ballroom, disappearing no one knew how or where, and dropping one of her glass slippers behind her in her flight.

The King's son had remained inconsolable until he chanced to pick up the little glass slipper, which he carried away in his pocket and was seen to take out continually, and look at affectionately, with the air of a man very much in love; in fact, from his behaviour during the remainder of the evening all the Court and the royal family were sure that he was desperately in love with the wearer of the little glass slipper.

Cinderella listened in silence, turning her face to the kitchen fire, and perhaps it was that which made her look so rosy; but nobody ever noticed or admired her at home; so it did not signify, and next morning she went to her weary work again just as before.

A few days after the whole city was attracted by the sight of a herald going round with a little glass slipper in his hand, publishing, with a flourish of trumpets, that the King's son ordered this to be fitted on the foot of every lady in the kingdom, and that he wished to marry the lady whom it fitted best, or to whom it and the fellow-slipper belonged. Princesses, duchesses, countesses, and simple gentlewomen all tried it on, but, being a fairy slipper, it fitted nobody; and, besides, nobody could produce its fellow-slipper, which lay all the time safely in the pocket of Cinderella's old woollen gown.

At last the herald came to the house of the two sisters, and though they well knew neither of themselves was the beautiful lady they made every attempt to get their clumsy feet into the glass slipper, but in vain.

"Let me try it on," said Cinderella from the chimney-corner.

"What, you?" cried the others, bursting into shouts of laughter; but Cinderella only smiled and held out her hand.

Her sisters could not prevent her, since the command was that every maiden in the city should try on the slipper, in order that no chance might be left untried, for the prince was nearly breaking his heart; and his father and mother were afraid that, though a prince, he would actually die for love of the beautiful unknown lady.

So the herald bade Cinderella sit down on a three-legged stool in the kitchen, and he himself put the slipper on her pretty little foot. It fitted exactly. She then drew from her pocket the fellow-slipper, which she also put on, and stood up. With the touch of the magic shoes all her dress was changed likewise. No longer was she the poor, despised cinder-wench, but the beautiful lady whom the King's son loved.

Her sisters recognized her at once. Filled with astonishment, mingled with no little alarm, they threw themselves at her feet, begging her pardon for all their former unkindness. She raised and embraced them, telling them she forgave them with all her heart, and only hoped they would love her always. Then she departed with the herald to the King's palace, and told her whole story to His Majesty and the royal family. They were not in the least surprised, for everybody believed in fairies, and everybody longed to have a fairy godmother.

As for the young prince, he found her more lovely and lovable than ever, and insisted upon marrying her immediately. Cinderella never went home again, but she sent for her two sisters to the palace, and married them shortly after to two rich gentlemen of the Court.

The Fisherman and His Wife [1]

There was once a fisherman and his wife. They lived together in a vinegar jug close by the sea, and the fisherman went there every day and fished: and he fished and he fished.

So he sat there one day at his fishing and always looked into the clear water: and he sat and he sat.

Then down went the hook, deep down, and when he pulled it up, there he had a big golden fish. And the fish said to him, "Listen, fisher, I beg of you, let me live. I am not a real fish; I am an enchanted Prince. How would it help you if you killed me? I wouldn't taste good to you anyway—put me back into the water and let me swim."

"Nu," said the man, "you needn't make so many words about it. A fish that can talk—I would surely have let him swim anyway."

With that he put him back into the clear water, and the fish went down and left a long streak of blood after him. And the fisher got up and went home to his wife in the vinegar jug.

"Husband," said the wife, "haven't you caught anything today?"

"Nay," said the man. "I caught a golden fish who said he was an enchanted Prince, so I let him swim again."

"But didn't you wish yourself something?" asked the wife.

"Nay," said the man. "What could I have wished?"

"Ach!" said the wife. "Here we live in a vinegar jug that smells so sour and is so dark: you could have wished us a little hut. Go there now and tell him—tell him we want a little hut. He will do that, surely."

"Ach!" said the man. "Why should I go there?"

"Ei!" said the wife. "After all, you caught him and let him swim again, didn't you? He will do that surely; go right there."

The man still didn't want to go, but he did not want to go against his wife's wishes either, and so he went off to the sea. As he came there, the sea was all green and yellow and not at all so clear any more. So he went and stood and said:

Manye, Manye, Timpie Tee,
Fishye, Fishye in the sea,
Ilsebill my wilful wife
Does not want my way of life.

Now the fish came swimming along and said, "Nu, what does she want then?"

"Ach!" said the man. "After all, I caught you and let you go. Now my wife says I should really have wished myself something. She doesn't want to live in the vinegar jug any more; she would dearly like to have a hut."

[1] From "Tales From Grimm," translated by Wanda Gåg, illustrations from drawings by Wanda Gåg

"Go there," said the fish. "She has that now."

So the man went home and his wife wasn't sitting in the vinegar jug any more, but there stood a little hut and she was sitting in front of it on a bench. She took his hand and said to him, "Just come in. See, now isn't that much better?"

So they went in, and in the hut was a little hall and a parlor; also a sleeping room in which stood their bed. And a kitchen and dining room, with the best of utensils laid out in the nicest way: pewter and brassware and all that belonged there. In back of the hut was a little yard with chickens and ducks, and a garden with vegetables and fruit.

"See," said the wife, "isn't that neat?"

"Yes," said the man, "and so let it be. Now we will live right contentedly."

"Nu, we'll think about that," said the wife.

With that they ate something and went to bed.

· · · · ·

So that went on for about eight or fourteen days, when the wife said: "Listen, man, the hut is much too small, and the yard and garden are so tiny. The fish might really have given us a bigger house. I want to live in a stone mansion. Go to the fish, he must give us a mansion."

"Ach, wife," said the man. "The hut is good enough—why should we want to live in a mansion?"

"Go there," said the wife. "The fish can easily do that much."

"Nay, wife," said the man, "the fish has already given us the hut. I don't want to go there again; it might displease the fish."

"Go!" said the wife. "He can do that right well and will do it gladly; you just go there."

The man's heart became heavy and he didn't want to go. He said to himself, "That is not right," but he went there anyway.

When he came to the sea, the water was all purple and gray and thick, and not green and yellow any more, but it was still quiet. So he went and stood and said:

Manye, Manye, Timpie Tee,
Fishye, Fishye in the sea,
Ilsebill my wilful wife
Does not want my way of life.

"Nu, what does she want then?" asked the fish.

"Ach!" said the man. "She wants to live in a big stone mansion."

"Go there then," said the fish, "she is standing in front of the door."

So the man left and thought he would go home, but when he reached it, there was a big stone mansion, and his wife was standing on the steps, just ready to go in. She took him by the hand and said, "Just come inside."

That he did, and in the mansion was a big hall with marble floors, and there were

238

so many many servants, and they tore open the big doors. The walls were all bright, and covered with fine tapestries, and the rooms were full of golden chairs and tables. Crystal chandeliers hung from the ceilings, all the parlors and chambers were covered with carpets, and food and the best of wines stood on the tables so that they were ready to break.

In back of the mansion was a big courtyard with horse and cow stables, and carriages of the very best. Also there was a marvelous big garden with the most beautiful flowers and fine fruit trees. And a park—at least a half a mile long—in it were stags and deer and rabbits and all that one could ever wish for oneself.

"See?" said the wife, "isn't that beautiful?"

"Oh yes," said the man, "and so let it be. Now we will live in the beautiful mansion and be well satisfied."

"Nu, we'll think that over and sleep on it," said the wife.

With that they went to bed.

· · · · ·

The next morning the wife woke up first. It was just daybreak, and she saw from her bed the wonderful land lying before her. The man was still sleeping, so she nudged him in his side with her elbow and said, "Man, get up and just look out of the window. See? Couldn't one become King over all that land? Go to the fish—we want to be King."

"Ach, wife!" said the man. "Why should we want to be King? I don't want to be King."

"Nu," said the wife, "if *you* don't want to be King, *I* want to be King. Go to the fish and tell him I want to be King."

"Ach, wife!" said the man, "that I don't want to tell the fish."

"Why not?" said the wife. "Go right straight there. I must be King!"

So the man went there and was right dismayed. "That is not right and is not right," he thought. He did not want to go but he went anyway. And as he came to

the shore, there it was all blackish grey and the water foamed up from the bottom and it smelled all rotten. So he went and stood and said:

Manye, Manye, Timpie Tee,
Fishye, Fishye in the sea,
Ilsebill my wilful wife
Does not want my way of life.

"Nu, what does she want then?" asked the fish.

"Ach!" said the man. "She wants to be King."

"Go there then—she is all that," said the fish.

So the man went, and when he came to the mansion it had become a big castle. It had a high tower with wonderful trimmings on it, and a sentry stood before the door, and there were so many many soldiers with drums and trumpets! And as he came into the castle, he found that everything was made of marble and gold, with velvet covers and big golden tassels. Then the doors of the hall opened. There was all the court, and his wife sat on a high throne of gold and diamonds. She had a crown of pure gold on her head, and a scepter of gold and jewels in her hand. On both sides of her stood six maidens in a row, each always one head smaller than the other.

So he went and stood there and said, "Oh wife, are you now King?"

"Yes," said the wife. "Now I am King."

So he stood there and looked at her, and when he had looked at her like that for a while, he said, "Ach wife, how nice it is that you are King! Now we have nothing more to wish for."

"Nay, man," said the wife and looked all restless. "There isn't enough to do. To me the time seems so long—I can't stand that any more. Go there to the fish. King I am, now I must also become Emperor."

"Ach wife!" said the man. "Why should you want to be Emperor?"

"Man," said she, "go to the fish. I want to be Emperor!"

"Ach wife!" said the man. "I don't want to tell that to the fish. He can't make an Emperor—that he cannot and cannot do."

"What!" said the wife. "I am King and you are my man. Will you go there right away? If he can make a King, he can make an Emperor. I want and want to be Emperor. Go there right now!"

So he had to go, but he became all scared. And as he went along like that, he thought to himself, "That doesn't and doesn't go right. Emperor is too much to ask for—the fish will get tired in the end."

With that he came to the sea. It was all black and thick, and began to ferment so that it made bubbles, and such a wild wind blew over it that the man was horrified. So he went and stood and said:

Manye, Manye, Timpie Tee,
Fishye, Fishye in the sea,
Ilsebill my wilful wife
Does not want my way of life.

"Nu, what does she want then?" asked the fish.

"Ach fish!" said the man, "she wants to be Emperor."

"Go there then," said the fish. "She is all that."

So the man went, and when he came there, the whole castle was made of polished marble with alabaster statues and golden decorations. In front of the door soldiers were marching, and they blew their trumpets and beat their drums and kettle drums. In the castle, barons and earls and dukes were walking around as servants: they opened the doors for him which were of pure gold. And when he came inside, there sat his wife on a throne which was made all of one piece of gold and was about two miles high. She wore a big golden crown which was three ells high and was set with brilliants and carbuncles. In one hand she held the scepter and in the other hand she had the imperial globe. On both sides of the throne stood the gentlemen-at-arms in two rows, one always smaller than the next: from the biggest giant who was two miles high, to the smallest dwarf who was only as big as my little finger. And in front of her stood so many many Princes and Kings!

So the man went and stood and said, "Wife, are you now Emperor?"

"Yes," said she, "I am Emperor."

So he stood there and looked at her right well, and after he had looked at her like that for a while, he said, "Ach wife, how nice it is now that you are Emperor."

"Man!" she said. "Why are you standing there like that? I am Emperor but now I want to become Pope. Go to the fish."

"Ach wife!" said the man. "What do you ask of me? You can't become Pope. There is only one Pope in Christendom; surely the fish can't make that."

"Man," said she, "I want to be Pope. Go right there. Even today I must become Pope."

"Nay, wife," said the man, "that I don't want to tell him; that won't go right, that is too much—the fish can't make you a Pope."

"Man, what chatter!" said the wife. "If

he can make an Emperor, he can make a
Pope as well. Get along. I am Emperor
and you are my man—will you go there
now?"

At that he was frightened and went
there; but he felt all faint, and shook and
quaked, and his knees and calves became
flabby. And now such a big wind blew
over the land, and the clouds flew so that
it grew as dark as though it were evening.
The leaves blew from the trees, the water
splashed against the shore, and worked
and churned as though it were boiling.
And far away he saw the ships; they were
in trouble, and tossed and leaped on the
billows. The sky was still a little blue in
the middle, but at the sides it was coming
up right red as in a heavy storm.

So he went there in despair, and stood
in terror and said:

Manye, Manye, Timpie Tee,
Fishye, Fishye in the sea,
Ilsebill my wilful wife
Does not want my way of life.

"Nu, what does she want then?" asked
the fish.

"Ach," said the man, "she wants to be
Pope."

"Go there then," said the fish. "She is
that now."

· · · · ·

So he went, and when he came home it
was like a big church with palaces all
around it. There he pushed his way

241

through the crowd: inside everything was lit up with thousands and thousands of candles. His wife was dressed in pure gold and sat on an even higher throne than before and now she wore three big golden crowns, and all around her there was so much pomp and grandeur! On both sides of her, there stood two rows of candles: from the tallest, as thick as a tower, down to the smallest kitchen candle. And all the Emperors and Kings were down before her on their knees.

"Wife," said the man, and looked at her right well, "are you now Pope?"

"Yes," said she, "I am Pope."

So he went and stood and looked at her, and it was just as though he looked at the sun. After he had looked at her for a while, he said, "Ach wife, how nice it is now that you are Pope."

But she sat there stiff as a tree and did not stir or move herself. Then he said, "Well, wife, now that you are Pope you will have to be satisfied. You can't become anything more."

"That I will think over," said the wife.

With that they went to bed, but the wife was not satisfied, and her greediness did not let her sleep. She was always wondering what else she could become.

The man slept right well and soundly— he had done much running that day—but the wife could not sleep and tossed herself from one side to the other all through the night and wondered what else she could become, but could think of nothing higher.

With that the sun began to rise, and as she saw the rosy dawn she leaned over one end of the bed and looked out of the window. And when she saw the sun coming up: "Ha!" she thought, "couldn't I, too, make the sun and moon go up?"

"Man," she said, and poked him in the ribs with her elbow, "wake up, and go there to the fish. I want to be like God."

The man was still half asleep but he was so alarmed by this, that he fell out of bed. He thought he had not heard a-right and

rubbed his eyes and said, "Ach wife, what are you saying?"

"Man," said she, "if I can't make the sun and moon rise and have to sit here and see that the sun and moon are going up, I can't stand that, and I won't have a peaceful moment until I can make them go up myself."

Then she looked at him in such a horrible way that a shudder ran over him.

"Go right there," she said, "I want to be like God."

"Ach wife!" said the man, and fell before her on his knees. "That the fish can't do. Emperor and Pope he can make. I beg of you, be satisfied and stay Pope."

At that she became furious and her hair flew wildly about her head. She lifted up her tunic and gave him a kick with her foot and screamed, "I can't stand it and I can't stand it any longer! Will you go?"

So he pulled on his trousers and ran away as though he were mad. But outside there was a storm and it raged so that he could hardly stay on his feet. The houses and the trees blew over and the mountains quaked. The big rocks broke off and rolled into the sea, and the sky was pitch black, and it thundered and lightened, and the sea went up into big black waves as high as church towers and mountains, and they all had a white crown of foam on their tops. So he screamed out and could hardly hear his own voice:

Manye, Manye, Timpie Tee!
Fishye, Fishye in the sea!
Ilsebill my wilful wife
Does not want my way of life.

"Nu, what does she want then?" asked the fish.

"Ach!" said the man. "She wants to make the sun and moon rise. She wants to be like God."

"Go home then," said the fish, "she's back in her vinegar jug again."

And there they are both sitting to this day.

The Three Aunts[1]

Once on a time there was a poor man who lived in a hut far away in the wood and got his living by shooting. He had an only daughter, and she was both fair and pretty. As the mother had died when she was a child, and now she was half grown, the daughter said she would go out into the world and learn to earn her bread.

"Well, my daughter," said the father, "true enough, you have learned nothing here but how to pluck birds and roast them, but still you may as well try to earn your bread."

So the lass went off to seek a place, and when she had gone a little while, she came to the king's house. There she stayed and got a place, and the queen thought so much of her that the other maids got envious of her. So they made up their minds to tell the queen how the lassie said she was good to spin a pound of flax in twenty-four hours, for the queen was a great housewife and thought much of all kinds of handiwork.

"Well, what you have said you shall also do," said the queen; "but you may have a little longer time if you choose."

Now the poor lassie dared not say she had never spun in all her life, but she only begged for a room to herself. That she got, and the wheel and the flax were brought up to her. There she sat crying and ill at ease and was at her wit's end. She pulled the wheel this way and that, and twisted and turned it about, but she made a poor hand of it, for she had never even seen a spinning wheel in her life.

But all at once, as she sat there, in came an old woman to her.

"What ails you, child?" she said.

"Ah!" said the lassie. "It's no good to tell you; you'll never be able to help me."

"Don't be too sure about that," said the old woman. "Maybe I know how to help you after all."

Well, thought the lassie to herself, I may as well tell her. And so she told her how her fellow-servants had given out that she was good to spin a pound of flax in twenty-four hours.

"And here am I, poor me, shut up to spin all that heap in a day and a night, when I have never even seen a spinning wheel in all my born days."

"Well, child, that's all the same," said the old woman. "If you'll call me Aunt on your wedding day, I'll spin this flax for you; and so you may just go away and lie down to sleep."

Yes, the lassie was willing enough, and off she went and lay down to sleep.

Next morning when she awoke, there lay all the flax spun on the table, and that so clean and fine no one had ever seen such even and pretty yarn. The queen was so happy over the nice yarn she had got that she was even fonder of the lassie than before. But the other maids were still more envious, and hit on telling the queen how the lassie had said she was good to weave the yarn she had spun in twenty-four hours. Again the queen said well, what she had said she should also do, but if she couldn't quite finish it in twenty-four hours, she wouldn't be too hard upon her, she might have a little longer time. This time, too, the lassie dared not say no, but begged for a room to herself, and then she would try. There she sat again, sobbing and crying, and not knowing which way to turn, when another old woman came in and asked:

"What ails you, child?"

At first the lassie wouldn't say, but at last she told her why she was so sad.

"Well, well," said the old woman, "never mind! If you'll call me Aunt on your wedding day, I'll weave this yarn for you; and so you may just go to bed, and lie down to sleep."

[1] From "East of the Sun and West of the Moon," by Ingri and Edgar Parin d'Aulaire, illustration from a drawing by Ingri and Edgar Parin d'Aulaire

Yes, the lassie was willing enough, so she went and lay down to sleep. When she awoke, there lay the piece of linen on the table, woven so neat and close, no woof could be better. So the lassie took the piece and brought it to the queen, who was very happy to get such beautiful linen and became even fonder of the lassie than ever before. But as for the others, they grew still more bitter against her, and thought of nothing but how to find out something to tell about her.

At last they told the queen the lassie had said she was good to make up the piece of linen into shirts in twenty-four hours. Well, all happened as before; the lassie dared not say she couldn't sew, so she was shut up again in a room by herself, and there she sat in tears and grief. But then came another old woman who said she would sew the shirts for her if she would call her Aunt on her wedding day. The lassie was only too glad to do this, and then she did as the old woman told her, and went and lay down to sleep.

Next morning when she woke, she found the piece of linen made up into shirts that lay on the table—and such beautiful work no one had ever set eyes on, and more than that, the shirts were all marked and ready to wear. When the queen saw this work, she was so happy at the way in which it was sewn that she clapped her hands, and said:

"Such sewing I have never had, nor even seen, in all my born days."

And after that she was as fond of the lassie as of her own child, and she said to her:

"If you'd like to have the prince for your husband, you shall have him; for you will never need to hire work-women. You can sew and spin and weave all yourself."

So, as the lassie was pretty and the prince liked her well, the wedding soon came on. But no sooner had the prince sat down with the bride to the bridal feast, then in came an ugly old hag with a long nose—I'm sure it was three ells long.

So up got the bride and made a curtsy, and said:

"Good day, my aunt."

"Is that an aunt of my bride?" said the prince.

Yes, she was!

"Well, then, she'd better sit down with us to the feast," said the prince; but, to tell you the truth, both he and the rest thought she was a loathsome woman to have next you.

But just then in came another ugly old hag. She had a seat so broad and so fat that she was just able to squeeze in through the door. Up jumped the bride in a trice, and greeted her with: "Good day, my aunt!"

And the prince asked again if that were the aunt of his bride. They both said yes; so the prince said, if that were so, she too had better sit down with them to the feast.

But they had scarce taken their seats before another ugly old hag came in, with eyes as large as saucers, and so red and bleared 'twas gruesome to look at her. But up jumped the bride again, with her "Good day, my aunt." And her, too, the prince asked to sit down. But he was far from happy and he thought to himself:

"Heaven shield me from the kind of aunts my bride has!" So when he had sat awhile, he could not keep his thoughts to himself any longer, but asked:

"But how in all the world can my bride, who is such a lovely lassie, have such loathsome, misshapen aunts?"

"I'll soon tell you that," said the first. "I was just as pretty as your bride, when I was her age; but the reason why I've got this long nose is that I have always been sitting and poking and nodding over my spinning, and so my nose got stretched and stretched, until it got as long as you now see it."

"And I," said the second, "ever since I was young, I have sat and shoved back-

wards and forwards on the weaving bench, and that's how my seat has got so broad and big as you now see it."

"And I," said the third, "ever since I was little, I have sat and stared and sewn, and sewn and stared, night and day; and that's why my eyes have got so ugly and red, and now there's no help for them."

"So! So!" said the prince. "I am glad I came to know this; for if folk can get so ugly and loathsome by all this, then my bride shall neither spin nor weave nor sew again in all her days."

The Half-Chick[1]

There was once upon a time a handsome, black Spanish hen, who had a large brood of chickens. They were all fine, plump little birds, except the youngest who was quite unlike his brothers and sisters. This one looked just as if he had been cut in two. He had only one leg, and one wing, and one eye and he had half a head and half a beak. His mother shook her head sadly as she looked at him and said:

"My youngest born is only a half-chick. He can never grow up a tall handsome cock like his brothers. They will go out into the world and rule over poultry yards of their own. But this poor little fellow will always have to stay at home with his mother." And she called him Medio Pollito, which is Spanish for half-chick.

Now though Medio Pollito was such an odd, helpless-looking little thing, his mother soon found he was not at all willing to remain under her wing and protection. Indeed, in character he was as unlike his brothers and sisters as he was in appearance. They were good, obedient chickens, and when the old hen called them, they chirped and ran back to her side. But Medio Pollito had a roving spirit in spite of his one leg, and when his mother called him to return to the coop, he pretended he could not hear because he had only one ear.

When she took the whole family out for a walk in the fields, Medio Pollito would hop away by himself and hide among the Indian corn. Many an anxious moment his brothers and sisters had looking for him, while his mother ran to and fro cackling in fear and dismay.

As he grew older he became more self-willed and disobedient. His manner to his mother was often rude and his temper to the other chickens disagreeable.

One day he had been out for a longer expedition than usual in the fields. On his return he strutted up to his mother with a peculiar little hop and kick which was his way of walking and, cocking his one eye at her in a very bold way, he said:

"Mother, I am tired of this life in a dull farmyard, with nothing but a dreary maize field to look at. I'm off to Madrid to see the king."

"To Madrid, Medio Pollito!" exclaimed his mother. "Why, you silly chick, it would be a long journey for a grown-up cock; a poor little thing like you would be tired out before you had gone half the distance. No, no, stay at home with your mother and some day, when you are bigger, we will go on a little journey together."

But Medio Pollito had made up his mind. He would not listen to his mother's advice, nor to the prayers and entreaties of his brothers and sisters.

"What is the use of our crowding each other in this poky little place?" he said. "When I have a fine courtyard of my own at the king's palace, I shall perhaps ask some of you to come and pay me a short visit." And scarcely waiting to say good-bye to his family, away he stumped down the high road that led to Madrid.

"Be sure you are kind and civil to everyone you meet," called his mother, running after him. But he was in such a hurry to be off he did not wait to answer her or even to look back.

A little later in the day, as he was taking a short cut through a field, he passed a stream. Now the stream was choked and overgrown with weeds and water plants so its waters could not flow freely.

"Oh, Medio Pollito!" it cried, as the half-chick hopped along its banks. "Do come and help me by clearing away these weeds."

"Help you, indeed!" exclaimed Medio Pollito, tossing his head and shaking the

[1]From the "Green Fairy Book," edited by Andrew Lang. Illustration by Debi Sussman

few feathers in his tail. "Do you think I have nothing to do but waste my time on such trifles? Help yourself, and don't trouble busy travelers. I am off to Madrid to see the king." And hoppity-kick, hoppity-kick, away stumped Medio Pollito.

A little later he came to a fire that had been left by some gypsies in a wood. It was burning very low and would soon be out.

"Oh, Medio Pollito," cried the fire, in a weak wavering voice as the half-chick approached, "in a few minutes I shall go quite out unless you put some sticks and dry leaves upon me. Do help me or I shall die!"

"Help you, indeed!" answered Medio Pollito. "I have other things to do. Gather sticks for yourself and don't trouble me. I am off to Madrid to see the king." And hoppity-kick, hoppity-kick, away stumped Medio Pollito.

The next morning, as he was nearing Madrid, he passed a large chestnut tree in whose branches the wind was caught and entangled.

"Oh, Medio Pollito," called the wind, "do hop up here and help me get free of these branches. I cannot come away and it is so uncomfortable."

"It is your own fault for going there," answered Medio Pollito. "I can't waste all my morning stopping here to help you. Just shake yourself off and don't hinder me, for I am off to Madrid to see the king." And hoppity-kick, hoppity-kick, away stumped Medio Pollito in great glee, for the towers and roofs of Madrid were now in sight.

When he entered the town he saw before him a great splendid house, with soldiers standing before the gates. This he knew must be the royal palace, and he determined to hop up to the front gate and wait there until the king came out. But as he was hopping past one of the back windows, the king's cook saw him.

"Here is the very thing I want," he exclaimed, "for the king has just sent a mes-

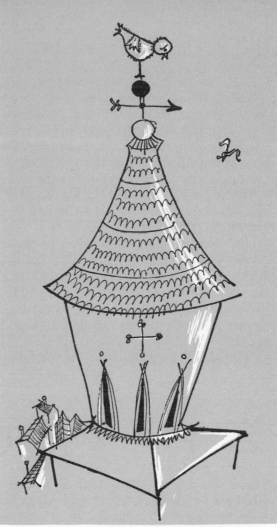

sage that he must have chicken broth for his dinner!" And opening the window he stretched out his arm, caught Medio Pollito, and popped him into the broth pot standing near the fire. Oh, how wet and clammy the water felt as it went over Medio Pollito's head, making his feathers cling to his side.

"Water, water," he cried out in his despair, "do have pity upon me and do not wet me like this."

"Ah, Medio Pollito," replied the water, "you would not help me when I was a little stream away in the fields and now you must be punished."

Then the fire began to burn and scald Medio Pollito. He hopped from one side of the pot to the other, trying to get away from the heat, and crying out in pain:

"Fire, fire! Do not scorch me like this. You cannot think how it hurts."

"Ah, Medio Pollito," answered the fire, "you would not help me when I was dying in the wood. You are being punished."

At last, just when the pain was so great Medio Pollito thought he must die, the cook lifted up the lid of the pot to see if the broth was ready for the king's dinner.

"Look here," he cried in horror, "this chicken is quite useless! It is burned to a cinder. I can't send it up to the royal table." And opening the window he threw Medio Pollito out into the street. But the wind caught him up and whirled him through the air so quickly Medio Pollito could scarcely breathe, and his heart beat against his side till he thought it would break.

"Oh, wind," he gasped out, "if you hurry me along like this you will kill me. Do let me rest a moment, or—" But he was so breathless he could not finish his sentence.

"Ah, Medio Pollito," replied the wind, "when I was caught in the branches of the chestnut tree you would not help me. Now you are punished." And he swirled Medio Pollito over the roofs of the houses till they reached the highest church in the town, and there he left him fastened to the top of the steeple.

And there stands Medio Pollito to this day. If you go to Madrid and walk through the streets till you come to the highest church, you will see Medio Pollito perched on his one leg on the steeple, with his one wing drooping at his side, and gazing sadly out of his one eye over the town.

The Sleeping Beauty [1]

There was once a King and his Queen, who had no children, which grieved them more than can be imagined. They went to all the healing waters in the world; they made vows; they went on pilgrimages; they did everything they could think of: but it was all to no good.

At last, however, the Queen did have a baby—a little girl. There was a fine christening party; and all the fairies in the kingdom (there were seven of them) were made godmothers to the Princess, so that each of them could give her a gift, as was the custom of fairies at that time, and so she was endowed with every good quality imaginable. After the baptism itself, all the guests came back to the King's palace, where there was a great banquet in honour of the fairies. Each of them sat at table, and a rich cloth was spread for her, and on it a golden casket containing a knife, fork, and spoon of fine gold, all studded with diamonds and rubies. But just as every one had sat down, in came an old fairy who had not been invited because for more than fifty years she had not come out of her tower, so that every one thought she must be dead or else under a spell.

The King had a place laid for her; but they could not manage to find a golden casket, such as the others had, because only the set of seven had been made. The old fairy thought she was being slighted, so she grumbled to herself in a threatening way. One of the younger fairies sitting beside her heard this, and fearing that she might be giving the little Princess some unlucky gift, went and hid behind the curtains when the banquet was over, so as to be the last to speak, and thus be able to put right, as far as she could, any harm that the old fairy might do.

Now the fairies began to present their gifts to the Princess. The youngest granted her this boon—that she should be the most beautiful girl in the world; the next, that she should be the wittiest; the third, that whatever she did, she should do most

[1] From "Fairy Tales of Long Ago," edited by M. C. Carey, illustration from a drawing by D. J. Watkins-Pitchford

gracefully; the fourth, that she should dance perfectly; the fifth, that she should sing like a nightingale; and the sixth, that she should be able to play sweetly on all kinds of musical instruments.

Now it was the old fairy's turn; wagging her head more in spite than from old age, she said that the Princess would prick herself with a distaff, and that would be the death of her. Everybody shuddered at this terrible gift, and all burst into tears. At that moment the young fairy stepped out from behind the curtains and said in a loud voice: "Take courage, Your Majesties; your daughter will not die: true, I have not the power to undo completely what my elder sister has prophesied, and the Princess will indeed prick her hand with a distaff—but, far from dying of it, she will only fall into a deep sleep which shall last a hundred years, at the end of which time a king's son shall come and wake her."

The King tried to avert the ill-fortune promised by the old fairy, by at once having it proclaimed that no one was allowed to spin with a distaff, or to have a distaff in their house, on pain of death.

After fifteen or sixteen years, the King and Queen having gone to stay in one of their country houses, it chanced that the little Princess, roaming about the palace and wandering from room to room and from floor to floor, came to the top of one of the towers, and found a little attic, where a kindly old woman was sitting spinning. For this old woman had never heard of the King's orders against the use of the distaff.

"What are you doing, my good woman?" asked the Princess.

"Why, spinning, my pretty dear," answered the old woman, who did not know who her visitor was.

"How nice it looks!" said the Princess. "How do you do it? Here, let me have it, to see if I can do it as well."

No sooner had she taken hold of the distaff than she pricked her hand, because she was rather hasty and snatched, and be-cause, anyhow, the fairies would have it so; and down she fell in a faint. The kind old woman was in a taking; she shouted for help: people came running from all directions, dashed water over the Princess, undid her stays, chafed her hands, and rubbed her temples with Hungary water; but nothing would bring her round.

Meanwhile the King had come home; hearing the noise he rushed up the tower, and seeing what had happened remembered what the fairies had promised. Rightly guessing that there was no help for it since what the fairies foretell must be, he had the Princess carried to the finest room in the palace, and laid on a bed all hung with gold and silver brocade. She looked like an angel, she was so beautiful; for her faint had not faded the bright colours of her complexion; her cheeks were the colour of pale pink carnations, and her lips like coral; only her eyes were closed; they could still hear her breathing softly, so at any rate she could not be dead. The King ordered his people to leave her in peace, till the hour should come for her to awake.

The good fairy who had saved her life by ordering her to sleep for a hundred years was in the kingdom of Mataquin, twelve thousand leagues away, when the accident happened; but she was told of it within the instant by a little dwarf in seven-league boots (that is, boots in which one can walk seven leagues at a stride). The fairy set out at once, and arrived in an hour, driving a chariot drawn by dragons, all of fire.

The King came out and gave her his arm as she dismounted from the chariot. She said he had done all for the best. But as she thought of everything beforehand, it struck her that the Princess would be very lonely all alone in that great palace when she at last awoke; so this is what she did. She touched everything in the palace with her magic wand, except the King and Queen—the governesses, the maids of honour, the waiting gentlewomen, the gentlemen of the bedchamber, the officers, the stewards, the cooks, the scullions, the grooms, the guards, the ushers, the pages, the footmen; she touched all the horses in the stables, and the stable-boys too, the mastiffs in the yard and Pouffle, the Princess's little lap-dog, who was curled up on her bed. As soon as she touched them they all fell asleep, never to wake until their mistress did, so as to be always ready to serve her when she should have need of them. Even the spit in front of the kitchen fire, on which partridges and pheasants were roasting, stopped turning, and the fire died down. It was all done in a moment; for fairies are fast workers when they choose.

Then the King and Queen, having kissed their dear child without waking her, left the palace and forbade any one to go near it. Indeed it was not necessary to forbid it; for in a matter of minutes there grew up round the borders of the park such a quantity of trees both great and small, of briars and brambles all twined together, that neither man nor beast could get through it: so that nothing was left to sight, even from a great way off, but the tops of the palace towers. No one doubted that the fairy had done this on purpose, so that the Princess would not be bothered with sightseers during her long sleep.

A hundred years went by. Another royal family came to the throne, and the son of the King who was then reigning was out hunting near the old palace. He asked what were the towers he could see above the tops of that great thick wood. Every one answered according to what he had heard tell; some saying that it was an old haunted castle; others that it was the place where the local witches held their meetings; but the most common opinion was that a great ogre lived there, and that he carried off thither all the children he could catch, to eat them at his ease without being followed, for he alone was able to force his way through the wood.

The Prince did not know what to be-

lieve; but just then an old countryman up and said: "Your Highness, it's more nor fifty years gone since I heard my old father say that there was a Princess in that castle, the prettiest that ever was seen; and she was bound to sleep there a hundred years, and be awakened by the King's son, who was the one for her."

Hearing this the young Prince felt himself all on fire. In a flash he determined to fulfil the prophecy; and, spurred on by love and glory, he resolved to see for himself how things stood. No sooner had he advanced on the wood than all the briars and brambles and all the great trees bent back to let him pass. He walked towards the palace along a great avenue of trees, surprised to see that none of his servants could follow, because the trees had closed up behind him as soon as he had passed by. None the less he went on, for a young Prince in love is always brave.

He came into a great forecourt, where all that met his eyes at first sight was enough to freeze his blood. There was a frightful silence; the appearance of death was everywhere; bodies of men and animals, seemingly dead, were stretched all round. But he could tell by the red noses and beery complexions of the ushers that they were only asleep. The goblets in their hands still held a few drops of wine to show that they had fallen asleep while drinking.

He went on into a great courtyard paved all in marble, and up a staircase into a guard-room, where the guards were drawn up with their muskets on their shoulders, all snoring away. He passed through room after room full of ladies and gentlemen in waiting, all fast asleep, some sitting and some on their feet. At last he came to a room all over gilt; there on a bed with all its curtains drawn back, he saw the most beautiful sight of his whole life: a Princess who seemed to be about fifteen or sixteen years old who had something mysteriously splendid, and as it were shining, about her. Trembling all over he came nearer to ad-

mire her, and fell on his knees beside her. At that moment the spell ceased to work; the Princess awoke, and bending on him what I must call a loving glance indeed, considering it was the first time she had set eyes on him, said: "Is it you, my Prince? You have been a long time coming."

The Prince was overjoyed to hear this, and delighted with the way in which she spoke it, so that he could not think how to express his joy and gratitude; he assured her that he loved her better than he did himself. The other things he told her were rather confusing; they cried a good deal, and were tongue-tied with love. He was in even greater confusion than she was, and no wonder; she had had time to think over what she would say, for it seems (though history tells us nothing of this) that the good fairy had arranged for her to have pleasant dreams during her long sleep. They talked for four hours without getting to the end of half the things they meant to tell each other.

Meanwhile the palace had come to life at the same time as the Princess, and every one bethought himself of going about his business. But as not every one was in love, they felt ravenously hungry. The maid of honour was as hungry as any of them, and losing her patience called out to her mistress that dinner was ready. The Prince helped the Princess to rise: she was already dressed in magnificent clothes, but he had the sense not to tell her that she was wearing his grandmother's fashions, with a high neckline; she was none the less beautiful for that.

They went into the dining-room all hung with mirrors, where dinner was served by the officers of her household, while a band of violins and hautboys played quaint old music most sweetly—tunes that had not been heard for a hundred years. Afterwards the chaplain married them in the palace chapel without delay, and they lived happily ever after.

The Golden Basket [1]

LUDWIG BEMELMANS

Celeste stood on her right, Melisande close to her left; in the center, seated on a platform behind her desk, which was crammed with bills and slips of paper, was Madame ter Meulen.

The little girls looked deeply into her eyes, and Madame ter Meulen felt the tender pressure of four little hands. They straightened the lace on her collar and wound up her wrist watch. At last she took off her glasses and said, "Yes, he may go, but he must do his history first."

Down the stairs came a determined voice:

"The history of Bruges begins in the ninth century with Baldwin of the Iron Arm, so called because he always appeared in armor and even slept in it.

"In 860 he married Judith, daughter of Charles the Bald, King of France, who conferred the province of Flanders upon his son-in-law.

"Baldwin died in 879 and was succeeded by his son, Baldwin the Bald."

The little girls told Madame ter Meulen that they had never heard better history; every date was absolutely correct.

And so it was arranged that tomorrow, the day Mr. Coggeshall had to go to Brussels, Monsieur ter Meulen would go with Jan and the two little girls to have a look at the boat. "You may have the day off," said Madame to Jan, "but before you go, the garden has to be carried out and watered."

This garden was planted in small boxes with handles to carry them. It moved in and out of the house every day and was made up of four little hedges of ivy, two bay trees, and two geraniums.

These boxes were placed around a plot in front of the hotel, and within this happy frame stood tables and chairs. An awning covered them.

Early the next morning all this was finished. Jan brought a hose from the kitchen and connected it to a faucet on the outside of the hotel. In a little while Madame ter Meulen came to inspect the dripping garden and behind her came Jan's father. Monsieur ter Meulen wore plain clothes. He looked like somebody else until he spoke and said, "I am ready."

He had a thin cane and balanced a little hat on top of his head. The hat seemed to slip and he constantly reached for it. He was ill at ease, feeling for an apron that was not there, going through unaccustomed pockets, and twisting his watch chain. He held his cane like a ladle or a carving knife, pointing up instead of down.

Madame came and kissed her husband. "Here, Papa, take my watch; yours is broken." Monsieur ter Meulen and the children started to cross the cobbled square. Their shadows ran around them as they turned into the Street of the Pelican. Suddenly Papa thought of something. He walked back to the corner where Madame was still looking out of the window. He shouted to her: "How does he want the fish tonight, Monsieur in number eight?"

"Butter with parsley," answered Madame.

"With pommes soufflées?" asked Monsieur.

"Yes," came the answer, "with pommes soufflées."

"What time?"

"At seven they will eat."

"We must be back at five then."

"Yes, at five, Papa."

"Fine."

"Au revoir, mon petit chou." "Mon petit chou," my little cabbage, was Madame's name for Monsieur ter Meulen, but she used it only in tender moments, never in business.

Monsieur ter Meulen had taken along two small packages. "A little repast," he

[1] From "The Golden Basket," by Ludwig Bemelmans, illustrations from drawings by Ludwig Bemelmans

explained, "in case we all get hungry. And I brought a small bottle of wine for myself.

"I wonder," said Monsieur ter Meulen, "whether it would not be nicer to go out to the windmills, or watch the swans, or perhaps take a carriage and ride around a little."

"No, no!" The little girls came near and looked at Monsieur ter Meulen. He melted immediately—he even hurried. Jan was far ahead. He opened the little door to the garden, and there was the boat!

Not a toy, but a little barge made of real wood, heavy and solid!

"It must have a name," said Jan, "and I thought it would be nice to call it *Melisande* on one side and *Celeste* on the other. Let us christen it right away, right now."

Papa took the little bottle away from his eager son. "Later," he said; "first let us see if it really is a boat, that is, can it swim?"

With a colored piece of chalk Melisande wrote her name on one side and Celeste on the other. Later the names would be painted on properly. And now came the big moment.

Jan rolled a few round logs under the boat while his father held up one end. The little girls carried the oars. A man came down the canal in a rowboat, and they waited to let him pass. "Now Papa, you push in the center, Melisande on the right, Celeste on the left. One, two, three—umph."

There she was, with Jan sitting on the little bench in the center. It was a boat, he had made it himself, and it was more interesting and wonderful than anything that floated and called itself a ship.

Jan pulled on the right oar. The craft obeyed, and came close to the edge of the canal where Papa held it. Was it safe? One small pearl of water squeezed itself into the boat. It ran around and rested in a corner. No other drop followed it. The boat is water-tight; now they can get in,

Melisande and Celeste in front. "Papa, will you take the seat at the back? I will row for the first half hour. The bottle, Papa, and don't forget the lunch. Melisande, the camera . . ."

"Celeste, you are sitting on my side of the boat," said Melisande. "Look at the name."

Has there ever been a boat in which people have not tried to change places? But even that could be done. "And now we are off!"

"To the left, ladies and gentlemen, is the church of Saint Sauveur—we have seen it often and even from a boat, but it was never so beautiful as now. The bridge we are going under is the Pont des Augustins. And over there is the Quai de Rosaire. The fellow with the green cap who is staring at us is my classmate, Pieter Gheldere. Is everyone watching us? Would they all like to have a boat like this? I guess they would. Pieter is going away and making believe he has not even seen it."

"Melisande, will you take a picture of Jan? Now, hold still—don't row, and look this way." Click! "We have it!"

"Here comes the most beautiful of all our bridges, with Saint Nepomuc standing in the center of it. And there, coming over the bridge, is Monsieur the Mayor of Bruges."

Monsieur ter Meulen, the humble pro-

prietor and chef of the Panier d'Or, saw him first. He forgot that he was in a boat on the water. He stood up, and with a wide sweep of his arm, reached for his hat and bowed deeply.

Monsieur the Mayor also reached for his hat; he held it in mid-air for a second and then dropped it. His face became the mirror of the accident that had taken place below. Without a moment's hesitation he cleared the railing of the bridge and leaped into the canal to join Celeste and Melisande, Jan and Monsieur ter Meulen, who had disappeared under the boat as it upset and threw the little girls in a wide circle over the head of the sinking proprietor of the Panier d'Or. Their sailor hats had come off and fallen on the frightened heads of two swans that tried to get away. The birds raced under the bridge with them, the two ribbons with the golden names of a British battleship trailing behind them.

There was much confusion and much gurgling, there were many bubbles, and then everyone appeared unharmed. The canal is shallow—the water reached to the elbow of Monsieur ter Meulen, to the rosette of the Legion of Honor in the buttonhole of His Excellency the Mayor, and to the ears of the children.

The boat was floating upside down. Two men were busy getting it out of the water. A crowd gathered; a sergeant of police wrote in a little book; the swans sat frightened under the bridge and read inside the hats: "Harrods, Ltd., London"— which of course they did not understand.

"Monsieur the Mayor, I believe this is your hat. My own—there, will you catch it, Melisande? And my cane—be quick, Jan, it's floating away. The lunch is under the boat, the bottle at the bottom. Too bad, but let it go."

Because they were in the habit of greeting each other on the street, Monsieur ter Meulen and Monsieur van der Vichte bowed to each other in the water, wished each other a good afternoon, and in parting raised their dripping hats in a polite good-by.

The Angel [1]

HANS CHRISTIAN ANDERSEN

"Whenever a good child dies, an angel of God comes down from heaven, takes the dead child in his arms, spreads out his great white wings, and flies with him over all the places which the child has loved during his life. Then he gathers a large handful of flowers which he carries up to the Almighty, that they may bloom more brightly in heaven than they do on earth. And the Almighty presses the flowers to His heart, but He kisses the flower that pleases Him best, and it receives a voice and is able to join the song of the chorus of bliss."

These words were spoken by an angel of God as he carried a dead child up to heaven, and the child listened as if in a dream. Then they passed over well-known spots where the little one had often played, and through beautiful gardens full of lovely flowers.

"Which of these shall we take with us to heaven to be transplanted there?" asked the angel.

Close by grew a slender, beautiful rose-bush, but some wicked hand had broken the stem, and the half-opened rosebuds hung all faded and withered on the trailing branches.

"Poor rosebush!" said the child. "Let us take it with us to heaven, that it may bloom above in God's garden."

The angel took up the rosebush. Then he kissed the child and the little one half-opened his eyes. The angel gathered also some beautiful flowers, as well as a few humble buttercups and heartsease.

"Now we have flowers enough," said the child, but the angel only nodded. He did not fly upward to heaven.

It was night and quite still in the great town. Here they remained, and the angel hovered over a small narrow street in which lay a large heap of straw, ashes, and sweepings from houses of people who had moved away. There lay fragments of plates, pieces of plaster, rags, old hats, and other rubbish. Amidst all of this confusion, the angel pointed to the pieces of a broken flowerpot, and to a lump of earth which had fallen out of it. The earth had been kept from falling to pieces by the roots of a withered field flower which had been thrown amongst the rubbish.

"We will take this with us," said the angel. "I will tell you why as we fly along."

And as they flew the angel related the history.

"Down in that narrow lane, in a low cellar, lived a poor sick boy. He had been afflicted from his childhood, and even in his best days he could just manage to walk up and down the room on crutches once or twice, but no more. During some days in summer the sunbeams would lie on the floor of the cellar for about half an hour. In this spot the poor sick boy would sit warming himself in the sunshine and watching the red blood through his delicate fingers as he held them before his face. Then he would say he had been out, though he knew nothing of the green forest in its spring verdure till a neighbor's son brought him a green bough from a beech tree. This he would place over his head, and fancy that he was in the beechwood while the sun shone and the birds caroled gaily. One spring day the neighbor's boy brought him some field flowers, and among them was one to which the roots still adhered. This he carefully planted in a flowerpot, and placed in a window seat near his bed. And the flower had been planted by a fortunate hand, for it grew, put forth fresh shoots, and blossomed every year. It became a splendid flower garden to the sick boy, and his little treasure upon earth. He watered it and cherished it, and took care it should have the benefit of every sunbeam that found its way into the cellar, from the earliest morning ray to the evening sunset. The

[1] From "Andersen's Fairy Tales," translated by Mrs. E. V. Lucas and Mrs. H. B. Paull, illustration by Arthur Szyk

flower entwined itself even in his dreams. For him it bloomed; for him it spread its perfume. And it gladdened his eyes, and to the flower he turned, even in death, when the Lord called him. He has been one year with God. During that time the flower has stood in the window, withered and forgotten, till cast out among the sweepings into the street, on the day the lodgers moved. And this poor flower, withered and faded as it is, we have added to our nosegay, because it gave more real joy than the most beautiful flower in the garden of a queen."

"But how do you know all this?" asked the child whom the angel was carrying to heaven.

"I know it," said the angel, "because I was the poor sick boy who walked upon crutches, and I know my own flower well."

Then the child opened his eyes and looked into the glorious happy face of the angel, and at the same moment they found themselves in that heavenly home where all is happiness and joy. And God pressed the dead child to His heart, and wings were given him so that he could fly with the angel, hand in hand. Then the Almighty pressed all the flowers to His heart. But He kissed the withered field flower and it received a voice. Then it joined in the song of the angels, who surrounded the throne, some near, and others in a distant circle, but all equally happy. They all joined in the chorus of praise, both great and small—the good, happy child and the poor field flower, that once lay withered and cast away on a heap of rubbish in a narrow dark street.

The Jungle Book

RUDYARD KIPLING

HOW MOWGLI ENTERED THE WOLF PACK [1]

It was seven o'clock of a very warm evening in the Seeonee hills when Father Wolf woke up from his day's rest, scratched himself, yawned, and spread out his paws one after the other to get rid of the sleepy feeling in their tips. Mother Wolf lay with her big gray nose dropped across her four tumbling, squealing cubs, and the moon shone into the mouth of the cave where they all lived.

"Augrh!" said Father Wolf. "It is time to hunt again." He was going to spring downhill when a little shadow with a bushy tail crossed the threshold and whined: "Good luck go with you, O Chief of the Wolves. And good luck and strong white teeth go with the noble children that they may never forget the hungry in this world."

It was the jackal—Tabaqui, the Dishlicker—and the wolves of India despise Tabaqui because he runs about making mischief, and telling tales, and eating rags and pieces of leather from the village rubbish heaps. But they are afraid of him too, because Tabaqui, more than anyone else in the jungle, is apt to go mad, and then he forgets that he was ever afraid of anyone, and runs through the forest biting everything in his way. Even the tiger runs and hides when little Tabaqui goes mad, for madness is the most disgraceful thing that

[1] From "The Jungle Book," by Rudyard Kipling, illustrations by Fritz Eichenberg

can overtake a wild creature. We call it hydrophobia, but they call it *dewanee*—the madness—and run."

"Enter, then, and look," said Father Wolf stiffly, "but there is no food here."

"For a wolf, no," said Tabaqui, "but for so mean a person as myself a dry bone is a good feast. Who are we, the *Gidur-log* [the jackal people], to pick and choose?" He scuttled to the back of the cave, where he found the bone of a buck with some meat on it, and sat cracking the end merrily.

"All thanks for this good meal," he said, licking his lips. "How beautiful are the noble children! How large are their eyes! And so young too! Indeed, indeed, I might have remembered that the children of kings are men from the beginning."

Now, Tabaqui knew as well as anyone else that there is nothing so unlucky as to compliment children to their faces. It pleased him to see Mother and Father Wolf look uncomfortable.

Tabaqui sat still, rejoicing in the mischief that he had made, and then he said spitefully:

"Shere Khan, the Big One, has shifted his hunting grounds. He will hunt among these hills for the next moon, so he has told me."

Shere Khan was the tiger who lived near the Waingunga River, twenty miles away.

"He has no right!" Father Wolf began angrily—"By the Law of the Jungle he has no right to change his quarters without due warning. He will frighten every head of game within ten miles, and I—I have to kill for two, these days."

"His mother did not call him Lungri [the Lame One] for nothing," said Mother Wolf quietly. "He has been lame in one foot from his birth. That is why he has only killed cattle. Now the villagers of the Waingunga are angry with him, and he has come here to make *our* villagers angry. They will scour the jungle for him when he is far away, and we and our children must run when the grass is set alight. In-

deed, we are very grateful to Shere Khan!"

"Shall I tell him of your gratitude?" said Tabaqui.

"Out!" snapped Father Wolf. "Out and hunt with thy master. Thou hast done harm enough for one night."

"I go," said Tabaqui quietly. "Ye can hear Shere Khan below in the thickets. I might have saved myself the message."

Father Wolf listened, and below in the valley that ran down to a little river he heard the dry, angry, snarly, singsong whine of a tiger who has caught nothing and does not care if all the jungle knows it.

"The fool!" said Father Wolf. "To begin a night's work with that noise! Does he think that our buck are like his fat Waingunga bullocks?"

"H'sh. It is neither bullock nor buck he hunts tonight," said Mother Wolf. "It is Man."

The whine had changed to a sort of humming purr that seemed to come from every quarter of the compass. It was the noise that bewilders woodcutters and gypsies sleeping in the open, and makes them run sometimes into the very mouth of the tiger.

"Man!" said Father Wolf, showing all his white teeth. "Faugh! Are there not enough beetles and frogs in the tanks that he must eat Man, and on our ground too!"

The Law of the Jungle, which never orders anything without a reason, forbids every beast to eat Man except when he is killing to show his children how to kill, and then he must hunt outside the hunting grounds of his pack or tribe. The real reason for this is that man-killing means, sooner or later, the arrival of white men on elephants, with guns, and hundreds of brown men with gongs and rockets and torches. Then everybody in the jungle suffers. The reason the beasts give among themselves is that Man is the weakest and most defenseless of all living things, and it is unsportsmanlike to touch him. They say too—and it is true—that man-eaters become mangy, and lose their teeth.

The purr grew louder, and ended in the

full-throated "Aaarh!" of the tiger's charge.

Then there was a howl—an untigerish howl—from Shere Khan. "He has missed," said Mother Wolf. "What is it?"

Father Wolf ran out a few paces and heard Shere Khan muttering and mumbling as he tumbled about in the scrub.

"The fool has had no more sense than to jump at a woodcutter's campfire, and has burned his feet," said Father Wolf with a grunt. "Tabaqui is with him."

"Something is coming uphill," said Mother Wolf, twitching one ear. "Get ready."

The bushes rustled a little in the thicket, and Father Wolf dropped with his haunches under him, ready for his leap. Then, if you had been watching, you would have seen the most wonderful thing in the world—the wolf checked in mid-spring. He made his bound before he saw what it was he was jumping at, and then he tried to stop himself. The result was that he shot up straight into the air for four or five feet, landing almost where he left ground.

"Man!" he snapped. "A man's cub. Look!"

Directly in front of him, holding on by a low branch, stood a naked brown baby who could just walk—as soft and as dimpled a little atom as ever came to a wolf's cave at night. He looked up into Father Wolf's face and laughed.

"Is that a man's cub?" said Mother Wolf. "I have never seen one. Bring it here."

A wolf accustomed to moving his own cubs can, if necessary, mouth an egg without breaking it, and though Father Wolf's jaws closed right on the child's back not a tooth even scratched the skin as he laid it down among the cubs.

"How little! How naked, and—how bold!" said Mother Wolf softly. The baby was pushing his way between the cubs to get close to the warm hide. "Ahai! He is taking his meal with the others. And so this is a man's cub. Now, was there ever a wolf that could boast of a man's cub among her children?"

"I have heard now and again of such a thing, but never in our Pack or in my time," said Father Wolf. "He is altogether without hair, and I could kill him with a touch of my foot. But see, he looks up and is not afraid."

The moonlight was blocked out of the mouth of the cave, for Shere Khan's great square head and shoulders were thrust into the entrance. Tabaqui, behind him, was squeaking: "My lord, my lord, it went in here!"

"Shere Khan does us great honor," said Father Wolf, but his eyes were very angry. "What does Shere Khan need?"

"My quarry. A man's cub went this way," said Shere Khan. "Its parents have run off. Give it to me."

Shere Khan had jumped at a woodcutter's campfire, as Father Wolf had said, and was furious from the pain of his burned feet. But Father Wolf knew that the mouth of the cave was too narrow for a tiger to come in by. Even where he was, Shere Khan's shoulders and forepaws were cramped for want of room, as a man's would be if he tried to fight in a barrel.

"The Wolves are a free people," said Father Wolf. "They take orders from the Head of the Pack, and not from any striped cattle-killer. The man's cub is ours—to kill if we choose."

"Ye choose and ye do not choose! What talk is this of choosing? By the bull that I killed, am I to stand nosing into your dog's den for my fair dues? It is I, Shere Khan, who speak!"

The tiger's roar filled the cave with thunder. Mother Wolf shook herself clear of the cubs and sprang forward, her eyes, like two green moons in the darkness, facing the blazing eyes of Shere Khan.

"And it is I, Raksha [The Demon], who answers. The man's cub is mine, Lungri —mine to me! He shall not be killed. He shall live to run with the Pack and to hunt with the Pack; and in the end, look you, hunter of little naked cubs—frog-eater—fish-killer—he shall hunt *thee*! Now get hence, or by the Sambhur that I killed (*I eat no starved cattle*), back thou goest to thy mother, burned beast of the jungle, lamer than ever thou camest into the world! Go!"

Father Wolf looked on amazed. He had almost forgotten the days when he won Mother Wolf in fair fight from five other wolves, when she ran in the Pack and was not called The Demon for compliment's sake. Shere Khan might have faced Father Wolf, but he could not stand up against Mother Wolf, for he knew that where he was she had all the advantage of the ground, and would fight to the death. So he backed out of the cave mouth growling, and when he was clear he shouted:

"Each dog barks in his own yard! We

will see what the Packs will say to this fostering of man-cubs. The cub is mine, and to my teeth he will come in the end, O bush-tailed thieves!"

Mother Wolf threw herself down panting among the cubs, and Father Wolf said to her gravely:

"Shere Khan speaks this much truth. The cub must be shown to the Pack. Wilt thou still keep him, Mother?"

"Keep him!" she gasped. "He came naked, by night, alone and very hungry; yet he was not afraid! Look, he has pushed one of my babes to one side already. And that lame butcher would have killed him and would have run off to the Waingunga while the villagers here hunted through all our lairs in revenge! Keep him? Assuredly I will keep him. Lie still, little frog. O thou Mowgli—for Mowgli

261

the Frog I will call thee—the time will come when thou wilt hunt Shere Khan as he has hunted thee."

"But what will our Pack say?" said Father Wolf.

The Law of the Jungle lays down very clearly that any wolf may, when he marries, withdraw from the Pack he belongs to. But as soon as his cubs are old enough to stand on their feet he must bring them to the Pack Council, which is generally held once a month at full moon, in order that the other wolves may identify them. After that inspection the cubs are free to run where they please, and until they have killed their first buck no excuse is accepted if a grown wolf of the Pack kills one of them. The punishment is death where the murderer can be found; and if you think for a minute you will see that this must be so.

Father Wolf waited till his cubs could run a little, and then on the night of the Pack Meeting took them and Mowgli and Mother Wolf to the Council Rock—a hilltop covered with stones and boulders where a hundred wolves could hide. Akela, the great gray Lone Wolf, who led all the Pack by strength and cunning, lay out at full length on his rock, and below him sat forty or more wolves of every size and color, from badger-colored veterans who could handle a buck alone to young black three-year-olds who thought they could. The Lone Wolf had led them for a year now. He had fallen twice into a wolf trap in his youth, and once he had been beaten and left for dead; so he knew the manners and customs of men. There was very little talking at the Rock. The cubs tumbled over each other in the center of the circle where their mothers and fathers sat, and now and again a senior wolf would go quietly up to a cub, look at him carefully, and return to his place on noiseless feet. Sometimes a mother would push her cub far out into the moonlight to be sure that he had not been overlooked. Akela from his rock would cry: "Ye know

the Law—ye know the Law. Look well, O Wolves!" And the anxious mothers would take up the call: "Look—look well, O Wolves!"

At last—and Mother Wolf's neck bristles lifted as the time came—Father Wolf pushed "Mowgli the Frog," as they called him, into the center, where he sat laughing and playing with some pebbles that glistened in the moonlight.

Akela never raised his head from his paws, but went on with the monotonous cry: "Look well!" A muffled roar came up from behind the rocks—the voice of Shere Khan crying: "The cub is mine. Give him to me. What have the Free People to do with a man's cub?" Akela never even twitched his ears. All he said was: "Look well, O Wolves! What have the Free People to do with the orders of any save the Free People? Look well!"

There was a chorus of deep growls, and a young wolf in his fourth year flung back Shere Khan's question to Akela: "What have the Free People to do with a man's cub?" Now, the Law of the Jungle lays down that if there is any dispute as to the right of a cub to be accepted by the Pack, he must be spoken for by at least two members of the Pack who are not his father and mother.

"Who speaks for this cub?" said Akela. "Among the Free People who speaks?" There was no answer and Mother Wolf got ready for what she knew would be her last fight, if things came to fighting.

Then the only other creature who is allowed at the Pack Council—Baloo, the sleepy brown bear who teaches the wolf cubs the Law of the Jungle: old Baloo, who can come and go where he pleases because he eats only nuts and roots and honey—rose upon his hind quarters and grunted.

"The man's cub—the man's cub?" he said. "I speak for the man's cub. There is no harm in a man's cub. I have no gift of words, but I speak the truth. Let him run with the Pack, and be entered with the others. I myself will teach him."

"We need yet another," said Akela. "Baloo has spoken, and he is our teacher for the young cubs. Who speaks besides Baloo?"

A black shadow dropped down into the circle. It was Bagheera the Black Panther, inky black all over, but with the panther markings showing up in certain lights like the pattern of watered silk. Everybody knew Bagheera, and nobody cared to cross his path; for he was as cunning as Tabaqui, as bold as the wild buffalo, and as reckless as the wounded elephant. But he had a voice as soft as wild honey dripping from a tree, and a skin softer than down.

"O Akela, and ye the Free People," he purred, "I have no right in your assembly, but the Law of the Jungle says that if there is a doubt which is not a killing matter in regard to a new cub, the life of that cub may be bought at a price. And the Law does not say who may or may not pay that price. Am I right?"

"Good! Good!" said the young wolves, who are always hungry. "Listen to Bagheera. The cub can be bought for a price. It is the Law."

"Knowing that I have no right to speak here, I ask your leave."

"Speak then," cried twenty voices.

"To kill a naked cub is shame. Besides, he may make better sport for you when he is grown. Baloo has spoken in his behalf. Now to Baloo's word I will add one bull, and a fat one, newly killed, not half a mile from here, if ye will accept the man's cub according to the Law. Is it difficult?"

There was a clamor of scores of voices, saying: "What matter? He will die in the winter rains. He will scorch in the sun. What harm can a naked frog do us? Let him run with the Pack. Where is the bull, Bagheera? Let him be accepted." And then came Akela's deep bay, crying: "Look well—look well, O Wolves!"

Mowgli was still deeply interested in the pebbles, and he did not notice when the wolves came and looked at him one by one. At last they all went down the hill for the dead bull, and only Akela, Bagheera, Baloo, and Mowgli's own wolves were left. Shere Khan roared still in the night, for he was very angry that Mowgli had not been handed over to him.

"Ay, roar well," said Bagheera, under his whiskers, "for the time will come when this naked thing will make thee roar to another tune, or I know nothing of man."

"It was well done," said Akela. "Men and their cubs are very wise. He may be a help in time."

"Truly, a help in time of need; for none can hope to lead the Pack forever," said Bagheera.

Akela said nothing. He was thinking of the time that comes to every leader of every pack when his strength goes from him and he gets feebler and feebler, till at last he is killed by the wolves and a new leader comes up—to be killed in his turn.

"Take him away," he said to Father Wolf, "and train him as befits one of the Free People."

And that is how Mowgli was entered into the Seeonee Wolf Pack for the price of a bull and on Baloo's good word.

Snow White and the Seven Dwarfs [1]

On a winter's day many years ago, a Queen sat sewing at her palace window. Through the window, framed in black ebony, she saw the gleaming white snow.

Suddenly the Queen pricked her finger, and three tiny drops of blood appeared.

"I wish I had a baby," thought the Queen, "with skin as white as this snow, lips as red as this blood, and hair as black as the ebony of the window frame."

Soon afterwards her wish came true. A lovely little daughter was born to the Queen. She had skin as white as snow, lips as red as blood, and hair as black as ebony. She was named Snow White.

A few years later the Queen died, and the King married again. The new Queen was very proud and vain. She thought herself the most beautiful woman in the world. She had a magic mirror, and every day she would look into it and ask,

"Magic mirror on the wall,
Who is the fairest of us all?"

And the mirror would reply,

"Thou art the fairest, Lady Queen."

But as Snow White grew up, she became more and more lovely. Soon she was more beautiful than the Queen, her stepmother.

One day the Queen stood as usual before her mirror, and asked,

"Magic mirror on the wall,
Who is the fairest of us all?"

This time the mirror answered,

"Oh, Lady Queen, thou still art fair,
But none to Snow White can compare."

The stepmother Queen flew into a rage. She called one of the King's huntsmen to her and said, "Take Snow White out into the forest and kill her. Bring back her heart, so that I will know you have obeyed me."

But when they reached the forest, the huntsman could not bear to kill the lovely girl. "Run away and hide," he said to Snow White. Then he killed a wild animal and took its heart back to the wicked Queen.

Snow White, left alone in the forest, wandered along until she came to a little cottage. She knocked at the door and, when there was no answer, she opened the door and went in.

There she saw a little table neatly set with seven little white cups and saucers. Along the wall there were seven little beds. They looked so inviting that Snow White lay down on one of the beds and fell sound asleep.

This was the home of the Seven Dwarfs, and soon they returned from the mountains. When they lit the candles, they saw Snow White asleep on the bed. "How beautiful she is," they said softly, so as not to disturb her. And they let her sleep there until morning.

The next day the Seven Dwarfs crowded around Snow White. "Who are you?" they asked. "How did you get here?"

Snow White told the Dwarfs about her wicked stepmother, and how the huntsman had spared her life. "Now I am without a home," she said.

"Would you like to live with us?" asked the Dwarfs. "You could sew and mend, and keep everything tidy."

This made Snow White very happy. "Oh, thank you," she said. "I could want nothing better." So she stayed and took care of the home of the Seven Dwarfs.

Off in the palace, the stepmother thought that Snow White was dead. But one day she went to her mirror as usual and asked,

"Magic mirror on the wall,
Who is the fairest of us all?"

The mirror answered,

[1] A fairy tale by the Brothers Grimm. Illustration by Art Seiden

"Oh, Lady Queen, thou still art fair,
  But none to Snow White can compare;
  Deep within the forest glen,
  She lives with seven little men."

The Queen was furious. She decided to kill Snow White herself. Taking off her palace gown, she dressed herself as a peddler woman. Then she set out for the forest with a basket of fruit on her arm. In the basket was a fine rosy apple, filled with magic poison.

When she came to the cottage, the wicked stepmother found Snow White at the window, darning a little sock.

"Good day, pretty maid," said the disguised stepmother. "I have some nice apples to sell." She held up the shiny red apple that was poisoned.

The Seven Dwarfs had warned Snow White not to let anybody in while they were away in the mountains. So she said,

"I cannot let you in." But the apple looked so fresh and inviting that she reached out and took it. No sooner had she taken her first bite, than she fell on the floor in a dead faint.

The stepmother laughed as she hurried back through the woods. "Now I am the fairest in the land," she said to herself.

It was a sad sight that met the Dwarfs when they returned to the cottage. Their beloved Snow White was lying quiet and still on the floor. They wept, but try as they might they could not bring her back to life.

Snow White looked so beautiful that the Dwarfs decided to place her in a glass case. Then they carried her to a hilltop, where they took turns keeping watch.

One day, a handsome Prince from a far country rode by. He looked at the lovely girl in the glass case, and fell in love with her. He begged the Dwarfs to let him

take Snow White with him. "I cannot live without her," he pleaded. The Dwarfs gave their consent.

As the Prince lifted the case, the piece of poisoned apple fell out of Snow White's lips. She came to life again, and sat up.

"How did I get here? And who are you?" she said to the Prince. The Prince and the Dwarfs were overcome with joy. They told her all that had happened.

Then the Prince fell on his knees before Snow White. "Will you come with me and be my bride?" he asked. And so charming did he look that Snow White said, "Yes." Then Snow White thanked the Dwarfs for all that they had done for her, and rode off with the Prince.

A great wedding feast was proclaimed. The palace was decked with brilliant lights, velvet drapes and gorgeous flowers. Snow White's stepmother was among the people invited to the wedding. She did not know that Snow White was to be the Prince's bride.

After dressing herself in her finest clothes, the stepmother Queen went to her mirror, and asked,

> "Magic mirror on the wall,
> Who is the fairest of us all?"

The mirror replied,

> "Oh, Queen, thou hast a beauty rare,
> But Snow White, the Prince's bride, is still more fair."

The Queen turned pale in amazement and rage. She struck at the magic mirror. And as the mirror fell to the floor in fragments, the wicked stepmother fell dead. Never again would she harm Snow White.

The wedding feast was very gay, and the dancing and festivities lasted all through the night. And Snow White and the Prince lived happily ever after.

The Story of Aladdin, or the Wonderful Lamp [1]

There lived in ancient times in the capital of China a tailor named Mustapha, who was so poor that he could scarcely support his wife and son. Now his son, whose name was Aladdin, was idle and careless and disobedient to his father and mother, and he played from morning till night in the streets with other bad and idle lads. His father was so much troubled that he became ill and died in a few months.

As Aladdin was one day playing with his vagabond associates, a stranger, passing by, stood and regarded him earnestly. This stranger was a sorcerer, an African magician. Taking Aladdin aside from his companions, he said, "Boy, is not thy father called Mustapha the tailor?" "Yes," answered the boy, "but he is now dead."

At these words the African magician kissed him and cried, "I am thine uncle. I have been abroad for many years, and now I am come home." Then, he gave him a small handful of money, saying, "Go, O my son, to thy mother, and tell her that I will visit her to-morrow."

As soon as the African magician had departed Aladdin ran to his mother overjoyed. "Mother," he said, "I have met my uncle!" "No, my son," answered his mother, "thou hast no uncle by thy father's side or mine." Then Aladdin related to her all that the African magician had told him.

The next day Aladdin's mother made ready a repast, and when night came the African magician entered, laden with wine and various fruits. He saluted Aladdin's mother, and shed tears, and lamented that he had not arrived in time to see his brother Mustapha. "I have been forty years absent from my country," said the wily magician, "travelling in the Indies, Persia, Arabia, Syria, and Egypt."

Then he turned to Aladdin, and asked him what trade or occupation he had chosen. At this question Aladdin hung down his head, blushing and abashed, while his mother replied that he was an idle fellow, living on the streets. "This is not well," said the magician. "If thou hast no desire to learn a handicraft I will take a shop for thee, and furnish it with fine linens and rich stuffs." Aladdin's mother, who had not till then believed that the magician was the brother of her husband, now could no longer doubt. She thanked him for his kindness to Aladdin.

The next day the African magician came again, and took Aladdin to a merchant, who provided the lad with a rich and handsome suit, after which the magician took him to visit the principal shops, where they sold the richest stuffs and linens. He showed him also the largest and finest mosques, and entertained him at the most frequented inns. Then the magician escorted Aladdin to his mother, who, when she saw her son so magnificently attired, bestowed a thousand blessings upon his benefactor.

Aladdin rose early the next morning, and dressed himself in his elegant new garments. Soon after this the African magician entered the house and said, "Come, my dear son, and I will show thee fine things to-day!" He then led the lad out of the city, enticing him beyond the gardens, across the country, until they arrived

[1] From "The Arthur Rackham Fairy Book," selected by Arthur Rackham, illustrations from drawings by Arthur Rackham and H. J. Ford

at some mountains. He amused Aladdin all the way by relating to him pleasant stories, and feasting him with cakes and fruit.

When at last they arrived at a valley between two mountains of great height the magician said to Aladdin, "We will go no farther. I will now show thee some extraordinary things. While I strike a light do thou gather up loose sticks for a fire." Aladdin collected a pile of sticks, and the African magician set fire to them, and when they began to burn he muttered several magical words, and cast a perfume upon the fire. Immediately a great smoke arose, and the earth, trembling, opened and uncovered a stone with a brass ring fixed in the middle.

Aladdin became so frightened at what he saw that he would have run away, but the magician caught hold of him, and gave him such a box on the ear that he knocked him down. Aladdin rose up trembling, and with tears in his eyes inquired what he had done to merit such a punishment. "I have my reasons," answered the magician harshly. "Thou seest what I have just done! But, my son," continued he, softening, "know that under this stone is hidden a treasure destined to be thine. It will make thee richer than the greatest monarch in the world. Fate decrees that no one but thou may lift the stone or enter the cave, but to do this successfully thou must promise to obey my instructions."

Aladdin was amazed, and said quickly, "Command me, Uncle, for I promise to obey." The magician then directed him to take hold of the ring and lift the stone, and to pronounce at the same time the names of his father and grandfather. Aladdin did as he was bidden, and raised the heavy stone with ease, and laid it on one side. When the stone was pulled up there appeared a cave with steps to go farther down.

"Observe, my son," said the African magician, "what I direct. Descend, and at the bottom of these steps thou wilt find a

door open. Beyond the door are three great halls. Tuck up thy vest, and pass through them without stopping. Above all things do not touch the walls, for if thou do so thou wilt die instantly.

"At the end of the third hall thou wilt find a door which opens into a garden planted with fine trees, loaded with fruits. Walk directly across the garden to a terrace, where thou wilt see a niche, and in that niche a lighted lamp. Take down the lamp, pour out the oil, and bring it to me. If thou shouldst wish for any of the fruits of the garden thou mayest gather as much as thou pleasest."

The magician then took a ring from his finger, and placed it upon Aladdin's hand, telling him that it would preserve him from all evil. Aladdin sprang into the cave, descended the steps, and found the three halls just as the African magician had described. He passed through, crossed the garden, took down the lamp from the niche, poured out the oil, and placed it in his bosom.

But as he came down from the terrace he stopped to observe the fruits. All the trees were loaded with extraordinary fruits of different colours. The white were pearls, the clear and transparent diamonds, the red rubies, the green emeralds, the blue turquoises, the purple amethysts, and those that were yellow sapphires. Aladdin was altogether ignorant of their worth, yet he was so pleased with the variety of bright colours of the seeming fruits that he gathered some of every sort.

Aladdin then returned to the mouth of the cave, where the magician was expecting him with the utmost impatience. Now the African magician intended, as soon as he should receive the lamp from Aladdin, to push the lad back into the cave, so that there should remain no witness of the affair. But Aladdin refused to give up the lamp until he was out of the cave. The magician, provoked at this refusal, flew into a rage, threw some incense into the fire, pronounced two magical words, and instantly the stone which had covered the mouth of the cave moved back into its place. Then the African magician, having lost all hope of obtaining the wonderful lamp, returned that same day to Africa.

When Aladdin found himself thus buried alive he cried, and called out to his uncle that he was ready to give him the lamp, but in vain, since his cries could not be heard.

He then sat down upon the steps, without any hopes of ever seeing the light again.

Aladdin remained in this state for two days, without eating or drinking. On the third day, clasping his hands in despair, he accidentally rubbed the ring which the magician had placed upon his finger. Immediately a Genie of enormous size and frightful aspect rose out of the earth, his head reaching the roof of the cave, and said to him, "What wouldest thou have? I will obey thee as thy slave, and the slave of all who may possess the ring on thy finger, I and the other slaves of that ring!"

Aladdin answered without hesitation, "Whoever thou art, deliver me from this place!" He had no sooner spoken these words than he found himself on the very spot where the magician had caused the earth to open.

Thankful to find himself safe, he quickly made his way home. When he reached his mother's door the joy at seeing her and the weakness due to lack of food made him faint. His mother did all she could to bring him to himself, and the first words he spoke were, "Pray, Mother, give me something to eat." His mother brought what she had, and set it before him.

Aladdin then related to his mother all that had happened to him, and showed her the transparent fruits of different colours which he had gathered in the garden. But though these fruits were precious stones, brilliant as the sun, the mother was ignorant of their worth, and she laid them carelessly aside.

Aladdin slept very soundly till the next morning, but on waking he found that there was nothing to eat in the house, nor any money with which to buy food.

"Alas, my son," said his mother, "I have not a bit of bread to give thee, but I have a little cotton which I have spun, and I will go and sell it." "Mother," replied Aladdin, "keep thy cotton for another time, and give me the lamp I brought home with me yesterday. I will go and sell it."

Aladdin's mother brought the lamp, and

as it was very dirty she took some fine sand and water to clean it, but she no sooner began to rub than in an instant a hideous Genie, of gigantic size, appeared before her, and said in a voice like thunder, "What wouldest thou have? I am ready to obey thee as thy slave, and the slave of all those who hold the lamp in their hands, I and the other slaves of the lamp!"

Aladdin's mother, terrified at the sight of the Genie, fainted, but Aladdin snatched the lamp out of her hand, and said to him, "I am hungry. Bring me something to eat." The Genie disappeared immediately, and in an instant returned with a large silver tray, holding twelve covered dishes of the same metal, which contained the most delicious viands, six large white bread cakes, two flagons of wine, and two silver cups. All these he placed upon a carpet, and disappeared.

Aladdin fetched some water and sprinkled it in his mother's face, and she recovered. Great was her surprise to see the dishes, and to smell the savoury odour which exhaled from them. When, however, Aladdin informed her that they were brought by the Genie whom she had seen she was greatly alarmed, and urged him to sell the enchanted lamp and have nothing to do with the Genie. "With thy leave, Mother," answered Aladdin, "I will keep the lamp, as it has been of service to us. Let us make profitable use of it, without exciting the envy and jealousy of our neighbours. However, since the Genie frightens thee I will take the lamp out of thy sight, and put it where I may find it when I want it." His mother, convinced by his arguments, said he might do as he wished, but for herself she would have nothing to do with Genii.

The mother and son then sat down to breakfast, and they found that they had enough food left for dinner and supper, and also for two meals for the next day. By the following night they had eaten all the provisions the Genie had brought, and the next day Aladdin, putting one of the silver dishes under his vest, went to the silver market and sold it. Before returning home he called at the baker's and bought bread, and on his return gave the rest of the money to his mother, who went and purchased provisions enough to last for some time.

After this manner they lived, till Aladdin had sold all the dishes and the silver tray. When the money was spent he had recourse again to the lamp. He took it in his hand, rubbed it, and immediately the Genie appeared, and said, "What wouldst thou have? I am ready to obey thee as thy slave, and the slave of all those who hold that lamp in their hands, I and the other slaves of the lamp!" "I am hungry," said Aladdin. "Bring me something to eat." The Genie immediately disappeared, and instantly returned with a tray containing the same number of dishes as before, and he set them down and vanished. And when the provisions were gone Aladdin sold the tray and dishes as before. Thus he and his mother continued to live for some time, and though they had an inexhaustible treasure in their lamp they dwelt quietly with frugality.

Meanwhile by his acquaintance among the jewellers, Aladdin came to know that the fruits which he had gathered in the subterranean garden, instead of being coloured glass, were jewels of inestimable value.

One day Aladdin heard an order proclaimed, commanding the people to close their shops and houses and to keep within doors while the Princess Badroulboudour, the Sultan's daughter, went to the baths and returned. Aladdin became filled with curiosity to see the face of the Princess. So he placed himself behind the outer door of the bath, which was so situated that he could not fail to see her.

He had not long to wait before the Princess came, and he could see her plainly through a chink in the door without being discovered. She was attended by a great crowd of ladies, and slaves, and eunuchs, who walked on each side and behind her. When she came near to the door of the bath she took off her veil, and Aladdin saw her face. She was the most beautiful young woman in the world, and Aladdin became filled with admiration and love.

After the Princess had passed by, Aladdin returned home in a state of great dejection, which he could not conceal from his mother. She inquired the cause, and Aladdin told her all that had occurred, saying, "This, my mother, is the cause of my melancholy! I love the Princess more than I can express, I cannot live without the beautiful Badroulboudour, and I am resolved to ask her in marriage of the Sultan, her father."

Aladdin's mother burst into a loud laugh. "Alas, my son," she said, "what art thou thinking of? Thou must be mad to talk thus!" "I assure thee, my mother," replied Aladdin, "that I am not mad, but I am resolved to demand the Princess in marriage, and I will expect thee to use thy persuasion with the Sultan." "I go to the Sultan?" answered his mother, amazed and surprised. "I assure thee I cannot undertake such an errand. And who art thou, my son," continued she, "to think of the Sultan's daughter? Hast thou forgotten that thy father was one of the poorest tailors in the city? How can I open my mouth to make such a proposal to the Sultan? His majestic presence and the lustre of his Court would confound me! Besides, no one ever asks a favour of the Sultan without taking him a fitting present."

Aladdin replied, "Would not those fruits that I brought home from the subterranean garden make an acceptable present? For what thou and I took for coloured glass are really jewels of inestimable value, and I am persuaded that they will be favourably received by the Sultan. Thou hast a large porcelain dish fit to hold them; fetch it, and let us see how the stones will look when we have arranged them according to their different colours." Aladdin's mother brought the porcelain dish, and he arranged the jewels on it according to his fancy.

The next morning Aladdin's mother took the porcelain dish, in which were the jewels, and set out for the Sultan's palace. She entered the audience chamber, and placed herself just before the Sultan, the Grand Vizier, and the great lords of the Court, who sat in council, but she did not venture to declare her business, and when the audience chamber closed for the day she returned home. The next morning she again repaired to the audience chamber, and left it when it closed without having dared to address the Sultan, and she continued to do thus daily, until at last one morning the chief officer of the Court approached her, and at a sign from him she followed him to the Sultan's throne, where he left her.

Aladdin's mother saluted the Sultan, and he said to her, "My good woman, I have observed thee for a long time. What business brings thee hither?"

Aladdin's mother then told him about Aladdin's love for the Princess, and she ended by formally demanding the Princess in marriage for her son. After which she took the porcelain dish and presented it to the Sultan.

The Sultan's amazement and surprise were inexpressible when he saw so many large, beautiful, and valuable jewels. After he had admired and handled all the jewels one by one he turned to his Grand Vizier, and said, "What sayest thou to such a present? Is it not worthy of the Princess my daughter?"

These words agitated the Grand Vizier, for the Sultan had intended to bestow the Princess his daughter upon the Vizier's son. Therefore, the Vizier whispered in his ear and said, "I cannot but own that the present is worthy of the Princess, but I beg thee to grant me three months' delay, and before the end of that time I hope that my son may be able to make a nobler present than Aladdin, who is an entire stranger to thy Majesty."

The Sultan granted his request, and, turning to Aladdin's mother, said to her, "My good woman, go home and tell thy son that I agree to the proposal thou hast made me, but that I cannot marry the Princess my daughter until the end of three months. At the expiration of that time come again." Aladdin's mother, overjoyed at these words, hastened home and informed Aladdin of all the Sultan had said. Aladdin thought himself the most happy of all men at hearing this news.

When two of the three months were passed his mother one evening, finding no oil in the house, went out to purchase some. She found in the city a general rejoicing. The shops were decorated, the streets were crowded. Aladdin's mother asked the oil-merchant what was the meaning of all this festivity. He answered. "To-night the Grand Vizier's son is to marry the Princess Badroulboudour, the Sultan's daughter!"

Aladdin's mother hastened home, and related the news to Aladdin. He was thunderstruck on hearing her words, and, hastening to his chamber, closed the door, took the lamp in his hand, rubbed it in the same place as before, and immediately the Genie appeared.

"Genie," said Aladdin, "I have demanded the Princess Badroulboudour in marriage of the Sultan her father. He promised her to me, only requiring three months' delay. But instead of keeping his word he has this night married her to the Grand Vizier's son. What I require of thee is this: as soon as the bride and bridegroom are alone bring them both hither."

"Master," said the Genie, "I hear and obey!" The Genie then disappeared, flew to the palace, took up the bed with the bride and bridegroom in it, returned, and set it down in Aladdin's room. The Genie then took up the bridegroom, who was trembling with fear, and shut him up in a dark closet. Aladdin approached the Princess and said most respectfully, "Adorable Princess, thou art here in safety! The Sultan thy father promised thee in marriage to me, and as he has now broken his word I am thus forced to carry thee away, in order to prevent thy marriage with the Grand Vizier's son. Sleep in peace until morning, when I will restore thee to the Sultan thy father." Having thus reassured the Princess, Aladdin laid himself down and slept until morning.

Aladdin had no occasion the next morning to summon the Genie, who appeared at the hour appointed. He brought the bridegroom from the closet, and, placing him beside the Princess, transported the bed to the royal palace. The bridegroom, pale and trembling with fear, sought the Sultan, related to him all that had happened, and implored him to break off his marriage with the Princess. The Sultan did so, and commanded all rejoicings to cease.

Aladdin waited until the three months were completed, and the next day sent his mother to the palace to remind the Sultan of his promise. The Sultan no sooner saw her than he remembered her business, and as he did not wish to give his daughter to a stranger thought to put her off by a request impossible of fulfilment. "My good woman," he said, "it is true that sultans should keep their promises, and I am willing to do so as soon as thy son shall send me forty trays of massy gold, full of the same sort of jewels thou hast already made me a present of. The trays must be carried by a like number of black slaves, who shall be led by as many young and handsome white slaves magnificently dressed."

Aladdin's mother hastened home, laughing within herself at her son's foolish ambition. She then gave him an exact account of what the Sultan had said to her, and the conditions on which he consented to the marriage. Aladdin immediately retired to his room, took the lamp, and rubbed it. The Genie appeared, and with the usual salutation offered his services. "Genie," said Aladdin, and he described the Sultan's wishes. "Go and fetch me this present as soon as possible."

In a short time the Genie returned with forty black slaves, each bearing upon his head a heavy tray of pure gold, full of pearls, diamonds, rubies, emeralds, and every sort of precious stone, all larger and more beautiful than those already pre-sented to the Sultan. These, together with the white slaves, quite filled the house.

Aladdin found his mother in great amazement at seeing so many people and such vast riches. "Mother," he said, "I would have you return to the palace with this present as a dowry, that the Sultan may judge by the rapidity with which I fulfil his demands of the ardent and sincere love I have for the Princess his daughter."

The procession of slaves and the humble mother proceeded through the streets; and the people ran together to see so extraordinary and magnificent a spectacle. At length they arrived at the Sultan's palace, and the first slave, followed by the rest, advanced into the audience chamber, where the Sultan was seated on his throne, surrounded by his viziers and the chief officers of the Court.

Aladdin's mother advanced to the foot of the throne and prostrated herself before the Sultan. When he cast his eyes on the forty trays filled with the most precious and brilliant jewels and gazed upon the fourscore slaves so richly attired he no longer hesitated, as the sight of such immense riches and Aladdin's quickness in satisfying his demand easily persuaded him that the young man would make a most desirable son-in-law. Therefore he said to Aladdin's mother, "Go and tell thy son that I wait with open arms to embrace him."

Aladdin's mother hastened home and informed her son of this joyful news. He, enraptured at the prospect of his marriage with the Princess, retired to his chamber, again rubbed the lamp, and the obedient Genie appeared as before. "Genie," said Aladdin, "provide me with the richest and most magnificent raiment ever worn by a king, and with a charger that surpasses in beauty the best in the Sultan's stable, with a saddle, bridle, and other caparisons worth a million of gold pieces. I want also twenty slaves, richly clothed, to walk by my side and follow me, and twenty more to go before me in two ranks. Besides these, bring my mother six female slaves to attend her, as richly dressed as any of the Princess Badroulboudour's, each carrying a dress fit for a sultan's wife. I want also ten thousand pieces of gold in ten purses. Go, and make haste." The Genie presented all these to Aladdin and disappeared.

Of the ten purses Aladdin took four, which he gave to his mother; the other six he left in the hands of the slaves who brought them, with an order to throw the gold by handfuls among the people as they went to the Sultan's palace. The six slaves who carried the purses he ordered likewise to march before him, three on the right hand and three on the left.

Aladdin then clad himself in his new garments, and, mounting his charger, began the march to the Sultan's palace. The streets through which he passed were instantly filled with a vast concourse of people, who rent the air with their acclamations. When he arrived at the palace everything was prepared for his reception.

The marriage feast was begun, and the Sultan ordered that the contract of marriage between the Princess Badroulboudour and Aladdin should be immediately drawn up; then he asked Aladdin if he wished the ceremony solemnized that day. To which Aladdin answered, "Though great is my impatience, I beg leave to defer it until I have built a palace fit to receive the Princess; therefore, I pray thee, give me a spot of ground near thy palace where I may build." "My son," said the Sultan, "take what ground thou thinkest proper." And he embraced Aladdin, who took his leave with as much politeness as though he had always lived at Court.

As soon as Aladdin reached home he dismounted, retired to his own chamber, took the lamp, and called the Genie as before. "Genie," said Aladdin, "I would have thee build me as soon as possible a palace near the Sultan's fit to receive my wife, the Princess Badroulboudour. Build it of porphyry, jasper, lapis lazuli, or the finest marbles of various colours. On the terraced roof build me a large hall, crowned with a dome. Let the walls be of massy gold and silver. On each of the four sides of this hall let there be six windows. Leave one window lattice unfinished, but enrich all the others with diamonds, rubies, and emeralds. I would have also a spacious garden and a treasury full of gold and silver. There must be kitchens, offices, storehouses, and stables full of the finest horses. I want also male and female slaves and equerries and grooms. Come and tell me when all is finished."

The next morning before break of day the Genie presented himself to Aladdin, and said, "Master, thy palace is finished. Come and see if it pleaseth thee." Aladdin had no sooner signified his consent than the Genie transported him thither in an instant, and led him through richly furnished apartments, and Aladdin found nothing but what was magnificent. "Genie," he said, "there is only one thing wanting, which I forgot to mention, that is a carpet of fine velvet for the Princess to walk upon, between my palace and the Sultan's." The Genie disappeared, and instantly a carpet of fine velvet stretched across the park to the door of the Sultan's palace.

Aladdin's mother, dressed in her most sumptuous garments, and attended by six female slaves, who were clad richly and magnificently, went in stately procession across the park. She was received at the palace with great honour, and the Sultan immediately ordered bands to play. In the joyous city the merchants began to adorn their shops and houses with fine carpets and silks, and to prepare illuminations for the coming festival.

When night arrived the Princess took tender leave of her father, and, accompanied by Aladdin's mother, set out across the velvet carpet, amid the sound of trumpets and lighted by a thousand torches. Aladdin received her with joy, and led her into the large, illuminated hall, where was spread a magnificent repast.

The next morning Aladdin mounted and went in the midst of a large troop of slaves to the Sultan's palace. The Sultan received him with honours, and Aladdin then said, "I entreat thee to partake of a repast in the Princess's palace, attended by thy Grand Vizier and all thy Court." The Sultan consented with pleasure, and, followed by all the lords of his Court, accompanied Aladdin.

The nearer the Sultan approached Aladdin's palace the more he was struck with its beauty. But when he came into the hall of the four-and-twenty windows enriched with diamonds, rubies, emeralds, all large and perfect stones, he was so much surprised that he remained for some time motionless. "This palace," exclaimed he, "is surely one of the wonders of the world!"

The Sultan examined and admired all the windows, but on counting them he found that there were but three-and-twenty so richly adorned, and that the four-and-twentieth was left imperfect, and in great astonishment he inquired the reason of this. "It was by my orders that the workmen left it thus," said Aladdin, "since I wished that thou shouldst have the glory of finishing this hall." The Sultan was much pleased with this compliment, and immediately ordered his jewellers and goldsmiths to complete the four-and-twentieth window. The jewellers worked steadily for a whole month, but could not finish half the window, although they used all the jewels the Sultan had and borrowed from the Vizier.

Aladdin, who knew that all the Sultan's endeavours to complete the window were in vain, sent for the jewellers and goldsmiths, and commanded them not only to desist, but to undo the work they had done, and to return the jewels to the Sultan and to the Grand Vizier. They undid in a few hours what they had accomplished in a month, and retired, leaving Aladdin alone in the hall. He took the lamp, which he carried about with him, rubbed it, and the Genie appeared. "Genie," said Aladdin, "I order thee to complete the four-and-twentieth window." And immediately the window became perfect like the others.

Scarcely was the window completed before the Sultan arrived to question Aladdin as to why the jewellers and goldsmiths had desisted from their work. Aladdin received him at the door, and conducted him directly to the hall, where he was amazed to see the window perfect like the rest. "My son," exclaimed the Sultan, embracing him, "what a man thou art to do all this in the twinkling of an eye! Verily, the more I know thee the more I admire thee!" And he returned to his palace content.

After this Aladdin lived in great state. He visited mosques, attended prayers, and returned the visits of the principal lords of the Court. Every time he went out he caused two slaves, who walked by the side of his horse, to throw handfuls of money among the people as he passed through the streets and the squares; and no one came to his palace gates to ask alms but returned satisfied with his liberality, which gained him the love and blessings of the people.

Aladdin had conducted himself in this manner for several years when the African magician became curious to know whether he had perished in the subterranean garden. He employed his magic arts to discover the truth, and he found that Aladdin, instead of having perished miserably in the cave, had made his escape, and was living splendidly, and that he was in possession of the wonderful lamp, and had married a princess. The magician no sooner learned this than his face became inflamed with anger, and he cried out in a rage, "This miserable tailor's son has discovered the secret and the virtue of the lamp! I will, however, prevent his enjoying it long!"

The next morning he mounted a horse, set forward, and never stopped until he arrived at the capital of China, where he took up his residence at an inn.

The next day he ascertained by the means of his magic arts that Aladdin was absent on the hunt, and that the lamp was in the palace. He then went to a coppersmith's and bought a dozen copper lamps. These he placed in a basket, and went directly to Aladdin's palace. As he approached he began crying out, "Who will change old lamps for new ones? Who will change old lamps for new ones?" And

all who passed by thought him a madman or a fool to offer to change new lamps for old.

Now the Princess Badroulboudour, who was in the hall with the four-and-twenty windows, heard a man crying, "Who will change old lamps for new ones?" and, remembering the old lamp which Aladdin had laid upon a shelf before he went to the chase, the Princess, who knew not the value of the lamp, commanded a eunuch to take it and make the exchange. The eunuch did so, and the African magician, as soon as he saw the lamp, snatched it eagerly from his hand, and gave him a new one in its place.

The magician then hastened away until he reached a lonely spot in the country, when he pulled the lamp out of his bosom and rubbed it. At that summons the Genie appeared, and said, "What wouldst thou have? I am ready to obey thee as thy slave, and the slave of all those who hold that lamp in their hands, I and the other slaves of the lamp!" "I command thee," replied the magician, "to transport me immediately, and the palace which thou and the other slaves of the lamp have built in this city, with all the people in it, to Africa." The Genie disappeared, and immediately the magician, and the palace, and all its inhabitants, were lifted up and transported from the capital of China and set down in Africa.

As soon as the Sultan arose the next morning he went to the window to contemplate and admire Aladdin's palace. When he looked that way instead of a palace he saw an empty space. His amazement was so great that he remained for some time turning his eyes towards the spot, and at last convinced that no palace stood opposite his own he returned to his apartment and ordered his Grand Vizier to be sent for.

The Grand Vizier came with much precipitation. "Tell me," said the Sultan, "what has become of Aladdin's palace." "His palace!" exclaimed the Vizier. "Is it not in its usual place?" "Go to my window," answered the Sultan, "and tell me if thou canst see it." The Grand Vizier went to the window, where he was struck with no less amazement than the Sultan had been. "Well," said the Sultan, "hast thou seen Aladdin's palace?" "Alas," answered the Grand Vizier, "it has vanished completely! I have always thought that the edifice, which was the object of thy admiration, with all its immense riches, was the work of magic and a magician."

At these words the Sultan flew into a passion. "Where is that impostor, that wicked wretch," cried he, "that I may have his head taken off immediately? Go thou, bring him to me loaded with chains!" The Grand Vizier hastened to obey these orders, and commanded a detachment of horse to meet Aladdin returning from the chase, and to arrest him and bring him before the Sultan.

The detachment pursued their orders, and about five or six leagues from the city met Aladdin returning from the chase. Without explanation they arrested him, and fastened a heavy chain about his neck, and one around his body, so that both his arms were pinioned to his sides. In this state they carried him before the Sultan, who ordered him to be put to death immediately. But a multitude of people had followed Aladdin as he was led in chains through the city, and they threatened a riot if any harm should befall him. The Sultan, terrified at this menace, ordered the executioner to put up his scimitar, and to unbind Aladdin.

When Aladdin found himself at liberty he turned towards the Sultan, and said, "I know not what I have done to lose thy favour. Wilt thou not tell me what crime I have committed?" "Your crime, perfidious wretch!" answered the Sultan. "Dost thou not know it? Where is thy palace? What has become of the Princess my daughter?" Aladdin looked from the window, and, perceiving the empty spot where his palace had stood, was thrown into such confusion and amazement that he could

not return one word of answer. At length, breaking the silence, he said, "I know not whither my palace has vanished. Neither can I tell thee where it may be. Grant me but forty days in which to make inquiry, and if at the end of that time I have not the success I wish I will offer my head at the foot of thy throne, to be disposed of at thy pleasure." "Go," said the Sultan. "I give thee the forty days thou askest for, but if thou dost not find my daughter thou shalt not escape my wrath. I will find thee out in whatsoever part of the world thou mayest conceal thyself, and I will cause thy head to be struck off!"

Aladdin went out of the Sultan's presence in great humiliation, and filled with confusion. For three days he wandered about the city making inquiries, but all in vain: he could find no trace of the vanished palace. At last he wandered into the country, and at the approach of night came to the banks of a river, where he sat down to rest. Clasping his hands in despair, he accidentally rubbed the ring which the African magician had placed upon his finger before he went into the cave and down the steps to fetch the precious lamp. Immediately the same Genie appeared whom he had seen in the cave where the magician had left him. "What wouldest thou have?" said the Genie. "I am ready to obey thee as thy slave, and the slave of any who wears that ring, I and the other slaves of the ring!"

Aladdin, agreeably surprised at an apparition he so little expected, replied, "Save my life, Genie, by showing me the place where the palace I caused to be built now stands, or immediately transport it back where it first stood." "What thou commandest is not in my power," answered the Genie. "I am only the slave of the ring. Thou must address thyself to the slave of the lamp." "If that be the case," replied Aladdin, "I command thee by the power of the ring to transport me to the spot where my palace stands, in what part of the world soever it may be, and set me down under

the window of the Princess Badroulboudour."

These words were no sooner out of his
mouth than the Genie transported him into
Africa, to the middle of a large plain, where
his palace stood, and, placing him exactly
under the window of the Princess Badroulboudour's apartment, left him. The next
morning when the Princess looked out of
her window she perceived Aladdin sitting
beneath it. Scarcely believing her eyes,
she opened the window and motioned to
him to come up. Aladdin hastened to her
apartment, and it is impossible to express
the joy of both at seeing each other after
so cruel a separation.

After embracing and shedding tears of joy they sat down, and Aladdin said, "I beg of thee, Princess, both for thine own sake and the Sultan thy father's and mine, tell me what became of an old lamp which I left upon a shelf in my robing-room when I departed for the chase?" "Alas, dear husband," answered the Princess, "I was afraid our misfortune might be owing to that lamp, and what grieves me most is that I have been the cause of it!" "Princess," replied Aladdin, "do not blame thyself, but tell me what has happened, and into whose hands it has fallen."

The Princess then related how she had changed the old lamp for a new, and how the next morning she had found herself in an unknown country, which she was told was Africa by the traitor who had transported her hither by his magic arts. She also told how the wicked magician visited her daily, forcing upon her his unwelcome attentions, and how he daily tried to persuade her to take him for a husband in the place of Aladdin. "And," added the Princess, "he carries the wonderful lamp carefully wrapped in his bosom, and this I can assure thee of, because he pulled it out before me and showed it to me in triumph."

"Princess," said Aladdin, "this magician is a most perfidious wretch, and I have here the means to punish him, and to deliver thee from both thine enemy and mine. To accomplish this thou must obey my directions most carefully. When the African magician comes to-night place this powder in his cup of wine, offer him the cup, and he will esteem it so great a favour that he will not refuse, but will eagerly quaff it off. No sooner will he have drunk than thou wilt see him fall backwards." After the Princess had agreed to the measures proposed by Aladdin he took his leave.

When the evening arrived the magician came at the usual hour, and as soon as he was seated the Princess handed him a cup of wine, in which the powder had been dissolved. The magician reclined his head back to show his eagerness, drank the wine to the very last drop, turned his eyes in his head, and fell to the floor dead. At a signal from the Princess Aladdin entered the hall, and he requested her to retire immediately to her own apartment.

When the Princess, her women and eunuchs, were gone out of the hall Aladdin shut the door, and, going to the magician, opened his vest, took out the lamp, which was carefully wrapped up, and unfolded and rubbed it, whereupon the Genie immediately appeared. "Genie," said Aladdin, "transport this palace instantly to China, to the place from whence it was brought hither." Immediately the palace was lifted up and transported to China.

The morning of the return of Aladdin's palace the Sultan stood at his window absorbed in grief. He cast his eyes towards the spot where the palace had once stood, and which he now expected to find vacant, but to his surprise and amazement there stood Aladdin's palace in all its former grandeur. He immediately ordered a horse to be saddled and bridled and brought to him without delay, which he mounted that instant, thinking that he could not make haste enough to reach the palace.

Aladdin received the Sultan at the foot of the great staircase, helped him to dismount, and led him into the Princess's apartment. The happy father embraced her with his face bathed in tears of joy, and the Princess related to him all that had happened to her from the time the palace was transported to Africa to the death of the African magician.

Aladdin ordered the magician's body to be removed, and in the meantime the Sultan commanded the drums, trumpets, cymbals, and other instruments of music to announce his joy to the public, and a festival of ten days to be proclaimed for the return of the Princess and Aladdin.

Little Lisa[1]

Once upon a time there was a little girl whose name was Lisa. She lived with her father and mother in a little red house in Delecarlia, Sweden.

Little Lisa's mother made her a beautiful orange-colored dress. With it she wore a red-striped apron, a little red hood, and a blue scarf. Her father bought her a pair of red shoes and a most beautiful parasol to go with the dress.

How lovely Little Lisa looked with all her new things!

"I am the prettiest girl in all Sweden," thought Little Lisa.

One day Lisa's mother said, "Put on your pretty dress and your new shoes, for today you are going to visit your grandmother. I have baked this cake for her. Follow the main road straight through the forest and you will soon be there." Little Lisa was delighted; she clapped her hands in joy, for wasn't she going, all alone, to visit her grandmother who lived far away in the big forest? She might even stay overnight with Granny who told such wonderful fairy tales!

So Lisa promised to be careful to follow the main road, and kissing her mother good-bye, with her basket on her arm, she started off.

It was cool and pleasant in the forest, and Little Lisa enjoyed listening to the songs of the birds. After she had been walking a while she saw some wild strawberries, growing by the roadside.

"How delicious! I am so thirsty," said Little Lisa as she stooped to pick them. How wonderful they tasted as she ate and ate. On and on she went; the farther she went, the bigger and the redder were the strawberries. Soon she was deep in the woods. Too late she remembered that she had promised her mother not to leave the road.

"Whatever shall I do?" cried the frightened little girl.

Just then she heard a deep growl, and looking up, saw a great big bear walking towards her.

"Grr! Grr! I am going to eat you," said the bear.

"Oh, please don't, dear Uncle Bear," begged Little Lisa. "I will gladly give you my beautiful red-striped apron and my blue scarf if you will only let me go."

"Very well," said the bear. "If you will give me your apron and your blue scarf, I won't eat you."

So Little Lisa gave the big bear her red-striped apron and her blue scarf, and the bear trundled along, singing to himself, "Now I am the prettiest bear in the whole forest."

Poor Little Lisa. Her tears fell fast. And there were so many trees she didn't know which way to turn!

All of a sudden she heard a terrible howl, and there, right in front of her, stood a big wolf, smacking his lips greedily.

"Ha! Ha! I am going to eat you," said the wolf.

[1] From "Fairy Tales from the North," retold by Einar Nerman, illustrations by Einar Nerman

"Please, oh, please don't dear Uncle Gray," said Little Lisa. "I will give you my beautiful orange dress if you will only let me go."

"But, the dress is too small for me," answered the wolf.

"Perhaps you can use it for a headdress," said Little Lisa.

"That is not a bad idea," said the wolf, as he put it on his head; and walking proudly away, he said to himself, "Now I am the most beautiful wolf in the whole, big forest."

Little Lisa continued on her way. "If I can only find my way home, I won't mind," she sighed.

But once again she heard a strange noise. This time it was a big red fox that stood right in front of her.

"Aha! What a fine meal! Don't move, for I am going to eat you," said the fox.

"No, please don't, dear Mr. Fox," said Little Lisa. "I will gladly give you my beautiful blue parasol if you will only let me go."

"Well," said the fox, "that is a pretty blue parasol. Give it to me and I will let you go."

So Little Lisa gave him her beautiful blue parasol and Mr. Fox ran happily away, saying to himself:

"I am now the finest fox in the whole, big forest."

Poor Little Lisa, how she cried! All she had left were the little red hood, and her pretty red shoes. She had given away all her other things. She had even lost her basket! She must have forgotten to pick it up when the bear frightened her. As the shadows grew darker and darker in the big black forest, she tried hard to be brave and to keep on walking. The stars twinkled brightly in the black sky while the Old Man in the Moon smiled kindly down on her. Tired out, she sat down on a big stone to rest. She thought of all the beautiful clothes she had had to give away; she thought of her mother at home in the cozy cottage; she thought of her grand-mother, watching and waiting for her to come. And there she was, lost in the great big forest. Poor Little Lisa! How she cried!

Suddenly, she heard a little voice near her say,

"Why are you crying, little girl?"

There, close to her feet, sat a cunning little rabbit.

"If you don't answer me," said the rabbit, flapping his long, pink ears, "I must run away, for I am in a hurry. Ha! What nice shoes you have. Would you give them to me to help me run faster?"

"Take them, take them, dear Mr. Bunny," said Little Lisa. "All my other beautiful clothes are now gone, so I won't need the shoes. Take them and put them on your hind feet." And she gave Mr. Bunny her pretty red shoes.

"Many thanks," said the rabbit, as he put on the red shoes. "You are certainly a very nice little girl. And because you are such a good little girl, you may get up on my back, and you will see how fast we can travel."

So Little Lisa climbed up on his back, and away they went like the wind. You can be sure Little Lisa held on tight. She didn't want to fall off.

As they galloped happily along, the silence of the deep forest was broken by a terrible noise.

"Oh!" cried Little Lisa. "I think that must be the bear, the wolf, and the fox, who are coming to eat me up. Hurry, hurry."

"Don't be afraid, Little Lisa," said the rabbit. "If you hold on tight, nobody can catch us. I can run faster than anyone in the whole forest. But first let's look and make sure just what it is all about," said the rabbit. So saying, they hid behind a big tree.

Little Lisa peeped out and what do you think she saw? There stood the bear, the wolf, and the fox, quarreling as to which of them was the most beautiful animal in the whole forest. Furiously and loudly they argued. In their anger they tore off their clothes in order to be better able to fight.

Mr. Fox, who was very clever, started to run round and round a big tree. Mr. Bear and Mr. Wolf followed. Mr. Bear grabbed hold of Mr. Fox's tail and Mr. Fox took hold of Mr. Wolf's tail; Mr. Wolf, in turn, took hold of Mr. Bear's little, short tail, and so round and round, and faster and faster went the three!

But while they were chasing one another in this way, Little Lisa sneaked up and grabbed all her clothes. "If you don't want my beautiful clothes, I might as well take them back," she said. But the bear, the

wolf, and the fox were too busy growling at each other to notice her. They became more and more angry. "Brr, brr! Grr, grr! Growl, growl!" Faster and faster they ran. They ran so fast, that Little Lisa could hardly see them. They had no time to look around. Quickly Little Lisa put on her clothes, and, taking her parasol, ran to Mr. Bunny, who was waiting for her behind the tree.

"I think we'd better hurry away before they see us," said Little Lisa, as she climbed up on the back of Mr. Bunny.

"If you run straight home to Mother and Father, I will give you some hot waffles with jam," said she coaxingly.

"That sounds good to me," said Mr. Bunny, running faster than ever.

It wasn't long before they arrived home. You can imagine how surprised Little Lisa's mother was when she caught sight of her little daughter, riding on Mr. Bunny's back. And she was even more surprised when Little Lisa told her all that had happened to her in the big forest.

"You see what happens, when you don't obey? You shouldn't have left the main road, Little Lisa," said her mother. But because she was so happy to have her home again, she forgave her and said: "Let's have a party to celebrate your safe return and as long as you have promised Mr. Bunny waffles and jam I think we might make it a real waffle party."

And so she lighted the stove and soon the smell of delicious waffles filled the house. She made piles and piles of them and when they were ready, Little Lisa and Father and Mother and the friendly little Mr. Bunny sat down to supper. How wonderful they tasted and how they ate and ate!

To tell the truth, Mr. Bunny ate fifty-nine waffles; Lisa's mother ate seventy; her father eighty-two and, as for Little Lisa, she was so very, very hungry that she ate one hundred and thirty-three waffles!

Can you believe it?

Puss in Boots[1]

A miller who was dying divided all his property between his three children. This was a very simple matter, as he had nothing to leave but his mill, his ass, and his cat; so he made no will, and called in no lawyer, for he would probably have taken a large slice out of these poor possessions. The eldest son took the mill, the second the ass, while the third was obliged to content himself with the cat, at which he grumbled very much. "My brothers," said he, "by putting their property together may gain an honest livelihood, but there is nothing left for me except to die of hunger; unless, indeed, I were to kill my cat and eat him, and make a coat out of his skin, which would be very scanty clothing."

The cat, who heard the young man talking to himself, looked at him with a grave and wise air, and said, "Master, I think you had better not kill me. I shall be much more useful to you alive."

"How so?" asked his master.

"You have but to give me a sack and a pair of boots such as gentlemen wear when they go shooting, and you will find you are not so ill off as you suppose."

Now, though the young miller did not put much faith in the cat's words, he thought it rather surprising that a cat should speak at all. And he had before now seen him show so much cleverness in catching rats and mice that it seemed well to trust him a little further, especially as, poor young fellow, he had nobody else to trust.

When the cat got his boots he drew them on with a grand air. Then, slinging his sack over his shoulder and drawing the cords of it round his neck, he marched bravely to a rabbit-warren hard by, with which he was well acquainted. Putting some bran and lettuces into his bag, and stretching himself out beside it as if he were dead, he waited for some fine, fat young rabbit to peer into the sack to eat the food that was inside. This happened very shortly, for there are plenty of foolish young rabbits in every warren; and when one of them, who really was a splendid fat fellow, put his head inside, Master Puss drew the cords immediately, and took him and killed him without mercy. Then, very proud of his prey, he marched direct up to the palace, and begged to speak with the King. He was desired to ascend to the apartment of his Majesty, where, making a low bow, he said, "Sire, here is a magnificent rabbit from the warren of my lord

[1] From "The Arthur Rackham Fairy Book," selected by Arthur Rackham. Illustrations from drawings by Walter Crane

the Marquis of Carabas, which he has desired me to offer humbly to your Majesty."

"Tell your master," replied the King, "that I accept his present, and am very much obliged to him."

Another time Puss went and hid himself and his sack in a wheat-field, and there caught two splendid fat partridges in the same manner as he had done the rabbit. When he presented them to the King, with a similar message as before, his Majesty was so pleased that he ordered the cat to be taken down into the kitchen and given something to eat and drink.

One day, hearing that the King was intending to take a drive by the river with his daughter, the most beautiful princess in the world, Puss said to his master, "Sir, if you would only follow my advice your fortune is made. You have only to go and bathe in the river at a place which I shall show you, and leave all the rest to me. Only remember that you are no longer yourself, but my lord the Marquis of Carabas."

The miller's son agreed, not that he had any faith in the cat's promise, but because he no longer cared what happened.

While he was bathing the King and all the Court passed by, and were startled to hear loud cries of "Help! Help! My lord the Marquis of Carabas is drowning!" The King put his head out of the carriage, and saw nobody but the cat who had at different times brought him so many presents of game; however, he ordered his guards to go quickly to the help of my lord the Marquis of Carabas. While they were pulling the unfortunate marquis out of the water the cat came up bowing to the side of the King's carriage, and told a long and pitiful story about some thieves, who, while his master was bathing, had come and carried away all his clothes, so that it would be impossible for him to appear before his Majesty and the illustrious princess.

"Oh, we will soon remedy that," answered the King kindly, and immediately ordered one of the first officers of the household to ride back to the palace with all speed and bring back the most elegant supply of clothes for the young gentleman, who kept in the background until they arrived. Then, being handsome and well made, his new clothes became him so well that he looked as if he had been a marquis all his days, and advanced with an air of respectful ease to offer his thanks to his Majesty.

The King received him courteously, and the princess admired him very much. Indeed, so charming did he appear to her that she persuaded her father to invite him into the carriage with them, which, you may be sure, the young man did not refuse. The cat, delighted at the success of his scheme, went away as fast as he could, and ran so swiftly that he kept a long way ahead of the royal carriage. He went on and on till he came to some peasants who were mowing in a meadow. "Good people," said he, in a very firm voice, "the King is coming past here shortly, and if you do not say that the field you are mowing belongs to my lord the Marquis of Carabas you shall all be chopped as small as mincemeat."

"Yes, sire," he answered. "It is not a bad meadow, take it altogether."

Then the cat came to a wheat-field, where the reapers were reaping with all their might. He bounced in upon them: "The King is coming past to-day, and if you do not tell him that this wheat belongs to my lord the Marquis of Carabas I will have you every one chopped as small as mincemeat."

The reapers, very much alarmed, did as they were told, and the King congratulated the marquis upon possessing such beautiful fields, laden with such an abundant harvest.

They drove on, the cat always running before and saying the same thing to everybody he met—that they were to declare the whole country belonged to his master; so that even the King was astonished at

So when the King drove by and asked whose meadow it was where there was such a splendid crop of hay, the mowers all answered in trembling tones that it belonged to my lord the Marquis of Carabas.

"You have very fine land, marquis," said his Majesty to the miller's son.

the vast estate of my lord the Marquis of Carabas.

But now the cat arrived at a great castle where dwelt an ogre, to whom belonged all the land through which the King had been passing. He was a cruel tyrant, and his tenants and servants were terribly afraid of him. This accounted for their being so ready to say whatever they were told to say by the cat, who had taken pains to find out all about the ogre. So, putting on the boldest face he could assume, Puss marched up to the castle with his boots on, and asked to see the owner of it, saying that he was on his travels, but did not wish to pass so near the castle of such a noble gentleman without paying his respects to him. When the ogre heard this message he went to the door, received the cat as civilly as an ogre can, and begged him to walk in and repose himself.

"Thank you, sir," said the cat; "but first I hope you will satisfy a traveller's curiosity. I have heard in far countries of your many remarkable qualities, and especially how you have the power to change yourself into any sort of beast you choose —a lion, for instance, or an elephant."

"That is quite true," replied the ogre. "And lest you should doubt it I will immediately become a lion."

He did so; and the cat was so frightened that he sprang up to the roof of the castle and hid himself in the gutter—a proceeding rather inconvenient, on account of his boots, which were not exactly fitted to walk with upon tiles. At length, perceiving that the ogre had resumed his original form, he came down again stealthily, and confessed that he had been very much frightened.

"But, sir," said he, "it may be easy enough for such a big gentleman as you to change himself into a large animal; I do not suppose you can become a small one —a rat or mouse, for instance. I have heard that you can; still, for my part, I consider it quite impossible."

"Impossible?" cried the other indignantly. "You shall see!" And immediately the cat saw the ogre no longer, but a little mouse running along on the floor.

This was exactly what he wanted; and he did the most natural thing a cat could do in the circumstances—he sprang upon the mouse and gobbled it up in a trice. So there was an end of the ogre.

By this time the King had arrived opposite the castle, and was seized with a strong desire to enter it. The cat, hearing the noise of the carriage-wheels, ran forward in a great hurry, and, standing at the gate, said in a loud voice, "Welcome, sire, to the castle of my lord the Marquis of Carabas."

"What," cried his Majesty, very much surprised, "does the castle also belong to you? Truly, marquis, you have kept your secret well up to the last minute. I have never seen anything finer than this courtyard and these battlements. Indeed, I have nothing like them in the whole of my dominions."

The marquis, without speaking, helped the princess to descend, and, standing aside, that the King might enter first—for he had already acquired all the manners of a Court—followed his Majesty to the great hall, where a magnificent collation had been spread for the ogre and some of his friends. Without more delay they all sat down to feast.

The King, charmed with the good qualities of the Marquis of Carabas—and likewise his wine, of which he had drunk six or seven cups—said, bowing across the table at which the princess and the miller's son were talking very confidentially together, "It rests with you, marquis, whether you will not become my son-in-law."

"I shall be only too happy," said the Marquis, very readily, and the princess's eyes declared the same.

So they were married the very next day, and took possession of the ogre's castle, and of everything that had belonged to him.

As for the cat, he became at once a grand personage, and had never any need to run after mice, except for his own amusement.

The Wizard of Oz

L. FRANK BAUM

DISCOVERY OF OZ, THE TERRIBLE [1]

The four travelers walked up to the great gate of Emerald City and rang the bell. After ringing several times it was opened by the same Guardian of the Gates they had met before.

"What! Are you back again?" he asked in surprise.

"Do you not see us?" answered the Scarecrow.

"But I thought you had gone to visit the Wicked Witch of the West."

"We did visit her," said the Scarecrow.

"And she let you go again?" asked the man, in wonder.

"She could not help it, for she is melted," explained the Scarecrow.

"Melted! Well, that is good news, indeed," said the man. "Who melted her?"

"It was Dorothy," said the Lion gravely.

"Good gracious!" exclaimed the man, and he bowed very low indeed before her.

Then he led them into his little room and locked the spectacles from the great box on all their eyes, just as he had done before. Afterward they passed on through the gate into the Emerald City, and when the people heard from the Guardian of the Gates that they had melted the Wicked Witch of the West they all gathered around the travelers and followed them in a great crowd to the Palace of Oz.

The soldier with the green whiskers was still on guard before the door, but he let them in at once, and they were again met by the beautiful green girl, who showed each of them to their old rooms at once, so they might rest until the Great Oz was ready to receive them.

The soldier had the news carried straight to Oz that Dorothy and the other travelers had come back again, after destroying the Wicked Witch; but Oz made no reply. They thought the Great Wizard would send for them at once, but he did not. They had no word from him the next day, nor the next, nor the next. The waiting was tiresome and wearing, and at last they grew vexed that Oz should treat them in so poor a fashion, after sending them to undergo hardships and slavery. So the Scarecrow at last asked the green girl to take another message to Oz, saying if he did not let them in to see him at once they would call the Winged Monkeys to help them, and find out whether he kept his promises or not. When the Wizard was given this message he was so frightened that he sent word for them to come to the Throne Room at four minutes after nine o'clock the next morning. He had once met the Winged Monkeys in the Land of the West, and he did not wish to meet them again.

The four travelers passed a sleepless night, each thinking of the gift Oz had promised to bestow on him. Dorothy fell asleep only once, and then she dreamed she was in Kansas, where Aunt Em was telling her how glad she was to have her little girl at home again.

Promptly at nine o'clock the next morning the green-whiskered soldier came to them, and four minutes later they all went into the Throne Room of the Great Oz.

Of course each one of them expected to see the Wizard in the shape he had taken before, and all were greatly surprised when they looked about and saw no one

[1] From "The Wizard of Oz." by L. Frank Baum, illustration from drawing by W. W. Denslow

at all in the room. They kept close to the door and closer to one another, for the stillness of the empty room was more dreadful than any of the forms they had seen Oz take.

Presently they heard a Voice, seeming to come from somewhere near the top of the great dome, and it said, solemnly:

"I am Oz, the Great and Terrible. Why do you seek me?"

They looked again in every part of the room, and then, seeing no one, Dorothy asked, "Where are you?"

"I am everywhere," answered the Voice, "but to the eyes of common mortals I am invisible. I will now seat myself upon my throne, that you may converse with me." Indeed, the Voice seemed just then to come straight from the throne itself; so they walked toward it and stood in a row while Dorothy said:

"We have come to claim our promise, O Oz."

"What promise?" asked Oz.

"You promised to send me back to Kansas when the Wicked Witch was destroyed," said the girl.

"And you promised to give me brains," said the Scarecrow.

"And you promised to give me a heart," said the Tin Woodman.

"And you promised to give me courage," said the Cowardly Lion.

"Is the Wicked Witch really destroyed?" asked the Voice, and Dorothy thought it trembled a little.

"Yes," she answered, "I melted her with a bucket of water."

"Dear me," said the Voice, "how sudden! Well, come to me tomorrow, for I must have time to think it over."

"You've had plenty of time already," said the Tin Woodman angrily.

"We shan't wait a day longer," said the Scarecrow.

"You must keep your promises to us!" exclaimed Dorothy.

The Lion thought it might be as well to frighten the Wizard, so he gave a large, loud roar, which was so fierce and dreadful that Toto jumped away from him in alarm and tipped over the screen that stood in a corner. As it fell with a crash they looked that way, and the next moment all of them were filled with wonder. For they saw, standing in just the spot the screen had hidden, a little old man, with a bald head and a wrinkled face, who seemed to be as much surprised as they were. The Tin Woodman, raising his ax, rushed toward the little man and cried out, "Who are you?"

"I am Oz, the Great and Terrible," said the little man, in a trembling voice, "but don't strike me—please don't—and I'll do anything you want me to."

Our friends looked at him in surprise and dismay.

"I thought Oz was a great Head," said Dorothy.

"And I thought Oz was a lovely Lady," said the Scarecrow.

"And I thought Oz was a terrible Beast," said the Tin Woodman.

"And I thought Oz was a Ball of Fire," exclaimed the Lion.

"No; you are all wrong," said the little man meekly. "I have been making believe."

"Making believe!" cried Dorothy. "Are you not a great Wizard?"

"Hush, my dear," he said; "don't speak so loud, or you will be overheard—and I should be ruined. I'm supposed to be a great Wizard."

"And aren't you?" she asked.

"Not a bit of it, my dear; I'm just a common man."

"You're more than that," said the Scarecrow, in a grieved tone; "you're a humbug."

"Exactly so!" declared the little man, rubbing his hands together as if it pleased him. "I am a humbug."

"But this is terrible," said the Tin Woodman; "how shall I ever get my heart?"

"Or I my courage?" asked the Lion.

"Or I my brains?" wailed the Scarecrow, wiping the tears from his eyes.

"My dear friends," said Oz, "I pray you not to speak of these little things. Think of me, and the terrible trouble I'm in at being found out."

"Doesn't anyone else know you're a humbug?" asked Dorothy.

"No one knows it but you four—and myself," replied Oz. "I have fooled everyone so long that I thought I should never be found out. It was a great mistake my ever letting you into the Throne Room. Usually I will not see even my subjects, and so they believe I am something terrible."

"But, I don't understand," said Dorothy, in bewilderment. "How was it that you appeared to me as a great Head?"

"That was one of my tricks," answered Oz. "Step this way, please, and I will tell you all about it."

He led the way to a small chamber in the rear of the Throne Room, and they all followed him. He pointed to one corner, in which lay the Great Head, made out of many thicknesses of paper, and with a carefully painted face.

"This I hung from the ceiling by a wire,"

said Oz. "I stood behind the screen and pulled a thread, to make the eyes move and the mouth open."

"But how about the voice?" she inquired.

"Oh, I am a ventriloquist," said the little man, "and I can throw the sound of my voice wherever I wish, so that you thought it was coming out of the Head. Here are the other things I used to deceive you." He showed the Scarecrow the dress and the mask he had worn when he seemed to be the lovely Lady; and the Tin Woodman saw that his terrible Beast was nothing but a lot of skins, sewn together, with slats to keep their sides out. As for the Ball of Fire, the false Wizard had hung that also from the ceiling. It was really a ball of cotton, but when oil was poured upon it the ball burned fiercely.

"Really," said the Scarecrow, "you ought to be ashamed of yourself for being such a humbug."

"I am—I certainly am," answered the little man sorrowfully; "but it was the only thing I could do. Sit down, please, there are plenty of chairs; and I will tell you my story."

So they sat down and listened while he told the following tale:

"I was born in Omaha—"

"Why, that isn't very far from Kansas!" cried Dorothy.

"No; but it's farther from here," he said, shaking his head at her sadly. "When I grew up I became a ventriloquist, and at that I was very well trained by a great master. I can imitate any kind of a bird or beast." Here he mewed so like a kitten that Toto pricked up his ears and looked everywhere to see where she was. "After a time," continued Oz, "I tired of that, and became a balloonist."

"What is that?" asked Dorothy.

"A man who goes up in a balloon on circus day, so as to draw a crowd of people together and get them to pay to see the circus," he explained.

"Oh," she said, "I know."

"Well, one day I went up in a balloon and the ropes got twisted, so that I couldn't come down again. It went way up above the clouds, so far that a current of air struck it and carried it many, many miles away. For a day and a night I traveled through the air, and on the morning of the second day I awoke and found the balloon floating over a strange and beautiful country.

"It came down gradually, and I was not hurt a bit. But I found myself in the midst of a strange people, who, seeing me come from the clouds, thought I was a great Wizard. Of course I let them think so, because they were afraid of me, and promised to do anything I wished them to.

"Just to amuse myself, and keep the good people busy, I ordered them to build this City, and my Palace; and they did it all willingly and well. Then I thought, as the country was so green and beautiful, I would call it the Emerald City, and to make the name fit better I put green spectacles on all the people, so that everything they saw was green."

"But isn't everything here green?" asked Dorothy.

"No more than in any other city," replied Oz; "but when you wear green spectacles, why of course everything you see looks green to you. The Emerald City was built a great many years ago, for I was a young man when the balloon brought me here, and I am a very old man now. But my people have worn green glasses on their eyes so long that most of them think it really is an Emerald City, and it certainly is a beautiful place, abounding in jewels and precious metals, and every good thing that is needed to make one happy. I have been good to the people, and they like me; but ever since this Palace was built I have shut myself up and would not see any of them.

"One of my greatest fears was the Witches, for while I had no magical powers at all I soon found out that the Witches were really able to do wonderful things. There were four of them in this country, and they ruled the people who live in the North and South and East and West. Fortunately, the Witches of the North and South were good, and I knew they would do me no harm; but the Witches of the East and West were terribly wicked, and had they not thought I was more powerful than they themselves, they would surely have destroyed me. As it was, I lived in deadly fear of them for many years; so you can imagine how pleased I was when I heard your house had fallen on the Wicked Witch of the East. When you came to me I was willing to promise anything if you would only do away with the other Witch; but, now that you have melted her, I am ashamed to say that I cannot keep my promises."

"I think you are a very bad man," said Dorothy.

"Oh, no, my dear; I'm really a very good man; but I'm a very bad Wizard, I must admit."

"Can't you give me brains?" asked the Scarecrow.

"You don't need them. You are learning something every day. A baby has brains, but it doesn't know much. Experience is the only thing that brings knowledge, and the longer you are on earth the more experience you are sure to get."

"That may all be true," said the Scarecrow, "but I shall be very unhappy unless you give me brains."

The false Wizard looked at him carefully.

"Well," he said with a sigh, "I'm not much of a magician, as I said; but if you will come to me tomorrow morning, I will stuff your head with brains. I cannot tell you how to use them, however; you must find that out for yourself."

"Oh, thank you—thank you!" cried the Scarecrow. "I'll find a way to use them, never fear!"

"But how about my courage?" asked the Lion anxiously.

"You have plenty of courage, I am sure," answered Oz. "All you need is confidence in yourself. There is no living thing that is not afraid when it faces danger. True courage is in facing danger when you are afraid, and that kind of courage you have in plenty."

"Perhaps I have, but I'm scared just the same," said the Lion. "I shall really be very unhappy unless you give me the sort of courage that makes one forget he is afraid."

"Very well; I will give you that sort of courage tomorrow," replied Oz.

"How about my heart?" asked the Tin Woodman.

"Why, as for that," answered Oz, "I think you are wrong to want a heart. It makes most people unhappy. If you only knew it, you are in luck not to have a heart."

"That must be a matter of opinion," said the Tin Woodman. "For my part, I will bear all the unhappiness without a murmur, if you will give me the heart."

"Very well," answered Oz meekly. "Come to me tomorrow and you shall have a heart. I have played Wizard for so many years that I may as well continue the part a little longer."

"And now," said Dorothy, "how am I to get back to Kansas?"

"We shall have to think about that," replied the little man. "Give me two or three days to consider the matter and I'll try to find a way to carry you over the desert. In the meantime you shall all be treated as my guests, and while you live in the Palace my people will wait upon you and obey your slightest wish. There is only one thing I ask in return for my help— such as it is. You must keep my secret and tell no one I am a humbug."

They agreed to say nothing of what they had learned, and went back to their rooms in high spirits. Even Dorothy had hope that "The Great and Terrible Humbug," as she called him, would find a way to send her back to Kansas, and if he did she was willing to forgive him everything.

Alice in Wonderland

LEWIS CARROLL

DOWN THE RABBIT HOLE [1]

Alice was beginning to get very tired of sitting by her sister on the bank, and of having nothing to do; once or twice she had peeped into the book her sister was reading, but it had no pictures or conversations in it, "and what is the use of a book," thought Alice, "without pictures or conversations?"

So she was considering in her own mind (as well as she could, for the hot day made her feel very sleepy and stupid) whether the pleasure of making a daisy chain would be worth the trouble of getting up and picking the daisies, when suddenly a white rabbit with pink eyes ran close by her.

There was nothing so *very* remarkable in that; nor did Alice think it so *very* much out of the way to hear the Rabbit say to itself, "Oh, dear! Oh, dear! I shall be too late!" (when she thought it over afterward it occurred to her that she ought to have wondered at this, but at the time it all seemed quite natural); but when the Rabbit actually *took a watch out of its waistcoat pocket,* and looked at it, and then hurried on, Alice started to her feet, for it flashed across her mind that she had never before seen a rabbit with either a waistcoat pocket or a watch to take out of it, and, burning with curiosity, she ran across the field after it, and was just in time to see it pop down a large rabbit hole under the hedge.

In another moment down went Alice after it, never once considering how in the world she was to get out again.

The rabbit hole went straight on like a tunnel for some way, and then dipped suddenly down, so suddenly that Alice had not a moment to think about stopping herself before she found herself falling down what seemed to be a very deep well.

Either the well was very deep, or she fell very slowly, for she had plenty of time as she went down to look about her, and to wonder what was going to happen next. First she tried to look down and make out what she was coming to, but it was too dark to see anything; then she looked at the sides of the well, and noticed that they were filled with cupboards and bookshelves; here and there she saw maps and pictures hung upon pegs. She took down a jar from one of the shelves as she passed; it was labeled "ORANGE MARMALADE," but to her great disappointment it was empty; she did not like to drop the jar for fear of killing somebody underneath, so managed to put it into one of the cupboards as she fell past it.

"Well!" thought Alice to herself, "after such a fall as this, I shall think nothing of tumbling downstairs! How brave they'll all think me at home! Why, I wouldn't say anything about it even if I fell off the top of the house!" (Which was very likely true.)

Down, down, down. Would the fall *never* come to an end? "I wonder how many miles I've fallen by this time?" she said aloud. "I must be getting somewhere near the center of the earth. Let me see: that would be four thousand miles down, I think" (for, you see, Alice had learned several things of this sort in her lessons

[1] From "Alice in Wonderland," by Lewis Carroll, illustrated by Sir John Tenniel

in the schoolroom, and though this was not a *very* good opportunity for showing off her knowledge, as there was no one to listen to her, still it was good practice to say it over)—"yes, that's about the right distance—but then I wonder what Latitude or Longitude I've got to?" (Alice had not the slightest idea what Latitude was, or Longitude either, but she thought they were nice grand words to say.)

Presently she began again. "I wonder if I shall fall right *through* the earth! How funny it'll seem to come out among the people that walk with their heads downward! The Antipathies, I think" (she was rather glad there *was* no one listening this time, as it didn't sound at all the right word); "but I shall have to ask them what the name of the country is, you know. Please, ma'am, is this New Zealand or Australia?" (and she tried to curtsy as she spoke—fancy *curtsying* as you're falling through the air! Do you think you could manage it?) "And what an ignorant little girl she'll think me for asking! No, it'll never do to ask; perhaps I shall see it written up somewhere."

Down, down, down. There was nothing else to do, so Alice soon began talking again. "Dinah'll miss me very much tonight, I should think!" (Dinah was the cat.) "I hope they'll remember her saucer of milk at teatime. Dinah, my dear! I wish you were down here with me! There are no mice in the air, I'm afraid, but you might catch a bat, and that's very like a mouse, you know. But do cats eat bats, I wonder?" And here Alice began to get rather sleepy, and went on saying to herself, in a dreamy sort of way, "Do cats eat bats? Do cats eat bats?" and sometimes, "Do bats eat cats?" for, you see, as she couldn't answer either question, it didn't much matter which way she put it. She felt that she was dozing off, and had just begun to dream that she was walking hand in hand with Dinah, and was saying to her very earnestly, "Now, Dinah, tell me the truth, did you ever eat a bat?" when suddenly, thump! thump! down she came upon a heap of sticks and dry leaves, and the fall was over.

Alice was not a bit hurt, and she jumped up onto her feet in a moment; she looked up, but it was dark overhead; before her was another long passage, and the White Rabbit was still in sight, hurrying down it. There was not a moment to be lost: away went Alice like the wind, and was just in time to hear it say, as it turned a corner, "Oh, my ears and whiskers, how late it's getting!" She was close behind it

when she turned the corner, but the Rabbit was no longer to be seen: she found herself in a long, low hall, which was lit up by a row of lamps hanging from the roof.

There were doors all round the hall, but they were all locked, and when Alice had been all the way down one side and up the other, trying every door, she walked sadly down the middle, wondering how she was ever to get out again.

Suddenly she came upon a little three-legged table, all made of solid glass; there was nothing on it but a tiny golden key, and Alice's first idea was that this might belong to one of the doors of the hall; but, alas! either the locks were too large, or the key was too small, but at any rate it would not open any of them. However, on the second time round she came upon a low curtain she had not noticed before, and behind it was a little door about fifteen inches high; she tried the little golden key in the lock, and to her great delight it fitted!

Alice opened the door and found that it led into a small passage, not much larger than a rat hole; she knelt down and looked along the passage into the loveliest garden you ever saw. How she longed to get out of that dark hall, and wander about among those beds of bright flowers and those cool fountains. But she could not even get her head through the doorway. "And even if my head would go through," thought poor Alice, "it would be of very little use without my shoulders. Oh, how I wish I could shut up like a telescope! I think I could, if I only knew how to begin." For, you see, so many out-of-the-way things had happened lately that Alice had begun to think that very few things indeed were really impossible.

There seemed to be no use in waiting by the little door, so she went back to the table, half hoping she might find another key on it, or at any rate a book of rules for shutting people up like telescopes: this time she found a little bottle on it ("which certainly was not here before," said Alice), and tied round the neck of the bottle was a paper label with the words "DRINK ME" beautifully printed on it in large letters.

It was all very well to say "Drink me," but the wise little Alice was not going to do *that* in a hurry. "No, I'll look first," she said, "and see whether it's marked '*poison*' or not," for she had read several nice little stories about children who had got burnt, and eaten up by wild beasts, and other unpleasant things, all because they *would* not remember the simple rules their friends had taught them, such as, that a red-hot poker will burn you if you hold it too long; and that if you cut your finger *very* deeply with a knife it usually bleeds; and she had never forgotten that if you drink much from a bottle marked "poison," it is almost certain to disagree with you sooner or later.

However, this bottle was *not* marked "poison," so Alice ventured to taste it, and finding it very nice (it had, in fact, a sort of mixed flavor of cherry tart, custard, pineapple, roast turkey, toffy, and hot buttered toast), she very soon finished it off.

"What a curious feeling!" said Alice. "I must be shutting up like a telescope."

And so it was, indeed; she was now only ten inches high, and her face brightened up at the thought that she was now the right size for going through the little door into that lovely garden. First, however, she waited for a few minutes to see if she was going to shrink any further; she felt a little nervous about this, "for it might end, you know," said Alice to herself, "in my going out altogether, like a candle. I wonder what I should be like then?" And she tried to fancy what the flame of a candle looks like after the candle is blown out, for she could not remember ever having seen such a thing.

After a while, finding that nothing more happened, she decided on going into the garden at once; but, alas for poor Alice! when she got to the door, she found she had forgotten the little golden key, and when she went back to the table for it, she found she could not possibly reach it. She could see quite plainly through the glass, and she tried her best to climb up one of the legs of the table, but it was too slippery, and when she had tired herself out with trying, the poor little thing sat down and cried.

"Come, there's no use in crying like that!" said Alice to herself rather sharply; "I advise you to leave off this minute!" She generally gave herself very good advice (though she very seldom followed it), and sometimes she scolded herself so severely as to bring tears into her eyes, and once she remembered trying to box her own ears for having cheated herself in a game of croquet she was playing against herself; for this curious child was very fond of pretending to be two people. "But it's no use now," thought poor Alice, "to pretend to be two people! Why, there's hardly enough of me left to make *one* respectable person!"

Soon her eye fell on a little glass box that was lying under the table: she opened it, and found in it a very small cake, on which the words "EAT ME" were beautifully marked in currants. "Well, I'll eat it," said Alice, "and if it makes me grow larger, I can reach the key; and if it makes me grow smaller, I can creep under the door; so either way I'll get into the garden, and I don't care which happens!"

She ate a little bit, and said anxiously to herself, "Which way? Which way?" holding her hand on the top of her head to feel which way it was growing, and she was quite surprised to find that she remained the same size; to be sure, this is what generally happens when one eats cake, but Alice had got so much into the way of expecting nothing but out-of-the-way things to happen that it seemed quite dull and stupid for life to go on in the common way.

So she set to work, and very soon finished off the cake.

THE POOL OF TEARS[1]

"Curiouser and curiouser!" cried Alice (she was so much surprised that for the moment she quite forgot how to speak good English); "now I'm opening out like the largest telescope that ever was! Good-by, feet!" (For when she looked down at her feet, they seemed to be almost out of sight, they were getting so far off.) "Oh, my poor little feet, I wonder who will put on your shoes and stockings for you now, dears? I'm sure *I* shan't be able! I shall be a great deal too far off to trouble myself about you: you must manage the best way you can—but I must be kind to them," thought Alice, "or perhaps they won't walk the way I want to go! Let me see: I'll give them a new pair of boots every Christmas."

And she went on planning to herself how she would manage it. "They must go by the carrier," she thought; "and how funny it'll seem, sending presents to one's own feet! And how odd the directions will look:

> *Alice's Right Foot, Esq.,*
> *Hearthrug,*
> *near the Fender*
> *(with Alice's love).*

"Oh, dear, what nonsense I'm talking!" Just at this moment her head struck against the roof of the hall: in fact she was now rather more than nine feet high, and she at once took up the little golden key and hurried off to the garden door.

Poor Alice! It was as much as she could do, lying down on one side, to look through into the garden with one eye; but to get through was more hopeless than ever; she sat down and began to cry again.

"You ought to be ashamed of yourself," said Alice, "a great girl like you" (she might well say this), "to go on crying in this way! Stop this moment, I tell you!" But she went on all the same, shedding gallons of tears, until there was a large pool all around her, about four inches deep and reaching half down the hall.

After a time she heard a little pattering of feet in the distance, and she hastily dried her eyes to see what was coming. It was the White Rabbit returning, splendidly dressed, with a pair of white kid gloves in one hand and a large fan in the other: he came trotting along in a great hurry, muttering to himself as he came, "Oh, the Duchess, the Duchess! Oh, won't she be savage if I've kept her waiting!" Alice felt so desperate that she was ready to ask help of anyone; so, when the Rabbit came near her, she began in a low timid voice, "If you please, sir—" The Rabbit started violently, dropped the white kid gloves and the fan, and scurried away into the darkness as hard as he could go.

[1] From "Alice in Wonderland," by Lewis Carroll, illustrated by Sir John Tenniel

Alice took up the fan and gloves, and, as the hall was very hot, she kept fanning herself all the time she went on talking: "Dear, dear! How queer everything is to-day! And yesterday things went on just as usual. I wonder if I've been changed in the night? Let me think: was I the same when I got up this morning? I almost think I can remember feeling a little different. But if I'm not the same, the next question is, Who in the world am I? Ah, *that's* the great puzzle!" And she began thinking over all the children she knew that were of the same age as herself, to see if she could have been changed for any of them.

"I'm sure I'm not Ada," she said, "for her hair goes in such long ringlets, and mine doesn't go in ringlets at all; and I'm sure I can't be Mabel, for I know all sorts of things, and she, oh! she knows such a very little! Besides, *she's* she, and *I'm* I, and—oh, dear, how puzzling it all is! I'll try if I know all the things I used to know. Let me see: four times five is twelve, and four times six is thirteen, and four times seven is—oh, dear! I shall never get to twenty at that rate! However, the Multiplication Table doesn't signify; let's try Geography. London is the capital of Paris, and Paris the capital of Rome, and Rome— no, *that's* all wrong, I'm certain! I must have been changed for Mabel! I'll try and say 'How doth the little—'" and she crossed her hands on her lap, as if she were saying lessons, and began to repeat it, but her voice sounded hoarse and strange, and the words did not come the same as they used to do:

"How doth the little crocodile
  Improve his shining tail,
And pour the waters of the Nile
  On every golden scale!

How cheerfully he seems to grin,
  How neatly spreads his claws,
And welcomes little fishes in
  With gently smiling jaws!"

"I'm sure those are not the right words," said poor Alice, and her eyes filled with tears again as she went on, "I must be Mabel after all, and shall have to go and live in that poky little house, and have next to no toys to play with, and oh! ever so many lessons to learn! No, I've made up my mind about it: if I'm Mabel, I'll stay down here! It'll be no use their putting their heads down and saying, 'Come up again, dear!' I shall only look up and say, 'Who am I, then? Tell me that first, and then, if I like being that person, I'll come up; if not, I'll stay down here till I'm somebody else'—but, oh, dear!" cried Alice, with a sudden burst of tears, "I do wish they *would* put their heads down! I am so *very* tired of being all alone here!"

As she said this she looked down at her hands, and was surprised to see that she had put on one of the Rabbit's little white kid gloves while she was talking. "How *can* I have done that?" she thought. "I must be growing small again." She got up and went to the table to measure herself by it, and found that, as nearly as she could guess, she was now about two feet high, and was going on shrinking rapidly; she soon found out that the cause of this was the fan she was holding, and she dropped it hastily, just in time to save herself from shrinking away altogether.

"That *was* a narrow escape!" said Alice, a good deal frightened at the sudden change, but very glad to find herself still in existence; "and now for the garden!" and she ran with all speed back to the little door; but, alas! the little door was shut again and the little golden key was lying on the glass table as before, "and things are worse than ever," thought the poor child, "for I never was so small as this before, never! And I declare it's too bad, that it is!"

As she said these words her foot slipped, and in another moment, splash! she was up to her chin in salt water. Her first idea was that she had somehow fallen into the sea, "and in that case I can go back by railway," she said to herself. (Alice had been to the seaside once in her life, and had come to the general conclusion that wherever you go to on the English coast you find a number of bathing machines in the sea, some children digging in the sand with wooden spades, then a row of lodging houses, and behind them a railway station.) However, she soon made out that she was in the pool of tears which she had wept when she was nine feet high.

"I wish I hadn't cried so much!" said Alice, as she swam about, trying to find her way out. "I shall be punished for it now, I suppose, by being drowned in my own tears! That *will* be a queer thing, to be sure! However, everything is queer today."

Just then she heard something splashing about in the pool a little way off, and she swam nearer to make out what it was; at first she thought it must be a walrus or hippopotamus, but then she remembered how small she was now, and she soon made out that it was only a mouse, that had slipped in like herself.

"Would it be of any use, now," thought Alice, "to speak to this mouse? Everything is so out-of-the-way down here that I should think very likely it can talk; at any rate, there's no harm in trying." So she began: "O Mouse, do you know the way out of this pool? I am very tired of swimming about here, O Mouse!" (Alice thought this must be the right way of speaking to a mouse: she had never done such a thing before, but she remembered having seen in her brother's Latin Grammar, "A mouse—of a mouse—to a mouse—a mouse—O mouse!") The Mouse looked at her rather inquisitively, and seemed to her to wink with one of its little eyes, but it said nothing.

"Perhaps it doesn't understand English," thought Alice; "I dare say it's a French mouse, come over with William the Conqueror." (For, with all her knowledge of history, Alice had no very clear notion how long ago anything had happened.)

So she began again: *"Où est ma chatte?"* which was the first sentence in her French lesson book. The Mouse gave a sudden leap out of the water, and seemed to quiver all over with fright. "Oh, I beg your pardon!" cried Alice hastily, afraid that she had hurt the poor animal's feelings. "I quite forgot you didn't like cats."

"Not like cats!" cried the Mouse in a shrill, passionate voice. "Would *you* like cats if you were me?"

"Well, perhaps not," said Alice in a soothing tone; "don't be angry about it. And yet I wish I could show you our cat Dinah; I think you'd take a fancy to cats if you could only see her. She is such a dear quiet thing," Alice went on, half to herself, as she swam lazily about in the pond, "and she sits purring so nicely by the fire, licking her paws and washing her face—and she is such a nice soft thing to nurse—and she's such a capital one for catching mice—Oh, I beg your pardon!" cried Alice again; for this time the Mouse was bristling all over, and she felt certain it must be really offended. "We won't talk about her any more if you'd rather not."

"We, indeed!" cried the Mouse, who was trembling down to the end of his tail. "As if *I* would talk on such a subject! Our family always *hated* cats—nasty, low, vulgar things! Don't let me hear the name again!"

"I won't, indeed!" said Alice, in a great hurry to change the subject of conversation. "Are you—are you fond—of—of dogs?" The Mouse did not answer, so Alice went on eagerly: "There is such a nice little dog near our house I should like to show you! A little bright-eyed terrier, you know, with oh! such long curly brown hair! And it'll fetch things when you throw them, and it'll sit up and beg for its dinner, and all sorts of things—I can't remember half of them—and it belongs to a farmer, you know, and he says it's so useful it's worth a hundred pounds! He says it kills all the rats and—Oh, dear!"

cried Alice in a sorrowful tone, "I'm afraid I've offended it again." For the Mouse was swimming away from her as hard as it could go, and making quite a commotion in the pool as it went.

So she called softly after it, "Mouse, dear! Do come back again, and we won't talk about cats or dogs either, if you don't like them!" When the Mouse heard this it turned and swam slowly back to her; its face was quite pale (with passion, Alice thought), and it said in a low, trembling voice, "Let us get to the shore, and then I'll tell you my history, and you'll understand why it is I hate cats and dogs."

It was high time to go, for the pool was getting quite crowded with the birds and animals that had fallen into it. There was a Duck and a Dodo, a Lory and an Eaglet, and several other curious creatures. Alice led the way, and the whole party swam to the shore.

The Shy Little Horse [1]

MARGARET WISE BROWN

Once upon a time in a barnyard there was a shy little horse. Every time he heard anyone coming, he ran away. Not so the donkey, not so the pig.

The old gray donkey rolled his eyes and lowered his head, put forward his ears, and then trotted over to see who the visitor was. And the old fat pig, if she wasn't eating, wallowed over to the side of her pen and grunted at the visitor. But the little horse was shy. He galloped away and his mother galloped with him to the far end of the field.

Then one day a visitor came to the barnyard. The visitor was a tall man with a mustache.

The donkey saw him coming and ran to the fence and stuck forward his long ears and rolled his big brown jack-rabbit eyes. But the visitor didn't pay any attention to the donkey. The old pig blinked at him, and the chickens scratched about as though there were only chickens in the barnyard. But the visitor didn't even see the old pig and the chickens. The visitor was looking at the shy little horse.

And that shy little horse just lowered his head and kicked up his heels and galloped away.

Now this visitor had come just to see the shy little horse. But every time the man got near him, the little horse kicked up his heels and away he flew across the field. And his mother galloped with him and stayed by his side.

But the tall man with the mustache knew a lot about shy little horses. So he just went and leaned against the fence and

[1] From "The Fish With the Deep Smile," by Margaret Wise Brown. Illustrations by Hamilton Greene

whistled away to himself and didn't look at the shy little horse any more.

Now that funny little horse saw the man do this and he heard him whistling. The shy little horse lowered his head and nibbled the green grass. The man didn't move and kept on whistling. The shy little horse kicked up his heels and ran farther down the field and nibbled some more grass and peeked at the man. The man didn't move and kept on whistling. Then the shy little horse nibbled some grass nearer to the man. The man didn't move and kept on whistling. What a funny man, thought the shy little horse. Why doesn't he chase me and try to get me in a corner and put a halter over my head? The man didn't move and kept on whistling.

By this time the little horse was so curious he was nearly popping inside. He had never seen a man like this before. All the other men had chased him into a corner and caught him and put a halter over his head. He was quite near to the man now, and he stood there ready to leap away and gallop to the far ends of the field. The man didn't move and kept on whistling. The shy little horse nosed nearer and nearer. The whistling tickled his ears in a way he liked. And he liked the man to stand so still he could get a good look at him.

Then the man moved just a tiny little bit. He uncurled his fingers, and on the palm of his hand were two square lumps of sugar. The shy little horse's mother stepped nearer to the man, almost right up to him. The man didn't move and kept on whistling. This was a wonderful thing. The old mother horse stepped right up to the man and buried her nose in his hand and took one lump of sugar and stepped back and chewed it. Then she stepped up and took the other lump of sugar. The man didn't move and kept on whistling. Then after a while he walked out of the field the way he had come and went away.

The next day he came back, and he stood there whistling and he gave the mother horse another lump of sugar. The third day when he came, he walked right over to the mother horse and put a halter over her head and gave her a lump of sugar. Then he led her out of the field, and the shy little horse followed after, close to his mother's side. The man led the mother horse and the shy little horse right down the road where the little horse had never been before.

Way down the road they went, until they came to a small dirt road. The man turned up the dirt road, and the shy little horse's brand new hooves didn't make clicking noises any more on the dirt, they just made soft little thuds. They went up the dirt road to a long white house with a big white stable with green doors and windows.

And out from the house came a shy little boy and looked at the shy little horse.

For the tall man with the mustache was the father of the shy little boy, and he had bought the shy little horse for the little boy's very own. The little boy's mother came out of the house and said what a beautiful young horse it was. And the little boy said, "Some day I will ride him."

It wasn't so long before the shy little boy had taught the shy little horse to eat sugar out of his own hand. And the shy little horse and the shy little boy grew up together, and it wasn't long—maybe a year or two, for there was plenty of time—before the little boy had grown old enough to ride the shy little horse and the shy little horse had grown large enough to carry the little boy on his back.

They rode all over the country, the boy and his horse, and after a while they weren't even shy any more. They jumped fences and galloped across the grassy fields.

The Golden Goose [1]

There was once a man who had three sons, the youngest of whom was called Simpleton. He was scorned and despised by the others and kept in the background.

The eldest son was going into the forest to cut wood, and, before he started, his mother gave him a nice sweet cake and a bottle of wine to take with him so that he might not suffer from hunger or thirst.

In the wood he met a little old gray man, who bade him good day and said, "Give me a bit of the cake in your pocket, and let me have a drop of your wine. I am so hungry and thirsty."

But the clever son said, "If I give you my cake and wine, I shan't have enough for myself. Be off with you!"

He left the little man standing there and went on his way. But he had not been long at work, cutting down a tree, before he made a false stroke. He dug the ax into his own arm and he was obliged to go home to have it bound up.

Now this was no accident. It was

[1] A fairy tale by the Brothers Grimm. Illustration from a drawing by L. Leslie Brooke

brought about by the little old gray man.

The second son now had to go into the forest to cut wood, and like the eldest, his mother gave him a sweet cake and a bottle of wine. In the same way the little gray man met him and asked for a piece of his cake and a drop of his wine. But the second son made the same sensible answer, "If I give you any, I shall have the less for myself. Be off and out of my way!" And he went on.

His punishment, however, was not long delayed. After a few blows at the tree, he hit his own leg and had to be carried home.

Then Simpleton said, "Let me go to cut the wood, father."

But his father said, "Your brothers have only come to harm by it. You had better leave it alone. You know nothing about it." But Simpleton begged so hard to be allowed to go that at last his father said, "Well, off you go then. You will be wiser when you have hurt yourself."

His mother gave him a cake which was mixed only with water and baked in the ashes, and a bottle of sour beer. When he reached the forest, like the others he met the little gray man.

"Give me a bit of the cake in your pocket and a drop of your wine. I am so hungry and thirsty," said the little man.

Simpleton answered, "I only have a cake baked in the ashes, and some sour beer. But if you like such fare, we will sit down and eat it together."

So they sat down. But when Simpleton pulled out his cake it was a nice sweet cake, and his sour beer was turned into good wine. So they ate and drank, and the little man said, "As you have such a good heart and are willing to share your goods, I will give you good luck. There stands an old tree. Cut it down and you will find something at the roots."

So saying, he disappeared without giving Simpleton any further directions.

Simpleton cut down the tree, and when it fell, lo and behold! a goose was sitting among the roots, and its feathers were of pure gold. He picked it up and took it with him to an inn where he meant to stay the night. The landlord had three daughters, who saw the goose and were very curious as to what kind of bird it could be, and wanted to get one of its golden feathers.

The eldest thought, "There will soon be some opportunity for me to pull out one of the feathers." And when Simpleton went outside, she took hold of its wing to pluck out a feather, but her hand stuck fast and she could not get away.

Soon afterwards, the second sister came up, meaning also to pluck out one of the golden feathers. But she had hardly touched her sister when she found herself held fast.

Finally the third one came with the same intention, but the others screamed out, "Keep away! For goodness' sake, keep away!"

But she, not knowing why she was to keep away, thought, "Why should I not be there if they are there?"

So she ran up. But as soon as she touched her sisters she had to stay hanging on to them, and they all had to pass the night like this.

In the morning, Simpleton took up the goose under his arm without noticing the three girls hanging on behind. They had to keep running behind, dodging his legs right and left.

In the middle of the fields they met the parson, who when he saw the procession cried out, "For shame, you bold girls! Why do you run after the lad like that? Do you call that proper behavior?"

Then he took hold of the hand of the youngest girl to pull her away. But no sooner had he touched her than he felt himself held fast, and he too had to run behind.

Soon afterwards the sexton came up and, seeing his master the parson treading on the heels of the three girls, cried out in amazement, "Hallo, your reverence!

Lo and behold! a goose was sitting there

Where are you going so fast? Don't forget that we have a christening!"

So saying, he plucked the parson by the sleeve and soon found that he could not get away.

As this party of five, one behind the other, tramped on, two peasants came along the road, carrying their hoes. The parson called them and asked them to set the sexton and himself free, but as soon as ever they touched the sexton they were held fast. So now there were seven people running behind Simpleton and his goose.

By and by they reached a town where a king ruled whose only daughter was so solemn that nothing and nobody could make her laugh. So the King had proclaimed that whoever could make her laugh should marry her.

When Simpleton heard this he took his goose, with all his following, before her, and when she saw these seven people running one behind another, she burst into fits of laughter and seemed as if she could never stop. Thereupon Simpleton asked her in marriage. But the King did not like him for a son-in-law and made all sorts of conditions. First, he said Simpleton must bring him a man who could drink up a cellarful of wine.

Then Simpleton at once thought of the little gray man who might be able to help him, and he went out to the forest to look for him. On the very spot where the tree that he had cut down had stood, he saw a man sitting with a very sad face.

Simpleton asked him what was the matter and he answered, "I am so thirsty, and I can't quench my thirst. I hate cold water, and I have already emptied a cask of wine. But what is a drop like that on a burning stone?"

"Well, there I can help you," said Simpleton. "Come with me and you shall soon have enough to drink and to spare."

He led him to the King's cellar, and the man started upon the great casks. And he drank and drank till his sides ached, and by the end of the day the cellar was empty.

Then again Simpleton demanded his bride. But the King was annoyed that a wretched fellow called "Simpleton" should have his daughter and he made new conditions. He was now to find a man who could eat up a mountain of bread.

Simpleton did not reflect long, but went straight to the forest. And there in the selfsame place sat a man tightening a strap round his body and making a very miserable face.

He said, "I have eaten up a whole ovenful of rolls. But what is the good of that when anyone is as hungry as I am? I am never satisfied. I have to tighten my belt every day if I am not to die of hunger."

Simpleton was delighted and said, "Get up and come with me. You shall have enough to eat."

And he took him to the court, where the King had caused all the flour in the kingdom to be brought together and a huge mountain of bread to be baked. The man from the forest sat down before it and began to eat, and at the end of the day the whole mountain had disappeared.

Now for the third time Simpleton asked for his bride. But again the King tried to find an excuse, and demanded a ship which could sail on land as well as at sea.

"As soon as you sail up in it, you shall have my daughter," he said.

Simpleton went straight to the forest, and there sat the little gray man to whom he had given his cake. The little man said, "I have eaten and drunk for you, and now I will give you the ship, too. I do it all because you were merciful to me."

Then he gave him the ship which could sail on land as well as at sea, and when the King saw it he could no longer withhold his daughter. The marriage was celebrated, and at the King's death Simpleton inherited the kingdom, and lived long and happily with his wife.

The Adventures of Peter Cottontail

THORNTON W. BURGESS

PETER FINDS A NAME [1]

Peter Rabbit had quite lost his appetite. When Peter forgets to eat, you may make up your mind that Peter has something very important to think about. At least, he has something on his mind that he thinks is important. The fact is, Peter had fully made up his mind to change his name.

He thought Peter Rabbit too common a name. But when he tried to think of a better one, he found that no name that he could think of really pleased him any more. So he thought and he thought and he thought and he thought. And the more he thought the less appetite he had.

From "The Adventures of Peter Cottontail," by Thornton W. Burgess, illustrations from drawings by Harrison Cady

Now Jimmy Skunk was the only one to whom Peter had told how discontented he was with his name, and it was Jimmy who had suggested to Peter that he change it. Jimmy thought it a great joke, and he straightway passed the word along among all the little meadow and forest people that Peter Rabbit was going to change his name. Everybody laughed and chuckled over the thought of Peter Rabbit's foolishness, and they planned to have a great deal of fun with Peter as soon as he should tell them his new name.

Peter was sitting on the edge of the Old Briar-patch one morning when Ol' Mistah Buzzard passed, flying low. "Good mo'ning, Brer Cottontail," said Ol' Mistah Buzzard, with a twinkle in his eye.

At first Peter didn't understand that Ol' Mistah Buzzard was speaking to him, and by the time he did it was too late to reply, for Ol' Mistah Buzzard was way, way up in the blue, blue sky.

"Cottontail, Cottontail," said Peter over and over to himself and began to smile. Every time he said it he liked it better. "Cottontail, Peter Cottontail! How much better sounding that is than Peter Rabbit! That sounds as if I really were somebody. Yes, Sir, that's the very name I want. Now I must send word to all my friends that hereafter I am no longer Peter Rabbit, but Peter Cottontail."

Peter kicked up his heels in just the funny way he always does when he is pleased. Suddenly he remembered that such a fine, long, high-sounding name as Peter Cottontail demanded dignity. So he stopped kicking up his heels and began to practice putting on airs. But first he called to the Merry Little Breezes and told them about his change of name and asked them to tell all his friends that in the future he would not answer to the name of Peter Rabbit, but only to the name of Peter Cottontail. He was very grave and earnest and important as he explained it to the Merry Little Breezes. The Merry Little Breezes kept their faces straight while he

was talking, but as soon as they had left him to carry his message they burst out laughing. It was such a joke!

And they giggled as they delivered this message to each of the little forest and meadow people:

"Peter Rabbit's changed his name.
In the future without fail
You must call him, if you please,
Mr. Peter Cottontail."

While they were doing this, Peter was back in the Old Briar-patch practicing new airs and trying to look very high and mighty and important, as became one with such a fine-sounding name as Peter Cottontail.

The Adventures of Pinocchio

C. COLLODI

PINOCCHIO'S NOSE GROWS LONGER [1]

As soon as the three doctors had left the room, the Fairy went to Pinocchio's bed and, touching him on the forehead, noticed that he was burning with fever.

She took a glass of water, put a white powder into it, and, handing it to the Marionette, said lovingly to him:

"Drink this, and in a few days you'll be up and well."

Pinocchio looked at the glass, made a wry face, and asked in a whining voice: "Is it sweet or bitter?"

"It is bitter, but it is good for you."

"If it is bitter, I don't want it."

"Drink it!"

"I don't like anything bitter."

"Drink it and I'll give you a lump of sugar to take the bitter taste from your mouth."

"Where's the sugar?"

"Here it is," said the Fairy, taking a lump from a golden sugar bowl.

"I want the sugar first, then I'll drink the bitter water."

"Do you promise?"

"Yes."

The Fairy gave him the sugar and Pinocchio, after chewing and swallowing it in a twinkling, said, smacking his lips:

"If only sugar were medicine! I should take it every day."

"Now keep your promise and drink these few drops of water. They'll be good for you."

Pinocchio took the glass in both hands and stuck his nose into it. He lifted it to his mouth and once more stuck his nose into it.

"It is too bitter, much too bitter! I can't drink it."

"How do you know, when you haven't even tasted it?"

"I can imagine it. I smell it. I want another lump of sugar, then I'll drink it."

The Fairy, with all the patience of a good mother, gave him more sugar and again handed him the glass.

"I can't drink it like that," the Marionette said, making more wry faces.

"Why?"

"Because that feather pillow on my feet bothers me."

The Fairy took away the pillow.

"It's no use. I can't drink it even now."

"What's the matter now?"

"I don't like the way that door looks. It's half open."

The Fairy closed the door.

"I won't drink it," cried Pinocchio, bursting out crying. "I won't drink this awful water. I won't. I won't! No, no, no, no!"

[1] From "The Adventures of Pinocchio," by C. Collodi, illustrated by Attilio Mussino

"My boy, you'll be sorry."

"I don't care."

"You are very sick."

"I don't care."

"In a few hours the fever will take you far away to another world."

"I don't care."

"Aren't you afraid of death?"

"Not a bit. I'd rather die than drink that awful medicine."

At that moment, the door of the room flew open and in came four Rabbits as black as ink, carrying a small black coffin on their shoulders.

"What do you want from me?" asked Pinocchio.

"We have come for you," said the largest Rabbit.

"For me? But I'm not dead yet!"

"No, not dead yet; but you will be in a few moments since you have refused to take the medicine which would have made you well."

"Oh, Fairy, my Fairy," the Marionette cried out, "give me that glass! Quick, please! I do not want to die! No, no, not yet—not yet!"

And holding the glass with two hands, he swallowed the medicine at one gulp.

"Well," said the four Rabbits, "this time we have made the trip for nothing."

And turning on their heels, they marched solemnly out of the room, carrying their little black coffin and muttering and grumbling between their teeth.

In a twinkling, Pinocchio felt fine. With one leap he was out of bed and into his clothes.

The Fairy, seeing him run and jump around the room gay as a bird on wing, said to him:

"My medicine was good for you, after all, wasn't it?"

"Good indeed! It has given me new life."

"Why, then, did I have to beg you so hard to make you drink it?"

"I'm a boy, you see, and all boys hate medicine more than they do sickness."

"What a shame! Boys ought to know, after all, that medicine, taken in time, can save them from much pain and even from death."

"Next time I won't have to be begged so hard. I'll remember those black Rabbits with the black coffin on their shoulders and I'll take the glass and pouf!—down it will go!"

"Come here now and tell me how it came about that you found yourself in the hands of the Assassins."

"It happened that Fire Eater gave me five gold pieces to give to my Father, but on the way, I met a Fox and a Cat, who asked me, 'Do you want the five pieces to become two thousand?' And I said, 'Yes.' And they said, 'Come with us to the Field of Wonders.' And I said, 'Let's go.' Then they said, 'Let us stop at the Inn of the Red Lobster for dinner and after midnight we'll set out again.' We ate and went to sleep. When I awoke they were gone and I started out in the darkness all alone. On the road I met two Assassins dressed in black coal sacks, who said to me, 'Your money or your life!' and I said, 'I haven't any money'; for, you see, I had put the money under my tongue. One of them tried to put his hand in my mouth and I bit it off and spat it out; but it wasn't a

hand, it was a cat's paw. And they ran after me and I ran and ran, till at last they caught me and tied my neck with a rope and hanged me to a tree, saying, 'Tomorrow we'll come back for you and you'll be dead and your mouth will be open, and then we'll take the gold pieces that you have hidden under your tongue.'"

"Where are the gold pieces now?" the Fairy asked.

"I lost them," answered Pinocchio, but he told a lie, for he had them in his pocket.

As he spoke, his nose, long though it was, became at least two inches longer.

"And where did you lose them?"

"In the wood near by."

At this second lie, his nose grew a few more inches.

"If you lost them in the near-by wood," said the Fairy, "we'll look for them and find them, for everything that is lost there is always found."

"Ah, now I remember," replied the Marionette, becoming more and more confused. "I did not lose the gold pieces, but I swallowed them when I drank the medicine."

At this third lie, his nose became longer than ever, so long that he could not even turn around. If he turned to the right, he knocked it against the bed or into the windowpanes; if he turned to the left, he struck the walls or the door; if he raised it a bit, he almost put the Fairy's eyes out.

The Fairy sat looking at him and laughing.

"Why do you laugh?" the Marionette asked her, worried now at the sight of his growing nose.

"I am laughing at your lies."

"How do you know I am lying?"

"Lies, my boy, are known in a moment. There are two kinds of lies, lies with short legs and lies with long noses. Yours, just now, happen to have long noses."

Pinocchio, not knowing where to hide his shame, tried to escape from the room, but his nose had become so long that he could not get it out of the door.

Crying as if his heart would break, the Marionette mourned for hours over the length of his nose. No matter how he tried, it would not go through the door. The Fairy showed no pity toward him, as she was trying to teach him a good lesson, so that he would stop telling lies, the worst habit any boy may acquire. But when she saw him, pale with fright and with his eyes half out of his head from terror, she began to feel sorry for him and clapped her hands together. A thousand woodpeckers flew in through the window and settled themselves on Pinocchio's nose. They pecked and pecked so hard at that enormous nose that in a few moments, it was the same size as before.

"How good you are, my Fairy," said Pinocchio, drying his eyes, "and how much I love you!"

"I love you, too," answered the Fairy, "and if you wish to stay with me, you may be my little brother and I'll be your good little sister."

Copper-toed Boots

MARGUERITE DE ANGELI

FUN WITH THE CALF[1]

Shad slammed the kitchen door and threw down the pan in which he had carried the potato parings for the chickens. Then he set the pail of drinking water on the shelf with a thud. He was still *mad*. Miss McKinnon had kept him an hour after school, and made him do sum after sum. Ma called to him from the other room, where she was setting the table for supper.

"Wash good, now, and don't wipe all the dirt on the towel!" she said. "Cousin Lija's here. He's just stepped over to say 'Hello' to Miz Scott."

"Yes, Ma," said Shad putting the tin basin in the wooden sink, and beginning to pump. Pa had just had the cistern rain water pumped in that spring. Shad thought how much carrying of water it saved. He could smell the delicious odor of the potatoes, and hear their gentle *sissing* in the iron pan.

Shad dabbled his hands in the water round and round. He was wishing he knew some way to make the teacher feel like he did. He could hear the scratch of the slate pencil yet! Shad didn't like examples. And the slate pencil set his teeth on edge. Uhh! He swished the water around the basin.

"Are you using soap?" Ma called again. "I don't hear any squish of soap suds!"

"Yes, Ma," Shad answered as he reached for the soap. He was just going to dry his hands on the roller towel when Ma called again, and came to the kitchen door.

"Tuck in your shirt, and wash your face, too. Mind! No streaks down the sides!" Ma went to the stove to turn over the browning potatoes, and to lift the lid where

dandelion greens were boiling with salt pork.

Shad buried his face in a handful of soap suds. He even washed back of his ears. He thought he might as well, then Ma would let him alone. Will came in the back door with an armful of wood, which he threw down with a clatter into the wood box by the stove.

"You didn't give those little biddies any water! I had to do it," he said to Shad.

Will was Shad's older brother. Not much older, only two years, but enough so that Will thought it was a great deal. He brushed the wood chips from his clothes, and went to wash. Shad was drying his hands on the towel that hung back of the door, when Cousin Lija came in. He made believe he didn't know that Shad was behind the door, and pushed it back as far as it would go, squeezing Shad to the wall.

"Seems as if this door won't open like it should," he said, then suddenly let go so that Shad sat down, plump! on the floor. They all laughed. There was always nonsense when Cousin Lija came. He never sent any word that he was coming, but just happened in, sure of a welcome. He was always shabby, but shining clean. Shad thought his cheeks looked like those blush apples Ma used for apple sauce. He was full of fun, and Ma said he was a saint. Shad didn't know what a saint was, but he knew he did love to have Cousin Lija come.

Then Pa came in.

"Hello! Well, well, when did you get here?" he said to Cousin Lija.

"You're just in time!" said Ma. "Every-

[1] From "Copper-toed Boots," by Marguerite de Angeli, illustrations from drawings by Marguerite de Angeli

312

thing is ready for supper." She stooped down to lift a rhubarb pie from the oven, and began to dish up the food.

"I guess there's plenty of room," she said. "I didn't put another leaf in the table. It's more cozy this way."

"Oh, plenty of room, plenty of room," said Cousin Lija. "Now, I remember"— he winked at Pa, and Shad knew there was a story coming—"how we used to have so much company we had to take turns sitting down to table, and Paw used to get 'em to sleep one by one, and then stand 'em up in the corner." They all laughed again.

When they were nearly through eating, Pa, who was the leader of the town's singing society, said, "One of you boys will have to go out to Mr. Tyler's after supper, and tell him to come to the singing practice tonight, instead of tomorrow night.

He's bass solo, and we need him. Concert's next week."

"I can't do it, Pa. I've got a whole lot of jography to write, and then my examples to do," said Will.

"I'll go, I'll go!" said Shad. It was fun to go somewhere after supper. Pa never let the boys play out after supper, except a little while in the summer.

"Put your jacket on," said Ma. "It's chilly after dark. And hurry back. Hear?"

"Yes, Ma," said Shad, scooting out before she had a chance to tell him to go alone. Ma said he always got into mischief when Ash Tomlinson went with him on an errand. Shad was around the corner and whistling for Ash in less time than it takes to tell about it. Ash came out with a piece of cake in his hand.

"Want to go with me out to Josh Tyler's? Pa sent me on an errand."

They heard the birds and saw the tulips in bloom

"Wait till I ask Josie. Ma's not home," said Ash, cramming the rest of the cake in his mouth.

He came out in a moment, and they set off toward Main Street. It was just after sunset, and the streets were empty. Birds were making sleepy sounds as they settled for the night and Tuttle's cow was lowing in the pasture. The cool green of the sky was reflected in little pools on the ruts of the road, left by the rain of the morning. It made the houses a pure white against the dark of trees and bushes. The trees cast no shadow now because the sun was gone, and the new leaves glistened with moisture. Tulips were in bloom, and they could smell the lilies of the valley in Whites' garden as they passed.

The Whites' was one of the oldest houses in town. Shad had heard Pa tell about the Whites and the Harts coming to Michigan about forty years before, when there was nothing there but a wilderness, and Michigan wasn't even a state. It was good farming land, and there was plenty of wood for the cutting. They had come in a covered wagon, and had slept the first night under an oak that still stood in the meadow down by the lumber yard. Then people had come from Connecticut, and from Massachusetts, from New York State, and from Canada, to settle in this town that was now the county seat, Lapeer.

Pa had come from England by way of Canada, where he had married Ma. They had come to this new little town on the Flint River where Pa had set up his blacksmith shop, just off Neppessing Street. Of course every one except the Indians pronounced it "Nipsing." There was plenty of work for a smith, with people coming in from all around the country, but not much money. Often Pa had to take things in trade for his work, as did every one else. It was part of living in a new place, and fun, too, Shad thought.

As he and Ash stepped off the sidewalk, where it ended out beyond the school, Shad felt the water seep through his shoes where the soles were thin. He looked down at Ash's feet.

"Got my feet wet," he said. "Wish't I had a pair of boots like yours."

Ash looked proudly down at his sturdy leather boots. They had copper toes, and came nearly to his knees. He swung his shoulders, and took longer strides. Ash was a little older than Shad, and stocky and red-headed. Shad was as tall, though he was slender. Shad could step out as well as Ash or better, and soon they had reached Tyler's house, delivered their message, and were on their way back, taking the long way round the farm this time. As they reached Mr. Tyler's pasture lot, they heard a calf bawling, and found him halfway over the stump fence, caught in the twisted roots.

Ash climbed up on one side of him, and Shad on the other, and pulled the frightened calf out of the tangle. Then Ash said, "We ought to have some fun with him. What shall we do? Shall we tie him in the school yard? That would be fun!"

"Oh! *I* know what we'll do with him!" said Shad. "Tie him here for now, then tonight, when everybody's asleep, we'll come back and get him, and just you wait till that Miss McKinnon sees what fun it is to keep *me* after school to do examples! We'll show her!" Shad made the knot fast to the fence, with the calf standing outside the pasture.

It was nearly dark, and on a lonely road, so Shad was sure no one would find him. As they went along home, he and Ash whispered and giggled at Shad's plan. Lights glowed from the windows as they passed. The young frogs were trilling, and, as Shad left Ash and turned in the walk, Pa was just leaving for singing society.

"I'll be late, Maggie," he said. "So don't wait up." Ma was mending under the lamp, and Will sat scratching his head as if that would solve his arithmetic problem.

"Where's Cousin Lija?" asked Shad.

"He's gone," said Ma. "Caleb Hicks had

to drive over to Columbiaville, and Lija thought he might as well go along. He was going that way. Now you and Will get to bed." Ma bit off the thread, and folded up the shirt she was mending.

"Look, Ma," said Shad, "I've got a hole right through my shoe, and it's nearly through the other one, too. I got my feet wet."

"'Sakes alive!" said Ma. "Through *again?* Well, I guess you'll have to wear your Sunday ones till these are mended. You put them on in the morning. Then, if they give out, you'll have to go barefoot. Come now, to bed!"

"Aw, Ma! Can't I have a pair of copper-toed boots? Ash has 'em. Please, Ma!"

Ma took up the lamp, and led the way. "Pa can't get you any boots now. He's got all he can do with payments on the house and everything. Will, put away your book and slate, and come along."

They had their usual argument about who was taking up the most room in the bed, but Will was finally asleep. Shad lay waiting; and hoping that Ma would soon go to bed and to sleep, too.

His leg was cramped. Then his elbow itched, and he wanted to turn over, but was afraid Will would wake, so he lay quiet. Shad lay quiet so long that *he* almost went to sleep, too. Then he heard Ma get up from her chair, and walk into the bedroom. He heard the rustling of her petticoats as she undressed. He heard her yawn, and the creaking of the spring as she crept into bed. Then all was still. It wasn't much longer before he heard a low whistle. He raised up and listened. Yes, there it was again. He slipped out of bed, and tiptoed to the window. There was Ash standing below in the moonlight.

Shad drew on his trousers and socks, picked up his shoes and jacket, and went softly down the stair well. The last step creaked, and Shad stood still for a moment to see if Ma had wakened, but he could hear her slow, quiet breathing, and knew she was asleep. He went to the side door,

and slid back the bolt. He turned the knob carefully, closing the door with scarcely a sound. Two more steps took him off the porch and onto the grass, where Ash was waiting.

Shad put on his shoes and jacket, then the two boys went out into the road so their footsteps wouldn't sound on the board sidewalk. They did not speak, for fear of being heard, but went down the road and away from the house as quickly as possible. Shad knew he must either get back before Pa got home, or wait long enough to be sure that he was in bed and asleep.

They talked in excited whispers, and put their hands over their mouths when they had to laugh at the fun they were going to have. Many of the houses were dark, as most people went early to bed, but there was a light in the Tavern, so they kept still until they turned the corner at the school.

"I only hope that old calf is still there," said Shad then. "Let's run. Nobody will hear us now."

He was off down the muddy road, with Ash keeping up as best he could. The calf was still there, and, when they untied him, wanted to *stay* there. He didn't want to go at all, but they pushed him and pulled him, and got him along some way. Back they went to the school house, and up the walk. Shad had to get behind and push to get him up the steps. The door wasn't locked, but, when they finally got the balky calf inside, he wouldn't go any further. They had to almost carry him up to the second floor. There they stopped to rest. They sat on the floor, and laughed till their sides ached to think how funny it would

be when the calf was discovered in the morning. The calf began to bawl again in such strange surroundings, so Shad got up, and tried to lead him up the stairs to the belfry. He balked. Ash pushed from behind, and, by much tugging and pulling, they got the poor frightened animal to the top. There they left him, shut the door, and ran down through the school, and out onto the road. Shad turned.

"Hark!" he said. "Hear him bawl! But nobody else can hear him; the houses are too far away. Now, after Joe gets through ringing the bell in the morning, you slip up there, and tie his tail to the bell rope."

"*Me!*" said Ash. "Not *much!* I have enough trouble with Teacher as it is. This is *your* idea. You can do the tying. But I'd just like to see her face when the fun begins! Ho! Ho! Ho!"

Ash laughed so loud, Shad said, "Shhhh! You'll have the whole town out to see what's going on. Well, I suppose I'll have to do the tying, then, but you've got to stand by me. You're in this, too!"

"Oh, you can slip into your seat just as *easy!*" said Ash. "Teacher will never think it's you! She might think *I* did it, but I can say I didn't *tie* the calf. Of course, I don't have to tell her what I did do. She might think Bill Noggles did it. He's always doing something."

Shad thought it really did sound easy, and they stopped again to laugh, and slap their knees to think of a *calf* in the school belfry!

"We'd better hurry," said Shad. "I don't want to run into Pa. I guess he'll be kinda late getting home from the singing practice, 'cause this is the last one before the concert, but I guess we've been a pretty long time." Ash thought *his* father and mother might be just coming home, too, so they stopped their fooling, and went along quickly.

They met no one. The house was dark and still as Shad went in. He listened as he tiptoed past the bedroom door, but couldn't hear Pa. He was in time and safe!

The Story of Babar

JEAN DE BRUNHOFF

Illustrations from drawings by Jean de Brunhoff

In the great forest a little elephant is born. His name is Babar.

His mother loves him very much. She rocks him to sleep with her trunk while singing softly to him. Babar grows bigger. He plays with the other little elephants. He is a good little elephant.

One day Babar is riding happily on his mother's back. A wicked hunter, hiding behind some bushes, shoots at them. The hunter runs up to catch poor Babar. Babar runs away because he is afraid of the hunter.

After several days, he comes to a town.

He hardly knows what to make of it, because this is the first time that he has seen so many houses.

So many things are new to Babar! He is especially interested in two very well dressed gentlemen he notices on the street.

He says to himself: "I would like to have some fine clothes, too! I wonder how I can get them?"

Luckily, a very rich Old Lady who has always been fond of little elephants understands right away that he is longing for a fine suit. As she likes to make people happy, she gives him her purse.

Babar says to her politely: "Thank you, Madam."

Without wasting any time, Babar goes into a big store. He enters the elevator. It is great fun to ride up and down in this funny box. He rides all the way up ten times and all the way down ten times. He does not want to stop, but the elevator boy finally says to him: "This is not a toy, Mr. Elephant. You must get out and do your shopping. Look, here comes the floor-walker."

Babar then buys himself a shirt with a collar and tie, a suit of a becoming shade of green, then a handsome derby hat, and also shoes with spats.

Well satisfied with his purchases, and feeling very elegant indeed, Babar now goes to the photographer to have his picture taken.

Babar dines with his friend, the Old Lady. She thinks he looks very smart in his new clothes.

After dinner, because he is tired, he goes to bed and falls asleep very quickly.

Babar now lives at the Old Lady's house. In the mornings, he does setting-up exercises with her, and then he takes his bath.

He goes out for an automobile ride every day. The Old Lady has given him the car. She gives him whatever he wants.

A learned professor gives him lessons. Babar pays attention and does well in his work. He is a good pupil and makes rapid progress.

In the evening, after dinner, he tells the Old Lady's friends all about his life in the great forest.

However, Babar is not quite happy, for he misses playing in the great forest with his little cousins and his friends, the monkeys.

He often stands at the window, thinking sadly of his childhood, and cries when he remembers his mother.

Two years pass. One day, while out walking, he sees two little elephants coming toward him.

"Why," he says in astonishment to the Old Lady, "it's Arthur and Celeste, my little cousins!"

Babar kisses them affectionately and hurries off with them to buy them some fine clothes.

Meanwhile, in the forest, the elephants are calling, and hunting high and low for Arthur and Celeste, and their mothers are very worried. Fortunately, in flying over the town, an old marabou bird has seen them, and comes back quickly to tell the news.

The mothers of Arthur and Celeste come to the town to fetch them. They are very happy to have Arthur and Celeste back, but they scold them just the same, because they ran away.

Babar makes up his mind to go back with Arthur and Celeste and their mothers to see the great forest again.

They are all ready to start. Babar kisses the Old Lady good-by. He promises to come back some day. He will never forget her.

Alas, this very day, the King of the elephants has eaten a bad mushroom, and he becomes so ill that he dies.

After the funeral the three oldest elephants hold a meeting to choose a new King.

Just then they hear a noise. They turn around. Guess what they see! Babar arriving in his car, and all the elephants running and shouting.

"Here they are! Here they are!" they cry.

"Hello, Babar! Hello, Arthur! Hello, Celeste!"

"What beautiful clothes! What a beautiful car!"

Then Cornelius, the oldest of all the elephants, speaks. "My good friends," he says, "since Babar has just returned from the big city and has learned so much, living among men, let us crown him King." All the other elephants agree, and eagerly they await Babar's reply.

"I want to thank you, one and all," says

Babar. "Celeste and I are going to be married, and if I become your King—she will be your Queen."

"Long live Queen Celeste! Long live King Babar!" cry all the elephants. And thus it is that Babar becomes King.

"You have good ideas," Babar says to Cornelius. "I will therefore make you a general, and when I get my crown, I will give you my hat. In a week I shall marry Celeste. We will then have a splendid party in honor of our marriage and our coronation."

Then, turning to the birds, Babar asks them to go and invite all the animals to the party.

The wedding guests begin to arrive for the festivities.

There is a celebration in the forest. After the wedding and coronation, everyone dances merrily.

At last the festivities are over. King Babar and Queen Celeste are very happy. The guests have gone home, happy, too, though tired from too much dancing. They will long remember this great celebration.

And now King Babar and Queen Celeste, both eager for further adventures, set out on their honeymoon in a gorgeous yellow balloon.

New World for Nellie

ROWLAND EMETT

Illustration from a drawing by Rowland Emett

Tucked away in a forgotten corner of England, where the main lines never go, was a railroad that had seen better days. There was only one rusty old engine called Nellie, and two coaches. Once a day and twice a week it steamed down the Cloud Cuckoo Valley to the sea, carrying hens and pigs on Wednesday-market-day, and taking people to see the paddle boats on Saturday afternoon. Albert Funnel, the driver, and Frederick Firedoor, the guard-fireman-and-porter, were always getting into trouble with the station master because they *would* keep stopping the train to pick wild flowers for Nellie's window box.

They always seemed to arrive at the grade crossing when someone else had got there first, and what with one thing and another the railroad was in a pretty fine muddle, and there was quite a lot of grumbling up and down the line.

Albert and Frederick felt quite upset because nobody appreciated them, and one evening they made up their minds to leave home.

When the Night Mail stopped for his usual chat and a smoke, he told them of all sorts of exciting places and gave them a wonderful idea. So they collected four signals, some grey goose feathers, and an old pair of Albert's overalls and set to work.

When they had finished, they were astonished to find they had a beautiful flying machine, so they packed their bag, took some clean collars and their old brown teapot, and left Buttergoose Hill and Duckwallow Marsh far behind, to the great surprise of everybody at Starfish Point.

They went past the lightship on Dogfish Ledge, and on toward the sinking sun until there was nothing to see but sea and sky and seagulls. One night when they had only three clean collars and two spoonfuls of tea left, they found themselves above a strange and wonderful city full of buildings which seemed to reach the sky. One or two of them actually *scraped*. Through a break in the clouds below them, Albert was overjoyed to see some rails and, by letting out some steam a bit at a time and taking a tuck in the sail, he managed to bring Nellie down onto them. They soon discovered they were on a breathtaking railway indeed for it went all round the rooftops and chimney pots and never came near the ground at all!

They were glad to get off at the very first opportunity, and seeing an open skylight they went in and found themselves on a great marble staircase. Frederick was so jumpy he blew the whistle, and immediately a door flew open and they were surrounded by the Philharmonic-symphonic Orchestra and their leader, Signor Piccolino Tromboli. He was in a muddle with his music, and THAT, he said, was the very note he had been searching for all day. He implored them to stay and help with his concert and promised them a private box, and coffee and ice cream in the intermission. Albert and Frederick agreed, and unscrewed all the noisy bits of Nellie and shared them out among the musicians. The people were so charmed they demanded an encore, and Signor Tromboli played *The Runaway Train.*

After the concert they all put Nellie together again, and Signor Tromboli presented her with a solid silver flute and kept her old brass whistle as a keepsake. The musicians reluctantly said good-bye and told them how to get to the proper railroad tracks. When they got there, Albert took out his compass to find some tracks going south, which had always been his favorite direction. They took Nellie down to the tracks, but were most upset to find she wouldn't fit and while they were wondering whatever to do they were gently scooped up by the cowcatcher of the El-mer K. Pheffenfeifer, which was just pull-ing out for the Deep South. They made themselves comfortable and settled down quite happily, lulled by the clanging of the great brass bell, which reminded them of the bell buoy on Dogfish Ledge.

When they came to the Deep South, Al-bert and Frederick immediately fell in love with the paddle boats because they all had *two* long funnels each. The captain of one was sitting on a log by himself looking miserable, and he told them that evening there was going to be a Grand Torchlight Race for 10,000 dollars. He had made up his mind to win, but his paddle boat had mysteriously sunk in the night. Albert and Frederick put their heads together and they all went up a little secret bayou and spent the afternoon with hammers and string.

That evening a wonderful new stern-wheeler left all the others absolutely *no-where* and carried off the prize of 10,000 silver dollars!

The next morning, after sharing the prize with Captain Ezra, they went back to the railroad and suddenly thought out an ex-cellent way to make Nellie fit on the tracks.

One afternoon, going through a rocky kind of country, they saw a nasty-looking man tying the Sheriff's beautiful daughter Poppy to the rails, right in the path of the Westbound Limited, which was thunder-ing down the track! Losing no time, they rushed to the rescue, stopping the train, and smothering the villain with damp steam, soot and cinders. A crowd of angry script-writers and directors rushed up, and said Nellie had entirely spoiled the movie they were making and *ruined* their card-board engine, which had taken them two weeks to make! They chased Nellie over the Kittybreath Creek through the Cats-paw Hills, right into the heart of the Smoky Patch Mountains, where there had been a small Gold Rush.

The head miner, Abner Nugget, told Al-bert that everybody was *quite* worn out with working the mines, and worse still, when Saturday nights came round, they were all too tired to have any dancing and fun. Nellie soon altered things, and with Frederick playing *Clementine* and *She'll Be Comin' Round the Mountain* on the silver flute, the miners were able to have Saturday-night fun all day long.

They stayed until everybody was rich and happy, and when they said good-bye all the miners followed them down to the tracks where the Fast Through Freight to Codfish Cape was waiting for some more steam. Abner gave them a small presenta-tion sack of gold dust, made a farewell speech, and then suddenly decided to go with them. The Brakeman agreed to give them all a lift if they would help with the brakes, and Nellie had a wonderful time steaming up and down the catwalk of the Fast Through Freight, adjusting the brake-wheels.

When the train stopped at Codfish Cape, they felt quite homesick because the light-house and fishing nets made them think of Starfish Point, and they suddenly wished they were back home at Duckwallow Marsh. They spoke to some divers who were mending a telegraph cable in the bay, and they said it went to England, and there *couldn't* be a quicker way home, now, could there? And in exchange for the sack of gold dust, the Head Diver fitted them out for the journey. With a warning to look out for swordfish, and to be *sure* and take the left-hand fork at Devilfish Deeps, they set out for home. . . .

From Buttergoose Hill to Duckwallow Marsh things were in a dreadful state. No-body had been able to go to market, and the hens and pigs were all over the place, when one afternoon William Flatfish saw a funnel breaking the quiet surface of Starfish Bay. The news spread like wildfire, and everybody came to welcome Nellie home. They vowed they would never grumble again, and the station master was so pleased, he promised to have Nellie painted up in everybody's favorite colors immediately. Frederick and Albert asked Abner Nugget to live with them forever, if only he would start a small gold mine at the bottom of the garden, so that there would always be money on hand for improvements and brass-polish.

So now, once a day and twice a week, there is great excitement through the Cloud Cuckoo Valley and along Duckwallow Marsh, and when they hear that silver whistle blow, everybody stops to gaze with admiration at the smartest train in the whole country, and wave to Nellie, who went adventuring in the New World and came home to fame and fortune.

The Wind in the Willows

KENNETH GRAHAME

MR. TOAD [1]

It was a bright morning in the early part of summer; the river had resumed its wonted banks and its accustomed pace, and a hot sun seemed to be pulling everything green and bushy and spiky up out of the earth towards him, as if by strings. The Mole and the Water Rat had been up since dawn very busy on matters connected with boats and the opening of the boating season; painting and varnishing, mending paddles, repairing cushions, hunting for missing boathooks, and so on; and were finishing breakfast in their little parlour and eagerly discussing their plans for the day, when a heavy knock sounded at the door.

"Bother!" said the Rat, all over egg. "See who it is, Mole, like a good chap, since you've finished."

The Mole went to attend the summons, and the Rat heard him utter a cry of surprise. Then he flung the parlour door open, and announced with much importance, "Mr. Badger!"

This was a wonderful thing, indeed, that the Badger should pay a formal call on them, or indeed on anybody. He generally had to be caught, if you wanted him badly, as he slipped quietly along a hedgerow of an early morning or a late evening, or else hunted up in his own house in the middle of the wood, which was a serious undertaking.

The Badger strode heavily into the room, and stood looking at the two animals with an expression full of seriousness. The Rat let his egg-spoon fall on the table-cloth, and sat open-mouthed.

"The hour has come!" said the Badger at last with great solemnity.

"What hour?" asked the Rat uneasily, glancing at the clock on the mantelpiece.

"*Whose* hour, you should rather say," replied the Badger. "Why, Toad's hour! The hour of Toad! I said I would take him in hand as soon as the winter was well over, and I'm going to take him in hand to-day!"

"Toad's hour, of course!" cried the Mole delightedly. "Hooray! I remember now! *We'll* teach him to be a sensible Toad!"

"This very morning," continued the Badger, taking an arm-chair, "as I learnt last night from a trustworthy source, another new and exceptionally powerful motor-car will arrive at Toad Hall on approval or return. At this very moment, perhaps, Toad is busy arraying himself in those singularly hideous habiliments so dear to him, which transform him from a (comparatively) good-looking Toad into an Object which throws any decent-minded animal that comes across it into a violent fit. We must be up and doing, ere it is too late. You two animals will accompany me instantly to Toad Hall, and the work of rescue shall be accomplished."

"Right you are!" cried the Rat, starting up. "We'll rescue the poor unhappy animal! We'll convert him! He'll be the most converted Toad that ever was before we've done with him!"

They set off up the road on their mis-

[1] From "The Wind in the Willows," by Kenneth Grahame, illustrated by Ernest H. Shepard

sion of mercy, Badger leading the way. Animals when in company walk in a proper and sensible manner, in single file, instead of sprawling all across the road and being of no use or support to each other in case of sudden trouble or danger.

They reached the carriage-drive of Toad Hall to find, as the Badger had anticipated, a shiny new motor-car, of great size, painted a bright red (Toad's favourite colour), standing in front of the house. As they neared the door it was flung open, and Mr. Toad, arrayed in goggles, cap, gaiters, and enormous overcoat, came swaggering down the steps, drawing on his gauntleted gloves.

"Hullo! come on, you fellows!" he cried cheerfully on catching sight of them. "You're just in time to come with me for a jolly—to come for a jolly—for a—er—jolly—"

His hearty accents faltered and fell away as he noticed the stern unbending look on the countenances of his silent friends, and his invitation remained unfinished.

The Badger strode up the steps. "Take him inside," he said sternly to his companions. Then, as Toad was hustled through the door, struggling and protesting, he turned to the chauffeur in charge of the new motor-car.

"I'm afraid you won't be wanted to-day," he said. "Mr. Toad has changed his mind. He will not require the car. Please understand that this is final. You needn't wait." Then he followed the others inside and shut the door.

"Now, then!" he said to the Toad, when the four of them stood together in the hall, "first of all, take those ridiculous things off!"

"Shan't!" replied Toad, with great spirit. "What is the meaning of this gross outrage? I demand an instant explanation."

"Take them off him, then, you two," ordered the Badger briefly.

They had to lay Toad out on the floor, kicking and calling all sorts of names, before they could get to work properly. Then

the Rat sat on him, and the Mole got his motor-clothes off him bit by bit, and they stood him up on his legs again. A good deal of his blustering spirit seemed to have evaporated with the removal of his fine panoply. Now that he was merely Toad, and no longer the Terror of the Highway, he giggled feebly and looked from one to the other appealingly, seeming quite to understand the situation.

"You knew it must come to this, sooner or later, Toad," the Badger explained severely. "You've disregarded all the warnings we've given you, you've gone on squandering the money your father left you, and you're getting us animals a bad name in the district by your furious driving and your smashes and your rows with the police. Independence is all very well, but we animals never allow our friends to make fools of themselves beyond a certain limit; and that limit you've reached. Now, you're a good fellow in many respects, and I don't want to be too hard on you. I'll make one more effort to bring you to reason. You will come with me into the smoking-room, and there you will hear some facts about yourself; and we'll see whether you come out of that room the same Toad that you went in."

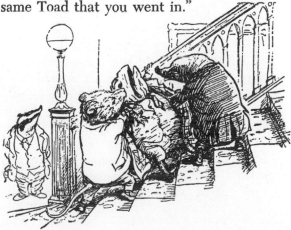

He took Toad firmly by the arm, led him into the smoking-room, and closed the door behind them.

"*That's* no good!" said the Rat contemptuously. "*Talking* to Toad'll never cure him. He'll *say* anything."

They made themselves comfortable in arm-chairs and waited patiently. Through the closed door they could just hear the long continuous drone of the Badger's voice, rising and falling in waves of oratory; and presently they noticed that the sermon began to be punctuated at intervals by long-drawn sobs, evidently proceeding from the bosom of Toad, who was a soft-hearted and affectionate fellow, very easily converted—for the time being—to any point of view.

After some three-quarters of an hour the door opened, and the Badger reappeared, solemnly leading by the paw a very limp and dejected Toad. His skin hung baggily about him, his legs wobbled, and his cheeks were furrowed by the tears so plentifully called forth by the Badger's moving discourse.

"Sit down there, Toad," said the Badger kindly, pointing to a chair. "My friends," he went on, "I am pleased to inform you that Toad has at last seen the error of his ways. He is truly sorry for his misguided conduct in the past, and he has undertaken to give up motor-cars entirely and for ever. I have his solemn promise to that effect."

"That is very good news," said the Mole gravely.

"Very good news indeed," observed the Rat dubiously, "if only—*if* only—"

He was looking very hard at Toad as he said this, and could not help thinking he perceived something vaguely resembling a twinkle in that animal's still sorrowful eye.

"There's only one thing more to be done," continued the gratified Badger. "Toad, I want you solemnly to repeat, before your friends here, what you fully admitted to me in the smoking-room just now. First, you are sorry for what you've done, and you see the folly of it all?"

There was a long, long pause. Toad looked desperately this way and that, while the other animals waited in grave silence. At last he spoke.

"No!" he said a little sullenly, but stoutly; "I'm *not* sorry. And it wasn't folly at all! It was simply glorious!"

"What?" cried the Badger, greatly scandalized. "You backsliding animal, didn't you tell me just now, in there—"

"O, yes, yes, in *there*," said Toad impatiently. "I'd have said anything in *there*. You're so eloquent, dear Badger, and so moving, and so convincing, and put all your points so frightfully well—you can do what you like with me in *there*, and you know it. But I've been searching my mind since, and going over things in it, and I find that I'm not a bit sorry or repentant really, so it's no earthly good saying I am; now, is it?"

"Then you don't promise," said the Badger, "never to touch a motor-car again?"

"Certainly not!" replied Toad emphatically. "On the contrary, I faithfully promise that the very first motor-car I see, poop-poop! off I go in it!"

"Told you so, didn't I?" observed the Rat to the Mole.

"Very well, then," said the Badger firmly, rising to his feet. "Since you won't yield to persuasion, we'll try what force can do. I feared it would come to this all along. You've often asked us three to come and stay with you, Toad, in this handsome house of yours; well, now we're going to. When we've converted you to a proper point of view we may quit, but not before. Take him upstairs, you two, and lock him up in his bedroom, while we arrange matters between ourselves."

"It's for your own good, Toady, you know," said the Rat kindly, as Toad, kicking and struggling, was hauled up the stairs by his two faithful friends. "Think what fun we shall all have together, just as we used to, when you've quite got over this—this painful attack of yours!"

"We'll take great care of everything for you till you're well, Toad," said the Mole; "and we'll see your money isn't wasted, as it has been."

"No more of those regrettable incidents with the police, Toad," said the Rat, as they thrust him into his bedroom.

"And no more weeks in hospital, being ordered about by female nurses, Toad," added the Mole, turning the key on him.

They descended the stair, Toad shouting abuse at them through the keyhole; and the three friends then met in conference on the situation.

"It's going to be a tedious business," said the Badger, sighing. "I've never seen Toad so determined. However, we will see it out. He must never be left an instant unguarded. We shall have to take it in turns to be with him, till the poison has worked itself out of his system."

They arranged watches accordingly. Each animal took it in turns to sleep in Toad's room at night, and they divided the day up between them. At first Toad was undoubtedly very trying to his careful guardians. When his violent paroxysms possessed him he would arrange bedroom chairs in rude resemblance of a motor-car and would crouch on the foremost of them, bent forward and staring fixedly ahead, making uncouth and ghastly noises, till the climax was reached, when, turning a com-

plete somersault, he would lie prostrate amidst the ruins of the chairs, apparently completely satisfied for the moment. As time passed, however, these painful seizures grew gradually less frequent, and his friends strove to divert his mind into fresh channels. But his interest in other matters did not seem to revive, and he grew apparently languid and depressed.

One fine morning the Rat, whose turn it was to go on duty, went upstairs to relieve Badger, whom he found fidgeting to be off and stretch his legs in a long ramble round his wood and down his earths and burrows. "Toad's still in bed," he told the Rat, outside the door. "Can't get much out of him, except, 'O, leave him alone, he wants nothing, perhaps he'll be better presently, it may pass off in time, don't be unduly anxious,' and so on. Now, you look out, Rat! When Toad's quiet and submissive, and playing at being the hero of a Sunday-school prize, then he's at his artfullest. There's sure to be something up. I know him. Well, now I must be off."

"How are you to-day, old chap?" inquired the Rat cheerfully, as he approached Toad's bedside.

He had to wait some minutes for an answer. At last a feeble voice replied, "Thank you so much, dear Ratty! So good of you to inquire! But first tell me how you are yourself, and the excellent Mole?"

"O, *we're* all right," replied the Rat. "Mole," he added incautiously, "is going out for a run round with Badger. They'll be out till luncheon-time, so you and I will spend a pleasant morning together, and I'll do my best to amuse you. Now jump up, there's a good fellow, and don't lie moping there on a fine morning like this!"

"Dear, kind Rat," murmured Toad, "how little you realise my condition, and how very far I am from 'jumping up' now—if ever! But do not trouble about me. I hate being a burden to my friends, and I do not expect to be one much longer. Indeed, I almost hope not."

"Well, I hope not, too," said the Rat

heartily. "You've been a fine bother to us all this time, and I'm glad to hear it's going to stop. And in weather like this, and the boating season just beginning! It's too bad of you, Toad! It isn't the trouble we mind, but you're making us miss such an awful lot."

"I'm afraid it *is* the trouble you mind, though," replied the Toad languidly. "I can quite understand it. It's natural enough. You're tired of bothering about me. I mustn't ask you to do anything further. I'm a nuisance, I know."

"You are, indeed," said the Rat. "But I tell you, I'd take any trouble on earth for you, if only you'd be a sensible animal."

"If I thought that, Ratty," murmured Toad, more feebly than ever, "then I would beg you—for the last time, probably—to step round to the village as quickly as possible—even now it may be too late—and fetch the doctor. But don't you bother. It's only a trouble, and perhaps we may as well let things take their course."

"Why, what do you want a doctor for?" inquired the Rat, coming closer and examining him. He certainly lay very still and flat, and his voice was weaker and his manner much changed.

"Surely you have noticed of late—" murmured Toad. "But no—why should you? Noticing things is only a trouble. To-morrow, indeed, you may be saying to yourself, 'O, if only I had noticed sooner!

If only I had done something!' But no; it's a trouble. Never mind—forget that I asked."

"Look here, old man," said the Rat, beginning to get rather alarmed, "of course I'll fetch a doctor to you, if you really think you want him. But you can hardly be bad enough for that yet. Let's talk about something else."

"I fear, dear friend," said Toad, with a sad smile, "that 'talk' can do little in a case like this—or doctors either, for that matter; still, one must grasp at the slightest straw. And, by the way—while you are about it —I *hate* to give you additional trouble, but I happen to remember that you will pass the door—would you mind at the same time asking the lawyer to step up? It would be a convenience to me, and there are moments—perhaps I should say there is *a* moment—when one must face disagreeable tasks, at whatever cost to exhausted nature!"

"A lawyer! O, he must be really bad!" the affrighted Rat said to himself, as he hurried from the room, not forgetting, however, to lock the door carefully behind him.

Outside, he stopped to consider. The other two were far away, and he had no one to consult.

"It's best to be on the safe side," he said on reflection. "I've known Toad fancy himself frightfully bad before, without the slightest reason; but I've never heard him ask for a lawyer! If there's nothing really the matter, the doctor will tell him he's an old ass, and cheer him up; and that will be something gained. I'd better humour him and go; it won't take very long." So he ran off to the village on his errand of mercy.

The Toad, who had hopped lightly out of bed as soon as he heard the key turned in the lock, watched him eagerly from the window till he disappeared down the carriage-drive. Then, laughing heartily, he dressed as quickly as possible in the smartest suit he could lay hands on at the moment, filled his pockets with cash which he took from a small drawer in the dressing-table, and next, knotting the sheets from his bed together and tying one end of the improvised rope round the central mullion of the handsome Tudor window which formed such a feature of his bedroom, he scrambled out, slid lightly to the ground, and, taking the opposite direction to the Rat, marched off light-heartedly, whistling a merry tune.

It was a gloomy luncheon for Rat when the Badger and the Mole at length returned, and he had to face them at table with his pitiful and unconvincing story. The Badger's caustic, not to say brutal, remarks may be imagined, and therefore passed over; but it was painful to the Rat that even the Mole, though he took his friend's side as far as possible, could not help saying, "You've been a bit of a duffer this time, Ratty! Toad, too, of all animals!"

"He did it awfully well," said the crestfallen Rat.

"He did *you* awfully well!" rejoined the Badger hotly. "However, talking won't mend matters. He's got clear away for the time, that's certain; and the worst of it is, he'll be so conceited with what he'll think is his cleverness that he may commit any folly. One comfort is, we're free now, and needn't waste any more of our precious time doing sentry-go. But we'd better continue to sleep at Toad Hall for a while longer. Toad may be brought back at any moment—on a stretcher, or between two policemen."

So spoke the Badger, not knowing what the future held in store, or how much water, and of how turbid a character, was to run under bridges before Toad should sit at ease again in his ancestral Hall.

Meanwhile, Toad, gay and irresponsible, was walking briskly along the high road, some miles from home. At first he had taken bypaths, and crossed many fields, and changed his course several times, in case of pursuit; but now, feeling by this time safe from recapture, and the sun smiling brightly on him, and all Nature joining

in a chorus of approval to the song of self-praise that his own heart was singing to him, he almost danced along the road in his satisfaction and conceit.

"Smart piece of work that!" he remarked to himself, chuckling. "Brain against brute force—and brain came out on the top—as it's bound to do. Poor old Ratty! My! won't he catch it when the Badger gets back! A worthy fellow, Ratty, with many good qualities, but very little intelligence and absolutely no education. I must take him in hand some day, and see if I can make something of him."

Filled full of conceited thoughts such as these he strode along, his head in the air, till he reached a little town, where the sign of "The Red Lion," swinging across the road half-way down the main street, reminded him that he had not breakfasted that day, and that he was exceedingly hungry after his long walk. He marched into the inn, ordered the best luncheon that could be provided at so short a notice, and sat down to eat it in the coffee-room.

He was about half-way through his meal when an only too familiar sound, approaching down the street, made him start and fall a-trembling all over. The poop-poop! drew nearer and nearer, the car could be heard to turn into the inn-yard and come to a stop, and Toad had to hold on to the leg of the table to conceal his overmastering emotion. Presently the party entered the coffee-room, hungry, talkative, and gay, voluble on their experiences of the morning and the merits of the chariot that had brought them along so well. Toad listened eagerly, all ears, for a time; at last he could stand it no longer. He slipped out of the room quietly, paid his bill at the bar, and as soon as he got outside sauntered round quietly to the inn-yard. "There cannot be any harm," he said to himself, "in my only just *looking* at it!"

The car stood in the middle of the yard, quite unattended, the stable-helps and other hangers-on being all at their dinner. Toad walked slowly round it, inspecting, criticizing, musing deeply.

"I wonder," he said to himself presently, "I wonder if this sort of car *starts* easily?"

Next moment, hardly knowing how it came about, he found he had hold of the handle and was turning it. As the familiar sound broke forth, the old passion seized on Toad and completely mastered him, body and soul. As if in a dream he found himself, somehow, seated in the driver's seat; as if in a dream, he pulled the lever and swung the car round the yard and out through the archway; and, as if in a dream, all sense of right and wrong, all fear of obvious consequences, seemed temporarily suspended. He increased his pace, and as

the car devoured the street and leapt forth on the high road through the open country, he was only conscious that he was Toad once more, Toad at his best and highest, Toad the terror, the traffic-queller, the Lord of the lone trail, before whom all must give way or be smitten into nothingness and everlasting night. He chanted as he flew, and the car responded with sonorous drone; the miles were eaten up under him as he sped he knew not whither, fulfilling his instincts, living his hour, reckless of what might come to him.

· · · · ·

"To my mind," observed the Chairman of the Bench of Magistrates cheerfully, "the *only* difficulty that presents itself in this otherwise very clear case is, how we can possibly make it sufficiently hot for the incorrigible rogue and hardened ruffian whom we see cowering in the dock before us. Let me see: he has been found guilty, on the clearest evidence, first, of stealing a valuable motor-car; secondly, of driving to the public danger; and, thirdly, of gross impertinence to the rural police. Mr. Clerk, will you tell us, please, what is the very stiffest penalty we can impose for each of these offences? Without, of course, giving the prisoner the benefit of any doubt, because there isn't any."

The Clerk scratched his nose with his pen. "Some people would consider," he

328

observed, "that stealing the motor-car was the worst offence; and so it is. But cheeking the police undoubtedly carries the severest penalty; and so it ought. Supposing you were to say twelve months for the theft, which is mild; and three years for the furious driving, which is lenient; and fifteen years for the cheek, which was pretty bad sort of cheek, judging by what we've heard from the witness-box, even if you only believe one-tenth part of what you heard, and I never believe more myself—those figures, if added together correctly, tot up to nineteen years—"

"First-rate!" said the Chairman.

"—So you had better make it a round twenty years and be on the safe side," concluded the Clerk.

"An excellent suggestion!" said the Chairman approvingly. "Prisoner! Pull yourself together and try and stand up straight. It's going to be twenty years for you this time. And mind, if you appear before us again, upon any charge whatever, we shall have to deal with you very seriously!"

Then the brutal minions of the law fell upon the hapless Toad; loaded him with chains, and dragged him from the Court House, shrieking, praying, protesting; across the market-place, where the playful populace, always as severe upon detected crime as they are sympathetic and helpful when one is merely "wanted," assailed him with jeers, carrots, and popular catch-words; past hooting school children, their innocent faces lit up with the pleasure they ever derive from the sight of a gentleman in difficulties; across the hollow-sounding drawbridge, below the spiky portcullis, under the frowning archway of the grim old castle, whose ancient towers soared high overhead; past guardrooms full of grinning soldiery off duty, past sentries who coughed in a horrid sarcastic way, because that is as much as a sentry on his post dare do to show his contempt and abhorrence of crime; up time-worn winding stairs, past men-at-arms in casquet and

corselet of steel, darting threatening looks through their vizards; across courtyards, where mastiffs strained at their leash and pawed the air to get at him; past ancient warders, their halberds leant against the wall, dozing over a pasty and a flagon of brown ale; on and on, past the rack-chamber and the thumbscrew-room, past the turning that led to the private scaffold, till they reached the door of the grimmest dungeon that lay in the heart of the innermost keep. There at last they paused, where an ancient gaoler sat fingering a bunch of mighty keys.

"Oddsbodikins!" said the sergeant of police, taking off his helmet and wiping his forehead. "Rouse thee, old loon, and take over from us this vile Toad, a criminal of deepest guilt and matchless artfulness and resource. Watch and ward him with all thy skill; and mark thee well, greybeard, should aught untoward befall, thy old head shall answer for his—and a murrain on both of them!"

The gaoler nodded grimly, laying his withered hand on the shoulder of the miserable Toad. The rusty key creaked in the lock, the great door clanged behind them; and Toad was a helpless prisoner in the remotest dungeon of the best-guarded keep of the stoutest castle in all the length and breadth of Merry England.

Manners Can Be Fun

MUNRO LEAF

PLAYING [1]

When I play with other boys we take turns doing the things we want to do. If we are playing games, we follow the rules. One of us doesn't always try to change things so that he will win. We play for fun.

When I play with other girls we share our things and take turns doing what we like to most. We don't whine and cry, or quarrel when we don't have everything our way, and go home angry.

There are some people we don't like to play with—and here they are!

[1] From "Manners Can Be Fun," by Munro Leaf, illustrated by Munro Leaf

Uncle Remus: His Songs and His Sayings

JOEL CHANDLER HARRIS

THE WONDERFUL TAR-BABY STORY [1]

"Didn't the fox *never* catch the rabbit, Uncle Remus?" asked the little boy the next evening.

"He come mighty nigh it, honey, sho's you born—Brer Fox did. One day atter Brer Rabbit fool 'im wid dat calamus root, Brer Fox went ter wuk en got 'im some tar, en mix it wid some turkentime, en fix up a contrapshun wat he call a Tar-Baby, en he tuck dish yer Tar-Baby en he sot 'er in de big road, en den he lay off in de bushes fer to see what de news wuz gwineter be. En he didn't hatter wait long, nudder, kaze bimeby here come Brer Rabbit pacin' down de road—lippity-clippity, clippity-lippity—dez ez sassy ez a jay-bird. Brer Fox, he lay low. Brer Rabbit come prancin' 'long twel he spy de Tar-Baby, en den he fotch up on his behime legs like he wus 'stonished. De Tar-Baby, she sot dar, she did, en Brer Fox, he lay low.

"'Mawnin'!' sez Brer Rabbit, sezee—'nice wedder dis mawnin',' sezee.

"Tar-Baby ain't sayin' nothin', en Brer Fox, he lay low.

"'How duz yo' sym'tums seem ter segashuate?' sez Brer Rabbit, sezee.

"Brer Fox, he wink his eye slow, en lay low, en de Tar-Baby, she ain't sayin' nothin'.

"'How you come on, den? Is you deaf?' sez Brer Rabbit, sezee. 'Kaze if you is, I kin holler louder,' sezee.

"Tar-Baby stay still, en Brer Fox, he lay low.

"'Youer stuck up, dat's w'at you is,' says Brer Rabbit, sezee, 'en I'm gwineter kyore you, dat's w'at I'm a gwineter do,' sezee.

[1] From "Uncle Remus: His Songs and His Sayings," by Joel Chandler Harris, illustrated by A. B. Frost

"Brer Fox, he sorter chuckle in his stummick, he did, but Tar-Baby ain't sayin' nothin'.

" 'I'm gwineter larn you howter talk ter 'specttubble fokes ef hit's de las' ack,' sez Brer Rabbit, sezee. 'Ef you don't take off dat hat en tell me howdy, I'm gwineter bus' you wide open,' sezee.

"Tar-Baby stay still, en Brer Fox, he lay low.

"Brer Rabbit keep on axin' 'im, en de Tar-Baby, she keep on sayin' nothin', twel present'y Brer Rabbit draw back wid his fis', he did, en blip he tuck 'er side er de head. Right dar's whar he broke his merlasses jug. His fis' stuck, en he can't pull loose. De tar hilt 'im. But Tar-Baby, she stay still, en Brer Fox, he lay low.

" 'Ef you don't lemme loose, I'll knock you agin,' sez Brer Rabbit, sezee, en wid dat he fotch 'er a wipe wid de udder han', en dat stuck. Tar-Baby, she ain't sayin' nothin', en Brer Fox, he lay low.

" 'Tu'n me loose, fo' I kick de natal stuffin' outen you,' sez Brer Rabbit, sezee. but de Tar-Baby, she ain't sayin' nothin'.

She des hilt on, en den Brer Rabbit lose de use er his feet in de same way. Brer Fox, he lay low. Den Brer Rabbit squall out dat ef de Tar-Baby don't tu'n 'im loose he butt 'er cranksided. En den he butted, en his head got stuck. Den Brer Fox, he sa'ntered fort', lookin' des ez innercent ez one er yo' mammy's mockin'-birds.

" 'Howdy, Brer Rabbit,' sez Brer Fox, sezee. 'You look sorter stuck up dis mawnin',' sezee, en den he rolled on de groun', en laughed en laughed twel he couldn't laugh no mo'. 'I speck you'll take dinner wid me dis time, Brer Rabbit. I done laid in some calamus root, en I ain't gwineter take no skuse,' sez Brer Fox, sezee."

Here Uncle Remus paused, and drew a two-pound yam out of the ashes.

"Did the fox eat the rabbit?" asked the little boy to whom the story had been told.

"Dat's all de fur de tale goes," replied the old man. "He mout, en den again he moutent. Some say Jedge B'ar come long en loosed 'im—some say he didn't. I hear Miss Sally callin'. You better run 'long."

Rabbit Hill

ROBERT LAWSON

DIVIDING NIGHT [1]

The days lengthened and the sun climbed higher and with the lengthening days the spirits of the Little Animals also rose. In the garden long rows of brilliant green vegetables were thrusting their way up. The lawns were now rich carpets of new grass, very smooth and beautiful, for the Mole, ashamed of his destructive rampage, had kept strictly away from them. Each evening Father inspected the bluegrass. It was slow growing and would not amount to much this year, but next summer—Oh my! From his burrow entrance Porkey surveyed the flourishing field of buckwheat with great satisfaction.

In the chicken-run countless baby chicks ran and scratched and peeped endlessly while the mother hens chuckled and scolded. Phewie and the Gray Fox often paused there in the early evenings to look over the prospects, but Phewie was so satisfied by Sulphronia's generosity in the matter of garbage that his interest in live chicken was rapidly waning. He had even persuaded the Fox to sample a bit of her cookery. The Fox at first had scorned the idea, saying he preferred his chicken fresh, but after trying a Southern-fried chicken wing, as Sulphronia fried it, he had been quite won over and now usually joined Phewie in his midnight feasts.

Each evening the Animals inspected the

[1] From "Rabbit Hill," by Robert Lawson, illustrations from drawings by Robert Lawson

333

garden. The seed packets placed on sticks at the ends of the rows were all gone over carefully with many *Oh's* and *Ah's* at the brightly colored pictures. Little Georgie, of course, had to read them for Uncle Analdas who had always mislaid his specs.

Each Animal made notes on the vegetables available and his family's tastes and needs in preparation for Dividing Night.

That long-awaited occasion arrived and passed off with less controversy than usual, for the garden was so large that there seemed to be ample for all, even the most finicky.

It was a bright moonlit night and every Animal on the Hill had gathered to present his claims. Phewie and the Gray Fox acted as judges, for not being vegetarians they could be trusted to make fair and disinterested decisions. Father, of course, made most of the speeches.

One question arose which had never come up at any former Dividing Night. Willie Fieldmouse and his relatives, grateful for the Folks' rescue of Willie from the rain barrel, proposed that a small portion of the garden be set aside for the exclusive use of the household. Mother warmly seconded this, for she had been most touched by the sign on the driveway. There was considerable debate, but Porkey seemed to represent the opinion of the majority when he said, "Let them take their chances along with the rest of us. Folks don't respect our claims, so why should we give *them* special privileges. 'Tain't democratic." So the motion was voted down.

To some present Uncle Analdas' claims seemed a little extravagant. After all, he was not a regular resident of the Hill, but since he was the guest of Father and Mother, both of whom were highly regarded, there was no open comment, although there was a bit of spiteful gossip behind cupped paws.

On the whole the meeting was most pleasant and orderly, very different from

some of the former ones, when the meager, ill-kept gardens of the previous Folks had led to a great deal of wrangling.

Father voiced this thought in his closing speech. "We seem," he said, "to be blessed with most generous, well-bred and kindly Folks. Their present plantings promise the most bountiful garden with which we have been favored in many years. I hope, therefore, that it is not necessary to impress on any of you the desirability of adhering strictly to those rules and regulations which have always been observed here on the Hill.

"Each Animal's allotment shall be for his and his family's exclusive use and enjoyment; anyone encroaching on property not his own risks banishment from our community.

"In the event that the Folks should take an undue quantity of vegetables from any one Animal's holding, our Board of Relief will assign him additional space.

"Finally, *nothing is to be touched until Midsummer's Eve*. This rule is of the utmost importance for we have learned by long experience that premature inroads on the crops only result in hardship for everyone. By allowing them to approach maturity a far more plentiful supply will be available for all. I hope that you will all use that patience and self-restraint for which the Animals of our Hill have long been noted and that those of us whose duty it is to see that these regulations are enforced will not be called upon to invoke any disciplinary measures. May I also remind you, Porkey, and you, Foxy, that this prohibition applies to buckwheat, chickens and ducks, as well as vegetables?"

"It's all right with *me*," Phewie piped up. "Ain't no closed season on garbidge. Come on, Foxy, this is fried chicken night. I move the meetin's adjourned."

The Animals all wandered home from the meeting in a most contented mood. A group of the young ones were singing "Happy days are here again." Of course it was quite a wait to Midsummer's Eve, but the fields were green now, there was plenty of natural provender, and the garden promised a really bumper crop. The housewives were all planning their preserving and canning. Mother broached the subject of a new storage room which she had long desired. Uncle Analdas could help with the excavating and Little Georgie had become quite handy with tools now, so he could build the shelves. Little Georgie had been sent to the Fat-Man-at-the-Crossroads for some items overlooked in the morning's marketing, and seated before the burrow, Mother went on outlining her plans for the storeroom.

How the Rhinoceros Got His Skin[1]

RUDYARD KIPLING

Once upon a time, on an uninhabited island on the shores of the Red Sea, there lived a Parsee from whose hat the rays of the sun were reflected in more-than-oriental splendour. And the Parsee lived by the Red Sea with nothing but his hat and his knife and a cooking-stove of the kind that you must particularly never touch. And one day he took flour and water and currants and plums and sugar and things, and made himself one cake which was two feet across and three feet thick. It was indeed a Superior Comestible (*that's* magic), and he put it on the stove because *he* was allowed to cook on that stove, and he baked it and he baked it till it was all done brown and smelt most sentimental. But just as he was going to eat it there came down to the beach from the Altogether Uninhabited Interior one Rhinoceros with a horn on his nose, two piggy eyes, and few manners. In those days the Rhinoceros's skin fitted him quite tight. There were no wrinkles in it anywhere. He looked exactly like a Noah's Ark Rhinoceros, but of course much bigger. All the same, he had no manners then, and he has no manners now, and he never will have any manners. He said, "How!" and the Parsee left that cake and climbed to the top of a palm tree with nothing on but his hat, from which the rays of the sun were always reflected in more-than-oriental splendour. And the Rhinoceros upset the oil-stove with his nose, and the cake rolled on the sand, and he spiked that cake on the horn of his nose, and he ate it, and he went away, waving his tail, to the desolate and Exclusively Uninhabited Interior which abuts on the islands of Mazanderan, Socotra, and the Promontories of the Larger Equinox. Then the Parsee came down from his palm-tree and put the stove on its legs and recited the following *Sloka*, which, as you have not heard, I will now proceed to relate:—

Them that takes cakes
Which the Parsee-man bakes
Makes dreadful mistakes.

And there was a great deal more in that than you would think.

Because, five weeks later, there was a heat wave in the Red Sea, and everybody took off all the clothes they had. The Parsee took off his hat; but the Rhinoceros took off his skin and carried it over his shoulder as he came down to the beach to bathe. In those days it buttoned underneath with three buttons and looked like a waterproof. He said nothing whatever about the Parsee's cake, because he had eaten it all; and he never had any manners, then, since, or henceforward. He waddled

[1] From "Just So Stories," by Rudyard Kipling. Illustrations by Art Seiden

straight into the water and blew bubbles through his nose, leaving his skin on the beach.

Presently the Parsee came by and found the skin, and he smiled one smile that ran all round his face two times. Then he danced three times round the skin and rubbed his hands. Then he went to his camp and filled his hat with cake-crumbs, for the Parsee never ate anything but cake, and never swept out his camp. He took that skin, and he shook that skin, and he scrubbed that skin, and he rubbed that skin just as full of old, dry, stale, tickly cake-crumbs and some burned currants as ever it could *possibly* hold. Then he climbed to the top of his palm-tree and waited for the Rhinoceros to come out of the water and put it on.

And the Rhinoceros did. He buttoned it up with the three buttons, and it tickled like cake-crumbs in bed. Then he wanted to scratch, but that made it worse; and then he lay down on the sands and rolled and rolled and rolled, and every time he rolled the cake crumbs tickled him worse and worse and worse. Then he ran to the palm-tree and rubbed and rubbed and rubbed himself against it. He rubbed so much and so hard that he rubbed his skin into a great fold over his shoulders, and another fold underneath, where the buttons used to be (but he rubbed the buttons off), and he rubbed some more folds over his legs. And it spoiled his temper, but it didn't make the least difference to the cake-crumbs. They were inside his skin and they tickled. So he went home, very angry indeed and horribly scratchy; and from that day to this every rhinoceros has great folds in his skin and a very bad temper, all on account of the cake-crumbs inside.

But the Parsee came down from his palm-tree, wearing his hat, from which the rays of the sun were reflected in more-than-oriental splendour, packed up his cooking-stove, and went away in the direction of Orotavo, Amygdala, the Upland Meadows of Anantarivo, and the Marshes of Sonaput.

Augustus Goes South[1]

LE GRAND

The flickering orange light of the fire threw fantastic shadows which raced across the tree trunks. The popping and snapping of the wood was the only sound that broke the silence.

Augustus and Albert sat beside the fire, feeling pleasantly excited and adventurous at the prospect of spending the night alone in the woods.

"Gee, this is swell," said Augustus, leaning back against a tree trunk and stretching as if the sense of freedom that he felt was too big and he had to stretch to take it all in.

"Yes—swell," agreed Albert, absently slapping at a spot on his ankle that suddenly itched.

"Umff," sputtered Augustus, slapping at his ankles too. "Mosquitoes!"

There was a whining drone near his face and he slapped at it. Across from him he could see Albert slapping too.

"Boy," said Augustus. "These swamp mosquitoes are big!"

Albert threw some green leaves on the fire to make a heavy smoke. That helped some but still the sound of slapping went on steadily.

"They'll eat us alive," muttered Augustus. "We'd better make a hut."

"Take too long," said Albert. "And besides I've got a better idea. See the hollow trunk in that big old fallen tree?"

Augustus looked at the hollow tree trunk and grinned.

"Sure," he said. "That's a hut all made for us."

"Yes," said Albert. "We can cover the front with palmettos. That'll keep the mosquitoes out. Come on, let's get some palmettos."

He took a stick from the fire for a torch and they left the circle of firelight and pushed through the bushes to a palmetto thicket.

"Look out for snakes," said Albert. "This swamp is full of water moccasins. And they're bad!"

He broke off a long pole and beat the bushes ahead to scare away any snakes that might be lurking in the darkness.

Back they floundered with a big load of palmetto fronds and poles. They built up the space in front of the tree trunk, weaving the long fan-shaped clusters of palmetto into a solid wall except for a small opening directly in front of the fire. More green branches on the fire sent up thick clouds of smoke which curled back into the opening and drove most of the mosquitoes out.

Sometimes when the smoke swirled in too thickly, it almost drove Albert and Augustus out too. Except for that, it was strangely cozy in the tree trunk. Although there was room for both of them, the smallness of the space made them feel snug and safe and pleasant.

Augustus and Albert lay on their stomachs, facing the opening and watched the flickering firelight shift across the palmetto screen.

As he thought of the ruined buildings in the darkness just beyond, Augustus' imagination pictured them as they had been long ago when he felt sure there had been a pirate village here.

"Look there," he said to Albert, and pointed out at the darkness. "Probably right out there is where the pirates were. Maybe so close we could touch them if they were there now!"

Albert looked uneasily beyond the circle of light from the fire. The shadows were dark and mysterious under the trees and when the flames flickered the shadows

---

[1] From "Augustus Goes South," by Le Grand, illustrations from drawings by Le Grand

seemed to come alive, moving stealthily back and forth and sometimes closing in around the tree-trunk hut.

"Maybe—maybe they weren't quite that close," mumbled Albert, as he drew a little farther back from the opening.

"Oh yes, they were!" insisted Augustus. "Right out there—why, we'd be right in the middle of them!"

Suddenly Augustus remembered a picture he had seen of a cruel scowling pirate face. Until that moment he had been thinking of the bright-colored clothes and gold sparkling in the firelight.

"Well," he went on, "maybe they *were* a little farther off." As he thought of that fiercely scowling face, he shifted a little farther back in the tree trunk. "Maybe they were way down at the other end of the island!" he said suddenly.

"Yes," agreed Albert warmly. "Why, maybe they weren't even on this island at all. Probably it was some other island!"

The shadows towered high as the fire burned lower and lower. There was no wood left to build it up and neither Augustus nor Albert made a move to get any more.

"I guess we'd better go to sleep when the fire burns out," said Albert nervously.

"Yeh," said Augustus, but he didn't sound at all sleepy.

The shadows moved in closer and closer. A hollow hooting sound began off in the woods. The sound was faint and far off at first but it grew steadily louder. Other hollow voices joined in and the mingled sounds rose to a wild fierce clamor that beat through the darkness in gusty waves.

"It's—it's just owls," said Albert, but he could feel the back of his neck prickling.

"Yeh, just owls," said Augustus, but that didn't make the wild screaming any less scary.

"Anyway, I don't believe in ghosts," said Albert suddenly, although no one had said anything about ghosts.

"No," agreed Augustus much louder than was necessary. "Who'd believe all those

old stories about pirate ghosts haunting the places where their treasure is buried? Huh! I guess I wouldn't."

The fire was very low now, just a dim red glow too weak to keep back the shadows that hovered right at the open end of the log.

"They say that ghosts are all white," said Albert suddenly.

"Ye—yeh," said Augustus, staring hard into the blackness.

"Huh," said Albert, "who'd believe that?"

"Huh, I betcha I wouldn't," said Augustus firmly.

"It's getting kind of dark," said Albert.

"Yeh," said Augustus. "Course that doesn't make any difference."

After a while Augustus said, "Maybe it might get cold before morning. I guess we'd better keep the fire going after all."

The wild racket of the owls had died away. In the silence the small rustling night noises of the woods seemed very loud.

Albert had been thinking for some time that almost anything would be better than just lying there in the dark.

"All right," he said, "let's get some wood."

They squeezed out through the narrow opening together. Scuttling past the tiny red spark that was all that was left of the fire, they headed for the woods. Augustus had a hatchet and Albert had the shovel

which he held out in front of him for some reason that was not quite clear, since they were going for wood.

The moon was not up but the faint light of the stars gleamed coldly on the water. Once they stopped and looked around as a new strange noise made their hair rise.

"Oh, that's just a branch rubbing against another one," said Albert.

"Yeh," said Augustus. "Anyway ghosts wouldn't make much noise—even if there were ghosts."

"N—no," said Albert. "They're just kind of white and still-like."

"Yeh," said Augustus. "Just white an—" He stopped suddenly and grabbed Albert's arm. "L—l—look!" he quavered.

Something white gleamed against the darkness beyond!

For what seemed like an hour Augustus held tightly to Albert and Albert held onto Augustus. They didn't move. Neither did the white thing.

"Who—who's there?" stammered Augustus.

There was no answer.

The white thing seemed to grow brighter, shining through the darkness like a steadily increasing white light. Suddenly Augustus was aware that the moon had risen and was gradually lighting the trees and rocks all around. The white thing still hadn't moved and Augustus felt a little bolder.

"Who's there?" he called again.

And again there was no answer.

Suddenly Augustus' fright began to turn to anger. He began to feel angry at himself for being so scared.

"I'll show you," he shouted. He raised

the hatchet over his head and threw it at the glowing white shape ahead.

The hatchet struck with a sharp clattering noise. It didn't sound at all like a ghost; it sounded more like a pile of rocks.

Augustus crept cautiously ahead. He reached the edge of the woods. The white shape was just ahead of him. Beside him he could feel Albert. Albert still had the shovel; he reached out and poked at the white thing. Small pieces of white fell from the rest and rolled away.

"Aw," said Augustus, "it's only some ol' white rocks with the moon shining on them."

Albert reached down and picked something up. He held it up to the light of the moon and gasped.

"Augustus," he said excitedly, "it's a shell —that thing is a big shell pile—the kind *Grandpère* says the treasures are buried in!"

"Yay," shouted Augustus. "I knew. I knew it—I knew it all the time!"

He grabbed the shovel and started to dig furiously. The shells were hard to dig away and Augustus made little progress in the dark.

He tripped over the handle of the shovel and sat down hard. Albert said, "Let's wait until morning. We couldn't see what we found even if we found it. And besides we'd probably miss it in the dark, anyway."

Augustus was impatient to go on, but after trying to dig again, he realized it was hopeless.

"All right," he said. "Let's make a big fire and sit up the rest of the night. We'll watch so no one else can come along and get the treasure."

They dragged a huge load of wood back to the hollow tree and built the fire up into a blaze so big it lighted up the whole end of the island.

Too excited now to be scared, Augustus and Albert lay in the hollow tree and waited impatiently for morning.

"Now remember—no sleeping," said Augustus. "It'd be a fine thing, wouldn't it, if somebody came along and dug up our treasure after we almost found it—and us asleep!"

Although Albert agreed not to sleep, he tried reasonably to point out that people didn't usually roam around in the swamps at night.

"Who'd be likely to come digging around here on a dark night like this?" he asked.

"Well, finding treasure is a mighty funny thing," said Augustus. "You can't ever tell what might happen."

It was snug and comfortable in the tree trunk. The sides reflected the cheerful orange glow of the firelight.

Through the opening in the palmetto screen the pleasantly pungent odor of wood smoke mingled with the fresh damp earthy smell of the woods at night.

Morning seemed a long time coming.

"Remember—no sleeping," said Augustus.

Albert didn't answer. Augustus looked at him. Albert was asleep.

"Oh well," thought Augustus, "I'll let him sleep a while."

The sound of the frogs was soothing and monotonous, like the drip of rain on a roof, Augustus thought. He remembered how pleasant it was to be half-asleep in the houseboat while the rain dripped steadily.

The firelight wavered as the fire burned lower. The flames died, leaving a bed of glowing coals. Gradually the glow of the coals dimmed. Pale moonlight flooded the open space in front of the tree trunk, replacing the warm fireglow. Occasionally there was a thin faint splashing as a fish jumped out of water. The last of the glowing coals winked out. Augustus did not build up the fire. Augustus was asleep.

The deep calm of the woods lay undisturbed over the moon-silvered swamp.

The sky was red and gold with the glow of a bright sunrise when the squall of a blue jay woke Albert. He rubbed his eyes, looked around, then jumped up.

"Hey, wake up," he shouted, and while Augustus yawned and blinked at him, Albert picked up the shovel and ran toward the pile of shells.

Augustus followed him and they took turns digging. It was hard work. The shells overlapped so that the shovel didn't go very far into the pile no matter how hard they pushed. There was a place near the center of the pile where the shells were sunk in a hollow and Augustus said that showed where the treasure was buried. Using the shovel like a scoop, they dragged shells down the side of the pile, gradually getting farther into the hollow place.

After they had dug for what seemed like a long time without finding anything, Albert stopped to rest and stare gloomily at the shell pile.

"You know," he said, "not all these shell piles have treasure in them."

Even Augustus looked discouraged, but he gritted his teeth and said, "No, I guess not, but if there's any treasure in this one I'll find it if I have to dig clear to China. Gimme that shovel! We'll see."

They went on digging, taking turns with the shovel as the sun rose higher and drops of sweat glistened on their foreheads.

"Uh!" said Albert suddenly as his shovel hit something that was not shells.

He dug again and this time Augustus heard the muffled scraping sound that was altogether different from the sharp clatter of the shells.

"What is it?" whispered Augustus.

"Don't know," whispered Albert. "It doesn't feel like a wooden chest though."

Augustus ran to help and pulled at the shells with his hands while Albert dug with the shovel.

"It feels like cloth," said Albert wonderingly as he scraped the shovel around in the hole.

"Huh," said Augustus, "it can't be. Who ever heard of pirates burying treasure in cloth?"

He stretched his arm down into the hole and felt around with his hand.

"It *is* cloth," he muttered as his fingers scraped over something soft but scratchy.

They dug harder than ever, and the sound of the shells rolling down the side of the pile was like the clink of gold pieces.

"Guess we can get it now," said Albert, reaching down in the hole. Augustus got into the hole and pushed.

"All together now when I count three," he said. He braced himself and counted, "One, Two, *Three*—uh!"

"It's coming," gasped Albert. "Keep pushing."

"Here it comes," grunted Augustus, as the shells fell away and up came a big canvas bag.

With their eyes wide with excitement Albert and Augustus stood for a moment looking down at the bag.

"Why," said Albert. "Why, look—it's a mailbag."

Augustus just gaped at the bag, reading the words U. S. MAIL that were printed across it.

"But it's a new mailbag," said Augustus. "How could the pirates have buried it?"

Albert stood looking at the mailbag and scratching his ear as he always did when he was puzzled.

"The pirates didn't do it," he said finally. "Anyway, not those old pirates." He looked all around, staring anxiously into the dim shadows in the woods. "Augustus," he whispered, "this must be one of Mr. Thibodaux's mailbags and I bet he's been robbed!"

Augustus had been fumbling at the mailbag and now he succeeded in opening it. There were no letters in it, but down in the bottom Augustus felt some square packages wrapped in paper. He dumped them out and tore away the paper coverings.

"Look!" he gasped. "Money!"

Albert's mouth popped open and he whistled shrilly through his teeth. The package was full of paper money.

"We'd better get out of here quick," whispered Augustus.

Peter and the Wolf

SERGE PROKOFIEFF

Illustrated by Warren Chappell

Early one morning Peter opened the gate and went out into the big green meadow. On the branch of a birch tree sat a little bird,—Peter's friend. When he saw Peter he chirped at him gaily, "All's quiet here."

Soon a duck came waddling around. She was very happy to see that Peter had not closed the gate, and so decided to have a nice swim in the deep pond in the meadow.

As soon as the little bird saw the duck, he flew down and settled himself in the grass beside her. Shrugging his shoulders he said, "What kind of a bird are *you* if you can't fly?" To which the duck replied, "What kind of a bird are *you* if you can't swim?" and dived into the pond.

They argued and argued, the duck swimming in the pond, the little bird hopping back and forth along the bank. Suddenly, something caught Peter's eye. It was a cat crawling through the grass. The cat said to herself, "The bird is busy arguing. If I could only have him for my dinner!" Stealthily she crept toward him on her velvet paws. "Oh, look out!" cried Peter.

Quickly the bird flew up into the tree while the duck quacked angrily at the cat —from the middle of the pond. The cat crawled round and round the tree and thought, "Is it worth climbing up so high? By the time I get there the bird will have flown away."

All at once Grandpapa came out. He

was angry because Peter had gone to the meadow. "The meadow is a dangerous plàce," he cried. "What if a wolf should come out of the forest?—What would you do then?" Peter paid no attention to Grandpapa's words. Boys like Peter are not afraid of wolves. Grandpapa took Peter by the hand, led him home—and locked the gate.

No sooner had Peter gone than a big grey wolf *did* come out of the forest. In a twinkling the cat sprang up into the tree. The duck quacked and in her great excitement, jumped out of the pond. No matter how hard the duck tried to run, she couldn't escape the wolf. He was getting nearer and nearer. He was catching up with her—there—he got her—and swallowed her with a single gulp!

And now this is how things stood: the cat was sitting on one branch up in the tree,—the bird was sitting on another,—not too close to the cat,—while the wolf walked round and round the tree, looking at them both with greedy eyes.

In the meantime, Peter, without the slightest fear, stood behind the closed gate, watching all that was going on. Presently, he ran into the house, found a strong rope, hurried back and climbed up the high stone wall. One of the branches of the tree around which the wolf was pacing, stretched out over this high wall. Grabbing hold of this branch, Peter climbed over into the tree.

He said to the bird, "Fly down and circle around the wolf's head, but take care that he doesn't catch you!" The bird almost touched the wolf's head with his wings, while the wolf snapped furiously at him from this side—and that. How that bird did worry the wolf! And oh! how the wolf tried to catch him! But the bird was far too clever for him.

Meanwhile, Peter had made a lasso, and letting it down very carefully—he caught the wolf by the tail and pulled with all his might. Feeling himself caught, the wolf began to jump wildly, trying to get loose. But Peter had tied the other end of the rope to the tree, and the wolf's jumping only made the rope tighter around his tail!

Just then, who should come out of the woods but the hunters who were following the wolf's trail, and shooting as they came. From his perch in the tree Peter cried out to them: "You don't need to shoot. The bird and I have already caught him! Please help us take him to the zoo."

The hunters were only too willing. And now you can just imagine the triumphant procession! Peter at the head—after him the hunters, leading the wolf—and winding up the procession, Grandpapa and the cat. Grandpapa shook his head reprovingly. "This is all very well, but what if Peter had *not* caught the wolf,—what then!" Above them flew the little bird, merrily chirping, "Aren't we smart, Peter and I? See what *we* have caught." And if you had listened very carefully, you could have heard the duck quacking away inside the wolf, because in his haste the wolf had swallowed her whole—and the duck was still alive.

The Horse Who Lived Upstairs

PHYLLIS McGINLEY

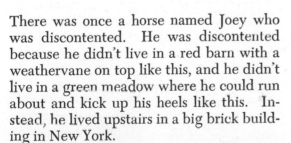

Illustration from a drawing by Helen Stone

There was once a horse named Joey who was discontented. He was discontented because he didn't live in a red barn with a weathervane on top like this, and he didn't live in a green meadow where he could run about and kick up his heels like this. Instead, he lived upstairs in a big brick building in New York.

Joey worked for Mr. Polaski who sold fruits and vegetables to city people. Joey pulled the vegetable wagon through the city streets. And in New York, there isn't room for barns or meadows.

So every night when Joey came home, he stepped out from the shafts of the wagon, and into an elevator, and up he went to his stall on the fourth floor of the big brick building. It was a fine stall and Joey was very comfortable there. He had plenty of oats to eat and plenty of fresh straw to lie on. He even had a window to look out of. But still Joey was discontented.

"How I long to sip fresh water from a babbling brook!" he often exclaimed. And then he would sniff discontentedly at the old bathtub near the elevator which served him as a watering trough.

It wasn't that he had to work hard. Mr. Polaski was kind to him and brought him home at five o'clock every day.

In the winter Joey had a blanket to wear on his back to keep him warm. And in the summer time Mr. Polaski got him a hat to wear on his head to keep him cool. And every day he had many interesting adventures. Sometimes he met a Policeman who gave him sugar. Sometimes ladies patted him on the nose and fed him carrots. He was introduced to the high-bred horses who drew the hansom cabs along the Plaza. He saw the children playing in the playgrounds and the parks. But it made no difference to Joey. "This is no life for a horse," he used to say to the Percheron who lived in the next stall to him. "We city horses don't know what real living is. I want to move to the country and sleep in a red barn with a weathervane on top, and kick up my heels in a green meadow."

So how happy he was when one day Mr. Polaski said to him, "Joey, I think I could sell more vegetables if I drove a truck. I will miss you, Joey, but you will like it on the farm where I am going to send you."

The next morning a big motor van rolled up. Joey got inside, and away he went to the country. Of course he said goodbye to the Percheron. "Goodbye, Joey," called his friend. "I hope you will be contented on the farm."

When Joey reached the country, sure enough, there was the barn with its weathervane, and there was the meadow. "This is the life!" cried Joey to himself. But poor Joey! The barn was cold in winter and hot in summer. He didn't have a blanket and he didn't have a hat. And he had very little time to kick up his heels in the green meadow, for all day long he pulled a plow through the earth. A plow is harder to pull than a wagon, and besides, the farmer worked from sunrise to sundown instead of the eight hours Joey was used to. Sometimes they forgot to put fresh straw in his stall, and nobody thought to give him sugar or carrots. There were plenty of children but they climbed on his back and teased him when he wanted to eat. And instead of the Percheron, there was a cross old gray horse next door to him, who looked down his nose at Joey because Joey knew so little about farm life.

One day, when he wasn't pulling a plow, because it was Sunday, Joey saw several people picnicking in the meadow. He decided to join them, for they looked as if they came from the City, and he thought they might have a lump of sugar in one of their pockets.

When he reached the spot they had gone for a walk, so he ate up their lunch. When they came back, they were very angry and Joey was shut up in his stall for the rest of the day. He didn't even have a window to look out of. He was lonely for his friends, the Policeman, and the ladies who patted him on the nose. He was lonely for the high-bred horses, and all the interesting sights of the City. "I don't think I belong in the country after all," sighed Joey. "I am now more discontented than ever."

Next day he heard the honk of a horn. He looked from the door of the barn, and whom should he see but Mr. Polaski, getting out of the truck!

"I have come for Joey," Mr. Polaski told the farmer. "I cannot get any more tires for my truck, so I think I will sell fruit and vegetables from my wagon again."

My goodness, but Joey was happy! He went back to the City with Mr. Polaski and got into the elevator and up he went to the fourth floor of the big brick building. There was his stall, and there was the window for him to look out of. And there was the friendly Percheron. "Welcome back, Joey," exclaimed the Percheron. "I have missed you. The Policeman has missed you. The lady customers have missed you, and so have the children in the playgrounds and the parks. Tell me, how did you like the country?" "The country is all right for country animals," Joey said, "but I guess I am just a City horse at heart." And he was never discontented again.

Bambi

FELIX SALTEN

YOUNG BAMBI LEARNS ABOUT FOREST LIFE [1]

In early summer the trees stood still under the blue sky, held their limbs outstretched and received the direct rays of the sun. On the shrubs and bushes in the undergrowth, the flowers unfolded their red, white and yellow stars. On some the seed pods had begun to appear again. They perched innumerable on the fine tips of the branches, tender and firm and resolute, and seemed like small, clenched fists. Out of the earth came whole troops of flowers, like motley stars, so that the soil of the twilit forest floor shone with a silent, ardent, colorful gladness. Everything smelled of fresh leaves, of blossoms, of moist clods and green wood. When morning broke, or when the sun went down, the whole woods resounded with a thousand voices, and from morning till night, the bees hummed, the wasps droned, and filled the fragrant stillness with their murmur.

These were the earliest days of Bambi's life. He walked behind his mother on a narrow track that ran through the midst of the bushes. How pleasant it was to walk there. The thick foliage stroked his flanks softly and bent supplely aside. The track appeared to be barred and obstructed in a dozen places and yet they advanced with the greatest ease. There were tracks like this everywhere, running criss-cross through the whole woods. His mother knew them all, and if Bambi sometimes stopped before a bush as if it were an impenetrable green wall, she always found where the path went through, without hesitation or searching.

Bambi questioned her. He loved to ask his mother questions. It was the pleasant-est thing for him to ask a question and then to hear what answer his mother would give. Bambi was never surprised that question after question should come into his mind continually and without effort. He found it perfectly natural, and it delighted him very much. It was very delightful, too, to wait expectantly till the answer came. If it turned out the way he wanted, he was satisfied. Sometimes, of course, he did not understand, but that was pleasant also because he was kept busy picturing what he had not understood, in his own way. Sometimes he felt very sure that his mother was not giving him a complete answer, was intentionally not telling him all she knew. And, at first, that was very pleasant, too. For then there would remain in him such a lively curiosity, such suspicion, mysteriously and joyously flashing through him, such anticipation, that he would become anxious and happy at the same time, and grow silent.

Once he asked, "Whom does this trail belong to, Mother?"

His mother answered, "To us."

Bambi asked again, "To you and me?"

"Yes."

"To us two?"

"Yes."

"Only to us two?"

"No," said his mother, "to us deer."

"What are deer?" Bambi asked, and laughed.

His mother looked at him from head to foot and laughed too. "You are a deer and I am a deer. We're both deer," she said. "Do you understand?"

Bambi sprang into the air for joy. "Yes,

[1] From "Bambi," by Felix Salten, illustrations from drawings by Kurt Wiese

I understand," he said. "I'm a little deer and you're a big deer, aren't you?"

His mother nodded and said, "Now you see."

But Bambi grew serious again. "Are there other deer besides you and me?" he asked.

"Certainly," his mother said. "Many of them."

"Where are they?" cried Bambi.

"Here, everywhere."

"But I don't see them."

"You will soon," she said.

"When?" Bambi stood still, wild with curiosity.

"Soon." The mother walked on quietly. Bambi followed her. He kept silent for he was wondering what "soon" might mean. He came to the conclusion that "soon" was certainly not "now." But he wasn't sure at what time "soon" stopped being "soon" and began to be a "long while." Suddenly he asked, "Who made this trail?"

"We," his mother answered.

Bambi was astonished. "We? You and I?"

The mother said, "We, we . . . we deer."

Bambi asked, "Which deer?"

"All of us," his mother said sharply.

They walked on. Bambi was in high spirits and felt like leaping off the path, but he stayed close to his mother. Something rustled in front of them, close to the ground. The fern fronds and wood-lettuce concealed something that advanced in violent motion. A threadlike, little cry shrilled out piteously; then all was still. Only the leaves and the blades of grass shivered back into place. A ferret had caught a mouse. He came slinking by, slid sideways, and prepared to enjoy his meal.

"What was that?" asked Bambi excitedly.

"Nothing," his mother soothed him.

"But," Bambi trembled, "but I saw it."

"Yes, yes," said his mother. "Don't be frightened. The ferret has killed a mouse."

But Bambi was dreadfully frightened. A vast, unknown horror clutched at his heart. It was long before he could speak again. Then he asked, "Why did he kill the mouse?"

"Because," his mother hesitated. "Let us walk faster," she said as though something had just occurred to her and as though she had forgotten the question. She began to hurry. Bambi sprang after her.

A long pause ensued. They walked on quietly again. Finally Bambi asked anxiously, "Shall we kill a mouse, too, sometime?"

"No," replied his mother.

"Never?" asked Bambi.

"Never," came the answer.

"Why not?" asked Bambi, relieved.

"Because we never kill anything," said his mother simply.

Bambi grew happy again.

Loud cries were coming from a young ash tree which stood near their path. The mother went along without noticing them, but Bambi stopped inquisitively. Overhead two jays were quarreling about a nest they had plundered.

"Get away, you murderer!" cried one.

"Keep cool, you fool," the other answered, "I'm not afraid of you."

"Look for your own nests," the first one shouted, "or I'll break your head for you." He was beside himself with rage. "What vulgarity!" he chattered, "what vulgarity!"

The other jay had spied Bambi and fluttered down a few branches to shout at him. "What are you gawking at, you freak?" he screamed.

Bambi sprang away terrified. He reached his mother and walked behind her again, frightened and obedient, thinking she had not noticed his absence.

After a pause he asked, "Mother, what is vulgarity?"

"I don't know," said his mother.

Bambi thought a while; then he began again. "Why were they both so angry with each other, Mother?" he asked.

"They were fighting over food," his mother answered.

"Will we fight over food, too, sometime?" Bambi asked.

"No," said his mother.

Bambi asked, "Why not?"

"Because there is enough for all of us," his mother replied.

Bambi wanted to know something else. "Mother," he began.

"What is it?"

"Will we be angry with each other sometime?" he asked.

"No, child," said his mother, "we don't do such things."

They walked along again. Presently it grew light ahead of them. It grew very bright. The trail ended with the tangle of vines and bushes. A few steps more and they would be in the bright open space that spread out before them. Bambi wanted to bound forward, but his mother had stopped.

"What is it?" he asked impatiently, already delighted.

"It's the meadow," his mother answered.

"What is a meadow?" asked Bambi insistently.

His mother cut him short. "You'll soon find out for yourself," she said. She had become very serious and watchful. She stood motionless, holding her head high and listening intently. She sucked in deep breathfuls of air and looked very severe.

"It's all right," she said at last, "we can go out."

Bambi leaped forward, but his mother barred the way.

"Wait till I call you," she said. Bambi obeyed at once and stood still. "That's right," said his mother, to encourage him, "and now listen to what I am saying to you." Bambi heard how seriously his mother spoke and felt terribly excited.

"Walking on the meadow is not so simple," his mother went on. "It's a difficult and dangerous business. Don't ask me why. You'll find that out later on. Now do exactly as I tell you to. Will you?"

"Yes," Bambi promised.

"Good," said his mother, "I'm going out alone first. Stay here and wait. And don't take your eyes off me for a minute. If you see me run back here, then turn round and run as fast as you can. I'll catch up with you soon." She grew silent and seemed to be thinking. Then she went on earnestly, "Run anyway as fast as your legs will carry you. Run even if something should happen . . . even if you should see me fall to the ground. . . . Don't think of me, do you understand? No matter what you see or hear, start running right away and just as fast as you possibly can. Do you promise me to do that?"

"Yes," said Bambi softly. His mother spoke so seriously.

She went on speaking. "Out there if

I should call you," she said, "there must be no looking around and no questions, but you must get behind me instantly. Understand that. Run without pausing or stopping to think. If I begin to run, that means for you to run too, and no stopping until we are back here again. You won't forget, will you?"

"No," said Bambi in a troubled voice.

"Now I'm going ahead," said his mother, and seemed to become calmer.

She walked out. Bambi, who never took his eyes off her, saw how she moved forward with slow, cautious steps. He stood there full of expectancy, full of fear and curiosity. He saw how his mother listened in all directions, saw her shrink together, and shrank together himself, ready to leap back into the thickets. Then his mother grew calm again. She stretched herself. Then she looked around satisfied and called, "Come!"

Bambi bounded out. Joy seized him with such tremendous force that he forgot his worries in a flash. Through the thicket he could see only the green tree-tops overhead. Once in a while he caught a glimpse of the blue sky.

Now he saw the whole heaven stretching far and wide and he rejoiced without knowing why. In the forest he had seen only a stray sunbeam now and then, or the tender, dappled light that played through the branches. Suddenly he was standing in the blinding hot sunlight whose boundless power was beaming upon him. He stood in the splendid warmth that made him shut his eyes but which opened his heart.

Bambi was as though bewitched. He was completely beside himself with pleasure. He was simply wild. He leaped into the air three, four, five times. He had to do it. He felt a terrible desire to leap and jump. He stretched his young limbs joyfully. His breath came deeply and easily. He drank in the air. The sweet smell of the meadow made him so wildly happy that he had to leap into the air.

Bambi was a child. If he had been a human child he would have shouted. But he was a young deer, and deer cannot shout, at least not the way human children do. So he rejoiced with his legs and with his whole body as he flung himself into the air. His mother stood by and was glad. She saw that Bambi was wild. She watched how he bounded into the air and fell again awkwardly, in one spot. She saw how he stared around him, dazed and bewildered, only to leap up over and over again. She understood that Bambi knew only the narrow deer tracks in the forest and how his brief life was used to the limits of the thicket. He did not move from one place because he did not understand how to run freely around the open meadow.

So she stretched out her forefeet and bent laughingly towards Bambi for a moment. Then she was off with one bound, racing around in a circle so that the tall grass stems swished.

Bambi was frightened and stood motionless. Was that a sign for him to run back to the thicket? His mother had said to him, "Don't worry about me no matter what you see or hear. Just run as fast as you can." He was going to turn around and run as she had commanded him to, but his mother came galloping up suddenly. She came up with a wonderful swishing sound and stopped two steps from him. She bent towards him, laughing as she had at first and cried, "Catch me." And in a flash she was gone.

Bambi was puzzled. What did she mean? Then she came back again running so fast that it made him giddy. She pushed his flank with her nose and said quickly, "Try to catch me," and fled away.

Bambi started after her. He took a few steps. Then his steps became short bounds. He felt as if he were flying without any effort on his part. There was a space under his hoofs, space under his bounding feet, space and still more space. Bambi was beside himself with joy.

The swishing grass sounded wonderful

to his ears. It was marvelously soft and as
fine as silk where it brushed against him.
He ran round in a circle. He turned and
flew off in a new circle, turned around
again and kept running.

His mother was standing still, getting
her breath again. She kept following
Bambi with her eyes. He was wild.

Suddenly the race was over. He
stopped and came up to his mother, lifting his hoofs elegantly. He looked joyfully
at her. Then they strolled contentedly
side by side.

Since he had been in the open, Bambi
had felt the sky and the sun and the green
meadow with his whole body. He took
one blinding, giddy glance at the sun,
and he felt its rays as they lay warmly on
his back.

Presently he began to enjoy the meadow
with his eyes also. Its wonders amazed
him at every step he took. You could not
see the tiniest speck of earth the way you
could in the forest. Blade after blade of
grass covered every inch of the ground.
It tossed and waved luxuriantly. It bent
softly aside under every footstep, only to
rise up unharmed again. The broad green
meadow was starred with white daisies,
with the thick, round red and purple clover
blossoms and bright, golden dandelion
heads.

"Look, look, Mother!" Bambi exclaimed.
"There's a flower flying."

"That's not a flower," said his mother,
"that's a butterfly."

Bambi stared at the butterfly, entranced.
It had darted lightly from a blade of grass
and was fluttering about in its giddy way.
Then Bambi saw that there were many
butterflies flying in the air above the
meadow. They seemed to be in a hurry
and yet moved slowly, fluttering up and
down in a sort of game that delighted him.
They really did look like gay flying flowers
that would not stay on their stems but had
unfastened themselves in order to dance
a little. They looked, too, like flowers that
come to rest at sundown but have no fixed

places and have to hunt for them, dropping
down and vanishing as if they really had
settled somewhere, yet always flying up
again, a little way at first, then higher and
higher, and always searching farther and
farther because all the good places have
already been taken.

Bambi gazed at them all. He would
have loved to see one close by. He wanted
to see one face to face but he was not able
to. They sailed in and out continually.
The air was aflutter with them.

When he looked down at the ground
again he was delighted with the thousands
of living things he saw stirring under his
hoofs. They ran and jumped in all directions. He would see a wild swarm of
them, and the next moment they had disappeared in the grass again.

"Who are they, Mother?" he asked.

"Those are ants," his mother answered.

"Look," cried Bambi, "see that piece
of grass jumping. Look how high it can
jump!"

"That's not grass," his mother explained,
"that's a nice grasshopper."

"Why does he jump that way?" asked
Bambi.

"Because we're walking here," his
mother answered, "he's afraid we'll step
on him."

"O," said Bambi, turning to the grasshopper who was sitting on a daisy; "O,"
he said again politely, "you don't have to
be afraid; we won't hurt you."

"I'm not afraid," the grasshopper replied in a quavering voice; "I was only frightened for a moment when I was talking to my wife."

"Excuse us for disturbing you," said Bambi shyly.

"Not at all," the grasshopper quavered. "Since it's you, it's perfectly all right. But you never know who's coming and you have to be careful."

"This is the first time in my life that I've ever been on the meadow," Bambi explained; "my mother brought me. . . ."

The grasshopper was sitting with his head lowered as though he were going to butt. He put on a serious face and murmured, "That doesn't interest me at all. I haven't time to stand here gossiping with you. I have to be looking for my wife. Hopp!" And he gave a jump.

"Hopp!" said Bambi in surprise at the high jump with which the grasshopper vanished.

Bambi ran to his mother. "Mother, I spoke to him," he cried.

"To whom?" his mother asked.

"To the grasshopper," Bambi said, "I spoke to him. He was very nice to me. And I like him so much. He's so wonderful and green and you can see through his sides. They look like leaves, but you can't see through a leaf."

"Those are his wings," said his mother.

"O," Bambi went on, "and his face is so serious and wise. But he was very nice to me anyhow. And how he can jump! 'Hopp!' he said, and he jumped so high I couldn't see him any more."

They walked on. The conversation with the grasshopper had excited Bambi and tired him a little, for it was the first time he had ever spoken to a stranger. He felt hungry and pressed close to his mother to be nursed.

Then he stood quietly and gazed dreamily into space for a little while with a sort of joyous ecstasy that came over him every time he was nursed by his mother. He noticed a bright flower moving in the tangled grasses. Bambi looked more closely at it. No, it wasn't a flower, but a butterfly. Bambi crept closer.

The butterfly hung heavily to a grass stem and fanned its wings slowly.

"Please sit still," Bambi said.

"Why should I sit still? I'm a butterfly," the insect answered in astonishment.

"O, please sit still, just for a minute," Bambi pleaded, "I've wanted so much to see you close to. Please."

"Well," said the butterfly, "for your sake I will, but not for long."

Bambi stood in front of him. "How beautiful you are!" he cried fascinated; "how wonderfully beautiful, like a flower!"

"What?" cried the butterfly, fanning his wings, "did you say like a flower? In my circle it's generally supposed that we're handsomer than flowers."

Bambi was embarrassed. "O, yes," he stammered, "much handsomer, excuse me, I only meant . . ."

"Whatever you meant is all one to me," the butterfly replied. He arched his thin body affectedly and played with his delicate feelers.

Bambi looked at him enchanted. "How elegant you are!" he said. "How elegant and fine! And how splendid and white your wings are!"

The butterfly spread his wings wide apart, then raised them till they folded together like an upright sail.

"O," cried Bambi, "I know that you are handsomer than the flowers. Besides, you can fly and the flowers can't because they grow on stems, that's why."

The butterfly spread his wings. "It's enough," he said, "that I can fly." He soared so lightly that Bambi could hardly see him or follow his flight. His wings moved gently and gracefully. Then he fluttered into the sunny air.

"I only sat still that long on your account," he said balancing in the air in front of Bambi. "Now I'm going."

That was how Bambi found the meadow.

The Good Master

KATE SEREDY

THE RIDING LESSON [1]

Nobody ever found out just what had happened between Kate and Father that night, nobody ever spoke about it. Jancsi knew she didn't get a licking—lickings were noisy affairs. But for a few days peace and serenity reigned. Kate was left alone with Mother in the daytime. Mother never complained about her. Jancsi and Father were very busy. They had hired men to do the plowing and planting. Jancsi had full charge of the three milking cows, the pigs, and the poultry. At the crack of dawn he was up. He milked and fed the cows and strained the milk. Then he took corn and swill to the pigs, mush to the chickens. Next he drove the ducks and geese to a grassy inclosure with a brook running through it. On nice days he led the cows to a small pasture close to the barn. If breakfast wasn't ready, he helped Father in the stables. After breakfast Father rode out to the herds. His herds were scattered over a vast area. Horses across the river to the north, sheep to the south. They had to be far away from each other because sheep ruin the grass for horses, cropping it too close to the ground. The men who took care of the herds lived in little huts close to the corrals. Sometimes Jancsi rode along with Father. He loved the days when he was allowed to do so. The herdsmen were his friends; they told him stories, taught him to whittle, to play the tilinkó, rope a wild horse, and clip sheep. Best of all Jancsi loved the times when they were so far away from home that Father decided to stay overnight. They cooked supper on an open fire and ate it crouching around the embers, singing, swapping stories, or talking about the animals. Here he was one of the men and they never made him feel that he was just a young boy. Later on they made bunks right out in the open field, under the starry sky. The herdsmen had great big coats, called "bunda." The bunda is made of sheepskin, and the herdsmen wear it all the year round. They say it keeps them warm in the winter, when they wear it with the furry side in. With furry side out, it keeps them cool in the summer. "My bunda is my house," they say, and that is true. No icy blast penetrates it, no rain soaks through it. Jancsi loved to snuggle down into the furry warmth of this great coat; loved the keen smell of grass, the stir of animals close by, the song of the nightingale, the friendly companionship of it all.

On the days when he had to stay home, life wasn't so interesting before Kate came. Chopping wood, helping Mother in the dairy, carrying water, had been his share.

The first few days after Kate's hectic arrival the relation between the cousins was rather strained. Kate couldn't get over the funny "petticoats" Jancsi was wearing. Catching her amused glances, Jancsi paid her back by gazing solemnly at the rafters, muttering something about "outlandish rats that get into people's sausages." Finally it was Kate who broke the ice. One afternoon she was waiting at the gate when Father and Jancsi returned from the day's ride. Jancsi was riding his favorite, a skittish two-year-old horse. It was dancing and prancing now, eager to get to the stable and hungry for its oats. Kate followed them and watched Jancsi unsaddle the horse and feed it.

From "The Good Master," by Kate Seredy, illustrations from drawings by Kate Seredy

"He's beautiful. May I pat his neck?" she asked.

"Watch out, he's ticklish," warned Jancsi.

"Takes a real boy to ride a horse like you do," said Kate with admiration, but hastened to add, "even if you do wear petticoats."

"Petticoats! Can't you see they're split?" Jancsi demonstrated, spreading his pleated pants.

"M-m-m," said Kate. "Do you think I could ride if I split my skirts?"

"I could teach you, Kate. I bet you'd make a good rider with your long legs."

"Will you, Jancsi? Honest? And then I could ride with you and Uncle instead of messing around with old embroideries, trying to be good."

"Well . . . maybe you could. I'll teach you anyway," promised Jancsi.

Next day Father rode alone. Jancsi was working like fury, trying to finish his chores quickly. He had a surprise for Kate. There were twelve brand-new ducklings in the poultry yard. He finished his work quicker than he expected. Mother was in the vegetable patch, spading up the soil for her seedlings. He walked back to the house and called Kate. She emerged from the bedroom, walking primly and awkwardly. She looked like a very, very good little girl! The warning flashed through Jancsi's mind: "When she looks like an angel, she is contemplating something disastrous." He made up his mind to be extra careful.

He took her to the chicken coop first. He showed her the nests where the hens were sitting on eggs. Kate was bound to break some eggs to see whether there were really little chicks inside. Only his solemn promise that he would call her when the chickens began to break through saved the lives of several future chicks.

The pigsty was a total failure as an entertainment. Kate just held her nose and walked away. Then Jancsi took her to see the cows.

"Can you ride a cow?" asked Kate.

Jancsi laughed. "No, you silly, they're milk cows."

"Milk cows? Don't tell me stories, they're chocolate cows. Why, they're all brown!"

When she finally understood that you have to milk a cow to get milk, she didn't want to believe it. "Why," she said, "milk grows in bottles!" But she wasn't interested enough to argue about it—she hated milk.

The geese and ducks were more interesting to her. She giggled at the funny way the ducks waddled and shook their tails. When Jancsi finally took her to see the baby ducks, Kate clapped her hands, exclaimed over them. She was fairly dancing with joy.

"See, they're only a day old, but they can swim like nobody's business," explained Jancsi proudly. Kate wanted to pick them up, but he told her that she must never handle very young animals; they might die. Surprisingly Kate listened to him. She said: "You know what they are like? Like little bunches of dandelions, all yellow and fuzzy. Let's pick dandelions and make believe they're duckies."

When they had a heap of the fuzzy yellow flowers, they sat down on the bank and tied them into small bunches. Kate threw some of them into the brook, where they floated, looking surprisingly like the ducklings. Then something unexpected happened. The mother duck got very excited, cocked her head to one side, then the other side. She peered at these yellow bunches suspiciously. Then she began to swim toward them, quack-quacking loudly.

"Look, Kate!" exclaimed Jancsi. "She thinks the flowers are baby ducks. Oh, how funny!"

It was funny indeed. Poor mother duck called and scolded, she tried to round up her strange brood, all in vain. The dandelions floated serenely down the brook. She got mad and pecked at one of the bunches, which promptly came to pieces.

She was frantic now. She kept turning this way, that way, not knowing what had happened.

Kate and Jancsi rolled on the grass; they were weak with laughter. Then something caught Jancsi's eye. He sat up and gazed at Kate who was lying on her stomach, kicking her legs, giggling and moaning in her amusement. There was something very wrong with Kate's costume. Her dark blue skirt was spread out on both sides on the grass, but there wasn't any skirt on Kate proper, only long white bloomers. He shook her shoulder. "Kate! What—what happened to your dress?"

Kate turned her head and peered at herself. "I split my skirt because you said you'd teach me to ride," she announced calmly. She scrambled to her feet, dragging the horrified Jancsi with her. "Come on to the stable, let's start the lesson."

Jancsi was too shocked. "But, Kate, your good dress. It's ruined!"

"Phoo. Your petticoats are split and they aren't ruined," scoffed Kate.

"But you're a girl—it looks awful queer," mumbled Jancsi, trailing reluctantly after her. He wished Father would come home so he could put off the riding lesson. He picked an old fat mare for Kate. He was just puttering around with the saddles, playing for time. She watched him with interest, asking questions about saddle, harness, reins. Then Jancsi led out the horses and, casting a last hopeful glance toward the gate, gave up waiting for Father. He proceeded to show Kate how to mount. He did it first, then dismounted again, and, holding both reins, explained every move.

"Stand at the left side of the horse. Put your left hand on the pommel, your right hand on the stirrup to steady it. Step in the stirrup with your left foot and swing over the saddle." He made Kate mount and dismount several times. Then he handed her the reins, and mounted his own horse.

They started walking the horses slowly around the yard. "Please, Kate," Jancsi said, seeing her excited face and gleaming eyes, "please, Kate, don't scream. It frightens the horses. Just in case anything should happen, kick loose from the stirrups and jump."

Kate nodded her head solemnly, clinging to the pommel with both hands.

"Let go of the pommel," instructed Jancsi. "Only gypsies ride that way. Sit up straight."

"But the horse keeps bobbing up and down, and I'm so high up," complained Kate, eying the ground suspiciously.

"High up! You were higher up on the rafters," giggled Jancsi.

"They didn't bob!" was the troubled answer.

It took quite a while before Kate got used to the bobbing and learned to sit straight and loose. Then she rewarded Jancsi with a gleaming smile. "I got it. Let's go fast now."

"Not today, Kate, you'll be sore all over anyway, not being used to the saddle."

But Kate wouldn't dismount. She coaxed and begged and wheedled until Jancsi made the horses trot. This was as far as he would go, however. He stopped the horses in spite of her dark and sulky look.

"Whee-ee!" She let out a long, loud scream. Jancsi's horse immediately went into the most violent action. He turned round and round like a spinning top. He dug his hoofs in the ground, trying to throw Jancsi. He rose on his hind legs,

thrashing the air viciously with his front hoofs. Jancsi clung to the plunging animal, talking to him in a soft, reassuring voice. He finally succeeded in bringing the horse to a shivering stop. Dismounting he looked around for Kate. The incredible child sat on her old mare, watching him with great interest.

"You screaming monkey," panted Jancsi. "Just you wait till I go riding with you again. Get off that horse!"

Kate didn't seem to notice that he was mad. "Gee, Jancsi, but you can ride! It was wonderful. This old armchair"—pointing to her horse—"just stood here while you had all the fun. Let me ride your horse now."

Jancsi, slightly pacified by her admiration, suddenly smiled. "If you dismount and walk over here, I'll let you." This wasn't a rash promise. He knew what would happen. Kate rolled off her horse —and just crumpled on the ground.

"My legs," she cried. "I haven't any legs!"

"Come on, Kate, walk over here!" teased Jancsi.

"Don't grin at me, I can't stand up. Oooh, I hurt all over!" moaned Kate.

"You sit there then until somebody picks you up," said Jancsi, leaving the puzzled Kate to rub her numb legs.

He was just putting away the saddles when Father rode in. Jancsi saw him stop and talk to Kate. He was laughing when he came into the stable.

"How long did you keep her in the saddle, anyway?" he asked.

Jancsi told him the story of the afternoon—except about the split skirt. He was very uneasy about that.

On their way back to the house, Father picked Kate up and carried her in. In the kitchen he put her on her shaking feet. Mother, who was bending over a pot of stew, turned around to greet them.

"Supper's ready," she started to say, but suddenly threw up her hands. "Oh, my goodness gracious! What did you do to the child?" The split skirt was in full evidence now. Kate, balancing stiffly and awkwardly, was a queer sight indeed. She wasn't disturbed, however. "Had to split it to ride like Jancsi," she said.

"Split it? On purpose? Why, you look positively indecent, Kate," exclaimed Mother. "Hurry up and change your dress."

"Can't hurry and haven't any other dress!" was the calm answer.

"Well, then sit down. I'm ashamed to see such lack of modesty," cried Mother.

"Can't sit, either!" wailed Kate.

Poor Kate. She had to eat her supper, balancing on her unsteady pins, conscious of the amused glances of Father and Jancsi and the shocked looks of Mother. It was a willing and meek Kate who was carried to bed right after supper.

When Mother returned to the kitchen, Father said: "We'd better lend her Jancsi's outgrown clothes."

Jancsi approved of the idea. Mother was doubtful, but finally agreed that, Kate being what she was, she would be much better off in pants.

Winnie-the-Pooh

A. A. MILNE

IN WHICH EEYORE LOSES A TAIL AND POOH FINDS ONE [1]

The Old Grey Donkey, Eeyore, stood by himself in a thistly corner of the forest, his front feet well apart, his head on one side, and thought about things. Sometimes he thought sadly to himself, "Why?" and sometimes he thought, "Wherefore?" and sometimes he thought, "Inasmuch as which?"—and sometimes he didn't quite know what he *was* thinking about. So when Winnie-the-Pooh came stumping along, Eeyore was very glad to be able to stop thinking for a little, in order to say "How do you do?" in a gloomy manner to him.

"And how are you?" said Winnie-the-Pooh.

Eeyore shook his head from side to side.

"Not very how," he said. "I don't seem to have felt at all how for a long time."

"Dear, dear," said Pooh, "I'm sorry about that. Let's have a look at you."

So Eeyore stood there, gazing sadly at the ground, and Winnie-the-Pooh walked all round him once.

"Why, what's happened to your tail?" he said in surprise.

"What *has* happened to it?" said Eeyore.

"It isn't there!"

"Are you sure?"

"Well, either a tail *is* there or it isn't there. You can't make a mistake about it. And yours *isn't* there!"

[1] From "Winnie-the-Pooh," by A. A. Milne, illustrated by Ernest H. Shepard

"Then what is?"

"Nothing."

"Let's have a look," said Eeyore, and he turned slowly round to the place where his tail had been a little while ago, and then, finding that he couldn't catch it up, he turned round the other way, until he came back to where he was at first, and then he put his head down and looked between his front legs, and at last he said, with a long, sad sigh, "I believe you're right."

"Of course I'm right," said Pooh.

"That Accounts for a Good Deal," said Eeyore gloomily. "It Explains Everything. No Wonder."

"You must have left it somewhere," said Winnie-the-Pooh.

"Somebody must have taken it," said Eeyore. "How Like Them," he added, after a long silence.

Pooh felt that he ought to say something helpful about it, but didn't quite know what. So he decided to do something helpful instead.

"Eeyore," he said solemnly, "I, Winnie-the-Pooh, will find your tail for you."

"Thank you, Pooh," answered Eeyore. "You're a real friend," said he. "Not like Some," he said.

So Winnie-the-Pooh went off to find Eeyore's tail.

It was a fine spring morning in the forest as he started out. Little soft clouds played happily in a blue sky, skipping from time to time in front of the sun as if they had come to put it out, and then sliding away suddenly so that the next might have his turn. Through them and between them the sun shone bravely; and a copse which had worn its firs all the year round seemed old and dowdy now beside the new green lace which the beeches had put on so prettily. Through copse and spinney marched Bear; down open slopes of gorse and heather, over rocky beds of streams, up steep banks of sandstone into the heather again; and so at last, tired and hungry, to the Hundred Acre Wood. For it was in the Hundred Acre Wood that Owl lived.

"And if anyone knows anything about anything," said Bear to himself, "it's Owl who knows something about something," he said, "or my name's not Winnie-the-Pooh," he said. "Which it is," he added. "So there you are."

Owl lived at The Chestnuts, an old-world residence of great charm, which was grander than anybody else's, or seemed so to Bear, because it had both a knocker *and* a bell-pull. Underneath the knocker there was a notice which said:

PLES RING IF AN RNSER IS REQIRD.

Underneath the bell-pull there was a notice which said:

PLEZ CNOKE IF AN RNSR IS NOT REQID.

These notices had been written by Christopher Robin, who was the only one in the forest who could spell; for Owl, wise though he was in many ways, able to read and write and spell his own name WOL, yet somehow went all to pieces over delicate words like MEASLES and BUTTERED TOAST.

Winnie-the-Pooh read the two notices very carefully, first from left to right, and afterwards, in case he had missed some of it, from right to left. Then, to make quite sure, he knocked and pulled the knocker, and he pulled and knocked the bell-rope, and he called out in a very loud voice, "Owl! I require an answer! It's Bear speaking." And the door opened, and Owl looked out.

"Hallo, Pooh," he said. "How's things?"

"Terrible and Sad," said Pooh, "because Eeyore, who is a friend of mine, has lost his tail. And he's Moping about it. So could you very kindly tell me how to find it for him?"

"Well," said Owl, "the customary procedure in such cases is as follows."

"What does Crustimoney Proseedcake mean?" said Pooh. "For I am a Bear of Very Little Brain, and long words Bother me."

"It means the Thing to Do."

"As long as it means that, I don't mind," said Pooh humbly.

"The thing to do is as follows. First, Issue a Reward. Then—"

"Just a moment," said Pooh, holding up his paw. "*What* do we do to this—what you were saying? You sneezed just as you were going to tell me."

"I *didn't* sneeze."

"Yes, you did, Owl."

"Excuse me, Pooh, I didn't. You can't sneeze without knowing it."

"Well, you can't know it without something having been sneezed."

"What I *said* was, 'First *Issue* a Reward.'"

"You're doing it again," said Pooh sadly.

"A Reward!" said Owl very loudly. "We write a notice to say that we will give a large something to anybody who finds Eeyore's tail."

"I see, I see," said Pooh, nodding his head. "Talking about large somethings," he went on dreamily, "I generally have a small something about now—about this time in the morning," and he looked wistfully at the cupboard in the corner of Owl's parlour; "just a mouthful of condensed milk or whatnot, with perhaps a lick of honey—"

"Well, then," said Owl, "we write out this notice, and we put it up all over the forest."

"A lick of honey," murmured Bear to himself, "or—or not, as the case may be." And he gave a deep sigh, and tried very hard to listen to what Owl was saying.

But Owl went on and on, using longer and longer words, until at last he came back to where he started, and he explained that the person to write out this notice was Christopher Robin.

"It was he who wrote the ones on my front door for me. Did you see them, Pooh?"

For some time now Pooh had been saying "Yes" and "No" in turn, with his eyes shut, to all that Owl was saying, and having said, "Yes, yes," last time, he said "No, not at all," now, without really knowing what Owl was talking about.

"Didn't you see them?" said Owl, a little surprised. "Come and look at them now."

So they went outside. And Pooh looked at the knocker and the notice below it, and he looked at the bell-rope and the notice below it, and the more he looked at the bell-rope, the more he felt that he had seen something like it, somewhere else, sometime before.

"Handsome bell-rope, isn't it?" said Owl.

Pooh nodded.

"It reminds me of something," he said, "but I can't think what. Where did you get it?"

"I just came across it in the Forest. It was hanging over a bush, and I thought at first somebody lived there, so I rang it, and nothing happened, and then I rang it again very loudly, and it came off in my hand, and as nobody seemed to want it, I took it home, and—"

"Owl," said Pooh solemnly, "you made a mistake. Somebody did want it."

"Who?"

"Eeyore. My dear friend Eeyore. He was—he was fond of it."

"Fond of it?"

"Attached to it," said Winnie-the-Pooh sadly.

So with these words he unhooked it, and carried it back to Eeyore; and when Christopher Robin had nailed it on in its right place again, Eeyore frisked about the forest, waving his tail so happily that Winnie-the-Pooh came over all funny, and had to hurry home for a little snack of something to sustain him. And, wiping his mouth half an hour afterwards, he sang to himself proudly:

Who found the Tail?
  "I," said Pooh,
"At a quarter to two
    (Only it was quarter to
      eleven really),
  I found the Tail!"

And To Think That I Saw It on Mulberry Street

DR. SEUSS

Illustration from a drawing by Dr. Seuss

When I leave home to walk to school,
Dad always says to me,
"Marco, keep your eyelids up
And see what you can see."

But when I tell him where I've been
And what I think I've seen,
He looks at me and sternly says,
"Your eyesight's much too keen.

"Stop telling such outlandish tales.
Stop turning minnows into whales."

. . . . . .

Now, what can I say
When I get home today?

All the long way to school
And all the way back,
I've looked and I've looked
And I've kept careful track,
But all that I've noticed,
Except my own feet,
Was a horse and a wagon
On Mulberry Street.
That's nothing to tell of,
That won't do, of course . . .
Just a broken-down wagon
That's drawn by a horse.

That *can't* be my story. That's only a *start*.
I'll say that a ZEBRA was pulling that cart!
And that is a story that no one can beat,
When I say that I saw it on Mulberry
    Street.
Yes, the zebra is fine,
But I think it's a shame,
Such a marvelous beast
With a cart that's so tame.
The story would really be better to hear
If the driver I saw were a charioteer.
A gold and blue chariot's *something* to
    meet,
Rumbling like thunder down Mulberry
    Street!

No, it won't do at all . . .
A zebra's too small.

A reindeer is better;
He's fast and he's fleet,
And he'd look mighty smart
On old Mulberry Street.

Hold on a minute!
There's something wrong!
A reindeer hates the way it feels
To pull a thing that runs on wheels.
He'd be much happier, instead,
If he could pull a fancy sled.

Hmmmm . . . A reindeer and
    sleigh . . .

Say—*any*one could think of *that*,
Jack or Fred or Joe or Nat—
Say, even Jane could think of *that*.

But it isn't too late to make one little
    change.
A sleigh and an ELEPHANT! *There's*
    something strange!

I'll pick one with plenty of power and size,
A blue one with plenty of fun in his eyes.
And then, just to give him a little more
    tone,
Have a Rajah, with rubies, perched high on
    a throne.
Say! That makes a story that *no one* can
    beat,
When I say that I saw it on Mulberry
    Street.

But now I don't know . . .
It still doesn't seem right.

An elephant pulling a thing that's so
    light
Would whip it around in the air like a
    kite.
But he'd look simply grand
With a great big brass band!

A band that's so good should have someone
    to hear it,
But it's going so fast that it's hard to keep
    near it.
I'll put on a trailer! I know they won't
    mind
If a man sits and listens while hitched on
    behind.

But now is it fair? Is it fair what I've
    done?
I'll bet those wagons weigh more than a
    ton.
That's really too heavy a load for *one* beast;
I'll give him some helpers. He needs two,
    at least.

But now what worries me is this . . .
Mulberry Street runs into Bliss.
Unless there's something I can fix up,
There'll be an *awful* traffic mix-up!
It takes Police to do the trick,
To guide them through where traffic's
    thick—
It takes Police to do the trick.
They'll never crash now. They'll race at
    top speed
With Sergeant Mulvaney, himself, in the
    lead.

The Mayor is there
And he thinks it is grand,
And he raises his hat
As they dash by the stand.

The Mayor is there
And the Aldermen too,
All waving big banners
Of red, white and blue.

And that is a story that NO ONE can beat
When I say that I saw it on Mulberry
    Street!

With a roar of its motor an airplane ap-
    pears
And dumps out confetti while everyone
    cheers.
And that makes a story that's really not
    bad!
But it still could be better. Suppose that
    I add . . .
. . . A Chinaman
Who eats with sticks. . . .
A big Magician
Doing tricks . . .
A ten-foot beard
That needs a comb. . . .
No time for more,
I'm almost home.

. . . . .

I swung 'round the corner
And dashed through the gate,
I ran up the steps
And I felt simply GREAT!

FOR I HAD A STORY THAT NO ONE
    COULD BEAT!
AND TO THINK THAT I SAW IT ON
    MULBERRY STREET!

But Dad said quite calmly,
"Just draw up your stool
And tell me the sights
On the way home from school."

There was so much to tell, I JUST
    COULDN'T BEGIN!
Dad looked at me sharply and pulled at his
    chin.
He frowned at me sternly from there in his
    seat,
"Was there nothing to look at . . . no peo-
    ple to greet?
Did *nothing* excite you or make your heart
    beat?"

"Nothing," I said, growing red as a beet,
"But a plain horse and wagon on Mulberry
    Street."

Black Beauty

ANNA SEWELL

A STORMY DAY [1]

One day late in the autumn, my master had a long journey to go on business. I was put into the dogcart, and John went with his master. I always liked to go in the dogcart, it was so light, and the high wheels ran along so pleasantly. There had been a great deal of rain, and now the wind was very high and blew the dry leaves across the road in a shower. We went along merrily till we came to the toll bar and the low wooden bridge. The river banks were rather high, and the bridge, instead of rising, went across just level, so that in the middle, if the river was full, the water would be nearly up to the woodwork and planks; but as there were good substantial rails on each side, people did not mind it.

The man at the gate said the river was rising fast, and he feared it would be a bad night. Many of the meadows were under water, and in one low part of the road, the water was halfway up to my knees; the bottom was good, and master drove gently, so it was no matter.

When we got to the town, of course I had a good bait, but as the master's business engaged him a long time we did not start for home till rather late in the afternoon. The wind was then much higher, and I heard the master say to John, he had never been out in such a storm; and so I thought, as we went along the skirts of a wood, where the great branches were swaying about like twigs, and the rushing sound was terrible.

"I wish we were well out of this wood," said my master.

"Yes, sir," said John, "it would be rather awkward if one of these branches came down upon us."

The words were scarcely out of his mouth, when there was a groan, and a crack, and a splitting sound, and tearing, crashing down among the other trees came an oak, torn up by the roots, and it fell right across the road just before us. I will never say I was not frightened, for I was. I stopped still, and I believe I trembled; of course I did not turn round or run away; I was not brought up to that. John jumped out and was in a moment at my head.

"That was a very near touch," said my master. "What's to be done now?"

"Well, sir, we can't drive over that tree nor yet get round it; there will be nothing for it, but to go back to the four crossways, and that will be a good six miles before we get round to the wooden bridge again; it will make us late, but the horse is fresh."

So back we went and round by the crossroads; but by the time we got to the bridge it was very nearly dark. We could just see that the water was over the middle of it; but as that happened sometimes when the floods were out, master did not stop. We were going along at a good pace, but the moment my feet touched the first part of the bridge I felt sure there was something wrong. I dare not go forward, and I made a dead stop. "Go on, Beauty," said my master, and he gave me a touch with the whip, but I dare not stir; he gave me a sharp cut, I jumped, but I dare not go forward.

"There's something wrong, sir," said John, and he sprang out of the dogcart and came to my head and looked all about. He tried to lead me forward. "Come on, Beauty, what's the matter?" Of course I could not tell him, but I knew very well that the bridge was not safe.

Just then the man at the tollgate on the other side ran out of the house, tossing a torch about like one mad.

"Hoy, hoy, hoy, halloo, stop!" he cried.

1 From "Black Beauty," by Anna Sewell, illustrated by Fritz Eichenberg

"What's the matter?" shouted my master.

"The bridge is broken in the middle, and part of it is carried away; if you come on you'll be into the river."

"Thank God!" said my master. "You Beauty!" said John, and took the bridle and gently turned me round to the right-hand road by the riverside. The sun had set some time, the wind seemed to have lulled off after that furious blast which tore up the tree. It grew darker and darker, stiller and stiller. I trotted quietly along, the wheels hardly making a sound on the soft road. For a good while neither master nor John spoke, and then master began in a serious voice. I could not understand much of what they said, but I found they thought, if I had gone on as the master wanted me, most likely the bridge would have given way under us, and horse, chaise, master and man would have fallen into the river; and as the current was flowing very strongly, and there was no light and no help at hand, it was more than likely we should all have been drowned. Master said God had given men reason, by which they could find out things for themselves, but He had given animals knowledge which did not depend on reason, and which was much more prompt and perfect in its way, and by which they had often saved the lives of men. John had many stories to tell of dogs and horses, and the wonderful things they had done; he thought people did not value their animals half enough, nor make friends of them as they ought to do. I am sure he makes friends of them if ever a man did.

At last we came to the Park gates, and found the gardener looking out for us. He said that mistress had been in a dreadful way ever since dark, fearing some accident had happened, and that she had sent James off on Justice, the roan cob, towards the wooden bridge to make inquiry after us.

We saw a light at the hall door and at the upper windows, and as we came up mistress ran out, saying, "Are you really safe, my dear? Oh! I have been so anxious, fancying all sorts of things. Have you had no accident?"

"No, my dear; but if your Black Beauty had not been wiser than we were, we should all have been carried down the river at the wooden bridge." I heard no more, as they went into the house, and John took me to the stable. Oh! what a good supper he gave me that night, a good bran mash and some crushed beans with my oats, and such a thick bed of straw, and I was glad of it, for I was tired.

Raggedy Andy Stories

JOHNNY GRUELLE

RAGGEDY ANDY'S SMILE [1]

Raggedy Andy's smile was gone.

Not entirely, but enough so that it made his face seem onesided.

If one viewed Raggedy Andy from the left side, one could see his smile.

But if one looked at Raggedy Andy from the right side, one could not see his smile. So Raggedy Andy's smile was gone.

It really was not Raggedy Andy's fault.

He felt just as happy and sunny as ever.

And perhaps would not have known the difference had not the other dolls told him he had only one half of his cheery smile left.

Nor was it Marcella's fault. How was she to know that Dickie would feed Raggedy Andy orange juice and take off most of his smile?

[1] From "Raggedy Andy Stories," by Johnny Gruelle, illustrated from drawings by Johnny Gruelle

And besides taking off one half of Raggedy Andy's smile, the orange juice left a great brown stain upon his face.

Marcella was very sorry when she saw what Dickie had done.

Dickie would have been sorry, too, if he had been more than two years old, but when one is only two years old, he has very few sorrows.

Dickie's only sorrow was that Raggedy Andy was taken from him, and he could not feed Raggedy Andy more orange juice.

Marcella kissed Raggedy Andy more than she did the rest of the dolls that night, when she put them to bed, and this made all the dolls very happy.

It always gave them great pleasure when any of their number was hugged and kissed, for there was not a selfish doll among them.

Marcella hung up a tiny stocking for each of the dollies, and placed a tiny little china dish for each of the penny dolls beside their little spool box bed.

For, as you probably have guessed, it was Christmas eve, and Marcella was in hopes Santa Claus would see the tiny stockings and place something in them for each dollie.

Then when the house was very quiet, the French doll told Raggedy Andy that most of his smile was gone.

"Indeed!" said Raggedy Andy. "I can still feel it! It must be there!"

"Oh, but it really is gone!" Uncle Clem said. "It was the orange juice!"

"Well, I still feel just as happy," said Raggedy Andy, "so let's have a jolly game of some sort! What shall it be?"

"Perhaps we had best try to wash your face!" said practical Raggedy Ann. She always acted as a mother to the other dolls when they were alone.

"It will not do a bit of good!" the French doll told Raggedy Ann, "for I remember I had orange juice spilled upon a nice white frock I had one time, and the stain would never come out!"

"That is too bad!" Henny, the Dutch doll,

said. "We shall miss Raggedy Andy's cheery smile when he is looking straight at us!"

"You will have to stand on my right side, when you wish to see my smile!" said Raggedy Andy, with a cheery little chuckle 'way down in his soft cotton inside.

"But I wish everyone to understand," he went on, "that I am smiling just the same, whether you can see it or not!"

And with this, Raggedy Andy caught hold of Uncle Clem and Henny, and made a dash for the nursery door, followed by all the other dolls.

Raggedy Andy intended jumping down the stairs, head over heels, for he knew that neither he, Uncle Clem nor Henny would break anything by jumping down stairs.

But just as they got almost to the door, they dropped to the floor in a heap, for there, standing watching the whole performance, was a man.

All the dolls fell in different attitudes, for it would never do for them to let a real person see that they could act and talk just like real people.

Raggedy Andy, Uncle Clem and Henny stopped so suddenly they fell over each other and Raggedy Andy, being in the lead and pulling the other two, slid right through the door and stopped at the feet of the man.

A cheery laugh greeted this and a chubby hand reached down and picked up Raggedy Andy and turned him over.

Raggedy Andy looked up into a cheery little round face, with a little red nose and red cheeks, and all framed in white whiskers which looked just like snow.

Then the little round man walked into the nursery and picked up all the dolls and looked at them. He made no noise when he walked, and this was why he had taken the dolls by surprise at the head of the stairs.

The little man with the snow-white whiskers placed all the dolls in a row and from a little case in his pocket he took a tiny bottle and a little brush. He dipped the little brush in the tiny bottle and touched all the dolls' faces with it.

He had purposely saved Raggedy Andy's face until the last. Then, as all the dolls watched, the cheery little white-whiskered man touched Raggedy Andy's face with the magic liquid, and the orange juice stain disappeared, and in its place came Raggedy Andy's rosy cheeks and cheery smile.

And, turning Raggedy Andy so that he could face all the other dolls, the cheery little man showed him that all the other dolls had new rosy cheeks and newly-painted faces. They all looked just like new dollies. Even Susan's cracked head had been made whole.

Henny, the Dutch doll, was so surprised he fell over backward and said, "Squeek!"

When the cheery little man with the white whiskers heard this, he picked Henny up and touched him with the paint brush in the center of the back, just above the place where Henny had the little mechanism which made him say "Mamma" when he was new. And when the little man touched Henny and tipped him forward and backward, Henny was just as good as new and said "Mamma" very prettily.

Then the little man put something in each of the tiny doll stockings, and something in each of the little china plates for the two penny dolls.

Then, as quietly as he had entered, he left, merely turning at the door and shaking his finger at the dolls in a cheery, mischievous manner.

Raggedy Andy heard him chuckling to himself as he went down the stairs.

Raggedy Andy tiptoed to the door and over to the head of the stairs.

Then he motioned for the other dolls to come.

There, from the head of the stairs, they watched the cheery little white-whiskered man take pretty things from a large sack and place them about the chimneyplace.

"He does not know that we are watching him," the dolls all thought, but when the little man had finished his task, he turned quickly and laughed right up at the dolls, for he had known that they were watching him all the time.

Then, again shaking his finger at them in his cheery manner, the little white-whiskered man swung the sack to his shoulder, and with a whistle such as the wind makes when it plays through the chinks of a window, he was gone—up the chimney.

The dolls were very quiet as they walked back into the nursery and sat down to think it all over, and as they sat there thinking, they heard out in the night the "tinkle, tinkle, tinkle" of tiny sleigh bells, growing fainter and fainter as they disappeared in the distance.

Without a word, but filled with a happy wonder, the dolls climbed into their beds, just as Marcella had left them, and pulled the covers up to their chins.

And Raggedy Andy lay there, his little shoe button eyes looking straight towards the ceiling and smiling a joyful smile—not a "half smile" this time, but a "full size smile."

The Velveteen Rabbit

MARGERY WILLIAMS BIANCO

HOW TOYS BECOME REAL [1]

There was once a velveteen rabbit, and in the beginning he was really splendid. He was fat and bunchy, as a rabbit should be; his coat was spotted brown and white, he had real thread whiskers, and his ears were lined with pink sateen. On Christmas morning, when he sat wedged in the top of the Boy's stocking, with a sprig of holly between his paws, the effect was charming.

There were other things in the stocking, nuts and oranges and a toy engine, and chocolate almonds and a clockwork mouse, but the Rabbit was quite the best of all. For at least two hours the Boy loved him, and then Aunts and Uncles came to dinner, and there was a great rustling of tissue paper and unwrapping of parcels, and in the excitement of looking at all the new presents the Velveteen Rabbit was forgotten.

For a long time he lived in the toy cupboard or on the nursery floor, and no one thought very much about him. He was naturally shy, and being only made of velveteen, some of the more expensive toys quite snubbed him. The mechanical toys were very superior, and looked down upon every one else; they were full of modern ideas, and pretended they were real. The model boat, who had lived through two seasons and lost most of his paint, caught the tone from them and never missed an opportunity of referring to his rigging in technical terms. The Rabbit could not claim to be a model of anything, for he didn't know that real rabbits existed; he thought they were all stuffed with sawdust like himself, and he understood that sawdust was quite out-of-date and should never be mentioned in modern circles. Even Timothy, the jointed wooden lion, who was made by the disabled soldiers, and should have had broader views, put on airs and pretended he was connected with Government. Between them all the poor little Rabbit was made to feel himself very insignificant and commonplace, and the only person who was kind to him at all was the Skin Horse.

The Skin Horse had lived longer in the nursery than any of the others. He was so old that his brown coat was bald in patches and showed the seams underneath, and most of the hairs in his tail had been pulled out to string bead necklaces. He was wise, for he had seen a long succession of mechanical toys arrive to boast and swagger, and by-and-by break their mainsprings and pass away, and he knew that they were only toys, and would never turn into anything else. For nursery magic is very strange and wonderful, and only those playthings that are old and wise and experienced like the Skin Horse understand all about it.

"What is REAL?" asked the Rabbit one day, when they were lying side by side near the nursery fender, before Nana came to tidy the room. "Does it mean having things that buzz inside you and a stick-out handle?"

"Real isn't how you are made," said the Skin Horse. "It's a thing that happens to you. When a child loves you for a long, long time, not just to play with, but REALLY loves you, then you become Real."

"Does it hurt?" asked the Rabbit.

[1] From "The Velveteen Rabbit," by Margery Williams Bianco, illustration from a drawing by William Nicholson

"Sometimes," said the Skin Horse, for he was always truthful. "When you are Real you don't mind being hurt."

"Does it happen all at once, like being wound up," he asked, "or bit by bit?"

"It doesn't happen all at once," said the Skin Horse. "You become. It takes a long time. That's why it doesn't often happen to people who break easily, or have sharp edges, or who have to be carefully kept. Generally, by the time you are Real, most of your hair has been loved off, and your eyes drop out and you get loose in the joints and very shabby. But these things don't matter at all, because once you are Real you can't be ugly, except to people who don't understand."

"I suppose you *are* Real?" said the Rabbit. And then he wished he had not said it, for he thought the Skin Horse might be sensitive. But the Skin Horse only smiled.

"The Boy's Uncle made me Real," he said. "That was a great many years ago; but once you are Real you can't become unreal again. It lasts for always."

The Rabbit sighed. He thought it would be a long time before this magic called Real happened to him. He longed to be-

come Real, to know what it felt like; and yet the idea of growing shabby and losing his eyes and whiskers was rather sad. He wished that he could become it without these uncomfortable things happening to him.

There was a person called Nana who ruled the nursery. Sometimes she took no notice of the playthings lying about, and sometimes, for no reason whatever, she went swooping about like a great wind and hustled them away in cupboards. She called this "tidying up," and the playthings all hated it, especially the tin ones. The Rabbit didn't mind it so much, for wherever he was thrown he came down soft.

One evening, when the Boy was going to bed, he couldn't find the china dog that always slept with him. Nana was in a hurry, and it was too much trouble to hunt for china dogs at bedtime, so she simply looked about her, and seeing that the toy cupboard door stood open, she made a swoop.

"Here," she said, "take your old Bunny! He'll do to sleep with you!" And she dragged the Rabbit out by one ear, and put him into the Boy's arms.

That night, and for many nights after, the Velveteen Rabbit slept in the Boy's bed. At first he found it rather uncomfortable, for the Boy hugged him very tight, and sometimes he rolled over on him, and sometimes he pushed him so far under the pillow that the Rabbit could scarcely breathe. And he missed, too, those long moonlight hours in the nursery, when all the house was silent, and his talks with the Skin Horse. But very soon he grew to like it, for the Boy used to talk to him, and made nice tunnels for him under the bed-clothes that he said were like the burrows the real rabbits lived in. And they had splendid games together, in whispers, when Nana had gone away to her supper and left the night-light burning on the mantelpiece. And when the Boy dropped off to sleep, the Rabbit would snuggle down close under his little warm chin and

dream, with the Boy's hands clasped close round him all night long.

And so time went on, and the little Rabbit was very happy—so happy that he never noticed how his beautiful velveteen fur was getting shabbier and shabbier, and his tail coming unsewn, and all the pink rubbed off his nose where the Boy had kissed him.

Spring came, and they had long days in the garden, for wherever the Boy went the Rabbit went too. He had rides in the wheelbarrow, and picnics on the grass, and lovely fairy huts built for him under the raspberry canes behind the flower border. And once, when the Boy was called away suddenly to go out to tea, the Rabbit was left out on the lawn until long after dusk, and Nana had to come and look for him with the candle because the Boy couldn't go to sleep unless he was there. He was wet through with the dew and quite earthy from diving into the burrows the Boy had made for him in the flower bed, and Nana grumbled as she rubbed him off with a corner of her apron.

"You must have your old Bunny!" she said. "Fancy all that fuss for a toy!"

The Boy sat up in bed and stretched out his hands.

"Give me my Bunny!" he said. "You mustn't say that. He isn't a toy. He's REAL!"

When the little Rabbit heard that he was happy, for he knew that what the Skin Horse had said was true at last. The nursery magic had happened to him, and he was a toy no longer. He was Real. The Boy himself had said it.

That night he was almost too happy to sleep, and so much love stirred in his little sawdust heart that it almost burst. And into his boot-button eyes, that had long ago lost their polish, there came a look of wisdom and beauty, so that even Nana noticed it next morning when she picked him up, and said, "I declare if that old Bunny hasn't got quite a knowing expression!"

The Lion-Hearted Kitten[1]

PEGGY BACON

Once there was a striped kitten with yellow eyes and a black nose. He was only a very little kitten but he had the heart of a lion. He was as brave as he could be, and one day he started out to conquer the world. The path he took led through a big black wood, and down this path the kitten stalked very proudly, with his head held high as possible.

Pretty soon, along came a big gray wolf.

"Grumble tumble in the jungle, I'm hungry!" growled the wolf, for this is what the wolves say when they are going to eat you up.

Now it is all very well to be brave in a crisis, but it is even better to be clever too. This the kitten knew, so without showing any fear he said boldly:

"O Mr. Wolf, I was just looking for you. My great-aunt the tigress told me to ask you the way to roast lamb. She says you know so much more about such things than she."

The wolf was impressed and a little flattered. But he was also a bit suspicious of this small kitten, and so he said:

"Tell your great-aunt the tigress that I roast lamb the same way that I roast kitten."

This really frightened the kitten, but he pretended great unconcern and retorted:

"Of course, Mr. Wolf, if you really wish me to tell her that, I will do so; but my great-aunt the tigress is rather short of temper and she might take offense at what you say; she has kittens of her own and a great many little nieces and nephews."

"Hmmm," murmured the wolf gazing

[1] From "The Lion-Hearted Kitten, and Other Stories," by Peggy Bacon, illustrations from drawings by Peggy Bacon

thoughtfully at the kitten who had begun to wash its face, "you may tell her that roast lamb tastes nice with sage and onions." He turned and ran into the wood.

The kitten trotted on along the path and suddenly around a corner he came face to face with a great big enormous snake who was hanging from the branch of a tree just over the path.

"Hiss swish, wish a dish for dinner!" hissed the snake, for that is what the snakes say when they are going to eat you up.

"O Miss Boa Constrictor," cried the kitten (for that was the snake's name), "I have been looking for you everywhere. My great-aunt the tigress wishes to know the best way to catch birds. She says that you are so clever at it, and she would be much obliged for some advice on the subject."

Now snakes catch little creatures by staring in their eyes till they are so frightened they dare not move; the boa constrictor said:

"Watch me and I'll show you," for she thought the little kitten looked quite fat and delicious.

But the kitten was far too wise for that, so he simply looked hard beyond the snake and called out:

"Well, I do declare, if that isn't my great-aunt the tigress herself coming this way now!"

The snake whipped round quickly for fear the tigress was creeping up behind

her, and while she looked back, the kitten escaped into the wood.

The brave little kitten ran on and on till by and by very suddenly round a big tree he came face to face with the tigress herself.

This time the kitten for all his courage was much alarmed. His breath came fast and his heart beat rapidly, but his wits did not forsake him.

"O Aunty Tigress," he gasped, "I have been hunting and hunting for you till I am all out of breath. My mother, the golden tigress of the next forest but one, wishes to know what it is your kittens eat which makes them so big and fat. She is worried about me because I am so very small."— After this speech the kitten held his breath, waiting for the tigress to reply.

For a long time the tigress looked at the kitten and sniffed at the kitten and put her head on one side and considered the kitten. And after a while she came to the conclusion that this kitten certainly did look quite like her kittens save for size; and since her own children had grown up and left home she decided it would be nice to adopt another; so giving the kitten a motherly lick of a large kind she said:

"You certainly are much too small, and if you will come home with me I will feed you up and fatten you up and see what I can do."

Away they walked together, the kitten not without misgivings, going through the big black wood till they came to the tigress' cave. There the tigress gave the kitten all kinds of meat and bones; and sure enough the kitten began to grow, and he grew and grew and grew until he got to be about as big as a cat. The tigress was then well satisfied, for she said: "You are now exactly the size of my own kittens; this diet has agreed with you."

And so the kitten continued to live happily in the cave cared for and protected by the tigress, but he never grew to be any bigger than a cat.

Rapunzel[1]

There was once a man and his wife who had long wished in vain for a child, and at last they had reason to hope that heaven would grant their wish. There was a little window at the back of their house, which overlooked a beautiful garden full of lovely flowers and shrubs. It was, however, surrounded by a wall, and nobody dared to enter, because it belonged to a witch who was feared by everybody.

One day the woman, standing at this window and looking into the garden, saw a bed planted with beautiful rampion. It looked so fresh and green that she longed to eat some of it. This longing increased every day; and as she knew it could never be satisfied, she began to look pale and miserable and to pine away. Then her husband was alarmed and said, "What ails you, my dear wife?"

"Alas!" she answered. "If I cannot get any of the rampion to eat from the garden behind our house, I shall die."

Her husband, who loved her, thought, "Before you let your wife die you must fetch her some of that rampion, cost what it may." So in the twilight he climbed over the wall into the witch's garden, hastily picked a handful of rampion, and took it back to his wife. She immediately prepared it and ate it very eagerly. It was so very, very nice that the next day her longing for it increased threefold. She could have no peace unless her husband fetched her some more. So in the twilight he set out again, but when he got over the wall he was terrified to see the witch before him.

"How dare you come into my garden like a thief and steal my rampion?" she said, with angry looks. "It shall be the worse for you!"

"Alas!" he answered. "Be merciful to me. I am only here from necessity. My wife sees your rampion from the window, and she has such a longing for it that she would die if she could not get some of it."

The anger of the witch abated and she said to him, "If it is as you say, I will allow you to take away with you as much rampion as you like, but on one condition. You must give me the child which your wife is about to bring into the world. I will care for it like a mother, and all will be well with it."

In his fear the man consented to everything. And when the baby was born, the witch appeared, gave it the name of Rapunzel (rampion), and took it away with her.

Rapunzel was the most beautiful child under the sun. When she was twelve years old, the witch shut her up in a tower which stood in a wood. It had neither staircase nor doors, but only a little window quite high up in the wall.

When the witch wanted to enter the tower, she stood at the foot of it and cried, "Rapunzel, Rapunzel, let down your hair!"

Rapunzel had splendid long hair, as fine as spun gold. As soon as she heard the voice of the witch, she unfastened her plaits and twisted her hair round a hook by the window. It fell twenty ells downwards, and the witch climbed up by it.

It happened a couple of years later that the King's son rode through the forest and came close to the tower. From thence he heard a song so lovely that he stopped to listen. It was Rapunzel who in her loneli-

[1] A fairy tale by the Brothers Grimm. Illustration from a drawing by H. J. Ford.

ness made her sweet voice resound to pass away the time. The King's son wanted to join her, and he sought for the door of the tower but there was none to find.

He rode home, but the song had touched his heart so deeply that he went into the forest every day to listen to it. Once when he was hidden behind a tree he saw a witch come to the tower and call out, "Rapunzel, Rapunzel, let down your hair!"

Then Rapunzel lowered her plaits of hair and the witch climbed up to her. "If that is the ladder by which one ascends," he thought, "I will try my luck myself." And the next day, when it began to grow dark, he went to the tower and cried, "Rapunzel, Rapunzel, let down your hair!"

The hair fell down and the King's son climbed up it.

At first Rapunzel was terrified, for she had never set eyes on a man before. But the King's son talked to her kindly, and told her that his heart had been so deeply touched by her song that he had no peace and was obliged to see her. Then Rapunzel lost her fear. And when he asked her if she would have him for her husband, and she saw that he was young and handsome, she thought, "He will love me better than old Mother Gothel." So she said, "Yes," and laid her hand in his. She said, "I will gladly go with you, but I do not know how I am to get down from this tower. When you come, will you bring a skein of silk with you every time? I will twist it into a ladder, and when it is long enough I will descend by it, and you can take me away with you on your horse."

She arranged with him that he should come and see her every evening, for the old witch came in the daytime.

The witch discovered nothing till suddenly Rapunzel said to her, "Tell me, Mother Gothel, how can it be that you are so much heavier to draw up than the young prince who will be here before long?"

"Oh, you wicked child, what do you say? I thought I had separated you from all the world, and yet you have deceived me." In her rage she seized Rapunzel's beautiful hair, twisted it twice round her left hand, snatched up a pair of shears, and cut off the plaits, which fell to the ground. She was so merciless that she took poor Rapunzel away into a wilderness, where she forced her to live in the greatest grief and misery.

In the evening of the day on which she had banished Rapunzel, the witch fastened the plaits which she had cut off to the hook by the window. And when the Prince came and called:

"Rapunzel, Rapunzel, let down your hair!"

—she lowered the hair. The Prince climbed up, but there he found, not his beloved Rapunzel, but the witch, who looked at him with angry and wicked eyes.

"Ah!" she cried mockingly, "you have come to fetch your ladylove, but the pretty bird is no longer in her nest. And she can sing no more, for the cat has seized her and it will scratch your own eyes out too. Rapunzel is lost to you. You will never see her again."

The Prince was beside himself with grief, and in his despair he sprang out of the window. He was not killed, but his eyes were scratched out by the thorns among which he fell. He wandered about blind in the wood and had nothing but roots and berries to eat. He did nothing but weep and lament over the loss of his beloved wife Rapunzel. In this way he wandered about for some years, till at last he reached the wilderness where Rapunzel had been living very sadly in great poverty.

He heard a voice which seemed very familiar to him and he went towards it. Rapunzel knew him at once and fell weeping upon his neck. Two of her tears fell upon his eyes, and they immediately grew quite clear and he could see as well as ever.

He took her to his kingdom, where he was received with joy, and they lived long and happily together.

Heidi

JOHANNA SPYRI

IN THE PASTURE [1]

Heidi was awakened early in the morning by a loud whistle; and when she opened her eyes, sunshine was pouring through the round window on her bed and the hay close by, so that everything about shone like gold. Heidi looked round her in amazement and did not know where she was.

Then she heard her grandfather's deep voice outside, and everything came back to her mind—where she had come from, and that now she was up on the Alm with her grandfather and no longer with old Ursel. Ursel was always cold, so that she liked to sit by the kitchen fire or by the stove in her chamber. Heidi had been obliged to stay very near, so that the old woman could see where she was, because she was deaf and could not hear her. This had often been very tiresome to Heidi, who longed to run outside.

So she was very glad when she awoke in her new home and remembered how many strange things she had seen the day before and what she would see again that day, especially Schwänli and Bärli.

Heidi jumped quickly out of bed and in a few minutes had put on all that she wore the day before; it was very little. Then she climbed down the ladder and ran out in front of the hut. There already stood the goatherd Peter with his flock, and the grandfather was bringing Schwänli and Bärli out of the shed to join the other goats. Heidi ran up to him to say good morning to him and the goats.

"Would you like to go to the pasture, too?" asked the grandfather. Heidi was pleased with the idea and jumped for joy.

"But first wash and be clean, or else the sun will laugh at you when it is shining so brightly up there and sees that you are dirty; see, everything is ready for you."

The grandfather pointed to a large tub full of water standing before the door in the sunshine. Heidi ran to it and splashed and rubbed until she was all shining. Meanwhile the grandfather went into the hut and called to Peter:

"Come here, general of the goats, and bring your haversack with you."

Peter, surprised, obeyed the call and brought along the little bag in which he carried his scanty dinner.

"Open it," said the old man; and he put in a large piece of bread and an equally large piece of cheese. Peter opened his round eyes as wide as possible in his amazement, for both pieces were half as large again as what he had brought for his own dinner.

"Now in goes the little bowl," continued the uncle, "for the child cannot drink the way you do, right from the goat; she doesn't know how. Milk two bowlfuls at noon for her, as she is to go with you and stay until you come down again; take care that she doesn't fall over the rocks; do you hear?"

Heidi came running up.

"Can the sun laugh at me now, grandfather?" she asked eagerly. In her fear of the sun she had rubbed her face, neck, and arms so vigorously with the coarse towel her grandfather had hung by the water tub that she looked as red as a lobster. Her grandfather smiled.

"No; now he has nothing to laugh at," he admitted. "But tonight, when you come

[1] From "Heidi," by Joanna Spyri, illustration from a drawing by Gustaf Tenggren

home, you must go in all over, like a fish; for after running about like the goats you will have black feet. Now you can march along."

So she went merrily up the Alm. The wind in the night had blown away the last clouds; the sky was everywhere a deep blue, and in the midst stood the sun, shining on the green mountain; all the blue and yellow flowers opened their cups and looked up with gladness. Heidi jumped here and there and shouted for joy; for there were whole troops of delicate primroses together, and yonder it was blue with gentians, and everywhere in the sunshine smiled and nodded the tender-leaved golden rockroses. Heidi was so charmed by all these glistening, nodding flowers that she entirely forgot the goats and even Peter. She ran far ahead and then off on one side, for it shone red here and yellow there and enticed her in every direction. Wherever she went she picked quantities of the flowers and put them into her apron, for she wanted to carry them all home and put them into the hay in her sleeping room, that it might look there as it did here.

So Peter had to look everywhere; and his round eyes, which did not move quickly from one place to another, had more work than they could well manage, for the goats were as bad as Heidi. They ran hither and thither, and he was obliged to whistle and shout and swing his rod continually in order to drive all the stragglers together.

"Where have you gone now, Heidi?" he called almost angrily.

"Here," sounded from some unseen place. Peter could see no one, for Heidi was sitting on the ground behind a knoll, which was thickly covered with fragrant wild flowers. The whole air round was filled with the sweet odor, and Heidi had never breathed anything so delicious before. She sat down among the flowers and drew in long breaths of the perfume.

"Come along!" called Peter again. "You must not fall down over the cliffs; the uncle charged me not to let you."

"Where are the cliffs?" asked Heidi without stirring from the place, for every breath of wind brought the sweet fragrance to her with increasing charm.

"Up there, 'way up; we have still a long way to go; so come along now! And up at the top sits the old robber-bird croaking."

That succeeded. Heidi immediately jumped up and ran to Peter with her apron full of flowers.

"You have enough now," he said, when they were once more climbing together. "Besides, you'll stay here forever, and if you pick them all you won't have any to-morrow."

The last reason convinced Heidi; besides, her apron was already so full that there was hardly room for more. So she went along with Peter; and the goats behaved better and hurried along without delay, for they smelt the good herbage in the distance on the high pasture land.

The pasture where Peter usually went with his goats for the day lay at the foot of the high cliff. The lower part of this was covered with bushes and fir trees, but it rose toward heaven quite bald and steep. On one side of the mountain there were deep abysses. The grandfather was quite right in warning Peter about them.

When Peter reached this spot on the heights, he took off his bag and laid it carefully in a little hollow in the ground. He knew that the wind often rushed across in strong gusts, and he did not wish to see his precious possessions roll down the mountain. Then he stretched himself out on the ground in the sunny pasture to rest.

In the meantime Heidi had taken off her apron, rolled it up tightly with the flowers inside, and laid it close to the lunch bag. Then she sat down beside Peter and looked round her. The valley lay far below in the full morning sunshine. In front of her Heidi saw a great wide field of snow, stretching high up into the deep blue sky; on the left stood an enormous mass of rock, on each side of which a higher tower of bald, jagged cliffs rose into the sky and looked very sternly down on Heidi. The child sat as still as a mouse; everywhere there was a great, deep stillness; only the wind passed very softly and gently over the tender bluebells and the radiant golden rockroses, which were everywhere gaily nodding to and fro on their slender stems. Peter had gone to sleep after his labor, and the goats were climbing among the bushes.

She drank in the golden sunlight, the fresh air, the delicate fragrance of the flowers, and desired nothing more than to remain there forever.

Then she heard above her a loud, shrill screaming and croaking, and as she looked up into the air the largest bird she had ever seen in her life was flying round on wide, outstretched wings and coming back in wider circles and screaming loud and piercingly over her head.

"Peter! Peter! Wake up!" cried Heidi at the top of her voice. "See, there is the robber-bird! See! see!"

Peter jumped up at the call and looked with Heidi at the bird, which was flying higher and higher in the blue sky. Finally it disappeared over the gray cliffs.

"Where has he gone now?" asked Heidi, who had watched the bird eagerly.

"Home to his nest," was Peter's answer.

"Is his home 'way up there? Oh, how lovely to be so high up! Why does he scream so?" asked Heidi again.

"Because he can't help it," explained Peter.

"Let us climb up there and see where his home is," proposed Heidi.

"Oh! oh! oh!" burst out Peter, uttering each exclamation with stronger disapproval. "No goat can get there, and the uncle said you must not fall over the cliff."

Then Peter suddenly began such a whistling and calling that Heidi did not know what was going to happen; but the goats must have understood the sound, for one after another they came jumping down until the whole flock was assembled on the green slope, some nibbling the spicy stalks, others running to and fro, and still others amusing themselves by butting one another with their horns.

Heidi jumped up and ran round among the goats. It was new and extremely amusing to her to see how the little creatures leaped about and played together, and Heidi made the personal acquaintance of each, for every one had a quite distinct individuality and its own peculiar ways.

Meanwhile Peter had brought out the bag and nicely arranged all four of the pieces of bread and cheese on the ground in a square, the larger pieces on Heidi's side, the smaller ones on his side. Then he took the little bowl and milked sweet, fresh milk from Schwänli into it and placed it in the middle of the square. Then he called Heidi, but he had to call longer for her than for the goats, because she was so interested and pleased with the playing and frolicking of her new playmates that she saw and heard nothing else.

But Peter knew how to make himself understood. He called till he made the rocks above echo; and Heidi appeared, and the table he had laid looked so inviting that she danced round it for joy.

"Stop jumping; it is time to eat," said Peter. "Sit down and begin."

Heidi sat down.

"Is the milk mine?" she asked, looking with satisfaction at the neat square and the bowl in the middle.

"Yes," answered Peter, "and the two large pieces of bread and cheese are yours, too; and when you have drunk all the milk, you can have another bowlful from Schwänli, and then it is my turn."

"And where will you get your milk?" Heidi wanted to know.

"From my goat—from Schnecke. Go to eating!" commanded Peter once more.

Heidi began with her milk, and as soon as she set down her empty bowl Peter rose and filled it again. Heidi broke some of her bread into it; the rest, a piece still larger than all Peter's bread, she handed over to him, with all her large portion of cheese, and said:

"You may have that. I have enough."

Peter looked at Heidi in speechless amazement, for never in his life had he been able to say such a thing or give anything away. He hesitated a little, for he could not really believe that Heidi was in earnest. She went on offering the bread and cheese, and when he did not take it, she laid it down on his knee. Then he saw that she meant it for him, seized the prize, nodded his thanks, and then made the most satisfactory dinner of his goatherd life. Meantime Heidi watched the goats.

"What are their names, Peter?" she asked.

He knew them all well enough and could keep them in his head all the better because he had little else to store away there. So he began and without hesitation named one after the other, pointing to each one as he did so.

There was the big Türk with his powerful horns. He was always trying to butt all the others, and if he came near, most of them ran away and would have nothing to do with their rough comrade. The brave Distelfinck, a slender, nimble little goat, was the only one that did not avoid him, but often ran at him three or four times in succession so swiftly and skillfully that the big Türk would stand still in astonishment and make no further attack; for Distelfinck looked very warlike and had sharp horns.

Then there was the little white Schneehöpli, always bleating so touchingly, so beseechingly, that Heidi ran to her again and again and put her arms round her head to comfort her. But now the child hurried to her once more, for her mournful young voice was again raised in appeal. Heidi threw her arm round the little creature's neck and asked quite sympathetically:

"What is the matter, Schneehöpli? Why do you cry so?"

The goat trustingly pressed close to Heidi's side and became perfectly quiet.

Peter called out from where he was sitting, with frequent interruptions while he took a bite and a swallow:

"She does so because the old one doesn't come with her any more. They sold her and sent her to Maienfeld day before yesterday; so she doesn't come up on the Alm any longer."

"Who is the old one?" asked Heidi.

"Why, the mother, of course," was the reply.

"Where is the grandmother?" asked Heidi again.

"Hasn't any."

"And the grandfather?"

"Hasn't any."

"You poor Schneehöpli," said Heidi, drawing the little creature tenderly toward her. "Don't cry so any more, for, you see, I will come with you every day, and then you won't be alone; and if you want anything, you can come to me."

Schneehöpli rubbed her head contentedly against Heidi's shoulder and bleated no more.

By far the prettiest and cleanest of the goats were Schwänli and Bärli, who were decidedly superior in their behavior, and usually went their own way; they especially avoided the troublesome Türk and treated him with scorn.

The animals had begun to climb up to the bushes again, each one after his own fashion: some leaping carelessly over everything, others cautiously seeking out the good herbs as they went along, while Türk tried his horns here and there—first in one place and then in another.

Schwänli and Bärli climbed prettily and gracefully, and whenever they found fine bushes, there they stationed themselves and nibbled them. Heidi stood with her hands behind her back, watching them all with the closest attention.

"Peter," she said to the boy, who had thrown himself down again on the ground, "the prettiest of them all are Schwänli and Bärli."

"Of course they are," was the reply. "The Alm-Uncle brushes and washes them and gives them salt and has the best shed."

Suddenly Peter jumped up and fairly

leaped after the goats. Heidi ran after him; she felt that something must have happened, and she could not remain behind. Peter ran through the midst of the goats to the side of the mountain, where the rocks descended steep and bare far below, and where a careless goat, going near, might easily fall over and break all its bones. He had seen the venturesome Distelfinck jumping along in that direction; he reached there just in time, for at that instant the little goat came to the very edge of the precipice. Just as it was falling, Peter flung himself down on the ground and managed to seize one of its legs and hold it fast. Distelfinck bleated with anger and surprise, to be held so by his leg, and struggled obstinately onward. Peter screamed, "Heidi, help me!" for he couldn't get up and was almost pulling off Distelfinck's leg. Heidi was already there and instantly understood their sorry plight. She quickly pulled up from the ground some fragrant herbs and held them under Distelfinck's nose and said soothingly:

"Come, come, Distelfinck, you must be sensible! See, you might fall off and break your bones, and that would give you frightful pain."

The goat quickly turned round and eagerly nibbled the herbs from Heidi's hand. Meanwhile Peter had succeeded in getting on his feet and had seized the cord which held the bell round Distelfinck's neck. Heidi seized it on the opposite side, and the two together led the runaway back to the peacefully feeding flock.

When Peter had the goat in safety once more, he raised his rod to beat him soundly as a punishment, and Distelfinck timidly drew back, for he saw what was going to happen. But Heidi cried:

"No, Peter! no, you must not beat him! See how frightened he is!"

"He deserves it," snarled Peter and was going to strike the goat. But Heidi seized his arm and cried indignantly:

"You shall not do it; it will hurt him! Let him alone!"

Peter looked in astonishment at the commanding Heidi, whose black eyes snapped at him. He hesitatingly dropped his rod.

"He can go if you will give me some of your cheese again tomorrow," said Peter, yielding; for he wanted some reward for his fright.

"You may have it all—the whole piece—tomorrow and every day; I do not want it," said Heidi. "And I will give you a good part of my bread, too, as I did today. But then you must never beat Distelfinck, nor Schneehöpli, nor any of the goats."

"It's all the same to me," remarked Peter; and this was as good as a promise with him. Then he let the culprit go, and the happy Distelfinck leaped high in the air and then bounded back into the flock.

Thus the day had passed away unnoticed, and the sun was just ready to go down behind the mountains. Heidi sat down on the ground again and silently gazed at the bluebells and the rockroses glowing in the evening light; and all the grass seemed tinted with gold, and the cliffs above began to gleam and sparkle. Suddenly Heidi jumped up and exclaimed:

"Peter! Peter! it's on fire! It's on fire! All the mountains are burning, and the big snow field over there is on fire, and the sky! Oh, see! see! The high cliff is all burning! Oh, the beautiful fiery snow! Peter get up! See! the fire reaches up to the robber-bird! Look at the rocks! See the fir trees! Everything, everything is on fire!"

"It's always so," said Peter good-naturedly, peeling the bark from his rod. "But it is no fire."

"What is it, then?" asked Heidi, running back and forth in order to look on every side; for she could not see enough, it was so beautiful everywhere.

"It comes so of itself," explained Peter.

"Oh, see! see!" cried Heidi in great excitement. "Suddenly it grows rosy red! Look at the snow and the high, pointed rocks! What are their names, Peter?"

"Mountains don't have names," he replied.

"Oh, how lovely! See the snow all rosy red! And oh, on the rocks above there are ever and ever so many roses! Oh, now they are turning gray! Oh! Oh! Now it is all gone! It is all gone, Peter!" And Heidi sat down on the ground and looked as distressed as if everything were really coming to an end.

"It will be just the same again tomorrow," explained Peter. "Get up! We must go home now."

Peter whistled and called the goats together, and they started on the homeward journey.

"Will it be like that every day—every day when we go to the pasture?" asked Heidi, listening eagerly for some decided assurance as she walked by Peter's side.

"Usually," was the reply,

"But really tomorrow again?" she wanted to know.

"Yes; yes, tomorrow, certainly!" assured Peter.

Then Heidi was happy once more, but she had received so many impressions, and so many things were going round in her mind, that she was perfectly silent until they reached the hut and saw her grandfather. He was sitting under the fir trees, where he had also made a seat and was in the habit of waiting there in the evening for his goats.

Heidi ran straight up to him, followed by Schwänli and Bärli; for the goats knew their master and their shed. Peter called out to Heidi:

"Come again tomorrow! Good night!"

Heidi darted back, gave Peter her hand, and assured him that she would accompany him again; then she sprang into the midst of the departing flock, threw her arms once more round Schneehöpli's neck, and said confidingly:

"Sleep well, Schneehöpli, and remember that I will go with you again tomorrow and that you must never bleat so mournfully again."

Schneehöpli seemed pleased and looked thankfully into Heidi's face and then leaped gaily after the other goats.

Heidi came back under the fir trees.

"Oh, grandfather, it was so beautiful!" she exclaimed even before she had reached him—"the fire and the roses on the cliffs and the blue and yellow flowers; and see what I have brought you!"

Whereupon Heidi shook all her wealth of flowers out of her folded apron in front of her grandfather. But what a sight the poor little flowers made! Heidi no longer recognized them. They were all like hay, and not a single cup was open.

"Oh, grandfather, what is the matter with them?" cried Heidi, quite shocked. "They were not like that; why do they look so now?"

"They like to stand out in the sunshine and not to be shut up in your apron," said the grandfather.

"Then I will never bring any more home. But, grandfather, what made the robber-bird scream so?" asked Heidi urgently.

"You must jump into the water now, while I go to the shed and fetch the milk; afterward we will go into the house together and have supper. Then I will tell you about it."

So it was; and later, when Heidi sat on her high stool before her little bowl of milk, next her grandfather, she again asked the question:

"Why did the robber-bird keep croaking and screaming so, grandfather?"

"He is mocking at the people down below, because so many sit together in the villages and make one another wicked. So he mocks at them: 'It would be much better for you to leave one another and let each go his own way and climb up to some mountaintop, as I do!'"

The grandfather spoke so wildly that the robber-bird's screaming came back to Heidi's mind still more forcefully.

"Why have the mountains no names, grandfather?" asked Heidi again.

"They have names," he replied, "and if you can describe one to me so that I can recognize it, I will tell you what it is called."

Then Heidi described the rocky mountain, with its two high towers, just as she had seen it, and the grandfather, well pleased, said:

"Very good! I know it; it is called Falknis. Did you see any more?"

Then Heidi described the mountain with the big snow field, which had been on fire, then turned rose color, and then suddenly grew pale and wan.

"I know that, too," said the grandfather. "That is the Scesaplana. So it pleased you up in the pasture, did it?"

Then Heidi told him about everything that had happened—how lovely it had been; and she asked her grandfather to tell her where the fire at evening had come from, for Peter could not tell her.

"You see," the grandfather explained, "the sun does it. When he says good night to the mountains, he sends to them his most beautiful rays so that they may not forget him until he comes back in the morning."

This pleased Heidi, and she could hardly wait for another day to come so that she could go up to the pasture and see once more how the sun said good night to the mountains. But first she had to go to sleep, and she slept soundly the whole night long on her bed of hay and dreamed of bright shining mountains and their red roses, in the midst of which Schneehöpli merrily ran and jumped.

Amahl and the Night Visitors

GIAN-CARLO MENOTTI

THE THREE KINGS ARRIVE [1]

At the sound of the knock, Amahl's mother awoke with a start but didn't move from her bed on the bench. "Amahl," she said drowsily, "go and see who's knocking at the door."

"Yes, Mother." He went to the door and opened it a crack, his heart thudding in his chest. He closed the door quickly and rushed to his mother.

"Mother, Mother, Mother, come with me.

I want to be sure that you see what I see."

His mother raised herself on her elbow.

"What is the matter with you now?

What is all this fuss about?

Who is it, then?"

Amahl was shaking with excitement. "Mother—" he stopped. He hardly dared tell her what he had seen. "Outside the door there is"—he swallowed and went on with an effort—"there is a king with a crown."

His mother gazed toward the roof and asked the heavens,

"What shall I do with this boy,

What shall I do?

If you don't learn to tell the truth,

I'll have to spank you!"

There was another knock at the door and she sighed and sank back on the sheepskins. She told Amahl severely,

"Go back and see who it is

and ask what they want."

Amahl hurried to the door and again opened it just a crack and stared. He hobbled back to his mother.

"Mother, Mother, Mother, come with me.

I want to be sure that you see what I see."

His mother shook her head at him and asked,

"What is the matter with you now?

[1] From "Amahl and the Night Visitors" by Gian-Carlo Menotti, illustrated by Roger Duvoisin. Whittlesey House, McGraw-Hill Book Company, Inc. Copyright, 1952, by G. Schirmer, Inc.

What is all this fuss about?"

Amahl gazed at her desperately.

"Mother—I didn't tell the truth before."

His mother smiled at him.

"That's a good boy."

Amahl gulped hurriedly,

"There is not a king outside."

His mother almost laughed.

"I should say not!"

Amahl blurted,

"There are *two* kings!"

His mother sat up and wailed to the roof again,

"What shall I do with this boy,
what shall I do, what shall I do?
Hurry back and see who it is,
and don't you dare make up tales!"

Amahl rushed to the door once more and rushed back, crying,

"Mother, Mother, Mother, come with
    me.
If I tell you the truth
I know you won't believe me."

His mother said shortly, "Try it for a change."

"But you won't believe me," Amahl protested.

"I'll believe you if you tell the truth."

"Sure enough," Amahl said, knowing now that he wasn't dreaming, "there are not two kings outside."

"That is surprising," replied his mother sarcastically.

Amahl tried to keep from grinning at her in triumph.

"The kings are three
and one of them is black."

Angry at last, his mother sat up.

"Oh! What shall I do with this boy!
If you were stronger, I'd like to whip
    you!"

"I knew it," Amahl murmured to himself.

His mother arose wearily from the bench. She pushed Amahl aside.

"I'm going to the door myself, and then, young man, you'll have to reckon with me!"

She went with determination toward the door and Amahl limped close behind her. As the door swung open and she saw the three kings standing there in all their splendor, she caught her breath. She bowed to them in utter amazement.

"Good evening," said the tall king with sweet blue eyes and a long white beard. "I am King Melchior." He wore rich robes trimmed with ermine, and silver slippers, and his voice was majestic but very kindly.

"Good evening," said a black king softly. "I am King Balthazar." He, too, was tall, but dark-bearded, and he wore robes of gold and scarlet and leopard skin.

"Good evening," said the third king. "I am Kaspar."

Amahl wanted to laugh with delight. Kaspar's robes, while they were rich, didn't fit him very well, and his crown was askew on his head as if he had just slapped it on any old way. His shoes didn't match either—one was gold and the other was purple.

Amahl whispered triumphantly to his mother, "What did I tell you?"

"Noble sires," she said in an awed voice.

The black king, Balthazar, asked gently,

"May we rest a while in your house
and warm ourselves by your fireplace?"

Amahl's mother answered humbly,

"I am a poor widow.
A cold fireplace and a bed of straw
are all I have to offer you.
To these you are welcome."

King Kaspar, who seemed to be a little deaf, cupped his ear. "What did she say?"

Balthazar answered him. "That we are welcome."

Kaspar smiled down at Amahl and his mother. Amahl clapped his hands with excitement. "Oh, thank you, thank you, thank you!" exclaimed Kaspar.

Then the three kings said together, "Thank you!"

WE THANK THEE

Ralph Waldo Emerson

Illustration by Flora Smith

For flowers that bloom about our feet;
For tender grass, so fresh and sweet;
For song of bird and hum of bee;
For all things fair we hear or see—
　　Father in Heaven, we thank Thee!

For blue of stream, for blue of sky;
For pleasant shade of branches high;
For fragrant air and cooling breeze;
For beauty of the blowing trees—
　　Father in Heaven, we thank Thee!

For mother-love, for father-care;
For brothers strong and sisters fair;
For love at home and school each day;
For guidance lest we go astray—
　　Father in Heaven, we thank Thee!

For Thy dear, everlasting arms,
That bear us o'er all ills and harms;
For blessed words of long ago,
That help us now Thy will to know—
　　Father in Heaven, we thank Thee!

GOD IS SO GOOD

Jane Taylor

God is so good that He will hear
　　Whenever children humbly pray;
He always lends a gracious ear
　　To what the youngest child may say.

His own most Holy Book declares
　　He loves good little children still;
And that He listens to their prayers,
　　Just as a tender father will.

GOD BLESS THIS FOOD

God bless this food, and bless us all,
And keep us safe, whate'er befall,
　　For Jesus' sake.

GOD'S BLESSING

God bless the master of this house,
　　God bless the mistress too,
And all the little children
　　That round the table go.

WHERE THE BEE SUCKS

William Shakespeare

Where the bee sucks, there suck I.
In a cowslip's bell I lie;
There I couch when owls do cry.
On the bat's back I do fly
After summer merrily.
Merrily, merrily, shall I live now
Under the blossom that hangs on the
    bough.

THE CHAMBERED NAUTILUS

Oliver Wendell Holmes

This is the ship of pearl, which, poets feign,
    Sails the unshadowed main,—
    The venturous bark that flings
On the sweet summer wind its purpled
    wings
In gulfs enchanted, where the Siren sings,
    And coral reefs lie bare,
Where the cold sea-maids rise to sun their
    streaming hair.

Its webs of living gauze no more unfurl;
    Wrecked is the ship of pearl!
    And every chambered cell,
Where its dim dreaming life was wont to
    dwell,
As the frail tenant shaped his growing
    shell,
    Before thee lies revealed,—
Its irised ceiling rent, its sunless crypt un-
    sealed!

Year after year beheld the silent toil
    That spread his lustrous coil;
    Still, as the spiral grew,
He left the past year's dwelling for the
    new,
Stole with soft step its shining archway
    through,
    Built up its idle door,
Stretched in his last-found home, and knew
    the old no more.

Thanks for the heavenly message brought
    by thee,
    Child of the wandering sea,
    Cast from her lap, forlorn!
From thy dead lips a clearer note is born
Than ever Triton blew from wreathèd
    horn!
    While on mine ear it rings,
Through the deep caves of thought I hear
    a voice that sings—

Build thee more stately mansions, O my
    soul,
    As the swift seasons roll!
    Leave thy low-vaulted past!
Let each new temple, nobler than the last,
Shut thee from heaven with a dome more
    vast,
    Till thou at length art free,
Leaving thine outgrown shell by life's
    unresting sea!

Illustrations by Flora Smith

FAIRY SONG

John Keats

Illustration by Charles Folkard

Shed no tear! O, shed no tear!
The flower will bloom another year.
Weep no more! O, weep no more!
Young buds sleep in the root's white core.
Dry your eyes! Oh! dry your eyes!
For I was taught in Paradise
To ease my breast of melodies—
        Shed no tear.
Overhead! look overhead!
'Mong the blossoms white and red—
Look up, look up. I flutter now
On this flush pomegranate bough.
See me! 'tis this silvery bell
Ever cures the good man's ill.
Shed no tear! O, shed no tear!
The flowers will bloom another year.
Adieu, adieu—I fly, adieu,
I vanish in the heaven's blue—
        Adieu, adieu!

THE DAISY'S SONG
SELECTED STANZAS

John Keats

The sun, with his great eye,
Sees not so much as I;
And the moon, all silver-proud
Might as well be in a cloud.

And O the spring—the spring!
I lead the life of a king!
Couch'd in the teeming grass,
I spy each pretty lass.

I look where no one dares,
And I stare where no one stares,
And when the night is nigh
Lambs bleat my lullaby.

THE MOUNTAIN
AND THE SQUIRREL

Ralph Waldo Emerson

Illustration from a drawing by Jessie Wilcox Smith

The mountain and the squirrel
Had a quarrel,
And the former called the latter "Little
   prig;"
Bun replied,
"You are doubtless very big;
But all sorts of things and weather
Must be taken in together
To make up a year,
And a sphere.
And I think it no disgrace
To occupy my place.
If I'm not so large as you,
You are not so small as I,
And not half so spry:
I'll not deny you make
A very pretty squirrel track.
Talents differ; all is well and wisely put;
If I cannot carry forests on my back,
Neither can you crack a nut."

THE OPEN ROAD

Walt Whitman

Afoot and light-hearted, I take to the open
   road,
Healthy, free, the world before me,
The long brown path before me, leading
   wherever I choose.

Henceforth I ask not good-fortune, I myself am good-fortune,
Henceforth I whimper no more, postpone
   no more, need nothing,
Done with indoor complaints, libraries,
   querulous criticisms,
Strong and content, I travel the open road.

A GARDEN
SELECTED STANZAS

Percy Bysshe Shelley

A sensitive plant in a garden grew,
And the young winds fed it with silver
   dew,
And it opened its fan-like leaves to the
   light,
And closed them beneath the kisses of
   night.

And the Spring arose on the garden fair,
And the Spirit of Love fell everywhere;
And each flower and herb on Earth's dark
   breast
Rose from the dreams of its wintry nest.

LOVELIEST OF TREES

A. E. Housman

Illustration by Flora Smith

Loveliest of trees, the cherry now
Is hung with bloom along the bough,
And stands about the woodland ride
Wearing white for Eastertide.

Now, of my threescore years and ten,
Twenty will not come again,
And take from seventy springs a score,
It only leaves me fifty more.

And since to look at things in bloom
Fifty springs are little room,
About the woodlands I will go
To see the cherry hung with snow.

SEA-FEVER

John Masefield

I must go down to the seas again, to the
    lonely sea and the sky,
And all I ask is a tall ship and a star to
    steer her by,
And the wheel's kick and the wind's song
    and the white sail's shaking,
And a grey mist on the sea's face and a
    grey dawn breaking.

I must go down to the seas again, for the
    call of the running tide
Is a wild call and a clear call that may not
    be denied;
And all I ask is a windy day with the white
    clouds flying,
And the flung spray and the blown spume,
    and the sea-gulls crying.

I must go down to the seas again, to the
    vagrant gypsy life,
To the gull's way and the whale's way
    where the wind's like a whetted knife;
And all I ask is a merry yarn from a laugh-
    ing fellow-rover,
And quiet sleep and a sweet dream when
    the long trick's over.

THE DAFFODILS

William Wordsworth

I wandered lonely as a cloud
    That floats on high o'er vales and hills,
When all at once I saw a crowd,
    A host of golden daffodils;
Beside the lake, beneath the trees,
Fluttering and dancing in the breeze.

Continuous as the stars that shine
    And twinkle on the milky way,
They stretched in never-ending line
    Along the margin of a bay:
Ten thousand saw I at a glance,
Tossing their heads in sprightly dance.

The waves beside them danced, but they
    Outdid the sparkling waves in glee:
A poet could not but be gay,
    In such a jocund company:
I gazed—and gazed—but little thought
What wealth the show to me had brought:

For oft when on my couch I lie
    In vacant or in pensive mood,
They flash upon that inward eye
    Which is the bliss of solitude,
And then my heart with pleasure fills
And dances with the daffodils.

LOCHINVAR

Walter Scott

O, young Lochinvar is come out of the
    west,
Through all the wide Border his steed was
    the best,
And save his good broadsword he weapons
    had none;
He rode all unarmed, and he rode all
    alone.
So faithful in love, and so dauntless in war,
There never was knight like the young
    Lochinvar.

He stayed not for brake, and he stopped
    not for stone,
He swam the Eske river where ford there
    was none;
But, ere he alighted at Netherby gate,
The bride had consented, the gallant came
    late:
For a laggard in love, and a dastard in war,
Was to wed the fair Ellen of brave
    Lochinvar.

So boldly he entered the Netherby hall,
Among bride's-men and kinsmen, and
    brothers and all;
Then spoke the bride's father, his hand on
    his sword
(For the poor craven bridegroom said
    never a word),
"O come ye in peace here, or come ye in
    war,
Or to dance at our bridal, young Lord
    Lochinvar?"

"I long wooed your daughter, my suit you
    denied;—
Love swells like the Solway, but ebbs like
    its tide—
And now I am come, with this lost love of
    mine,
To lead but one measure, drink one cup
    of wine.
There are maidens in Scotland more lovely
    by far,

That would gladly be bride to the young
    Lochinvar."

The bride kissed the goblet; the knight
    took it up,
He quaffed off the wine, and he threw
    down the cup,
She looked down to blush, and she looked
    up to sigh,
With a smile on her lips and a tear in her
    eye.
He took her soft hand, ere her mother
    could bar,—
"Now tread we a measure!" said young
    Lochinvar.

So stately his form, and so lovely her face,
That never a hall such a galliard did grace;
While her mother did fret, and her father
    did fume,
And the bridegroom stood dangling his
    bonnet and plume;
And the bride-maidens whispered, "'Twere
    better by far
To have matched our fair cousin with
    young Lochinvar."

One touch to her hand, and one word in
    her ear,
When they reached the hall door, and the
    charger stood near;
So light to the croupe the fair lady he
    swung,
So light to the saddle before her he sprung!
"She is won! we are gone, over bank, bush,
    and scaur;
They'll have fleet steeds that follow,"
    quoth young Lochinvar.

There was mounting 'mong Græmes of the
    Netherby clan;
Forsters, Fenwicks, and Musgraves, they
    rode and they ran;
There was racing, and chasing, on Can-
    nobie Lee,
But the lost bride of Netherby ne'er did
    they see.
So daring in love, and so dauntless in war,
Have ye e'er heard of gallant like young
    Lochinvar?

THE PIPER

William Blake

Illustration by Flora Smith

Piping down the valleys wild,
 Piping songs of pleasant glee,
On a cloud I saw a child,
 And he laughing said to me:

"Pipe a song about a lamb!"
 So I piped with merry cheer.
"Piper, pipe that song again";
 So I piped: he wept to hear.

"Drop thy pipe, thy happy pipe;
 Sing thy songs of happy cheer!"
So I sang the same again,
 While he wept with joy to hear.

"Piper, sit thee down and write
 In a book that all may read."
So he vanished from my sight;
 And I plucked a hollow reed,

And I made a rural pen,
 And I stained the water clear,
And I wrote my happy songs
 Every child may joy to hear.

CASABIANCA

Felicia Dorothea Hemans

The boy stood on the burning deck,
 Whence all but him had fled;
The flame that lit the battle's wreck,
 Shone round him o'er the dead.

Yet beautiful and bright he stood,
 As born to rule the storm;
A creature of heroic blood,
 A proud, though childlike form.

The flames roll'd on—he would not go
 Without his father's word;
That father, faint in death below,
 His voice no longer heard.

He call'd aloud—"Say, father, say
 If yet my task be done!"
He knew not that the chieftain lay
 Unconscious of his son.

"Speak, father!" once again he cried,
 "If I may yet be gone!"
And but the booming shots replied,
 And fast the flames roll'd on.

Upon his brow he felt their breath,
 And in his waving hair;
And look'd from that lone post of death,
 In still, yet brave despair;

And shouted but once more aloud,
 "My father! must I stay?"
While o'er him fast, thro' sail and shroud,
 The wreathing fires made way.

They wrapt the ship in splendour wild,
 They caught the flag on high,
And stream'd above the gallant child,
 Like banners in the sky.

There came a burst of thunder sound—
 The boy—oh! where was he?
Ask of the winds that far around
 With fragments strewed the sea,

With mast, and helm, and pennon fair,
 That well had borne their part;
But the noblest thing that perished there
 Was that young faithful heart.

PAUL REVERE'S RIDE

Henry Wadsworth Longfellow

Illustration by Flora Smith

Listen, my children, and you shall hear
Of the midnight ride of Paul Revere,
On the eighteenth of April, in Seventy-
    five;
Hardly a man is now alive
Who remembers that famous day and year.

He said to his friend, "If the British march
By land or sea from the town to-night,
Hang a lantern aloft in the belfry arch
Of the North Church tower as a signal
    light,—
One, if by land, and two, if by sea;
And I on the opposite shore will be,
Ready to ride and spread the alarm
Through every Middlesex village and farm,
For the country folk to be up and to arm."

Then he said, "Good night!" and with
    muffled oar
Silently rowed to the Charlestown shore,
Just as the moon rose over the bay,
Where swinging wide at her moorings lay
The Somerset, British man-of-war;
A phantom ship, with each mast and spar
Across the moon like a prison bar,
And a huge black hulk, that was magnified
By its own reflection in the tide.

Meanwhile, his friend, through alley and
    street,
Wanders and watches with eager ears,
Till in the silence around him he hears
The muster of men at the barrack door,
The sound of arms, and the tramp of feet,
And the measured tread of the grenadiers,
Marching down to their boats on the shore.

Then he climbed the tower of the Old
    North Church,
By the wooden stairs, with stealthy tread,
To the belfry-chamber overhead,
And startled the pigeons from their perch

On the sombre rafters, that round him
    made
Masses and moving shapes of shade,—
By the trembling ladder, steep and tall,
To the highest window in the wall,
Where he paused to listen and look down
A moment on the roofs of the town,
And the moonlight flowing over all.

Beneath, in the churchyard, lay the dead,
In their night-encampment on the hill,
Wrapped in silence so deep and still
That he could hear, like a sentinel's tread,
The watchful night-wind, as it went
Creeping along from tent to tent,
And seeming to whisper, "All is well!"
A moment only he feels the spell
Of the place and the hour, and the secret
    dread
Of the lonely belfry and the dead;
For suddenly all his thoughts are bent
On a shadowy something far away,
Where the river widens to meet the bay,—
A line of black that bends and floats
On the rising tide, like a bridge of boats.

Meanwhile, impatient to mount and ride,
Booted and spurred, with a heavy stride
On the opposite shore walked Paul Revere.
Now he patted his horse's side,
Now gazed at the landscape far and near,
Then, impetuous, stamped the earth,
And turned and tightened his saddle-girth;
But mostly he watched with eager search
The belfry-tower of the Old North Church,
As it rose above the graves on the hill,
Lonely and spectral and sombre and still.
And lo! as he looks, on the belfry's height
A glimmer, and then a gleam of light!
He springs to the saddle, the bridle he
    turns,
But lingers and gazes, till full on his sight
A second lamp in the belfry burns!

A hurry of hoofs in a village street,
A shape in the moonlight, a bulk in the
    dark,
And beneath, from the pebbles, in passing,
    a spark

Struck out by a steed flying fearless and
 fleet:
That was all! And yet, through the gloom
 and the light,
The fate of a nation was riding that night;
And the spark struck out by that steed, in
 his flight,
Kindled the land into flame with its heat.

He has left the village and mounted the
 steep,
And beneath him, tranquil and broad and
 deep,
Is the Mystic, meeting the ocean tides;
And under the alders that skirt its edge,
Now soft on the sand, now loud on the
 ledge,
Is heard the tramp of his steed as he rides.

It was twelve by the village clock,
When he crossed the bridge into Medford
 town.
He heard the crowing of the cock,
And the barking of the farmer's dog,
And felt the damp of the river's fog,
That rises after the sun goes down.

It was one by the village clock,
When he galloped into Lexington.
He saw the gilded weathercock
Swim in the moonlight as he passed,
And the meeting-house windows, blank
 and bare,
Gaze at him with a spectral glare,
As if they already stood aghast
At the bloody work they would look upon.

It was two by the village clock,
When he came to the bridge in Concord
 town.
He heard the bleating of the flock,
And the twitter of birds among the trees,
And felt the breath of the morning breeze
Blowing over the meadows brown.
And one was safe and asleep in his bed
Who at the bridge would be first to fall,
Who that day would be lying dead,
Pierced by a British musket-ball.

You know the rest. In the books you have
 read,
How the British Regulars fired and fled,—
How the farmers gave them ball for ball,
From behind each fence and farm-yard
 wall,
Chasing the red-coats down the lane,
Then crossing the fields to emerge again
Under the trees at the turn of the road,
And only pausing to fire and load.

So through the night rode Paul Revere;
And so through the night went his cry of
 alarm
To every Middlesex village and farm,—
A cry of defiance and not of fear,
A voice in the darkness, a knock at the
 door,
And a word that shall echo forevermore!
For, borne on the night-wind of the Past,
Through all our history, to the last,
In the hour of darkness and peril and need,
The people will waken and listen to hear
The hurrying hoof-beats of that steed,
And the midnight message of Paul Revere.

SONG OF THE BROOK

Alfred, Lord Tennyson

Illustration by Flora Smith

I come from haunts of coot and hern,
  I make a sudden sally,
And sparkle out among the fern,
  To bicker down a valley.

By thirty hills I hurry down,
  Or slip between the ridges,
By twenty thorps, a little town,
  And half a hundred bridges.

Till last by Philip's farm I flow
  To join the brimming river,
For men may come and men may go,
  But I go on for ever.

I chatter over stony ways,
  In little sharps and trebles,
I bubble into eddying bays,
  I babble on the pebbles.

With many a curve my banks I fret
  By many a field and fallow,
And many a fairy foreland set
  With willow-weed and mallow.

I chatter, chatter, as I flow
  To join the brimming river,
For men may come and men may go,
  But I go on for ever.

I wind about, and in and out,
  With here a blossom sailing,
And here and there a lusty trout,
  And here and there a grayling.

And here and there a foamy flake
  Upon me, as I travel
With many a silvery waterbreak
  Above the gravel,

And draw them all along, and flow
  To join the brimming river,
For men may come and men may go,
  But I go on for ever.

I steal by lawns and grassy plots,
  I slide by hazel covers;
I move the sweet forget-me-nots
  That grow for happy lovers.

I slip, I slide, I gloom, I glance,
  Among my skimming swallows;
I make the netted sunbeam dance
  Against my sandy shallows.

I murmur under moon and stars
  In brambly wildernesses;
I linger by my shingly bars;
  I loiter round my cresses;

And out again I curve and flow
  To join the brimming river,
For men may come and men may go,
  But I go on for ever.

DREAM-SONG

Walter de la Mare

Illustration by Pamela Bianco

Sunlight, moonlight,
 Twilight, starlight—
Gloaming at the close of day,
 And an owl calling,
 Cool dews falling
In a wood of oak and may.

Lantern-light, taper-light,
 Torchlight, no-light:
Darkness at the shut of day,
 And lions roaring,
 Their wrath pouring
In wild waste places far away.

Elf-light, bat-light,
 Touchwood-light and toad-light,
And the sea a shimmering gloom of grey,
 And a small face smiling
 In a dream's beguiling
In a world of wonders far away.

SOME ONE

Walter de la Mare

Illustration by Pamela Bianco

Some one came knocking
 At my wee, small door;
Some one came knocking,
 I'm sure—sure—sure;
I listened, I opened,
 I looked to left and right,
But nought there was a-stirring
 In the still dark night;
Only the busy beetle
 Tap-tapping in the wall,
Only from the forest
 The screech-owl's call,
Only the cricket whistling
 While the dewdrops fall,
So I know not who came knocking,
 At all, at all, at all.

Aesop's Fables

THE HORSE AND THE LION

Illustration from a drawing by Fritz Kredel

The lion was hungry. Hunting had not been too good during the past week. He was sitting by the roadside feeling sorry for himself when a handsome horse came trotting past. The lion's mouth watered as he thought what a wonderful dinner that horse would make if only he could catch him.

The lion just couldn't get his mind off that horse. So he let it be noised about that he had become a wonderful doctor who could heal any animal's complaint.

A day or two later the horse, pretending that he had a thorn in one hoof, came to the lion's den for help. The lion licked his chops. This was the chance he had been looking for. He asked the horse to raise one of his hind feet so he could make an examination. Solicitously, in his best bedside manner, he bent his head as though to examine the ailing hoof.

Just as he was ready to spring, the horse let go with his upraised hoof. There was a sickening thud as hoof met nose. And the last thing the lion remembered was a whinny of laughter as the horse galloped away toward the forest.

Application: THE BEST LAID-OUT SCHEME OFTEN HAS A KICKBACK.

THE GOOSE WITH THE GOLDEN EGGS

Illustration by Boris Artzybasheff

A farmer went to the nest of his goose to see whether she had laid an egg. To his surprise he found, instead of an ordinary goose egg, an egg of solid gold. Seizing the golden egg he rushed to the house in great excitement to show it to his wife.

Every day thereafter the goose laid an egg of pure gold. But as the farmer grew rich he grew greedy. And thinking that if he killed the goose he could have all her treasure at once, he cut her open only to find—nothing at all.

Application: THE GREEDY WHO WANT MORE LOSE ALL.

THE LEOPARD AND THE FOX

Illustration by Boris Artzybasheff

The leopard, one day, took it into his head to value himself upon the great variety and beauty of his spots. Truly he saw no reason why even the lion should take place before him, since he could not show so beautiful a skin. As for the rest of the wild beasts of the forest, he treated them all, without distinction, in the most haughty, disdainful manner. But the fox, being among them, went up to him and with a great deal of spirit and resolution told him that he was mistaken in the value he was pleased to set upon himself, since persons of judgment were not used to form their opinion of merit from an outside appearance, but by considering the good qualities and endowments with which the mind was stored.

Application: HOW MUCH MORE PLEASING AND POWERFUL WOULD BEAUTY PROVE IF IT WERE NOT SO FREQUENTLY SPOILED BY THE AFFECTATION AND CONCEIT OF ITS POSSESSOR.

THE KID AND THE WOLF

Illustration by Percy J. Billinghurst

There was once a very active kid who would leave the other goats in the farm-yard below and climb onto the steep roof of the farmhouse.

"Look at me, mother," he would call down. "You are afraid to come up here where I am." The other goats paid very little attention to the boasting kid, but one day a wolf passed by the farmhouse. He gave one look at the kid on the rooftree and would have passed by since it was easy to see that here was one dinner that was safe out of his reach. But the kid jeered and bleated: "Why don't you try to come up and catch me, coward?"

The wolf stopped, looked up again, and called back: "It is not you who call me coward, but the place on which you are standing."

Application: IF YOU MUST REVILE YOUR NEIGHBOR, MAKE CERTAIN FIRST THAT HE CANNOT REACH YOU.

400

THE PIED PIPER OF HAMELIN

Robert Browning

Illustrations by Arthur Rackham

Hamelin Town's in Brunswick
By famous Hanover city;
  The river Weser, deep and wide,
  Washes its walls on the southern side;
  A pleasanter spot you never spied;

But, when begins my ditty,
  Almost five hundred years ago,
  To see the townsfolk suffer so
    From vermin was a pity.
                Rats!

They fought the dogs, and killed the cats,
  And bit the babies in the cradles,
And ate the cheeses out of the vats,
  And licked the soup from the cook's own
    ladles,
Split open the kegs of salted sprats,
Made nests inside men's Sunday hats,
And even spoiled the women's chats,
  By drowning their speaking
  With shrieking and squeaking
In fifty different sharps and flats.

At last the people in a body
  To the Town Hall came flocking:
" 'Tis clear," cried they, "our Mayor's a
  noddy;
  And as for our Corporation—shocking
To think that we buy gowns lined with
  ermine
For dolts that can't or won't determine
What's best to rid us of our vermin!
You hope, because you're old and obese,
To find in the furry civic robe ease?
Rouse up, sirs! Give your brain a rack-
  ing
To find the remedy we're lacking,
Or, sure as fate, we'll send you pack-
  ing!"
At this the Mayor and Corporation
Quaked with a mighty consternation.

An hour they sat in council,
  At length the Mayor broke silence:
"For a guilder I'd my ermine gown sell;
  I wish I were a mile hence!
It's easy to bid one rack one's brain—
I'm sure my poor head aches again
I've scratched it so, and all in vain,
  Oh for a trap, a trap, a trap!"
Just as he said this, what should hap
At the chamber door but a gentle tap?
  "Bless us," cried the Mayor, "what's
    that?"

(With the Corporation as he sat,
Looking little though wondrous fat;
Nor brighter was his eye, nor moister,
Than a too-long-opened oyster,
Save when at noon his paunch grew muti-
  nous
For a plate of turtle green and glutinous),
  "Only a scraping of shoes on the mat?
  Anything like the sound of a rat
  Makes my heart go pit-a-pat!"

"Come in!"—the Mayor cried, looking
  bigger:
And in did come the strangest figure.
His queer long coat from heel to head
Was half of yellow and half of red;

And he himself was tall and thin,
With sharp blue eyes, each like a pin,
And light loose hair, yet swarthy skin,
No tuft on cheek nor beard on chin,
But lips where smiles went out and in—
There was no guessing his kith and kin!
And nobody could enough admire
The tall man and his quaint attire.
Quoth one: "It's as my great grandsire,
Starting up at the Trump of Doom's tone,
Had walked this way from his painted tombstone."

He advanced to the council-table:
And, "Please, your honours," said he, "I'm able,
By means of a secret charm, to draw

All creatures living beneath the sun,
That creep, or swim, or fly, or run,
After me so as you never saw!
And I chiefly use my charm
On creatures that do people harm,
The mole, and toad, and newt, and
    viper;
And people call me the Pied Piper."
(And here they noticed round his neck
    A scarf of red and yellow stripe,
To match with his coat of the selfsame
    cheque;

And at the scarf's end hung a pipe;
And his fingers, they noticed, were ever
    straying
As if impatient to be playing
Upon this pipe, as low it dangled
Over his vesture so old-fangled.)
    "Yet," said he, "poor piper as I am,
    In Tartary I freed the Cham,
    Last June, from his huge swarms of
        gnats;
    I eased in Asia the Nizam
    Of a monstrous brood of vampire bats:

And, as for what your brain bewilders,
If I can rid your town of rats
Will you give me a thousand guilders?"
"One? fifty thousand!"—was the exclamation
Of the astonished Mayor and Corporation.

Into the street the Piper stept,
  Smiling first a little smile,
As if he knew what magic slept
  In his quiet pipe the while;
Then, like a musical adept,
To blow the pipe his lips he wrinkled,
And green and blue his sharp eyes twinkled
  kled
Like a candle-flame where salt is sprinkled;
  kled;
And ere three shrill notes the pipe uttered,
  tered,
You heard as if an army muttered;

And the muttering grew to a grumbling;
And the grumbling grew to a mighty
  rumbling;
And out of the house the rats came
  tumbling.
Great rats, small rats, lean rats, brawny
  rats,
Brown rats, black rats, gray rats, tawny
  rats,
Grave old plodders, gay young friskers,
  Fathers, mothers, uncles, cousins,
Cocking tails and pricking whiskers,
  Families by tens and dozens,
Brothers, sisters, husbands, wives—
Followed the Piper for their lives.
From street to street he piped advancing,
  ing,
And step by step they followed dancing,
Until they came to the river Weser
Wherein all plunged and perished
—Save one, who, stout as Julius Cæsar,
Swam across and lived to carry
(As he the manuscript he cherished)
To Rat-land home his commentary,
Which was, "At the first shrill notes of
  the pipe,
I heard a sound as of scraping tripe,
And putting apples, wondrous ripe,
Into a cider press's gripe;
And a moving away of pickle-tub-
  boards,
And a leaving ajar of conserve cup-
  boards,
And a drawing the corks of train-oil-
  flasks,
And a breaking the hoops of butter
  casks;
And it seemed as if a voice
(Sweeter far than by harp or by psaltery
Is breathed) called out, Oh, rats! re-
  joice!
The world is grown to one vast dry-
  saltery!
To munch on, crunch on, take your
  nuncheon,
Breakfast, supper, dinner, luncheon!
And just as a bulky sugar puncheon,
All ready staved, like a great sun shone
Glorious scarce an inch before me,

Just as methought it said, come, bore me!
—I found the Weser rolling o'er me."

You should have heard the Hamelin people
Ringing the bells till they rocked the
    steeple.
  "Go," cried the Mayor, "and get long
    poles!
  Poke out the nests and block up the
    holes!
  Consult with carpenters and builders,
  And leave in our town not even a trace
  Of the rats!"—when suddenly up the
    face
Of the Piper perked in the market-place,
With a, "First, if you please, my thousand
    guilders!"

A thousand guilders! The Mayor looked
    blue;
So did the Corporation too.
For council dinners made rare havoc
With Claret, Moselle, Vin-de-Grave, Hock;
And half the money would replenish
Their cellar's biggest butt with Rhenish.
To pay this sum to a wandering fellow
With a gipsy coat of red and yellow!
  "Beside," quoth the Mayor, with a know-
    ing wink,
  "Our business was done at the river's
    brink;
  We saw with our eyes the vermin sink,
  And what's dead can't come to life, I
    think.
  So, friend, we're not the folks to shrink

From the duty of giving you something
    to drink,
And a matter of money to put in your
    poke,
But, as for the guilders, what we spoke
Of them, as you very well know, was in
    joke.
Besides, our losses have made us thrifty;
A thousand guilders! Come, take fifty!"

The Piper's face fell, and he cried,
"No trifling! I can't wait, beside!
I've promised to visit by dinnertime
Bagdad, and accepted the prime
Of the Head Cook's pottage, all he's
    rich in,
For having left the Caliph's kitchen,
Of a nest of scorpions no survivor—
With him I proved no bargain-driver,
With you, don't think I'll bate a stiver!
And folks who put me in a passion
May find me pipe to another fashion."
"How?" cried the Mayor, "d'ye think I'll
    brook
Being worse treated than a Cook?
Insulted by a lazy ribald
With idle pipe and vesture piebald?
You threaten us, fellow? Do your worst,
Blow your pipe there till you burst!"

Once more he stept into the street;
    And to his lips again
Laid his long pipe of smooth straight cane;
    And ere he blew three notes (such sweet
Soft notes as yet musicians cunning
    Never gave the enraptured air),
There was a rustling, that seemed like a
    bustling
Of merry crowds justling, at pitching and
    hustling,
Small feet were pattering, wooden shoes
    clattering,
Little hands clapping, and little tongues
    chattering,
And, like fowls in a farmyard when barley
    is scattering,
Out came the children running.
All the little boys and girls,
With rosy cheeks and flaxen curls,
And sparkling eyes and teeth like pearls,

Tripping and skipping, ran merrily after
The wonderful music with shouting and
    laughter.
The Mayor was dumb, and the Council
    stood
As if they were changed into blocks of
    wood,
Unable to move a step, or cry
To the children merrily skipping by—
And could only follow with the eye
That joyous crowd at the Piper's back.
But how the Mayor was on the rack,

And the wretched Council's bosoms beat,
As the Piper turned from the High Street
To where the Weser rolled its waters
Right in the way of their sons and daugh-
    ters!
However, he turned from South to West,
And to Koppelberg Hill his steps ad-
    dressed,
And after him the children pressed;
Great was the joy in every breast.
    "He never can cross that mighty top!
    He's forced to let the piping drop,

And we shall see our children stop!"
When lo! as they reached the mountain's
  side,
A wondrous portal opened wide,
As if a cavern was suddenly hollowed;
And the Piper advanced and the children
  followed,
And when all were in to the very last,
The door in the mountain-side shut fast.
Did I say all? No! one was lame,
And could not dance the whole of the way;

And in after years, if you would blame
His sadness, he was used to say:
  "It's dull in our town since my play-
    mates left;
  I can't forget that I'm bereft
  Of all the pleasant sights they see,
  Which the Piper also promised me;
  For he led us, he said, to a joyous land,
  Joining the town and just at hand,
Where waters gushed and fruit trees grew,
And flowers put forth a fairer hue,

And everything was strange and new.
The sparrows were brighter than peacocks
    here,
And their dogs outran our fallow deer,
And honey-bees had lost their stings;
And horses were born with eagle's wings;
And just as I became assured
My lame foot would be speedily cured,
The music stopped, and I stood still,
And found myself outside the Hill,
Left alone against my will,
To go now limping as before,
And never hear of that country more!"

Alas, alas for Hamelin!
    There came into many a burgher's pate
    A text which says, that Heaven's Gate
    Opes to the Rich at as easy rate
As the needle's eye takes a camel in!

The Mayor sent East, West, North and
    South,
To offer the Piper by word of mouth,
    Wherever it was men's lot to find him,
Silver and gold to his heart's content,
If he'd only return the way he went,
    And bring the children all behind him.
But when they saw 'twas a lost endeavour,
And Piper and dancers were gone forever
They made a decree that lawyers never
    Should think their records dated duly

If, after the day of the month and year,
These words did not as well appear,
    "And so long after what happened here
    On the twenty-second of July,
    Thirteen hundred and seventy-six:"
And the better in memory to fix
The place of the Children's last retreat,
They called it, the Pied Piper's street—
Where any one playing on pipe or tabor,
Was sure for the future to lose his labour.
Nor suffered they hostelry or tavern
    To shock with mirth a street so solemn;
But opposite the place of the cavern
    They wrote the story on a column,
And on the great church window painted
The same, to make the world acquainted
How their children were stolen away;
And there it stands to this very day.
And I must not omit to say
That in Transylvania there's a tribe
Of alien people that ascribe
The outlandish ways and dress,
On which their neighbours lay such stress,
To their fathers and mothers having risen
Out of some subterraneous prison,
Into which they were trepanned
Long time ago in a mighty band
Out of Hamelin town in Brunswick land,
But how or why they don't understand.

So, Willy, let you and me be wipers
Of scores out with all men—especially
    pipers,
And, whether they pipe us free from rats
    or from mice,
If we've promised them aught, let us keep
    our promise.

The Adventures of Huckleberry Finn

MARK TWAIN

"BETTER LET BLAME' WELL ALONE" [1]

It must 'a' been close on to one o'clock when we got below the island at last, and the raft did seem to go mighty slow. If a boat was to come along we was going to take to the canoe and break for the Illinois shore; and it was well a boat didn't come, for we hadn't ever thought to put the gun in the canoe, or a fishing line, or anything to eat. We was in ruther too much of a sweat to think of so many things. It warn't good judgment to put *everything* on the raft.

If the men went to the island I just expect they found the campfire I built, and watched it all night for Jim to come. Anyways, they stayed away from us, and if my building the fire never fooled them it warn't no fault of mine. I played it as low-down on them as I could.

When the first streak of day began to show we tied up to a towhead in a bend on the Illinois side, and hacked off cottonwood branches with the hatchet, and covered up the raft with them so she looked like there had been a cave-in in the bank there. A towhead is a sand bar that has cottonwoods on it as thick as harrow teeth.

We had mountains on the Missouri shore and heavy timber on the Illinois side, and the channel was down the Missouri shore at that place, so we warn't afraid of anybody running across us. We laid there all day, and watched the rafts and steamboats spin down the Missouri shore, and upbound steamboats fight the big river in the middle. I told Jim all about the time I had jabbering with that woman; and Jim said she was a smart one, and if she was to start after us herself *she* wouldn't set down and watch a campfire—no, sir, she'd fetch a dog. Well, I said, why couldn't she tell her husband to fetch a dog? Jim said he bet she did think of it by the time the men was ready to start, and he believed they must 'a' gone uptown to get a dog and so they lost all that time, or else we wouldn't be here on a towhead sixteen or seventeen mile below the village—no, indeedy, we would be in that same town again. So I said I didn't care what was the reason they didn't get us as long as they didn't.

When it was beginning to come on dark we poked our heads out of the cottonwood thicket, and looked up and down and across; nothing in sight; so Jim took up some of the top planks of the raft and built a snug wigwam to get under in blazing weather and rainy, and to keep the things dry. Jim made a floor for the wigwam, and raised it a foot or more above the level of the raft, so now the blankets and all the traps was out of reach of steamboat waves. Right in the middle of the wigwam we made a layer of dirt about five or six inches deep with a frame around it for to hold it to its place; this was to build a fire on in sloppy weather or chilly; the wigwam would keep it from being seen. We made an extra steering oar, too, because one of the others might get broke on a snag or something. We fixed up a short forked stick to hang the old lantern on, because we must always light the lantern whenever we see a steamboat coming downstream, to keep from getting run over; but we wouldn't have to light it for upstream boats unless we see we was in what they call a "crossing"; for the river was pretty high yet, very low banks being still a little under water; so upbound boats didn't always run the channel, but hunted easy water.

This second night we run between seven

1 From "The Adventures of Huckleberry Finn," by Mark Twain, illustrated by Donald McKay

and eight hours, with a current that was making over four mile an hour. We catched fish and talked, and we took a swim now and then to keep off sleepiness. It was kind of solemn, drifting down the big, still river, laying on our backs looking up at the stars, and we didn't ever feel like talking loud, and it warn't often that we laughed—only a little kind of a low chuckle. We had mighty good weather as a general thing, and nothing ever happened to us at all—that night, nor the next, nor the next.

Every night we passed towns, some of them away up on black hillsides nothing but just a shiny bed of lights; not a house could you see. The fifth night we passed St. Louis, and it was like the whole world lit up. In St. Petersburg they used to say there was twenty or thirty thousand people in St. Louis, but I never believed it till I see that wonderful spread of lights at two o'clock that still night. There warn't a sound there; everybody was asleep.

Every night now I used to slip ashore toward ten o'clock at some little village, and buy ten or fifteen cents' worth of meal or bacon or other stuff to eat; and sometimes I lifted a chicken that warn't roosting comfortable, and took him along. Pap always said, take a chicken when you get a chance, because if you don't want him yourself you can easy find somebody that does, and a good deed ain't ever forgot. I never see pap when he didn't want the chicken himself, but that is what he used to say, anyway.

Mornings before daylight I slipped into cornfields and borrowed a watermelon, or a mushmelon, or a punkin, or some new corn, or things of that kind. Pap always said it warn't no harm to borrow things if you was meaning to pay them back sometime; but the widow said it warn't anything but a soft name for stealing, and no decent body would do it. Jim said he reckoned the widow was partly right and pap was partly right; so the best way would be for us to pick out two or three things from the list and say we wouldn't borrow them any more—then he reckoned it wouldn't be no harm to borrow the others. So we talked it over all one night, drifting along down the river, trying to make up our minds whether to drop the watermelons, or the cantelopes, or the mushmelons, or what. But toward daylight we got it all settled satisfactory, and concluded to drop crabapples and p'simmons. We warn't feeling just right before that, but it was all comfortable now. I was glad the way it come out, too, because crabapples ain't ever good and the p'simmons wouldn't be ripe for two or three months yet.

We shot a waterfowl now and then that got up too early in the morning or didn't go to bed early enough in the evening. Take it all round, we lived pretty high.

The fifth night below St. Louis we had a big storm after midnight, with a power of thunder and lightning, and the rain poured down in a solid sheet. We stayed in the wigwam and let the raft take care of itself. When the lightning glared out we could see a big straight river ahead, and high, rocky bluffs on both sides. By and by says I, "Hel-*lo*, Jim, looky yonder!" It was a steamboat that had killed herself on a rock. We was drifting straight down for her. The lightning showed her very distinct. She was leaning over, with part of her upper deck above water, and you could see every little chimbly guy clean and clear, and a chair by the big bell, with an old slouch hat hanging on the back of it, when the flashes come.

Well, it being away in the night and stormy, and all so mysterious-like, I felt just the way any other boy would 'a' felt when I seen that wreck laying there so mournful and lonesome in the middle of the river. I wanted to get aboard of her and slink around a little, and see what there was there. So I says:

"Le's land on her, Jim."

But Jim was dead against it at first. He says:

"I doan' want to go fool'n' 'long er no

wrack. We's doin' blame' well, en we better let blame' well alone, as de good book says. Like as not dey's a watchman on dat wrack."

"Watchman your grandmother," I says; "there ain't nothing to watch but the texas and the pilothouse; and do you reckon anybody's going to resk his life for a texas and a pilothouse such a night as this, when it's likely to break up and wash off down the river any minute?" Jim couldn't say nothing to that, so he didn't try. "And besides," I says, "we might borrow something worth having out of the captain's stateroom. Seegars, *I* bet you—and cost five cents apiece, solid cash. Steamboat captains is always rich, and get sixty dollars a month, and *they* don't care a cent what a thing costs, you know, long as they want it. Stick a candle in your pocket; I can't rest, Jim, till we give her a rummaging. Do you reckon Tom Sawyer would ever go by this thing? Not for pie, he wouldn't. He'd call it an adventure—that's what he'd call it; and he'd land on that wreck if it was his last act. And wouldn't he throw style into it?—wouldn't he spread himself, nor nothing? Why, you'd think it was Christopher C'lumbus discovering Kingdom Come. I wish Tom Sawyer *was* here."

Jim he grumbled a little, but give in. He said we mustn't talk any more than we could help, and then talk mighty low. The lightning showed us the wreck again just in time, and we fetched the stabboard derrick, and made fast there.

The deck was high out here. We went sneaking down the slope of it to labboard, in the dark, towards the texas, feeling our way slow with our feet, and spreading our hands out to fend off the guys, for it was so dark we couldn't see no sign of them. Pretty soon we struck the forward end of the skylight, and clumb onto it; and the next step fetched us in front of the captain's door, which was open, and by Jimminy, away down through the texas hall we see a light! and all in the same second we seem to hear low voices in yonder!

Jim whispered and said he was feeling powerful sick, and told me to come along. I says, all right, and was going to start for the raft; but just then I heard a voice wail out and say:

"Oh, please don't, boys; I swear I won't ever tell!"

Another voice said, pretty loud:

"It's a lie, Jim Turner. You've acted this way before. You always want more'n your share of the truck, and you've always got it, too, because you've swore 't if you didn't you'd tell. But this time you've said it jest one time too many. You're the meanest,

411

treacherousest hound in this country."

By this time Jim was gone for the raft. I was just a-biling with curiosity; and I says to myself, Tom Sawyer wouldn't back out now, and so I won't either; I'm a-going to see what's going on here. So I dropped on my hands and knees in the little passage, and crept aft in the dark till there warn't but one stateroom betwixt me and the cross hall of the texas. Then in there I see a man stretched on the floor and tied hand and foot, and two men standing over him, and one of them had a dim lantern in his hand, and the other one had a pistol. This one kept pointing the pistol at the man's head on the floor, and saying:

"I'd *like* to! And I orter, too—a mean skunk!"

The man on the floor would shrivel up and say, "Oh, please don't, Bill; I hain't ever goin' to tell."

And every time he said that the man with the lantern would laugh and say:

"'Deed you *ain't!* You never said no truer thing 'n that, you bet you." And once he said: "Hear him beg! and yit if we hadn't got the best of him and tied him he'd 'a' killed us both. And what *for?* Jist for noth'n'. Jist because we stood on our *rights*—that's what for. But I lay you ain't a-goin' to threaten nobody any more, Jim Turner. Put *up* that pistol, Bill."

Bill says:

"I don't want to, Jake Packard. I'm for killin' him—and didn't he kill old Hatfield jist the same way—and don't he deserve it?"

"But I don't *want* him killed, and I've got my reasons for it."

"Bless yo' heart for them words, Jake Packard! I'll never forget you long's I live!" says the man on the floor, sort of blubbering.

Packard didn't take no notice of that, but hung up his lantern on a nail and started toward where I was, there in the dark, and motioned Bill to come. I crawfished as fast as I could about two yards, but the boat slanted so that I couldn't

make very good time; so to keep from getting run over and catched I crawled into a stateroom on the upper side. The man came a-pawing along in the dark, and when Packard got to my stateroom, he says:

"Here—come in here."

And in he come, and Bill after him. But before they got in I was up in the upper berth, cornered, and sorry I come. Then they stood there, with their hands on the ledge of the berth, and talked. I couldn't see them, but I could tell where they was by the whisky they'd been having. I was glad I didn't drink whisky; but it wouldn't made much difference anyway, because most of the time they couldn't 'a' treed me because I didn't breathe. I was too scared. And, besides, a body *couldn't* breathe and hear such talk. They talked low and earnest. Bill wanted to kill Turner. He says:

"He's said he'll tell, and he will. If we was to give both our shares to him *now* it wouldn't make no difference after the row and the way we've served him. Shore's you're born, he'll turn state's evidence; now you hear *me*. I'm for putting him out of his troubles."

"So'm I," says Packard, very quiet.

"Blame it, I'd sorter begun to think you wasn't. Well, then, that's all right. Le's go and do it."

"Hold on a minute; I hain't had my say yit. You listen to me. Shooting's good, but there's quieter ways if the things *got* to be done. But what *I* say is this: it ain't good sense to go court'n' around after a halter if you can git at what you're up to in some way that's jist as good and at the same time don't bring you into no resks. Ain't that so?"

"You bet it is. But how you goin' to manage it this time?"

"Well, my idea is this: we'll rustle around and gather up whatever pickin's we've overlooked in the staterooms, and shove for shore and hide the truck. Then we'll wait. Now I say it aint' a-goin' to be more'n two hours befo' this wrack breaks

up and washes off down the river. See? He'll be drownded, and won't have nobody to blame for it but his own self. I reckon that's a considerable sight better 'n killin' of him. I'm unfavorable to killin' a man as long as you can git aroun' it; it ain't good sense, it ain't good morals. Ain't I right?"

"Yes, I reck'n you are. But s'pose she *don't* break up and wash off?"

"Well, we can wait the two hours anyway and see, can't we?"

"All right, then; come along."

So they started, and I lit out, all in a cold sweat, and scrambled forward. It was dark as pitch there; but I said, in a kind of a coarse whisper, "Jim!" and he answered up, right at my elbow, with a sort of a moan, and I says:

"Quick, Jim, it ain't no time for fooling around and moaning; there's a gang of murderers in yonder, and if we don't hunt up their boat and set her drifting down the river so these fellows can't get away from the wreck there's one of 'em going to be in a bad fix. But if we find their boat we can put *all* of 'em in a bad fix—for the sheriff'll get 'em. Quick—hurry! I'll hunt the labboard side, you hunt the stabboard. You start at the raft, and—"

"Oh, my lordy, lordy! *Raf'?* Dey ain' no raf' no mo'; she done broke loose en gone!—en here we is!"

Well, I catched my breath and most fainted. Shut up on a wreck with such a gang as that! But it warn't no time to be sentimentering. We'd *got* to find that boat now—had to have it for ourselves. So we went a-quaking and shaking down the stabboard side, and slow work it was, too —seemed a week before we got to the stern. No sign of a boat. Jim said he didn't believe he could go any farther—so scared he hadn't hardly any strength left, he said. But I said, come on, if we get left on this wreck we are in a fix, sure. So on we prowled again. We struck for the stern of the texas, and found it, and then scrabbled along forwards on the skylight, hanging on from shutter to shutter, for the edge of the skylight was in the water. When we got pretty close to the cross-hall door there was the skiff, sure enough! I could just barcly see her. I felt ever so thankful. In another second I would 'a' been aboard of her, but just then the door opened. One of the men stuck his head out only about a couple of foot from me, and I thought I was gone; but he jerked it in again, and says:

"Heave that blame lantern out o' sight, Bill!"

He flung a bag of something into the boat, and then got in himself and set down. It was Packard. Then Bill *he* come out and got in. Packard says, in a low voice:

"All ready—shove off!"

I couldn't hardly hang on to the shutters, I was so weak. But Bill says:

"Hold on—'d you go through him?"

"No. Didn't you?"

"No. So he's got his share o' the cash yet."

"Well, then, come along; no use to take truck and leave money."

"Say, won't he suspicion what we're up to?"

"Maybe he won't. But we got to have it anyway. Come along."

So they got out and went in.

The door slammed to because it was on the careened side; and in a half second I was in the boat, and Jim come tumbling after me. I out with my knife and cut the rope, and away we went!

We didn't touch an oar, and we didn't speak nor whisper, nor hardly even breathe. We went gliding swift along, dead silent, past the tip of the paddlebox, and past the stern; then in a second or two more we was a hundred yards below the wreck, and the darkness soaked her up, every last sign of her, and we was safe, and knowed it.

When we was three or four hundred yards downstream we see the lantern show like a little spark at the texas door for a second, and we knowed by that that the rascals had missed their boat, and was beginning to understand that they was in just as much trouble now as Jim Turner was.

Then Jim manned the oars, and we took out after our raft. Now was the first time that I begun to worry about the men—I reckon I hadn't had time to before. I begun to think how dreadful it was, even for murderers, to be in such a fix. I says to myself, there ain't no telling but I might come to be a murderer myself yet, and then how would I like it? So says I to Jim:

"The first light we see we'll land a hundred yards below it or above it, in a place where it's a good hiding place for you and the skiff, and then I'll go and fix up some kind of a yarn, and get somebody to go for that gang and get them out of their scrape, so they can be hung when their time comes."

Treasure Island

ROBERT LOUIS STEVENSON

THE TREASURE HUNT [1]

"Jim," said Silver, when we were alone, "if I saved your life, you saved mine; and I'll not forget it. I seen the doctor waving you to run for it—with the tail of my eye, I did; and I seen you say no, as plain as hearing. Jim, that's one to you. This is the first glint of hope I had since the attack failed, and I owe it you. And now, Jim, we're to go in for this here treasure hunting, with sealed orders too, and I don't like it; and you and me must stick close, back to back like, and we'll save our necks in spite o' fate and fortune."

Just then a man hailed us from the fire that breakfast was ready, and we were soon seated here and there about the sand over biscuit and fried junk. They had lit a fire fit to roast an ox; and it was now grown so hot that they could only approach it from the windward, and even there not without precaution. In the same wasteful spirit, they had cooked, I suppose, three times more than we could eat; and one of them, with an empty laugh, threw what was left into the fire, which blazed and roared again over this unusual fuel. I

[1] From "Treasure Island," by Robert Louis Stevenson. Illustrations from drawings by N. C. Wyeth and Norman Price

never in my life saw men so careless of the morrow; hand to mouth is the only word that can describe their way of doing. And what with wasted food and sleeping sentries, though they were bold enough for a brush and be done with it, I could see their entire unfitness for anything like a prolonged campaign.

Even Silver, eating away, with Captain Flint upon his shoulder, had not a word of blame for their reckessness. And this the more surprised me, for I thought he had never shown himself so cunning as he did then.

"Aye, mates," said he, "it's lucky you have Barbecue to think for you with this here head. I got what I wanted, I did. Sure enough they have the ship. Where they have it, I don't know yet; but once we hit the treasure, we'll have to jump about and find out. And then, mates, us that has the boats, I reckon, has the upper hand."

Thus he kept running on, with his mouth

full of the hot bacon: thus he restored their hope and confidence and, I more than suspect, repaired his own at the same time.

"As for hostage," he continued, "that's his last talk, I guess, with them he loves so dear. I've got my piece o' news, and thanky to him for that, but it's over and done. I'll take him in a line when we go treasure hunting, for we'll keep him like so much gold, in case of accidents, you mark, and in the meantime. Once we got the ship and treasure both, and off to sea like jolly companions, why, then, we'll talk Mr. Hawkins over, we will, and we'll give him his share, to be sure, for all his kindness."

It was no wonder the men were in a good humor now. For my part I was horribly cast down. Should the scheme he had now sketched prove feasible, Silver, already doubly a traitor, would not hesitate to adopt it. He had still a foot in either camp, and there was no doubt he would prefer wealth and freedom with the pirates to a bare escape from hanging, which was the best he had to hope on our side.

Nay, and even if things so fell out that he was forced to keep his faith with Dr. Livesey, even then what danger lay before us! What a moment that would be when the suspicions of his followers turned to certainty, and he and I should have to fight for dear life—he, a cripple, and I, a boy—against five strong and active seamen!

Add to this double apprehension the mystery that still hung over the behavior of my friends; their unexplained desertion of the stockade; their inexplicable cession of the chart; or, harder still to understand, the doctor's last warning to Silver, "Look out for squalls when you find it"; and you will readily believe how little taste I found in my breakfast, and with how uneasy a heart I set forth behind my captors on the quest for treasure.

We made a curious figure, had anyone been there to see us: all in soiled sailor clothes, and all but me armed to the teeth. Silver had two guns slung about him—one before and one behind—besides the great cutlass at his waist and a pistol in each pocket of his square-tailed coat. To complete his strange appearance, Captain Flint sat perched upon his shoulder and gabbling odds and ends of purposeless sea talk. I had a line about my waist, and followed obediently after the sea cook, who held the loose end of the rope, now in his free hand, now between his powerful teeth. For all the world I was led like a dancing bear.

The other men were variously burdened: some carrying picks and shovels—for that had been the very first necessary they brought ashore from the *Hispaniola;* others laden with pork, bread, and brandy for the midday meal. All the stores, I observed, came from our stock; and I could see the truth of Silver's words the night before. Had he not struck a bargain with the doctor, he and his mutineers, deserted by the ship, must have been driven to subsist on clear water and the proceeds of their hunting. Water would have been little to their taste; a sailor is not usually a good shot; and besides all that, when they were so short of eatables, it was not likely they would be very flush of powder.

Well, thus equipped, we all set out—even the fellow with the broken head, who should certainly have kept in shadow—and straggled, one after another, to the beach, where the two gigs awaited us. Even these bore trace of the drunken folly of the pirates, one in a broken thwart, and both in their muddy and unbailed condition. Both were to be carried along with us, for the sake of safety; and so, with our numbers divided between them, we set forth upon the bosom of the anchorage.

As we pulled over, there was some discussion on the chart. The red cross was, of course, far too large to be a guide; and the terms of the note on the back, as you will hear, admitted of some ambiguity. They ran, thus:

*Tall tree, Spyglass shoulder, bearing
a point to the N. of N.N.E.*
  Skeleton Island E.S.E. and by E.
Ten feet.

A tall tree was thus the principal mark.
Now, right before us, the anchorage was
bounded by a plateau from two to three
hundred feet high, adjoining on the north
the sloping southern shoulder of the Spyglass, and rising again toward the south
into the rough, cliffy eminence called the
Mizzenmast Hill. The top of the plateau
was dotted thickly with pine trees of vary-
ing height. Every here and there, one of a
different species rose forty or fifty feet
clear above its neighbors, and which of
these was the particular "tall tree" of Captain Flint could only be decided on the
spot, and by the readings of the compass.

Yet, although that was the case, every
man on board the boats had picked a
favorite of his own ere we were halfway
over, Long John alone shrugging his
shoulders and bidding them wait till they
were there.

We pulled easily, by Silver's directions,
not to weary the hands prematurely; and,
after quite a long passage, landed at the
mouth of the second river—that which
runs down a woody cleft of the Spyglass.
Thence, bending to our left, we began to
ascend the slope toward the plateau.

At the first outset, heavy, miry ground
and a matted, marshy vegetation, greatly
delayed our progress; but by little and
little the hill began to steepen and become
stony under foot, and the wood to change
its character and to grow in a more open
order. It was, indeed, a most pleasant
portion of the island that we were now
approaching. A heavy-scented broom and
many flowering shrubs had almost taken
the place of grass. Thickets of green nutmeg were dotted here and there with the
red columns and the broad shadow of the
pines, and the first mingled their spice
with the aroma of the others. The air,
besides, was fresh and stirring, and this,
under the sheer sunbeams, was a wonderful refreshment to our senses.

The party spread itself abroad, in a fan
shape, shouting and leaping to and fro.
About the center, and a good way behind
the rest, Silver and I followed—I tethered
by my rope, he plowing, with deep pants,
among the sliding gravel. From time to
time, indeed, I had to lend him a hand or
he must have missed his footing and fallen
backward down the hill.

We had thus proceeded for about half a mile, and were approaching the brow of the plateau, when the man upon the farthest left began to cry aloud, as if in terror. Shout after shout came from him, and the others began to run in his direction.

"He can't 'a' found the treasure," said old Morgan, hurrying past us from the right, "for that's clean a-top."

Indeed, as we found when we also reached the spot, it was something very different. At the foot of a pretty big pine, and involved in a green creeper, which had even partly lifted some of the smaller bones, a human skeleton lay, with a few shreds of clothing, on the ground. I believe a chill struck for a moment to every heart.

"He was a seaman," said George Merry, who, bolder than the rest, had gone up close and was examining the rags of clothing. "Leastways, this is good sea cloth."

"Aye, aye," said Silver, "like enough; you wouldn't look to find a bishop here, I reckon. But what sort of a way is that for bones to lie? 'Tain't in natur'."

Indeed, on a second glance, it seemed impossible to fancy that the body was in a natural position. But for some disarray (the work, perhaps, of the birds that had fed upon him or of the slow-growing creeper that had gradually enveloped his remains), the man lay perfectly straight—his feet pointing in one direction, his hands, raised above his head like a diver's, pointing directly in the opposite.

"I've taken a notion into my old numskull," observed Silver. "Here's the compass; there's the tiptop p'int o' Skeleton Island, stickin' out like a tooth. Just take a bearing, will you, along the line of them bones."

It was done. The body pointed straight in the direction of the island, and the compass read duly E.S.E. and by E.

"I thought so," cried the cook; "this here is a p'inter. Right up there is our line for the Pole Star and the jolly dollars. But, by thunder! if it don't make me cold inside to think of Flint. This is one of *his* jokes, and no mistake. Him and these six was alone here; he killed 'em, every man; and this one he hauled here and laid down by compass, shiver my timbers! They're long bones, and the hair's been yellow. Aye, that would be Allardyce. You mind Allardyce, Tom Morgan?"

"Aye, aye," returned Morgan, "I mind him; he owed me money, he did, and took my knife ashore with him."

"Speaking of knives," said another, "why don't we find his'n lying round? Flint warn't the man to pick a seaman's pocket; and the birds, I guess, would leave it be."

"By the powers, and that's true!" cried Silver.

"There ain't a thing left here," said Merry, still feeling round among the bones, "not a copper doit nor a baccy box. It don't look nat'ral to me."

"No, by gum, it don't," agreed Silver; "not nat'ral nor not nice, says you. Great guns! messmates, but if Flint was living, this would be a hot spot for you and me. Six they were, and six are we; and bones is what they are now."

"I saw him dead with these here deadlights," said Morgan. "Billy took me in. There he laid, with penny pieces on his eyes."

"Dead—aye, sure enough he's dead and gone below," said the fellow with the bandage; "but if ever sperrit walked, it would be Flint's. Dear heart, but he died bad, did Flint!"

"Aye, that he did," observed another; "now he raged, and now he hollered for the rum, and now he sang. 'Fifteen Men' were his only song, mates, and I tell you true I never rightly liked to hear it since. It was main hot, and the windy was open, and I hear that old song comin' out as clear as clear—and the death-haul on the man already."

"Come, come," said Silver, "stow this talk. He's dead, and he don't walk, that I know; leastways, he won't walk by day, and you may lay to that. Care killed a cat. Fetch ahead for the doubloons."

We started, certainly, but in spite of the hot sun and the staring daylight, the pirates no longer ran separate and shouting through the wood, but kept side by side and spoke with bated breath. The terror of the dead buccaneer had fallen on their spirits.

Partly from the damping influence of this alarm, partly to rest Silver and the sick folk, the whole party sat down as soon as they had gained the brow of the ascent.

The plateau being somewhat tilted toward the west, this spot on which we had paused commanded a wide prospect on either hand. Before us, over the treetops, we beheld the Cape of the Woods fringed with surf; behind, we not only looked down upon the anchorage and Skeleton Island, but saw—clear across the spit and the eastern lowlands—a great field of open sea upon the east. Sheer above us rose the Spyglass, here dotted with single pines, there black with precipices. There was no sound but that of the distant breakers, mounting from all round, and the chirp of countless insects in the brush. Not a man, not a sail upon the sea; the very largeness of the view increased the sense of solitude.

Silver, as he sat, took certain bearings with his compass.

"There are three 'tall trees,'" said he, "about in the right line from Skeleton Island. 'Spyglass shoulder,' I take it, means that lower p'int there. It's child's play to find the stuff now. I've half a mind to dine first."

"I don't feel sharp," growled Morgan. "Thinkin' o' Flint—I think it were—has done me."

"Ah, well, my son, you praise your stars he's dead," said Silver.

"He were an ugly devil," cried a third pirate, with a shudder; "that blue in the face, too!"

"That was how the rum took him," added Merry.

"Blue! well, I reckon he was blue. That's a true word."

Ever since they had found the skeleton and got upon this train of thought they had spoken lower and lower, and they had almost got to whispering by now, so that the sound of their talk hardly interrupted the silence of the wood. All of a sudden, out of the middle of the trees in front of us, a thin, high, trembling voice struck up the well-known air and words:

*"Fifteen men on the dead man's chest—
Yo-ho-ho, and a bottle of rum!"*

I never have seen men more dreadfully affected than the pirates. The color went from their six faces like enchantment; some leaped to their feet, some clawed hold of others; Morgan groveled on the ground.

"It's Flint, by—!" cried Merry.

The song had stopped as suddenly as it began—broken off, you would have said, in the middle of a note, as though someone had laid his hand upon the singer's mouth. Coming so far through the clear, sunny atmosphere among the green treetops, I thought it had sounded airily and sweetly; and the effect on my companions was the stranger.

"Come," said Silver, struggling with his ashen lips to get the word out, "this won't do. Stand by to go about. This is a rum start, and I can't name the voice: but it's someone skylarking—someone that's flesh and blood, and you may lay to that."

His courage had come back as he spoke, and some of the color to his face along with it. Already the others had begun to lend an ear to this encouragement, and were coming a little to themselves, when the same voice broke out again—not this time singing, but in a faint, distant hail, that echoed yet fainter among the clefts of the Spyglass.

"Darby M'Graw," it wailed—for that is the word that best describes the sound—"Darby M'Graw! Darby M'Graw!" again and again and again; and then rising a little higher, and with an oath that I leave out, "Fetch aft the rum, Darby!"

The buccaneers remained rooted to the ground, their eyes starting from their heads. Long after the voice had died away they still stared in silence, dreadfully, before them.

"That fixes it!" gasped one. "Let's go."

"They was his last words," moaned Morgan, "his last words aboveboard."

Dick had his Bible out and was praying volubly. He had been well brought up, had Dick, before he came to sea and fell among bad companions.

Still, Silver was unconquered. I could hear his teeth rattle in his head, but he had not yet surrendered.

"Nobody in this here island ever heard of Darby," he muttered; "not one but us that's here." And then, making a great effort, "Shipmates," he cried, "I'm here to get that stuff, and I'll not be beat by man nor devil. I never was feared of Flint in his life and, by the powers, I'll face him dead. There's seven hundred thousand pound not a quarter of a mile from here. When did ever a gentleman o' fortune show his stern to that much dollars, for a boozy old seaman with a blue mug—and him dead, too?"

But there was no sign of reawakening courage in his followers; rather, indeed, of growing terror at the irreverence of his words.

"Belay there, John!" said Merry. "Don't you cross a sperrit."

And the rest were all too terrified to reply. They would have run away severally had they dared, but fear kept them together, and kept them close by John, as if his daring helped them. He, on his part, had pretty well fought his weakness down.

"Sperrit? Well, maybe," he said. "But there's one thing not clear to me. There was an echo. Now, no man ever seen a sperrit with a shadow; well, then, what's he doing with an echo to him, I should like to know? That ain't in natur', surely?"

This argument seemed weak enough to me. But you can never tell what will af-fect the superstitious, and, to my wonder, George Merry was greatly relieved.

"Well, that's so," he said. "You've a head upon your shoulders, John, and no mistake. 'Bout ship, mates! This here crew is on a wrong tack, I do believe. And come to think on it, it was like Flint's voice, I grant you, but not just so clear-away like it, after all. It was liker somebody else's voice now —it was liker—"

"By the powers, Ben Gunn!" roared Silver.

"Aye, and so it were," cried Morgan, springing on his knees. "Ben Gunn it were!"

"It don't make much odds, do it, now?" asked Dick. "Ben Gunn's not here in the body, any more'n Flint."

But the older hands greeted this remark with scorn.

"Why, nobody minds Ben Gunn," cried Merry; "dead or alive, nobody minds him."

It was extraordinary how their spirits had returned and how the natural color had revived in their faces. Soon they were chatting together, with intervals of listening; and not long after, hearing no further sound, they shouldered the tools and set forth again, Merry walking first with Silver's compass to keep them on the right line with Skeleton Island. He had said the truth: dead or alive, nobody minded Ben Gunn.

Dick alone still held his Bible, and looked around him as he went, with fearful glances; but he found no sympathy, and Silver even joked him on his precautions.

"I told you," said he, "I told you you had sp'iled your Bible. If it ain't no good to swear by, what do you suppose a sperrit would give for it? Not that!" and he snapped his big fingers, halting a moment on his crutch.

But Dick was not to be comforted; indeed, it was soon plain to me that the lad was falling sick; hastened by heat, exhaustion, and the shock of his alarm, the fever predicted by Dr. Livesey was evidently growing swiftly higher.

It was fine open walking here, upon the summit; our way lay a little downhill, for, as I have said, the plateau tilted toward the west. The pines, great and small, grew wide apart; and even between the clumps of nutmeg and azalea wide-open spaces baked in the hot sunshine. Striking, as we did, pretty near northwest across the island, we drew, on the one hand, ever nearer under the shoulders of the Spyglass and, on the other, looked ever wider over that western bay where I had once tossed and trembled in the coracle.

The first of the tall trees was reached, and by the bearing proved the wrong one. So with the second. The third rose nearly two hundred feet into the air above a clump of underwood; a giant of a vegetable, with a red column as big as a cottage, and a wide shadow around in which a company could have maneuvered. It was conspicuous far to sea on both the east and west, and might have been entered as a sailing mark upon the chart.

But it was not its size that now impressed my companions; it was the knowledge that seven hundred thousand pounds in gold lay somewhere buried below its spreading shadow. The thought of the money, as they drew nearer, swallowed up their previous terrors. Their eyes burned in their heads; their feet grew speedier and lighter; their whole soul was bound up in that fortune, that whole lifetime of extravagance and pleasure, that lay waiting for each of them.

Silver hobbled, grunting, on his crutch; his nostrils stood out and quivered; he cursed like a madman when the flies settled on his hot and shiny countenance; he plucked furiously at the line that held me to him and, from time to time, turned his eyes upon me with a deadly look. Certainly he took no pains to hide his thoughts; and certainly I read them like print. In the immediate nearness of the gold, all else had been forgotten; his promise and the doctor's warning were both things of the past; and I could not doubt that he hoped to seize upon the treasure, find and board the *Hispaniola* under cover of night, cut every honest throat about that island, and sail away as he had at first intended, laden with crimes and riches.

Shaken as I was with these alarms, it was hard for me to keep up with the rapid pace of the treasure hunters. Now and again I stumbled, and it was then that Silver plucked so roughly at the rope and launched at me his murderous glances. Dick, who had dropped behind us and now brought up the rear, was babbling to himself both prayers and curses, as his fever kept rising. This also added to my wretchedness, and, to crown all, I was haunted by the thought of the tragedy that had once been acted on that plateau, when that ungodly buccaneer with the blue face— he who died at Savannah, singing and shouting for drink—had there, with his own hand, cut down his six accomplices. This grove, that was now so peaceful, must then have rung with cries, I thought; and even with the thought I could believe I heard it ringing still.

We were now at the margin of the thicket and more light shone through the trees.

"Huzza, mates, all together!" shouted Merry, and the foremost broke into a run.

And suddenly, not ten yards farther, we beheld them stop. A low cry arose. Silver doubled his pace, digging away with the foot of his crutch like one possessed; and next moment he and I had come also to a dead halt.

Before us was a great excavation, not very recent, for the sides had fallen in and grass had sprouted on the bottom. In this were the shaft of a pick broken in two and the boards of several packing cases strewn around. On one of these boards I saw, branded with a hot iron, the name *Walrus* —the name of Flint's ship.

All was clear to probation. The cache had been found and rifled: the seven hundred thousand pounds were gone!

There never was such an overturn in this world. Each of these six men was as though he had been struck. But with Silver the blow passed almost instantly. Every thought of his soul had been set fullstretch, like a racer, on that money. Well, he was brought up in a single second, dead; and he kept his head, found his temper, and changed his plan before the others had had time to realize the disappointment.

"Jim," he whispered, "take that, and stand by for trouble."

And he passed me a double-barreled pistol.

At the same time he began quietly moving northward, and in a few steps had put the hollow between us two and the other five. Then he looked at me and nodded, as much as to say, "Here is a narrow corner," as, indeed, I thought it was. His looks were now quite friendly; and I was so revolted at these constant changes that I could not forbear whispering, "So you've changed sides again."

There was no time left for him to answer in. The buccaneers, with oaths and cries, began to leap, one after another, into the pit, and to dig with their fingers, throwing the boards aside as they did so. Morgan found a piece of gold. He held it up with a spout of oaths. It was a two-guinea piece, and it went from hand to hand among them for a quarter of a minute.

"Two guineas!" roared Merry, shaking it at Silver. "That's your seven hundred thousand pounds, is it? You're the man for bargains, ain't you? You're him that never bungled nothing, you woodenheaded lubber!"

"Dig away, boys," said Silver, with the coolest insolence, "you'll find some pignuts and I shouldn't wonder."

"Pignuts!" repeated Merry in a scream. "Mates, do you hear that? I tell you, now, that man there knew it all along. Look in the face of him, and you'll see it wrote there."

"Ah, Merry," remarked Silver, "standing for cap'n again? You're a pushing lad, to be sure."

But this time everyone was entirely in Merry's favor. They began to scramble out of the excavation, darting furious glances behind them. One thing I observed, which looked well for us: they all got out upon the opposite side from Silver.

Well, there we stood, two on one side, five on the other, the pit between us, and nobody screwed up high enough to offer the first blow. Silver never moved; he watched them, very upright on his crutch, and looked as cool as ever I saw him. He was brave, and no mistake.

At last Merry seemed to think a speech might help matters.

"Mates," says he, "there's two of them alone there: one's the old cripple that brought us all here and blundered us down to this; the other's that cub that I mean to have the heart of. Now, mates—"

He was raising his arm and his voice, and plainly meant to lead a charge. But just then—crack! crack! crack!—three musket shots flashed out of the thicket. Merry tumbled head foremost into the excavation; the man with the bandage spun round like a teetotum and fell all his length upon his side, where he lay dead, but still twitching; and the other three turned and ran for it with all their might.

Before you could wink, Long John had fired two barrels of a pistol into the struggling Merry; and as the man rolled up his eyes at him in the last agony, "George," said he, "I reckon I settled you."

At the same moment, the doctor, Gray, and Ben Gunn joined us, with smoking muskets, from among the nutmeg trees.

"Forward!" cried the doctor. "Double quick, my lads. We must head 'em off the boats."

And we set off at a great pace, sometimes plunging through the bushes to the chest.

I tell you, but Silver was anxious to keep up with us. The work that man went through, leaping on his crutch till the muscles of his chest were fit to burst, was work no sound man ever equaled; and so thinks the doctor. As it was, he was already thirty yards behind us, and on the verge of strangling, when we reached the brow of the slope.

"Doctor," he hailed, "see there! No hurry!"

Sure enough there was no hurry. In a more open part of the plateau we could see the three survivors still running in the same direction as they had started, right for Mizzenmast Hill. We were already between them and the boats, and so we four sat down to breathe, while Long John, mopping his face, came slowly up with us.

"Thank ye kindly, doctor," says he. "You came in in about the nick, I guess, for me and Hawkins. And so it's you, Ben Gunn!" he added. "Well, you're a nice one, to be sure."

"I'm Ben Gunn, I am," replied the maroon, wriggling like an eel in his embarrassment. "And," he added, after a long pause, "how do, Mr. Silver? Pretty well, I thank ye, says you."

"Ben, Ben," murmured Silver, "to think as you've done me!"

The doctor sent back Gray for one of the pickaxes, deserted, in their flight, by the mutineers; and then as we proceeded leisurely downhill to where the boats were lying, related, in a few words, what had taken place. It was a story that interested Silver; and Ben Gunn, the half-idiot maroon, was the hero from beginning to end.

Ben, in his long, lonely wanderings about the island, had found the skeleton—it was he that had rifled it; he had found the treasure; he had dug it up (it was the haft of his pickax that lay broken in the excavation); he had carried it on his back, in many weary journeys, from the foot of the tall pine to a cave he had on the two-pointed hill at the northeast angle of the island, and there it had lain stored in safety since two months before the arrival of the *Hispaniola*.

When the doctor had wormed this secret from him, on the afternoon of the attack, and when next morning he saw the anchorage deserted, he had gone to Silver, given him the chart, which was now useless—given him the stores, for Ben Gunn's cave was well supplied with goats' meat salted by himself—given anything and everything to get a chance of moving in safety from the stockade to the two-pointed hill, there to be clear of malaria and keep a guard upon the money.

"As for you, Jim," he said, "it went against my heart, but I did what I thought best for those who had stood by their duty. And if you were not one of these, whose fault was it?"

That morning, finding that I was to be involved in the horrid disappointment he had prepared for the mutineers, he had run all the way to the cave and, leaving the squire to guard the captain, had taken Gray and the maroon, and started, making the diagonal across the island, to be at hand beside the pine. Soon, however, he saw that our party had the start of him; and Ben Gunn, being fleet of foot, had been dispatched in front to do his best alone. Then it had occurred to him to work upon the superstitions of his former shipmates; and he was so far successful that Gray and the doctor had come up and were already ambushed before the arrival of the treasure hunters.

"Ah," said Silver, "it were fortunate for me that I had Hawkins here. You would have let old John be cut to bits, and never given it a thought, doctor."

"Not a thought," replied Dr. Livesey cheerily.

And by this time we had reached the gigs. The doctor, with the pickax, demolished one of them, and then we all got aboard the other, and set out to go round by sea for North Inlet.

This was a run of eight or nine miles. Silver, though he was almost killed already with fatigue, was set to an oar, like the rest of us, and we were soon skimming swiftly over a smooth sea. Soon we passed out of the straits and doubled the southeast corner of the island, round which, four days ago, we had towed the *Hispaniola*.

As we passed the two-pointed hill we could see the black mouth of Ben Gunn's cave, and a figure standing by it, leaning on a musket. It was the squire, and we waved a handkerchief and gave him three cheers, in which the voice of Silver joined as heartily as any.

Three miles farther, just inside the

"I dare you to thank me!" cried the squire. "It is a gross dereliction of my duty. Stand back."

And thereupon we all entered the cave. It was a large, airy place, with a little spring and a pool of clear water, overhung with ferns. The floor was sand. Before a big fire lay Captain Smollett, and in a far corner, only duskily flickered over by the blaze, I beheld great heaps of coin and quadrilaterals built of bars of gold. That was Flint's treasure that we had come so far to seek, and that had cost already the lives of seventeen men from the *Hispaniola*. How many it had cost in the amassing, what blood and sorrow, what good ships scuttled on the deep, what brave men walking the plank blindfold, what shot of cannon, what shame and lies and cruelty, perhaps no man alive could tell. Yet there were still three upon that island—Silver, and old Morgan, and Ben Gunn—who had each taken his share in these crimes, as each had hoped in vain to share in the reward.

"Come in, Jim," said the captain. "You're a good boy in your line, Jim, but I don't think you and me'll go to sea again. You're too much of the born favorite for me. Is that you, John Silver? What brings you here, man?"

"Come back to my dooty, sir," returned Silver.

"Ah!" said the captain; and that was all he said.

What a supper I had of it that night, with all my friends around me; and what a meal it was, with Ben Gunn's salted goat, and some delicacies and a bottle of old wine from the *Hispaniola*. Never, I am sure, were people gayer or happier. And there was Silver, sitting back almost out of the firelight, but eating heartily, prompt to spring forward when anything was wanted, even joining quietly in our laughter—the same bland, polite, obsequious seaman of the voyage out.

mouth of North Inlet, what should we meet but the *Hispaniola*, cruising by herself. The last flood had lifted her, and had there been much wind, or a strong tide current, as in the southern anchorage, we should never have found her more, or found her stranded beyond help. As it was, there was little amiss beyond the wreck of the mainsail. Another anchor was got ready, and dropped in a fathom and a half of water. We all pulled round again to Rum Cove, the nearest point for Ben Gunn's treasure house; and then Gray, singlehanded, returned with the gig to the *Hispaniola*, where he was to pass the night on guard.

A gentle slope ran up from the beach to the entrance of the cave. At the top the squire met us. To me he was cordial and kind, saying nothing of my escapade, either in the way of blame or praise. At Silver's polite salute he somewhat flushed.

"John Silver," he said, "you're a prodigious villain and impostor—a monstrous impostor, sir. I am told I am not to prosecute you. Well, then, I will not. But the dead men, sir, hang about your neck like millstones."

"Thank you kindly, sir," replied Long John, again saluting.

Lassie Come-Home

ERIC KNIGHT

FREEDOM AGAIN AT LAST [1]

It was Lassie's time sense that did it—that curious sense in an animal which tells it exactly what time of the day it is.

For had it been any other part of the day, Lassie might have followed her lifetime training to obey a spoken order and returned to Hynes as he bid her. But she did not.

It had been while on one of the newly ordered walks, with Lassie going along obediently at Hynes's heel. The leash was about Lassie's neck, but she neither tugged ahead on it nor lingered behind so that it tugged at her. She was going as a well-trained dog should go, close at the left heel so that her head almost touched Hynes's knee.

Everything was orderly as could be wished—only that Hynes had not forgotten his resentment about being forced to take exercise himself so that Lassie could be kept in good fettle. He wanted to get back to his tea—and he still wanted to show Lassie "who was boss."

And so, quite needlessly, he suddenly tugged on the leash.

"Come along wiv yer, will yer?" he snapped.

Lassie felt the sudden tug on her neck and hesitated. She was only slightly puzzled. She knew from long training that she was doing exactly what was expected of her. Obviously, though, this man expected something else. She wasn't sure what it was.

So in that moment of indecision, she slackened her pace. Almost gladly Hynes noted this. He turned and yanked at the leash.

"Come on, now. Come on when I tell yer," he shouted.

Lassie backed away from the threatening tone. Hynes yanked again. Lassie did what any dog will do: she braced herself for the tug and lowered her head.

Hynes tugged harder. The leash slipped up over Lassie's head.

She was free!

In the split second that Hynes saw that, he acted according to his nature—but not according to his own knowledge as a dogman. He jumped to grab Lassie. It was exactly the wrong thing to do. For instinctively she jumped away to elude him.

Hynes's action had done only one thing. It had shown Lassie clearly that she wanted to keep away from him. Had he spoken to her in an ordinary manner, she might have come to him. In fact, if he had just ordered her to heel, she might have followed him back to the kennel held by nothing more than her trained habits of obedience to man.

[1] From "Lassie Come-Home," by Eric Knight, illustrated by Marguerite Kirmse

Hynes was enough of a dog-man, however, to understand this—to see that he had made a bad mistake, that if he moved menacingly again, he might frighten the dog even more. So he began to do what he should have done in the first place.

"Here, Lassie. Come here," he said.

Lassie stood in indecision. One instinct told her to obey. But the memory of the sudden leap at her was too fresh.

Hynes saw that. He lifted his voice in a high, wheedling tone which he thought might be alluring.

"Nice Lassie. Nice dog," he chanted. "Nice dog—now stay there. Don't you move, now. Stay there."

He half knelt, and snapped his fingers to hold the dog's attention. Imperceptibly, inch by inch, he crept nearer.

"Stand still, now," Hynes ordered.

The lifetime of training that Sam Carraclough had given Lassie seemed to have its effect now. For even though Lassie disliked Hynes, she had been schooled that she must obey human beings who spoke the words of command to her.

But there was another lifetime impulse that stirred her—although only faintly. It was the time sense.

Dimly, mistily, it began to waken in her. She did not know it or reason it or think it clearly as a man would. It began to grow in her faintly. It was only a weak stirring.

It was time—time to—time to . . .

She watched Hynes creeping nearer. Her head lifted a trifle.

It was time—time to—time to go . . .

Hynes edged himself nearer. In another second he would be near enough to grab the dog—to sink his fingers into the wealth of heavy mane and hang on until he could slip the guardian leash over her head again.

Lassie watched him. The stirring was becoming plainer.

It was time—time to go for . . .

Hynes gathered himself. As if sensing it, Lassie moved. Quickly she backed away two paces from the crawling man. She wanted to be free.

"Drat you," Hynes exploded.

As if he realized this mistake, he began all over again.

"Nice Lassie, now. Stand still, there. Stand still. Stay there."

Lassie was not listening to him now, however. With only a small part of her senses she was watching the man edging nearer. All the rest of her was increasingly intent upon the stirring that was becoming clearer and clearer. She wanted time. She felt somehow that if this man reached her, she would be disappointed once more.

She stepped back again. And just at that moment Hynes leaped. Lassie dodged aside.

Angrily Hynes stood erect. He walked toward her, speaking soothing words. Lassie backed away. Always she kept the same distance between Hynes and herself—the distance an animal knows so well—the distance which places it beyond the sudden reach of an enemy.

Her instinct was saying:

"Keep away from him. Do not let him reach you. For there is something—something else. It is time—time to go—time to go for the . . ."

And then, suddenly, in that second, Lassie knew. She knew as surely and irrevocably as the hands of a clock that point to five minutes to four.

It was time to go for the boy!

She wheeled and began trotting away—trotting as if she had but to go a few hundred yards. There was nothing to tell her that the rendezvous she would keep was hundreds of miles and scores of days away. There was only the plain, unadorned knowledge of a duty to be done. And she was going to do it as best she could.

But now, behind her, she heard Hynes. He was running, shouting. She broke from her trot into a gentle lope. She was not afraid. It was as if she knew surely that this two-footed creature could never catch up with her. She didn't even need to put on speed. Her thrown-back ears told her how near Hynes was. Then, too, dogs, like most other animals, have their eyes set much more at the side of their heads than do human beings, and thus are able to see behind them with only the slightest turn of the head.

Lassie did not seem to worry about Hynes. She just kept on going in her steady lope, down the path, over the lawn.

For a second, Hynes's heart leaped with hope. Perhaps, he thought, Lassie would head back to the kennels.

But the kennels, where she had been chained and penned, were not a home for Lassie. They were a hated place. And Hynes's hope died as he saw the collie turn down the gravel path toward the front gate.

Hynes's heart gave a leap again. The gate was always closed, and the walls about the "home" part of the estate were tall, frowning granite ones. Perhaps he could corner her yet.

Priscilla and her grandfather rode up the road from the fishing village and halted by the iron gate to the estate.

"I'll open it, Grandfather," the girl said.

She slipped lightly from her saddle as the Duke began bumbling in protest. But Priscilla knew she could dismount and mount again much more easily than her grandfather. For despite all the protests, he was an old man, and climbing up into the saddle of even the quietest horse was a task accompanied by much fuming and puffing and groaning.

Linking the reins over her crooked arm, the girl drew back the bolt and, putting her weight against the wrought-iron structure, she swung it slowly back on its hinges.

It was only then that she heard the noise. Looking up the path, she saw Hynes. He was racing toward her. Before him was the beautiful collie. And Hynes was shouting:

"Close that gate, Miss Priscilla! Close that gate! That collie's loose. Don't let 'er get hout! Close the gate!"

Priscilla looked about her. Before her was the great gate. All she needed to do was swing it shut, and Lassie was trapped inside the home grounds.

She looked up at her grandfather. He was unaware of all the stir. His deaf ears had not caught the high shoutings of Hynes.

Priscilla began to pull the gate. For a second she swung her weight back on it. She half heard her grandfather beginning to roar in puzzled protest. But then she forgot that, and she saw only one picture in her mind.

It was the picture of a village boy just a little taller than herself, standing beside the meshed wire of a run, saying to his dog: "Bide here forever and leave us be—and don't never come home no more." And she knew then that while the boy was saying it, every sense and part of him was crying out to say just the opposite.

So she stood, seeing the picture in her mind, listening to the words again as if they were spoken plainly. And still she had not closed the gate.

Her grandfather was still fuming, knowing something was happening that his aged senses could not grasp. Hynes was still screaming:

"Close that gate, Miss Priscilla. Close it!"

Priscilla stood in the moment of indecision, and then quickly she began swinging the gate wide open. There was a blur that flashed past her knees and then Priscilla stood, looking down the road, watching the dog go steadily at a lope as if it knew it had a long, long way to go. So she lifted her hand.

"Good-bye, Lassie," she said, softly. "Good-bye and—good luck!"

On his horse sat the Duke, not looking down the road at the collie, but staring at his granddaughter.

"Well, drat my buttons," he breathed. "Drat my buttons."

Robinson Crusoe

DANIEL DEFOE

ROBINSON CRUSOE ON THE DESOLATE ISLAND [1]

When I waked it was broad day, the weather clear, and the storm abated, so that the sea did not rage and swell as before; but that which surprised me most was that the ship was lifted off in the night from the sand where she lay by the swelling of the tide, and was driven up almost as far as the rock which I first mentioned, where I had been so bruised by the dashing me against it. This being within about a mile from the shore where I was, and the ship seeming to stand upright still, I wished myself on board, that, at least, I might save some necessary things for my use.

When I came down from my apartment in the tree, I looked about me again, and the first thing I found was the boat, which lay as the wind and the sea had tossed her, up upon the land, about two miles on my right hand. I walked as far as I could upon the shore to have got to her, but found a neck or inlet of water between me and the boat, which was about half a mile broad; so I came back for the present, being more intent upon getting at the ship, where I hoped to find something for my present subsistence.

A little after noon I found the sea very calm, and the tide ebbed so far out that I could come within a quarter of a mile of the ship, and here I found a fresh renewing of my grief; for I saw evidently, that if we had kept on board, we had been all safe, that is to say, we had all got safe on shore, and I had not been so miserable as to be left entirely destitute of all comfort and company, as I now was. This forced tears from my eyes again, but as there was little relief in that, I resolved, if possible, to get to the ship, so I pulled off my clothes, for the weather was hot to extremity, and took the water. But when I came to the ship, my difficulty was still greater to know how to get on board, for as she lay aground, and high out of the water, there was nothing within my reach to lay hold of. I swam round her twice, and the second time I spied a small piece of rope, which I wondered I did not see at first, hang down by the forechains so low, as that with great difficulty I got hold of it, and by the help of that rope got up into the forecastle of the ship. Here I found that the ship was bulged, and had a great deal of water in her hold, but that she lay so on the side of a bank of hard sand, or rather earth, that her stern lay lifted up upon the bank and her head low almost to the water. By this means all her quarter was free, and all that was in that part was dry; for you may be sure my first work was to search and to see what was spoiled and what was free. And first I found that all the ship's provisions were dry and untouched by the water; and being very well disposed to eat, I went to the bread room and filled my pockets with biscuit, and eat it as I went about other things, for I had no time to lose. I also found some rum in the great cabin, of which I took a large dram, and which I had indeed need enough of to spirit me for what was before me. Now I wanted nothing but a boat to furnish myself with many things which I foresaw would be very necessary to me.

It was in vain to sit still and wish for what was not to be had, and this extremity roused my application. We had several spare yards, and two or three large spars of wood, and a spare topmast or two in the ship. I resolved to fall to work with these, and flung as many of them overboard as I could manage for their weight, tying every one with a rope that they might not drive away. When this was done I went down the ship's side, and pulling them to me, I tied four of them fast together at both ends, as well as I could, in the form of a raft, and laying two or three short pieces of plank upon them crossways, I found I could walk upon it very well, but that it was not able to bear any great weight, the pieces being too light. So I went to work, and with the carpenter's saw I cut a spare topmast into three lengths, and added them to my raft, with a great deal of labor and pains; but hope of furnishing myself with necessaries encouraged me to go beyond what I should have been able to have done upon another occasion.

My raft was now strong enough to bear any reasonable weight. My next care was what to load it with, and how to preserve what I laid upon it from the surf of the sea; but I was not long considering this. I first laid all the planks or boards upon it that I could get, and having considered well what I most wanted, I first got three of the seamen's chests, which I had broken open and emptied, and lowered them down upon my raft. The first of these I filled with provisions, namely, bread, rice, three Dutch cheeses, five pieces of dried goat's flesh, which we lived much upon, and a little remainder of European corn which had been laid by for some fowls which we brought to sea with us, but the fowls were killed. There had been some barley and wheat together; but, to my great disappointment, I found afterwards that the rats had eaten or spoiled it all. As for liquors, I found several cases of bottles belonging to our skipper, in which were some cordial waters, and in all about five or six gallons of rack; these I stowed by themselves, there being no need to put them into the chest, nor no room for them. While I was doing this, I found the tide began to flow, though very calm; and I had the mortification to see my coat, shirt, and waistcoat which I had left on shore, upon the sand, swim away; as for my breeches, which were only linen and open-kneed, I swam on board in them and my stockings. However, this put me upon rummaging for clothes, of which I found enough, but took no more than I wanted for present use; for I had other things which my eye was more upon—as, first, tools to work with on shore; and it was after long searching that I found out the carpenter's chest, which was indeed a very useful prize to me, and much more valuable than a shiploading of gold would have been at that time. I got it down to my raft, even whole as it was, without losing time to look into it, for I knew in general what it contained.

My next care was for some ammunition and arms. There were two very good fowling pieces in the great cabin, and two pistols; these I secured first, with some powder horns, and a small bag of shot, and two old rusty swords. I knew there were three barrels of powder in the ship, but knew not where our gunner had stowed them; but with much search I found them, two of them dry and good, the third had taken water. Those two I got to my raft with the arms. And now I thought myself pretty well freighted, and began to think how I should get to shore with them, having neither sail, oar, nor rudder, and the least capful of wind would have overset all my navigation.

I had three encouragements: a smooth, calm sea, the tide rising and setting into the shore, and what little wind there was blew me towards the land. And thus, having found two or three broken oars belonging to the boat, and besides the tools which were in the chest, I found two saws, an axe, and a hammer, and with this cargo I put to sea. For a mile, or thereabouts, my raft went very well, only that I found it drive a little distant from the place where I had landed before, by which I perceived that there was some indraught of the water, and consequently I earnestly hoped to find some creek or river there, which I might make use of as a port to get to land with my cargo.

As I imagined, so it was. There appeared before me a little opening of the land, and I found a strong current of the tide set into it, so I guided my raft as well as I could to keep in the middle of the stream; but here I had like to have suffered a second shipwreck, which, if I had, I think verily would have broke my heart; for knowing nothing of the coast, my raft ran aground at one end of it upon a shoal, and not being aground at the other end, it wanted but a little that all my cargo had slipped off towards that end that was afloat, and so fallen into the water. I did my utmost, by setting my back against the chests, to keep them in their places, but could not thrust off the raft with all my strength, neither durst I stir from the posture I was in; but holding up the chests with all my might, stood in that manner near half an hour, in which time the rising of the water

brought me a little more upon a level; and a little after, the water still rising, my raft floated again, and I thrust her off with the oar I had into the channel; and then driving up higher, I at length found myself in the mouth of a little river, with land on both sides, and a strong current or tide running up. I looked on both sides for a proper place to get to shore, for I was not willing to be driven too high up the river, hoping in time to see some ship at sea, and therefore resolved to place myself as near the coast as I could.

At length I spied a little cove on the right shore of the creek, to which, with great pain and difficulty, I guided my raft, and at last got so near, as that, reaching ground with my oar, I could thrust her directly in. But here I had liked to have dipped all my cargo into the sea again; for that shore lying pretty steep, that is to say sloping, there was no place to land, but where one end of the float, if it run on shore, would lie so high, and the other sink lower as before, that it would endanger my cargo again. All that I could do was to wait till the tide was at the highest, keeping the raft with my oar like an anchor to hold the side of it fast to the shore, near a flat piece of ground, which I expected the water would flow over; and so it did. As soon as I found water enough (for my raft drew about a foot of water) I thrust her on upon that flat piece of ground, and there fastened or moored her by sticking my two broken oars into the ground; one on one side near one end, and one on the other side near the other end; and thus I lay till the water ebbed away, and left my raft and all my cargo safe on shore.

My next work was to view the country, and seek a proper place for my habitation, and where to stow my goods to secure them from whatever might happen. Where I was I yet knew not; whether on the continent or on an island, whether inhabited or not inhabited, whether in danger of wild beasts or not. There was a hill not above a mile from me, which rose up very steep and high, and which seemed to overtop some other hills which lay as in a ridge from it northward. I took out one of the fowling pieces, and one of the pistols, and a horn of powder, and thus armed, I traveled for discovery up to the top of that hill; where, after I had with great labor and difficulty got to the top, I saw my fate to my great affliction, namely, that I was in an island environed every way with the sea, no land to be seen, except some rocks which lay a great way off, and two small islands less than this, which lay about three leagues to the west.

I found also that the island I was in was barren, and, as I saw good reason to believe, uninhabited, except by wild beasts, of whom however I saw none; yet I saw abundance of fowls, but knew not their kinds, neither when I killed them could I tell what was fit for food, and what not. At my coming back, I shot at a great bird, which I saw sitting upon a tree on the side of a great wood—I believe it was the first gun that had been fired there since the creation of the world. I had no sooner fired, but from all parts of the wood there arose an innumerable number of fowls of many sorts, making a confused screaming, and crying every one according to his usual note; but not one of them of any kind that I knew. As for the creature I killed, I took it to be a kind of hawk, its color and beak resembling it, but had no talons or claws more than common; its flesh was carrion and fit for nothing.

Contented with this discovery, I came back to my raft, and fell to work to bring my cargo on shore, which took me up the rest of that day; and what to do with myself at night I knew not, nor indeed where to rest; for I was afraid to lie down on the ground, not knowing but some wild beast might devour me, though, as I afterwards found, there was really no need for those fears.

However, as well as I could, I barricaded myself round with the chests and boards that I had brought on shore, and made a kind of a hut for that night's lodging. As for food, I yet saw not which way to supply myself, except that I had seen two or three creatures, like hares, run out of the wood where I shot the bird.

I now began to consider that I might yet get a great many things out of the ship which would be useful to me, and particularly some of the rigging and sails, and such other things as might come to land, and I resolved to make another voyage on board the vessel, if possible; and as I knew that the first storm that blew must necessarily break her all in pieces, I resolved to set all other things apart till I got everything out of the ship that I could get. Then I called a council, that is to say, in my thoughts, whether I should take back the raft; but this appeared impracticable, so I resolved to go as before, when the tide was down, and I did so, only that I stripped before I went from my hut, having nothing on but a checkered shirt, and a pair of linen trousers, and a pair of pumps on my feet.

I got on board the ship, as before, and prepared a second raft, and having had experience of the first, I neither made this so unwieldy nor loaded it so hard; but yet I brought away several things very useful to me; as first, in the carpenter's stores, I found two or three bags full of nails and spikes, a great screw jack, a dozen or two of hatchets, and above all, that most useful thing called a grindstone. All these I se-

cured, together with several things belonging to the gunner, particularly two or three iron crows, and two barrels of musket bullets, seven muskets, and another fowling piece, with some small quantity of powder, a large bagful of small shot, and a great roll of sheet lead; but this last was so heavy, I could not hoist it up to get it over the ship's side.

Besides these things, I took all the men's clothes that I could find, and a spare foretopsail, hammock, and some bedding; and with this I loaded my second raft, and brought them all safe on shore, to my very great comfort.

I was under some apprehensions during my absence from the land, that at least my provisions might be devoured on shore; but when I came back I found no sign of any visitor, only there sat a creature like a wildcat upon one of the chests, which, when I came towards it, ran away a little distance, and then stood still. She sat very composed and unconcerned, and looked full in my face, as if she had a mind to be acquainted with me. I presented my gun at her, but as she did not understand it, she was perfectly unconcerned at it, nor did she offer to stir away; upon which I tossed her a bit of biscuit, though by the way I

was not very free of it, for my store was not great. However, I spared her a bit, I say, and she went to it, smelled it, ate it, and looked, as pleased, for more; but I thanked her, and could spare no more, so she marched off.

Having got my second cargo on shore, though I was fain to open the barrels of powder, and bring them by parcels (for they were too heavy, being large casks), I went to work to make me a little tent with the sail and some poles which I cut for that purpose; and into this tent I brought everything that I knew would spoil, either with rain or sun, and I piled all the empty chests and casks up in a circle round the tent, to fortify it from any sudden attempt, either from man or beast.

When I had done this, I blocked up the door of the tent with some boards within, and an empty chest set up on end without; and spreading one of the beds on the ground, laying my two pistols just at my head, and my gun at length by me, I went to bed for the first time, and slept very quietly all night, for I was very weary and heavy; for the night before I had slept little, and had labored very hard all day, as well to fetch all those things from the ship as to get them on shore.

I had the biggest magazine of all kinds now that ever were laid up, I believe, for one man, but I was not satisfied still; for while the ship sat upright in that posture, I thought I ought to get everything out of her that I could. So every day at low water I went on board, and brought away something or other; but particularly the third time I went, I brought away as much of the rigging as I could, as also all the small ropes and rope twine I could get, with a piece of spare canvas, which was to mend the sails upon occasion, and the barrel of wet gunpowder. In a word, I brought away all the sails first and last, only that I was fain to cut them in pieces, and bring as much at a time as I could; for they were no more useful to be sails, but as mere canvas only.

But that which comforted me more still was that, last of all, after I had made five or six such voyages as these, and thought I had nothing more to expect from the ship that was worth my meddling with; I say, after all this, I found a great hogshead of bread, and three large runlets of rum or spirits, and a box of sugar, and a barrel of fine flour. This was surprising to me, because I had given over expecting any more provisions, except what was spoiled by the water. I soon emptied the hogshead of that bread, and wrapped it up, parcel by parcel, in pieces of the sails, which I cut out; and, in a word, I got all this safe on shore also.

The next day I made another voyage. And now, having plundered the ship of what was portable and fit to hand out, I began with the cables; and cutting the great cable into pieces, such as I could move, I got two cables and a hawser on shore, with all the ironwork I could get; and having cut down the spritsailyard, and the mizzenyard, and everything I could to make a large raft, I loaded it with all those heavy goods and came away. But my good luck began now to leave me; for this raft was so unwieldy and so overladen that after I had entered the little cove, where I

had landed the rest of my goods, not being able to guide it so handily as I did the other, it overset, and threw me and all my cargo into the water. As for myself it was no great harm, for I was near the shore; but as to my cargo, it was a great part of it lost, especially the iron, which I expected would have been of great use to me. However, when the tide was out, I got most of the pieces of cable ashore, and some of the iron, though with infinite labor; for I was fain to dip for it into the water—a work which fatigued me very much. After this, I went every day on board and brought away what I could get.

I had been now thirteen days on shore, and had been eleven times on board the ship, in which time I had brought away all that one pair of hands could be well supposed capable to bring; though I believe verily, had the calm weather held, I should have brought away the whole ship, piece by piece. But preparing the twelfth time to go on board, I found the wind begin to rise; however, at low water I went on board, and though I thought I had rummaged the cabin so effectually, as that nothing more could be found, yet I discovered a locker with drawers in it, in one of which I found two or three razors, and one pair of large scissors, with some ten or a dozen of good knives and forks; in another I found about thirty-six pounds value in money, some European coin, some Brazil, some pieces of eight, some gold, some silver.

I smiled to myself at the sight of this money. "O Drug!" said I aloud, "what art thou good for? Thou art not worth to me, no, not the taking off the ground. One of these knives is worth all this heap. I have no manner of use for thee, even remain where thou art and go to the bottom, as a creature whose life is not worth saving." However, upon second thoughts, I took it away, and wrapping all this in a piece of canvas, I began to think of making another raft; but while I was preparing this, I found the sky overcast, and the wind began to

rise, and in a quarter of an hour it blew a fresh gale from the shore. It presently occurred to me that it was in vain to pretend to make a raft with the wind offshore, and that it was my business to be gone before the tide of flood began, otherwise I might not be able to reach the shore at all. Accordingly I let myself down into the water, and swam across the channel, which lay between the ship and the sands, and even that with difficulty enough, partly with the weight of things I had about me, and partly the roughness of the water; for the wind rose very hastily, and before it was quite high water it blew a storm.

But I was gotten home to my little tent, where I lay with all my wealth about me very secure. It blew very hard all that night, and in the morning when I looked out, behold no more ship was to be seen. I was a little surprised, but recovered myself with this satisfactory reflection, namely, that I had lost no time, nor abated any diligence, to get everything out of her that could be useful to me, and that indeed there was little left in her that I was able to bring away, if I had had more time.

I now gave over any more thoughts of the ship, or of anything out of her, except what might drive on shore from her wreck, as indeed divers pieces of her afterwards did; but those things were of small use to me.

My thoughts were now wholly employed about securing myself against either savages, if any should appear, or wild beasts, if any were in the island; and I had many thoughts of the method how to do this, and what kind of dwelling to make; whether I should make me a cave in the earth or a tent upon the earth; and, in short, I resolved upon both, of the manner, and description of which it may not be improper to give an account.

I soon found the place I was in was not for my settlement, particularly because it was upon a low moorish ground near the sea, and I believed would not be wholesome, and more particularly because there was no fresh water near it, so I resolved to find a more healthy and more convenient spot of ground.

I consulted several things in my situation which I found would be proper for me. Health, and fresh water, I just now mentioned; shelter from the heat of the sun; security from ravenous creatures, whether man or beast; a view to the sea, that if God sent any ship in sight, I might not lose any advantage for my deliverance, of which I was not willing to banish all my expectation yet.

In search of a place proper for this, I found a little plain on the side of a rising hill, whose front towards this little plain was steep as a houseside, so that nothing could come down upon me from the top; on the side of this rock there was a hollow place, worn a little way in, like the entrance or door of a cave; but there was not really any cave or way into the rock at all.

On the flat of the green, just before this hollow place, I resolved to pitch my tent. This plain was not above an hundred yards broad, and about twice as long, and lay like a green before my door, and at the end it descended irregularly every way down into the low grounds by the seaside. It was on the N.N.W. side of the hill, so that I was sheltered from the heat every day, till it came to a W. and by S. sun, or thereabouts, which in those countries is near the setting.

Before I set up my tent, I drew a half circle before the hollow place, which took in about ten yards in its semidiameter, from the rock, and twenty yards in its diameter, from its beginning and ending.

In this half circle I pitched two rows of strong stakes, driving them into the ground till they stood very firm, like piles, the biggest end being out of the ground about five foot and a half, and sharpened on the top. The two rows did not stand above six inches from one another.

Then I took the pieces of cable which I had cut in the ship, and laid them in rows one upon another, within the circle between these two rows of stakes, up to the top, placing other stakes in the inside, leaning against them, about two foot and a half high, like a spur to a post; and this fence was so strong that neither man nor beast could get into it or over it. This cost me a great deal of time and labor, especially to cut the piles in the woods, bring them to the place, and drive them into the earth.

The entrance into this place I made to be not by a door, but by a short ladder to go over the top; which ladder, when I was in, I lifted over after me, and so I was completely fenced in and fortified, as I thought, from all the world, and consequently slept secure in the night, which otherwise I could not have done; though, as it appeared afterward, there was no need of all this caution from the enemies that I apprehended danger from.

David Copperfield

CHARLES DICKENS

"BARKIS IS WILLING" [1]

On the last night of my restraint, I was awakened by hearing my own name spoken in a whisper. I started up in bed, and putting out my arms in the dark, said:

"Is that you, Peggotty?"

There was no immediate answer, but presently I heard my name again, in a tone so very mysterious and awful, that I think I should have gone into a fit, if it had not occured to me that it must have come through the keyhole.

I groped my way to the door, and putting my own lips to the keyhole, whispered:

"Is that you, Peggotty dear?"

"Yes, my own precious Davy," she replied. "Be as soft as a mouse, or the Cat'll hear us."

I understood this to mean Miss Murdstone, and was sensible of the urgency of the case; her room being close by.

"How's mamma, dear Peggotty? Is she very angry with me?"

I could hear Peggotty crying softly on her side of the keyhole, as I was doing on mine, before she answered. "No. Not very."

"What is going to be done with me, Peggotty dear? Do you know?"

"School. Near London," was Peggotty's answer. I was obliged to get her to repeat it, for she spoke it the first time quite down my throat, in consequence of my having forgotten to take my mouth away from the keyhole and put my ear there; and though her words tickled me a good deal, I didn't hear them.

"When, Peggotty?"

"To-morrow."

"Is that the reason why Miss Murdstone took the clothes out of my drawers?" which she had done, though I have forgotten to mention it.

"Yes," said Peggotty. "Box."

"Shan't I see mamma?"

"Yes," said Peggotty. "Morning."

Then Peggotty fitted her mouth close to the keyhole, and delivered these words through it with as much feeling and earnestness as a keyhole has ever been the medium of communicating, I will venture to assert; shooting in each broken little sentence in a convulsive little burst of its own.

"Davy, dear. If I ain't been azackly as intimate with you. Lately, as I used to be. It ain't because I don't love you. Just as well and more, my pretty poppet. It's because I thought it better for you. And for some one else besides. Davy, my darling, are you listening? Can you hear?"

"Ye—ye—ye—yes, Peggotty!" I sobbed.

[1] From "David Copperfield," by Charles Dickens. Illustrations by Jon Nielsen

"My own!" said Peggotty, with infinite compassion. "What I want to say, is. That you must never forget me. For I'll never forget you. And I'll take as much care of your mamma, Davy. As ever I took of you. And I won't leave her. The day may come when she'll be glad to lay her poor head. On her stupid, cross, old Peggotty's arm again. And I'll write to you, my dear. Though I ain't no scholar. And I'll— I'll—" Peggotty fell to kissing the keyhole, as she couldn't kiss me.

"Thank you, dear Peggotty!" said I. "Oh, thank you! Thank you! Will you promise me one thing, Peggotty? Will you write and tell Mr. Peggotty and little Em'ly, and Mrs. Gummidge and Ham, that I am not so bad as they might suppose, and that I sent 'em all my love—especially to little Em'ly? Will you, if you please, Peggotty?"

The kind soul promised, and we both of us kissed the keyhole with the greatest affection—I patted it with my hand, I recollect, as if it had been her honest face—and parted. From that night there grew up in my breast a feeling for Peggotty which I cannot very well define. She did not replace my mother; no one could do that; but she came into a vacancy in my heart, which closed upon her, and I felt towards her something I have never felt for any other human being. It was a sort of comical affection, too; and yet if she had died, I cannot think what I should have done, or how I should have acted out the tragedy it would have been to me.

In the morning Miss Murdstone appeared as usual, and told me I was going to school; which was not altogether such news to me as she supposed. She also informed me that when I was dressed, I was to come downstairs into the parlor, and have my breakfast. There I found my mother, very pale and with red eyes: into whose arms I ran, and begged her pardon from my suffering soul.

"Oh, Davy!" she said. "That you could hurt any one I love! Try to be better, pray to be better! I forgive you; but I am so grieved, Davy, that you should have such bad passions in your heart."

They had persuaded her that I was a wicked fellow, and she was more sorry for that than for my going away. I felt it sorely. I tried to eat my parting breakfast, but my tears dropped upon my bread-and-butter, and trickled into my tea. I saw my mother look at me sometimes, and then glance at the watchful Miss Murdstone, and then look down, or look away.

"Master Copperfield's box there!" said Miss Murdstone, when wheels were heard at the gate.

I looked for Peggotty, but it was not she; neither she nor Mr. Murdstone appeared. My former acquaintance, the carrier, was at the door; the box was taken out to his cart, and lifted in.

"Clara!" said Miss Murdstone, in her warning note.

"Ready, my dear Jane," returned my mother. "Good-by, Davy. You are going for your own good. Good-by, my child. You will come home in the holidays, and be a better boy."

"Clara!" Miss Murdstone repeated.

"Certainly, my dear Jane," replied my mother, who was holding me. "I forgive you, my dear boy. God bless you!"

"Clara!" Miss Murdstone repeated.

Miss Murdstone was good enough to take me out to the cart, and to say on the way that she hoped I would repent, before I came to a bad end; and then I got into the cart, and the lazy horse walked off with it.

We might have gone about half a mile, and my pocket-handkerchief was quite wet through, when the carrier stopped short.

Looking out to ascertain for what, I saw, to my amazement, Peggotty burst from a hedge and climb into the cart. She took me in both her arms, and squeezed me to her stays until the pressure on my nose was extremely painful, though I never thought of that till afterwards when I found it very tender. Not a single word did Peggotty speak. Releasing one of her arms, she put

it down in her pocket to the elbow, and brought out some paper bags of cakes which she crammed into my pockets, and a purse which she put into my hand, but not one word did she say. After another and a final squeeze with both arms, she got down from the cart and ran away; and my belief is, and has always been, without a solitary button on her gown. I picked up one, of several that were rolling about, and treasured it as a keepsake for a long time.

The carrier looked at me, as if to inquire if she were coming back. I shook my head, and said I thought not. "Then, come up," said the carrier to the lazy horse; who came up accordingly.

Having by this time cried as much as I possibly could, I began to think it was of no use crying any more, especially as nei-

ther Roderick Random, nor that Captain in the Royal British Navy had ever cried, that I could remember, in trying situations. The carrier seeing me in this resolution, proposed that my pocket-handkerchief should be spread upon the horse's back to dry. I thanked him, and assented; and particularly small it looked, under those circumstances.

I had now leisure to examine the purse. It was a stiff leather purse, with a snap, and had three bright shillings in it, which Peggotty had evidently polished up with whitening, for my greater delight. But its most precious contents were two half-crowns folded together in a bit of paper, on which was written, in my mother's hand, "For Davy. With my love." I was so overcome by this, that I asked the carrier to be so good as to reach me my pocket-handkerchief again; but he said he thought I had better do without it, and I thought I really had, so I wiped my eyes on my sleeve and stopped myself.

For good, too; though in consequence of my previous emotions, I was still occasionally seized with a stormy sob. After we had jogged on for some little time, I asked the carrier if he was going all the way?

"All the way where?" inquired the carrier.

"There," I said.

"Where's there?" inquired the carrier.

"Near London," I said.

"Why, that horse," said the carrier, jerking the rein to point him out, "would be deader than pork afore he got over half the ground."

"Are you only going to Yarmouth, then?" I asked.

"That's about it," said the carrier. "And there I shall take you to the stage-cutch, and the stage-cutch that'll take you to—wherever it is."

As this was a great deal for the carrier (whose name was Mr. Barkis) to say—he being, as I observed in a former chapter, of a phlegmatic temperament, and not at all conversational—I offered him a cake as a mark of attention, which he ate at one gulp, exactly like an elephant, and which made no more impression on his big face than it would have done on an elephant's.

"Did *she* make 'em, now?" said Mr. Barkis, always leaning forward, in his slouching way, on the footboard of the cart with an arm on each knee.

"Peggotty, do you mean, sir?"

"Ah!" said Mr. Barkis. "Her."

"Yes. She makes all our pastry and does all our cooking."

"Do she though?" said Mr. Barkis.

He made up his mouth as if to whistle, but he didn't whistle. He sat looking at the horse's ears, as if he saw something new there; and sat so for a considerable time. By-and-by, he said:

"No sweethearts, I b'lieve?"

"Sweetmeats did you say, Mr. Barkis?" For I thought he wanted something else to eat, and had pointedly alluded to that description of refreshment.

"Hearts," said Mr. Barkis. "Sweethearts; no person walks with her?"

"With Peggotty?"

"Ah!" he said. "Her."

"Oh, no. She never had a sweetheart."

"Didn't she, though?" said Mr. Barkis.

Again he made up his mouth to whistle, and again he didn't whistle, but sat looking at the horse's ears.

"So she makes," said Mr. Barkis, after a long interval of reflection, "all the apple parsties, and does all the cooking, do she?"

I replied that such was the fact.

"Well. I'll tell you what," said Mr. Barkis. "P'raps you might be writin' to her?"

"I shall certainly write to her," I rejoined.

"Ah!" he said, slowly turning his eyes towards me. "Well! If you was writin' to her, p'raps you'd recollect to say that Barkis was willin'; would you?"

"That Barkis was willing," I repeated innocently. "Is that all the message?"

"Ye—es," he said, considering. "Ye—es. Barkis is willin'."

"But you will be at Blunderstone again to-morrow, Mr. Barkis," I said, faltering a little at the idea of my being far away from it then, "and could give your own message so much better."

As he repudiated this suggestion, however, with a jerk of his head, and once more confirmed his previous request by saying, with profound gravity, "Barkis is willin'. That's the message," I readily undertook its transmission. While I was waiting for the coach in the hotel at Yarmouth that very afternoon, I procured a sheet of paper and an inkstand and wrote a note to Peggotty, which ran thus: "My dear Peggotty. I have come here safe. Barkis is willing. My love to mamma. Yours affectionately. P.S. He says he particularly wants you to know—*Barkis is willing.*"

The Adventures of Tom Sawyer

MARK TWAIN

THE GLORIOUS WHITEWASHER [1]

Saturday morning was come, and all the summer world was bright and fresh, and brimming with life. There was a song in every heart; and if the heart was young the music issued at the lips. There was cheer in every face and a spring in every step. The locust trees were in bloom and the fragrance of the blossoms filled the air. Cardiff Hill, beyond the village and above it, was green with vegetation; and it lay just far enough away to seem a Delectable Land, dreamy, reposeful, and inviting.

Tom appeared on the sidewalk with a bucket of whitewash and a long-handled brush. He surveyed the fence, and all gladness left him and a deep melancholy settled down upon his spirit. Thirty yards of board fence nine feet high. Life to him seemed hollow, and existence but a burden. Sighing he dipped his brush and passed it along the topmost plank; repeated the operation; did it again; compared the insignificant whitewashed streak with the far-reaching continent of unwhitewashed fence, and sat down on a tree-box discouraged. Jim came skipping out at the gate with a tin pail, and singing "Buffalo Gals." Bringing water from the town pump had always been hateful work in Tom's eyes before, but now it did not strike him so. He remembered that there was company at the pump. White, mulatto, and Negro boys and girls were always there waiting their turns, resting, trading playthings, quarreling, fighting, skylarking. And he remembered that, although the

[1] From "The Adventures of Tom Sawyer," by Mark Twain, illustrated by Donald McKay

pump was only a hundred and fifty yards off, Jim never got back with a bucket of water under an hour—and even then somebody generally had to go after him. Tom said:

"Say, Jim, I'll fetch the water if you'll whitewash some."

Jim shook his head and said:

"Can't, Marse Tom. Ole missis, she tole me I got to go an' git dis water an' not stop foolin' roun' wid anybody. She say she spec' Marse Tom gwine to ax me to whitewash, an' so she tole me go 'long an' 'tend to my own business—she 'lowed *she'd* 'tend to de whitewashin'."

"Oh, never you mind what she said, Jim. That's the way she always talks. Gimme the bucket—I won't be gone only a minute. *She* won't ever know."

"Oh, I dasn't, Marse Tom. Ole missis she'd take an' tar de head off'n me. 'Deed she would."

"*She!* She never licks anybody—whacks 'em over the head with her thimble—and who cares for that, I'd like to know. She talks awful, but talk don't hurt—anyways it don't if she don't cry. Jim, I'll give you a marvel. I'll give you a white alley!"

Jim began to waver.

"White alley, Jim! And it's a bully taw."

"My! Dat's a mighty gay marvel, *I* tell you! But Marse Tom I's powerful 'fraid ole missis—"

"And besides, if you will I'll show you my sore toe."

Jim was only human—this attraction was too much for him. He put down his pail, took the white alley, and bent over the toe with absorbing interest while the bandage was being unwound. In another moment he was flying down the street with his pail and a tingling rear, Tom was whitewashing with vigor, and Aunt Polly was retiring from the field with a slipper in her hand and triumph in her eye.

But Tom's energy did not last. He be-

gan to think of the fun he had planned for this day, and his sorrows multiplied. Soon the free boys would come tripping along on all sorts of delicious expeditions, and they would make a world of fun of him for having to work—the very thought of it burnt him like fire. He got out his worldly wealth and examined it—bits of toys, marbles, and trash; enough to buy an exchange of *work*, maybe, but not half enough to buy so much as half an hour of pure freedom. So he returned his straitened means to his pocket and gave up the idea of trying to buy the boys. At this dark and hopeless moment an inspiration burst upon him! Nothing less than a great, magnificent inspiration.

He took up his brush and went tranquilly to work. Ben Rogers hove in sight presently—the very boy, of all boys, whose ridicule he had been dreading. Ben's gait was the hop-skip-and-jump—proof enough that his heart was light and his anticipations high. He was eating an apple, and giving a long, melodious whoop, at intervals, followed by a deep-toned ding-dong-dong, ding-dong-dong, for he was personating a steamboat. As he drew near, he slackened speed, took the middle of the street, leaned far over to starboard and rounded to ponderously and with laborious pomp and circumstance—for he was personating the *Big Missouri*, and considered himself to be drawing nine feet of water. He was boat and captain and engine bells combined, so he had to imagine himself standing on his own hurricane deck giving the orders and executing them:

"Stop her, sir! Ting-a-ling-ling!" The headway ran almost out and he drew up slowly toward the sidewalk.

"Ship up to back! Ting-a-ling-ling!" His arms straightened and stiffened down his sides.

"Set her back on the stabboard! Ting-a-ling-ling! Chow! ch-chow-wow! Chow!" His right hand, meantime, describing stately circles—for it was representing a forty-foot wheel.

"Let her go back on the labboard! Ting-a-ling-ling! Chow-ch-chow-chow!" The left hand began to describe circles.

"Stop the stabboard! Ting-a-ling-ling! Stop the labboard! Come ahead on the stabboard! Stop her! Let your outside turn over slow! Ting-a-ling-ling! Chow-ow-ow! Get out that headline! *Lively* now! Come—out with your spring line—what 're you about there! Take a turn round that stump with the bight of it! Stand by that stage, now—let her go! Done with the engines, sir! Ting-a-ling-ling! *Sh't! sh't! sh't!*" (trying the gauge cocks).

Tom went on whitewashing—paid no attention to the steamboat. Ben stared a moment and then said:

"Hi-*yi! You're* up a stump, ain't you!"

No answer. Tom surveyed his last touch with the eye of an artist, then he gave his brush another gentle sweep and surveyed the result, as before. Ben ranged up alongside of him. Tom's mouth watered for the apple, but he stuck to his work. Ben said:

"Hello, old chap, you got to work, hey?"

Tom wheeled suddenly and said:

"Why, it's you, Ben! I warn't noticing."

"Say—*I'm* going in a-swimming, *I* am. Don't you wish you could? But of course you'd druther *work*—wouldn't you? Course you would!"

Tom contemplated the boy a bit, and said:

"What do you call work?"

"Why, ain't *that* work?"

Tom resumed his whitewashing, and answered carelessly:

"Well, maybe it is, and maybe it ain't. All I know is, it suits Tom Sawyer."

"Oh come, now, you don't mean to let on that you *like* it?"

The brush continued to move.

"Like it? Well, I don't see why I oughtn't to like it. Does a boy get a chance to whitewash a fence every day?"

That put the thing in a new light. Ben stopped nibbling his apple. Tom swept his brush daintily back and forth—stepped back to note the effect—added a touch here and there—criticized the effect again—Ben watching every move and getting more and more interested, more and more absorbed. Presently he said:

"Say, Tom, let *me* whitewash a little."

Tom considered, was about to consent; but he altered his mind:

"No—no—I reckon it wouldn't hardly do, Ben. You see, Aunt Polly's awful particular about this fence—right here on the street, you know—but if it was the back fence I wouldn't mind and *she* wouldn't. Yes, she's awful particular about this fence; it's got to be done very careful; I reckon there ain't one boy in a thousand, maybe two thousand, that can do it the way it's got to be done."

"No—is that so? Oh come, now—lemme just try. Only just a little—I'd let *you*, if you was *me*, Tom."

"Ben, I'd like to, honest Injun; but Aunt Polly—well, Jim wanted to do it, but she wouldn't let him; Sid wanted to do it, and she wouldn't let Sid. Now don't you see how I'm fixed? If you was to tackle this fence and anything was to happen to it—"

"Oh, shucks, I'll be just as careful. Now lemme try. Say—I'll give you the core of my apple."

"Well, here— No, Ben, now don't. I'm afeard—"

"I'll give you *all* of it!"

Tom gave up the brush with reluctance in his face, but alacrity in his heart. And while the late steamer *Big Missouri* worked and sweated in the sun, the retired artist sat on a barrel in the shade close by, dangled his legs, munched his apple, and planned the slaughter of more innocents. There was no lack of material; boys happened along every little while; they came to jeer, but remained to whitewash. By the time Ben was fagged out, Tom had traded the next chance to Billy Fisher for a kite, in good repair; and when *he* played out, Johnny Miller bought in for a dead rat and a string to swing it with—and so on, and so on, hour after hour. And when the

middle of the afternoon came, from being a poor poverty-stricken boy in the morning, Tom was literally rolling in wealth. He had, besides the things before mentioned, twelve marbles, part of a jew's-harp, a piece of blue bottle glass to look through, a spool cannon, a key that wouldn't unlock anything, a fragment of chalk, a glass stopper of a decanter, a tin soldier, a couple of tadpoles, six firecrackers, a kitten with only one eye, a brass doorknob, a dog collar—but no dog—the handle of a knife, four pieces of orange peel, and a dilapidated old window sash.

He had had a nice, good, idle time all the while—plenty of company—and the fence had three coats of whitewash on it! If he hadn't run out of whitewash, he would have bankrupted every boy in the village.

Tom said to himself that it was not such a hollow world, after all. He had discovered a great law of human action, without knowing it—namely, that in order to make a man or a boy covet a thing, it is only necessary to make the thing difficult to attain. If he had been a great and wise philosopher, like the writer of this book, he would now have comprehended that Work consists of whatever a body is *obliged* to do and that Play consists of whatever a body is not obliged to do. And this would help him to understand why constructing artificial flowers or performing on a treadmill is work, while rolling tenpins or climbing Mont Blanc is only amusement. There are wealthy gentlemen in England who drive four-horse passenger coaches twenty or thirty miles on a daily line, in the summer, because the privilege costs them considerable money; but if they were offered wages for the service, that would turn it into work and then they would resign.

The boy mused awhile over the substantial change which had taken place in his worldly circumstances, and then wended toward headquarters to report.

Tom presented himself before Aunt

Polly, who was sitting by an open window in a pleasant rearward apartment, which was bedroom, breakfast room, dining room, and library combined. The balmy summer air, the restful quiet, the odor of the flowers, and the drowsing murmur of the bees had had their effect, and she was nodding over her knitting—for she had no company but the cat, and it was asleep in her lap. Her spectacles were propped up on her gray head for safety. She had thought that of course Tom had deserted long ago, and she wondered at seeing him place himself in her power again in this intrepid way. He said: "Mayn't I go and play now, aunt?"

"What, a'ready? How much have you done?"

"It's all done, aunt."

"Tom, don't lie to me—I can't bear it."

"I ain't, aunt; it *is* all done."

Aunt Polly placed small trust in such evidence. She went out to see for herself; and she would have been content to find twenty per cent of Tom's statement true. When she found the entire fence whitewashed, and not only whitewashed but elaborately coated and recoated, and even a streak added to the ground, her astonishment was almost unspeakable. She said:

"Well, I never! There's no getting round it, you *can* work when you're a mind to, Tom." And then she diluted the compliment by adding, "But it's powerful seldom you're a mind to, I'm bound to say. Well, go 'long and play; but mind you get back sometime in a week, or I'll tan you."

She was so overcome by the splendor of his achievement that she took him into the closet and selected a choice apple and delivered it to him, along with an improving lecture upon the added value and flavor a treat took to itself when it came without sin through virtuous effort. And while she closed with a happy Scriptural flourish, he "hooked" a doughnut.

The Swiss Family Robinson

JOHANN WYSS

OUR FIRST HARVEST [1]

Late in the evening we heard the sounds of trampling hoofs, and presently Jack appeared, thundering along upon his two-legged steed, followed in the distance by Fritz and Franz. These latter carried upon their cruppers game bags, the contents of which were speedily displayed. Four birds, a kangaroo, twenty muskrats, a monkey, two hares, and half a dozen beaver rats were laid before me.

The boys seemed almost wild with excitement at the success of their expedition, and presently Jack exclaimed:

"Oh, father, you can't think what grand fun hunting on an ostrich is. We flew along like the wind. Sometimes I could scarcely breathe, we were going at such a rate, and was obliged to shut my eyes because of the terrific rush of air. Really, father, you must make me a mask with glass eyes to ride with, or I shall be blinded one of these fine days."

"Indeed!" replied I. "I must do no such thing."

"Why not?" asked he, with a look of amazement upon his face.

"For two reasons; firstly, because I do not consider that I *must* do anything that you demand; and, secondly because I think that you are very capable of doing it yourself. However, I must congratulate you upon your abundant supply of game. You must have indeed worked hard. Yet I wish that you would let me know when you intend starting on such a long expedition as this. You forget that though you yourselves know that you are quite safe, and that all is going on well, yet that we at home are quite in a constant state of anxiety. Now, off with you, and look to your

animals, and then you may find supper ready."

Presently the boys returned, and we prepared for a most appetizing meal which the mother set before us.

While we were discussing the roast pig, and washing it down with fragrant mead, Fritz described the day's expedition.

They had set their traps near Woodlands, and had there captured the muskrats, attracting them with small carrots, while with other traps, baited with fish and earth worms, they had caught several beaver rats and a duck-billed platypus. Hunting and fishing had occupied the rest of the day, and it was with immense pride that Jack displayed the kangaroo which he had run down with his swift courser.

We resolved to be up betimes the following morning, that we might attend to the preparation of the booty, and as I now noticed that the boys were all becoming extremely drowsy, I closed the day with evening devotions.

The number of creatures we killed rendered the removal of their skins a matter of no little time and trouble. It was not an agreeable task at any time, and when I saw the array of animals the boys had brought me to flay I determined to construct a machine which would considerably lessen the labor.

Among the ship's stores, in the surgeon's chest, I discovered a large syringe. This, with a few alterations, would serve my purpose admirably. Within the tube I first fitted a couple of valves, and then, perforating the stopper, I had in my possession a powerful air pump.

[1] From "The Swiss Family Robinson," by Johann Wyss, illustration from drawing by Lynd Ward

446

The boys stared at me in blank amazement when, armed with this instrument, I took up the kangaroo and declared myself ready to commence operations.

"Skin a kangaroo with a squirt?" said they, and a roar of laughter followed the remark.

I made no reply to the jests which followed, but silently hung the kangaroo by its hind legs to the branch of a tree. I then made a small incision in the skin, and inserting the mouth of the syringe forced air with all my might between the skin and the body of the animal. By degrees the hide of the kangaroo distended, altering the shape of the creature entirely.

Still I worked on, forcing yet more air until it had become a mere shapeless mass, and I soon found that the skin was almost entirely separated from the carcass. A bold cut down the belly, and a few touches here and there where the ligatures still bound the hide to the body, and the animal was flayed.

"What a splendid plan!" cried the boys. "But why should it do it?"

"For a most simple and natural reason," I replied. "Do you not know that the skin of an animal is attached to its flesh merely by slender and delicate fibers, and that between these exist thousands of little bladders or air chambers? By forcing air into these bladders the fibers are stretched, and at length, elastic as they are, cracked. The skin has now nothing to unite it to the body, and, consequently, may be drawn off with perfect ease."

The remaining animals were subjected to the same treatment, and, to my great joy, in a couple of days the skins were all off and being prepared for use.

I now summoned the boys to assist me in procuring blocks of wood for my crushing machine, and the following day we set forth with saws, ropes, axes, and other tools. We soon reached the tree I had selected for my purpose, and I began by sending Fritz and Jack up into the tree with axes to cut off the larger of the high branches so that, when the tree fell, it might not injure its neighbors. They then descended, and Fritz and I attacked the stem.

As the easiest and most speedy method we used a saw, such a one as is employed by sawyers in a saw pit, and Fritz taking one end and I the other, the tree was soon cut half through. We then adjusted ropes that we might guide its fall, and again began to cut. It was laborious work, but when I considered that the cut was sufficently deep we took the ropes and pulled with our united strength. The trunk cracked, swayed, tottered, and fell with a crash.

The boughs were speedily lopped off, and the trunk sawed into blocks four feet long.

To cut down and divide this tree had taken us a couple of days, and on the third we carted home four large and two small blocks, and with the vertebrae joints of the whale I, in a very short time, completed my machine.

While engaged on this undertaking I had paid little attention to our fields of grain, and, accordingly, great was my surprise when one evening the fowls returned, showing most evident indifference to their evening meal, and with their crops full. It suddenly struck me that these birds had come from the direction of our cornfield. I hurried off to see what damage they had done, and then found to my great joy that the grain was perfectly ripe.

The amount of work before us startled my wife. This unexpected harvest, which added reaping and threshing, to the fishing, salting, and pickling already on hand, quite troubled her.

"Only think," she said, "of my beloved potatoes and manioc roots! What is to become of them, I should like to know? It is time to take them up, and how to manage it, with all this press of work, I can't see."

"Don't be downhearted, wife," said I; "there is no immediate hurry about the manioc, and digging potatoes in this fine,

447

light soil is easy work compared to what it is in Switzerland, while as to planting more, that will not be necessary if we leave the younger plants in the ground. The harvest we must conduct after the Italian fashion, which, although anything but economical, will save time and trouble, and as we are to have two crops in the year, we need not to be too particular."

Without further delay, I commenced leveling a large space of firm, clayey ground to act as a threshing floor: it was well sprinkled with water, rolled, beaten, and stamped. As the sun dried the moisture it was watered anew, and the treatment continued until it became as flat, hard, and smooth as threshing floor needs to be.

Our largest wicker basket was then slung between Storm and Grumble; we armed ourselves with reaping hooks, and went forth to gather in the wheat in the simplest and most expeditious manner imaginable.

I told my reapers not to concern themselves about the length of the straw, but to grasp the wheat where it was convenient to them, without stooping. Each was to wind a stalk around his own handful, and throw it into the basket. In this way great labor was saved. The plan pleased the boys immensely, and in a short time the basket had been filled many times, and the field displayed a quantity of tall, headless stubble, which perfectly horrified the mother, so extravagant and untidy did she consider our work.

"This is dreadful!" cried she. "You have left numbers of ears growing on short stalks, and look at that splendid straw completely wasted! I don't approve of your Italian fashion at all."

"It is not a bad plan, I can assure you, wife, and the Italians do not waste the straw by not cutting it with the grain. Having more arable than pasture land, they use this high stubble for their cattle, letting them feed in it, and eat what grain is left. Afterward, allowing the grass to

grow up among it, they mow all together for winter fodder. And now for threshing, also in Italian fashion. We shall find that it spares our arms and backs as much in that as in reaping."

The little sheaves were laid in a large circle on the floor, the boys mounted Storm, Grumble, Lightfoot, and Hurricane, starting off at a brisk trot, with many a merry jest, and round they went, trampling and stamping out the grain, while dust and chaff flew in clouds about them.

From time to time the animals took mouthfuls of the tempting food they were beating out. We thought they well deserved it, and called to mind the command given to the Jews: "Thou shalt not muzzle the ox that treadeth out the corn."

After threshing, we proceeded to winnowing; by simply throwing the threshed corn with shovels high in the air when the land or sea breeze blew strong, the chaff and refuse was carried away by the wind and the grain fell to the ground.

During these operations our poultry paid the threshing floor many visits, testifying a lively interest in the success of our labors, and gobbling up the grain at such a rate that my wife was obliged to keep them at a reasonable distance. But I would not have them altogether stinted in the midst of our plenty. I said, "Let them enjoy themselves; what we lose in grain, we gain in flesh. I anticipate delicious chicken pie, roast goose, and boiled turkey!"

When our harvest stores were housed, we found that we had reaped sixty-, eighty-, even a hundredfold what had been sown. Our larder was truly filled with all manner of store.

Expecting a second harvest, we were constrained to prepare the field for sowing again, and immediately therefore commenced mowing down the stubble. While engaged in this, flocks of quails and partridges came to glean among the scattered ears. We did not secure any great number, but resolved to be prepared for them next season, and by spreading nets to catch them in large numbers.

My wife was satisfied when she saw the straw carried home and stacked. Our crop of maize, which of course had not been threshed like the other grain, afforded soft leaves which were used for stuffing mattresses, while the stalks, when burnt, left ashes so rich in alkali as to be especially useful.

I changed the crops sown on the ground to rye, barley, and oats, and hoped they would ripen before the rainy season.

Justin Morgan Had a Horse

MARGUERITE HENRY

THE PULLING BEE [1]

By the time spring came on, Joel and Miller Chase were friends. In the late afternoons, while Mistress Chase napped, the miller often gave Joel a whole hour to himself.

One afternoon early in May Joel stood looking out the inn door. Suddenly the yard began filling with big-faced dray horses and oxen, and men were gathering about a huge pine log.

"Is it a pulling bee?" asked Joel, turning to Miller Chase quickly.

"If Nathan Nye is about, looking mighty important and bossy, you can be expecting most anything. He was ever good at fixing contests."

"He's there!" exclaimed Joel. "And he's got tug chains."

"H'm," mused the miller, tapping his cheek, "if I was a boy now with no chores

[1] From "Justin Morgan Had a Horse," by Marguerite Henry, illustrations from drawings by Wesley Dennis

to do, it seems like I'd skedaddle right out there."

Joel grinned over his shoulder, and in no time at all he was helping Mister Nye fasten the tug chains to a big dappled mare.

The mare's owner, Abel Hooper, was too busy boasting to the farmers to be of any help. "A mighty lucky thing I'm first," he was saying. "Lucy and me'll pull this here piece a kindling to the sawmill in one pull. Then you can all hyper on home whilst it's still daylight."

But Abel Hooper had to eat his words, for Lucy barely caused the log to tremble.

One after another, the beasts had their turn, and no matter how whips cracked or masters yelled, the log seemed rooted to the earth.

"Folks, I guess it's up to the oxen now," Nathan Nye was saying, when into the yard came Evans riding Little Bub.

"Hey, Nathan," called Evans, "what's all the hullabaloo?"

"'Tis a pulling bee," answered Mister Nye, "but can't none of the beasts pull that there pine log to the sawmill in three pulls or less. Just look at Hooper's big mare! She's roaring from the try. And Biggle's gelding—his muscles are still a-hitching and a-twitching. Even Ezra Wiggins' beast failed. None of them can budge the log."

"None except my one-horse team!" crowed Evans.

Joel held his breath. He felt scared right down to his toes.

The crowd snickered. Then it hooted.

"*That* little flea? Why, he's just a sample of a horse. He ain't no bigger than a mouse's whisker! Besides, his tail is so long, he's liable to get all tangled up and break a leg."

Evans looked over the horseflesh. "Little Bub," he said slowly, "ain't exactly what you'd call a dray horse, but whatever he's hitched to generally has to come the first time trying."

"Take him on home," scoffed Nathan Nye. "When we have a contest for ponies, we'll be letting you know."

Above the man-talk Joel heard the sharp voice of Mistress Chase. "Boy! You come here!"

On his way in Joel stopped only long enough to press his face hard against Little Bub's nose.

At the door Mistress Chase handed him a kettle of hasty pudding and a long stick.

"Hang the kettle over the fire," she said, "and stir and stir until I tell you to quit."

"*Hasty* pudding!" muttered Joel to himself. "It beats me how it got its name!"

Evans strutted into the room just then. "Chase!" he called to the miller. "I'll wager a barrel of cider that my horse can move that pine log to the sawmill in two pulls. But first, pour me a mugful. I'm dying of thirst."

At sound of Evans' voice Joel almost upset the pudding.

"Boy!" shrilled Mistress Chase. "Mind

your work. Hasty pudding's not meant to feed the fire!"

For once Joel paid no heed. He tore across the room and grabbed Mister Evans by the sleeve.

"Mister Evans!" he cried. "Little Bub's been dragging logs all day. You hain't going to enter him in the pulling bee?"

Evans gulped his drink. "Go away, Joel," he snapped in annoyance. "When I want advice, I'll not ask it of a whipper-snapper."

The little horse meanwhile was feasting upon all the fresh green shoots within his range. They tasted juicy and delicious after the business of logging.

One by one the stars dusted the sky. Nathan Nye brought out a lanthorn so Mister Evans could see to fasten his tug-chains to the log.

Joel followed Evans about like a puppy. Evans stood it as long as he could. Finally he shoved the boy aside.

"A nettle hain't half as pesky as you," he growled. "Stand back or I'll clout you."

Now Evans was stepping off the ten rods from the log to the mill.

"Want to give up before you start?" scoffed Nathan Nye.

"No such a thing. Why, I'm actually ashamed to ask my horse to pull such a little log. Now if you'll find me three stout men to sit astride the log, why then I'll ask him."

Joel bit his lips to keep from crying out. He hid his face in the horse's tangled mane. "Oh, Bub, my poor little Bub," he choked, "none of the big creatures could budge the log, and now with three men besides. Oh Bub, Bub . . ."

Laughter rang up and down the valley. "Ho-ho-ho—that pint-sized cob to pull such a big log! Ho-ho . . ."

Nathan Nye had no trouble at all in finding three brawny volunteers. As the men straddled the log, they joked and laughed and poked one another in the ribs.

"Look to your feet, men!" warned Evans. "This horse means business. Something's got to give."

Nye held the lanthorn aloft. It lighted the circle of faces. They were tense with excitement. Some of the men were placing last-minute bets with one another. Some were whittling like mad. Others twirled their whips nervously. Joel was white with anger.

Nye repeated the warning. "Look to your feet, men!"

Someone tittered.

Evans felt to see if the little horse was hitched securely. Then, "Git up!" he roared, as he slashed the whip across Bub's back.

The little horse galvanized into action. First, he backed ever so slightly. Then his powerful neck bent low, as if to give every muscle a chance to get going. Now he was straining forward. You could see his muscles grow firm and swell up like rubber balls. You could see the white foam come out on his body.

Joel, too, was drenched in sweat. The silence was heavy, like a gray blanket.

At last there was the groaning of chains. The log trembled. Slowly it moved. It kept on moving. It was more than halfway to the saw!

The little horse stopped. His sides were heaving. Joel breathed in and out with the horse. He felt as if his lungs were on fire. There was no sound at all from the crowd. Overhead a baby robin, trying to get settled for the night, chirped insistently.

Now Evans commanded again. And again the horse went through the same motions. He backed slightly. He bent his head. He strained every muscle. Again the log was moving, moving, moving. This time it did not stop until it reached the sawmill!

And still nobody had made a sound. The three men were as silent as the log they sat upon. Only the horse's breathing pierced the quiet.

Then everyone began shouting at once. "Hooray for Morgan's colt! Hooray! Hooray! Hooray for the big-little horse."

Joel had his arms around Bub's neck. His whole body ached, as if he had moved the log himself. "It's over! It's over! You did it, Bub! You did it!" he kept repeating. Then he sobbed a little from exhaustion and relief.

The horse lipped Joel's cheek and neck. He almost tried to say, "It's all right, Joel; don't be taking it so hard." He was steaming and tired, but it was good to be near the boy again. It was good He nickered softly.

A Christmas Carol

CHARLES DICKENS

THE CHRISTMAS SPIRIT ENTERS SCROOGE [1]

"I don't know what to do!" cried Scrooge, laughing and crying in the same breath; and making a perfect Laocoön of himself with his stockings. "I am as light as a feather, I am as happy as an angel, I am as merry as a schoolboy. I am as giddy as a drunken man. A Merry Christmas to everybody! A Happy New Year to all the world. Hallo here! Whoop! Hallo!"

He had frisked into the sitting-room, and was now standing there: perfectly winded.

"There's the saucepan that the gruel was in!" cried Scrooge, starting off again, and frisking round the fireplace. "There's the door, by which the Ghost of Jacob Marley entered! There's the corner where the Ghost of Christmas Present sat! There's the window where I saw the wandering Spirits! It's all right, it's all true, it all happened. Ha, ha, ha!"

Really, for a man who had been out of practice for so many years, it was a splendid laugh, a most illustrious laugh. The father of a long, long line of brilliant laughs!

"I don't know what day of the month it is!" said Scrooge. "I don't know how long I've been among the Spirits. I don't know anything. I'm quite a baby. Never mind. I don't care. I'd rather be a baby. Hallo! Whoop! Hallo here!"

He was checked in his transports by the churches ringing out the lustiest peals he had ever heard. Clash, clang, hammer, ding, dong, bell. Bell, dong, ding, hammer, clang, clash! Oh, glorious, glorious!

Running to the window, he opened it, and put out his head. No fog, no mist; clear, bright, jovial, stirring, cold; cold, piping for the blood to dance to; golden sunlight; heavenly sky; sweet fresh air; merry bells. Oh, glorious. Glorious!

"What's to-day?" cried Scrooge, calling downward to a boy in Sunday clothes, who perhaps had loitered in to look about him.

"Eh?" returned the boy, with all his might of wonder.

"What's to-day, my fine fellow?" said Scrooge.

"To-day!" replied the boy. "Why, CHRISTMAS DAY."

"It's Christmas Day!" said Scrooge to himself. "I haven't missed it. The Spirits have done it all in one night. They can do anything they like. Of course they can. Of course they can. Hallo, my fine fellow?"

"Hallo!" returned the boy.

"Do you know the Poulterer's, in the next street but one, at the corner?" Scrooge inquired.

"I should hope I did," replied the lad.

"An intelligent boy!" said Scrooge. "A remarkable boy! Do you know whether they've sold the prize Turkey that was hanging up there? Not the little prize Turkey: the big one?"

"What, the one as big as me?" returned the boy.

"What a delightful boy!" said Scrooge. "It's a pleasure to talk to him. Yes, my buck!"

"It's hanging there now," replied the boy.

"Is it?" said Scrooge. "Go and buy it."

"Walk-ER!" exclaimed the boy.

"No, no," said Scrooge. "I am in earnest. Go and buy it, and tell 'em to bring it here, that I may give them the direction where to take it. Come back with the man, and

[1] From "A Christmas Carol," by Charles Dickens, illustrated by Francis D. Bedford

453

stood upon his legs, that bird. He would have snapped 'em short off in a minute, like sticks of sealing-wax.

"Why, it's impossible to carry that to Camden Town," said Scrooge. "You must have a cab."

The chuckle with which he said this, and the chuckle with which he paid for the turkey, and the chuckle with which he paid for the cab, and the chuckle with which he recompensed the boy, were only to be exceeded by the chuckle with which he sat down breathless in his chair again, and chuckled till he cried.

Shaving was not an easy task, for his hand continued to shake very much; and shaving requires attention, even when you don't dance while you are at it. But if he had cut the end of his nose off, he would have put a piece of sticking-plaster over it, and been quite satisfied.

He dressed himself "all in his best," and at last got out into the streets. The people were by this time pouring forth, as he had seen them with the Ghost of Christmas Present; and walking with his hands behind him, Scrooge regarded every one with a delighted smile. He looked so irresistibly pleasant, in a word, that three or four good-humoured fellows said, "Good morning, Sir! A Merry Christmas to you!" And Scrooge said often afterwards, that of all the blithe sounds he had ever heard, those were the blithest in his ears.

He had not gone far, when coming on towards him he beheld the portly gentleman, who had walked into his counting-house the day before and said, "Scrooge and Marley's, I believe?" It sent a pang across his heart to think how this old gentleman would look upon him when they met; but he knew what path lay straight before him, and he took it.

"My dear Sir," said Scrooge, quickening his pace, and taking the old gentleman by both his hands. "How do you do? I hope you succeeded yesterday. It was very kind of you. A Merry Christmas to you, Sir!"

"Mr. Scrooge?"

I'll give you a shilling. Come back with him in less than five minutes, and I'll give you half-a-crown!"

The boy was off like a shot. He must have had a steady hand at a trigger who could have got a shot off half so fast.

"I'll send it to Bob Cratchit's!" whispered Scrooge, rubbing his hands, and splitting with a laugh. "He shan't know who sends it. It's twice the size of Tiny Tim. Joe Miller never made such a joke as sending it to Bob's will be!"

The hand in which he wrote the address was not a steady one, but write it he did, somehow, and went down stairs to open the street door, ready for the coming of the poulterer's man. As he stood there, waiting his arrival, the knocker caught his eye.

"I shall love it, as long as I live!" cried Scrooge, patting it with his hand. "I scarcely ever looked at it before. What an honest expression it has in its face! It's a wonderful knocker!—Here's the Turkey. Hallo! Whoop! How are you! Merry Christmas!"

It *was* a Turkey! He could never have

the streets, and watched the people hurrying to and fro, and patted children on the head, and questioned beggars, and looked down into the kitchens of houses, and up to the windows; and found that everything could yield him pleasure. He had never dreamed that any walk—that anything—could give him so much happiness. In the afternoon, he turned his steps towards his nephew's house.

He passed the door a dozen times, before he had the courage to go up and knock. But he made a dash, and did it:—

"Is your master at home, my dear?" said Scrooge to the girl. Nice girl! Very.

"Yes, Sir."

"Where is he, my love?" said Scrooge.

"He's in the dining-room, Sir, along with mistress. I'll show you up stairs, if you please."

"Thank'ee. He knows me," said Scrooge, with his hand already on the dining-room lock. "I'll go in here, my dear."

He turned it gently, and sidled his face in, round the door. They were looking at the table (which was spread out in great array); for these young housekeepers are always nervous on such points, and like to see that everything is right.

"Fred!" said Scrooge.

Dear heart alive, how his niece by marriage started! Scrooge had forgotten, for the moment, about her sitting in the corner with the footstool, or he wouldn't have done it, on any account.

"Why, bless my soul!" cried Fred. "Who's that?"

"It's I. Your uncle Scrooge. I have come to dinner. Will you let me in, Fred?"

Let him in! It is a mercy he didn't shake his arm off. He was at home in five minutes. Nothing could be heartier. His niece looked just the same. So did Topper when *he* came. So did the plump sister, when *she* came. So did every one when *they* came. Wonderful party, wonderful games, wonderful unanimity, wonder-ful happiness!

"Yes," said Scrooge. "That is my name, and I fear it may not be pleasant to you. Allow me to ask your pardon. And will you have the goodness"—here Scrooge whispered in his ear.

"Lord bless me!" cried the gentleman, as if his breath were gone. "My dear Mr. Scrooge, are you serious?"

"If you please," said Scrooge. "Not a farthing less. A great many back-payments are included in it, I assure you. Will you do me that favour?"

"My dear Sir," said the other, shaking hands with him. "I don't know what to say to such munifi—"

"Don't say anything, please," retorted Scrooge. "Come and see me. Will you come and see me?"

"I will!" cried the old gentleman. And it was clear he meant to do it.

"Thank'ee," said Scrooge. "I am much obliged to you. I thank you fifty times. Bless you!"

He went to church, and walked about

My Friend Flicka

MARY O'HARA

TAMING THE COLT [1]

When Ken opened his eyes next morning and looked out he saw that the house was wrapped in fog. There had been no rain at all since the day a week ago when the wind had torn the "sprinkling system" to pieces and blown all the tattered clouds away. That was the day he had found Flicka. And it had been terribly hot since then. They had hardly been able to stand the sun out on the terrace. They had gone swimming in the pool every day. On the hills, the grass was turning to soft tan.

Now there were clouds and they had closed down. After a severe hot spell there often came a heavy fog, or hail, or even snow.

Standing at the window, Ken could hardly see the pines on the Hill opposite. He wondered if his father would go after the yearlings in such a fog as this—they wouldn't be able to see them; but at breakfast McLaughlin said there would be no change of plans. It was just a big cloud that had settled down over the ranch—it would lift and fall—perhaps up on Saddle Back it would be clear.

They mounted and rode out.

The fog lay in the folds of the hills. Here and there a bare summit was in sunshine, then a little farther on, came a smother of cottony white that soaked the four riders to the skin and hung rows of moonstones on the whiskers of the horses.

It was hard to keep track of each other. Suddenly Ken was lost—the others had vanished. He reined in Shorty and sat listening. The clouds and mist rolled around him. He felt as if he were alone in the world.

A bluebird, color of the deep blue wild delphinium that dots the plains, became interested in him, and perched on a bush near by; and as he started Shorty forward again, the bluebird followed along, hopping from bush to bush.

The boy rode slowly, not knowing in which direction to go. Then, hearing shouts, he touched heels to Shorty and cantered, and suddenly came out of the fog and saw his father and Tim and Ross.

"There they are!" said McLaughlin, pointing down over the curve of the hill. They rode forward and Ken could see the yearlings standing bunched at the bottom, looking up, wondering who was coming. Then a huge coil of fog swirled over them and they were lost to sight again.

McLaughlin told them to circle around, spread out fanwise on the far side of the colts, and then gently bear down on them so they would start towards the ranch. If the colts once got running in this fog, he said, there'd be no chance of catching them.

The plan worked well; the yearlings were not so frisky as usual, and allowed themselves to be driven in the right direction. It was only when they were on the County Road, and near the gate where Howard was watching, that Ken, whose eyes had been scanning the bunch, as they appeared and disappeared in the fog, realized that Flicka was missing.

McLaughlin noticed it at the same moment, and as Ken rode toward his father, McLaughlin turned to him and said, "She's not in the bunch."

They sat in silence a few moments while McLaughlin planned the next step. The yearlings, dispirited by the fog, nibbled languidly at the grass by the roadside. McLaughlin looked at the Saddle Back and Ken looked too, the passionate desire in his heart reaching out to pierce the fog

[1] From "My Friend Flicka," by Mary O'Hara

and the hillside and see where Flicka had hidden herself away. Had she been with the bunch when they first were found? Had she stolen away through the fog? Or hadn't she been there in the beginning? Had she run away from the ranch entirely, after her bad experience a week ago? Or—and this thought made his heart drop sickeningly—had she perhaps died of the hurts she had received when she broke out of the corral and was lying stark and riddled with ants and crawling things on the breast of one of those hills?

McLaughlin looked grim. "Lone wolf—like her mother," he said. "Never with the gang. I might have known it."

Ken remembered what the Colonel had said about the Lone Wolf type—it wasn't good to be that way.

"Well, we'll drive the yearlings back up," said Rob finally. "No chance of finding her alone. If they happen to pass anywhere near her, she's likely to join them."

They drove the yearlings back. Once over the first hill, the colts got running and soon were out of sight. The fog closed down again so that Ken pulled up, unable to see where he was going, unable to see his father, or Ross or Tim.

He sat listening, astonished that the sound of their hoofs had been wiped out so completely. Again he seemed alone in the world.

The fog lifted in front of him and showed him that he stood at the brink of a sharp drop, almost a precipice, though not very deep. It led down into a semicircular pocket on the hillside which was fed by a spring; there was a clump of young cottonwoods, and a great bank of clover dotted with small yellow blossoms.

In the midst of the clover stood Flicka, quietly feasting. She had seen him before he saw her and was watching him, her head up, clover sticking out of both sides of her mouth, her jaws going busily.

At sight of her, Ken was incapable of either thought or action.

Suddenly from behind him in the fog, he heard his father's low voice, "Don't move—"

"How'd she get in there?" said Tim.

"She scrambled down this bank. And she could scramble up again, if we weren't here. I think we've got her," said McLaughlin.

"Other side of that pocket the ground drops twenty feet sheer," said Tim. "She can't go down there."

Flicka had stopped chewing. There were still stalks of clover sticking out between her jaws, but her head was up and her ears pricked, listening, and there was a tautness and tension in her whole body.

Ken found himself trembling too.

"How're you going to catch her, Dad?" he asked in a low voice.

"I kin snag her from here," said Ross, and in the same breath McLaughlin answered, "Ross can rope her. Might as well rope her here as in the corral. We'll spread out in a semicircle above this bank. She can't get up past us, and she can't get down."

They took their positions and Ross lifted his rope off the horn of his saddle.

Ahead of them, far down below the pocket, the yearlings were running. A whinny or two drifted up, and the sound of their hoofs, muffled by the fog.

Flicka heard them too. Suddenly she was aware of danger. She leaped out of the clover to the edge of the precipice which fell away down the mountainside toward where the yearlings were running. But it was too steep and too high. She came straight up on her hind legs with a neigh of terror, and whirled back toward the bank down which she had slid to reach the pocket. But on the crest of it, looming uncannily in the fog, were four black figures—she screamed, and ran around the base of the bank.

Ken heard Ross's rope sing. It snaked out just as Flicka dove into the bank of clover. Stumbling, she went down and for a moment was lost to view.

"Goldarn—" said Ross, hauling in his

rope, while Flicka floundered up and again circled her small prison, hurling herself at every point, only to realize that there was no way out.

She stood over the precipice, poised in despair and frantic longing. There drifted up the sound of the colts running below. Flicka trembled and strained over the brink—a perfect target for Ross, and he whirled his lariat again. It made a vicious whine.

Ken longed for the filly to escape the noose—yet he longed for her capture. Flicka reared up, her delicate forefeet beat the air, then she leaped out; and Ross' rope fell short again as McLaughlin said, "I expected that. She's like all the rest of them."

Flicka went down like a diver. She hit the ground, her legs folded under her, then she rolled and bounced the rest of the way. It was exactly like the bronco that had climbed over the side of the truck and rolled down the forty-foot bank; and in silence the four watchers sat in their saddles waiting to see what would happen when she hit bottom—Ken already thinking of the Winchester, and the way the crack of it had echoed back from the hills.

Flicka lit, it seemed, on four steel springs that tossed her up and sent her flying down the mountainside—perfection of speed and power and action. A hot sweat bathed Ken from head to foot, and he began to laugh, half choking—

The wind roared down and swept up the fog, and it went bounding away over the hills, leaving trailing streamers of white in the gullies, and coverlets of cotton around the bushes. Way below, they could see Flicka galloping toward the yearlings. In a moment she joined them, and then there was just a many-colored blur of moving shapes, with a fierce sun blazing down, striking sparks of light off their glossy coats.

"Get going!" shouted McLaughlin. "Get around behind them. They're on the run now, and it's cleared—keep them run-

ning, and we may get them all in together, before they stop. Tim, you take the short way back to the gate and help Howard turn them and get them through."

Tim shot off toward the County Road and the other three riders galloped down and around the mountain until they were at the back of the band of yearlings. Shouting and yelling and spurring their mounts, they kept the colts running, circling them around toward the ranch until they had them on the County Road.

Way ahead, Ken could see Tim and Howard at the gate, blocking the road. The yearlings were bearing down on them. Now McLaughlin slowed up, and began to call, "Whoa, whoa—" and the pace decreased. Often enough the yearlings had swept down that road and through the gate and down to the corrals. It was the pathway to oats, and hay, and shelter from winter storms—would they take it now? Flicka was with them—right in the middle —if they went, would she go too?

It was all over almost before Ken could draw a breath. The yearlings turned at the gate, swept through, went down to the corrals on a dead run, and through the gates that Gus had opened.

Flicka was caught again.

Mindful that she had clawed her way out when she was corraled before, McLaughlin determined to keep her in the main corral into which the stable door opened. It had eight-foot walls of aspen poles. The rest of the yearlings must be manoeuvered away from her.

Now that the fog had gone, the sun was scorching, and horses and men alike were soaked with sweat before the chasing was over and, one after the other, the yearlings had been driven into the other corral, and Flicka was alone.

She knew that her solitude meant danger, and that she was singled out for some special disaster. She ran frantically to the high fence through which she could see the other ponies standing, and reared and clawed at the poles; she screamed, whirled,

458

circled the corral first in one direction, and then the other. And while McLaughlin and Ross were discussing the advisability of roping her, she suddenly espied the dark hole which was the open upper half of the stable door, and dove through it. McLaughlin rushed to close it, and she was caught—safely imprisoned in the stable.

The rest of the colts were driven away, and Ken stood outside the stable, listening to the wild hoofs beating, the screams, the crashes. His Flicka within there—close at hand—imprisoned. He was shaking. He felt a desperate desire to quiet her somehow, to *tell her*. If she only knew how he loved her, that there was nothing to be afraid of, that they were going to be friends—

Ross shook his head with a one-sided grin. "Sure a wild one," he said, coiling his lariat.

"Plumb loco," said Tim briefly.

McLaughlin said, "We'll leave her to think it over. After dinner, we'll come up and feed and water her and do a little work with her."

But when they went up after dinner, there was no Flicka in the barn. One of the windows above the manger was broken, and the manger was full of glass.

Staring at it, McLaughlin gave a short laugh. He looked at Ken. "She climbed into the manger—see? Stood on the feed box, beat the glass out with her front hoofs and climbed through."

The window opened into the Six Foot Pasture. Near it was a wagonload of hay. When they went around the back of the stable to see where she had gone they found her between the stable and the hay wagon, eating.

At their approach, she leaped away, then headed east across the pasture.

"If she's like her mother," said Rob, "she'll go right through the wire."

"Ay bet she'll go over," said Gus. "She yumps like a deer."

"No horse can jump that," said McLaughlin.

Ken said nothing because he could not speak. It was the most terrible moment of his life. He watched Flicka racing toward the eastern wire.

A few yards from it, she swerved, turned and raced diagonally south.

"It turned her! it turned her!" cried Ken, almost sobbing. It was the first sign of hope for Flicka. "Oh, Dad, she has got sense, she has! She has!"

Flicka turned again as she met the southern boundary of the pasture, again at the northern; she avoided the barn. Without abating anything of her whirlwind speed, following a precise, accurate calculation, and turning each time on a dime, she investigated every possibility. Then, seeing that there was no hope, she raced south towards the range where she had spent her life, gathered herself, and rose to the impossible leap.

Each of the men watching had the impulse to cover his eyes, and Ken gave a howl of despair.

Twenty yards of fence came down with her as she hurled herself through. Caught on the upper strands, she turned a complete somersault, landing on her back, her four legs dragging the wires down on top of her, and tangling herself in them beyond hope of escape.

"Damn the wire!" cursed McLaughlin. "If I could afford decent fences—"

Ken followed the men miserably as they walked to the filly. They stood in a circle watching while she kicked and fought and thrashed until the wire was tightly wound and tangled about her, piercing and tearing her flesh and hide. At last she was unconscious, streams of blood running on her golden coat, and pools of crimson widening on the grass beneath her.

With the wire cutters which Gus always carried in the hip pocket of his overalls, he cut the wire away; and they drew her into the pasture, repaired the fence, placed hay, a box of oats, and a tub of water near her, and called it a day.

"I doubt if she pulls out of it," said

McLaughlin briefly. "But it's just as well. If it hadn't been this way it would have been another. A loco horse isn't worth a damn."

Ken lay on the grass behind Flicka. One little brown hand was on her back, smoothing it, pressing softly, caressing. The other hand supported his head. His face hung over her.

His throat felt dry; his lips were like paper.

After a long while he whispered, "I didn't mean to kill you, Flicka—"

Howard came to sit with him, quiet and respectful as is proper in the presence of grief or mourning.

"Gee! Highboy was never like that," he said.

Ken made no answer to this. His eyes were on Flicka, watching her slow breathing. He had often seen horses down and unconscious. Badly cut with wire, too—they got well. Flicka could get well.

"Gosh! She's about as bad as Rocket," said Howard cheerfully.

Ken raised his head scowling. "Rocket! That old black hellion!"

"Well, Flicka's her child, isn't she?"

"She's Banner's child too—"

There were many air-tight compartments in Ken's mind. Rocket—now that she had come to a bad end—had conveniently gone into one of them.

After a moment Howard said,

"We haven't given our colts their workout today." He pulled up his knees and clasped his hands around them.

Ken said nothing.

"We're supposed to, you know—we gotta," said Howard. "Dad'll be sore at us if we don't."

"I don't want to leave her," said Ken, and his voice was strange and thin.

Howard was sympathetically silent. Then he said, "I could do your two for you, Ken—"

Ken looked up gratefully. "Would you, Howard? Gee—that'd be keen—"

"Sure I'll do all of 'em, and you can stay here with Flicka."

"Thanks." Ken put his head down on his hand again, and the other hand smoothed and patted the filly's neck.

"Gee, she was pretty," said Howard, sighing.

"What d'ya mean—was!" snapped Ken. "You mean she is—she's beautiful."

"I meant when she was running back there," said Howard hastily.

Ken made no reply. It was true. Flicka floating across the ravines was something quite different from the inert mass lying on the ground, her belly rounded up into a mound, her neck weak and collapsed on the grass, her head stretched out, homely and senseless.

"Just think," said Howard, "you could have had any one of the other yearlings. And I guess by this time, it would have been half tamed down there in the corral —probably tied to the post."

As Ken still kept silent, Howard got slowly to his feet. "Well, I guess I might as well go and do the colts," he said, and walked away. At a little distance he turned. "If Mother goes for the mail, do you want to go along?"

Ken shook his head.

When Howard was out of sight, Ken kneeled up and looked Flicka all over. He had never thought that, as soon as this, he would have been close enough to pat her, to caress her, to hold and examine her. He felt a passion of possession. Sick and half destroyed as she was, she was his own, and his heart was bursting with love of her. He smoothed her all over. He arranged her mane in more orderly fashion; he tried to straighten her head.

"You're mine now, Flicka," he whispered.

He counted her wounds. The two worst were a deep cut above the right rear hock, and a long gash in her chest that ran down into the muscle of the foreleg. Besides those, she was snagged with three-cornered tears through which the flesh pushed out, and laced with cuts and scratches with blood drying on them in rows of little black beads.

Ken wondered if the two bad cuts ought to be sewn up. He thought of Doc Hicks, and then remembered what his Dad had said: "You cost me money every time you turn around." No—Gus might do it— Gus was pretty good at sewing up animals. But Dad said best thing of all is usually to let them alone. They heal up. There was Sultan, hit by an automobile out on the highway; it knocked him down and took a big piece of flesh out of his chest and left the flap of skin hanging loose—and it all healed up of itself and you could only tell where the wound had been by the hair's being a different length.

The cut in Flicka's hind leg was awfully deep—

He put his head down against her and whispered again, "Oh, Flicka—I didn't mean to kill you."

After a few moments, "Oh, get well— get well—*get well*—"

And again, "Flicka, don't be so wild. *Be all right*, Flicka—"

Gus came out to him carrying a can of black grease.

"De Boss tole me to put some of dis grease on de filly's cuts, Ken—it helps heal 'em up."

Together they went over her carefully, putting a smear of the grease wherever they could reach a wound.

Gus stood looking down at the boy.

"D'you think she'll get well, Gus?"

"She might, Ken. I seen plenty horses hurt as bad as dot, and dey yust as good as ever."

"Dad said—" But Ken's voice failed him when he remembered that his father had said she might as well die, because she was loco anyway.

The Swede stood a moment, his pale blue eyes, transparent and spiritual, looking kindly down at the boy; then he went on down to the barn.

Every trace of fog and mist had van-

ished, and the sun was blazing hot. Sweltering, Ken got up to take a drink of water from the bucket left for Flicka. Then, carrying handfuls of water in his small cupped hands, he poured it on her mouth. Flicka did not move, and once again Ken took his place behind her, his hand on her neck, his lips whispering to her.

After a while his head sank in exhaustion to the ground. . . .

A roaring gale roused him and he looked up to see racing black clouds forming into a line. Blasts of cold wind struck down at the earth and sucked up leaves, twigs, tumbleweeds, in whorls like small cyclones.

From the black line in the sky, a fine icy mist sheeted down, and suddenly there came an appalling explosion of thunder. The world blazed and shuddered with lightning. High overhead was a noise like the shrieking of trumpets and trombones. The particles of fine icy mist beating down grew larger; they began to dance and bounce on the ground like little peas—like marbles—like ping-pong balls—

They beat upon Ken through his thin shirt and whipped his bare head and face. He kneeled up, leaning over Flicka, protecting her head with his folded arms. The hailstones were like ping-pong balls— like billiard balls—like little hard apples— like bigger apples—and suddenly, here and there, they fell as big as tennis balls, bouncing on the ground, rolling along, splitting on the rocks.

One hit Ken on the side of the face and a thin line of blood slid down his cheek with the water.

Running like a hare, under a pall of darkness, the storm fled eastward, beating the grass flat upon the hills. Then, in the wake of the darkness and the screaming wind and hail, a clear silver light shone out, and the grass rose up again, every blade shimmering.

Watching Flicka, Ken sat back on his heels and sighed. She had not moved.

A rainbow, like a giant compass, drew a

half circle of bright color around the ranch. And off to one side, there was a vertical blur of fire hanging, left over from the storm.

Ken lay down again close behind Flicka and put his cheek against the soft tangle of her mane.

When evening came, and Nell had called Ken and had taken him by the hand and led him away, Flicka still lay without moving. Gently the darkness folded down over her. She was alone, except for the creatures of the sky—the heavenly bodies that wheeled over her; the two Bears, circling around the North Star; the cluster of little Sisters clinging together as if they held their arms wrapped around each other; the eagle, Aquila, that waited till nearly midnight before his great hidden wings lifted him above the horizon; and right overhead, an eye as bright as a blue diamond beaming down, the beautiful star, Vega.

Less alive than they, and dark under their brilliance, the motionless body of Flicka lay on the blood-stained grass, earth-bound and fatal, every breath she drew a costly victory.

Toward morning, a half moon rode in the zenith.

A single, sharp, yapping bark broke the silence. Another answered, then another and another—tentative, questioning cries that presently became long quavering howls. The sharp pixie faces of a pack of coyotes pointed at the moon, and the howls trembled up through their long, tight-stretched throats and open, pulsating jaws. Each little prairie-wolf was allowed a solo, at first timid and wondering, then gathering force and impudence. Then they joined with each other and at last the troop was in full, yammering chorus, capering and malicious and thumbing noses and filling the air with sounds that raise the hair on human heads and put every animal on the alert.

Flicka came back to consciousness with a deep, shuddering sigh. She lifted her head and rolled over on her belly, drawing her legs under her a little. Resting so, she turned her head and listened. The yammer rose and fell. It was a familiar sound, she had heard it since she was born. The pack was across the stream on the edge of the woods beyond.

All at once, Flicka gathered herself, made a sudden, plunging effort, and gained her feet. It was not good for a filly to be helpless on the ground with a pack of coyotes near by. She stood swaying, her legs splayed out weakly, her head low and dizzy. It was minutes before balance came to her, and while she waited for it her nostrils flared, smelling water. *Water!* How near was it? Could she get to it?

She saw the tub and presently walked unsteadily over to it, put her lips in and drank. New life and strength poured into her. She paused, lifting her muzzle and mouthed the cold water, freshening her tongue and throat. She drank deeply again, then raised her head higher and stood with her neck turned, listening to the coyotes, until the sounds subsided, hesitated, died away.

She stood over the tub a long time. The pack yammered again, but the sound was like an echo, artless and hollow with distance, a mile away. They had gone across the valley for hunting.

A faint luminousness appeared over the earth and a lemon-colored light in the east. One by one the stars drew back, and the pale, innocent blue of the early-morning sky closed over them.

By the time Ken reached Flicka in the morning, she had finished the water, eaten some of the oats, and was standing broadside to the level sunlight, gathering in every ultra-violet ray, every infra-red, for the healing and the recreation her battered body needed.

The Merry Adventures of Robin Hood

HOWARD PYLE

ROBIN HOOD TURNS BUTCHER [1]

Now after all these things had happened, and it became known to Robin Hood how the Sheriff had tried three times to make him captive, he said to himself, "If I have the chance, I will make our worshipful Sheriff pay right well for that which he hath done to me. Maybe I may bring him some time into Sherwood Forest and have him to a right merry feast with us." For when Robin Hood caught a baron or a squire, or a fat abbot or bishop, he brought them to the greenwood tree and feasted them before he lightened their purses.

But in the meantime Robin Hood and his band lived quietly in Sherwood Forest, without showing their faces abroad, for Robin knew that it would not be wise for him to be seen in the neighborhood of Nottingham, those in authority being very wroth with him. But though they did not go abroad, they lived a merry life within the woodlands, spending the days in shooting at garlands hung upon a willow wand at the end of the glade, the leafy aisles ringing with merry jests and laughter: for whoever missed the garland was given a sound buffet, which, if delivered by Little John, never failed to topple over the unfortunate yeoman. Then they had bouts of wrestling and of cudgel play, so that every day they gained in skill and strength.

Thus they dwelt for nearly a year, and in that time Robin Hood often turned over in his mind many means of making an even score with the Sheriff. At last he began to fret at his confinement; so one day he took up his stout cudgel and set forth to seek adventure, strolling blithely along until he came to the edge of Sherwood. There, as he rambled along the sunlit road, he met a lusty young Butcher driving a fine mare and riding in a stout new cart, all hung about with meat. Merrily whistled the Butcher as he jogged along, for he was going to the market, and the day was fresh and sweet, making his heart blithe within him.

"Good morrow to thee, jolly fellow," quoth Robin, "thou seemest happy this merry morn."

"Ay, that am I," quoth the jolly Butcher, "and why should I not be so? Am I not hale in wind and limb? Have I not the bonniest lass in all Nottinghamshire? And lastly, am I not to be married to her on Thursday next in sweet Locksley Town?"

"Ha," said Robin, "comest thou from Locksley Town? Well do I know that fair place for miles about, and well do I know each hedgerow and gentle pebbly stream, and even all the bright little fishes therein, for there I was born and bred. Now, where goest thou with thy meat, my fair friend?"

"I go to the market at Nottingham Town to sell my beef and my mutton," answered the Butcher. "But who art thou that comest from Locksley Town?"

"A yeoman am I, good friend, and men do call me Robin Hood."

"Now, by Our Lady's grace," cried the Butcher, "well do I know thy name, and many a time have I heard thy deeds both

[1] From "The Merry Adventures of Robin Hood," by Howard Pyle, illustrated by Howard Pyle

sung and spoken of. But Heaven forbid that thou shouldst take aught of me! An honest man am I, and have wronged neither man nor maid; so trouble me not, good master, as I have never troubled thee."

"Nay, Heaven forbid, indeed," quoth Robin, "that I should take from such as thee, jolly fellow! Not so much as one farthing would I take from thee, for I love a fair Saxon face like thine right well; more especially when it cometh from Locksley Town, and most especially when the man that owneth it is to marry a bonny lass on Thursday next. But come, tell me for what price thou wilt sell me all of thy meat and thy horse and cart."

"At four marks do I value meat, cart, and mare," quoth the Butcher, "but if I do not sell all my meat I will not have four marks in value."

Then Robin Hood plucked the purse from his girdle, and quoth he, "Here in this purse are six marks. Now, I would fain be a butcher for the day and sell my meat in Nottingham Town. Wilt thou close a bargain with me and take six marks for thine outfit?"

"Now may the blessings of all the saints fall on thine honest head!" cried the Butcher right joyfully, as he leaped down from his cart and took the purse that Robin held out to him.

"Nay," quoth Robin, laughing loudly, "many do like me and wish me well, but few call me honest. Now get thee gone back to thy lass, and give her a kiss from me." So saying, he donned the Butcher's apron, and, climbing into the cart, he took the reins in his hand and drove off through the forest to Nottingham Town.

When he came to Nottingham, he entered that part of the market where butchers stood, and took up his inn in the best place he could find. Next, he opened his stall and spread his meat upon the bench, then, taking his cleaver and steel and clattering them together, he trolled aloud in merry tones:

"Now come, ye lasses, and eke, ye dames,
  And buy your meat from me;
For three pennyworths of meat I sell
  For the charge of one penny.

"Lamb have I that hath fed upon nought
  But the dainty daisies pied,
And the violet sweet, and the daffodil
  That grow fair streams beside.

"And beef have I from the heathery wolds,
  And mutton from dales all green,
And veal as white as a maiden's brow,
  With its mother's milk, I ween.

"Then come, ye lasses, and eke, ye dames,
  Come, buy your meat from me;
For three pennyworths of meat I sell
  For the charge of one penny."

Thus he sang blithely, while all who stood near listened amazedly. Then, when he had finished, he clattered the steel and cleaver still more loudly, shouting lustily, "Now, who'll buy? Who'll buy? Four fixed prices have I. Three pennyworths of meat I sell to a fat friar or priest for sixpence, for I want not their custom; stout aldermen I charge threepence, for it doth not matter to me whether they buy or not; to buxom dames I sell three pennyworths of meat for one penny, for I like their custom well; but to the bonny lass that hath a liking for a good tight butcher I charge nought but one fair kiss, for I like her custom the best of all."

Then all began to stare and wonder and crowd around, laughing, for never was such selling heard of in all Nottingham Town; but when they came to buy they found it as he had said, for he gave goodwife or dame as much meat for one penny as they could buy elsewhere for three, and when a widow or a poor woman came to him, he gave her flesh for nothing; but when a merry lass came and gave him a kiss, he charged not one penny for his meat; and many such came to his stall, for his eyes were as blue as the skies of June, and he laughed merrily, giving to each full measure. Thus he sold his meat so fast that no butcher that stood near him could sell anything.

Then they began to talk among themselves, and some said, "This must be some thief who has stolen cart, horse, and meat"; but others said, "Nay, when did ye ever see a thief who parted with his goods so freely and merrily? This must be some prodigal who hath sold his father's land, and would fain live merrily while the money lasts." And these latter being the greater number, the others came round, one by one, to their way of thinking.

Then some of the butchers came to him to make his acquaintance. "Come, brother," quoth one who was the head of them all, "we be all of one trade, so wilt thou go dine with us? For this day the Sheriff hath asked all the Butcher Guild to feast with him at the Guild Hall. There will be stout fare and much to drink, and that thou likest, or I much mistake thee."

"Now, beshrew his heart," quoth jolly Robin, "that would deny a butcher. And, moreover, I will go dine with you all, my sweet lads, and that as fast as I can hie." Whereupon, having sold all his meat, he closed his stall and went with them to the great Guild Hall.

There the Sheriff had already come in state, and with him many butchers. When Robin and those that were with him came in, all laughing at some merry jest he had been telling them, those that were near the Sheriff whispered to him, "Yon is a right mad blade, for he hath sold more meat for one penny this day than we could sell for three, and to whatsoever merry lass gave him a kiss he gave meat for nought." And others said, "He is some prodigal that hath sold his land for silver and gold, and meaneth to spend all right merrily."

Then the Sheriff called Robin to him, not knowing him in his butcher's dress, and made him sit close to him on his right hand; for he loved a rich young prodigal—especially when he thought that he might lighten that prodigal's pockets into his own most worshipful purse. So he made much of Robin, and laughed and talked with him more than with any of the others.

At last the dinner was ready to be served and the Sheriff bade Robin say grace, so Robin stood up and said, "Now Heaven bless us all and eke good meat and good sack within this house, and may all butchers be and remain as honest men as I am."

At this all laughed, the Sheriff loudest of all, for he said to himself, "Surely this is indeed some prodigal, and perchance I may empty his purse of some of the money that the fool throweth about so freely." Then he spake aloud to Robin, saying, "Thou art a jolly young blade, and I love thee mightily"; and he smote Robin upon the shoulder.

Then Robin laughed loudly too. "Yea," quoth he, "I know thou dost love a jolly blade, for didst thou not have jolly Robin Hood at thy shooting match and didst thou not gladly give him a bright golden arrow for his own?"

At this the Sheriff looked grave and all the guild of butchers too, so that none laughed but Robin, only some winked slyly at each other.

"Come, fill us some sack!" cried Robin. "Let us e'er be merry while we may, for man is but dust, and he hath but a span to live here till the worm getteth him, as our good gossip Swanthold sayeth; so let life be merry while it lasts, say I. Nay, never look down i' the mouth, Sir Sheriff. Who knows but that thou mayest catch Robin Hood yet, if thou drinkest less good sack and Malmsey, and bringest down the fat about thy paunch and the dust from out thy brain. Be merry, man."

Then the Sheriff laughed again, but not as though he liked the jest, while the butchers said, one to another, "Before Heaven, never have we seen such a mad rollicking blade. Mayhap, though, he will make the Sheriff mad."

"How now, brothers," cried Robin, "be merry! nay, never count over your far-

466

things, for by this and by that I will pay this shot myself, e'en though it cost two hundred pounds. So let no man draw up his lip, nor thrust his forefinger into his purse, for I swear that neither butcher nor Sheriff shall pay one penny for this feast."

"Now thou art a right merry soul," quoth the Sheriff, "and I wot thou must have many a head of horned beasts and many an acre of land, that thou dost spend thy money so freely."

"Ay, that have I," quoth Robin, laughing loudly again, "five hundred and more horned beasts have I and my brothers, and none of them have we been able to sell, else I might not have turned butcher. As for my land, I have never asked my steward how many acres I have."

At this the Sheriff's eyes twinkled, and he chuckled to himself. "Nay, good youth," quoth he, "if thou canst not sell thy cattle, it may be I will find a man that will lift them from thy hands; perhaps that man may be myself, for I love a merry youth and would help such a one along the path of life. Now how much dost thou want for thy horned cattle?"

"Well," quoth Robin, "they are worth at least five hundred pounds."

"Nay," answered the Sheriff slowly, and as if he were thinking within himself, "well do I love thee, and fain would I help thee along, but five hundred pounds in money is a good round sum; besides I have it not by me. Yet I will give thee three hundred pounds for them all, and that in good hard silver and gold."

"Now thou old miser!" quoth Robin, "well thou knowest that so many horned cattle are worth seven hundred pounds and more, and even that is but small for them, and yet thou, with thy gray hairs and one foot in the grave, wouldst trade upon the folly of a wild youth."

At this the Sheriff looked grimly at Robin. "Nay," quoth Robin, "look not on me as though thou hadst sour beer in thy mouth, man. I will take thine offer, for I and my brothers do need the money.

We lead a merry life, and no one leads a merry life for a farthing, so I will close the bargain with thee. But mind that thou bringest a good three hundred pounds with thee, for I trust not one that driveth so shrewd a bargain."

"I will bring the money," said the Sheriff. "But what is thy name, good youth?"

"Men call me Robert o' Locksley," quoth bold Robin.

"Then, good Robert o' Locksley," quoth the Sheriff, "I will come this day to see thy horned beasts. But first my clerk shall draw up a paper in which thou shalt be bound to the sale, for thou gettest not my money without I get thy beasts in return."

Then Robin Hood laughed again. "So be it," he said, smiting his palm upon the Sheriff's hand. "Truly my brothers will be thankful to thee for thy money."

Thus the bargain was closed, but many of the butchers talked among themselves of the Sheriff, saying that it was but a scurvy trick to beguile a poor spendthrift youth in this way.

The afternoon had come when the Sheriff mounted his horse and joined Robin Hood, who stood outside the gateway of the paved court waiting for him, for he had sold his horse and cart to a trader for two marks. Then they set forth upon their way, the Sheriff riding upon his horse and Robin running beside him. Thus they left Nottingham Town and traveled forward along the dusty highway, laughing and jesting together as though they had been old friends. But all the time the Sheriff said within himself, "Thy jest to me of Robin Hood shall cost thee dear, good fellow, even four hundred pounds, thou fool." For he thought he would make at least that much by his bargain.

So they journeyed onward till they came within the verge of Sherwood Forest, when presently the Sheriff looked up and down and to the right and to the left of him, and then grew quiet and ceased his laughter. "Now," quoth he, "may Heaven and its saints preserve us this day from a rogue men call Robin Hood."

Then Robin laughed aloud. "Nay," said he, "thou mayst set thy mind at rest, for well do I know Robin Hood and well do I know that thou art in no more danger from him this day than thou art from me."

At this the Sheriff looked askance at Robin, saying to himself, "I like not that thou seemest so well acquainted with this bold outlaw, and I wish that I were well out of Sherwood Forest."

But still they traveled deeper into the forest shades, and the deeper they went, the more quiet grew the Sheriff. At last they came to where the road took a sudden bend, and before them a herd of dun deer went tripping across the path. Then Robin Hood came close to the Sheriff and pointing his finger, he said, "These are my horned beasts, good Master Sheriff. How dost thou like them? Are they not fat and fair to see?"

At this the Sheriff drew rein quickly. "Now fellow," quoth he, "I would I were well out of this forest, for I like not thy company. Go thou thine own path, good friend, and let me but go mine."

But Robin only laughed and caught the Sheriff's bridle rein. "Nay," cried he, "stay awhile, for I would thou shouldst see my brothers, who own these fair horned beasts with me." So saying, he clapped his bugle to his mouth and winded three merry notes, and presently up the path came leaping fivescore good stout yeomen with Little John at their head.

"What wouldst thou have, good master?" quoth Little John.

"Why," answered Robin, "dost thou not see that I have brought goodly company to feast with us today? Fye, for shame! Do you not see our good and worshipful master, the Sheriff of Nottingham? Take thou his bridle, Little John, for he has honored us today by coming to feast with us."

Then all doffed their hats humbly, without smiling or seeming to be in jest, while Little John took the bridle rein and led the palfrey still deeper into the forest, all marching in order, with Robin Hood walking beside the Sheriff, hat in hand.

All this time the Sheriff said never a word but only looked about him like one suddenly awakened from sleep; but when he found himself going within the very depths of Sherwood his heart sank within him, for he thought, "Surely my three hundred pounds will be taken from me, even if they take not my life itself, for I have plotted against their lives more than once." But all seemed humble and meek and not a word was said of danger, either to life or money.

So at last they came to that part of Sherwood Forest where a noble oak spread its branches wide, and beneath it was a seat all made of moss, on which Robin sat down, placing the Sheriff at his right hand. "Now busk ye, my merry men all," quoth he, "and bring forth the best we have, both of meat and wine, for his worship the Sheriff hath feasted me in Nottingham Guild Hall today, and I would not have him go back empty."

All this time nothing had been said of the Sheriff's money, so presently he began to pluck up heart. "For," said he to himself, "maybe Robin Hood hath forgotten all about it."

Then, while beyond in the forest bright fires crackled and savory smells of sweetly roasting venison and fat capons filled the glade, and brown pasties warmed beside the blaze, did Robin Hood entertain the Sheriff right royally. First, several couples stood forth at quarterstaff, and so shrewd were they at the game, and so quickly did they give stroke and parry, that the Sheriff, who loved to watch all lusty sports of the kind, clapped his hands, forgetting where he was, and crying aloud, "Well struck! Well struck, thou fellow with the black beard!" little knowing that the man he called upon was the Tinker that tried to serve his warrant upon Robin Hood.

Then the best archers of the band set up

a fair garland of flowers at eightscore paces distance, and shot at it with the cunningest archery practice. But the Sheriff grew grave, for he did not like this so well, the famous meeting at the butts in Nottingham Town being still green in his memory, and the golden arrow that had been won there hanging close behind him. Then, when Robin saw what was in the Sheriff's mind, he stopped the sport, and called forth some of his band, who sang merry ballads, while others made music upon the harp.

When this was done, several yeomen came forward and spread cloths upon the green grass, and placed a royal feast; while others still broached barrels of sack and Malmsey and good stout ale, and set them in jars upon the cloth, with drinking horns about them. Then all sat down and feasted and drank merrily together until the sun was low and the half-moon glimmered with a pale light betwixt the leaves of the trees overhead.

Then the Sheriff arose and said, "I thank you all, good yeomen, for the merry entertainment ye have given me this day. Right courteously have ye used me, showing therein that ye have much respect for our glorious King and his deputy in brave Nottinghamshire. But the shadows grow long, and I must away before darkness comes, lest I lose myself within the forest."

Then Robin Hood and all his merry men arose also, and Robin said to the Sheriff, "If thou must go, worshipful sir, go thou must; but thou hast forgotten one thing."

"Nay, I forgot nought," said the Sheriff; yet all the same his heart sank within him.

"But I say thou hast forgot something," quoth Robin. "We keep a merry inn here in the green wood, but whoever becometh our guest must pay his reckoning."

Then the Sheriff laughed, but the laugh was hollow. "Well, jolly boys," quoth he, "we have had a merry time together today, and even if ye had not asked me, I would have given you a score of pounds for the sweet entertainment I have had."

"Nay," quoth Robin seriously, "it would ill beseem us to treat Your Worship so meanly. By my faith, Sir Sheriff, I would be ashamed to show my face if I did not reckon the King's deputy at three hundred pounds. Is it not so, my merry men all?"

Then "Ay!" cried all, in a loud voice.

"Three hundred devils!" roared the Sheriff. "Think ye that your beggarly feast was worth three pounds, let alone three hundred?"

"Nay," quoth Robin gravely. "Speak not so roundly, Your Worship. I do love thee for the sweet feast thou hast given me this day in merry Nottingham Town; but there be those here who love thee not so much. If thou wilt look down the cloth thou wilt see Will Stutely, in whose eyes thou hast no great favor; then two other stout fellows are there here that thou knowest not, that were wounded in a brawl nigh Nottingham Town, some time ago—thou wottest when; one of them was sore hurt in one arm, yet he hath got the use of it again. Good Sheriff, be advised by me; pay thy score without more ado, or maybe it may fare ill with thee."

As he spoke the Sheriff's ruddy cheeks grew pale, and he said nothing more but looked upon the ground and gnawed his nether lip. Then slowly he drew forth his fat purse and threw it upon the cloth in front of him.

"Now take the purse, Little John," quoth Robin Hood, "and see that the reckoning be right. We would not doubt our Sheriff, but he might not like it if he should find he had not paid his full score."

Then little John counted the money and found that the bag held three hundred pounds in silver and gold. But to the Sheriff it seemed as if every clink of the bright money was a drop of blood from his veins. And when he saw it all counted out in a heap of silver and gold, filling a wooden platter, he turned away and silently mounted his horse.

"Never have we had so worshipful a guest before!" quoth Robin, "and, as the day waxeth late, I will send one of my young men to guide thee out of the forest depths."

"Nay, Heaven forbid!" cried the Sheriff hastily. "I can find mine own way, good man, without aid."

"Then I will put thee on the right track mine own self," quoth Robin, and, taking the Sheriff's horse by the bridle rein, he led him into the main forest path. Then, before he let him go, he said, "Now, fare thee well, good Sheriff, and when next thou thinkest to despoil some poor prodigal, remember thy feast in Sherwood Forest. 'Ne'er buy a horse, good friend, without first looking into its mouth,' as our good gaffer Swanthold says. And so, once more, fare thee well." Then he clapped his hand to the horse's back, and off went nag and Sheriff through the forest glades.

Then bitterly the Sheriff rued the day that first he meddled with Robin Hood, for all men laughed at him and many ballads were sung by folk throughout the country, of how the Sheriff went to shear and came home shorn to the very quick. For thus men sometimes overreach themselves through greed and guile.

Penrod

BOOTH TARKINGTON

PENROD'S STORY ABOUT UNCLE JOHN [1]

Miss Spence—in the flesh—had directed toward the physical body of the absent Penrod an inquiry as to the fractional consequences of dividing seventeen apples, fairly, among three boys, and she was surprised and displeased to receive no answer although to the best of her knowledge and belief, he was looking fixedly at her. She repeated her question crisply, without visible effect; then summoned him by name with increasing asperity. Twice she called him, while all his fellow pupils turned to stare at the gazing boy. She advanced a step from the platform.

"Penrod Schofield!"

"Oh, my goodness!" he shouted suddenly. "Can't you keep still a *minute?*"

Miss Spence gasped. So did the pupils. The whole room filled with a swelling conglomerate *"O-o-o-o-h!"*

As for Penrod himself, the walls reeled with the shock. He sat with his mouth open, a mere lump of stupefaction. For the appalling words that he had hurled at the teacher were as inexplicable to him as to any other who heard them.

Nothing is more treacherous than the human mind. Even when patiently bullied into a semblance of order and training, it may prove but a base and shifty servant. And Penrod's mind was not his servant; it was a master, with the April wind's whims; and it had just played him a diabolical trick. The very jolt with which he came back to the schoolroom in the midst of his fancied flight jarred his day-dream utterly out of him; and he sat, open-mouthed in horror at what he had said.

The unanimous gasp of awe was protracted. Miss Spence, however, finally recovered her breath, and, returning deliberately to the platform, faced the school. "And then, for a little while," as pathetic stories sometimes recount, "everything was very still." It was so still, in fact, that Penrod's newborn notoriety could almost be heard growing. This grisly silence was at last broken by the teacher.

"Penrod Schofield, stand up!"

The miserable child obeyed.

"What did you mean by speaking to me in that way?"

[1] From "Penrod," by Booth Tarkington, illustrated by Gordon Grant

He hung his head, raked the floor with the side of his shoe, swayed, swallowed, looked suddenly at his hands with the air of never having seen them before, then clasped them behind him. The school shivered in ecstatic horror, every fascinated eye upon him; yet there was not a soul in the room but was profoundly grateful to him for the sensation—including the offended teacher herself. Unhappily, all this gratitude was unconscious and altogether different from the kind which results in testimonials and loving-cups. On the contrary!

"Penrod Schofield!"

He gulped.

"Answer me at once! Why did you speak to me like that?"

"I was—" He choked, unable to continue.

"Speak out!"

"I was just—thinking," he managed to stammer.

"That will not do," she returned sharply. "I wish to know immediately why you spoke as you did."

The stricken Penrod answered helplessly:

"Because I was just thinking."

Upon the very rack he could have offered no ampler truthful explanation. It was all he knew about it.

"Thinking what?"

"Just thinking."

Miss Spence's expression gave evidence that her power of self-restraint was undergoing a remarkable test. However, after taking counsel with herself, she commanded:

"Come here!"

He shuffled forward, and she placed a chair upon the platform near her own.

"Sit there!"

Then (but not at all as if nothing had happened), she continued the lesson in arithmetic. Spiritually the children may have learned a lesson in very small fractions indeed as they gazed at the fragment of sin before them on the stool of peni-

tence. They all stared at him attentively with hard and passionately interested eyes, in which there was never one trace of pity. It cannot be said with precision that he writhed; his movement was more a slow, continuous squirm, effected with a ghastly assumption of languid indifference; while his gaze, in the effort to escape the marble-hearted glare of his schoolmates, affixed itself with apparent permanence to the waistcoat button of James Russell Lowell just above the "U" in "Russell."

Classes came and classes went, grilling him with eyes. Newcomers received the story of the crime in darkling whispers; and the outcast sat and sat and sat, and squirmed and squirmed and squirmed. (He did one or two things with his spine which a professional contortionist would have observed with real interest.) And all this while of freezing suspense was but the criminal's detention awaiting trial. A known punishment may be anticipated with some measure of equanimity; at least, the prisoner may prepare himself to undergo it; but the unknown looms more monstrous for every attempt to guess it. Penrod's crime was unique; there were no rules to aid him in estimating the vengeance to fall upon him for it. What seemed most probable was that he would be expelled from the school in the presence of his family, the mayor, and council, and afterward whipped by his father upon the State House steps, with the entire city as audience by invitation of the authorities.

Noon came. The rows of children filed out, every head turning for a last unpleasingly speculative look at the outlaw. Then Miss Spence closed the door into the cloakroom and that into the big hall, and came and sat at her desk, near Penrod. The tramping of feet outside, the shrill calls and shouting and the changing voices of the older boys ceased to be heard—and there was silence. Penrod, still affecting to be occupied with Lowell, was conscious that Miss Spence looked at him intently.

"Penrod," she said gravely, "what excuse have you to offer before I report your case to the principal?"

The word "principal" struck him to the vitals. Grand Inquisitor, Grand Khan, Sultan, Emperor, Tsar, Cæsar Augustus—these are comparable. He stopped squirming instantly, and sat rigid.

"I want an answer. Why did you shout those words at me?"

"Well," he murmured, "I was just—thinking."

"Thinking what?" she asked sharply.

"I don't know."

"That won't do!"

He took his left ankle in his right hand and regarded it helplessly.

"That won't do, Penrod Schofield," she repeated severely. "If that is all the excuse you have to offer I shall report your case this instant!"

And she rose with fatal intent.

But Penrod was one of those whom the precipice inspires. "Well, I *have* got an excuse."

"Well"—she paused impatiently—"what is it?"

He had not an idea, but he felt one coming, and replied automatically, in a plaintive tone:

"I guess anybody that had been through what *I* had to go through, last night, would think they had an excuse."

Miss Spence resumed her seat, though with the air of being ready to leap from it instantly.

"What has last night to do with your insolence to me this morning?"

"Well, I guess you'd see," he returned, emphasizing the plantive note, "if you knew what *I* know."

"Now, Penrod," she said, in a kinder voice, "I have a high regard for your mother and father, and it would hurt me to distress them, but you must either tell me what was the matter with you or I'll have to take you to Mrs. Houston."

"Well, ain't I going to?" he cried, spurred by the dread name. "It's because I didn't sleep last night."

"Were you ill?" The question was put with some dryness.

He felt the dryness. "No'm; *I* wasn't."

"Then if someone in your family was so ill that even you were kept up all night, how does it happen they let you come to school this morning?"

"It wasn't illness," he returned, shaking his head mournfully. "It was lots worse'n anybody's being sick. It was—it was—well, it was jest awful."

"*What* was?" He remarked with anxiety the incredulity in her tone.

"It was about Aunt Clara," he said.

"Your Aunt Clara!" she repeated. "Do you mean your mother's sister who married Mr. Farry of Dayton, Illinois?"

"Yes—Uncle John," returned Penrod sorrowfully. "The trouble was about him."

Miss Spence frowned a frown which he

rightly interpreted as one of continued suspicion. "She and I were in school together," she said. "I used to know her very well, and I've always heard her married life was entirely happy. I don't—"

"Yes, it was," he interrupted, "until last year when Uncle John took to running with travelling men—"

"What?"

"Yes'm." He nodded solemnly. "That was what started it. At first he was a good, kind husband, but these travelling men would coax him into a saloon on his way home from work, and they got him to drinking beer and then ales, wines, liquors, and cigars—"

"Penrod!"

"Ma'am?"

"I'm not inquiring into your Aunt Clara's private affairs; I'm asking you if you have anything to say which would palliate—"

"That's what I'm tryin' to *tell* you about, Miss Spence," he pleaded,—"if you'd jest only let me. When Aunt Clara and her little baby daughter got to our house last night—"

"You say Mrs. Farry is visiting your mother?"

"Yes'm—not just visiting—you see, she *had* to come. Well of course, little baby Clara, she was so bruised up and mauled, where he'd been hittin' her with his cane—"

"You mean that your uncle had done such a thing as *that!*" exclaimed Miss Spence, suddenly disarmed by this scandal.

"Yes'm, and mamma and Margaret had to sit up all night nursin' little Clara—and *Aunt* Clara was in such a state *somebody* had to keep talkin' to *her*, and there wasn't anybody but me to do it, so I—"

"But where was your father?" she cried.

"Ma'am?"

"Where was your father while—"

"Oh—papa?" Penrod paused, reflected; then brightened. "Why, he was down at the train, waitin' to see if Uncle John would try to follow 'em and make 'em come home so's he could persecute 'em some more. I wanted to do that, but they said if he did come I mightn't be strong enough to hold him and—" The brave lad paused again, modestly. Miss Spence's expression was encouraging. Her eyes were wide with astonishment, and there may have been in them, also, the mingled beginnings of admiration and self-reproach. Penrod, warming to his work, felt safer every moment.

"And so," he continued, "I had to sit up with Aunt Clara. She had some pretty big bruises, too, and I had to—"

"But why didn't they send for a doctor?" However, this question was only a flicker of dying incredulity.

"Oh, they didn't want any *doctor*," exclaimed the inspired realist promptly. "They don't want anybody to *hear* about it because Uncle John might reform—and then where'd he be if everybody knew he'd been a drunkard and whipped his wife and baby daughter?"

"Oh!" said Miss Spence.

"You see, he used to be upright as anybody," he went on explanatively. "It all begun—"

"Began, Penrod."

"Yes'm. It all commenced from the first day he let those travelling men coax him into the saloon." Penrod narrated the downfall of his Uncle John at length. In detail he was nothing short of plethoric; and incident followed incident, sketched with such vividness, such abundance of colour, and such verisimilitude to a drunkard's life as a drunkard's life should be, that had Miss Spence possessed the rather chilling attributes of William J. Burns himself, the last trace of skepticism must have vanished from her mind. Besides, there are two things that will be believed of any man whatsoever, and one of them is that he has taken to drink. And in every sense it was a moving picture which, with simple but eloquent words, the virtuous Penrod set before his teacher.

His eloquence increased with what it fed on; and as with the eloquence so with self-reproach in the gentle bosom of the teacher. She cleared her throat with difficulty once or twice, during his description of his ministering night with Aunt Clara. "And I said to her, 'Why, Aunt Clara, what's the use of takin' on so about it?' And I said, 'Now, Aunt Clara, all the crying in the world can't make things any better.' And then she'd just keep catchin' hold of me, and sob and kind of holler, and I'd say, 'Don't cry, Aunt Clara—*please* don't cry.'"

Then, under the influence of some fragmentary survivals of the respectable portion of his Sunday adventures, his theme became more exalted; and, only partially misquoting a phrase from a psalm, he related how he had made it of comfort to Aunt Clara, and how he had besought her to seek Higher guidance in her trouble.

The surprising thing about a structure such as Penrod was erecting is that the taller it becomes the more ornamentation it will stand. Gifted boys have this faculty of building magnificence upon cobwebs—and Penrod was gifted. Under the spell of his really great performance, Miss Spence gazed more and more sweetly upon the prodigy of spiritual beauty and goodness before her, until at last, when

Penrod came to the explanation of his "just thinking," she was forced to turn her head away.

"You mean, dear," she said gently, "that you were all worn out and hardly knew what you were saying?"

"Yes'm."

"And you were thinking about all those dreadful things so hard that you forgot where you were?"

"I was thinking," he said simply, "how to save Uncle John."

And the end of it for this mighty boy was that the teacher kissed him!

Lad: A Dog

ALBERT PAYSON TERHUNE

"QUIET!" [1]

To Lad the real world was bounded by The Place. Outside, there were a certain number of miles of land and there were an uncertain number of people. But the miles were uninspiring, except for the cross-country tramp with the Master. And the people were foolish and strange folk who either stared at him—which always annoyed Lad—or else tried to pat him; which he hated. But The Place was —The Place.

Always, he had lived on The Place. He felt he owned it. It was assuredly his to enjoy, to guard, to patrol from high road to lake. It was his world.

The denizens of every world must have

[1] From "Lad: A Dog," by Albert Payson Terhune

at least one deity to worship. Lad had one: the Master. Indeed, he had two: the Master and the Mistress. And because the dog was strong of soul and chivalric, withal, and because the Mistress was altogether lovable, Lad placed her altar even above the Master's. Which was wholly as it should have been.

There were other people at The Place—people to whom a dog must be courteous, as becomes a thoroughbred, and whose caresses he must accept. Very often, there were guests, too. And from puppyhood, Lad had been taught the sacredness of the Guest Law. Civilly, he would endure the pettings of these visiting outlanders. Gravely, he would shake hands with them, on request. He would even permit them to paw him or haul him about, if they were of the obnoxious, dog-mauling breed. But the moment politeness would permit, he always withdrew, very quietly, from their reach and, if possible, from their sight as well.

Of all the dogs on The Place, big Lad alone had free run of the house, by day and by night.

He slept in a "cave" under the piano. He even had access to the sacred dining-room, at mealtimes—where always he lay to the left of the Master's chair.

With the Master, he would willingly unbend for a romp at any or all times. At the Mistress' behest he would play with all the silly abandon of a puppy; rolling on the ground at her feet, making as though to seize and crush one of her little shoes in his mighty jaws; wriggling and waving his legs in air when she buried her hands in the masses of his chest-ruff; and otherwise comporting himself with complete loss of dignity.

But to all except these two, he was calmly unapproachable. From his earliest days he had never forgotten he was an aristocrat among inferiors. And, calmly aloof, he moved among his subjects.

Then, all at once, into the sweet routine of the House of Peace, came Horror.

It began on a blustery, sour October day. The Mistress had crossed the lake to the village, in her canoe, with Lad curled up in a furry heap in the prow. On the return trip, about fifty yards from shore, the canoe struck sharply and obliquely against a half-submerged log that a fall freshet had swept down from the river above the lake. At the same moment a flaw of wind caught the canoe's quarter. And, after the manner of such eccentric craft, the canvas shell proceeded to turn turtle.

Into the ice-chill waters splashed its two occupants. Lad bobbed to the top, and glanced around at the Mistress to learn if this were a new practical joke. But, instantly, he saw it was no joke at all, so far as she was concerned.

Swathed and cramped by the folds of her heavy outing skirt, the Mistress was making no progress shoreward. And the dog flung himself through the water toward her with a rush that left his shoulders and half his back above the surface. In a second he had reached her and had caught her sweater-shoulder in his teeth.

She had the presence of mind to lie out straight, as though she were floating, and to fill her lungs with a swift intake of breath. The dog's burden was thus made infinitely lighter than if she had struggled or had lain in a posture less easy for towing. Yet he made scant headway, until she wound one hand in his mane, and, still lying motionless and stiff, bade him loose his hold on her shoulder.

In this way, by sustained effort that wrenched every giant muscle in the collie's body, they came at last to land.

Vastly rejoiced was Lad, and inordinately proud of himself. And the plaudits of the Master and the Mistress were music to him. Indefinably, he understood he had done a very wonderful thing and that everybody on The Place was talking about him, and that all were trying to pet him at once.

This promiscuous handling he began to

find unwelcome. And he retired at last to his "cave" under the piano to escape from it. Matters soon quieted down; and the incident seemed at an end.

Instead, it had just begun.

For, within an hour, the Mistress—who, for days had been half-sick with a cold—was stricken with a chill, and by night she was in the first stages of pneumonia.

Then over The Place descended Gloom. A gloom Lad could not understand until he went upstairs at dinner-time to escort the Mistress, as usual, to the dining-room. But to his light scratch at her door there was no reply. He scratched again and presently the Master came out of the room and ordered him downstairs again.

Then from the Master's voice and look, Lad understood that something was terribly amiss. Also, as she did not appear at dinner and as he was for the first time in his life forbidden to go into her room, he knew the Mistress was the victim of whatever mishap had befallen.

A strange man, with a black bag, came to the house early in the evening; and he and the Master were closeted for an interminable time in the Mistress' room. Lad had crept dejectedly upstairs behind them; and sought to crowd into the room at their heels. The Master ordered him back and shut the door in his face.

Lad lay down on the threshold, his nose to the crack at the bottom of the door, and waited. He heard the murmur of speech. Once he caught the Mistress' voice—changed and muffled and with a puzzling new note in it—but undeniably the Mistress'. And his tail thumped hopefully on the hall floor. But no one came to let him in. And, after the mandate to keep out, he dared not scratch for admittance.

The doctor almost stumbled across the couchant body of the dog as he left the room with the Master. Being a dog-owner himself, the doctor understood and his narrow escape from a fall over the living obstacle did not irritate him. But it reminded him of something.

"Those other dogs of yours outside there," he said to the Master, as they went down the stairs, "raised a fearful racket when my car came down the drive, just now. Better send them all away somewhere till she is better. The house must be kept perfectly quiet."

The Master looked back, up the stairway; at its top, pressed close against the Mistress' door, crouched Lad. Something in the dog's heartbroken attitude touched him.

"I'll send them over to the boarding-kennels in the morning," he answered. "All except Lad. He and I are going to see this through, together. He'll be quiet, if I tell him to."

All through the endless night, while the October wind howled and yelled around the house, Lad lay outside the sick-room door, his nose between his absurdly small white paws, his sorrowful eyes wide open, his ears alert for the faintest sound from the room beyond.

Sometimes, when the wind screamed its loudest, Lad would lift his head—his ruff a-bristle, his teeth glinting from under his upcurled lip. And he would growl a throaty menace. It was as though he heard, in the tempest's racket, the strife of evil gale-spirits to burst in through the rattling windows and attack the stricken Mistress. Perhaps—well, perhaps there are things visible and audible to dogs; to which humans are blind and deaf. Or perhaps there are not.

Lad was there when day broke and when the Master, heavy-eyed from sleeplessness, came out. He was there when the other dogs were herded into the car and carried away to the boarding-kennels.

Lad was there when the car came back from the station, bringing to The Place an angular, wooden-faced woman with yellow hair and a yellower suitcase—a horrible woman who vaguely smelled of disinfectants and of rigid Efficiency, and who presently approached the sick-room clad and capped in stiff white. Lad hated her.

He was there when the doctor came for his morning visit to the invalid. And again he tried to edge his own way into the room, only to be rebuffed once more.

"This is the third time I've nearly broken my neck over that miserable dog," chidingly announced the nurse, later in the day, as she came out of the room and chanced to meet the Master on the landing. "Do please drive him away. *I've* tried to do it, but he only snarls at me. And in a dangerous case like this—"

"Leave him alone," briefly ordered the Master.

But when the nurse, sniffing, passed on, he called Lad over to him. Reluctantly, the dog quitted the door and obeyed the summons.

"Quiet!" ordered the Master, speaking very slowly and distinctly. "You must keep quiet. *Quiet!* Understand?"

Lad understood. Lad always understood. He must not bark. He must move silently. He must make no unnecessary sound. But, at least, the Master had not forbidden him to snarl softly and loathingly at that detestable white-clad woman every time she stepped over him.

So there was one grain of comfort.

Gently, the Master called him downstairs and across the living-room, and put him out of the house. For, after all, a shaggy eighty-pound dog is an inconvenience stretched across a sick-room doorsill.

Three minutes later, Lad had made his way through an open window into the cellar and thence upstairs; and was stretched out, head between paws, at the threshold of the Mistress' room.

On his thrice-a-day visits, the doctor was forced to step over him, and was man enough to forbear to curse. Twenty times a day, the nurse stumbled over his massive, inert body, and fumed in impotent rage. The Master, too, came back and forth from the sick-room, with now and then a kindly word for the suffering collie, and again and again put him out of the house. But always Lad managed, by hook or

crook, to be back on guard within a minute or two. And never once did the door of the Mistress' room open that he did not make a strenuous attempt to enter.

Servants, nurse, doctor, and Master repeatedly forgot he was there, and stubbed their toes across his body. Sometimes their feet drove agonizingly into his tender flesh. But never a whimper or growl did the pain wring from him. *"Quiet!"* had been the command, and he was obeying.

And so it went on, through the awful days and the infinitely worse nights. Except when he was ordered away by the Master, Lad would not stir from his place at the door. And not even the Master's authority could keep him away from it for five minutes a day.

The dog ate nothing, drank practically nothing, took no exercise; moved not one inch, of his own will, from the doorway. In vain did the glories of autumn woods call to him. The rabbits would be thick, out yonder in the forest, just now. So would the squirrels—against which Lad had long since sworn a blood-feud (and one of which it had ever been his futile life ambition to catch).

For him, these things no longer existed. Nothing existed; except his mortal hatred of the unseen Something in that forbidden room—the Something that was seeking to take the Mistress away with It. He yearned unspeakably to be in that room to guard her from her nameless Peril. And they would not let him in—these humans.

Wherefore he lay there, crushing his body close against the door and—waiting.

And, inside the room, Death and the Napoleonic man with the black bag fought their "no-quarter" duel for the life of the still, little white figure in the great white bed.

One night, the doctor did not go home at all. Toward dawn the Master lurched out of the room and sat down for a moment on the stairs, his face in his hands. Then and then only, during all that time of watching, did Lad leave the doorsill of his own accord.

Shaky with famine and weariness, he got to his feet, moaning softly, and crept over to the Master; he lay down beside him, his huge head athwart the man's knees; his muzzle reaching timidly toward the tight-clenched hands.

Presently the Master went back into the sick-room. And Lad was left alone in the darkness—to wonder and to listen and to wait. With a tired sigh he returned to the door and once more took up his heartsick vigil.

Then—on a golden morning, days after, the doctor came and went with the look of a Conqueror. Even the wooden-faced nurse forgot to grunt in disgust when she stumbled across the dog's body. She almost smiled. And presently the Master came through the doorway. He stopped at sight of Lad, and turned back into the room. Lad could hear him speak. And he heard a dear, *dear* voice make answer; very weakly, but no longer in that muffled and foreign tone which had so frightened him. Then came a sentence the dog could understand.

"Come in, old friend," said the Master, opening the door and standing aside for Lad to enter.

At a bound, the collie was in the room. There lay the Mistress. She was very thin, very white, very feeble. But she was there. The dread Something had lost the battle.

Lad wanted to break forth into a peal of ecstatic barking that would have deafened every one in the room. The Master read the wish and interposed, "*Quiet!*"

Lad heard. He controlled the yearning. But it cost him a world of will-power to do it. As sedately as he could force himself to move, he crossed to the bed.

The Mistress was smiling at him. One hand was stretched weakly forth to stroke him. And she was saying almost in a whisper, "Lad! Laddie!"

That was all. But her hand was petting him in the dear way he loved so well. And the Master was telling her all over again how the dog had watched outside her door. Lad listened—not to the man's praise, but to the woman's caressing whisper—and he quivered from head to tail. He fought furiously with himself once again, to choke back the rapturous barking that clamored for utterance. He knew this was no time for noise. Even without the word of warning, he would have known it. For the Mistress was whispering. Even the Master was speaking scarce louder.

But one thing Lad realized: the black danger was past. The Mistress was alive! And the whole house was smiling. That was enough. And the yearning to show, in noise, his own wild relief, was all but irresistible. Then the Master said:

"Run on, Lad. You can come back by-and-by."

And the dog gravely made his way out of the room and out of the house.

The minute he was out-of-doors, he proceeded to go crazy. Nothing but sheer mania could excuse his actions during the rest of that day. They were unworthy of a mongrel puppy. And never before in all his blameless, stately life had Lad so grossly misbehaved as he now proceeded to do. The Mistress was alive. The Horror was past. Reaction set in with a rush. As I have said, Lad went crazy.

Peter Grimm, the Mistress' cynical and temperamental gray cat, was picking its dainty way across the lawn as Lad emerged from the house.

Ordinarily, Lad regarded Peter Grimm with a cold tolerance. But now, he dashed at the cat with a semblance of stark wrath. Like a furry whirlwind he bore down upon the amazed feline. The cat, in dire offense, scratched his nose with a quite unnecessary virulence and fled up a tree, spitting and yowling, tail fluffed out as thick as a man's wrist.

Seeing that Peter Grimm had resorted to unsportsmanly tactics by scrambling whither he could not follow, Lad remembered the need for silence and forbore to bark threats at his escaped victim. Instead, he galloped to the rear of the house where stood the dairy.

The dairy door was on the latch. With his head Lad butted it open and ran into the stone-floored room. A line of full milkpans were ranged side by side on a shelf. Rising on his hind legs and bracing his forepaws on the shelf, Lad seized edges of the deep pans, one after another, between his teeth, and, with a succession of sharp jerks brought them one and all clattering to the floor.

Scampering out of the dairy, ankle deep in a river of spilled milk, and paying no heed to the cries of the scandalized cook, he charged forth in the open again. His eye fell on a red cow, tethered by a long chain in a pasture-patch beyond the stables.

She was an old acquaintance of his, this cow. She had been on The Place since before he was born. Yet, to-day Lad's spear knew no brother. He tore across the lawn and past the stables, straight at the astonished bovine. In terror, the cow threw up her tail and sought to lumber away at top speed. Being controlled by her tether she could run only in a wide circle. And around and around this circle Lad drove the bellowing brute as fast as he could make her run, until the gardener came panting to her relief.

But neither the gardener nor any other living creature could stay Lad's rampage that day. He fled merrily up to the Lodge at the gate, burst into its kitchen and through to the refrigerator. There, in a pan, he found a raw leg of mutton. Seizing this twelve-pound morsel in his teeth and dodging the indignant housewife, he careered out into the highway with his prize, dug a hole in the roadside ditch and was gleefully preparing to bury the mutton therein, when its outraged owner rescued it.

A farmer was jogging along the road behind a half-dozing horse. A painful nip on the rear hind leg turned the nag's drowsy jog into a really industrious effort at a runaway. Already, Lad had sprung clear of the front wheel. As the wagon bumped past him, he leaped upward; deftly caught a hanging corner of the lap-robe and hauled it free of the seat.

Robe in mouth, he capered off into a field; playfully keeping just out of the reach of the pursuing agrarian; and at last he deposited the stolen treasure in the heart of a bramble-patch a full half-mile from the road.

Lad made his way back to The Place by a wide detour that brought him through the grounds of a neighbor of the Master's.

This neighbor owned a dog—a mean-eyed, rangy and mangy pest of a brute that Lad would ordinarily have scorned to notice. But, most decidedly, he noticed the dog now. He routed it out of its kennel and bestowed upon it a thrashing that brought its possessor's entire family shrieking to the scene of conflict.

Courteously refusing to carry the matter further, in face of a half-dozen shouting humans, Lad cantered homeward.

From the clothes-line, on the drying-ground at The Place, fluttered a large white object. It was palpably a nurse's uniform—palpably *the* nurse's uniform. And Lad greeted its presence there with a grin of pure bliss.

In less than two seconds the uniform was off the line, with three huge rents marring its stiff surface. In less than thirty seconds, it was reposing in the rich black mud on the verge of the lake, and Lad was rolling playfully on it.

Then he chanced to remember his long-neglected enemies, the squirrels, and his equally-neglected prey, the rabbits. And he loped off to the forest to wage gay warfare upon them. He was gloriously, idiotically, criminally happy. And, for the time, he was a fool.

All day long, complaints came pouring

in to the Master. Lad had destroyed the whole "set" of cream. Lad had chased the red cow till it would be a miracle if she didn't fall sick of it. Lad had scared poor dear little Peter Grimm so badly that the cat seemed likely to spend all the rest of its nine lives squalling in the treetop and crossly refusing to come down.

Lad had spoiled a Sunday leg of mutton, up at the Lodge. Lad had made a perfectly respectable horse run madly away for nearly twenty-five feet, and had given the horse's owner a blasphemous half-mile run over a plowed field after a cherished and ravished lap-robe. Lad had well-nigh killed a neighbor's particularly killable dog. Lad had wantonly destroyed the nurse's very newest and most expensive uniform. All day it was Lad—Lad—Lad!

Lad, it seemed, was a storm-center, whence radiated complaints that ran the whole gamut from tears to lurid profanity; and, to each and every complaint, the Master made the same answer:

"Leave him alone. We're just out of hell—Lad and I! He's doing the things I'd do myself, if I had the nerve."

Which, of course, was a manifestly asinine way for a grown man to talk.

Long after dusk, Lad pattered meekly home, very tired and quite sane. His spell of imbecility had worn itself out. He was once more his calmly dignified self, though not a little ashamed of his babyish pranks, and mildly wondering how he had come to behave so.

Still, he could not grieve over what he had done. He could not grieve over anything just yet. The Mistress was alive! And while the craziness had passed, the happiness had not. Tired, drowsily at peace with all the world, he curled up under the piano and went to sleep.

He slept so soundly that the locking of the house for the night did not rouse him. But something else did. Something that occurred long after everyone on The Place was sound asleep. Lad was joyously pursuing, through the forest aisles of dreamland, a whole army of squirrels that had not sense enough to climb trees—when in a moment, he was wide awake and on guard. Far off, very far off, he heard a man walking.

Now, to a trained dog there is as much difference in the sound of human footfalls as, to humans, there is a difference in the aspect of human faces. A belated countryman walking along the highway, a furlong distant, would not have awakened Lad from sleep. Also, he knew and could classify, at any distance, the footsteps of everyone who lived on The Place. But the steps that had brought him wide awake and on the alert to-night, did not belong to one of The Place's people; nor were they the steps of anybody who had a right to be on the premises.

Someone had climbed the fence, at a distance from the drive, and was crossing the grounds, obliquely, toward the house. It was a man, and he was still nearly two hundred yards away. Moreover, he was walking stealthily; and pausing every now and then as if to reconnoiter.

No human, at that distance, could have heard the steps. No dog could have helped hearing them. Had the other dogs been at home instead of at the boarding-kennels, The Place would by this time have been re-echoing with barks. Both scent and sound would have given them ample warning of the stranger's presence.

To Lad, on the lower floor of the house, where every window was shut, the aid of scent was denied. Yet his sense of hearing was enough. Plainly, he heard the softly advancing steps—heard and read them. He read them for an intruder's—read them for the steps of a man who was afraid to be heard or seen, and who was employing all the caution in his power.

A booming, trumpeting bark of warning sprang into Lad's throat—and died there. The sharp command "*Quiet!*" was still in force. Even in his madness, that day, he had uttered no sound. He strangled back the tumultuous bark and listened in silence. He had risen to his feet and had come out from under the piano. In the middle of the living-room he stood, head lowered, ears pricked. His ruff was abristle. A ridge of hair rose grotesquely from the shaggy mass of coat along his spine. His lips had slipped back from his teeth. And so he stood and waited.

The shuffling, soft steps were nearer now. Down through the trees they came, and then onto the springy grass of the lawn. Now they crunched lightly on the gravel of the drive. Lad moved forward a little and again stood at attention.

The man was climbing to the veranda. The vines rustled ever so slightly as he brushed past them. His footfall sounded lightly on the veranda itself.

Next there was a faint clicking noise at the old-fashioned lock of one of the bay windows. Presently, by half-inches, the window began to rise. Before it had risen an inch, Lad knew that the trespasser was no one with whose scent he was familiar.

Another pause, followed by the very faintest scratching, as the man ran a knife-blade along the crack of the inner wooden blinds in search of the catch.

The blinds parted slowly. Over the windowsill the man threw a leg. Then he stepped down noiselessly into the room.

He stood there a second, evidently listening.

And, before he could stir or breathe, something in the darkness hurled itself upon him.

Without so much as a growl of warning, eighty pounds of muscular, hairy energy smote the man full in the chest. A set of hot-breathing jaws flashed for his jugular vein, missed it by a half-inch, and the graze left a red-hot searing pain along the man's throat. In the merest fraction of a moment, the murderously snapping jaws sank into the thief's shoulder. It is collie custom to fight with a running accompaniment of snarling growls. But Lad did not give voice. In total silence he made his

onslaught. In silence, he sought and gained his hold.

The intruder was less considerate of the Mistress' comfort. With a screech that would have waked every mummy in Egypt, he reeled back, under that first unseen impact, lost his balance and crashed to the hardwood floor, overturning a table and a lamp in his fall. Certain that a devil had attacked him there in the black darkness, the man gave forth yell after yell of mortal terror. Frantically, he strove to push away his assailant and his clammy hand encountered a mass of fur.

The thief had heard that all the dogs on The Place had been sent away because of the Mistress' illness. Hence his attempt at burglary. Hence also, his panic fear when Lad had sprung on him.

But with the feel of the thick warm fur, the man's superstitious terror died. He knew he had roused the house; but there was still time to escape if he could rid himself of this silent, terrible creature. He staggered to his feet. And, with the knife he still clutched, he smote viciously at his assailant.

Because Lad was a collie, Lad was not killed then and there. A bulldog or a bull-terrier, attacking a man, seeks for some convenient hold. Having secured that hold—be it good or bad—he locks his jaws and hangs on. You can well-nigh cut his head from his body before he will let go. Thus, he is at the mercy of any armed man who can keep cool long enough to kill him.

But a collie has a strain of wolf in his queer brain. He seeks a hold, it is true. But at an instant's notice, he is ready to shift that hold for a better. He may bite or slash a dozen times in as many seconds and in as many parts of the body. He is everywhere at once—he is nowhere in particular. He is not a pleasant opponent.

Lad did not wait the thief's knife to find his heart. As the man lunged, the dog transferred his profitless shoulderhold to a grip on the stabbing arm. The knife blade plowed an ugly furrow along his side. And the dog's curved eye-tooth slashed the man's arm from elbow to wrist, clean through to the bone.

The knife clattered to the floor. The man wheeled and made a leap for the open window; he had not cleared half the space when Lad bounded for the back of his neck. The dog's upper set of teeth raked the man's hard skull, carrying away a handful of hair and flesh; and his weight threw the thief forward on hands and knees again. Twisting, the man found the dog's furry throat; and with both hands sought to strangle him; at the same time backing out through the window. But it is not easy to strangle a collie. The piles of tumbled ruff-hair form a protection no other breed of dog can boast. Scarcely had the hands found their grip when one of them was crushed between the dog's vise-like jaws.

The thief flung off his enemy and turned to clear the veranda at a single jump. But before he had half made the turn, Lad was at his throat again, and the two crashed through the vines together and down onto the driveway below. The entire combat had not lasted for more than thirty seconds.

The Master, revolver and flashlight in hand, ran down to find the living-room amuck with blood and with smashed furniture, and one of the windows open. He flashed the electric ray through the window. On the ground below, stunned by striking against a stone jardinière in his fall, the thief sprawled senseless upon his back. Above him was Lad, his searching teeth at last having found their coveted throat-hold. Steadily, the great dog was grinding his way through toward the jugular.

There was a deal of noise and excitement and light after that. The burglar was trussed up and the local constable was summoned by telephone. Everybody seemed to be doing much loud talking.

Lad took advantage of the turmoil to slip back into the house and to his "cave" under the piano; where he proceeded to lick solicitously the flesh wound on his left side.

He was very tired; and he was very unhappy and he was very much worried. In spite of all his own precautions as to silence, the thief had made a most ungodly lot of noise. The commandment *"Quiet!"* had been fractured past repair. And, somehow, Lad felt to blame for it all. It was really his fault—and he realized it now—that the man had made such a racket. Would the Master punish him? Perhaps. Humans have such odd ideas of Justice. He—

Then it was that the Master found him; and called him forth from his place of refuge. Head adroop, tail low, Lad crept out to meet his scolding. He looked very much like a puppy caught tearing a new rug.

But suddenly, the Master and everyone else in the room was patting him and telling him how splendid he was. And the Master had found the deep scratch on his side and was dressing it, and stopping every minute or so, to praise him again. And then, as a crowning reward, he was taken upstairs for the Mistress to stroke and make much of.

When at last he was sent downstairs again, Lad did not return to his piano-lair. Instead, he went out-of-doors and away from The Place. And, when he thought he was far enough from the house, he solemnly sat down and began to bark.

It was good—*passing* good—to be able to make a noise again. He had never before known how needful to canine happiness a bark really is. He had long and pressing arrears of barks in his system. And thunderously he proceeded to divest himself of them for nearly half an hour.

Then, feeling much, *much* better, he ambled homeward, to take up normal life again after a whole fortnight of martyrdom.

Paul Bunyan and His Great Blue Ox

WALLACE WADSWORTH

THE HIRSUTE BUNYAN [1]

PAUL BUNYAN was of tremendous size and strength, the strongest man that ever swung an ax. He had curly black hair which his loving wife used to comb for him every morning with a great crosscut saw, after first parting it nicely with a broadax, and a big black beard that was as long as it was wide and as wide as it was long. He was rather proud of this beard, and took great care of it. Several times every day he would pull up a young pine tree by the roots and use its stiff branches in combing and brushing it smooth.

[1] From "Paul Bunyan and His Great Blue Ox," by Wallace Wadsworth, illustrated by Richard Bennett

Little Women

LOUISA M. ALCOTT

PLAYING PILGRIMS [1]

"Christmas won't be Christmas without any presents," grumbled Jo, lying on the rug.

"It's so dreadful to be poor!" sighed Meg, looking down at her old dress.

"I don't think it's fair for some girls to have plenty of pretty things, and other girls nothing at all," added little Amy, with an injured sniff.

"We've got father and mother and each other," said Beth contentedly, from her corner.

The four young faces on which the firelight shone brightened at the cheerful words, but darkened again as Jo said sadly:

"We haven't got father, and shall not have him for a long time." She didn't say "perhaps never," but each silently added it, thinking of father far away, where the fighting was.

Nobody spoke for a minute; then Meg said in an altered tone:

"You know the reason mother proposed not having any presents this Christmas was because it is going to be a hard winter for everyone; and she thinks we ought not to spend money for pleasure, when our men are suffering so in the army. We can't do much, but we can make our little sacrifices, and ought to do it gladly. But I am afraid I don't"; and Meg shook her head as she thought regretfully of all the pretty things she wanted.

"But I don't think the little we should spend would do any good. We've each got a dollar, and the army wouldn't be much helped by our giving that. I agree not to expect anything from mother or you, but I do want to buy 'Undine and Sintram' for myself; I've wanted it so long," said Jo, who was a bookworm.

"I have planned to spend mine in new music," said Beth, with a little sigh, which no one heard but the hearth brush and kettle holder.

"I shall get a nice box of Faber's drawing pencils; I really need them," said Amy decidedly.

"Mother didn't say anything about our money, and she won't wish us to give up everything. Let's each buy what we want, and have a little fun; I'm sure we work hard enough to earn it," cried Jo, examining the heels of her shoes in a gentlemanly manner.

"I know I do—teaching those tiresome children nearly all day, when I'm longing to enjoy myself at home," began Meg, in the complaining tone again.

"You don't have half such a hard time as I do," said Jo. "How would you like to be shut up for hours with a nervous, fussy old lady, who keeps you trotting, is never satisfied, and worries you till you're ready to fly out of the window or cry?"

"It's naughty to fret; but I do think washing dishes and keeping things tidy is the worst work in the world. It makes me cross; and my hands get so stiff, I can't practice well at all"; and Beth looked at her rough hands with a sigh that anyone could hear that time.

"I don't believe any of you suffer as I do," cried Amy; "for you don't have to go to school with impertinent girls, who plague you if you don't know your lessons, and laugh at your dresses, and label your father if he isn't rich, and insult you when your nose isn't nice."

"If you mean *libel*, I'd say so, and not talk about *labels*, as if papa was a pickle bottle," advised Jo, laughing.

[1] From "Little Women," by Louisa M. Alcott, illustration from a drawing by Jessie Wilcox Smith

484

"I know what I mean, and you needn't be *statirical* about it. It's proper to use good words, and improve your *vocabilary*," returned Amy, with dignity.

"Don't peck at one another, children. Don't you wish we had the money papa lost when we were little, Jo? Dear me, how happy and good we'd be, if we had no worries!" said Meg, who could remember better times.

"You said, the other day, you thought we were a deal happier than the King children, for they were fighting and fretting all the time, in spite of their money."

"So I did, Beth. Well, I think we are; for, although we do have to work, we make fun for ourselves, and are a pretty jolly set, as Jo would say."

"Jo does use such slang words!" observed Amy, with a reproving look at the long figure stretched on the rug. Jo immediately sat up, put her hands in her pockets, and began to whistle.

"Don't, Jo; it's so boyish!"

"That's why I do it."

"I detest rude, unladylike girls!"

"I hate affected, niminy-piminy chits!"

" 'Birds in their little nests agree,' " sang Beth, the peacemaker, with such a funny face that both sharp voices softened to a laugh, and the "pecking" ended for that time.

"Really, girls, you are both to be blamed," said Meg, beginning to lecture in her elder-sisterly fashion. "You are old enough to leave off boyish tricks, and to behave better, Josephine. It didn't matter so much when you were a little girl; but now you are so tall, and turn up your hair, you should remember that you are a young lady."

"I'm not! And if turning up my hair makes me one, I'll wear it in two tails till I'm twenty," cried Jo, pulling off her net, and shaking down a chestnut mane. "I hate to think I've got to grow up, and be Miss March, and wear long gowns, and look as prim as a China aster! It's bad enough to be a girl, anyway, when I like

boys' games and work and manners! I can't get over my disappointment in not being a boy; and it's worse than ever now, for I'm dying to go and fight with papa, and I can only stay at home and knit, like a poky old woman!" And Jo shook the blue army sock till the needles rattled like castanets, and her ball bounded across the room.

"Poor Jo! It's too bad, but it can't be helped; so you must try to be contented with making your name boyish, and playing brother to us girls," said Beth, stroking the rough head at her knee with a hand that all the dishwashing and dusting in the world could not make ungentle in its touch.

"As for you, Amy," continued Meg, "you are altogether too particular and prim. Your airs are funny now; but you'll grow up an affected little goose, if you don't take care. I like your nice manners and refined ways of speaking, when you don't try to be elegant; but your absurd words are as bad as Jo's slang."

"If Jo is a tomboy and Amy a goose, what am I, please?" asked Beth, ready to share the lecture.

"You're a dear, and nothing else," answered Meg warmly; and no one contradicted her, for the "Mouse" was the pet of the family.

As young readers like to know "how people look," we will take this moment to give them a little sketch of the four sisters, who sat knitting away in the twilight, while the December snow fell quietly without, and the fire crackled cheerfully within. It was a comfortable old room, though the carpet was faded and the furniture very plain; for a good picture or two hung on the walls, books filled the recesses, chrysanthemums and Christmas roses bloomed in the windows, and a pleasant atmosphere of home peace pervaded it.

Margaret, the eldest of the four, was sixteen, and very pretty, being plump and fair, with large eyes, plenty of soft, brown hair, a sweet mouth, and white hands, of which she was rather vain. Fifteen-year-old Jo was very tall, thin, and brown, and reminded one of a colt; for she never seemed to know what to do with her long limbs, which were very much in her way. She had a decided mouth, a comical nose, and sharp, gray eyes, which appeared to see everything, and were by turns fierce, funny, or thoughtful. Her long, thick hair was her one beauty; but it was usually bundled into a net, to be out of her way. Round shoulders had Jo, big hands and feet, a flyaway look to her clothes, and the uncomfortable appearance of a girl who was rapidly shooting up into a woman, and didn't like it. Elizabeth—or Beth, as everyone called her—was a rosy, smooth-haired, bright-eyed girl of thirteen, with a shy manner, a timid voice, and a peaceful expression, which was seldom disturbed. Her father called her "Little Tranquillity," and the name suited her excellently; for she seemed to live in a happy world of her own, only venturing out to meet the few whom she trusted and loved. Amy, though the youngest, was a most important person—in her own opinion at least. A regular snow-maiden, with blue eyes, and yellow hair curling on her shoulders, pale and slender, and always carrying herself like a young lady mindful of her manners. What the characters of the four sisters were we will leave to be found out.

The clock struck six; and, having swept up the hearth, Beth put a pair of slippers down to warm. Somehow the sight of the old shoes had a good effect upon the girls; for mother was coming, and everyone brightened to welcome her. Meg stopped lecturing, and lighted the lamp, Amy got out of the easy chair without being asked, and Jo forgot how tired she was as she sat up to hold the slippers nearer to the blaze.

"They are quite worn out; Marmee must have a new pair."

"I thought I'd get her some with my dollar," said Beth.

"No, I shall!" cried Amy.

"I'm the oldest," began Meg, but Jo cut in with a decided—

"I'm the man of the family now papa is away, and I shall provide the slippers, for he told me to take special care of mother while he was gone."

"I'll tell you what we'll do," said Beth; "let's each get her something for Christmas, and not get anything for ourselves."

"That's like you, dear! What will we get?" exclaimed Jo.

Everyone thought soberly for a minute; then Meg announced, as if the idea was suggested by the sight of her own pretty hands, "I shall give her a nice pair of gloves."

"Army shoes, best to be had," cried Jo.

"Some handkerchiefs, all hemmed," said Beth.

"I'll get a little bottle of cologne; she likes it, and it won't cost much, so I'll have some left to buy my pencils," added Amy.

"How will we give the things?" asked Meg.

"Put them on the table, and bring her in and see her open the bundles. Don't you remember how we used to do on our birthdays?" answered Jo.

"I used to be so frightened when it was my turn to sit in the big chair with the crown on, and see you all come marching round to give the presents, with a kiss. I liked the things and the kisses, but it was dreadful to have you sit looking at me while I opened the bundles," said Beth, who was toasting her face and the bread for tea, at the same time.

"Let Marmee think we are getting things for ourselves, and then surprise her. We must go shopping tomorrow afternoon, Meg; there is so much to do about the play for Christmas night," said Jo, marching up and down, with her hands behind her back and her nose in the air.

"I don't mean to act any more after this time; I'm getting too old for such things," observed Meg, who was as much a child as ever about "dressing-up" frolics.

"You won't stop, I know, as long as you can trail round in a white gown with your hair down, and wear gold-paper jewelry.

Meg, Jo, Beth, and Amy

You are the best actress we've got, and there'll be an end of everything if you quit the boards," said Jo. "We ought to rehearse tonight. Come here, Amy, and do the fainting scene, for you are as stiff as a poker in that."

"I can't help it; I never saw anyone faint, and I don't choose to make myself all black and blue, tumbling flat as you do. If I can go down easily, I'll drop; if I can't, I shall fall into a chair and be graceful; I don't care if Hugo does come at me with a pistol," returned Amy, who was not gifted with dramatic power, but was chosen because she was small enough to be borne out shrieking by the villain of the piece.

"Do it this way: clasp your hands so, and stagger across the room, crying frantically, 'Roderigo! save me! save me!'" and away went Jo with a melodramatic scream which was truly thrilling.

Amy followed, but she poked her hands out stiffly before her, and jerked herself along as if she went by machinery; and her "Ow!" was more suggestive of pins being run into her than of fear and anguish. Jo gave a despairing groan, and Meg laughed outright, while Beth let her bread burn as she watched the fun, with interest.

"It's no use! Do the best you can when the time comes, and if the audience laugh, don't blame me. Come on, Meg."

Then things went smoothly, for Don Pedro defied the world in a speech of two pages without a single break; Hagar, the witch, chanted an awful incantation over her kettleful of simmering toads, with weird effect; Roderigo rent his chains asunder manfully, and Hugo died in agonies of remorse and arsenic, with a wild "Ha! ha!"

"It's the best we've had yet," said Meg, as the dead villain sat up and rubbed his elbows.

"I don't see how you can write and act such splendid things, Jo. You're a regular Shakespeare!" exclaimed Beth, who firmly believed that her sisters were gifted with wonderful genius in all things.

"Not quite," replied Jo modestly. "I do think 'The Witch's Curse, an Operatic Tragedy,' is rather a nice thing; but I'd like to try Macbeth, if we only had a trap door for Banquo. I always wanted to do the killing part. 'Is that a dagger that I see before me?'" muttered Jo, rolling her eyes and clutching at the air, as she had seen a famous tragedian do.

"No, it's the toasting fork, with mother's shoe on it instead of the bread. Beth's stage-struck!" cried Meg, and the rehearsal ended in a general burst of laughter.

"Glad to find you so merry, my girls," said a cheery voice at the door, and actors and audience turned to welcome a tall, motherly lady, with a "can-I-help-you" look about her which was truly delightful. She was not elegantly dressed, but a noble-looking woman, and the girls thought the gray cloak and unfashionable bonnet covered the most splendid mother in the world.

"Well, dearies, how have you got on today? There was so much to do, getting the boxes ready to go tomorrow, that I didn't come home to dinner. Has anyone called, Beth? How is your cold, Meg? Jo, you look tired to death. Come and kiss me, baby."

While making these maternal inquiries Mrs. March got her wet things off, her warm slippers on, and sitting down in the easy chair, drew Amy to her lap, preparing to enjoy the happiest hour of her busy day. The girls flew about, trying to make things comfortable, each in her own way. Meg arranged the tea table; Jo brought wood and set chairs, dropping, overturning, and clattering everything she touched; Beth trotted to and fro between parlor and kitchen, quiet and busy; while Amy gave directions to everyone, as she sat with her hands folded.

As they gathered about the table, Mrs. March said, with a particularly happy face, "I've got a treat for you after supper."

A quick, bright smile went round like a streak of sunshine. Beth clapped her hands, regardless of the biscuit she held, and Jo tossed up her napkin, crying, "A letter! a letter! Three cheers for father!"

"Yes, a nice long letter. He is well, and thinks he shall get through the cold season better than we feared. He sends all sorts of loving wishes for Christmas, and an especial message to you girls," said Mrs. March, patting her pocket as if she had got a treasure there.

"Hurry and get done! Don't stop to quirk your little finger, and simper over your plate, Amy," cried Jo, choking in her tea, and dropping her bread, butter side down, on the carpet, in her haste to get at the treat.

Beth ate no more, but crept away, to sit

in her shadowy corner and brood over the delight to come, till the others were ready.

"I think it was so splendid in father to go as a chaplain when he was too old to be drafted, and not strong enough for a soldier," said Meg warmly.

"Don't I wish I could go as a drummer, a *vivan*—what's its name?—or a nurse, so I could be near him and help him," exclaimed Jo, with a groan.

"It must be very disagreeable to sleep in a tent, and eat all sorts of bad-tasting things, and drink out of a tin mug," sighed Amy.

"When will he come home, Marmee?" asked Beth, with a little quiver in her voice.

"Not for many months, dear, unless he is sick. He will stay and do his work faithfully as long as he can, and we won't ask for him back a minute sooner than he can be spared. Now come and hear the letter."

They all drew to the fire, mother in the big chair with Beth at her feet, Meg and Amy perched on either arm of the chair, and Jo leaning on the back, where no one would see any sign of emotion if the letter should happen to be touching. Very few letters were written in those hard times that were not touching, especially those which fathers sent home. In this one little was said of the hardships endured, the dangers faced, or the homesickness conquered; it was a cheerful, hopeful letter, full of lively descriptions of camp life, marches, and military news; and only at the end did the writer's heart overflow with fatherly love and longing for the little girls at home.

"Give them all my dear love and a kiss. Tell them I think of them by day, pray for them by night, and find my best comfort in their affection at all times. A year seems very long to wait before I see them, but remind them that while we wait we may all work, so that these hard days need not be wasted. I know they will remember all I said to them, that they will be loving children to you, will do their duty faithfully, fight their bosom enemies bravely, and conquer themselves so beautifully that when I come back to them I may be fonder and prouder than ever of my little women."

Everybody sniffed when they came to that part; Jo wasn't ashamed of the great tear that dropped off the end of her nose, and Amy never minded the rumpling of her curls as she hid her face on her mother's shoulder and sobbed out. "I *am* a selfish girl! but I'll truly try to be better, so he mayn't be disappointed in me by and by."

"We all will!" cried Meg. "I think too much of my looks, and hate to work, but won't any more, if I can help it."

"I'll try and be what he loves to call me, a 'little woman,' and not be rough and wild; but do my duty here instead of wanting to be somewhere else," said Jo, thinking that keeping her temper at home was a much harder task than facing a rebel or two down South.

Beth said nothing, but wiped away her tears with the blue army sock, and began to knit with all her might, losing no time in doing the duty that lay nearest her, while she resolved in her quiet little soul to be all that father hoped to find her when the year brought round the happy coming home.

Mrs. March broke the silence that followed Jo's words, by saying in her cheery voice, "Do you remember how you used to play Pilgrim's Progress when you were little things? Nothing delighted you more than to have me tie my piece bags on your backs for burdens, give you hats and sticks and rolls of paper, and let you travel through the house from the cellar, which was the City of Destruction, up, up, to the housetop, where you had all the lovely things you could collect to make a Celestial City."

"What fun it was, especially going by the lions, fighting Apollyon, and passing through the Valley where the hobgoblins were!" said Jo.

"I liked the place where the bundles fell off and tumbled downstairs," said Meg.

"My favorite part was when we came out on the flat roof where our flowers and arbors and pretty things were, and all stood and sung for joy up there in the sunshine," said Beth, smiling, as if that pleasant moment had come back to her.

"I don't remember much about it, except that I was afraid of the cellar and the dark entry, and always liked the cake and milk we had up at the top. If I wasn't too old for such things, I'd rather like to play it over again," said Amy, who began to talk of renouncing childish things at the mature age of twelve.

"We never are too old for this, my dear, because it is a play we are playing all the time in one way or another. Our burdens are here, our road is before us, and the longing for goodness and happiness is the guide that leads us through many troubles and mistakes to the peace which is a true Celestial City. Now, my little pilgrims, suppose you begin again, not in play, but in earnest, and see how far on you can get before father comes home."

"Really, mother? Where are our bundles?" asked Amy, who was a very literal young lady.

"Each of you told what your burden was just now, except Beth; I rather think she hasn't got any," said her mother.

"Yes, I have; mine is dishes and dusters, and envying girls with nice pianos, and being afraid of people."

Beth's bundle was such a funny one that everybody wanted to laugh; but nobody did, for it would have hurt her feelings very much.

"Let us do it," said Meg thoughtfully. "It is only another name for trying to be good, and the story may help us; for though we do want to be good, it's hard work, and we forget, and don't do our best."

"We were in the Slough of Despond to-night, and mother came and pulled us out as Help did in the book. We ought to have our roll of directions, like Christian. What shall we do about that?" asked Jo, delighted with the fancy which lent a little romance to the very dull task of doing her duty.

"Look under your pillows, Christmas morning, and you will find your guidebook," replied Mrs. March.

They talked over the new plan while old Hannah cleared the table; then out came the four little workbaskets, and the needles flew as the girls made sheets for Aunt March. It was uninteresting sewing, but tonight no one grumbled. They adopted Jo's plan of dividing the long seams into four parts, and calling the quarters Europe, Asia, Africa, and America, and in that way got on capitally, especially when they talked about the different countries as they stitched their way through them.

At nine they stopped work, and sung, as usual, before they went to bed. No one but Beth could get much music out of the old piano; but she had a way of softly touching the yellow keys, and making a pleasant accompaniment to the simple songs they sung. Meg had a voice like a flute, and she and her mother led the little choir. Amy chirped like a cricket, and Jo wandered through the airs at her own sweet will, always coming out at the wrong place with a croak or a quaver that spoilt the most pensive tune. They had always done this from the time they could lisp,

"Crinkle, crinkle, 'ittle 'tar,"

and it had become a household custom, for the mother was a born singer. The first sound in the morning was her voice, as she went about the house singing like a lark; and the last sound at night was the same cheery sound, for the girls never grew too old for that familiar lullaby.

Gulliver's Travels

JONATHAN SWIFT

THE EMPEROR OF LILLIPUT [1]

When I found myself on my feet, I looked about me, and must confess I never beheld a more entertaining prospect. The country round appeared like a continued garden, and the enclosed fields, which were generally forty feet square, resembled so many beds of flowers. These fields were intermingled with woods of half a stang, and the tallest trees, as I could judge, appeared to be seven feet high. I viewed the town on my left hand, which looked like the painted scene of a city in a theater.

The Emperor was already descended from the tower, and advancing on horseback toward me, which had like to have cost him dear. The beast, though very well trained, yet wholly unused to such a sight, which appeared as if a mountain moved before him, reared up on his hinder feet: but that prince, who is an excellent horseman, kept his seat, till his attendants ran in and held the bridle, while his Majesty had time to dismount. When he alighted, he surveyed me round with great admiration, but kept without the length of my chain.

He ordered his cooks and butlers, who were already prepared, to give me victuals and drink, which they pushed forward in a sort of vehicle upon wheels till I could reach them. I took these vehicles, and soon emptied them all. Twenty of them were filled with meat, and ten with liquor. Each of the former afforded me two or three good mouthfuls, and I emptied the liquor of ten vessels, which was contained in earthen vials, into one vehicle, drinking it off at a draught; and so I did with the rest.

The Empress and young princes of the

blood of both sexes, attended by many ladies, sat at some distance in their chairs. But upon the accident that happened to the Emperor's horse, they alighted, and came near his person, which I am now going to describe. He was taller by almost the breadth of my nail than any of his court, which alone was enough to strike an awe into the beholders. His features were strong and masculine, with an Austrian lip

[1] From "Gulliver's Travels," by Jonathan Swift, illustrations by Aldren Watson

and arched nose, his complexion olive, his countenance erect, his body and limbs well proportioned, all his motions graceful, and his deportment majestic. He was then past his prime, being twenty-eight years and three-quarters old, of which he had reigned about seven, in great felicity, and generally victorious.

For the better convenience of beholding him, I lay on my side, so that my face was parallel to his, and he stood but three yards off. However, I have had him since many times in my hand, and therefore cannot be deceived in the description. His dress was very plain and simple, and the fashion of it between the Asiatic and the European. But he had on his head a light helmet of gold, adorned with jewels, and a plume on the crest. He held his sword drawn in his hand, to defend himself, if I should happen to break loose. It was almost three inches long, the hilt and scabbard were gold enriched with diamonds. His voice was shrill, but very clear and articulate, and I could distinctly hear it when I stood up. The ladies and courtiers were all most magnificently clad, so that the spot they stood upon seemed to resemble a petticoat spread on the ground, embroidered with figures of gold and silver.

His Imperial Majesty spoke often to me, and I returned answers, but neither of us could understand a syllable. There were several of his priests and lawyers present (as I conjectured by their habits) who were commanded to address themselves to me. I spoke to them in as many languages as I had the least smattering of, which were High and Low Dutch, Latin, French, Spanish, Italian, and Lingua Franca; but all to no purpose.

After about two hours the court retired, and I was left with a strong guard, to prevent the impertinence and probably the malice of the rabble, who were very impatient to crowd about me as near as they dared. Some of them had the impudence to shoot their arrows at me as I sat on the ground by the door of my house, whereof one very narrowly missed my left eye. But the colonel ordered six of the ringleaders to be seized, and thought no punishment so proper as to deliver them bound into my hands. Some of his soldiers accordingly did, pushing them forward with the butt ends of their pikes into my reach. I took them all in my right hand, put five of them into my coat pocket, and as to the sixth, I made a countenance as if I would eat him alive. The poor man squalled terribly, and the colonel and his officers were in much pain, especially when they saw me take out my penknife. But I soon put them out of fear; for immediately cutting the strings he was bound with, I set him gently on the ground, and away he ran. I treated the rest in the same manner, taking them one by one out of my pocket, and I observed both the soldiers and people were highly pleased of my clemency.

Toward night I with some difficulty got into my house, where I lay on the ground, and continued to do so about a fortnight; during which time the Emperor gave orders to have a bed prepared for me. Six hundred beds of the common measure were brought in carriages, and worked up in my house. A hundred and fifty of their beds sewn together made up the breadth and length, and these were four double, which however kept me but very indifferently from the hardness of the floor, that was of smooth stone. By the same computation they provided me with sheets, blankets, and coverlets, tolerable enough for one who had been so long inured to hardships.

As the news of my arrival spread through the kingdom, it brought prodigious numbers of rich, idle, and curious people to see me; so that the villages were almost emptied. Great neglect of tillage and household affairs must have ensued, if his Imperial Majesty had not provided, by several proclamations and orders of state, against this inconvenience. He directed that those who had already beheld me should return home, and not presume to come within

fifty yards of my house without license from court, whereby the secretaries of state got considerable fees.

In the meantime, the Emperor held frequent councils to debate what course should be taken with me. I was afterward assured by a particular friend, a person of great quality, that the court was under many difficulties concerning me. They apprehended my breaking loose, that my diet would be very expensive, and might cause a famine. Sometimes they determined to starve me, or at least to shoot me in the face and hands with poisoned arrows, which would soon dispatch me. But again they considered that the stench of so large a carcass might produce a plague in the metropolis, and probably spread through the whole kingdom.

In the midst of these consultations, sev-eral army officers went to the door of the great council chamber. Two of them being admitted, they gave an account of my behavior to the six criminals above mentioned, which made so favorable an impression in the breast of his Majesty and the whole board in my behalf that an imperial commission was issued out, obliging all the villages nine hundred yards round the city, to deliver every morning six beeves, forty sheep, and other victuals for my sustenance; together with a proportionable quantity of bread, and wine, and other liquors for the due payment of which his Majesty gave assignments upon his treasury. For this prince lives chiefly upon his own demesnes, seldom raising any subsidies upon his subjects.

An establishment was also made of six hundred persons to be my domestics, who had board-wages allowed for their maintenance, and tents built for them very conveniently on each side of my door. It was likewise ordered that three hundred tailors should make me a suit of clothes after the fashion of the country; that six of his Majesty's greatest scholars should be employed to instruct me in their language; and, lastly, that the Emperor's horses, and those of the nobility, and troops of guards, should be frequently exercised in my sight, to accustom themselves to me.

All these orders were duly put in execution, and in about three weeks I made great progress in learning their language; during which time the Emperor frequently honored me with his visits, and was pleased to assist my masters in teaching me.

We began already to converse together in some fashion; and the first words I learned were to express my desire that he would please give me my liberty, which I every day repeated on my knees. His answer, as I could apprehend it, was that this must be a work of time, not to be thought on without the advice of his council, and that first I must *Lumos kelmin pesso desmar lon Emposo;* that is, swear a peace with him and his kingdom. Meanwhile, I should be used with all kindness, and he advised me to acquire, by my patience and discreet behavior, the good opinion of himself and his subjects.

He desired I would not take it ill if he gave orders to certain proper officers to search me; for probably I might carry about me several weapons, which must needs be dangerous things, if they answered the bulk of so prodigious a person. I said his Majesty should be satisfied, for I was ready to strip myself, and turn out my pockets before him. This I delivered part in words, and part in signs. He replied, that by the laws of the kingdom I must be searched by two of his officers. He said that he knew this could not be done without my consent and assistance; but that he had so good an opinion of my generosity and justice as to trust their persons in my hands. Whatever they took from me should be returned when I left the country, or paid for at the rate which I would set upon them.

I took up the two officers in my hands, put them into my coat pockets, and then into every other pocket about me, except my two fobs, and another secret pocket I had no mind should be searched, wherein I had some little necessaries that were of no consequence to any but myself. In one of my fobs there was a silver watch, and in the other a small quantity of gold in a purse. These gentlemen, having pen, ink, and paper about them, made an exact inventory of everything they saw; and when they were through, desired I would set them down, that they might deliver it to the Emperor. This inventory I afterward translated into English, and is word for word as follows:

In the right coat pocket of the Great Man-Mountain after the strictest search, we found only one great piece of coarse cloth, large enough to be a foot cloth for your Majesty's chief room of state. In the left pocket we saw a huge silver chest, with a cover of the same metal, which we the searchers were not able to lift. We desired it should be opened, and one of us stepping into it, found himself up to the midleg in a sort of dust, some part whereof flying up to our faces, set us both sneezing for several times together.

In his right waistcoat pocket we found a prodigious bundle of white thin substances, folded one over another, about the bigness of three men, tied with a strong cable, and marked with black figures; which we humbly conceive to be writings, every letter almost half as large as the palm of our hands. In the left there was a sort of engine, from the back of which were extended twenty long poles, resembling the palisados before your Majesty's court; wherewith we conjecture the Man-Mountain combs his head, for we did not always trouble him with questions, because we found it a great difficulty to make him understand us.

In the large pocket on the right side of his breeches we saw a hollow pillar of iron, about the length of a man, fastened to a strong piece of timber, larger than the pillar; and upon one side of the pillar were huge pieces of iron sticking out, cut into strange figures, which we know not what to make of. In the left pocket, another engine of the same kind.

In the smaller pocket on the right side were several round flat pieces of white and red metal, of different bulk. Some of the white, which seemed to be silver, were so large and heavy that my comrade and I could hardly lift them. In the left pocket were two black pillars irregularly shaped. We could not, without difficulty, reach the top of them as we stood at the bottom of his pocket. One of them was covered, and seemed all of a piece. But at the upper end of the other, there appeared a white round substance, about twice the bigness of our heads. Within each of these was enclosed a prodigious plate of steel; which, by our orders, we obliged him to show us, because we apprehended they might be dangerous engines. He took them out of their cases, and told us that in his own country his practice was to shave his beard with one of these, and to cut his meat with the other.

There were two pockets which we could not enter: these he called his fobs. They were two large slits cut into the top of his breeches, but squeezed close by the pressure of his belly.

Out of the right fob hung a great silver chain, with a wonderful kind of engine at the bottom. We directed him to draw out whatever was fastened to that chain; which appeared to be a globe, half silver, and half of some transparent metal. On the transparent side we saw certain strange figures circularly drawn, and thought we could touch them, till we found our fingers stopped by that lucid substance. He put this engine to our ears, which made an incessant noise like that of a watermill. We conjecture it is either some unknown

animal, or the god that he worships; but we are more inclined to the latter opinion, because he assured us that he seldom did anything without consulting it. He called it his oracle, and said it pointed out the time for every action of his life.

From the left fob he took out a net almost large enough for a fisherman, but contrived to open and shut like a purse and serve him for the same use. We found therein several massy pieces of yellow metal, which, if they be real gold, must be of immense value.

Having thus, in obedience to your Majesty's commands, diligently searched all his pockets, we observed a girdle about his waist made of the hide of some prodigious animal; from which, on the left side, hung a sword of the length of five men; and on

the right, a bag or pouch divided into two cells, each cell capable of holding three of your Majesty's subjects. In one of these cells were several globes or balls of a most ponderous metal, about the bigness of our heads, and requiring a strong hand to lift them. The other cell contained a heap of certain black grains, but of no great bulk or weight, for we could hold above fifty of them in the palms of our hands.

This is an exact inventory of what we found about the body of the Man-Mountain, who used us with great civility and due respect to your Majesty's commission. Signed and sealed on the fourth day of the eighty-ninth moon of your Majesty's auspicious reign.

CLEFREN FRELOCK
MARSI FRELOCK

When this inventory was read over to the Emperor, he directed me, although in very gentle terms, to deliver up the several particulars. He first called for my scimitar, which I took out, scabbard and all. In the meantime he ordered three thousand of his choicest troops to surround me at a distance, with their bows and arrows just ready to discharge: but I did not observe it, for my eyes were wholly fixed upon his Majesty.

He then desired me to draw my scimitar, which, although it had got some rust by the sea water, was in most parts exceeding bright. I did so, and immediately all the troops gave a shout between terror and surprise; for the sun shone clear, and the reflection dazzled their eyes as I waved the scimitar to and fro in my hand. His Majesty, who is a most magnanimous prince, was less daunted than I could expect. He ordered me to return it into the scabbard, and cast it on the ground as gently as I could, about six feet from the end of my chain.

The next thing he demanded was one of the hollow iron pillars, by which he meant my pocket pistols. I drew it out, and at his desire, as well as I could, expressed to him the use of it. Charging it only with powder, I first cautioned the Emperor not to be afraid, and then I let it off in the air. The astonishment here was much greater than at the sight of my scimitar. Hundreds fell down as if they had been struck dead; and even the Emperor, although he stood his ground, could not recover himself in some time.

I delivered up both my pistols in the same manner as I had done my scimitar, and then my pouch of powder and bullets; begging him that the former might be kept from the fire, for it would kindle with the smallest spark, and blow his Imperial palace into the air. I likewise delivered up my watch, which the Emperor was very curious to see, and commanded two of his tallest yeomen of the guards to bear it on a pole upon their shoulders, as draymen in England do a barrel of ale. He was amazed at the continual noise it made, and the motion of the minute hand, which he could easily discern. He asked the opinions of his learned men about him, which were various and remote, as the reader may well imagine; although indeed I could not very perfectly understand them. I then gave up my silver and copper money, my purse with nine large pieces of gold, and some smaller ones; my knife and razor, my comb and silver snuffbox, my handkerchief and journal book. My scimitar, pistols, and pouch were conveyed in carriages to his Majesty's stores; but the rest of my goods were returned me.

I had, as I before observed, one private pocket which escaped their search, wherein there was a pair of spectacles (which I sometimes use for the weakness of my eyes), a pocket perspective, and several other little conveniences. These being of no consequence to the Emperor, I did not think myself bound in honor to discover, and I apprehended they might be lost or spoiled if I ventured them out of my possession.

The Story of King Arthur and His Knights

HOW KING ARTHUR WAS WEDDED IN ROYAL STATE AND HOW THE ROUND TABLE WAS ESTABLISHED [1]

And now was come the early fall of the year; that pleasant season when the meadow-land and the wold were still green with summer that had only just passed; when the sky likewise was as of summer-time—extraordinarily blue and full of large floating clouds; when a bird might sing here and another there, a short song in memory of spring-time, when all the air was tempered with warmth and yet the leaves were everywhere turning brown and red and gold, so that when the sun shone through them it was as though a cloth of gold, broidered with brown and crimson and green, hung above the head. At this season of the year it is exceedingly pleasant to be a-field among the nut-trees with hawk and hound, or to travel abroad in the yellow world, whether it be a-horse or a-foot.

Now this was the time of year in which had been set the marriage of King Arthur and the Lady Guinevere at Camelot, and at that place was extraordinary pomp and glory of circumstance. All the world was astir and in a great ferment of joy, for everybody was exceedingly glad that King Arthur was to have him a Queen.

In preparation for that great occasion the town of Camelot was bedight very magnificently, for the stony street along which the Lady Guinevere must come to the royal castle of the King was strewn thick with fresh-cut rushes smoothly laid. Moreover it was in many places spread with carpets of excellent pattern such as might be fit to lay upon the floor of some goodly hall. Likewise all the houses along the way were hung with fine hangings of woven texture interwoven with threads of azure and crimson, and everywhere were flags and banners afloat in the warm and gentle breeze against the blue sky, wherefore that all the world appeared to be alive with bright colors, so that when one looked adown that street, it was as though one beheld a crooked path of exceeding beauty and gayety stretched before him.

Thus came the wedding-day of the King —bright and clear and exceedingly radiant.

King Arthur sat in his hall surrounded by his Court awaiting news that the Lady Guinevere was coming thitherward. And it was about the middle of the morning when there came a messenger in haste riding upon a milk-white steed. And the raiment of that messenger and the trappings of his horse were all of cloth of gold embroidered with scarlet and white, and the tabard of the messenger was set with many jewels of various sorts so that he glistened from afar as he rode, with a singular splendor of appearance.

So this herald-messenger came straight into the castle where the King abided waiting, and he said: "Arise, my lord King, for the Lady Guinevere and her Court draweth nigh unto this place."

Upon this the King immediately arose with great joy, and straightway he went forth with his Court of Knights, riding in great state. And as he went down that

[1] From "The Story of King Arthur and His Knights," by Howard Pyle, illustrated by Howard Pyle

litter wherein the Princess lay. And the framework of that litter was of richly gilded wood, and its curtains and its cushions were of crimson silk embroidered with threads of gold. And behind the litter there rode in gay and joyous array, all shining with many colors, the Court of the Princess—her damsels in waiting, gentlemen, ladies, pages, and attendants.

So those parties of the King and the Lady Guinevere drew nigh together until they met and mingled the one with the other.

Then straightway King Arthur dismounted from his noble horse and, all clothed with royalty, he went afoot unto the Lady Guinevere's litter, whiles Sir Gawaine and Sir Ewaine held the bridle of his horse. Thereupon one of her pages drew aside the silken curtains of the Lady Guinevere's litter, and King Leodegrance gave her his hand and she straightway descended therefrom, all embalmed, as it were, in exceeding beauty. So King Leodegrance led her to King Arthur, and King Arthur came to her and placed one hand beneath her chin and the other upon her head and inclined his countenance and kissed her upon her smooth cheek—all warm and fragrant like velvet for softness, and without any blemish whatsoever. And when he had thus kissed her upon the cheek, all those who were there lifted up their voices in great acclaim, giving loud voice of joy that those two noble souls had thus met together.

Thus did King Arthur give welcome unto the Lady Guinevere and unto King Leodegrance her father upon the highway beneath the walls of the town of Camelot, at the distance of half a league from that place. And no one who was there ever forgot that meeting, for it was full of extraordinary grace and noble courtliness.

Then King Arthur and his Court of Knights and nobles brought King Leodegrance and the Lady Guinevere with great ceremony unto Camelot and unto the royal castle, where apartments were

marvelously adorned street, all the people shouted aloud as he passed by, wherefore he smiled and bent his head from side to side; for that day he was passing happy and loved his people with wonderful friendliness.

Thus he rode forward unto the town gate, and out therefrom, and so came thence into the country beyond where the broad and well-beaten highway ran winding down beside the shining river betwixt the willows and the osiers.

And, behold! King Arthur and those with him perceived the Court of the Princess where it appeared at a distance, wherefore they made great rejoicing and hastened forward with all speed. And as they came nigh, the sun falling upon the apparels of silk and cloth of gold, and upon golden chains and the jewels that hung therefrom, all of that noble company that surrounded the Lady Guinevere her litter flashed and sparkled with surpassing radiance.

For seventeen of the noblest knights of the King's Court, clad in complete armor, and sent by him as an escort unto the lady, rode in great splendor, surrounding the assigned to all, so that the entire place was alive with joyousness and beauty.

And when high noon had come, the entire Court went with great state and ceremony unto the cathedral, and there, surrounded with wonderful magnificence, those two noble souls were married by the Archbishop.

And all the bells rang right joyfully, and all the people who stood without the cathedral shouted with loud acclaim, and lo! the King and the Queen came forth all shining, like unto the sun for splendor and like unto the moon for beauty.

In the castle a great noontide feast was spread, and there sat thereat four hundred, eighty and six lordly and noble folk— kings, knights, and nobles—with queens and ladies in magnificent array. And near to the King and the Queen there sat King Leodegrance and Merlin, and Sir Ulfius, and Sir Ector the trustworthy, and Sir Gawaine, and Sir Ewaine, and Sir Kay, and King Ban, and King Pellinore and many other famous and exalted folk, so that no man had ever beheld such magnificent courtliness as he beheld at that famous wedding-feast of King Arthur and Queen Guinevere.

And that day was likewise very famous in the history of chivalry, for in the afternoon the famous Round Table was established, and that Round Table was at once the very flower and the chiefest glory of King Arthur's reign.

For about mid of the afternoon the King and Queen, preceded by Merlin and followed by all that splendid Court of kings, lords, nobles and knights in full array, made progression to that place where Merlin, partly by magic and partly by skill, had caused to be builded a very wonderful pavilion above the Round Table where it stood.

And when the King and the Queen and the Court had entered in thereat they were amazed at the beauty of that pavilion, for they perceived, as it were, a great space that appeared to be a marvelous land of Fay. For the walls were all richly gilded and were painted with very wonderful figures of saints and of angels, clad in ultramarine and crimson, and all those saints and angels were depicted playing upon various musical instruments that appeared to be made of gold. And overhead the roof of the pavilion was made to represent the sky, being all of cerulean blue sprinkled over with stars. And in the midst of that painted sky was an image, as it were, of the sun in his glory. And under foot was a pavement all of marble stone, set in squares of black and white, and blue and red, and sundry other colors.

In the midst of the pavilion was a Round Table with seats thereat exactly sufficient for fifty persons, and at each of the fifty places was a chalice of gold filled with fragrant wine, and at each place was a paten of gold bearing a manchet of fair white bread. And when the King and his Court entered into the pavilion, lo! music began of a sudden for to play with a wonderful sweetness.

Then Merlin came and took King Arthur by the hand and led him away from Queen

Guinevere. And he said unto the King, "Lo! this is the Round Table."

Then King Arthur said, "Merlin, that which I see is wonderful beyond the telling."

After that Merlin discovered unto the King the various marvels of the Round Table, for first he pointed to a high seat, very wonderfully wrought in precious woods and gilded so that it was exceedingly beautiful, and he said, "Behold, lord King, yonder seat is hight the 'Seat Royal,' and that seat is thine for to sit in." And as Merlin spake, lo! there suddenly appeared sundry letters of gold upon the back of that seat, and the letters of gold read the name,

ARTHUR, KING.

And Merlin said, "Lord, yonder seat may well be called the center seat of the Round Table, for, in sooth, thou art indeed the very center of all that is most worthy of true knightliness. Wherefore that seat shall be called the center seat of all the other seats."

Then Merlin pointed to the seat that stood opposite to the Seat Royal, and that seat also was of a very wonderful appearance as afore told in this history. And Merlin said unto the King: "My lord King, that seat is called the Seat Perilous, for no man but one in all this world shall sit therein, and that man is not yet born upon the earth. And if any other man shall dare to sit therein that man shall either suffer death or a sudden and terrible misfortune for his temerity. Wherefore that seat is called the Seat Perilous."

"Merlin," quoth the King, "all that thou tellest me passeth the bound of understanding for marvelousness. Now I do beseech thee in all haste for to find forthwith a sufficient number of knights to fill this Round Table so that my glory shall be entirely complete."

Then Merlin smiled upon the King, though not with cheerfulness, and said, "Lord, why art thou in such haste? Know

that when this Round Table shall be entirely filled in all its seats, then shall thy glory be entirely achieved and then forthwith shall thy day begin for to decline. For when any man hath reached the crowning of his glory, then his work is done and God breaketh him as a man might break a chalice from which such perfect ichor hath been drunk that no baser wine may be allowed to defile it. So when thy work is done and ended shall God shatter the chalice of thy life."

Then did the King look very steadfastly into Merlin's face, and said, "Old man, that which thou sayest is ever of great wonder, for thou speakest words of wisdom. Ne'theless, seeing that I am in God His hands, I do wish for my glory and for His good will to be accomplished even though He shall then entirely break me when I have served His purposes."

"Lord," said Merlin, "thou speakest like a worthy king and with a very large and noble heart. Ne'theless, I may not fill the Round Table for thee at this time. For, though thou hast gathered about thee the very noblest Court of Chivalry in all of Christendom, yet are there but two and thirty knights here present who may be considered worthy to sit at the Round Table."

"Then, Merlin," quoth King Arthur, "I do desire of thee that thou shalt straightway choose me those two and thirty."

"So will I do, lord King," said Merlin.

Then Merlin cast his eyes around and lo! he saw where King Pellinore stood at a little distance. Unto him went Merlin and took him by the hand. "Behold, my lord King," quoth he. "Here is the knight in all the world next to thyself who at this time is most worthy for to sit at this Round Table. For he is both exceedingly gentle of demeanor unto the poor and needy and at the same time is so terribly strong and skillful that I know not whether thou or he is the more to be feared in an encounter of knight against knight."

Then Merlin led King Pellinore forward

and behold! upon the high seat that stood upon the left hand of the Royal Seat there appeared of a sudden the name,

PELLINORE.

And the name was emblazoned in letters of gold that shone with extraordinary luster. And when King Pellinore took his seat, great and loud acclaim long continued was given him by all those who stood round about.

Then after that Merlin had thus chosen King Arthur and King Pellinore he chose out of the Court of King Arthur the following knights, two and thirty in all, and these were the knights of great renown in chivalry who did first establish the Round Table. Wherefore they were surnamed "The Ancient and Honorable Companions of the Round Table."

To begin, there was Sir Gawaine and Sir Ewaine, who were nephews unto the King, and they sat nigh to him upon the right hand; there was Sir Ulfius (who held his seat but four years and eight months unto the time of his death, after which Sir Geheris—who was esquire unto his brother, Sir Gawaine—held that seat); and there was Sir Kay the Seneschal, who was foster brother unto the King; and there was Sir Baudwain of Britain (who held his seat but three years and two months until his death, after the which Sir Agravaine held that seat); and there was Sir Pellias and Sir Geraint and Sir Constantine, son of Sir Caderes the Seneschal of Cornwall (which same was king after King Arthur); and there was Sir Caradoc and Sir Sagramore, surnamed the Desirous, and Sir Dinadan and Sir Dodinas, surnamed the Savage, and Sir Bruin, surnamed the Black, and Sir Meliot of Logres, and Sir Aglaval and Sir Durnore, and Sir Lamorac (which three young knights were sons of King Pellinore), and there was Sir Griflet and Sir Ladinas and Sir Brandiles and Sir Persavant of Ironside, and Sir Dinas of Cornwall, and Sir Brian of Listinoise, and Sir Palomides and Sir Degraine and Sir Epinogres, the son of the King of North Umberland and brother unto the enchantress Vivien, and Sir Lamiel of Cardiff, and Sir Lucan the Bottler and Sir Bedevere his brother (which same bare King Arthur unto the ship of Fairies when he lay so sorely wounded nigh unto death after the last battle which he fought). These two and thirty knights were the Ancient Companions of the Round Table, and unto them were added others until there were nine and forty in all, and then was added Sir Galahad, and with him the Round Table was made entirely complete.

Now as each of these knights was chosen by Merlin, lo! as he took that knight by the hand, the name of that knight suddenly appeared in golden letters, very bright and shining, upon the seat that appertained to him.

But when all had been chosen, behold! King Arthur saw that the seat upon the right hand of the Seat Royal had not been filled, and that it bare no name upon it. And he said unto Merlin: "Merlin, how is this, that the seat upon my right hand hath not been filled, and beareth no name?"

And Merlin said: "Lord, there shall be a name thereon in a very little while, and he who shall sit therein shall be the greatest knight in all the world until that the knight cometh who shall occupy the Seat Perilous. For he who cometh shall exceed all other men in beauty and in strength and in knightly grace."

And King Arthur said: "I would that he were with us now." And Merlin said: "He cometh anon."

Thus was the Round Table established with great pomp and great ceremony of estate. For first the Archbishop of Canterbury blessed each and every seat, progressing from place to place surrounded by his Holy Court, the choir whereof singing most musically in accord, whiles others swung censers from which there ascended an exceedingly fragrant vapor of frankincense, filling that entire pavilion with an odor of Heavenly blessedness.

And when the Archbishop had thus blessed every one of those seats, the chosen knight took each his stall at the Round Table, and his esquire came and stood behind him, holding the banneret with his coat-of-arms upon the spear-point above the knight's head. And all those who stood about that place, both knights and ladies, lifted up their voices in loud acclaim.

Then all the knights arose, and each knight held up before him the cross of the hilt of his sword, and each knight spake word for word as King Arthur spake. And this was the covenant of their Knighthood of the Round Table: That they would be gentle unto the weak; that they would be courageous unto the strong; that they would be terrible unto the wicked and the evil-doer, that they would defend the helpless who should call upon them for aid; that all women should be held unto them sacred; that they would stand unto the defense of one another whensoever such defense should be required; that they would be merciful unto all men; that they would be gentle of deed, true in friendship, and faithful in love. This was their covenant, and unto it each knight sware upon the cross of his sword, and in witness thereof did kiss the hilt thereof. Thereupon all who stood thereabout once more gave loud acclaim.

Then all the knights of the Round Table seated themselves, and each knight brake bread from the golden paten, and quaffed wine from the golden chalice that stood before him, giving thanks unto God for that which he ate and drank.

Thus was King Arthur wedded unto Queen Guinevere, and thus was the Round Table established.

Pandora, The First Woman [1]

SALLY BENSON

Although Jupiter had punished Prometheus for stealing the divine fire from the chariot of the sun, he was not satisfied. He felt the gods should seek retaliation against Man for accepting the stolen gift. Summoning all the gods to the great hall, he asked them what they thought would plague and torment Man the most. It was decided, after many suggestions and arguments, that a woman might harry him and plant seeds of ambition and dissatisfaction in his breast. So, in much the same way as Prometheus had made Man, they brought clay from the earth and created a woman whom they named Pandora.

When she was given life, she was endowed by the gods with every gift; Venus bestowed beauty on her, Mercury gave her the art of persuasion, Apollo donated the love of music, and the Graces trained her in the social arts. Then, Vulcan fashioned an exquisite box of pure gold into which

[1] From "Stories of the Gods and Heroes," by Sally Benson, illustration from a drawing by Steele Savage

were put all the evils that have plagued mankind ever since—disease, famine, pestilence, fever, envy, greediness, gluttony, hatred and intolerance. It did not seem possible that a thing as lovely as the golden box could contain so many ills.

As they were about to close the box, the gods and goddesses regretted their hasty decision. And, although they were too proud to abandon the idea altogether, they added one beautiful gift that would lessen the pain caused by all the other disasters. This gift was called hope. The gods tucked it down into the bottom and cautioned Pandora not to open the box, which was intended as an offering to the man who took her in marriage.

Then, bidding her goodbye, they gave her to Mercury, Jupiter's messenger, who bore her away with him to the earth. Mercury left her with Epimetheus, who was so struck by her unusual beauty and grace that he gladly took her into his home.

Seeing the golden box under her arm, he asked her what it contained, and she answered that she did not know, exactly, but that she had been told to give it to the man she married. She placed it on a table and its brilliance lighted the entire room. Leaving Pandora alone, after cautioning her not to look at the contents of the chest until he asked the advice of his brother, Epimetheus traveled a whole day until he reached Mount Caucasus where Prometheus lay in chains. He related to him all that had happened, and Prometheus, suspecting a trick, told Epimetheus to hasten back and hide the box in a place so remote that no one could ever find it.

In the meantime, Pandora explored her new home. She picked flowers and scattered their petals, which were soft and fragrant under foot; she brought cold, sparkling water from the brook that roared over clean stones at the foot of the hill; she took honey from the bees and fruit from the trees. Each time she entered the house, the shining box caught her eye, and, more than once, she stopped to touch it, shake it, and wonder what it might hold. All day long she kept busy, until, as night drew near, she could find nothing else to do. Drawing a chair up to the table on which the box lay, she sat down, hypnotized by its beauty and glitter. Occasionally, she went to the door and looked in the distance to see if either Epimetheus or Man were approaching.

Finally, she took the box from the table and held it, turning it over and over, admiring its exquisite design. It was almost dark and she was all alone.

"Surely," she thought, "it can do no harm to open this lovely thing a mere crack and see what it contains. Is it a crown? A precious jewel? A magic cloak? A gift from the gods must be something both beautiful and rare."

The Furies, who were hovering about robed in invisibility, read her thoughts and stung her conscience with tiny pricks. She fumbled with the clasp on the box and loosened it. "Perhaps," she said to herself, "it is a robe of purest gold thread, embroidered with diamonds, rubies and sapphires. And if it is, it would be better if I opened the cask and wore the robe so that I will look more beautiful in Man's eyes."

As she thought this, the Furies stung her madly, but her curiosity was so great that she scarcely felt them. She opened the box a little, and peering in, saw nothing. Angry and emboldened, she opened it wider and saw what at first looked to be a brown, ugly cloud. The cloud moved and separated, and then, with a loud buzzing sound, hundreds of things resembling small insects escaped into the room. Terrified, she tried to close the box, but her hands shook and she could not manage the catch. It was almost empty when she finally slammed the lid, and only one thing remained. This was hope which had lain on the bottom.

She hurriedly placed the box on the table again and ran to the door to see if Epimetheus or Man were in sight. She looked around the room to make sure that none of the evils remained to be seen. She shook her robe in fear that some might lurk in its folds and she combed her hair free of them. Then, she set the table for supper, selecting the ripest fruits, the most delicious berries and the loveliest scented flowers. Pulling her chair far away from the table, she sat down to await Epimetheus and Man.

When they returned, they found her innocently busy mending their clothes. And she looked so beautiful sitting there, that Epimetheus almost forgot to ask her whether or not she had looked in the box. When he asked her, she pretended for a moment to have no idea what he meant. "The box?" she queried. "Oh, *that* one! It had slipped my mind entirely. Yes, I did open it a little, and there is a lovely, iridescent thing lying in it. It is more beautiful than the rarest jewel, and it is called hope."

"We will keep it there," Epimetheus told her.

She made no mention of the ugly, brown cloud composed of hundreds of ills that had flown out into the world, and it was some time before Epimetheus and Man knew that the box had contained anything but hope. When they did learn, Pandora had so endeared herself to them that they could not punish her. They looked at her sadly, unable to speak. Seeing the disapproval in their eyes, she tried to defend her disobedience. "It is true that I opened the box," she argued. "But it is also true that I allowed the evils to escape into the world. I brushed them from the room. They are not here and cannot harm us. And our house harbors only hope."

How Thor Found His Hammer [1]

HAMILTON WRIGHT MABIE

The frost-giants were always trying to get into Asgard. For more than half the year they held the world in their grasp, locking up the streams in their rocky beds, hushing their music and the music of the birds as well, and leaving nothing but a wild waste of desolation under the cold sky. They hated the warm sunshine which stirred the wild flowers out of their sleep, and clothed the steep mountains with verdure, and set all the birds a-singing in the swaying tree-tops. They hated the beautiful god Balder, with whose presence summer came back to the ice-bound earth, and, above all, they hated Thor, whose flashing hammer drove them back into Jotunheim, and guarded the summer sky with its sudden gleamings of power. So long as Thor had his hammer Asgard was safe against the giants.

One morning Thor started up out of a long, deep sleep, and put out his hand for the hammer; but no hammer was there. Not a sign of it could be found anywhere, although Thor anxiously searched for it. Then a thought of the giants came suddenly in his mind; and his anger rose till his eyes flashed like great fires, and his red beard trembled with wrath.

"Look, now, Loke," he shouted, "they have stolen Mjolner by enchantment, and no one on earth or in heaven knows where they have hidden it."

"We will get Freyja's falcon-guise and search for it," answered Loke, who was always quick to get into trouble or to get out of it again. So they went quickly to Folkvang and found Freyja surrounded by her maidens and weeping tears of pure gold, as she had always done since her husband went on his long journey.

"The hammer has been stolen by en-chantment," said Thor. "Will you lend me the falcon-guise that I may search for it?"

"If it were silver, or even gold, you should have it and welcome," answered Freyja, glad to help Thor find the wonderful hammer that kept them all safe from the hands of the frost-giants.

So the falcon-guise was brought, and Loke put it on and flew swiftly out of Asgard to the home of the giants. His great wings made broad shadows over the ripe fields as he swept along, and the reapers, looking up from their work, wondered what mighty bird was flying seaward. At last he reached Jotunheim, and no sooner had he touched ground and taken off the falcon-guise than he came upon the giant Thrym, sitting on a hill twisting golden collars for his dogs and stroking the long manes of his horses.

"Welcome, Loke," said the giant. "How fares it with the gods and the elves, and what has brought you to Jotunheim?"

"It fares ill with both gods and elves since you stole Thor's hammer," replied Loke, guessing quickly that Thrym was the thief; "and I have come to find where you have hidden it."

Thrym laughed as only a giant can when he knows he has made trouble for somebody.

"You won't find it," he said at last. "I have buried it eight miles under ground, and no one shall take it away unless he gets Freyja for me as my wife."

The giant looked as if he meant what he said, and Loke, seeing no other way of finding the hammer, put on his falcon-guise and flew back to Asgard. Thor was waiting to hear what news he brought, and both were soon at the great doors of Folkvang.

[1] From "Norse Stories," by Hamilton Wright Mabie. Illustration by Jon Nielsen

"Put on your bridal dress, Freyja," said Thor bluntly, after his fashion, "and we will ride swiftly to Jotunheim."

But Freyja had no idea of marrying a giant just to please Thor; and, in fact, that Thor should ask her to do such a thing threw her into such a rage that the floor shook under her angry tread, and her necklace snapped in pieces.

"Do you think I am a weak lovesick girl, to follow you to Jotunheim and marry Thrym?" she cried indignantly.

Finding they could do nothing with Freyja, Thor and Loke called all the gods together to talk over the matter and decide what should be done to get back the hammer. The gods were very much alarmed, because they knew the frost-giants would come upon Asgard as soon as they knew the hammer was gone. They said little, for they did not waste time with idle words, but they thought long and earnestly, and still they could find no way of getting hold of Mjolner once more. At last Heimdal, who had once been a Van, and could therefore look into the future, said: "We must have the hammer at once or Asgard will be in danger. If Freyja will not go, let Thor be dressed up and go in her place. Let keys jingle from his waist and a woman's dress fall about his feet. Put precious stones upon his breast, braid his hair like a woman's, hang the necklace around his neck, and bind the bridal veil around his head."

Thor frowned angrily. "If I dress like a woman," he said, "you will jeer at me."

"Don't talk of jeers," retorted Loke; "unless that hammer is brought back quickly, the giants will rule in our places."

Thor said no more, but allowed himself to be dressed like a bride, and soon drove off to Jotunheim with Loke beside him disguised as a servant-maid. There was never such a wedding journey before. They rode in Thor's chariot and the goats drew them, plunging swiftly along the way, thunder pealing through the mountains and the frightened earth blazing and smoking as they passed. When Thrym saw the bridal party coming he was filled with delight.

"Stand up, you giants," he shouted to his companions; "spread cushions upon the benches and bring in Freyja, my bride. My yards are full of golden-horned cows, black oxen please my gaze whichever way I look, great wealth and many treasures are mine, and Freyja is all I lack."

It was evening when the bride came driving into the giant's court in her blazing chariot. The feast was already spread against her coming, and with her veil modestly covering her face she was seated at the great table, Thrym fairly beside himself with delight. It wasn't every giant who could marry a goddess!

If the bridal journey had been so strange that any one but a foolish giant would have hesitated to marry a wife who came in such a turmoil of fire and storm, her conduct at the table ought certainly to have put Thrym on his guard; for never had a bride such an appetite before. The great tables groaned under the load of good things, but they were quickly relieved of their burden by the voracious bride. She ate a whole ox before the astonished giant had fairly begun to enjoy his meal. Then she devoured eight large salmon, one after the other; and having eaten up the part of the feast specially prepared for the hungry men, she turned upon the delicacies which had been made for the women, and especially for her own fastidious appetite.

Thrym looked on with wondering eyes, and at last, when she had added to these solid foods three whole barrels of mead, his amazement was so great that, his astonishment getting the better of his politeness, he called out, "Did any one ever see such an appetite in a bride before, or know a maid who could drink so much mead?"

Then Loke, who was playing the part of a serving-maid, thinking that the giant might have some suspicions, whispered to him, "Freyja was so happy in the thought of coming here that she has eaten nothing for eight whole days."

Thrym was so pleased at this evidence of affection that he leaned forward and raised the veil as gently as a giant could, but he instantly dropped it and sprang back the whole length of the hall before the bride's terrible eyes.

"Why are Freyja's eyes so sharp?" he called to Loke. "They burn me like fire."

"Oh," said the cunning serving-maid, "she has not slept for a week, so anxious has she been to come here, and that is why her eyes are so fiery."

Everybody looked at the bride and nobody envied Thrym. They thought it was too much like marrying a thunder-storm.

The giant's sister came into the hall just then, and seeing the veiled form of the bride sitting there went up to her and asked for a bridal gift. "If you would have my love and friendship give me those rings of gold upon your fingers."

But the bride sat perfectly silent. No one had yet seen her face or heard her voice.

Thrym became very impatient. "Bring in the hammer," he shouted, "that the bride may be consecrated, and wed us in the name of Var."

If the giant could have seen the bride's eyes when she heard these words he would have sent her home as quickly as possible, and looked somewhere else for a wife.

The hammer was brought and placed in the bride's lap, and everybody looked to see the marriage ceremony; but the wedding was more strange and terrible than the bridal journey had been. No sooner did the bride's fingers close round the handle of Mjolner than the veil which covered her face was torn off and there stood Thor, the giant-queller, his terrible eyes blazing with wrath.

The giants shuddered and shrank away from those flaming eyes, the sight of which they dreaded more than anything else in all the worlds; but there was no chance of escape. Thor swung the hammer round his head and the great house rocked on its foundations. There was a vivid flash of lightning, an awful crash of thunder, and the burning roof and walls buried the whole company in one common ruin.

Thrym was punished for stealing the hammer, his wedding guests got crushing blows instead of bridal gifts, and Thor and Loke went back to Asgard, where the presence of Mjolner made the gods safe once more.

Baucis and Philemon [1]

Once upon a time Jupiter, in human shape, visited Phrygia, and with him his son Mercury without his wings. They presented themselves, as weary travellers, at many a door seeking shelter, but found all closed, for it was late and the inhospitable inhabitants would not rouse themselves to open for them. At last a humble cottage received them, where Baucis and her husband, Philemon, had grown old together.

When the two heavenly guests crossed the humble threshold and bowed their heads to pass under the low door, the old man placed a seat, on which Baucis, bustling and attentive, spread a cloth, and begged them to sit down. Then she raked out the coals from the ashes and kindled up a fire, fed it with leaves and dry bark, and blew it into a flame. She brought out of a corner split sticks and dry branches, broke them up, and placed them under the kettle.

Her husband collected some pot-herbs in the garden, and she shred them from the stalks and prepared them for the pot. He reached down with a forked stick a flitch of bacon hanging in the chimney, cut a small piece, and put it in the pot to boil with the herbs.

Now, while the meal was being eaten, the old folks were astonished to see that the wine, as fast as it was poured out, renewed itself in the pitcher. Struck with terror, Baucis and Philemon recognized their heavenly guests, fell on their knees, and with clasped hands implored forgiveness for their poor entertainment. There was an old goose, which they kept as the guardian of their humble cottage, and they bethought them to make this sacrifice in honour of their guests.

But the goose, too nimble with the aid of feet and wings, eluded them and at last took shelter between the gods themselves. They forbade it to be slain and spoke these words: "We are gods. This inhospitable village shall pay the penalty of its impiety; you alone shall go free from punishment. Leave your house and come with us to the top of yonder hill."

They hastened to obey, and toiled up the steep ascent. They had reached to within an arrow's flight of the top when, turning their eyes below, they beheld all the country sunk in a lake, only their own house left standing. While they gazed with wonder at the sight and lamented the fate of their neighbours, that old house of theirs was changed into a temple.

Then spoke Jupiter: "Excellent old man, and woman worthy of such a husband, speak, tell us your wishes; what favour have you to ask of us?"

Philemon took counsel with Baucis a few moments; then they declared to the gods their wish. "We ask to be priests and guardians of your temple; and since we have passed our lives here in love and agreement, we wish that one and the same hour may take us both from life."

Their prayer was granted. They were the keepers of the temple as long as they lived. When grown very old, as they stood one day before the steps of the building, Baucis saw Philemon begin to put forth leaves, and old Philemon saw Baucis changing in the same manner. And now a leafy crown had grown over their heads. They exchanged parting words as long as they could speak. "Farewell, dear spouse," they said together, and at the same moment the bark closed over their mouths. The Tyanean shepherd still shows the two trees, standing side by side, made out of the two good old people.

[1] From "A Book of Myths, Selections from Bulfinch's Age of Fable," illustrated by Helen Sewell

TITLE INDEX

AUTHOR INDEX